Other novels by
Eugenia Price

STRANGER
IN
SAVANNAH

DOUBLEDAY

NEW YORK
LONDON
TORONTO
SYDNEY
AUCKLAND

STRANGER IN SAVANNAH

EUGENIA PRICE

PUBLISHED BY DOUBLEDAY

a division of Bantam Doubleday Dell Publishing Group, Inc.
666 Fifth Avenue, New York, New York 10103

DOUBLEDAY and the portrayal of an anchor with a dolphin
are trademarks of Doubleday, a division of
Bantam Doubleday Dell Publishing Group, Inc.

Library of Congress Cataloging-in-Publication Data

Price, Eugenia.
  Stranger in Savannah.

  The fourth and final book of the author's Savannah quartet.
  I. Title.
PS3566.R47S77   1989   813'.54   88-33546
ISBN 0-385-23069-9

Printed in the United States of America

May 1989

FIRST EDITION

BG

FOR

EILEEN HUMPHLETT

PART
I

January 1854–May 1854

O N E

J

       ust after first light in early January of the new year 1854, Natalie sensed from the odd, white glare as soon as her eyes flew open that it had snowed in the night. Her impulse was to leap out of bed, run to open the shutters, and fill her eyes with the clean, crystalline wonder of her world gone white outside along the high cliffs of the Etowah River in the Georgia upcountry. Instead she peered carefully at Burke, still sleeping beside her, then eased herself silently out of the warm bed into the icy room. A little cold never hurt anyone, she thought, hurrying in her bare feet to tilt the louvers of the shutters at their bedroom window just enough to see that inches of thick, glorious snow covered everything—Burke's woodpile in the corner of the still trackless front yard, her hydrangea bushes and the pine-straw walk out to the road that led to Miss Lib Stiles's house. Best of all, she liked the unpredictable way snow stacked itself on tree branches, sometimes in rounded heaps, sometimes in almost bladelike ridges of glistening flakes that didn't make it all the way to the ground.

There was far too much snow for Burke even to think of riding into Cartersville to work on the store he was building, and if she were to rescue her friend Mary Cowper Stiles from her parents' cruelty, *this was the day to try.* Burke would be at home to play with Callie before and after her lessons with Mary Cowper and Natalie would be free to undertake the vital mission she'd put off for weeks.

If I stall one more day, she told herself, still devouring the clean, white beauty through the barest slit in the shutter, I won't stand a chance of convincing Miss Lib. She's getting more and more distant every day and harder to talk to. Today, though, with Burke here to occupy Callie before her tutoring session, there'd be plenty of time to see Miss Lib alone while Uncle W.H. wrote his usual morning letters to politicians.

Natalie's only child, Callie, would be ten in July and her ears picked up everything said in her presence. Natalie had already bungled several chances to change Miss Lib's heartless bias during the hours when young, grieving Mary Cowper was busy teaching Callie at the Stiles house. Oh, she'd tried a time or two, but never all out because with her sharp ears, Callie could overhear, especially if Natalie and Miss Lib argued. Today, though, could be different. If she hurried her little family through breakfast and hustled herself down the road to the Stiles house, there would be plenty of time to corner Miss Lib alone.

Natalie did *not* want Callie to know about the terrible thing Mary Cowper's parents were doing to their daughter. For as long as possible, she meant to protect Callie from finding out how hard and unfair life could be. The girl adored Miss Lib and it was plain to both Natalie and Burke that Callie had a real crush on her beautiful young tutor. Why disillusion the child until she was old enough to understand that even the people she especially loved had faults? Natalie saw no fault in Mary Cowper, but finding out about her heartbreak would shatter Callie's heart if she knew. Burke thought Natalie overprotected their daughter and maybe he was right. Certainly Callie had shown no signs of being a fragile, timorous, pampered female child. She had hopped about and laughed her way all through her first decade as though she had been born with two good feet the same as other children. Natalie and Burke had held one good, frank talk with her about two years ago telling her straight out that she would always have a crippled foot. Callie's eyes had filled with quick tears which she'd as quickly wiped away and since then not one word of complaint had passed her lips. She hadn't even seemed to try harder not to limp. Callie had just gone on with her playtimes and chores and lessons, making jokes with her father and laughing and hugging them all as delightedly and with as much gusto as she'd always shown. She's tough in the right way, Natalie kept telling herself, but what Miss Lib was doing to Mary Cowper was too cruel even for Callie.

She turned from the window and glanced at Burke. He was still sound asleep, one big, powerful forearm thrown up over his golden head. I'll surprise him, she decided, and build up the fires myself this morning. Soundlessly she crept across the bedroom floor—Burke built the most creakless floors in the world—and into her kitchen, the rising sun already shafting its bright gold off the white magic outside. Burke also stacked split wood perfectly, so that she could select small, quick starting pieces of oak from his neat pile beside her kitchen fireplace without making any noise. Nothing tumbled when she slipped out enough sticks to cook breakfast. He'd banked the fire just right last night, too. No need for more than a few splinters of fat pine.

I guess I'll never put one splinter of pine on a fire as long as I live that I don't remember that dreadful day when I piled it on and burned down Burke's old Indian cabin outside Cassville, she thought, smiling, then frowning, because now that she'd learned how to keep house in the rugged upcountry, the memory embarrassed her. It also brought Indian Mary to mind. A day didn't pass that Natalie failed to think of Mary, living now in Natalie's parents' mansion on Reynolds Square in Savannah as Mrs. Jonathan Browning, the wife of Natalie's brother. Mary and I certainly changed places, she thought, giving the blaze two or three quick blasts from the bellows before heading back to build up the bedroom fire. I certainly had everything to learn about Mary's beloved Cherokee upcountry and she had it all to learn in Savannah society. I'm proud of us both. At least we didn't allow such a drastic change of cultures to keep us away from the men we loved. The thought sent a fresh burst of determination to accomplish what she meant to accomplish today with Miss Lib. She would simply confront her with the new evidence of how cruel and foolish both the Stiles parents had been to have forced Mary Cowper to break off her engagement to Stuart Elliott, the one young man she would ever love. Natalie's resolve firmed as she picked up an armful of split oak and slipped back into the bedroom just as Burke sat up in bed, sleepy-eyed, but obviously startled to see her busily doing his morning chores.

"What's wrong, Natalie? What are you doing?"

"Snow, Burke! It snowed in the night—six inches, I'm sure! I'm building our fires. What do you think I'm doing? I have to get outside in the middle of it—fast."

Out of bed too now in his nightshirt and bare feet, he caught her in his arms and held her against his warm body. "Shame on you. Building fires is my job! Get back under the covers. I don't want this house burned down!"

In response, she pulled his head down and kissed him. "I've learned perfectly well how to build a fire, sir, so no insinuations." Giving him another quick kiss on his nose, she broke away and leaped back into bed, glad to let him take care of the bedroom fireplace. "You can't ride to Cartersville today in all this snow," she said happily. "Isn't that marvelous? And hurry! Callie's going to come flying in here in a matter of minutes. Once that bright, snowy light hits her room, those eyes will be open and she'll be right here in bed with us. I want you to myself for two minutes anyway. Come on!"

"How old does Callie have to be," he asked, crawling back under the covers beside her, "before she realizes that now and then Mama and Papa need a little space—alone?"

She had no time to answer. No need to answer. Both were too busy holding, "smashing" closer and closer together beneath the thick covers, the bed still a little warm on the side where Burke had been sleeping. "Smashing" was Natalie's word for their seemingly futile attempts ever to get close enough. Even at the moments of their most ecstatic nearness, oneness, they had never seemed close enough for her or for Burke.

"Not close enough, Natalie—never close enough," he groaned.

"No. No, my darling, but at least it gives us something to keep trying for . . ."

"Yes," he murmured, his face buried in her neck. "Yes. I just hope we both live long enough to . . ."

"To get as close as we need to? We won't. No one could live long enough to get as close to you as I need to be." Then, abruptly she threw back the covers and sat up. "But there's always tonight, and right now there's a glorious snow outside and—"

"And," he laughed, "I hear Callie bumping her potty along closer to her bed so she won't freeze her feet on these cold floors."

"I must make her a hooked rug," Natalie said.

"She didn't even give us ten minutes alone today, did she?"

They listened to Callie's vigorous tinkle in the empty china chamber pot, then the now familiar one-sided thump as her crippled bare foot hit the floor.

"Listen," Natalie whispered. "She's peeping out her shutters right now!"

"Snow! Mama—Papa! It snowed last night," the child shouted from the adjoining room.

Both parents laughed, then steeled themselves for her mighty leap into their bed. In seconds she appeared, plopped on the bed, then wiggled her way under the covers between them where they all three squirmed and laughed and patted and hugged.

"Let me feel your feet, Callie," Natalie said. "They're like ice against my leg."

"Only one, Mama," Callie said casually. "My bumpy foot's always colder than the good one. Mary Cowper says that's circulation. She says the blood vessels in my bumpy foot must be turned crooked the same way my foot is." The girl sat up. "You can't go to work today, Papa, so we'll build a big, big snowman in our front yard! Remember? Like the one Uncle Jonathan showed me how to make when he and Aunt Mary and Grandpa and Grandma Browning were up here last winter. I wish they'd all come back, don't you?"

"Sure we do, honey," Burke said, scooting lower in the bed so the covers would reach over his shoulders with Callie in the middle now sitting bolt upright. "And you bet we'll build a snowman today."

"I've still got the old top hat Grandpa Mark gave me. Can we put that on him, too?"

"Oh, he wouldn't look dressed without his top hat," Burke said.

"Don't you wish Uncle Jonathan and Aunt Mary and my grandparents would come back up to see us, Mama?"

"Of course, darling, but right now, my mind's on making a quick breakfast so we can all get outdoors. Would you mind warmed-up biscuits just this once, Burke? I do have to get over to Miss Lib's house as soon as possible."

"Even before I go to my lessons, Mama?" Callie wanted to know.

"Even before that," Natalie said absently, climbing out of bed and quickly into her warm robe and slippers.

"Why, sweetheart?" Burke asked. "Why so early? Warmed-up biscuits are fine, but I thought sure you'd want to help us build our snowman."

"Oh, I'll be back long before you're finished."

"It only takes a little while, Mama," Callie said, "to roll snowballs big enough for his tummy and chest and head, and—"

"I know, but I have important business with Miss Lib Stiles and *it absolutely can't wait.*"

"I hope it isn't what I think it is, Natalie," Burke said, neither cross nor playful.

Halfway to the kitchen, Natalie turned back. "You'll know all about it in due time, darling," she said, and left the room.

"Mama likes secrets," Callie said, getting up. "Let's make up a secret, too, Papa. Even if she won't stay and play with us, we'll think up a secret kind of clothes to dress our snowman in."

"Better get washed and into some heavy clothes yourself, young lady. The house is far from warm yet." He grabbed her and pulled her back down beside him and made a few blow noises on her tummy the way he used to do when she was little.

Laughing loudly, Callie whacked him on his thick shoulder. "That still tickles and you're funny, Papa, but we've got to hurry. The snow might melt before we get out there." Now she pulled his head close to hers and whispered, "What is it you hope Mama won't do at Miss Lib's house?"

"I hear you whispering in there," Natalie called from the kitchen, where she was making cheerful, clattering sounds while she set the table.

"I guess we'll both find out in time," Burke whispered back to Callie.

"I said I heard you," Natalie called again, but the sudden sizzle of ham slices hitting the hot skillet made an answer unnecessary. "Get into something warm, Callie, and give me a hand watching the biscuits, will you? You can wash up and dress later."

"No, I can't, Mama. Papa and I need to be ready to get to work outside on our snowman just as soon as breakfast's over, so I'm going to wash and get dressed right this minute. Papa said to."

T W O

*L*eaving the breakfast dishes for her friend and house-keeper, Lorah Plemmons, who'd be along soon, Natalie bundled herself in the new cape her parents had just sent from Savannah and hurried across the front yard, where Burke and Callie were already at work on their snowman, Callie with her grandfather Browning's top hat perched jauntily on her own head. Barely slowing as she passed them, Natalie kept waving as she plodded through the snowy yard toward the road that led to Miss Lib's house. Both yelled for her to help as, together, husband and daughter rolled a bigger and bigger snowball, but she kept going, determined to keep her mind focused on the new persuasion she meant to use to convince Miss Lib that she was dead wrong to break her own daughter's heart.

The sight of Callie's twisted foot brought less pain to Natalie now than during the early years of the child's life, but seeing the clumsy way Callie managed that leg in order to stoop and roll snow beside her papa wrenched at her today. Miss Lorah Plemmons's daily manipulation which she'd kept up until after Callie's second birthday had helped enormously. The crippled foot turned only a little to one side now, but its ankle was so stiff even a simple activity like stooping to roll a snowball made the girl look so awkward that Natalie winced.

I'll certainly see to it that her little heart isn't hurt, though, she told

herself as she plowed along the road. If I ever know, as Miss Lib
certainly knows, that Callie loves a young man the way Mary Cowper
loves Stuart Elliott, I'll move heaven and earth to see that they're never
separated—not for one unnecessary minute. I can't do anything to help
Callie's clubfoot, but I can guard her heart. And I will. Oh, I will!

Before Burke joined Callie in the front yard a few minutes earlier,
he'd said almost sternly, "Don't butt in, Natalie. Whatever Miss Lib and
W.H. decide about their daughter's life is their business, not ours."

"I'm not butting," Natalie had flared, and honestly felt she wasn't.
For all her thirty-one years, Miss Lib and Uncle W.H. had been like her
family. After all, her papa once lived in the same house with Miss Lib
and the other Mackays when he first came to Savannah as a young man.
Miss Lib's mother, Miss Eliza Mackay, was her papa's closest friend to
this day and would always be. Miss Eliza was her mother's closest
friend, too. When she was just a young girl named Caroline Cameron,
who lived outside the city at Knightsford plantation, the Mackay house
had been her mama's Savannah home until she married Mark Browning.

"I'm not butting, Burke," she repeated aloud now, and plowed faster
through the drifted snow along the road that would pass Miss Lorah
Plemmons's pretty cottage Papa paid Burke to build for her. Even
though Miss Lorah's cottage had only four rooms, it was as carefully
and sturdily built as the Stiles mansion where Natalie was headed. One
of the thousands of reasons she loved Burke Latimer so, so deeply was
that he wouldn't have thought of building either house in a slipshod
manner. He'd put just as much care and skill into Miss Lorah's cottage as
into the imposing Stiles house.

She should be concentrating on her strategy with Miss Lib, but it
was hard to keep her mind off the beauty around her. In spite of three
years spent in a girls' seminary up North before she knew Burke, Natalie
was still thrilled by newly fallen snow. She didn't just make dents in it
either, by taking careful high steps as other people did. She *plowed,*
scuffing one booted foot after another, ripping the smooth white surface the way a plow ripped a field, because it was more fun to leave deep
furrows behind.

Bundled in the new Scottish plaid cape her mother had found at
Andrew Low's Emporium in Savannah, she hugged herself inside its
luxurious warmth, then shuddered because the cape had come from the
emporium of that rich, unromantic, stuffy old man Mary Cowper was
being forced to marry. Oh, Andrew Low was rather handsome in a
forbidding sort of way, with thick, dark red hair and beard and piercing

blue eyes, but he was forty-one and he certainly *wasn't* Stuart Elliott, the gorgeous *young* man Mary Cowper Stiles had loved since she was a schoolgirl. The only man she'd ever loved. The only man she would ever love. For all her adult life, Natalie had held one central belief: Nothing, *nothing* should ever be allowed to separate any two people who truly loved. Believing that and acting on it in spite of all objections and questions had brought her own eternal happiness with Burke, who, because he earned his living with his hands, hadn't been considered good enough for Mark Browning's only daughter either, but she'd married him anyway. She plowed faster, more determined than ever to turn stubborn Miss Lib around.

This minute, in one mittened hand, she clutched the letter Miss Eliza Mackay's daughter Kate had enclosed in her own latest letter—Natalie's new evidence that Miss Lib was wrong and was making a fool of herself to insist that her daughter marry a domineering old man. The whole argument was right there in black and white in the handwriting of Kate Mackay's longtime friend in South Carolina, feisty Miss Mary Elizabeth Huger. It stated plainly that people—the respected, *right* people—were making fun of Miss Lib and Uncle W.H. Burke had brought Kate Mackay's letter when he came home late yesterday from work on the store he was building in Cartersville. This morning Natalie fully intended to use the gossipy enclosure on Miss Lib, who had always cared terribly what other people thought, *if* they were the best people. The Hugers were the very best.

She was in sight of Miss Lorah's cozy yellow cottage. Woodsmoke was blowing in the rising wind from its fine brick chimney—the first brick one she'd ever had, Miss Lorah declared. Where she came from over in Ellijay, higher up in the Georgia mountains, people mostly had stick-and-mud chimneys. Abruptly, Natalie realized she had left her own cottage a little before eight-thirty and had only been on her way a few minutes. If she didn't stay long, there'd be time for a visit with her wise friend, Miss Lorah Plemmons. On impulse, she left the road, turned in at the cottage path, and headed for the narrow front porch.

<hr />

Yellow flowered sunbonnet on her head and bundled in the heavy folds of the warm green coat Miss Eliza Mackay had sent the last time Missy's family visited in the upcountry, Lorah Plemmons hurried to answer the knock at her front door.

"Heavenly days, child," she said to Natalie, "get inside! What in

tarnation are you doin' out in weather like this? I was just fixin' to leave
for your place. You had breakfast yet?"

"Oh, my, yes," Natalie said, warming her hands before the blazing
fire. "You know I always fix our breakfast. Take off your coat, Miss
Lorah. It's too cold outside for either of us to sit even for a few minutes
all bundled up. We'll freeze when we go out. I have to talk to you. It's
terribly important." She flung her own cape over a rocker and sat down
in it. "What I have to talk about is Miss Lib and what she's doing to poor
Mary Cowper."

Removing her own coat, Lorah took the rocker opposite. "What's
that in your hand, Missy?" Lorah asked, nodding toward the now quite
crumpled letter.

"It's my secret weapon," Natalie exclaimed. "I only got it yesterday
enclosed in a letter from Kate Mackay." She held out the single page.
"Here, I want you to read every word of it! I know I'll be more
convincing when I see Miss Lib this morning if I know you think this
letter will help break that stubborn streak she's caught in."

Lorah made no move toward the letter. "You know I never was one
to read other folks' mail."

"All right then, I'll read it to you. You won't be prying if *I* read it,
will you?"

Lorah couldn't help a small chuckle. "I reckon not. I know better
than to try to stop you."

"Good. First, you need to know that this is a letter from one of the
most socially acceptable families in the whole South—the Hugers of
South Carolina. Lifelong friends of the Mackays and the Stileses. People
Miss Lib pays attention to. People she admires and respects. Her
mother, Miss Eliza, and this lady's mother have been friends forever."

Still smiling, Lorah said, "That's a mighty long time."

"Now, don't say another word. Just listen to what Miss Mary Elizabeth Huger wrote to Kate Mackay: 'News has reached us here in South
Carolina through a friend of his first wife, the late Sarah Hunter Low,
that poor little Mary C. Stiles is definitely engaged now to Mr. Andrew
Low—a match made and approved of by Mary Cowper Stiles's parents,
who have shut the heartbroken damsel up in their castle by the Etowah
until Blue . . . or rather *Redbeard* comes back from England to claim
her. The young lady is pining away, looking out windows for someone
to come to her rescue. Alas, I fear no knight is bold enough to break a
lance with Redbeard, who, besides being favored by the parents, has red
gold for the winning.' " When Lorah just sat there silent, rocking,

Natalie repeated, "Did you take note, Miss Lorah, that I told you how highly Miss Lib Stiles regards the Hugers? That knowing Miss Mary Elizabeth Huger is being sarcastic about how she and Uncle W.H. are keeping Mary Cowper imprisoned could well turn Miss Lib around?"

"I took in every word you said, Missy."

"Well, did you really listen to what Miss Huger wrote?"

"I listened to that, too."

"Then, for heaven's sake, say something! I think what they're doing to Mary C. is mostly Miss Lib's fault. Oh, I know Uncle W.H. always needs more money and that he's partial to Andrew Low because he's British and rich and *old*. The Stileses are both getting old, too. Like old Redbeard Low. But it's cruel what they're doing, Miss Lorah! Mary Cowper loves Stuart Elliott and she'll never love anyone else. And don't tell me he's a young ne'er-do-well either, just because he likes his brandy and loses a little money gambling and the only thing he's proven himself to be is a crack shot, even better than Mary C. No one thought Burke was good enough for me, and look how happy we are. It didn't look right to older people like Mama and Papa either when Burke disappeared for a whole year after our shipwreck, but it didn't change the fact that Burke and I loved each other, did it? Stuart Elliott loves Mary Cowper, too. I had a long talk with him the last time he came here to see her and he says the only reason he's never settled down to a regular job is because everybody keeps telling him he's a wastrel—everybody except Mary C., who believes in him. Anyway, he's working every day now down in Savannah at the Bank of the State of Georgia as an assistant teller. Stuart's trying hard to show that he's worthy of Mary Cowper. He'd never worked at a regular position before in his life! Doesn't that tell you he's not a ne'er-do-well?"

Lorah thought briefly, then said, "It tells me he might be a spoiled rich boy."

"Nonsense. He isn't rich. At least Stuart himself isn't. The Elliotts and his stepfather's family, the Bullochs, *are* highly respected people, but, Miss Lorah, you're not thinking straight."

"I'm not?"

"There should be a law against parents deciding about two people who love each other!"

"Is that so?"

"Yes, it's so because Burke and I prove it. You know two people couldn't possibly be happier than we are and what makes Miss Lib's attitude so hard to understand is that she and William Mackay were the ones who convinced my parents that Burke and I should get married in the first place. Oh, I'd have married him anyway, but Miss Lib made a marvelous speech in our hotel back in Cassville the day before our wedding. She sat Mama and Papa down in chairs and convinced them that it shouldn't make any difference at all if Burke worked with his hands. Miss Lib did that and now look at the cruel, heartless way she's treating her own daughter!"

Lorah Plemmons got slowly to her feet and looked straight down at Natalie, still seated by the fire. "I may think a certain way about a thing, Missy, but unless somebody makes it my business, I just think. I don't talk."

"And you're not going to help me one bit to save Mary Cowper's happiness, is that what you're telling me? Don't you care that she'll have to spend the remainder of her life—years and years and years—married to a man old enough to be her father? Miss Lorah, she'll have to sleep beside that old man every night of her life! Being Mary Cowper, she'll try to be a good wife to him, which means she'll have to bear his children, and you know that a woman doesn't bear a man's children without—without letting him touch her and—"

"I have heard tell of that, yes, Missy."

On her feet now, Natalie snapped, "I didn't stop off here, when my time is so short, to have you treat me like a child!"

"I wasn't treating *you* any way," Lorah said evenly. "I just don't meddle in other people's business."

Her hand on Lorah's arms, Natalie pleaded, "Please listen! I don't think you've really been listening to anything I've said."

"It seems to me you haven't done a lot of listening to me over the years you and me's been together either, Missy. If you had been listening, you'd know I don't meddle for any reason."

"But you love Mary Cowper! I know you do."

"I love that pretty little thing so much sometimes I think my heart might break over her staying shut up in her room the way she does day after day, but I don't meddle."

Throwing her cape around her shoulders, Natalie said, "And you don't think I should either, is that what you're saying?"

"No, it's not," Lorah said, hauling on her own coat. "I don't meddle with your life either. I try to help all I can, but I don't meddle."

"Aren't friends supposed to help each other in times of trouble?" Natalie asked when they had left the house and were outside in the road about to separate, Lorah Plemmons to head for Natalie's cottage to clean up and Natalie to the Stiles house. "Oh, I know you're hired to be our housekeeper, but don't you help us too because we're all friends?"

"The best of friends. You and Mr. Burke are the best friends I ever had, I reckon."

"Then down in your heart, under that maddening way you have of twisting words around, you're really telling me to go ahead and do all I can to help Mary Cowper."

Holding the collar of the warm coat Eliza Mackay gave her high around her throat against the wind blowing off the icy river, Lorah said with a twinkle, "Missy, you just could be right." Tears that might have been partly caused by the wind brimmed in her eyes. "I know if anybody'd tried to keep me from marryin' up with my Luke, I'da kicked like a mule."

Lorah wasn't at all surprised when Missy threw both arms around her and gave her a quick hug.

"That's all I needed to know. Tell Burke and Callie I'll be home soon," the young woman said, and hurried away toward the Stiles place, its four tall chimneys pouring woodsmoke into the winter air. "The trouble is, though," she called back to Lorah, her voice barely audible over the wind, "poor Mary Cowper doesn't know how to fight back at all!"

Missy's right, Lorah thought, trudging through the deep snow toward the Latimer place. The Stiles girl had told Lorah herself she'd already bid her young man their last goodbye the day she broke off their engagement before Christmas. Mary Cowper had always minded her parents. Never did seem to think about being defiant with them. Not like Missy, who'd generally managed to talk her kind, warmhearted folks into most anything she had a mind to try. Mrs. Stiles and her husband had been kind to Lorah, but Miss Lib, as Missy called her, did have a streak of mule. As did Missy. Nobody may ever find out, Lorah decided, but sparks could fly this morning when Missy faces Mrs. Stiles with that gossipy letter from South Carolina. And I, for one, don't expect the letter to change anything.

THREE

One of the servants had swept the two front steps that led up onto the Stileses' wide veranda. Natalie stopped before knocking to stomp snow from her boots. No point in irritating Miss Lib, she thought, by tracking wet snow into her elegant parlor. Almost frightened by now at the prospect of confronting her friend on such a prickly subject, Natalie took time to breathe a prayer—the kind of prayer Burke called useless—that almost anyone but Miss Lib might open the door. To give her prayer added power, she crossed the fingers of her right hand inside her cape, further wrinkling the well-traveled page from the Huger letter.

Too quickly, the door opened and there stood Miss Lib—daring to smile at her—feigning surprise at such an early visit.

"Natalie, my dear! Come in out of the cold and wind. Look at you," she went on, Natalie thought with too much effusion. "Your new cape—hood and all—is covered with snow! It's stopped snowing. How did you get so much on you?"

Brushing at the long folds of the cape, Natalie added as courteously as her tangled emotions allowed, "The wind is blowing. It kept blowing snow down off the trees, and after all, I do live a couple of hundred yards away!"

"Of course," Miss Lib said, somewhat taken aback, Natalie thought, by her rather sharp response. "I suppose you came to see Mary Cowper," Miss Lib went on. "I'm sorry to say she's still upstairs in her room."

"Are you really sorry, Miss Lib?" Natalie asked, hanging the damp cape on a hall tree.

"Sorry about what?"

"That your only daughter is pining away in her room with a broken heart?"

Leaving her question on the air, Natalie followed Miss Lib into her handsome parlor furnished in the main with splendid tables and chairs and couches and gilded mirrors collected at great expense during the Stileses' tour of Europe at the end of Uncle W.H.'s service as chargé d'affaires in Vienna a few years ago. Some of the costly furnishings and carpets, even a large portion of the books lining the parlor walls, were still not paid for, Natalie knew. She also knew that Miss Lib and Uncle W.H. had always seemed unable to live within what Miss Eliza Mackay called "their means." No wonder they'd imprisoned Mary Cowper to keep her from marrying a *poor* young man. No one was as rich as old Andrew Low! The thought made Natalie feel as though someone had taken a bellows to her own anger. It caused dread to rise, too, because suddenly it seemed to her that in spite of how much everyone had always claimed to love sweet, submissive Mary Cowper Stiles, now only she, Natalie, was willing to fight for her right to happiness. Even Burke and Miss Lorah and good Miss Eliza Mackay were unwilling to buck Miss Lib's stubborn streak.

"Sit down, Miss Lib," she ordered.

Smiling as though genuinely amused that she was being commanded to sit down in her own parlor, the older woman obliged. "All right. I'm sitting, Natalie. What's this early-morning visit all about? What's that in your hand—a letter from Savannah?"

"It's a letter," she said, her voice deadly serious. "At least a part of a letter sent to me by your own sister, Kate. This, Miss Lib"—she held out the single crumpled page—"is from someone whose opinion should make a dent in you—even as much as you've changed."

"Natalie Latimer, I have not changed! You simply haven't grown up to your thirty years plus and, of course, I know exactly why you're here. As always, I'm glad to see you, but you might as well get it through your head that W.H. and I are *not* going to allow our daughter to marry into a life of poverty and heartache by tying herself to a worthless young scoundrel who acts as though he loves her only because he thinks her father is worth far more than he actually is!" Miss Lib rubbed her temples as though she had a headache. "I—I walked right into your trap, didn't I? Let you have it, as W.H. says, right between the eyes so now you can repeat your ridiculous notion that I've changed. By the way, any more talk on the subject of Mary Cowper's marriage is futile, but why don't you sit down, too, Natalie?"

"I think better standing up." She heard the ragged edge in her voice and smoothed it off abruptly. "Dear Miss Lib, you do respect the Hugers of South Carolina, don't you?" she asked quietly. "You and Uncle W.H. consider them among the best people, whose opinions really matter?"

"Why, of course we do. Our families have known one another for generations. But what on earth do the Hugers have to do with—"

"Plenty," Natalie said curtly. "Read this. Word of the dreadful thing you're doing to your only daughter has gotten all the way to South Carolina! Read what Mary Elizabeth Huger wrote and be honest with me. Doesn't it make you so ashamed of yourself you could die?"

Miss Lib took the letter, unfolded it slowly, smoothed it over her knee, and read in silence. Try as she did, Natalie could tell absolutely nothing of what Miss Lib was thinking by the look on her still beautiful, but now closed face. She wasn't even frowning. She was just reading—all the way to the end of the part about Mary Cowper and old Redbeard Andrew Low. Then she refolded the page, handed it back to Natalie, and stood up.

"Little Sinai has a sick child in the quarters this morning," she said politely. "I've promised to take over some turpentine and swab the child's throat. I'm sorry, but you'll have to excuse me. You're welcome to go up to Mary C.'s room and let her read this bit of ugly gossip from South Carolina, if you like. She knows already how you feel about her engagement to Mr. Low. And she *is* engaged to marry him, Natalie, just as soon as he's back from a business trip to Liverpool. She did indeed break off her foolish engagement to Stuart Elliott—two months ago. She is planning to become Mrs. Andrew Low. Mary Cowper isn't angry with her father and me either. She *knows* how you feel, how my mother and sisters feel, how William feels, but none of you has managed to turn her against her parents. Mary Cowper just isn't headstrong and rebellious the way . . ." Her voice wavered and Miss Lib looked out across the veranda, but said no more.

"The way I am, Miss Lib? Is that what you were about to say?"

"Mary C.'s father and I have always done only what we know to be best for her and her brothers. She knows this and trusts our judgment.

She is rather withdrawn these days, to be sure. I admit she does look out the windows a lot, but she'll get over that and she holds no ill feelings toward her father or me."

"That's because she can't!"

"What do you mean, she can't?"

"She's dead inside! Dead people don't feel anything. They—they just lie there and disintegrate! Is that what you want for your beautiful, suffering daughter, Miss Lib? Is it?"

"Suffering is what we mean to shield her *from*, Natalie."

From the hall tree where Miss Lib was taking down her own worn everyday cape, Natalie heard her friend's voice again—not quite so cold now, only courteous and formal. "I do apologize, Natalie, for dashing out this way, but I have to go. I promised Little Sinai to help with the sick child."

For a full minute or so after Miss Lib vanished out the front door, Natalie stood there, feeling the uncommon weakening desperation change to a far more familiar, far more manageable anger. Then, the old determination in full force again, she began to climb the stairs to the second floor of the handsome house which Burke had built with his own dear hands.

The door to Mary Cowper's room was closed again today, but Natalie, now so intimate with the grieving girl, turned the china knob softly and went on in, saying only, "It's Natalie."

Standing, as usual, at the same tall window that gave view out into the little grove where Natalie's infant son was buried, Mary Cowper did not turn around to face her, but said just above a whisper, "I—I've just found out this morning that I—have to see Stuart—one more time. I could tell by the tone of your voices, even with my door shut, that you were pleading with Mama downstairs. You might as well stop trying. She won't change her mind now. Not Mama."

For a long time neither spoke, then Natalie said, also just above a whisper—she and Mary Cowper often whispered these days—"I brought a page from a letter Mary Elizabeth Huger wrote to Kate Mackay. I let your mother read it. I was sure she'd be so humiliated that people like the Hugers were really making fun of her and Uncle W.H. that—"

"No!" Mary Cowper whirled around. "Nothing will ever change them and you make it harder for me when you keep trying, Natalie! I know you're the only one willing to stand up for me, but stop it, please. There's only one thing you can do to help."

"What?"

"Go with me to Savannah for a visit. Mama agrees I do need to do a lot of shopping before Mr. Low gets back in this country and you haven't been in Savannah once since you came up here to live. The best thing you can do for me is to be on that train beside me when I go. *I am going.* I have to see Stuart once more. There's something I have to tell him. Something I have to be sure he knows."

Without even remembering that she should ask Burke's permission, Natalie blurted, "You know I'll go with you! And you might as well know, too, that I'm not giving up. You're not married to old Andrew Low yet."

Mary Cowper was looking straight at her now, her eyes swollen, her lovely young face twisted and splotched, but still incredibly beautiful. "No, I'm not married to him yet, but I'm going to be. I've promised Mama and I—I don't have any strength against her. Somehow, though, I know I'll be all right if I can just see Stuart once more. I'll try even harder to memorize his face this time, the way his eyes crinkle when he laughs, his mouth, his fine straight nose. Can you understand that? Until this morning, I've just been—letting the pain control me. I haven't found a single way until now that I might be able to go through with my parents' plan—and not die in the process." She took a step toward Natalie. "But God did give us a way to remember. To remember so clearly that we can—almost believe we're being kissed by—other lips." A pathetic little note of hope was in her voice now. "I have a very fine memory, Natalie. I've always been quick to memorize anything. I just hadn't thought of how important it could be—until now."

When Natalie moved quickly toward her, arms out, Mary Cowper stepped away.

"All right," Natalie said finally. "We'll go to Savannah *if* you can convince your mother to let you go knowing Stuart's working there now. It's your job to wangle her permission, but I've just had another good, solid idea. Miss Lorah's on our side. Oh, she won't butt in, but if I ask her to, she'll go with us, and if she's along, I think Miss Lib will let you go."

Mary Cowper's large, dark eyes brightened. "Oh, yes! She trusts Miss Lorah. Are you sure she's on—our side? No, I've got to stop thinking that way! There can't be—sides. I've promised to obey my parents and I'm going to do it. But, yes, if Miss Lorah's along, I'm sure

Mama won't feel she has to go, too. Am I terrible not to want my own mother along?"

"You have no choice," Natalie said firmly. "If she went, everything would be spoiled. She wouldn't let you out of her sight long enough even to wave at Stuart across the street!"

For a time Mary Cowper paced nervously back and forth across her bedroom. Then she stopped pacing, a deep frown creasing her forehead. "Oh, Natalie, won't a man have to escort us there on the train? Do you suppose there's a chance Burke might do it?"

"No, I don't. He's got to finish that dumb store in Cartersville by March or break his contract. But what's wrong with your own brother, Henry? He's twenty now and Kate Mackay wrote that the Gordons are back in Savannah. Henry will jump at the chance to see Cliffie Gordon. You know he will."

She hadn't seen any but the sickliest smile on Mary Cowper's face in so long, Natalie couldn't help smiling herself when her friend's perfect features really did light up. "Natalie, you're wonderful! Henry's pretty stuffy. He thinks I'm stupid to have fallen in love with someone beneath me—oh, yes, Henry thinks just the way Mama does—but he is in love with Cliffie Gordon and I know he won't notice what I do once we get there. He'll have to ignore me, because I am not going to let anything stop me from seeing Stuart! And I want *time* with him, too. Not just a glimpse. It all came clear to me this morning before the sun came up. If I can be with him just once more, I'll—be able to—to—" Now she rushed to hug Natalie. "Put your arms around me and tell me my plan will work, please!"

"It will, Mary C.! You just watch me make it work. And you don't have to mention anything to your mother at all today. Let me convince Miss Lorah first. You'll need her promise to go when you bring up the plan with Miss Lib."

"Will Mrs. Plemmons agree?"

Natalie gave Mary Cowper a playful spank. "I'm her employer, don't forget."

Mary C. actually laughed a little. "She has a mind of her own, don't you forget."

"Burke will back me up."

"What if Burke won't let you go with me?"

"He doesn't *let* me do things! We discuss."

Fear flashed back into Mary Cowper's dark eyes. "What if he doesn't want you to go?"

"Oh, he won't want me to go. I already know that. Burke hates me out of his sight. I hate it when he's out of my sight, too, but we don't keep each other in jail."

"You think I'm in jail, don't you?"

"You are. And your mother is your jailer!"

"My papa agrees with her about—Mr. Low."

"Not really. I mean, with the proper persuasion, Uncle W.H. could be switched to our side."

"No, he couldn't."

"Why not?"

"He—he no longer has a good political base up here in the old Cherokee country."

"Nonsense. There are Democrats behind every tree up here!"

"Not the right kind, Papa says. He's a States' Rights Democrat. The people up here are mostly Union Democrats. They don't ever want to see the Union break up."

"Well, neither does Uncle W.H. I heard him tell Burke the other night that he hopes and prays that the Northern Democrats begin to see that strength lies in the union of all the states."

"I know, but—oh, Natalie, sometimes I think a lot boils down to the fact that Papa gets so nervous—almost angry—at the thought of abolition."

Natalie heaved a disgusted sigh. "Men are so stupid."

"Papa says he couldn't keep our land up here without our people. He agrees with the coastal planters in Savannah—in Chatham County—about keeping slavery. Mama says he could be elected to the State Legislature next year from Chatham County a lot easier than from up here in Cass. If—if I'm married to Andrew Low, I'd—I'd live in his fine house on Lafayette Square and Papa would have a family residence in Chatham County."

Natalie flounced across the room toward the door. "I refuse to believe anything so—so crass about Uncle W.H.! He's been far too busy writing his book on Austria for the last two years to think much about politics here. You can't accuse him of letting politics spoil your life! I thought you were loyal to your father."

"I am loyal to Papa. I wouldn't be willing to obey him and Mama if I weren't."

"Sometimes it's downright foolish to obey parents," Natalie said. "And this is one of those times."

"But—I have to obey them!"

"Why?"

"Because I just can't face the trouble I'd cause in our family if I–if I–"

She broke off in hard sobs and Natalie rushed back to her.

"Mary Cowper, listen to me. Your heart's too broken to think straight. You're even suspecting your own father of loving his political career more than he loves you and I know that can't be true!"

After a moment Mary C. got control enough to say, "Papa–loves me all right. Mama, too. I–I guess they're both just too old to remember how it was all those years ago when–they were young, and in love."

Natalie took a deep breath. "Mary Cowper, we have to keep first things first. I know you think you're going to give in to them, but this minute other things need to be thought through. You've made one excellent, quite sound decision. *You have to see Stuart again.* We're going to Savannah so you can do just that. For right now, that's the only thing we need to think about. Actually, if you want the truth, I was beginning to feel a little guilty for always making my parents come way up here to see me. Burke won't want me to go, but he'll understand. And we're going. Miss Lorah, too. I can manage her most of the time. We'll take Callie, of course, so I'll need Miss Lorah. And Henry will jump at the chance to see Cliffie Gordon. See how everything is falling into place? All you have to do is get your parents' permission. All you have to do is move one mountain. I'll move all the others."

Mary C. tried to smile. "It will be a mountain, all right, but I'll–try."

At the door, Natalie turned back to her. "I think you should know that I haven't given up on getting you married to Stuart."

"No! No, Natalie. Don't ever say that again!"

For a long moment, Natalie just looked at her. There was so much agony and pain in Mary Cowper's face, she looked almost old. Unable to think of anything to say that might help, Natalie quietly opened the door and left, closing it softly behind her.

FOUR

One of the things five-year-old Willow Browning liked best was to skip along beside Grandfather Mark all the way to the Savannah post office in the Customs House on Bull at Bay Street and all the way back to their handsome brick, Federal-styled house on Reynolds Square, where she lived with her mama and papa and Grandpa Mark and Grandma Caroline. Willow even liked going outside with Grandpa Mark on a freezing day like this one in January.

"We fooled 'em, didn't we, Grandpa?" she shouted up to him as they hurried around the corner into the familiar street where their house stood. "We fooled 'em, didn't we? Old Momie and old Grandmomie can't tell us what to do if it isn't what we want to do, can they?"

Laughing down at her, Grandfather Mark Browning squeezed the small hand he had scarcely let go since they left home half an hour earlier. "You sound more like your Aunt Natalie every day," he said. "I guess what you mean is that we're almost home again with the mail and neither of us froze to death."

"Old Momie said we'd freeze. Old Grandmomie Caroline said we'd freeze—straight!"

"Don't you mean—stiff, darling?" he asked. "I don't think your grandmother said we'd freeze *straight*. I think she must have said we'd freeze *stiff*. And we're not even brittle."

"What's brittle? What's brittle, Grandpa?"

"Well," he answered in his play-solemn voice, "brittle is—brittle."

"Like peanut brittle?" she asked, swinging hard on his hand.

"I guess so, yes. Anything that's really cold or that breaks easily is brittle."

"Brittle, brattle, brittle," she chanted. "Laugh some more! I like it when you laugh."

"I think your mother and grandmother thought we might turn into icicles and break on a cold day like this. But as you said, we fooled 'em." He tucked the bundle of letters they'd just picked up under one arm, leaving both hands free so he could pretend to examine Willow's mittened fingers. "See? You don't have a single brittle finger!"

Again her laughter pealed out into the cold morning air, and from sheer delight at being with him, she whacked him on the forearm.

"Now, that was exactly like your Aunt Natalie, young lady."

"Did Aunt Natalie hit people when she was little like me?"

"Indeed she did and it wasn't very ladylike either."

"We got a letter from Aunt Natalie," she reminded him, dancing along the street, still holding tightly to his hand.

"That's right, we did, and I can almost not wait till we get home so I can read it aloud to everybody."

"Does Aunt Natalie still hit people sometimes?"

"Oh, I don't think so. She's a grown-up lady. She may still want to now and then. I don't see her very often, you know."

"Aunt Natalie likes me!"

"She surely does. Everyone likes you, Miss Willow Browning."

"Do they like me because I'm so pretty with light curly hair like my mama's?"

"Well, your beauty is part of the reason, but people really like other people because there's good down inside."

"Oh, I'm good inside," the child announced. "I'm as good, Mama says, as my dead Cherokee grandmother. I'm named Willow like she was. Only Mama says Grandmother Green Willow had black, straight, Indian hair like my dead Uncle Ben."

"That's right, honey," he said.

"Is—sad what you are now, Grandpa?"

They had stopped before the steep stone steps that led up to their wide, white front door. "Do you want a ride, Willow?"

"Yes," she said, jumping up and down. "Give me a ride all the way to the top! I'll hit the door knocker myself!"

In the spacious entrance hall of the elegant, softly lighted house, Mary Browning had a little trouble persuading Willow to go upstairs with old Gerta, the German nurse, for a nap. Mary won the discussion with a promise to tell Willow when she woke up exactly what Aunt Natalie had written.

"The walk and the cold air made her sleepy," Mary explained, joining the older Brownings and her husband, Jonathan, in the ornate, handsomely corniced family drawing room for the sharing of the always welcome letter from Mary's old home in the upcountry of north Georgia. "I do hope Natalie has lots of news about how things are up there," she added, sitting on a footstool at Jonathan's feet. "I'm sure they've had snow at Etowah Cliffs this month. Snow is so beautiful."

"Don't tell me you miss snow, too, Mary dear," her mother-in-law said, shivering.

"You bet she misses it, Mama," Jonathan said with his gentle smile. "I heard her tell Miss Eliza last week she'd give almost anything to wake up to the world all white—just one morning."

"Miss Eliza laughed at me," Mary said cheerfully. "She also said I sounded like Natalie. Read Natalie's letter to us, Papa Mark!"

"Please do, Mark," Caroline said. "After all, when Natalie gets around to writing a letter, something is usually afoot. What's the date on it?"

"She wrote it on the tenth of January. Burke must have mailed it in Cartersville on the eleventh. This is only the sixteenth. Even counting last Saturday when the train doesn't run, that's pretty fast delivery, isn't it?"

"Yes, it is," Jonathan said. "But go on, read, sir. Read. I have to get back to the office."

His new gold spectacles in place, Mark began to read: " 'Dear One and All . . . I know I'm late as usual responding to your letter which we got right after Christmas, but Callie is still a handful and I've been so distressed over Mary Cowper—I'm still so distressed over her that I can't think straight enough to write anything very sensible.' "

"When was my sister *ever* 'very sensible'?" Jonathan asked with a grin. Then he apologized. "I shouldn't joke. We're all distressed for poor little Mary C. I know I am."

"Sh, darling," Mary whispered. "Let's just listen."

" 'It is absolutely cruel,' " Papa Mark went on reading, " 'what Miss

Lib and Uncle W.H. are doing to their helpless, heartbroken daughter, but when I see you, I'll go into more of the dreadful details. *We are coming to Savannah!'* "

Mama Caroline gasped. "Who's coming to Savannah? Surely not our daughter after all these years!"

"Hush, Mama," Jonathan said. "Let him finish."

" 'We are coming to Savannah soon, and when I say we, I mean Mary Cowper, Henry (to escort us), Miss Lorah, Callie, and your only daughter, Natalie Browning Latimer. A visit from me is long overdue and I absolutely have to do something to save my dear friend Mary C. from a fate far worse than sudden death.' "

"I knew it," Caroline said. "Something is afoot. I'm sorry for Mary Cowper, too, but her marriage to Andrew Low is certainly none of Natalie's business—or ours."

"At least Natalie will be right here in town, Mama. Whatever my sister has in mind," Jonathan said, "you'll have more than the usual control over her."

"What gave you the idea that anyone ever has control over Natalie, son?"

"Mr. Burke does pretty well," Mary offered. "At least most of the time."

"He's the only one," Mark said with a half-smile. "I wonder how Eliza Anne happened to agree to let Mary Cowper come with Natalie?"

"Why not read the remainder of the letter?" Caroline wanted to know. "Natalie might even tell us."

"I don't think so, darling," Papa Mark said, scanning the single-page. "There's only one more short paragraph and here it is: 'Of course, Mary Cowper and I will be doing a lot of shopping for her wedding, which, if I have anything to say about it, will be far different from the one Miss Lib's planning on. Our train will arrive on Friday, January 20, unless we have another heavy snow. My love to everyone and I'll see you soon, Natalie Browning Latimer.' "

"Is that all, Mark?"

"That's all. But, darling, what blessed news! Our little girl's coming to see us—and bringing Callie."

"And Miss Lorah," Mary breathed. "Oh, I'm so glad Miss Lorah will come! She never saw a city in her whole life before. She told me many times that she never expected to see a fine, big, bustling city like Savannah. I love Miss Lorah Plemmons so much!"

"And I might as well warn you," Jonathan said, "that I'm taking some time away from business to show her everything there is to see."

"Miss Eliza Mackay will want to go with you, Jonathan," Mary said eagerly. "She and Miss Lorah are close."

"Yes, yes, they seem to be," Caroline said with a slight frown, her mind, Mary thought, on what Natalie might be scheming about, not really on showing Miss Lorah anything.

When her mother-in-law stood up, Mary went to her. "Can I get something for you, Mama Caroline? Don't frown. I'll help with everything to do with their visit."

"I know you will, Mary, and there'll be a mountain of work. If they're all coming this Friday, there's not much time at all. You and I will have to plan menus, see that Gerta checks linens—the bed in our guest room needs a new slat. Mark, we'll have to entertain. That means guest lists to make. Oh, I hope it warms up outside. Shopping in this cold wind will be—"

"Wait a minute, dearest," Mark said, rising to take her arm. "Natalie and Miss Lorah won't expect such royal treatment, although I'm all for it. I just don't want you to get tired again. We can't take any chances on your congestion coming back."

Standing too now, Jonathan kissed Mary and hurried to the hall for his heavy coat. "That's right, Mama," he called back. "Sister won't even want any big dinners or—"

"Whether she wants them or not, I intend to entertain for her and for Mary Cowper. Miss Lorah, too, of course. Mark, don't be gone long. You and I have planning to do."

"I'll be home early, I promise, but I have to go now. William Mackay is dropping by the office to give me a ride in his carriage for my daily visit with Miss Eliza. I'll try to make the visit short." He kissed her lightly on the forehead. "No more frowns. We've too much to look forward to."

Poor Mama Caroline, Mary thought, as Jonathan and his father left the house. I wish she wouldn't worry so much about dinner parties and things. She's very good in her heart, but she worries about what Savannah people will say and this time I know she's uneasy that Miss Lorah might do wrong at the table as I did at my first dinner party. Miss Lorah might do wrong, but it won't worry her. She sees what people are, not what they do—right or wrong. Climbing the stairs to look in on Willow, she vowed to pray hard for Mama Caroline to enjoy the visit and count on Miss Eliza Mackay to smooth over the rough places. Miss Eliza *and*

Natalie. Oh, I'll hug Natalie a lot when she gets here. She's good now and my friend. The last time we visited her, she even hugged me back.

Standing beside Willow's tiny bed, Mary looked down at her sleeping daughter—curly-haired, so fair of skin—and marveled that the child had one drop of Cherokee blood coursing through her little veins. She did have, though, and she had Mary's Indian mother's name. Mama Caroline had objected only a little when she and Jonathan named their first child Willow and Mary knew her mother-in-law had agreed out of relief because the baby did not look Indian. She smiled to herself now, her thoughts leaping curiously to poor, pretty, young Mary Cowper Stiles, who had always been so kind to her even before she and Jonathan were married. It wasn't a bit like Natalie to leave Mr. Burke for only a family visit. She has a scheme for Mary C. Oh, dear. Only God knows what it is. She took a deep breath. But He does know. He does.

FIVE

"*Mama's going* to be overjoyed when she hears about our company from the upcountry," William said as he and Mark stepped onto the Mackay porch an hour or so later. "I expect the door's open. Mama'll be expecting us. My sisters are making calls this afternoon, both all gussied up in new duds from hat to shoes." Inside the front hall, he called, "Mama? Mark's here."

"Good of you to buy them both new outfits," Mark said, following William into the familiar house.

"You know Sarah never liked me much, but if I'd bought new Christmas duds for Kate and not for her, I'd never have heard the last of it."

"William? Mark? I'm in the parlor," Miss Eliza called. "Come in. I've been waiting for you."

They both embraced her and Miss Eliza gave Mark an extra squeeze and a pat. "Sit down, sit down. I think I must have been dozing," she apologized. "I should have met you on the porch. We need another log, William. Not a big one. I was reading today's *Georgian*," she went right on. "Trying to. Old ladies should not try to master that fine print. I always doze off." She motioned Mark toward her late husband's worn leather chair. "I was just trying to figure out the news about Senator Stephen Douglas's 'popular sovereignty' bill, Mark."

Mark and William exchanged grins as William tossed a short green oak log onto the fire. Both men were aware that she was comfortable enough with them to go right on with her thoughts as though they hadn't just come in.

"Since the Compromise of 1850," she mused, "we've had relative peace in the country over slavery, it seems to me. Why in the name of all that's sane and sensible do these men have to keep pushing to settle the Western territories so fast? Doesn't it just keep the whole trouble stirred up North and South? Southern planters want to push west the same as Northerners, you know. They'll want to take their people with them."

"I told you what I think, Mama," William said, using the old poker to settle the fresh log into place. "Senator Douglas has a good bill. It lets folks decide for themselves whether or not they take their own property west."

"I know what you think, William. I'm asking Mark. I can read what the South thinks about the Douglas bill. It's plainly in favor."

"I'm afraid I haven't had time to read the *Georgian* yet today," Mark said. "I know what they're calling Manifest Destiny—push west, push west—is sweeping the country. The need to decide whether a cross-country railroad will take the northern route to terminate in Chicago or the southern route to end in New Orleans could be at the heart of all the current argument. Of course, Douglas's bill would repeal the old Missouri Compromise since the Nebraska territory is north of 36° 30'. It could cause more trouble if the people who move west are allowed to decide for themselves whether to own slaves or not. The future is left up in the air. To me it plainly marks Kansas for slavery. But Douglas hasn't got his bill passed yet."

"I think Democrat Douglas wants to stir up a little interest in President Pierce's administration by all this," William said. "So far, except for prosperity, Pierce is flatter than a flitter as President." He laughed a little. "You can't tell me Douglas isn't looking toward a possible bid for the White House himself."

"New states and new territories are fine," Miss Eliza said, not really listening to William, "so long as organizing them doesn't stir up trouble over whether they're slave or free."

"That's like expecting water to run uphill, Mama."

As though William had said nothing, she went on, deep in her own thoughts. "I remember Robert Lee's words when he was here a few years ago. It's as though I can still see the dear boy, still hear what he said about Congress that night, right across the hall there in the dining room."

As though to humor her, William said, "We know Colonel Lee's low opinion of all politicians, Mama. But go on, tell us what you remember about that night."

"What I recall most plainly," she said, then stopped to give Mark an almost apologetic smile. "It was before poor Caroline lost control of herself over the ugly issue. Robert Lee spoke of the danger politicians face taking unto themselves the awesome task of passing or rejecting laws–laws that bless or rip apart people's daily lives. Lee hates the idea of being political, but he knows the risks politicians take. In spite of the quiet we've had since 1850, the Kansas-Nebraska bill could bring back the ugliness."

"You're borrowing trouble, Mama," William chided. "Even if he is chairman of the all-powerful Committee on Territories, Senator Douglas hasn't gotten his bill passed yet." William turned toward Mark. "Go on, tell her the good news!"

Beaming, Mark announced that he and Willow brought home a letter from Natalie this morning. "She's actually coming to Savannah!"

"Natalie's coming?" Miss Eliza's face lighted, then she frowned. "Oh, where are my manners, Mark? I'm so ashamed, dear boy. I must have fallen asleep trying to figure out Senator Douglas's bill and jumped right into it without even asking about anyone in your family. Is Mary all right today? Caroline? Jonathan? I take it little Willow is fine or she wouldn't have gone with you to the post office in this frigid weather . . ."

Reaching to pat her hand, Mark laughed. "They're all well, thank you. Miss Lorah Plemmons is also coming with Natalie, along with your granddaughter, Mary Cowper–and my other grandchild, Callie!"

"Why, that's the best news ever! *When*, Mark?"

"This Friday night." He glanced at the mantel clock. "Oh, say, I'd better get home. I promised Caroline not to stay long because she's already making guest lists." He gave Miss Eliza a sly grin. "You know Lorah Plemmons and my frontier daughter will both expect to be entertained like visiting royalty. Maybe I should say Natalie will be prepared to grit her teeth and go through several functions," he joked. "It's Miss Lorah who will be expecting them."

Mark couldn't remember when Miss Eliza had laughed so heartily. She was seventy-six and although quite well most of the time, he'd noticed lately that she seemed almost pensive. She was not pensive now.

The idea of Caroline getting all steamed up over fancy menus and guest lists for Miss Lorah Plemmons had struck her funny.

Still amused, Miss Eliza said, "Miss Lorah will come, I suppose, because Natalie wants her to, but she'd chuckle all over at the thought of poor Caroline fussing with dinner parties for her. Caroline only means to be doing the kind thing, though. I'll let you go, Mark. Caroline is a perfect hostess." When he stood, she took his hand. "Nothing's wrong to—occasion the sudden visit, is it?"

"Not with Natalie or Burke or Callie," he said, and stopped.

"Will Burke escort them?"

"Oh, I'm so excited, I forgot to tell you that your own grandson, Henry Stiles, is escorting them."

"Henry," she said, pleased. "My goodness, little Cliffie Gordon will be breathless over that bit of news when I tell her during my morning call tomorrow! Your father's hunch was right, William," she added, the faraway look again in her eyes. "You know he always said he had one of his hunches that someone in the Gordon family would marry a Mackay."

"I thought that was Mrs. Gordon's husband, W.W., who had that hunch, Mama."

She tossed her hand airily. "Well, maybe so. I tangle at times. No matter. The hunch was right. And oh, now they can at least have a good long visit together, Henry and Cliffie. Cliffie is really lovely these days. Mark, perhaps Caroline is thinking of giving a dinner party to announce their engagement!"

Mark laughed. "It could be that she is, even though those two have been engaged, according to Henry, for years."

Not looking at either of them again, Eliza Mackay said, "Eight years. Henry asked her to marry him when he was about twelve and Cliffie was seven or eight. Can you believe Henry is twenty and Cliffie sixteen?"

"This is all very pleasant," Mark said, "but I really must go." He bent to kiss Miss Eliza's graying, still curly hair. "Keep Senator Douglas in check now until I see you tomorrow, lovely lady."

"Be sure to read your copy of the *Georgian* today, Mark," she said. "I'm older than the country, you know, so I still tend to think that any decision the people make might be a good one. I do have some doubt, though, that letting *Southern* people decide whether or not the new territories are slave or free could cause a lot of our Northern friends to . . ."

"Get all riled up, Mama?" William asked, only half teasing. "They're already riled, but that doesn't stop me from hoping Douglas gets the bill through both houses. His 'popular sovereignty' would be a victory for us down here."

As though William had said nothing, Miss Eliza reached again for Mark's hand. "My mind flits about some, dear boy, and I know you do have to get home to Caroline, but—did Natalie say anything in her letter about my granddaughter, Mary Cowper, and—her marriage to Mr. Low?"

He had hoped the subject wouldn't come up. "Yes. Yes, she did. Natalie's got something up her sleeve, I'm afraid. You know she usually has."

He saw her look away again, as though sorting through her own thoughts. "Mary Cowper has always had a special place in my heart. There's just something so tender and sensitive about her. I—I wish the boy she loves were—a different sort of young man. I wish with all of me that Stuart Elliott were someone Eliza Anne and W.H. approved of."

Alone in the family drawing room with Caroline a short while later, Mark entered wholeheartedly into his wife's ideas for their social calendar. He longed for more family time without guests during Natalie's visit, but no longing of his had ever overshadowed his desire to please Caroline.

"You're being very patient about all this, Mark," she said, after tentative guest lists for high tea, a dinner party, and a large reception at the Pulaski Hotel had been jotted down. "Thank you. I'm sure they'll stay a few weeks. We'll have plenty of time just to be with Natalie and Callie. But isn't it too bad Mr. Low is still abroad? I'd so enjoy planning something in honor of Mary Cowper's engagement to such a prominent man."

"He won't be back until spring," Mark said, hoping not to have to discuss the prickly matter further. "Will you be helping Mary C. with trousseau shopping, dear?"

"Of course! Eliza Anne has written at length of her needs, of how much and how little the Stileses can spend. I'm sure, and so is Eliza Anne, that the Mackay sisters will insist upon being along when we shop, but as she reminded me, Sarah, in particular, has always thought W.H. to be far wealthier than he is. I think it was extremely hard for Eliza Anne not to come, too."

"I'm still surprised she didn't. Did she explain why?"

"Not very clearly. Something about granting Mary Cowper at least one desire of her heart. It seems the girl was quite adamant about wanting to feel grown-up now. Wanting to make her own trousseau choices. It's rather puzzling, really. And Eliza Anne did not elaborate."

An awkward silence fell between them. Not unpleasant, awkward. Mark's habit of the years took over. When one of those silences came, he had found it easier to let Caroline break it. They had seen eye to eye on most things—except the always incendiary issue of owning slaves. Caroline's strong defense of slavery had been the only subject which had meant trouble through the long years of their married life. She could no more change her feelings than he could change his own hatred of owning another human being. This matter had nothing to do with slavery, thank heaven. Still, he waited.

"I know what you're thinking, Mark."

He gave her a warm smile. "I'm not surprised. You have always known."

"You think Eliza Anne and W.H. are wrong to force their daughter to marry Andrew Low." When he said nothing, she sighed. "We can't let it come between us, my dear."

"How could it? It's certainly not our affair in any way."

"No, it isn't, but I know you think Mary Cowper should be allowed to marry that—Elliott boy, regardless of his questionable character."

"I don't think I've ever said as much."

"You don't need to. I know your tender, sympathetic heart. I also know that we permitted our own daughter to marry Burke when all signs pointed to disaster."

He laughed softly. "Aren't you glad we didn't meddle?"

"Yes. Burke's character wasn't in question, though. And don't remind me that Stuart Elliott is now a hardworking *assistant* bank teller. He's always drunk to excess and he does gamble. And he *is* only an assistant teller. How could he ever expect to support Mary Cowper, who's had everything she ever wanted?"

Now Mark sighed. "Everything except the one person she evidently wants to marry."

"We cannot know that's true! She's so . . ."

"Young? Not as young as Natalie when she knew she'd never love anyone but Burke."

"I was sure you'd say that. I also know Natalie has a reason for coming to Savannah aside from a visit to her parents. Mark, we can't allow her to interfere in any of this. Will you promise me you'll keep a close watch on her while they're all here? I know I'm being difficult to ask such a thing, but I also know how our daughter has kept you wrapped around her little finger all her life. I want you to make that promise. I . . ."

"Demand it?" he asked with another smile.

"No, I *beg* you not to let Natalie manipulate you again. She is set on rescuing Mary Cowper from Andrew Low and I don't want you involved in any way."

"Has Natalie told you that?"

"No, of course she hasn't. She wouldn't dare. She and I have a growing friendship by now, but it would never cross her mind to take me into her confidence on anything so–absurd as interfering in the wishes of the Stileses where their daughter's future is concerned. I want us to stay clear of it." When he again made no response, she added, "All right. Let's drop the subject. I've made myself plain–even if you haven't."

"Caroline," he said, his voice gentle, but now quite firm. "Do you hope Eliza Anne and W.H. succeed in their determination to marry the girl off to Andrew Low?"

"What I hope is entirely beside the point. What you and I do is not. I want us both to stay–acceptable in all this."

"And 'acceptable' means not to take Mary Cowper's feelings into consideration."

"That is not what I said! If her little heart is broken–even for a short time–I'll be ever so sorry. I just know that none of it is our affair."

SIX

Three seats in front of where Mary Cowper had chosen to sit alone with her tortured, excited thoughts, Natalie and Callie were looking out the window of the train when it chugged into the Central of Georgia station in Savannah on the clear Friday night of January 20. Wonder of wonders, Natalie thought, we're only about fifteen minutes late.

"Now, look carefully, Callie," she urged, when, hissing steam, its bell clanging, the engine ground to a stop before the low wooden station. "Grandfather Mark and Uncle Jonathan are surely out there waiting for us. Do you see them yet?"

"Yes, I see Grandpa Mark! I see Grandpa Mark, Mama—I see Uncle Jonathan, too. And a pretty lady! Who's she?"

"Well, move a little so I can get a good look. Oh, that's Henry's friend, Cliffie Gordon." Turning in her seat toward the one behind her where Henry and Miss Lorah had been sitting for the last fifty miles or so, Natalie shouted, "Henry! Your wish came true. Cliffie's out there—we see her!"

The young man responded with a big smile, as he climbed over Miss Lorah's knees and headed for the door of the coach.

"I wanta go with Henry," Callie yelled. "I wanta get off first with Henry!"

"Then go," Natalie laughed, "but do walk carefully. We've been sitting a long time, don't forget. Henry! Help Callie off the train. Those steps are too high for her."

"They are not," Callie shouted, already standing beside Henry waiting for the door to be opened. "I don't need any help! Grandpa will lift me down."

Natalie was up now in the narrow aisle beside Miss Lorah, looking first toward Callie, then back toward where Mary C. still sat huddled alone, not moving.

"I honestly think Callie forgets she's got a bad foot," Natalie muttered half to herself. "Are you terribly tired, Miss Lorah?"

"Haven't done a lick of work since late yesterday," the woman said, gathering up the various boxes and bundles piled around her feet. "Why would I be tired?" She stopped retying the string on the lunch box and looked up at Natalie. "I'm a little stiff, I reckon, but—mostly, I'm scared, Missy."

Natalie frowned. "Scared? Why on earth would you be scared?"

At work on the lunch-box string again, Miss Lorah said, "Wondering if I'll do right so far away from home around strangers."

Natalie laughed. "You? You're the last person I'd ever wonder about doing the right thing. Don't bother with that dumb box. It's got to be almost empty by now. Just leave it behind on the train."

"Two chicken legs left in it!" Miss Lorah chuckled. "Scrawny little legs. Nobody even tried to eat 'em. Most likely belonged to one of those little brown pullets that used to run all day long like there was a dog after 'em."

"We've got so much luggage, I insist you leave the lunch box here."

"Never was one to waste food," Miss Lorah said, pulling a tight knot in the string.

"My father and Jonathan are waiting for us. Henry and Callie are already outside, but, Miss Lorah, I want you to listen carefully. Put down that dumb lunch box! Are you listening?"

"I'm listenin'. Shoot."

"I need you right away—just as soon as we're off the train. I need you to keep Callie and Mary Cowper busy talking or something the minute we've all said hello—as soon as we set foot on that platform. We're here because of Mary Cowper, don't forget. It's very important that I have a few minutes alone with my father and Jonathan *before* we even get into Papa's carriage. Is that clear? I have to lay my plans to get Mary Cowper alone with Stuart and I'll need both Papa and my brother."

Still seated, Miss Lorah looked up at her and grinned, then said, "You're getting me mixed up in your scheme whether I want to or not, is that it?"

"Not at all. I'm in charge. Your part is just to keep Mary C. and Callie from interrupting me while I'm giving instructions to Papa and Jonathan."

"Poor little Mary Cowper's not going to bother you. It's Callie I'll have trouble keeping away from her grandpa."

"But you'll figure out something. You always do. Now, come on. It's time for us to get off. I'm going back to Mary Cowper, to tell her to stay close to you, no matter what."

Mark hugged his daughter until she pulled away, laughing, but he thought her laughter lacked its usual lilt. She seemed preoccupied. Glad to be back home, yes, but after a quick inquiry about the health of all the Mackays, her mother, Mary, little Willow, and a rather pointed and unnecessary suggestion that Henry and Cliffie wait together at the far end of the platform while bags were unloaded, Natalie pulled him and Jonathan to one side. When Callie broke away from Miss Lorah and ran to where the three stood, Natalie scolded her and sent her right back.

"But she's glad to see her old grandfather," Mark complained. "Can't what you have to say wait until we're in the carriage, Natalie?"

"No, it cannot."

"Papa," Jonathan teased, "haven't you met my sister yet? Funny, but I thought you knew her better than that. All right, Natalie, what's your plot this time? And hurry. Mama and Mary are waiting for us and we still have to take Mary Cowper to the Mackays on our way home."

"I know all that, Jonathan," Natalie said, annoyed. "But what I have to say is of the utmost importance."

"Oh, I'd never doubt that, Sister."

"Hush. If you want me to hurry, just hush. Papa, we have to act decisively and carefully in all we do—for poor Mary Cowper's sake."

"And just what is it we're doing?" Mark asked.

"She simply *has* to see Stuart Elliott *alone* and that means you'll have to use your influence at the bank so he can get free time. Lots of free time—several hours, maybe. So, first thing tomorrow morning, I want you to go to your bank—"

"My bank?" Mark interrupted. "I am on the board of directors, but the Bank of State of Georgia is far from *my* bank, darling. Besides, it's closed on Saturdays." He thought a minute. "Of course, I do know Elliott's boss."

"Then I want you to see him early Monday and tell him—well, tell him something about—oh, tell him anything that will get him to let Stuart leave work at least by noon Monday or no later than Tuesday. Tell him you need Stuart to—to—"

"To what?"

"Oh, Papa, don't be stubborn! Tell him you need him for anything that sounds plausible. I know. You and Stuart's father, Senator Elliott, were friends." She pursed her lips, thinking hard. "Tell him you need to have a fatherly talk with Stuart. That you promised his dead father—something like that should work fine."

Mark grinned at her. She hadn't changed much at all. Thirty-one-year-old Natalie still expected her father to handle everything, he thought, and was rather pleased. Surely her imagination was as wild as ever.

"Don't just smile, Papa! I'm sure whoever Stuart's boss is will let him go at once if you tell him you need to keep a promise to his father."

"And you don't think he might consider it a little strange that I've waited over a quarter of a century to have this fatherly talk with young Elliott? If I remember correctly, Senator Elliott died around 1828 or '30."

"This is certainly no time to be picky," Natalie scolded. "I'm sure you'll think of something. You've heard, as has everyone evidently but Miss Lib Stiles, that Stuart is really trying to live a responsible life now—he's working very, very hard at the bank, Mary Cowper says. Say you feel it's the right time for you to spend a few hours with him in order to —to encourage him in his admirable new resolve! There, how's that?"

"Well, I suppose it might work."

"Go on, Papa, give it a try," Jonathan urged. "You know Sister won't let up until you do."

Natalie gave her brother a quick kiss on the cheek, then threw her arms around Mark. "Oh, thank you, Papa! I can't wait to tell Mary Cowper that so far our plan is working just fine. Now, come on. We mustn't just stand here. It's highly important that we keep our arrival—all of it—running smoothly, so no one will suspect anything. Especially not Mama."

"We're not to mention any of this even to Mama?" Jonathan wanted to know.

"I said 'especially not Mama.' I'm sure she wants happiness for Mary Cowper as much as the three of us, but, well, in matters of parental affairs, Mama really can't be trusted. Miss Lib would draw and quarter me if she knew I was trying to help Mary Cowper and Mama always wants everyone's approval. Especially Miss Lib's."

After they left Mary Cowper, Henry, and Cliffie Gordon at the Mackay house on East Broughton, Natalie used every minute of her time on the drive to her family home on Reynolds Square convincing Jonathan to spend the entire day tomorrow—along with their mother and Callie—on a sightseeing tour with Miss Lorah. She was sure, dead sure, that Miss Lorah was on Mary Cowper's side in all this, but she was equally certain that the determined lady was not going to let it be known if she could help it. As her employer, Natalie informed her that she only expected her to be on hand to look after Callie and to want a tour of the city.

"Callie's never seen Savannah either," Natalie reminded her father and Jonathan. "So tomorrow, Papa, you can take care of business at the countinghouse. That way Jonathan will have a free day."

"I want Grandpa to go with us," Callie said, sleepy enough by now from the long trip not to be shouting her demands, but still definite. "I like you, Uncle Jonathan—but you come, too, Grandpa Mark. Miss Lorah, you want my grandfather to come, too, don't you?"

Lorah Plemmons said nothing.

"Someone has to take care of business, Callie," Mark said, entering in quite wonderfully, Natalie thought, as new plans formed in her busy mind. First thing tomorrow, she decided, I'll pay my respects to Miss Eliza and the Mackay sisters, give William his instructions in all this, and somehow find time alone to reassure Mary Cowper that our plan is working. That she *will* see Stuart again soon, and if I have anything to say about it, not for the last time either . . .

SEVEN

*A*fter breakfast on the following Monday, William Mackay left his mother's house with few questions asked because the merriment that goes with a visit was still in full sway. Having two of her grandchildren, Mary Cowper and her brother Henry, in the house had seemed a tonic for his mother. She was well for her years, but with no more exciting company than William and his two spinster sisters, Mama had tended at times to get a little vague. Not so with the young people there.

Of course, handsome Henry Stiles, a dead ringer for his father, hadn't been there much except to sleep. With Cliffie Gordon back in town after such a long time in the North, the attraction of the family had dimmed for him. He slept at the Mackay house, ate some meals there, but most of the time he was with the Gordon girl he planned to marry. There would be no problem with that marriage for sure. The Mackays, the Stileses, and the Gordons had been friends a long time. Today William's heart was heavy for Mary Cowper, especially since his talk with Natalie yesterday after church.

This was the second time William had gone looking for Stuart Elliott. The first time nearly ten years ago when Mary C. herself had begged him in a letter to find Stuart for her. To find him and assure him that she had been true to him for the more than two years she'd lived in

Vienna back in the days when her father was chargé d'affaires to Austria for President Polk. William had sneaked out of the house at night back then on some flimsy excuse and had found the young man a little drunk, gambling at the Savannah Men's Club. He was on his way to see Stuart today because Natalie had, "for old times' sake," so ordered.

In sight of the bank, William smiled, rather sadly, because for him sadness still, after nearly sixteen years, underlay everything. Sixteen years ago come June, his whole family—Virginia, his beloved wife, and his two children—had been lost at sea when the steamer *Pulaski* blew up. "Old times' sake" for William and Natalie would always matter to him, since Natalie, then only sixteen, had tried so desperately—tossing in the stormy sea herself—to save his infant son's life. Natalie Browning had always been a handful, but she would always hold a special place in William's heart. No one had thought it strange when, after Sunday dinner yesterday, Natalie had demanded that the two of them go for a walk alone. William had been sure that he was about to be given some Natalie orders. He was.

"I want you to go first thing Monday morning, William, to the Bank of the State of Georgia, where Stuart works," Natalie had said, "and tell him Mary Cowper is in town and that just as soon as I can manage everything, he'll be given time off from the bank to see her."

As usual, William's warning had gone unheeded: "Aren't you treading on dangerous ground, Natalie?"

"Not at all," she had said. "I'm rescuing Mary Cowper's future happiness! How would you have liked it if Miss Eliza and your father had forced you to marry someone else but Virginia? To marry an old woman who had nothing to offer you but money and—and the respect of Savannah's stupid business community?"

"There's nothing stupid about our business community," William had said, knowing she would also ignore that.

"Mary C. doesn't care about Andrew Low's old money or his old self or his fine new mansion on Lafayette Square! She's in love with Stuart Elliott. William, she loves him the way I love Burke, the way I know you still love Virginia!"

He did still love Virginia, would never, could never love another woman no matter how long he lived on this earth. And so he was heading for the bank today, to see the Elliott boy, to do what he could for Mary Cowper. Hard to believe his niece was twenty-one. William sensed that she did love Stuart Elliott. He also knew that Mary Cowper would go through with the wedding to Andrew Low because she wouldn't hurt her parents, wouldn't buck their demands. He also knew that if Eliza Anne and W.H. won out, if he and Natalie and Mary Cowper lost, the girl would do her level best to be a good wife to Low, a good mother to his two girls by his first wife—dead now for some five years. She would also do her best to be a good mother to any children she might give Low. Knowing Andrew as he did, William was also certain that poor little Mary Cowper wouldn't have many months of married life when she wasn't carrying a Low baby.

Climbing the bank steps, he breathed a wordless prayer that he'd find a way to know, even from the few minutes' talk he'd have with young Elliott, whether or not the boy really loved Mary Cowper. William had strong feelings that he did. One knowing look exchanged with Miss Lorah Plemmons at the dinner table yesterday made him think that the perceptive mountain lady, while seeming to hide behind her shyness at being in a bustling city like Savannah, was also rooting for Mary C. and young Elliott.

Along with Mark Browning, William, as a sizable stockholder in two southern railroads, including the Central of Georgia, was also a bank director and so was easily able to see Stuart Elliott alone in a storeroom at the rear of the bank.

"I'll get right to the point, Elliott," he said, sitting down on an empty crate. "Mary Cowper is in town. She got here late Friday with Natalie Browning Latimer, her child and housekeeper, and Mary C.'s brother Henry."

William's announcement plainly stunned the young man. For what seemed like more than a full minute, Stuart just stood there staring, seemingly unable to believe that Mary Cowper could be nearby.

Wanting more than ever to help the boy, William broke the silence: "Her parents did *not* come with her."

Stuart's relief showed only in the quick sag of his shoulders. It was cold in the storeroom, but tiny beads of perspiration broke on his upper lip. Slowly, he wiped his mouth with the back of his hand. He wiped it again, as though he needed more time to decide exactly what to say. William could not miss noticing how the young, slender hand trembled.

Finally Elliott spoke, almost in a whisper: "Why—why didn't she write me that she was coming?"

"I didn't ask about that," William said.

"But—Miss Lorah Plemmons's boy, Sam, always slipped my letters

to her—mailed hers to me—kept his promise to say nothing about them."
William waited patiently for Stuart to collect himself. "Back before
Mary Cowper went to Vienna, Sam was helping us out." An almost
pathetic half-smile softened the taut, handsome face. "You see, Mr.
Mackay, she traded Sam some of her prize arrowheads for the favors."

"Sam's a good fellow. Not too bright, I guess, but honest. Stuart?"

"Yes, sir?"

"You certainly look a lot better these days—healthier. Steady. I hear
you're doing well in your job here at the bank."

"Oh, I hope so! I'm really trying." A deep frown creased his forehead. "I don't know *why* I'm still trying, though. I've—already lost her."

For a long time, Stuart said nothing. William waited.

Then the boy turned abruptly to face him. "Mr. Mackay, sir, I know
I could—do anything for Mary Cowper—*anything*. Do you realize I
haven't had one single drink since early last spring because of her?
That's when she agreed to marry me. I just stopped cold turkey.
Stopped gambling, too. Began to save a little money after I got this job
as assistant teller." As though there was suddenly no more strength to
stand, he sank onto the big crate beside William. "Why do you think I go
on trying to change when I've lost my reason for living at all? Last fall
when I went up to Cass to see her, she broke our engagement." He gave
a bitter laugh. "I went in part to prove to her parents that I'd changed.
People in my hometown of Roswell were saying I looked better. Even
my stepfather said so. He and I almost—became friends." Stuart shook
his head slowly. "All the way on the train to Cassville, I had such high
hopes! I was sure the Stileses would begin to see that I did love her for
herself, that I'd do anything—anything to make her happy." For a long
moment, he fell silent, as though reliving the pain of his last visit to
Etowah Cliffs. "Oh, they were civil to me because they're—civilized
people. Poor Mary C. had to tell me herself that your sister and brother-
in-law were still forbidding her to marry me. Mr. Stiles, she said, offered
to tell me, but she wouldn't let me go through his kind of cold explanation." He was looking at William again, tears standing in his eyes. "She
wanted me to hear it from her. You see, she does love me, Mr. Mackay!"

William stood up. "I know she does, Stuart. I also know now for a
fact that you love her. I can't think of a way to let you know how sorry I
am about the way things turned out."

On his feet now, too, Stuart held out both hands, pleading. "Then
tell me—for God's sake, please tell me *why* did she come to Savannah?
Not to—taunt me. She loves me too much. But Mary Cowper doesn't

have the spine to go against her parents, so why did she come? She does love me." His face distorted with agony, he blurted quite loudly, "Even when she's forced to let—old man Low—violate her, she'll still love me! She'll be wanting me through every minute of his—"

"Stuart. Hush! If they're married, Low won't be violating her."

"Oh, yes, he will—because she loves *me!*"

His own heart torn by the boy's torment, William said, "I'm here this morning because Natalie claims that—that there's still some hope. I don't think there is, knowing my sister and her husband."

"Then, sir, why did you come?"

"I—I guess because I've always loved my niece, too. There's just something about her, a kind of sweetness, along with that strength in her that—"

"She doesn't have strength enough to buck her parents' dislike of me," Stuart interrupted.

"I know it looks that way. But it may take a lot more strength for people to do what they honestly feel they have to do than what they really *want* to do."

Now William fell silent. He hadn't yet been able to tell Stuart that Mary Cowper just had to see him once more. Holding her in his arms and then having to let her go could well drive the boy back to the brandy bottle—or worse. Cherokee Ben McDonald's suicide because he could never have Natalie shot like a bullet into William's mind. Still, he had to tell the young man. He'd promised Natalie to give Stuart the message.

"Mary Cowper came to Savannah, son, because she says she has to see you—once more. There's something she has to tell you." Stuart only stared at him. "Natalie hasn't given up hope," William went on. "She swears Mary C. has. What the poor girl thinks she needs to tell you, I haven't the faintest idea. Natalie doesn't seem a bit puzzled by it, but then, she's a woman, too. Can you—bear to see Mary Cowper again?"

Stuart turned his back, but said nothing.

"I—I feel sure I've never asked such a cruel thing of a man," William said at last. "I did promise, though. Maybe you're too young to understand how an old duffer about to turn fifty could love two young women like Natalie and Mary Cowper so much he'd dare ask such a mean favor." Until that second, his mission had not struck William as asking a favor of the boy. Now it did. "Stuart? Can you answer me? Could you bear to see her once more?"

Slowly, moving like an old man, Stuart turned around, actually steadying himself on the crate as he did so.

"Can you answer me, Stuart?"

"I have to—if she wants to see me," he whispered. "I'd do anything she asked. I can't help myself. But *how* do I see her? Where? When? It would have to be—in secret. I promised her father I'd never see her again . . ."

"Mark Browning made a promise to Natalie, too. He'll arrange with your employer for you to leave work at noon tomorrow. Natalie vows she'll clear the Browning house of everybody, including the servants. Mary Cowper will be there alone—waiting for you. The Brownings will be showing the city to Miss Lorah and their grandchild, Callie, then having dinner at our house. You and Mary C. should have two or three hours together. But, son, I want you to be sure about this. Can you go on here at the bank with your job, your own life, *after* you've seen her again?"

William's heart twisted at the boy's struggle to smile. "Sir, I can try. Who knows? Maybe, if there is a God, He'll strike me dead—right after I —lose her a second time. Then I won't have to try."

*R*ight after family breakfast the next morning, Natalie, on the pretext of indulging herself in a sentimental walk around the old neighborhood, managed to leave the Browning house by herself. Convincing Willow and Callie that she needed to go alone was even harder than convincing her mother, but she succeeded and a little before 9 A.M. she entered the Bank of the State of Georgia on Bryan Street and asked for Stuart Elliott.

As she watched him walk toward her across the big room, her own heart tightened. He looked so old! Oh, he was hurrying, his face expectant, but she saw no sign of happy anticipation as he strode toward her, both hands out.

"You did come," he gasped. "I had hoped you'd find a way to let me know about plans for this afternoon." The cynical laugh Miss Lib hated escaped him. "I didn't have much real hope—but here you are." He grasped her gloved hands.

"I told you before you left Cass that I'm on your side. I engineered this entire trip to Savannah for you and Mary Cowper."

"Was it your idea, Natalie?"

"No, it was hers. She simply had to see you again. I agreed. We're here. Mary Cowper will be at my family's house this afternoon waiting for you, Stuart, and she'll be alone. She and I have told the others she's visiting at the home of Anna Barnsley's aunt, Mrs. Taylor. You should have at least two, probably three hours alone with her. It's not very cold outside today, so I should be able to keep the sightseeing going for over an hour, then the whole lot of us will go to dinner with Miss Eliza at her house." She frowned, pulling her hands away. "We should appear to be having a business talk about banking or something."

He stepped back. "But how will I know exactly when it's safe to knock on your family's front door?"

"That's all arranged. Walk past once and make sure only one shutter in the drawing room at the front of the house is open. Just *one shutter*. Mary Cowper will have closed all the others as a signal to you. So, it's very simple. I can tell you're nervous and I certainly don't blame you, but you have to promise me one thing."

"Natalie, I'll promise anything!"

"Good. When you see Mary Cowper, *don't* look old and hopeless the way you looked just now when you crossed the lobby of this bank."

"But it *is* hopeless. Mr. William Mackay gave me no hope at all beyond—holding her in my arms just once more."

"Nonsense. Don't give up so easily. Be real with her. Tell her you can't live without her. That you agreed to let her break your engagement only because you were in enemy country—at her parents' house up in Cass. That you felt you didn't have a chance against their iron wills. But with her in Savannah on *your* territory, you don't intend to let her go again ever—not ever."

"Dear God, I wish I could take you seriously."

"You have to. If you love her you won't allow her to ruin her life—and yours—by marrying that rich old Andrew Low!"

"But she's *afraid* of her parents. She told me so herself."

"I don't care what she told you up there, this is today and she's here and she'll be waiting for you in less than three hours. Be strong, Stuart. You can save her, if you love her."

He was looking at Natalie now, his eyes wide. He was not daring or brash as he usually was, but wide-eyed, like a little boy, longing to believe. "Did—did she give you any hope, Natalie, that she'd—elope with me?" He grabbed her arm. "Tell me the truth. Did Mary Cowper give you any hope at all? Is that why you're here trying this risky business?"

With all her heart she longed to say yes. It was terribly important that Stuart go to Mary Cowper in a hopeful, confident state of mind. Her sweet friend was brave enough to face the horror of marrying a man she didn't love, but not once had Natalie ever known Mary Cowper to stand up to Miss Lib.

"I–I can't honestly say she told me she'd elope with you, but she *is* a woman now. Remind her of that. She's no longer a little girl and it's high time she stopped acting like one. Be strong, Stuart. Maybe you'd better use your arms more than you use words. Picture her lying beside that rich old man. Think of his hands on her–and be strong! Take what belongs to you. Mary Cowper *does* belong to you in her heart."

He turned away as though to hide his torment. "We'd never be welcome in her parents' home if she married me," he murmured. "That alone could end our love."

"Would it end your love for her?"

"No. Eventually, though, it could end hers for me. The Stiles family is–is like a fortress. Nothing penetrates it."

"But you will try?"

The smile he gave her was feeble, but it was a smile. "I'll try. Not because I'm strong. Because I can't help myself."

Back at her parents' house, Natalie went straight upstairs to the room her mother had prepared for Miss Lorah, knocked, then went on in without waiting.

"You don't mind if I barge right in, do you?" she asked, tossing her cape on the bed beside the new corset Miss Lib had made Lorah Plemmons buy in Cassville before they left.

Miss Lorah stood in the middle of the floor, clad only in her muslin underclothes, minus even one petticoat. Laughing, she said, "What if I did mind, Missy? You're here. I reckon you've seen me like this before. I was just standing here eyeing that–harness over there." She nodded toward the corset. "So far, I can't make head nor tail of it."

"You never wore a corset before?"

"That's right, but if you'll help me, I'm gonna wear it today or know the reason why. Did you enjoy your walk?"

Relieved to be reminded that she was supposed to have been strolling around on the unusually warm January day, recalling childhood memories in the neighborhood, Natalie said, "Oh, oh, yes. I most certainly did. I even went by my old school, Reverend White's Academy. Of course, I didn't go inside. I'm not that sentimental about school days, but I did pass by. It looked the same. Jonathan went there, too, when he was a boy."

Chuckling, Miss Lorah said, "Don't bother to try to fool me, Missy. Save your story for your parents. I know you didn't go out by yourself just to remember old times. Did you get everything worked out for Mary Cowper and her young man to see one another while we're out showing me the city?"

Hands on hips, Natalie said, "You're mean, Miss Lorah. You can be very mean, you know."

"I expect so."

Reaching for the corset, Natalie announced that she'd get even with her for being so smart as to catch on to where she'd really been this morning by lacing the harness up so tight there'd be no room even to chuckle. "You chuckle with your tummy anyway, did you know that?"

"Lord, help me," Miss Lorah said as Natalie slipped the corset over the graying head and began to pull at the long cotton laces. "Whew! Too tight!"

"Not yet—I'm just getting it into place. Now, take a deep breath and hold it."

After only two tightening yanks, Miss Lorah yelled, "Stop! Missy, do you hear me? You're pinchin' me in two!"

"I am not. If I know Mama, she'll want you to get out of the carriage at every fine church we pass, so you have to be dressed appropriately." Pulling with all her might so that she grunted when she spoke, Natalie explained: "Being in—Savannah—means—wearing one of these—torturous things—and that's that."

"Whoo-ee," Miss Lorah yelled. "Not one more yank, Missy. Do you hear me? Let go, let go . . ."

"Not yet. I have to tie the laces." That done, she laughed merrily. "Now, that wasn't so bad, was it? I won't guarantee it will be that comfortable all through our tour and dinner at Miss Eliza's, but—"

Standing stiff as a board, Miss Lorah looked down at where she was accustomed to finding her little round stomach. "Where'd it go? Untie me, Missy! You've got my stomach pushed against my backbone! How'm I supposed to get my breath all day?"

"Give yourself time to get used to it. Here, let me slip the corset cover and these petticoats over your head. Then once you see yourself in the new blue flowered dress Miss Lib bought for our trip, you'll see how lovely you look!"

Mumbling through the thick folds of petticoats as they came plummeting down over her head one at a time until there were four of them,

Miss Lorah said, "What's an old woman over fifty-five want with bein' lovely? I'll take my comfort any day."

She was fussing mightily, but Natalie noticed, as she slipped the new dress down over the upraised arms, that Miss Lorah was also laughing at herself. "There," Natalie said, reaching to tie the pale blue sash. "Now go sit down at the dressing table and I'll help you fix your hair."

"Fix my hair?" Miss Lorah gasped. "Child, if I can't pin up my own hair, I'd as soon be in my grave!"

Undeterred, Natalie began to brush the lightly wavy, graying hair, chattering away about how impressed Miss Lorah was going to be when she saw the new Customs House and Christ Church, where her family attended, but that best of all was the Independent Presbyterian Church, where Miss Eliza Mackay's husband had been a member. "They don't call people members in Christ Church," she rattled on. "They're communicants, but at Presbyterian and Methodist churches and I guess other kinds, too, people who go there are called members."

"I know a thing or two about church members," Miss Lorah said. Then she yelled. "You're scalping me, Missy!"

"I am not. Turn your head a little. I need to make a kind of puff over your ears. Right side first. Were you a member of a church in Ellijay? Miss Lib keeps worrying because there isn't an Episcopal church near enough for her to attend. When her father, Robert Mackay, died, they all went back to the Episcopal church here in Savannah. It's a most impressive building. It was designed by Mr. James Hamilton Couper of Hopeton plantation down the coast, but Papa and I always thought the steeple on the Independent Presbyterian Church was—"

"Would you hush long enough to tell me if Mary Cowper's gonna see her young man while we're out gettin' me used to being in a big city, Missy?"

"I was trying to keep your mind off them."

"I gathered that, but neither one of us—not you, not me—is gonna think about much else all day, so tell me the truth."

"Stuart's coming here a few minutes after noon. Mary Cowper will tell her grandmother, Miss Eliza, that she's visiting her old schoolmate Anna Barnsley. Mary Cowper has lots of Savannah friends. All Miss Lib's children were born here, you know."

"You're prattling again. What did you think?"

"About what?"

"Why, about her young man this morning. Is he going to mind you?"

Natalie patted the carefully pinned hair and studied it for a moment in the looking glass. "There. Aren't you a picture?"

"Pish-tush."

"Don't pish-tush me. Tell me the truth. I never saw you look so pretty! Did you?"

"Good as I can look, I reckon. At least maybe I won't put Miz Browning to shame if we happen to run into one of her high-toned friends. But that's not answering my question. How did the young feller seem to you? Course, you haven't said a word about it, but I know you did your best to talk him into eloping with Mary Cowper while we're here. Lord have mercy on us all!"

"I don't tell you much, because I've never had to. You already know. It's kind of eerie sometimes, did you know that?"

"Is that a yes answer? Does that mean he'll try to mind you? That he'll do his best to get her to—marry him before the older gentleman gets back from across the water?"

On a heavy sigh, Natalie said, "Yes. He doesn't have much hope, though. Oh, Miss Lorah, you pray. Maybe when we show you one of Savannah's churches this afternoon, you might pray that Mary Cowper will get up her nerve to do—what Stuart wants her to do. What she wants so desperately to do. Will you pray? Just to make sure, pray in both of the big churches!"

They were looking straight at each other in the looking glass. "In my way, I'm prayin' right now, Missy." The cheery smile came. "I was never in a big church in my whole life. I reckon God's never been penned up in one of them neither. Not even the one with the fine steeple you're so partial to."

NINE

The minute her eyes flew open that morning, Mary Cowper leaped from the bed she shared with her Aunt Kate at the old Mackay house and stood in a daze, struggling to orient herself to what the day might bring. For an instant, she thought she was alone, back at Etowah Cliffs in her own room. She wasn't. She was in Savannah. Not even alone. Aunt Kate Mackay was there, sound asleep on her side of the bed. No light showed at the window. It was still dark, winter dark, although not a bit cold. At least not cold as on a January morning in the upcountry.

Stuart.

Today was the day she would see Stuart, would see him, hear his voice, touch his face, feel his arms. Natalie had worked it all out. Natalie and dear Uncle William and Natalie's father, whom she'd always called Uncle Mark. Aunt Kate ripped out a short snore, then turned over. Was it still the middle of the night? It couldn't be. In the night, lying wide awake, struggling not to toss in the bed, Mary Cowper had heard her grandmother's parlor clock strike five times before she finally fell into a half-sleep. The room was still as dark as midnight, though, and she dared not light a candle to look at her watch. The last thing she remembered before she slept was that she needed to use the chamber pot. She'd do that now, so she'd have an excuse for being out of bed in case Aunt Kate woke up suddenly.

That done, she just stood in the middle of the floor wishing she could feel similar relief in her heart after today's meeting with Stuart.

Fully awake now, though exhausted, she rehearsed Natalie's plan. "I'll handle every single thing except your own story to your family about why you'll be away for most of the day, including dinner," Natalie had said. "Papa's arranged for Stuart to leave the bank right at twelve o'clock. Stuart will walk as fast as he can. That shouldn't take more than five minutes. I'll see that the house is empty of everyone, including Maureen and Gerta, by eleven-thirty."

Still standing on the floor, hands clenched, Mary Cowper wondered what might happen if someone at the Brownings' fell sick today. Miss Caroline or one of the white hired servants. Or little Willow or Callie. Her heart pounded so hard and fast, she marveled that Aunt Kate didn't wake up, wanting to know what was wrong, forcing her, as life always seemed to be forcing her, to act as though her heart wasn't full of pain and despair. Somehow she would have to get through the family talk and chatter at breakfast, would have to make herself eat something, to speak of how excited she was at the idea of spending most of the day with her old school friend Anna Barnsley, visiting in Savannah, too, at the house of her stern Aunt Charlotte. Mary Cowper had confided in Anna yesterday. Anna could be trusted utterly to keep her secret, but only God could prevent Charlotte Taylor from blabbing if, by chance, Grandmother Mackay or Aunt Kate or Aunt Sarah mentioned that they thought Mary Cowper and Anna had spent the day together at the old Scarbrough mansion on West Broad. Did she dare beg God to protect her, to help her act out such deceit? Did God ever help a deceitful person? Quickly, she pushed the question aside and prayed instead for Aunt Kate to wake up so the day could get started.

Daylight came awfully late in January. Maybe the day was farther along than she knew. It could be almost seven o'clock. Her legs and back and arms, even her fingers, began to feel numb with anxiety.

I should be wanting to hold back the minutes, she thought wildly. This day will be over soon enough. If I cling to each second of each minute right now, I'll still have it all to look forward to. I'll still know that there will be one more look at him, one more kiss, those strong, eager arms will hold me one more time—before I die.

Before I die.

It felt that way. Trying to die inside, so she would feel no more pain, had become her way of facing a whole lifetime with the elegant stranger, Andrew Low. She shuddered.

I'm going to obey my parents, dear Lord, she breathed. I am going to say goodbye forever to Stuart today, but I beg You to help me die inside when today is over . . . Please help me to be cheerful with Aunt Kate when she wakes up, with everyone at breakfast, and somehow help me get through this endless, long, long morning until time to–go to him. Help Stuart, too. Oh, if You don't help me at all, please, please help Stuart, who loves me as much as I love him. Make him strong and help him to believe, but still *accept,* what I have to tell him!

• • •

Alone, as Natalie promised, in the family drawing room of the Browning home, Mary Cowper stood back a little from the one window with the shutters open. Natalie had done everything right, even to slipping her a key to the front door, to making sure that the servants were gone. The gracious, well-designed, lavishly furnished house seemed larger than ever in the empty, tense silence as she waited, watching, straining for her first glimpse of the tall, lithe, dark-haired, hurrying figure of her beloved.

She took her eyes off the street just long enough to glance at the hall clock. Five minutes before twelve and Stuart couldn't leave the bank until noon. She should be rehearsing what she would say to him, but nothing came. Love, Natalie vowed, is strong enough to conquer anything, even time and distance. All right, she'd cling to that now. She'd will time to stop the very second he stepped into the entrance hall. Time did stop when a person died. She would die inside when he walked away from her later today, but the power of love for him would surely stop time while he was still there close enough to touch, to hear, to hold.

Once Stuart was gone, there would be no other way to move through the remainder of her life–except to die inside. Hearts are easier to hear than minds, she thought wildly, so at least for a while I'll listen only to my heart once he's here.

Once he's actually here—*in this room with me.*

• • •

She had no memory of running to open the wide front door. She realized only the hard, painful thump of her heart when his arms went around her again there in the front hallway.

Neither spoke one word as he pressed her hard against him, her own arms responding, drawing him closer—closer, unable as always to get him close enough. Finally, he kissed her, but unlike so many of his earlier kisses, this one was gentle, so tender, so full of yearning, she felt tears on her face. Her tears? His? And then, carefully, more tenderly than there would ever be words to describe, he led her as though she were a helpless child into the parlor and seated her on Miss Caroline's sofa. Quietly, he sat down beside her and began to study her face, to study it feature by feature, his dear hands holding both of hers.

Still neither had spoken. Irrelevantly, she noticed for the first time that he'd nicked his chin that morning while shaving. She reached to touch the tiny, clotted scratch. "You cut your chin, dearest . . ."

He only nodded and went on looking and looking as though his eyes had been starving for the sight of her through every moment since he'd ridden out of sight down the river road that took him to the train at Cassville after she'd sent him away forever a month before Christmas in the year just ended.

Suddenly, he smiled. His smile had always melted her, but this was a different smile. Stuart had changed. The new gentleness, the new quiet strength overwhelmed her. Overwhelmed her with a new longing to protect him, to help him. For the first time since her last sight of him, she thought now only of Stuart, not of the tragedy of her own life. She had no thought of herself now at all, only of Stuart—of the pain he would have to bear for all the days of his life without her. A longing to say something that might help him moved so stormily through her, she struggled for words. None came.

Only when he took her in his arms with the same new heartbreaking tenderness did she hear her own voice whisper brokenly, foolishly, "I'm —I'm so sorry you cut yourself."

And then they both laughed.

"So far," he said, teasing, "after all this time, your main concern seems to be the condition of my chin! Do you realize you haven't said one word about the rest of me?"

She tried to laugh. She wanted to. She'd always adored his little, lighthearted jokes, but instead she broke into hard, deep sobs and fell against him, as though begging him to rescue her.

For how long neither could have told, they clung together, murmuring each other's name over and over and over, begging, both begging the other to help.

Again, he was calling her Marysee, his special name for her. Not the usual Mary C., the abbreviation for her double name, but his endearing one-word Marysee. No one else ever called her Marysee. Only Stuart.

Her heart feeling as though it were being torn wide open, she pulled away, gasping, *"What are we going to do?* Stuart! *How* are we going to—do it?"

He got to his feet, walked to the one unshuttered window, and stood there in silence for so long, she grew anxious.

"Don't stand so close to that open window! Someone might see you."

When he turned slowly to look at her, she could have bitten off her tongue for what she'd just said. For what she'd inadvertently admitted—that she cared more about keeping her love for him hidden than she cared for his heart in what had to be one of its most helpless moments! She had begged him to tell her how they were going to go on living without each other, to tell *her* what to do—and then her cruel, thoughtless words had slapped him with the answer: They were going to say goodbye forever *today* because Mama wanted her to marry a man of wealth and prestige in the city and because Papa would be helped politically by the marriage.

She rushed to him, but before she could think how to tell him how sorry she felt, he grabbed her in his arms right in front of the open window onto Bryan Street and all of Reynolds Square and gasped roughly, "I'll tell you what we're going to do. We're going to get married right away!"

"No!"

"You want to. The only thing you really want, Marysee, is to marry me, to live out your life beside me, loving me, letting me love you!"

"Yes. Oh, yes, that's all I want—all I ever want, but—"

"We can go to a different part of the country. We won't have to face the wrath of your parents if you marry me and go West with me to begin a whole new life, to give me children who will grow up to be like you and me—fine and strong and good. They will grow up to be good like us because loving you has changed me. I'm good, too, now. Can't you tell I've changed?" He dropped his arms from around her, and held them out as though to prove his words. "Look at me. Can't you tell? Marysee, I haven't even had a drink of ale in months. I haven't gambled once. I'm doing well at the bank. And I did all that without knowing I'd ever lay eyes on you again! What could I amount to if you married me? *You* did all this for me, my dearest. You. I don't intend to let you go now that we're together again. I don't intend to let you marry that rich old animal, Andrew Low."

"He's not an animal!"

"I know better what he's like than you'll ever know if you have courage enough to follow your heart and marry me. Please, please let me save you from him, Marysee. *Please.*"

For all the time he was pleading with her, she grew dizzier and dizzier, as though all of her–body, soul, spirit–tilted wildly this way and that. Toward him helplessly–back again toward her mother, with even more helplessness. Seeing him again had seemed so right, so absolutely necessary. Natalie had been as certain as she that it had to be done. Everyone–Grandma Mackay, Uncle William, Burke, Miss Lorah, even though she wouldn't put it into words–everyone was on her side, according to Natalie, except Mama and Papa. She had been so sure that seeing him just one more time would keep the memory of Stuart's kisses on her mouth, his arms around her . . . would make it possible to obey Mama and Papa. At this moment, as he held her at arm's length so as to look straight into her eyes, she knew that she'd done the cruelest of things to the only man she'd ever love.

"I packed my few belongings, Marysee," he was saying. "I stayed late at the bank for the past two nights so I'd have my work done ahead. We can rent horses and ride as far toward Statesboro as we can tonight, then flag a train somewhere tomorrow. I've even packed blankets for us to sleep in the woods. It doesn't matter where, because we'll be together. I'll watch over you and take care of you and keep you safe and oh, dearest, I'll see to your happiness for as long as–"

"No!"

Her voice was so sharp, he stepped back as though she'd struck him. Stuart said nothing, he just stared at her unbelieving.

"I'd–I'd never be able to face Mama again," she said, and meant it, although every word sounded quite insane.

"You wouldn't have to face her–we'd be far, far away from Georgia!"

The Brownings' big clock in the hallway struck twice. Two o'clock already! "You'll have at least two or three hours alone," Natalie had said. Now there was only one . . . maybe. For the first time since he'd come, she noticed the relentless tick of the tall, graceful hall clock. Tick, tick, tick. Taking him away, taking Stuart away forever . . .

Since the one quick, startled step back, he hadn't moved toward touching her again. Silence is so much louder when a clock is ticking.

She was beginning to die right now, and like a train pulling away after a stop, her death was gathering speed.

After what seemed countless eternities stretching one after another, he spoke her name. Then, in a voice so hollow and defeated, she wouldn't have guessed it was Stuart's if she hadn't seen him form the words, he was saying, "You're—gone already, aren't you? You'll never love anyone but me, but you're—leaving, aren't you? Every time that clock ticks, you're going farther and farther away from me. I've—lost you, haven't I?"

"Oh, Stuart, *no*," she gasped, fighting tears. "You'll never lose me. That's—that's what I had to tell you today. Yes. I have to marry Mr. Low. I have to obey my parents. I can't break their hearts by running away with you, but I'll—never really leave you. Even if I—have his children, they will be—*yours*."

He pressed both hands over his eyes for a moment of what seemed to be some secret, dark realization—totally apart from her. Then, without touching her, without even looking at her again, he turned away, walked rapidly into the hall, and ran out the door, slamming it violently behind him.

From the window, she saw him pulling on his coat as he leaped down the steep front steps, but instead of heading back toward the bank, he crossed Reynolds Square until he reached the first big tree.

Never in her blackest moment had she known guilt or pain like this. She had been cruel to Stuart . . . to Stuart . . . to Stuart. No matter where he went or what he did for all the years of his life, no matter how often she prayed for him—even if he married someone else—he would always remember her as *cruel*.

Believing himself out of her sight, she saw him bury his face in his arms against the big oak tree and sob.

In the sterile aloneness of the empty house, Mary Cowper wept, too.

Emphie, Eliza Mackay's aging, still pole-thin servant, was clearing dinner plates from the table of happy, chattering guests—Miss Lorah Plemmons, Mark and Caroline Browning, Natalie, Jonathan and Mary—when there came a loud knock at the front door.

"Oh, my," Eliza said, starting at the sudden sound, "now who could that be? Were you expecting anyone, Kate, Sarah? William?" When they all said no, she began to fold her napkin carefully as though to answer the door herself.

"Keep your chair, Mama," Kate said. "I'll go,"

When Kate left the room, Natalie, whom Eliza had thought rather distracted throughout the meal, stood up. "You know, it could be Mary Cowper back from her visit with Anna Barnsley."

"Don't be rude, darling," Caroline scolded. "Sit back down until Miss Eliza is finished with her coffee. I'm sure Mary Cowper wouldn't knock on her own grandmother's front door."

"I'll overrule your mother this time," Mark said. "You're excused, Natalie. Mary Cowper and our daughter may have some secret young woman talk, darling." He smiled at his wife.

"I'm quite finished anyway," Eliza Mackay informed them, getting to her feet. "Let's go into the parlor."

"Good idea, Mama," Sarah said. "Whoever it is at the door can join us there."

Everyone held back until Miss Eliza had preceded them, and when she stopped in the front hall, they all stopped. They even stopped the pleasant, family-easy chatter to listen.

"Why, Charlotte Taylor!" Kate exclaimed from the front door. "What a pleasant surprise. Come in, come in. It's warmer than yesterday by far, but the wind's sharp."

"Only for a moment." The clipped, aristocratic voice of Charlotte Scarbrough Taylor reached everyone easily. "I just dropped by to invite my niece, Anna, and Mary Cowper for high tea this afternoon."

"Why, they aren't here right this minute, Mrs. Taylor," Eliza heard Natalie say in an almost comically elegant voice. "Who knows what those two old school chums might be up to on such a nice day?"

"Charlotte?" Eliza Mackay called, and began to move slowly toward the front door, where Charlotte Taylor still stood. "Do come in! I'd love to know what you've heard lately about your dear mother, Julia. Is she feeling any better?"

"Sorry, Mrs. Mackay, I haven't time for a visit, and yes, my mother is as well as could be expected, living off up there in the Cherokee wilds. Oh, I do apologize, young Mrs. Browning. I meant no offense, I assure you. I hadn't noticed you standing there in the shadows by your handsome husband."

Eliza Mackay turned to glance at Mary Browning, hoping perhaps that Mary hadn't heard Charlotte's crude slur on Mary's Cherokee blood.

Mary had heard, though, because she said easily, "Don't apologize, Mrs. Taylor. I understand the Savannah meaning of 'Cherokee wilds.' "

Charlotte Taylor, usually in control, seemed a bit taken aback, Eliza thought, but handled the awkward moment by responding tonelessly, "Well, I'm relieved to hear that."

"I don't believe you've met our dear friend Miss Lorah Plemmons, Charlotte," Eliza Mackay said, pulling Lorah's dress sleeve to get her to step forward a little. "Miss Lorah, this is the daughter of my lifelong friend, Julia Scarbrough. You've met Mrs. Scarbrough, I'm sure. She lives at the Barnsley estate only about twenty miles from Etowah Cliffs."

"Pleased to meet you, ma'am," Lorah Plemmons said, actually one of the few things she'd said throughout the meal except to murmur a time or two that the food was "mighty good."

"How do you do?" Charlotte Taylor's voice froze on the air. "Your housekeeper, Natalie?"

"And my best friend, outside of my husband," Natalie said with equal ice. "I'm sorry you can't stay for a visit, Mrs. Taylor," she went on, "but I certainly wouldn't worry about Anna and Mary Cowper. They're grown women, you know."

"Yes, Natalie, I do know, but grown women shouldn't lie. I was given to understand that they were both to take dinner here. Anna told me she was on her way here less than an hour ago."

"Less than an hour ago?" Sarah Mackay asked, stunned by the announcement. "Why, Mary Cowper told us when she left for your house right after eleven o'clock this morning that she was taking dinner with you and Anna and–"

"You must be mistaken, Sarah," Natalie broke in, looking in some desperation to Eliza Mackay for help.

"There's just been a little mix-up, I'm sure," Eliza said, perplexed herself, since she also believed her granddaughter to be at Charlotte Taylor's house with Anna. "Natalie's right, you know. Anna and Mary Cowper are both grown women now. They don't need to be looked after as though they were still little girls. Won't you change your mind and step in just for a cup of coffee, Charlotte? My old Hannah made a delicious apple pie. You could–"

"No, no, thank you very much, Mrs. Mackay." Turning abruptly, she walked onto the porch, only calling over her shoulder that she'd better find out what Anna was up to. Halfway down the front walk, they could all still hear her muttering angrily about having taken the long walk for nothing.

"Well, did you ever!" exclaimed Sarah Mackay, turning from the front door to her mother. "When Mary Cowper so plainly told us she was taking dinner and spending the afternoon at Mrs. Taylor's house with Anna Barnsley, why wouldn't Charlotte Taylor know it and *where* on earth do you suppose Mary Cowper is?"

In her cloak, tying on her hat, Natalie pushed past the group in the Mackay front hall, and through the door she flew, totally ignoring the calls and questions of her mother, Miss Eliza, and the Mackay sisters. Only Miss Lorah, Papa, Jonathan, and Mary exchanged knowing looks and kept silent.

T E N

*W*hen *Natalie,* quite out of breath and windblown, hurried up the front steps of her parents' home on Reynolds Square, she clung to her hope that the tryst had ended as she'd planned. She had run and walked as fast as she could all the way, believing the best. She even dared to hope that they'd already eloped. It was a minor matter that uppity Charlotte Taylor had let the cat out of the bag by exposing that Mary Cowper and Anna Barnsley had not been together. What mattered was that Mary C. and Stuart *had* been together for over two hours. Had been together as she still hoped and prayed they would always be. As any two lovers ought to be!

There probably will be no answer at all when I knock, she reassured herself at the top of the steep steps. I pray there isn't. If there's no one here, that means they're gone. The whole blessed truth can come out, so I won't even have to think of an excuse for Charlotte Taylor or anyone else.

She literally banged the heavy knocker and waited. When the weak, nervous voice from behind the closed door called, "Who is it, please?" her heart sank.

"It's Natalie, Mary Cowper! Let me in. I gave you my key."

Inside the warm, gracious entrance hall, she stared at her friend's brown eyes, the oddly expressionless face. Mary Cowper was just standing there, back straight, hands clenched, not even revealing by so much as a look what had happened between her and Stuart.

Instead of shaking the girl as she felt like doing, Natalie also just stood there returning the blank stare. Finally, she took Mary Cowper's hand and pulled her into the family drawing room.

"What happened?" Natalie demanded. "Mary Cowper Stiles—what happened? Is—is he gone?"

When her friend said not one word, showed not one change of expression, Natalie dropped the limp hand.

"Where's Stuart, Mary Cowper?"

The younger woman shook her head slowly, but said nothing.

"You don't know where he is? Don't you have any idea where he went?"

"I—I will never know where he is—ever again," Mary Cowper said at last, her voice surprisingly calm and controlled. "It's over. He's gone. I—sent him away and now—" A quick, jerky sob almost choked her. "And now, I need my mother! I need my mother more than I've ever needed her—ever in my whole life."

Natalie's mouth opened, but no words came. She could only stare unbelieving at the still lovely, but totally strange, unfamiliar face of the girl who had changed, it seemed, in a matter of hours from a warm, vibrant young woman into an aging replica of Miss Lib.

"What on earth could your mother do for you now?" Natalie asked after a heavy silence.

As she'd watched Miss Lib change, everything about Mary Cowper was changed now, too. Even her movements. Middle age had come over the way she held her back, her shoulders—the way she moved as she crossed the room to stand by that one unshuttered window.

"If Mama were here," Mary Cowper said, her voice almost matter-of-fact, "she could see for herself that I do have mettle." Turning to look straight at Natalie, she added, "I'm going to stay strong, too. I'll stay strong through all the years I'll be married to Mr. Low. I'll make Mama and Papa proud of me. You'll see, Natalie. You'll see."

Natalie felt as though her own heart would tear in two. In the face of the dreadful words Mary Cowper had just spoken, she had to use all the self-control she could muster not to give Mary Cowper the scolding of her life.

"I know how disappointed you are in me, Natalie," her friend was saying. "You've been so good to me—so good to Stuart. But I'm—strong now, I'm *strong*. I'm going to marry Mr. Low and—"

"You're going to shut your mouth and stop saying such crazy things!"

Natalie could hear the ugly screech of her own voice zinging around the tasteful elegance of her parents' drawing room, but she could no more have helped screeching than she could now—ever again—help Mary Cowper and Stuart!

Searching for a way to apologize for her outburst, Natalie heard herself ask tonelessly if Mary Cowper would mind if she found Stuart and tried to comfort him.

"Yes, I do mind," Mary C. said firmly. "He will have to learn to live like a—a civilized gentleman without me. I don't want you to see him, Natalie. You see, I—I hurt him terribly. He would only feel worse if he saw you again."

In desperation, Natalie plunged into the story of Charlotte Taylor's visit and the mess Mary Cowper had made for herself and for Anna Barnsley. Her own dreams for her young friend were so crushed, she found it impossible not to want to punish Mary C. in some way. "You'll have to come up with a mighty fancy, convincing story in order to allay all the questions you're going to be asked."

"No, I won't, Natalie. I'll just—tell everyone the truth. I'm through now having to lie and trick Mama. She's right, it's much better this way. I'll admit I've been with Stuart. That I sent him away. I'll call on Mrs. Taylor tomorrow and clear Anna Barnsley of her part in my deceit. Mama's right," she repeated. "It's much better to be aboveboard and honest and the only way to do that is never to disobey her and Papa."

For a long time, Natalie stood there, her eyes on the peacock pattern in her mother's silky oriental rug. Finally, she said, "Stuart isn't the only one who's lost you, I've lost you, too. You belong to Miss Lib and Uncle W.H. now, don't you?"

"If you don't want me—this way, I guess that's right."

Natalie did want her. She loved the pretty, spirited girl who had always made people so happy; wanted with all her heart to remain friends. But could she be friends with the stranger in the room with her now? As much a stranger as Miss Lib had seemed the snowy morning Natalie had begged her not to ruin Mary Cowper's life. Impossible. Oh, she would have to go on being neighborly with Miss Lib, would even try to enjoy her company as long as the subject of running other people's lives didn't come up. Burke always said well-bred people had an easier time pretending they felt one way when they knew they didn't.

Her breeding would help, she supposed, with both Miss Lib and Mary Cowper—even after Mary C. was Mrs. Andrew Low.

Natalie shuddered as she sank onto her mother's damask settee across the room from where Mary Cowper still stood by the window. A sickening weariness came over her and she leaned her head back and closed her eyes. The big hall clock Papa brought down from Philadelphia when he first built the Reynolds Square house started to tick so loudly she wondered irrelevantly why she hadn't noticed it before today. And then from the steps out front she heard the family returning from Miss Eliza's house.

"Your family's coming home, Natalie," Mary Cowper said from her place by the window. "I guess they'll have a lot of questions—especially after Anna's Aunt Charlotte blabbed."

On her feet, Natalie collected her cloak and hat and headed for the entrance hall. "I guess they will have. My mother will, I know. Papa and Jonathan and Mary know you saw Stuart." Her own voice sounded flat, expressionless. "I'm going upstairs before they get inside. You'll have to do your own explaining—about everything from now on. I'm through." Halfway up the curving stair, she called down, "Please see that Callie comes straight up to my room, will you? I don't want her to find out until she has to how an otherwise intelligent person like you can wreck her whole life without a single backward look!"

Mary Cowper was standing at the foot of the stairway and for a fleeting moment looked like Mary Cowper again. Their eyes met.

"Natalie, please," the girl pled in a small, desperate voice.

"Please—what, Mary Cowper?"

"Please understand that I dare not look back now. I'm far more afraid of one thought of Stuart—than of all the rest of my life."

"I can't believe that! Why? *Why?*"

Lifting her chin with resolve and determination, Mary Cowper answered, "Because *now*—I have Mama's blessing on my life. Somehow —*somehow* that will protect me. It's—got to."

ELEVEN

A week later, on Tuesday, the last day in January, a high tea, Caroline Browning's first scheduled event in Mary Cowper's honor, was just ending when Mark saw Miss Lorah peep around the wide doorway to the formal drawing room. He was talking business with the English merchant Charles Green, partner to Andrew Low. The negotiation by the firm of Andrew Low and Company of a cotton shipment was important, so important to the Browning firm that Jonathan had insisted upon his father's direct contact with the smooth-talking, diplomatic Green. But when Mark saw Miss Lorah wave to get his attention, then heard her "Ps-s-st!" he excused himself and joined her in the hall outside the drawing room.

"Hated to make a spectacle," Miss Lorah whispered, "but I figured you'd want to hear what I have to say." She paused long enough for her familiar chuckle, then added, "In spite of the fool I made of myself lettin' that cup of hot tea slide off my saucer onto Miss Caroline's good rug."

Patting her shoulder, Mark said with a smile, "Miss Lorah, if you tried from now till doomsday, you couldn't possibly make a fool of yourself."

"Knew I was bound to do something like that sooner or later," she said, blue eyes twinkling. "That's the slickest china anywhere! Least it seems to be when I get my old, horny hands on it."

"What's on your mind?" Mark asked, leading her to a quieter place away from where guests were collecting their wraps.

"Missy," she said, her smile gone now.

"Natalie? Did she send you to get me aside?"

"Good gracious, no! She'd throw a fit if she knew what I did."

"Well, is something wrong? Does my daughter need me?"

"I don't have to tell you how standoffish and distant she's been actin' ever since—ever since poor little Mary Cowper . . ." She broke off, staring at the wall beside where they stood, plainly embarrassed.

"Ever since Mary C. decided to obey her parents and marry Mr. Low," Mark finished for her. "Yes, I do know Natalie's been miserable. *Her* dreams got shattered, too." He sighed. "She's an incurable romantic, Miss Lorah. I'm sure she'd give almost anything to get back on the train and go home to Burke as fast as possible. She only came to Savannah to maneuver the Stiles girl into marriage with Stuart Elliott. Visiting her parents was merely a means to an end."

"I don't know as I'd say that, sir." She took a deep breath. "I just decided I'd best let you know what Mr. William Mackay's aimin' to do tomorrow morning."

"What, Miss Lorah? I thought sure Natalie's dark mood meant she'd given up on being a matchmaker. Please, tell me."

"I'm breakin' a hard-and-fast rule of mine to do it, mind you."

"I know, I know. You *do* mind your own business. But I should know. Evidently you agree or you wouldn't be here."

"I'm breakin' two rules all to smithereens. Tattlin' an' eavesdroppin' —both. I overheard Mr. Mackay and Missy talkin' about what he's plannin' to do tomorrow. Didn't mean to listen. I got wore out tryin' to keep up with all the fancy talk an' slipped upstairs to my room for a little peace an' quiet. Didn't quite shut my door all the way and there I sat hearin' every word Missy and Mr. Mackay said. They was in the upstairs hall—thinkin' nobody was anywhere near."

"Well, what were they saying?"

"Had to do with Mr. Mackay, once his mother had told him all that took place at her house with Mrs. Charlotte Taylor the afternoon Mr. Mackay happened to miss dinner. Well, once Mr. Mackay heard the story, got all the pieces together, he made up his mind that somebody oughta show a little interest in young Elliott, not just leave him out in the cold by hisself."

"So, he's appointed himself to see the boy?'

"Yes, sir."

"I—I think that's undoubtedly admirable, but, Miss Lorah, you called me aside just now because Natalie herself seemed to be on your mind. Did you overhear her say something that troubled you?"

"No, sir, and that's why I'm here buttin' in. Missy just stood there and listened to Mr. Mackay say what he was aimin' to do. For the longest time, she didn't utter one word."

"Is that what bothers you?"

"What bothers me is what she did finally say after Mr. William got through. You know I was the one that had to ease Missy out of the black time she had after she lost her first baby. I don't want to see her like that again ever, but, Mr. Mark, she told Mr. William not to mention another word about Mary Cowper Stiles or Stuart Elliott to her as long as he lived!"

"Did she explain why?"

"Yes, and that's what troubles me. She said she'd brought herself around to believe that her onetime friend Mary Cowper had *died!*"

"Died?"

"Died. Missy declared that only if Mary C. died inside her own heart would she ever be able to bear up bein' the wife of a man she didn't love. Missy is *mourning* her. She aims to go on mourning her. This ain't right. It ain't what you might call a healthy way for Missy to act!"

Mark ran both hands through his thick, gray-streaked dark hair. "No, it certainly is not," he sighed, "but what can I do about it, Miss Lorah? What can either of us do?"

"I guess not one blessed thing, but I made up my mind that, respectin' you the way I do, the least I could do was let you know the truth. You know Missy goes in spurts. She could go on grievin' over the Stiles girl for a time, then bust out with one of her big ideas on how to fix everything."

"But Andrew Low's partner, Mr. Green, just told me Low plans to return to Savannah late in April and schedule the wedding sometime in May. That doesn't leave Natalie much time to meddle."

"Did you feel like she was—meddlin'?"

"I'm of two minds on that, to be truthful. If it was meddling, I helped. I do thank you, though, Miss Lorah. I'm deeply grateful that you trusted me with this."

"I doubt that will stop me from wantin' to kick myself all over town later tonight when I'm in bed going over what I done."

"You did exactly right. I respect you, too. Tell me one more thing—are you glad William Mackay will try to talk to the Elliott boy tomorrow?"

Mark saw her cheerful smile light the aging face. "I'm *so glad,* sir, that if he hadn't made up his mind to do it, I mighta tried it myself! I spill tea, but I've always had a way with young folks. I won't see fifty again, but neither will I ever forget how it can hurt just bein' young."

"Sorry we haven't had time for a talk, William," Mark said as he stood beside Caroline bidding their guests goodbye at the front door. "Can you come by my office tomorrow?"

William nodded. "I've got a dinner engagement at the Pulaski House tomorrow at two o'clock. I can come after that."

Nothing in William's expression indicated that the dinner engagement might be more than business. "Then I'll look for you about four. Caroline will be shopping with Mary Cowper until late, I'm sure."

"Did I hear my name?" Caroline asked.

"Just that you'll be shopping for Mary C.'s trousseau until late tomorrow," Mark said, smiling at her. "Is Natalie going, too?"

"No," Caroline said, frowning. "I'd say the answer is definitely no. Our daughter's sulking. Natalie *sometimes* listens to you and William, Mark. I do wish you'd both try to convince her that, with the wedding at Etowah Cliffs, there's no graceful way she can refuse to be part of the plans. Mary Cowper even wants her to be her matron of honor!"

William smiled as he took Caroline's hand and said, "With all these folks trying to get out your front door, dear Caroline, I doubt now is the time to discuss Natalie or any of this mess."

Straightening her shoulders, Caroline said, "Of course not, William, but neither is it quite fair to Mary Cowper for any single one of us to spoil her wedding plans."

"I wasn't aiming to spoil anything," William said mildly.

"Nor I, darling," Mark whispered in Caroline's ear. "I'll see you tomorrow afternoon, William. Jonathan's already taken your mother and sisters out to your carriage. I'm sure they're chilly waiting for you."

Later that night, quietly talking in bed, Mark eased Caroline's head onto his shoulder. "Your first social event went extremely well, m'lady. As usual, I was proud of you. I thought Mary Cowper seemed pleased, too, didn't you?"

"As pleased as she could be with our daughter acting so surly. Mark, Natalie hasn't been in town but a little over a week and she's at her old tricks again. Is it something you and I do to her to cause her to revert to those spoiled-child ways?"

Toying with a dark curl not tucked under her nightcap, he didn't answer at once.

"Natalie was barely civil to Mary Cowper tonight at the girl's own prenuptial affair."

"I saw them talking several times," Mark said defensively. "Natalie even opened one or two wedding gifts for her and read the enclosures aloud."

"Natalie *is* well-bred. What I said was that she behaved in a barely civil manner. I do know what's eating her, you know. And once Mary Cowper and Mr. Low are living here in the city, I'm sure things will smooth out. It's just that I can't help wondering how Natalie will treat the girl once they're both back in Cass and Eliza Anne is burdened with all those wedding plans."

Mark paused. "I know her mother troubles you, but did you ever know a more charming, amenable little girl than Callie?" he asked. "Oh, she's spirited—almost as spirited as her mother was at ten, but you have to agree the child is enormously well behaved and courteous."

"You get better and better at changing the subject, don't you?" she asked pleasantly, moving still closer to him. " 'Blessed are the peacemakers.' You, my dear husband, are a peacemaker. And I'm not going to agitate over any of this. Do you believe me?"

"I believe everything you tell me."

"And I tell you that you have always been a peacemaker. A skillful one. I'm supposed to believe our daughter is *not* resorting to her spoiled-child ways because Callie's behavior proves that she's a good mother. Is that right?"

He laughed softly. "That's right."

"Could it be a little bit right for me to ask if being around us somehow brings back the old Natalie?"

He tightened his arm around her. "I'm sure you meant to say 'being around her father, who's always spoiled her.' "

"In part," she said, snuggling into the familiar curve of his body.

"If it helps any, I haven't discussed Mary Cowper's marriage to

Andrew Low once with Natalie since Mary Cowper sent Stuart Elliott away."

"You did help her plan that foolish meeting with the young man, though."

Mark yawned. "I did and I admitted it to you and to Miss Eliza." For a time, neither spoke. "I thought you were extremely kind about my having helped. Did I thank you for that?"

"No, but there was no need. Mark?"

"Hm?"

"I know you're sleepy, but I marvel at the way Mary Cowper is going ahead with the wedding plans—under the circumstances. Don't you?"

"I more than marvel. I think I worry some."

"For fear Natalie will still somehow manage to influence her?"

"I don't think so. I worry about Mary C.'s young heart. I also worry about the boy."

"Is Stuart Elliott still in Savannah?"

"As far as I know. He's doing well at the bank, I hear. I just wish the boy had a real friend he could count on. The very fact that Mary Cowper came to Savannah to see him had to raise his hopes. Now I try to imagine what torment it must be for him to wake up in the mornings."

"Do you suppose he'll start drinking again?"

"I have no idea." He held her against him. "I know I have no idea how I'd have managed through the years if I'd been forced to share my life with someone I didn't love."

"Are you referring to Stuart now or to Mary Cowper?"

"Maybe to them both."

"Young men heal quickly. Stuart will find someone else, I'm sure."

"Oh, he'll marry someday, I have no doubt." Mark sighed heavily. "And—of course, so will Mary Cowper."

"I predict she'll handle the circumstances of her life with great grace and strength."

"I agree she'll certainly try, but as Miss Lorah Plemmons said to me today, none of us should ever forget how much it hurts—just to be young."

TWELVE

*A*s William walked toward the bank to meet Stuart the next afternoon, he vowed he'd make every effort not to advise or even suggest that Stuart's life would someday begin to look up in spite of his broken heart. He would preach no sermons. He would rub no salt. He meant simply to do all he could to encourage the boy, to establish, if possible, some kind of friendship. Yesterday, when William invited him to dinner, Stuart had appeared in fair control of himself. There was no hint of liquor on his breath, a fact not always true of some Savannah gentlemen by midafternoon. Stuart had agreed to accept the invitation at once, but he had said little. In response to the question as to how he was faring, the young man had merely nodded.

Nearing the bank, William was annoyed by his own reluctance. Nobody looks forward to contact with a suffering man, he thought, and somehow he felt Stuart Elliott wasn't blaming *him* for what his sister, Eliza Anne, had forced upon Mary Cowper. William had long ago learned to get along with most people, particularly members of his own family, in spite of their quirks and foibles. His sister Sarah had taught him well here. Nothing Sarah might do would ever surprise William, but in his heart, although he wouldn't have admitted it, he had been surprised at Eliza Anne. Surprised and hurt, he thought, as he climbed the steps to the bank lobby. One thing he knew: He would not defend her with Stuart today or ever. That wasn't the reason he was making this effort with young Elliott. Any defense of Eliza Anne's actions would lead to criticism of Stuart himself. He had no intention of doing that. The boy used to drink too much—he gambled too much. The assistant teller's job was the first he'd ever kept. William understood why Eliza Anne and W.H. generally disapproved of him. Most respectable folks did in spite of the fact that he was the son of a United States senator from Georgia and his widowed mother had married prominent James Stephens Bulloch after the senator's death. Eliza Anne could be mulish. William knew that, but she'd had ample reason to object to the marriage. William, too, would have been concerned if his beloved niece had thrown in her lot quickly with Stuart and yet he felt obliged to offer the boy friendship. Because a man drank and gambled was no guarantee his heart couldn't break. Few good women ever really reformed a man just by marrying him and yet William's own broken heart at the death so many years ago of his young wife, Virginia, gave him sympathy for young Elliott now.

Entering the bank lobby, he thought honestly that his nagging concern for Stuart might be explainable only to Natalie. Well, so be it. He and Natalie were close and on the subject of love between a man and a woman, they saw eye to eye. That certainly had nothing to do with common sense. It had to do with believing almost like a religion, that when two people really love each other they should be together.

He'd been so deep in his own thoughts, Stuart Elliott was coming toward him across the bank lobby before William noticed. The two men shook hands and walked outside into the clear, mild morning of the first day of February.

Seated across from Mr. Mackay at a table for two in the dining room of the Pulaski House, Stuart made every effort to avoid looking straight at his puzzling dinner companion. He felt the man's goodwill—had felt it from their first conversation before he'd seen Mary Cowper again in Savannah—but he still hadn't figured out why Mrs. Stiles's brother would bother to invite him for a meal in public. Neither had mentioned Mary Cowper during their walk from the bank to the hotel. They'd said very little, in fact. Meeting and introducing Stuart's best friend, Robert Hutchinson, on the way had helped limber things up a bit, in spite of the fact that Bob Hutchinson hadn't been at all cordial. Why would he be? He was a loyal friend who had been slow to give up believing that in the end Mary Cowper would marry Stuart in outright defiance of her parents. Small wonder Bob was cool to her mother's brother.

When William Mackay ordered fried pork chops, potatoes, and string beans for them both, Stuart allowed himself a quick glance at the almost expressionless, now jowly face of the older man. Mackay was putting on weight. They exchanged half-smiles.

It must be a streak of sainthood in me, Stuart thought, that I don't dislike him. I don't. Maybe I don't like him either, but at least his taste in food is satisfactory and no one forced him to invite me. And he might— oh, he just might bring up—her name.

He felt like an idiot at such a thought. There was no reason in the wide, wide world for him to harbor one small shred of hope. Hope of any kind put him on dangerous, slippery ground. So little time had gone by since she'd crushed his last remaining dream. He hadn't yet learned how to sort out the difference between hope and the horror of life without her. Hope kept merging suddenly into despair, and despair into hope. He had no bearings. He was just muddling through the days and the endless, nearly sleepless nights. Oh, he'd even tried one night last week bringing a street woman home for company, but halfway through what was expected of him, he shoved her bodily, half dressed, out the door of his room and collapsed again into the old asinine sobbing.

"Would you like some mighty good blackberry preserves with your hot rolls when they bring 'em, Elliott? They make the preserves right here at the hotel. Good as homemade."

The commonplace question jerked Stuart back to the strange reality of where he was and with whom. What he really wanted was a stiff drink of brandy. "Uh, no, sir. On second thought, yes, sir. Good idea."

Mackay had a way of making a man look right at him when he spoke, so he was better off without a drink, since he fully intended to remain wary of their every exchange. He sipped scalding black coffee and watched Mackay methodically sweeten and then cream his own in silence. After a taste, finding it to his satisfaction, Mackay seemed deliberately to look out the window onto Bull Street. Stuart thought he, too, seemed wary, or maybe just reserved. Their meeting could be easy in no way for this brother of Eliza Anne Stiles, but Mackay had instigated it. For some crazy reason they were both here.

"Let's see," Mackay said at last, "you wouldn't remember your own father, Senator John Elliott, would you?"

"No, sir," Stuart said, relieved at the seemingly safe subject. "My father died when I was not quite a year old. I've always heard he was a strict man, but a strong senator." He tossed off what he hoped was a casual laugh. "Perhaps the mess I've made of my life is due to the fact that I didn't have a father." *That* kind of remark was exactly what Stuart had meant to avoid. It was stupidly personal. There was a quiet compelling about Mackay, though, that seemed to force him headlong into risky conversation. "What made you bring up my father, Mr. Mackay?"

From the floor beside his chair, Mackay picked up a folded copy of the *Georgian*. "I brought this for you, son," he said matter-of-factly. "I know how early you have to be at work at the bank. Thought maybe you didn't have time to pick up a copy. Go on, take it."

Mackay hadn't really answered his question. Reaching for the newspaper, Stuart felt suddenly anxious. "Is there something in there about me I need to read, sir? I've been revoltingly sober for a long time." He forced a grin. "I don't think I've committed any forgotten crime."

"Not a word about you," Mackay said, taking another sip of coffee. "With your own father once a United States senator, I thought you might be following the new ruckus going on up in Washington City."

"I didn't even know there was a—ruckus going on."

Mackay frowned slightly. "No, I suppose your mind's been on other things. You do know about Senator Stephen A. Douglas's bill to allow popular sovereignty in Kansas and Nebraska and—"

"Only vaguely. I know the bill will help the Southern slavery cause, but I'm not interested in politics." He stole a glance at Mackay, who seemed not at all surprised. "Does that bother you, sir, that I'm so lackadaisical about the welfare of our great expansionist country and its Manifest Destiny?"

"No. Guess I just took it for granted that you'd be interested, coming from your background. You're the namesake of the Revolutionary hero, your maternal grandfather, Daniel Stuart. No man loved his country more than he did."

"I know. I should know, I've heard it all my life from my blessed mother."

"Doesn't it make you proud?"

Stuart's guard was up now for sure. Mackay was probing to find out more about him, but why? What motive could he possibly have? What difference did it make what Stuart Elliott thought about anything? He felt Mackay's goodwill considerably less at this moment, sensing a sermon on the way against his reckless life. "Proud? Oh, I suppose I'm proud of old Grandfather Stuart, but history is a very long time ago, sir. I find it of minimal help with the—problems of today."

"You're kind of a rebel, aren't you, Elliott?"

"A rebel? I'm sure I am. At least, I've always been told that."

"They're beginning to call all of us Rebels down here in the South, you know. The self-righteous Northerners have been calling us that for some time."

Stuart grinned. "And—lords of the lash. I know, but I really hope you believe I don't care much one way or the other right now." In spite of himself, he knew he had again directed Mackay's thoughts to his own fresh heartbreak and he could have kicked himself.

A waiter brought their dinner and they both fell silent. Finally, after polite comments about the excellence of the food, Stuart swallowed a mouthful of pork and browned potatoes, then laid his fork down on his plate. "Why are we here—like this, Mr. Mackay?"

"No special reason," the older man answered, carefully cutting sections of pork from around the bone. "I just had you on my mind."

"I see." But he didn't see. Why was he on her Uncle William's mind? Could it, by a stretch of anyone's imagination, be true that William Mackay was actually on his side, as the beautiful Natalie Browning Latimer had declared herself to be?

"Heard some praise of your work at the bank's board of directors meeting not long ago, Elliott. Congratulations."

"Thank you."

"You plan to work your way up in the banking business?"

Stuart's best defense when in conversation with a respectable gentleman had always been to be glib. If possible, to frustrate the usual sermon. "Oh, I'd grab a promotion in a minute, providing a raise went with it."

Mackay looked at him so directly, Stuart had no choice but to return the look.

"Why do you ask, Mr. Mackay?"

"Just wondering. Looks as though you enjoy your dinner. I hope you do."

The conviction of Mackay's goodwill rushed back over Stuart. He felt tears sting his eyes and hated himself. It could be that this oddly reserved, kind man did understand. Would he wish later that he'd asked outright what William Mackay really felt about the way Mary Cowper had sold out to her parents? He knew about the tragic loss years ago of Mr. Mackay's entire little family in a now forgotten shipwreck. Stuart's own sister, Corrine, and her babies went down on the same boat. Mackay certainly seemed human. He could at least feel somewhat at ease with him—as he never could with the domineering Mr. Stiles. The man had evidently expected nothing more than a pleasant dinner engagement, had even made a futile effort to bring up the subject of North-South politics, had brought him a newspaper. Was William Mackay as guileless as he seemed? He couldn't be. He was the full brother of Mrs. W. H. Stiles! The momentary impulse to bare his heart to the older man vanished. He'd stay safely on the surface, where Mackay seemed quite willing to remain.

"Oh, I am enjoying my food, sir. Thank you. I do thank you very much for inviting me." In self-defense, he used his trusty trick of a smile and a cocked eyebrow. "I still wish I knew why."

"I told you. I had you on my mind."

In response, Stuart only frowned and concentrated on the rest of his meal.

After Mackay paid the bill, carefully counting out the exact amount, he fished a quarter tip from his pocket and they left the dining room.

On the street outside, they again shook hands. "You know where to find me if you've ever a mind to, son," Mr. Mackay said, and he said it without a single overtone that Stuart could sense. "I'm old enough to be your father. If you ever need me, Elliott, just whistle."

THIRTEEN

*A*s *Caroline* had predicted, Natalie's good manners did compel her to behave in a civilized manner through the remaining social events given by the Brownings and one or two other families during the unusually pleasant month of February. When Caroline called on Miss Eliza Mackay the week before their visitors were to return to the upcountry, Natalie had even gone shopping with her, the aunts, and Mary Cowper.

"I was really uneasy only once at Low's Emporium when Mary C. was selecting lace for her bridal veil," Caroline confided. "I felt almost sorry for Natalie, actually. She couldn't seem to bring herself even to look at that lace!"

"Is that when Sarah said Natalie just turned and walked away from all of you?" Miss Eliza asked.

"Yes. And when I followed her, there were tears standing in her eyes. My daughter is thirty-one years old. Why must she go on being such a romantic?"

Caroline caught the sly smile on her friend's face and returned it even before Miss Eliza had a chance to say, "Maybe because her mother and father are romantics, too."

"I suppose that's right. You have to admit, though, that I, at least try to—to . . ."

"Conform a bit?"

"Far more than her father prefers, I'm sure. I care so deeply about Mary Cowper's future happiness. Just as deeply as Mark cares, Miss Eliza, although you'd never know it to hear him . . ." She broke off.

"To hear him—what, Caroline?"

"I'd be more accurate if I said 'if you could hear his silences.' You know, Mark has a maddening habit of saying nothing when we don't see something exactly the same way. Even after all these years, I then feel properly guilty."

"Eliza Anne has managed to put us all in a tight, uncomfortable place, hasn't she? I understand why she's so determined not to see Mary Cowper marry Stuart, but—"

"But you don't understand why Eliza Anne is so dead set on forcing the child to marry Andrew Low."

"That's it. Still, it's a Stiles decision to make. And Eliza Anne is a Stiles now." For a time, Miss Eliza sat in her parlor rocker deep in thought. "You and Mark haven't had any real trouble over this, have you, Caroline?" she asked at last.

"No. Thank heaven, we've never had real trouble over anything but —the peculiar institution. Oh, Miss Eliza, I become so incensed on that subject. Mark is having to be careful with me over it again. Dear Jonathan brought up that Kansas-Nebraska bill at dinner yesterday."

"Yes. I know Senator Stephen Douglas is literally driving his bill through the Senate. William is all in favor of it because it leaves the slavery issue in the divided territories up to the people."

"And he thinks that will be good for the South. So do I."

"It certainly will make Kansas a slave state and Nebraska free. What worries me is that the bill doesn't say whether the people will decide in the territories or wait until and if the territories become states. Anything that makes for such confusion makes for future trouble." The two women again exchanged smiles. "You and I don't seem to have difficulty with the ugly issue." Miss Eliza added quickly, "I'm glad."

"So am I. Jonathan is sure there could be protest rallies and bitter debates in the House when the bill comes up there. Oh, Miss Eliza, why can't Northerners leave well enough alone down here?"

After a pause, Miss Eliza asked, "When will our upcountry visitors be leaving?"

Caroline laughed a bit ruefully. "You're as skillful as my husband at changing the subject. They leave the day after tomorrow. Henry is trying to persuade Natalie to stay another week. He hasn't seen nearly enough of Cliffie Gordon yet, but my daughter is determined to get back to Burke, so that settles that."

"And Mr. Low returns from Liverpool at the end of April. I suppose he'll be traveling to Cass soon after."

"For a wedding at Etowah Cliffs in May, I would think."

Eliza Mackay sighed deeply. "Yes, for a wedding in May . . ."

Burke met the returning travelers with his wagon at Cassville on March 3, and because Natalie insisted that Miss Lorah and Mary Cowper ride on the driver's seat with him, he managed to find out very little on the way back to Etowah Cliffs. After failing to get much specific response from Mary Cowper and only a very general report from Miss Lorah, he gave up and concentrated on driving the team over the bumpy road. From the wagon bed piled with trunks and boxes—with Natalie, Henry, and Callie riding the tailgate, legs swinging—there was anything but silence. They sang lustily, yelled or screamed at almost every sharp jostle, and yet Burke felt far from convinced that anyone was as carefree as each was pretending. Well, maybe Callie was. She'd almost hugged his neck off when they met beside the steaming train back at the Cassville station and for a minute he thought maybe she'd win her argument with Natalie about who would sit where. Plainly, Natalie did not want to sit beside Mary Cowper, though, and Burke was pretty sure of her reason. She'd written him only two short notes from Savannah with the "tragic news that Mary Cowper had thrown her life away." He knew how much Natalie cared, but he certainly hadn't expected her pique to last so long —over six weeks. Well, he'd find out soon enough once he'd delivered Henry and Mary Cowper and Miss Lorah.

Henry looked as distraught as any young man should who'd just said goodbye to his lady love, but the young man was trying hard to keep up with Callie's bursts of song. "Oh! Susannah" was filling the crisp early March air. Burke smiled to himself. His daughter would never be another Jenny Lind, but she was loud.

All through dinner at the Stileses and long after her regular bedtime, Callie regaled everyone who would listen and those who dozed off, as did Miss Lorah's Sam, with what seemed to her beaming father an endless round of talk about what she did in Savannah. Burke found himself surprisingly proud of the grown-up way Callie had evidently conducted herself at high tea, the formal dinner, and the Brownings' reception at the Pulaski House.

"You surprised me by asking Callie so many questions about poor Mama's social events," Natalie said when the two were finally alone on the sofa in their cottage parlor before a roaring fire.

"I did? Why? Here—kiss me before you answer."

After a long, deep kiss, their first real one, Natalie grabbed his face in her hands and declared, "I'm amazing! I really amaze myself."

"You amaze me, too."

"I know I do, but not as much as I amaze myself. How I managed to get through those insufferable weeks without you, I'll never know! Oh, Burke, it was dreadful—horrible."

"Your daughter had the time of her life."

"I know and she really was so grown-up and well behaved. Honestly, you'd never have known Callie hadn't been born in Savannah. She does have a streak of poor Mama in her I'd never seen before."

"*Poor* Mama?"

She sighed. "Yes. Sometimes I find Mama very hard to understand."

"I think that must be mutual," Burke said, winding a bright red curl above her ear around his finger.

"Oh, I know Mama's never understood me, but I saw a whole new side of her this time. She's never quite a grande dame. She fussed and stewed and pretended annoyance at every party she gave, but she reveled once they were underway. Under all that Savannah-lady behavior, though, I saw a side of Mama I hadn't seen."

"Want to tell me about it?"

He held her at arm's length and saw that she was frowning.

"Do you suppose I just hadn't noticed before? Or maybe I'm just beginning to see Miss Lib as she really is and that Mama looks good by contrast. She did all the expected, elegant things, Burke, but I saw a whole new side to Mama. She's going to accept old Andrew Low into the family circle because he's respected and prominent and filthy rich, but she's really heartbroken over what Miss Lib made Mary Cowper do. I know she is. I could—sense it. It all came clear to me on that tiresome train ride back here. In spite of the horror in Savannah, I think I glimpsed it there, too."

"What was so horrible? Miss Lorah and Henry seemed to enjoy themselves. Even Mary Cowper managed to put on a somewhat happy air at dinner tonight, I thought."

Natalie snorted.

"What does that mean?" Burke asked, smiling down at her.

"Stop grinning," she said. "Mary Cowper *died*. That 'happy air' you saw is her assumed role–a pretense she's forced herself to assume in order to keep moving around, acting alive when the truth is she's dead inside." She sat up alertly. "Do you know I saw *no sign* of life in her after she sent Stuart away? Not one!"

"Oh, come on, darling. You're exaggerating."

"I was there–I saw her. You didn't. And during the times when she was faking all that bride-to-be happiness, I began to notice something altogether new in Mama's face."

"I've always thought your mother was real. She's always struck me as kind, honest–honest about herself almost above everything. She can't help the way she feels about slavery and that's the only place she's any different from your father."

"Oh, I know all about that, and compared to Mary Cowper's tragedy, slavery is a side issue."

Burke shook his head. "I wish I could agree with you on that. I can tell you didn't read a single newspaper in Savannah. We're heading straight for bad trouble in this country."

"Foot," she said, annoyed, "I saw Mama's face when she looked at Mary Cowper and I honestly thought at times she might cry. And do you know she told me more than once how happy she is that I have you?"

He pulled her to him. "You have a wise, perceptive mother. No trickery. She's as honest a woman as I've ever known. Why, the last time they were up here she–she . . ." He stopped in midsentence.

"Burke, don't do that! I hate it when you start to say something and then cut it off. What were you going to say?"

"She and I happened to be alone on our front porch once and she told me all about the way she–broke down and became hysterical at dinner at the Mackays a few years ago when the Mexican War hero, Colonel Robert Lee, was there."

Natalie stared at him. "Mama told you *that?*"

"You knew about it, too?"

She nodded. "Papa told me long ago. It shattered him. He hates slavery the way you do–sometimes I think he hates it even more than you do and there he was trapped between his own beliefs and his love for Mama. Then, I pitied only Papa over that awful scene Mama pulled at the Mackays'. Now–now, I think I pity Mama, too. People can have dreadfully opposite feelings at one and the same time, can't they? More than opposite—contradictory!"

He held her head hard against his shoulder, one hand caressing the loved shape of it. "Oh, Natalie, Natalie . . . !"

Bolt upright again, she asked, her face concerned. "What did you mean by that 'Oh, Natalie'?"

"If you could only believe that—really believe it!"

"Didn't I just say I did?"

"Can't you see that's what Mary Cowper is trapped in? Can't you see that she's bleeding inside? Not dead, bleeding. She's as helpless as any rabbit with its leg caught in a steel trap. Her desire to please her parents is every bit as strong—evidently stronger than her desire to be with Stuart."

She jumped to her feet. "But it shouldn't be that way!"

"Maybe not, but it is."

"Anyway, I did see something I'd never seen before in Mama, Burke. I always loved her. I've always been terribly proud of her beauty, her charm and grace, but I saw—her heart this time and I liked what I saw. I even wish I'd found a way to tell her."

"You didn't?"

"No, but sometime I will. I know now I have to let her know. But how could Mary Cowper care more about Miss Lib than she does about Stuart? Aren't they two different kinds of love?"

"Of course they are. And if Miss Lib and W.H. didn't disapprove of Stuart so strongly, there'd be no problem. But the same line of reasoning applies to them. We're all a bundle of contradictions inside, Natalie. You are—I am."

"You are not!"

"Oh, yes, I am. You watch me squirm through my own contradictions if there is a war between the North and the South."

"Stop it! How could there be a war? It's all the same country. And don't explain how there could be. I refuse to listen. I'm—I'm trying to tell you about all the changes that are going on inside me and you have no right even to think of me in the same breath as politics!"

He laughed softly and reached for her hand. "That's right, I haven't. Sit back down with me, please."

Jumping back on the sofa almost as quickly as she'd leaped to her feet, Natalie threw both arms around him. "Help me, Burke! You've got to find a way to help me be—tender with Mary Cowper!"

"Oh, my darling, I want to! I want to," he murmured, smoothing her back. *"And* with Miss Lib." He could feel her body stiffen at that. "Yes, Miss Lib, too," he pressed the point. "You two have been friends—real friends for every day of your life until now. Don't you remember how she helped us persuade your parents when we got married in the little Cassville church?"

"I've tried that," she said almost tonelessly.

"And it doesn't help?"

"Mostly it just proves how much she's changed in her old age."

"How old is Miss Lib anyway?"

"Oh, forty-five or six, I guess. Just a little older than—old Redbeard Low!"

"I figured you'd bring him into it sooner or later."

"Burke, he and Mary Cowper have only been together at dumb old dinner parties. Can you believe that? Just two parties, in fact. Last year when she and Miss Lib and Uncle W.H. were in Savannah on some kind of legal business—and once he came up here, but that was three years ago, just two years after his first wife died. I don't think Mary C. has even been alone with him."

"Oh, she must have been at some point for him to want to marry her."

"That shows how little you know of the way those people live! He lost his first wife, he has two little girls, and he needs a woman in the house to look after them. The Stiles family is perfectly acceptable socially. He knows Uncle W.H. is a Southern Democrat who agrees with him politically about slavery and States' Rights and—"

Burke laughed. "Dearest, Andrew Low isn't even an American citizen! He's still a British subject."

"I just know that he and my father don't agree at all on American politics. Papa told me how Andrew Low threatened once to cut him off from the safe fund, some kind of arrangement rich men in Savannah have to rescue each other when they get in debt. Thank heaven, Papa didn't need his rotten money. Papa's business picked up, but old Redbeard is certainly no friend of Papa's and that puts him at the bottom of the heap in my opinion."

"How worried is your father these days over what Senator Douglas is trying to do in the Senate on the Kansas-Nebraska bill?"

"Papa and I don't waste our precious time together discussing things like that, Burke, and you know it. Kansas and Nebraska are both so far away—who cares?"

"A lot of people care, Natalie," he said in a solemn voice. "I care. I know most folks down here are sick and tired of the slavery issue and would rather leave well enough alone, but—"

"I'm one of them."

"I wish I could be."

"No, you don't. You and Papa are two of a kind."

"Then I'm in excellent company," he said with a wry smile. "I'd give a lot right now for a good, long talk with your father."

She snuggled down closer under his arm. "You're the two sweetest men on earth," she said. "Papa really tried to help save Mary Cowper. I meant to tell him how grateful I am—even if he failed."

"Sounds to me as though you need to see both your parents again. You must have left a lot unsaid."

"I did. Most of what I've told you just came to me on the train up here."

"Will they come up for the wedding?"

She took a deep, disgusted breath. "Oh, I suppose so. Mama would think Miss Lib might not approve if she didn't come."

"I think your mother will come only because she cares about the whole Stiles family."

Natalie lifted her face to kiss him. "Oh, Burke, thank you."

"For what?"

"For reminding me that I'm not as—dense about Mama as I used to be. I—I think I say nasty things like that from habit." She was silent for a time. Then, in a nervous, small-girl voice, she asked, "You don't suppose Callie will misunderstand *me* when I'm old, do you?"

"Of course she will! All children do at a certain age. Is our Mary doing as all right in Savannah society as Mrs. Jonathan Browning?"

"Mary's magnificent. Oh, she's still Mary—even a little bit Indian Mary still. Maybe more than a little bit, but that's just proof of how superficial society really is. I'm sure they gossip about her behind her back. Papa and Jonathan are rich enough, though, so that to her face they pretend to accept Mary." She thought a minute. "The same principle applies to old Redbeard Low."

"How well do you know the man, Natalie? Could you be even a little wrong about him? Maybe he isn't such a bad sort after all. Miss Lib and W.H. do love their daughter, you know."

"I'm not a bit wrong about him, Burke," she said, pulling him to his feet. "Old Redbeard Low despises my papa, just the way those high-and-mighty Savannah people despise little Mary. He treats him with courtesy only because Papa's almost as rich as he is."

"You can't leave him alone for a minute, can you?"

She gave him a light, teasing tap on the nose. "Not one more word, do you hear me? I need to be beside you again in our very own bed . . ."

FOURTEEN

The day after Andrew Low's return from England, Mark was dumbfounded to be invited to dine alone with Low at his relatively new home on Lafayette Square. The fine, stuccoed brick house, finished early in 1849, had been designed by the famous architect John Norris of New York, and although now nearly five years old, it was still the talk of Savannah because of its handsome classical design, its garden, and its elaborate exterior cast-iron railings enclosing the front and side balconies. In spite of their own prominence in the city, neither Mark nor Caroline had been invited to the Low house, but they knew of its expensive furnishings and that even the upstairs mantels were of black Egyptian marble.

On the warm, showery early May afternoon as his driver, Jupiter, drove him to Lafayette Square, Mark felt strangely anxious at the prospects of so much time alone with the gentleman who had been for years only a business associate. He and Low had never been friends. Mark would not forget the ruggedly handsome Scot's threats the day he, Charles Green, and the other members of the safe fund had discovered an abolitionist pamphlet on Mark's desk some five years ago, but time had eased the strains of that day. The Compromise of 1850 had also eased the strains between North and South over slavery. Neither man's mind had been changed. Mark still despised the ugly institution. Low strongly favored it. Mark smiled to himself as the carriage turned into the Abercorn Street side of Lafayette Square.

Low is richer than I, he thought, but he needs the South's cotton in order to stay that way. I need it, too, but my Yankee grandfather's Northern shipping interests insulate me from total dependency upon it. Would I feel as deeply as I do if my own wealth sank or swam on the future of the cotton market?

The question took the smile from his face, because he was dead sure of the answer: Yes, he would want emancipation in every state even if it cost his fortune. No man loved the city of Savannah more than he, but Aunt Nassie, who reared him, had nurtured his young mind with her staunch early abolitionism. The thought of one man owning another still repelled him, would always repel him.

Andrew Low's butler admitted Mark, and within seconds his sturdily built, bearded host, perhaps twenty years or so Mark's junior, strode into the ornate front room of the double parlors, their *café au lait* walls the perfect, subdued background for heavily carved woodwork and gleaming furniture.

Hand extended, Low greeted him warmly, his gruff voice seeming to exaggerate the Scottish burr still prominent in his speech. "Good of you to come, Browning. I trust Mrs. Browning understands my need for privacy with you, at least for this once. Sit down, sit down."

"My wife wouldn't expect to be invited on a business occasion," Mark said, taking a handsomely upholstered tapestry wing chair by the fire. "She sends her regards, of course."

Still standing, back to the fireplace, Low looked at Mark for a moment, his eyes intense beneath the heavy, dark red brows. "This—this isn't precisely a business meeting. I'm about to become a member of your, shall we say wider family circle, sir, and I felt a need to elevate our acquaintance from a mere business association to what might possibly turn out to be a friendship of sorts."

Mark smiled up at his host. If nothing else, Low was direct. "I see. Well, that sounds reasonable enough and I–I hope we succeed, Mr. Low." Deciding to be equally direct, Mark added, "I'd believed us to be friendly once, you know, until the day five or so years ago when you and the others in our safe fund called at my office to threaten me."

The merest hint of a smile played at Low's full mouth. "I suppose you're still clinging to your Northern ways."

"On the subject of slavery, yes."

"Look here, Browning, you're my senior by some years. I'm about to marry into the Stiles family. Wouldn't it be more appropriate for you to call me Andrew?"

"If you like."

"Yes. Thank you." Mark rather enjoyed the moment. He'd never known Andrew Low to appear ill at ease over anything. He seemed quite ill at ease now. Why? There was no doubt in anyone's mind that Andrew Low was a gentleman, known far and wide as domineering, sure of himself, in full charge at all times.

"I've been a very lonely man, Browning, for nearly five years. Ever since the death of my wife, Sarah. The letters and gestures of sympathy helped, of course, but I cared deeply for her and our two girls need a mother." Suddenly he sat down as though needing the support.

Mark nodded his understanding although Low was not looking at him. Of course the man had been lonely. He had been considered a wonderful provider for Sarah Hunter Low, had built this magnificent house for her, staffed it with slaves, furnished it with excellent taste, sparing no expense. But Mark had never once thought of Low's personal grief when she died. The realization shocked him.

"I'm deeply sorry for all those—lonely years," he said lamely. "You—you seldom give the impression of anything but being in full control. I hope you take no offense at that, Mr. Low."

"I do wish you'd call me Andrew."

"I apologize. It may take a little time—Andrew. You're younger than I, true, but Savannahians are a bit in awe of you."

"Not you, I'm certain."

"Any businessman respects the kind of success you enjoy."

"I suppose so, but success is a poor companion at times. It has never been known to fill an empty heart nor an empty bed."

"I'm sure it doesn't. Selfish of me, but I find myself hoping I go before my wife, Caroline." A rush of emotion resembling guilt came, but lingered only a moment. Why should he or anyone else in town feel guilty for not having detected this arrogant, powerful man's broken heart? It still seemed impossible that Andrew Low could love any woman as Mark loved Caroline.

"I need a wife," Low was saying, looking directly at him now. "I need to be a father again. I need the self-esteem fatherhood gives a man. My little girls need a woman's care and guidance. I need a hostess here in my house. I need a woman's sure hand with the servants. I need Miss

Mary Cowper Stiles very much. I don't know her well yet, but there will be time for that in the years to come." He smiled a little. "There's nothing wrong with my past middle-aged eyes. The young lady's a veritable beauty."

"I can certainly agree with you there, Andrew," Mark said, and felt much older just from having heard himself call this imposing man by his first name. "I'm sure you do have all those needs."

"I daresay Miss Stiles's needs will be met, too. And her father's. W. H. Stiles, according to his letters, is in a rather depressed state of mind these days."

"Oh, I thought he was deep in the finishing stages of his book on the Austrian revolution. I believe Harper and Brothers will publish it, perhaps next year."

"He is still at work on the book, but a book does end and the man is a bit at sea in the world of politics—his chief interest. Stiles is a devout Southern Democrat, you know, and even though I've just returned from abroad, I have learned of the gradual disintegration of the old Whig Party." He raised a hand, not finished. "I know Democrats should rejoice at the demise of their opponents, but far more disruptive political groups could replace the Whigs. Stiles is a traditional politician, Browning. He likes a sharply defined single opponent to demolish."

"I'm certainly no politician myself," Mark said carefully, "but I've heard there are some here in the First District, in Chatham County, who want W.H. to run for governor. I'd think that would stimulate him."

"It may. I doubt his chances, though, and anyway, the man's had a taste of national and international politics. His latest letter, which reached me here only yesterday, shows him to be intensely disturbed at the rising Northern opposition in Congress to the good efforts of Senator Stephen A. Douglas in behalf of his Kansas-Nebraska bill. The bill does favor the South, but I predict it will so anger the North, it could create more abolitionists in a few weeks than Garrison created in twenty years."

Low had been abroad for several months. Mark was amazed at his grasp of recent United States politics. The South certainly did favor the Douglas bill, but how could such a loose idea succeed? The deep division in the country looked more forbidding than ever to Mark.

Andrew Low got to his feet once more and stood peering down at him. "You'd rejoice, I suppose, at the creation of more abolitionists, Browning, as I would rejoice at the droves of slave owners who would surely move west in order to help create more slave land out there."

Low was not making a cutting remark. He was smiling as he spoke. "I could not possibly agree with you less where slavery is concerned," he went on, "but I do commend your courage in having stood steadfastly against it here in the heart of States' Rights Savannah. A lesser man would have buckled under the pressure I and the others in our safe fund put upon you a few years ago."

Low's tall butler announced dinner and the two men went together into the dining room, cheerful though rigidly formal with its light green walls and magnificently set table. Candlelight from the crystal chandelier gleamed off polished silver and crystal.

"An enormously pleasant room, Andrew," Mark said as he took his chair to Low's right. "I do like the color of the walls."

"My wife's choice. I'm not quite sure, but I believe the color is called celadon."

"That's right," Mark said, "it is." Not a highly tasteful reply, even a bit unkind, he supposed. He might have simply said nothing.

"One of my lifelong regrets," Low went on, "is that Sarah was desperately ill throughout the precious few months she lived in this house. I have no happy memories of her here. She was too ill."

While two women served their meal—roast beef, thick gravy, potatoes, lima beans, and hot rolls, following a rich soup course and oysters— far heavier food than Mark preferred, the two men carried on casual conversation, as Mark decided it was no wonder Andrew Low tended toward overweight. He was trying to like the man. He'd always respected Low's expertise as a merchant and shipowner, and at times today had even felt genuine pity for him. The somewhat pensive remark about having no happy memories of his first wife's short life in the Lafayette Square mansion touched Mark. Maybe one day they could be friends. His own views on slavery, unique in Savannah, had long ago schooled Mark to expect only casual men friends, except, of course, for William Mackay. He would try harder for a relationship with Low since the man did plan to marry Eliza Anne's daughter, but if it turned out to remain only superficial, Mark already knew how to handle that.

"Douglas's pro-Southern popular sovereignty bill has passed the Senate"—Low picked up the thread of their previous talk with ease—"but only the Almighty knows how bitter the House fight might become."

Unable to resist, Mark asked, "You called the bill pro-Southern, sir. Stephen A. Douglas is a Northerner who has never had the reputation of being anything but moderate. After all, he greatly helped Clay in getting through the Compromise of 1850. I suppose his agreement with

Breckinridge to include the outright repeal of the old Missouri Compromise did win a lot of Southerners."

"Of course it did, and the country's well rid of that unfortunate compromise, in my opinion," Low said, his tone of voice seeming to close off further discussion. He might just as well have said "–in my *dogmatic* opinion," Mark thought, suddenly devoid of the smattering of sympathy he'd felt for Low a few minutes earlier. The man had an infuriating way of flattening every impulse toward an understanding friendship. He seemed almost to enjoy the process.

"I feel W. H. Stiles, my future father-in-law, is genuinely worried about the inevitable increase of Northern resistance to us down here. That, to me at least, could account for his political restlessness right now. I can feel Stiles's longing to be back in Congress to help drive Douglas's bill through the House. The expansionist Know-Nothing Party is a dangerous development, Browning–from the point of view of any true Southerner." Looking directly at Mark now, Low smiled and held a forkful of beef in midair as he said in his most authoritative voice, "I would like to hear straight from your own lips, since we'll be in a sense family members soon, *what* you consider yourself. A Southerner? Certainly not. A Northerner? Certainly not. A Savannahian with Northern sympathies? Dangerous identity–more dangerous by the day if the news from Washington is any indication."

Mark returned his look, laid down his own fork, and said firmly, "I'm a citizen of the United States, Andrew, and–as you say–a Savannahian."

Low cut another bite of beef, chewed and swallowed it. "In short, a total contradiction, eh? Well, no matter."

Unable to let that pass, Mark asked, "No matter? How could it be of no matter with your opinions so strongly Southern, sir?"

"Simple. I keep separate compartments. You and I have an opportunity to build our relationship on a purely family basis. I know well how close you have always been to the Mackays, now the Stileses and so on. Do you not do that, too, Browning? Don't tell me you're so naïve as to allow your family ties to influence business or politics!"

Why his blunt, dogmatic statements rubbed Mark so much the wrong way, he couldn't have explained. He only knew they did. This minute, he *did not* like Andrew Low. Imagining this arrogant, domineering man married to gentle, loving little Mary Cowper was a near impossibility. Natalie is right, he thought, and looked at his watch, hoping for an excuse to leave early.

"We all know your wife is not in sympathy with your views on slavery," Low barreled ahead. "By 'we' I mean Savannahians who are anybody. I'd say you're an expert at keeping things in compartments. The lovely lady, Miss Caroline, has quite evidently not influenced you."

When Mark didn't comment at once, Low interjected, "I noticed you looked at your watch. You haven't been here quite an hour, you know."

It had seemed like two! "That's right," Mark said. "And I apologize. I've enjoyed my dinner so much and our talk—I thought perhaps more time had gone by than I suspected." That was a lie. "I do have a three-thirty appointment back at my countinghouse. And perhaps you're right about my keeping certain issues in separate compartments. At least, I keep them to myself. I love and respect my wife too much, I value her right to her opinion far too highly to . . ."

"To take any chances?" Low asked, an eyebrow cocked. "What could your wife possibly do to change your way of thinking where North and South are concerned? Have you given that any thought?"

"No, I haven't. I consider it not only personal but irrelevant. Certainly irrelevant to this conversation."

"I see. Then forgive me."

"Not at all, but I would like very much to know, Andrew, why you invited me here today. Is that too personal a question?"

The main course finished, Low leaned back in his chair. "I well may need you in the years ahead. The years of my married life to Miss Mary Cowper Stiles. I have every reason to believe that her parents are both delighted, happy, and certainly relieved to have their only daughter marry me. It is never foolish for an extravagant man like W. H. Stiles to fatten his coffers, to fall into a legitimate, legal Savannah residence should he decide to run again for office from Chatham County."

Mark found what he was hearing so hard to believe, he could only keep silent, his eyes on his own half-emptied dinner plate.

"Miss Stiles's beauty is indeed an inducement to me. I need a wife, my girls need a mother, I need a companion. Her youth, I might add, is an added inducement. I need more children. An heir. I—need her physical charms. I've been a very lonely man, Browning. A very, very lonely man. By marrying me, Miss Stiles will better herself, of course. She'll have every material benefit her heart can possibly desire. She will travel abroad and in the United States. Her place in Savannah, in Newport, in British society will be forever assured as Mrs. Andrew Low. To say nothing of the obvious benefits to her father—her family. Can I count on your support?"

Again, he tried to speak, but Mark could only stare at the man. The cold litany of benefits to warmhearted, innocent Mary Cowper and her father had been ticked off as a merchant would sell a line of dry goods or a shipment of cotton. First and foremost remained the passionate litany of what Andrew Low himself needed from being married to her! Low's eyes had burned with desire as he had ticked off his own need for her beauty, her youth—her physical charms.

"Perhaps you didn't hear my question," Low pressed. "Can I count on your support? W. H. Stiles will, in spite of the high esteem in which I hold his talents and political thought, need much help from me. The man is wise enough to realize that, thus joining his even wiser wife in seeing that Mary Cowper broke off her engagement to the young ne'er-do-well, Elliott. Do you care enough about W. H. Stiles and his—"

"Excuse me, Mr. Low," Mark interrupted. "You knew about Mary Cowper's engagement to young Elliott?"

Low threw back his head and laughed. "You don't think I've reached such a pinnacle in my life by ever buying a pig in a poke, do you now?" The laughter stopped. "I invited you here today to obtain, if possible, an answer to my question, sir. *Can I count on your support?*"

Mark waited for what he well knew was an unconscionably long time to respond, but he couldn't for the life of him think how to phrase an honest answer. Finally, just before the dinner plates were removed, he said, "You can count on my fairness, Andrew."

Obviously the response was not at all adequate. Neither man spoke during the time the Negro woman collected plates and the partially emptied silver bowls of vegetables. The instant she left the room, Low, as though there had been practically no interruption, said, "I see."

"I hope you do."

"For a man to promise *fairness* when his own views and loyalties are as contradictory as yours, Browning, falls somewhere quite short of a promise, I'd say."

The woman returned, a young helper behind her, bearing a high, layered chocolate cake, and before either man spoke again, dessert plates were laid with ample servings of the rich, moist cake.

"Thank you," Mark addressed the servant with a slight smile. "That looks delicious."

The delighted servant followed her helper out the swinging door, still beaming and bowing her pleasure. The tension in the elegant room heightened now, as Mark realized what he'd done. He was so accustomed to thanking—complimenting—his Irish Maureen and Miss Eliza's black Hannah, he had quite forgotten that Andrew Low undoubtedly preferred his servants to enter and depart without notice of any kind. He could feel Low's disapproval.

For a moment or two, they ate their dessert in silence. Then, as though trying a totally different tack, Low said almost anxiously, "You know Mary Cowper quite well, eh, Browning?"

"I feel I do, yes, sir."

"Then tell me, do you think she'll find me acceptable as a husband?"

How, Mark thought, could this enigmatic man dare to think of me as contradictory? Surely Andrew Low took the prize in contradictory behavior. Mark had been treated as any perfect gentleman would treat another. The meal was delicious, the service excellent. That he was supposed to feel honored as the only guest of the town's richest, most influential citizen was obvious. The truth was, he felt as though he'd been pummeled from one corner of the lovely room to another. "Do I— think she'll find you acceptable?" he repeated the question. "Mary Cowper is, even at her tender age, direct and honest. She has evidently made her choice. The girl will do all in her power to be a good, faithful, loyal wife to you."

"Splendid," Low said triumphantly. "There's one more thing, Browning. I was wondering if you'd mind writing a short letter to her— oh, simply telling her of our good talk, of my having honored you as my only dinner guest today and—" He broke off, toying with his fork, as though even he realized he'd gone too far.

Mark laid aside the heavy damask napkin. "No, Andrew, I couldn't do that. Mary Cowper and I have always had too close a friendship."

Quite cordially, Low remarked, "I don't believe in dueling, Browning, and surely that wasn't as insulting as it sounded."

"No, sir, it was not. I meant it. No matter how intimate our association might grow to be, I love Mary Cowper too much to interfere in any way." Both men stood up from the table. "I'm deeply grateful for the honor of dinner today, sir, and with all my heart, I wish you and your wife-to-be all joy and happiness and success."

"Thank you, Browning," he said, walking with Mark into the light-mustard-colored entrance hall, where his hat, cloak, and stick waited. "Perhaps if you don't feel free to say a good word in my behalf to Mary Cowper, you could find it in your heart to tell her of your admiration for the home over which she will preside?"

"When I see her, I certainly will do that," Mark said, brushing at his beaver hat. "Mrs. Browning and I will be going to Etowah Cliffs for the wedding. Is it May 17?"

"That's right. A Wednesday, I believe." Low smiled wryly. "Bishop Stephen Elliott will perform the wedding ceremony. No relation, though, to my predecessor."

"Bishop Elliott has been friends of the family for many years."

"So I understand." Low held out his hand. "Well, sir, it's been a pleasure and perhaps we'll see more of each other on an even more personal basis up in Cass next month. I hope I haven't appeared as nervous as a schoolboy."

Outside, the afternoon had cleared and the sun was shining. Mark was glad he'd instructed Jupiter not to return for him in the carriage. He needed time alone after being with such a thoroughly puzzling man. His visit with Andrew Low had certainly not been satisfactory, but he had managed to work his way through it. He still didn't like his host, but he felt he'd glimpsed a bit more of the man's curious nature.

Rounding the corner onto Bryan Street on the north side of Reynolds Square, he wished he'd stopped at Miss Eliza's house. Even a brief talk with her might have helped ease a little of his confusion about Low. Most of the time Miss Eliza was like a good, clear magnifying glass, bringing things into perspective for him. There really wasn't time, though. He did have an appointment back at the office. Mark and Caroline would not be taking the Central of Georgia to Cass until next week. There would be plenty of time to talk over Low's odd behavior with Miss Eliza, who was almost pathetically eager to be even a small part of the wedding plans. She had long ago decided her health would not permit her to go, but Mark knew her heart so well by now, he was aware of how much it meant to her just to discuss her granddaughter's dubious future with both him and Caroline. Was Mary Cowper's future as the wife of Andrew Low a matter for alarm? To Mark it was. He reluctantly admitted it to himself. Both Mackay sisters were going, of course, which meant William would be staying with Miss Eliza. William had traveled to Europe for a solitary holiday last year. He'd visited the Lees in Virginia, but Mark could see a big change in his old friend. Oh, William was still available when needed. He kept abreast of his now fairly wide business interests, he still gave his sister Sarah as good as she sent when she provoked it, but William seemed to be failing somehow. Certainly he was growing fat. Perhaps it was just as well that he had to stay in Savannah and miss the wedding. Any wedding was still hard for William and at times Mark still felt the burden of his old friend's grief.

A glance at his watch showed that he would have time to stop at home for a brief report to Caroline on the bewildering two hours spent with Andrew Low. He found her waiting for him, hoping he'd be able to stop.

Their grandchild, Willow, interrupted twice as they tried to converse alone in the family drawing room, but he found Caroline, in the few minutes they had together, more than understanding when he declared, "I can't even explain my feelings about the man to you, darling. One minute I pitied him—felt for his loneliness—the very next minute I felt downright hostile. The one thing that haunts me above all else is—what will Low be like alone with Mary Cowper? He scarcely knows her and yet he seems to have no doubts as to the rightness of the arrangement. They *will* have times alone like this, though, and for the life of me I can't imagine what it might be like! It's—it's almost as though he's made up his mind to buy a piece of valuable property or a shipment of cotton for the Liverpool market!"

"But what did he say that made you pity him?"

"His every mention of his first wife, Sarah, I think. Low's been lonely. I don't doubt that. He's human, after all. I don't recall thinking once while she was still alive, though, about whether or not they really loved each other, do you?"

"Come to think of it, no," Caroline said. "He was always the perfect gentleman. The first Mrs. Low was quiet, reserved, rather delicate, both physically and in her manner, but I don't think I'd call them up as one of the city's more devoted couples. Mary Cowper's far prettier, of course."

"And Low lusts after her! That I know."

"Mark! Did he say something to cause you to think that?"

"In a manner of speaking. The way he *looked* when he spoke of her told me far more."

"Oh, dear. He was married to Sarah Hunter Low barely five years and she had a child every year but two, of course. A little boy died when he was very small, as I remember." She reached for Mark's hand. "We're judging the man, darling."

"I know, but what's the difference whether a man is judged by his business dealings or by his private life?"

"That's the kind of question you should ask of Miss Eliza. I don't know the answer, but Mr. Low is beyond reproach in business, isn't he?"

"So far as I know," Mark said, getting to his feet. "I do have to get back to the office. No mail from Natalie, I guess."

"You know I'd have told you first thing."

"Well, at least she's agreed to be Mary Cowper's matron of honor."

"Do hurry home, Mark. I'll have had Jupiter drive me to the dressmaker's by the time you're back, to pick up Mary Cowper's bridal gown and the heavenly pale blue dress I had made for Natalie. I'm afraid we'll need to take an extra trunk just for those two gowns."

He kissed her briefly. "Aren't we taking a gown for Callie, too? After all, she's the flower girl at the wedding."

"No. Eliza Anne had that made up there."

"Will it meet your critical standard, do you think?"

"I'm sure it will. Whatever you think of her choice of a husband for her daughter, Eliza Anne does have excellent taste and little girls' dresses are simpler to make." She went to the door with him. "Now, do hurry home, please."

FIFTEEN

At midafternoon, Saturday, the thirteenth of May, four days before the wedding, the train carrying Mark and Caroline and the two Mackay sisters pulled into Cassville Station. Sarah Mackay spotted Callie first, waving from the station platform.

"I do believe that child's grown in the few weeks since we saw her last," Sarah exclaimed. "Look at her, Kate, she's almost as tall as her mother! Mark, look at your grandchild."

"I'm looking," he laughed, "and you may be right, Kate. Of course, her mother's never been very tall, but–"

"I declare, that child looks about to burst wide open," Sarah said, pulling Caroline toward the train window. "She's as pretty as a picture, too, isn't she?"

"We think so," Caroline said proudly. "I'm so glad Callie is a beautiful child. I once had a young friend whose mother outshone her by far and that's very hard on a girl. Mark, you and Burke must be sure all four of our trunks are unloaded if this thing ever jerks to a stop."

Callie reached them first, hip-hopping along the platform, both arms out, and right behind her came Burke and Natalie. Burke, Sarah thought, appeared quite pleased about something. His square, handsome, open face shone and he warmly took her hand as Natalie introduced her and Kate.

"It just doesn't seem possible," Natalie said, "that you three haven't met each other in all this time."

"I'm afraid I'm a real upcountry man," Burke said, not, Sarah thought, a bit apologetically. "We have a surprise for you," he went on to Mark and Caroline, pointing a short distance down the track. "Behold! Our new carriage."

Everyone exclaimed at the sight of Burke's very first gentleman's carriage–bright yellow, at Natalie's insistence, he explained, its shiny black top gleaming in the sunlight.

"Oh, it's a beautiful carriage," Caroline said, "but where will we all ride, Natalie?"

"Callie can sit in one of the seats inside with you and Papa, or on Papa's lap. Kate and Sarah in the other. I'll ride in the driver's seat with Burke, of course. In fact, I may drive!".

"Natalie!"

"Now, Mama, none of that. Burke can tell you I drive a team as expertly as he does. Come on," she urged, motioning them all toward the waiting carriage, the stamping, handsome matched pair of horses seeming eager to go. "New team, too. Didn't Burke make a good selection, Papa?"

"The horses look first-class to me," Mark said, as proud as if they belonged to him, Sarah thought, holding fast to Callie's hand.

"Don't forget, Mark," Caroline said, "we have four trunks plus six valises."

"*Four* trunks?" Natalie gasped. "I guarantee there won't be any fancy-dress balls up here. Why four trunks, Mama?"

"Why, we have Mary Cowper's bridal gown and your gorgeous gown."

Sarah saw Natalie give Burke what appeared to be a look of dismay. Burke registered nothing.

"How in the world will we get four trunks and all these people in one carriage, Burke?" Natalie demanded.

Grinning a little, Burke said, "I'm not quite sure, honey, but we'll find a way."

"Natalie, the bridal gown alone took up most of one trunk. You didn't want your own new dress crushed, did you? There was nothing to do but bring an extra . . ."

"And no chance to get a letter to you in time, Mama," Natalie said, frowning.

"Whatever for, dear?"

"I'm not going to be in the wedding."

Kate and Sarah exchanged horrified looks.

"Mary Cowper agrees finally that I shouldn't be her matron of honor feeling as I do, so she's chosen you, Sarah."

"*Me?*"

"Why not?"

"Natalie, I'm not beautiful *or* young!"

"What etiquette book says the matron of honor has to be? You're Mary C.'s aunt and you're not all that old, for goodness' sake. I think she made an excellent choice."

"But, Caroline," Sarah asked, still flabbergasted, "I'm so tall. Will the gown you had made for Natalie fit me?"

"It can be made to fit," Natalie said firmly.

"Well, I–I *was* bridesmaid for one of the Minis girls," Sarah said hesitantly, "but I just don't know."

"Why not, Sister?"

"Yes, why not?" Natalie pressed. "After all, you and Kate both seem to be all in favor of Mary Cowper marrying old Redbeard Low!"

"Natalie, that's enough," Caroline scolded.

"Do stop beating around the bush, Sister," Kate said. "It doesn't mean a thing, that old superstition about 'always a bridesmaid, never a bride'!"

"I didn't say it did."

"Sarah, you know perfectly well that I'm too plump to get into a gown designed for Natalie. If she refuses to stand up with poor little Mary Cowper, it certainly behooves you to take her place."

"You have to do it, Sarah," Natalie ordered. "There are no two ways about it. I–can't, so you must. Papa, you and Burke go for the baggage. It must be unloaded by now—even four whole trunks."

When the two men had hurried away toward the baggage truck, Sarah and Kate fell into animated conversation with Callie, leaving Natalie and her mother momentarily alone.

"I know what you're thinking, Mama, but don't spoil our friendship —yours and mine. I meant it when I said I *can't* be Mary C.'s matron of honor. And when you can't, you can't. It would be dishonest."

"That makes no sense whatever, and what would be dishonest about standing up with the person who considers you her best friend?"

"Because Mary Cowper doesn't consider me that anymore." Almost beseechingly, Natalie took a step toward her mother. "Mama, I agreed to do it at first because I thought I should, I guess. I do try sometimes to mind what people say—for your sake and Papa's."

"I know you do, darling."

"But the more I thought about it, the more certain I was that in a way I'd be lying if I stood there acting as though I was standing *with* her. I wouldn't be. To me, she's committed suicide just as surely as Ben McDonald did."

"Natalie!"

With surprising gentleness, Natalie went on, "You can 'Natalie' me all you want to, Mama, but I've seen Mary Cowper evening after evening, sitting alone on the front steps of Miss Eliza's veranda, her aloneness and heartbreak so plain, so awful, I had to stop walking over there. I couldn't stand looking at her anymore. She loves Stuart Elliott, she'll never love any other man, and in order to live as that old geezer's wife, she *has* to be dead inside."

"Does—does Eliza Anne know you're refusing to stand up with Mary Cowper?"

Natalie sighed. "Yes, she knows it now. I told her. She agreed on Sarah instead."

"Without any argument? How did she take it?"

"She's so determined to marry her daughter off to that rich old—old—Scotsman, she didn't have any choice but to agree."

"She didn't even argue with you?"

"Of course she argued, but Miss Lib knows me well enough by now to know that when I mean something, I mean it. I told her flat out that it wasn't that I didn't love Mary Cowper—it was that I couldn't, not wouldn't—couldn't do it. And, Mama, I *couldn't.*" With no warning, she threw both arms around her mother and wept.

On the day before the wedding, the women at Etowah Cliffs, even Natalie, flew around making garlands and wreaths, as well as supervising Eliza Anne's people. Every hour that passed raised the level of excitement and now and then tempers. Greenery could be cut and woven together early since most of it was cedar and pine and laurel, but early spring flowers, except those to be arranged in vases, could not be cut until late in the afternoon. Pink azalea, or wild honeysuckle as Miss Lorah called it, already spread the woods back of the river cliffs with vibrant color, but because flame azalea, which Eliza Anne wanted to use as a bower under which the bridal couple would stand, was so slow coming into bloom, she made countless trips to inspect buds during the final hours.

I'm so nervous, it might as well be my wedding, Eliza Anne thought, scurrying to inspect buds alone. Andrew Low certainly waited till the last minute to get here. The thought rather annoyed her, but she wasn't worried. Mr. Low's latest letter was most enthusiastic. He certainly had no doubts.

And *I know it's right.* I've never been more sure W.H. and I are doing the wise thing for her, but I know it's our doing, she admitted. Ours and Andrew Low's. None of it is easy. Natalie thinks I'm gloating. Well, I'm not. I'm just *sure* and W.H. is, too. Natalie created the most difficulty, of course, because she was never known to hide her feelings. I doubt that anyone else in our circle except Henry agrees. Still, the Brownings *had* come. And Eliza Anne's two spinster sisters, but the sisters' excitement and approval seemed to count for little since their normally dull lives, broken only by regular trips to the market and calls on the same Savannah friends, were easily brightened. Mark and Caroline had made not one word of protest, but they probably agreed with Natalie, especially Mark.

Her foot caught in a brambly blackberry hoop, as the memory of Mary Cowper's "confession" stabbed her memory. Why did it continue to bring pain? Any mother should be pleased that her daughter had chosen to tell her the whole truth, even to the part William and Mark had played in arranging the deceitful tryst in Savannah with that dreadful Elliott boy. Well, she was proud. Relieved, too. Mary Cowper had chosen to obey her and W.H. She was going to marry Andrew Low and would thereby want for nothing—ever. Her parents had seen to it that the child would be protected from anguish and poverty and a drunken husband for all the days of her life. As an old lady, their daughter would look back and thank them.

Up ahead in the area of woods near her house which they had long called the Park, she saw a blaze of flame color and gave thanks. The weather was fine—a warm afternoon today, another warm night, and there would be plenty of flame azaleas by tomorrow to form a splendid bower. How Mary Cowper loved the Park, she thought, hurrying to retrace her steps to the house to tell Little Sinai it was time to round up the children from the quarters so as to have them ready by four o'clock to begin cutting the pink azalea sprays. Tomorrow morning, Miss Lorah would supervise the actual making of the bower. Perhaps not too willingly. Eliza Anne had never been able to be sure Lorah Plemmons didn't feel in her heart that she and W.H. were pushing their daughter into heartbreak, but the woman would do a masterful job arranging the bright branches of blossoms into a perfect bridal bower.

Nearing her house, she gave thanks for the endless supply of dogwood spreading the woods with more white light than the Milky Way on a clear, blue-black mountain night. Her elegant house would be filled with flowers and festive food and wine and laughter. Her own gown had turned out rather well, she thought, glad again that she'd chosen the nearly flame azalea silk instead of yellow, as Natalie had urged. Natalie is always one-tracked, she reminded herself. Any time her pouting friend Natalie was invited to choose a color, it was yellow.

Climbing the back steps, she put aside how she and Natalie would get along once the wedding was over. It would undoubtedly be a prickly job patching up their damaged friendship. Inspecting the trays and trays of sugar cookies, cakes, and pies lining the counters in her large kitchen, she made herself dismiss the nagging thought that Natalie might just be right—that Mary Cowper's happiness would never depend upon wealth or the privilege of extensive travel or family. Eliza Anne's own happiness *was* dependent upon all those blessings. Her only daughter simply could not be that different, that rebellious against her own family background.

She hurried into the parlor to inspect the progress Miss Lorah and Natalie were making with the servants as they banked the mantel with cedar and magnolia leaves. The tall clock in the corner of the parlor struck three times. Oh, dear, Eliza Anne thought, Mr. Low and his business partner, Charles Green, will reach Cassville within the hour! She breathed a prayer that everything would go well, that Mary Cowper's wedding day would be a perfect memory for them all. So much to do yet, so much to plan. The thought of two such wealthy, prominent gentlemen as Andrew Low and Charles Green as guests in her house gave her a sense of both achievement and anxiety. It was kind of Burke to go for them in his new carriage. She was thankful W.H. had decided to go along. As much as she loved her husband, having him around the house on a day like this was almost too nerve-wracking.

If it had seemed at all plausible, Burke would have chosen to be almost anywhere else than on the driver's seat of his new carriage beside W. H. Stiles, en route to Cassville to meet the train that would bring Andrew Low and Charles Green for the wedding tomorrow. He was fond of

W.H. and glad to be asked to meet two such famous gentlemen in his new carriage instead of the Stileses' old one, but politics—the one subject he and W.H. usually avoided—had held sway over the first ten miles of the slow, tedious ride. Of course, no one expected to be for long in the company of W. H. Stiles without the subject of America's political future coming up, but Burke dodged it when possible since, in the main, he and W.H. could not have been farther apart. Stiles was not only a strong States' Rights Democrat with fiery pro-slavery convictions; he was also vigorously in favor of America's Manifest Destiny— steadily urging, working for an even more rapid expansion to the west. For mile after mile, Burke had mostly listened to the generally accepted Southern reasons for expansionism: prosperity, the addition of slave states in order to keep the South's predominance in the Senate, the new railroad that would one day connect the Atlantic to the Pacific.

Burke could manage all right while W.H. stayed on such generalities, but when he brought up the bitter human conflict raging in the country now—from pulpits, at political meetings, in the press—over Senator Douglas's Kansas-Nebraska bill, he began to feel uneasy. As with all Southerners, W. H. Stiles greatly favored the bill. Douglas, Burke knew, was neither strongly pro-slavery nor strongly anti-slavery. He was a compromiser, who had made a noble effort, before the bill passed the Senate back in January, just to ignore the Missouri Compromise—to leave the matter of slavery in the new territories up to the people who would move there. Northerners didn't like it, but were not unduly upset, since few could argue with the principle of "popular sovereignty." Congressional Southerners, on the other hand, had ganged up in their famous "F Street Mess" in Washington and formed a phalanx to strike the Missouri Compromise its deathblow. The Southerners had the votes, so Douglas reluctantly agreed to incorporate the repeal in his new bill. Burke could recall the very words Douglas had used when he relented: "I will incorporate it in my bill, though I know it will raise a hell of a storm!" With Douglas, it had not been a change of heart, but a clear recognition of where power lay in Congress. The senator's desire to move ahead with the new railroad, to expand the country, had won out. Burke did not agree that Stephen Douglas had relented in order to help his own future presidential chances. He knew Douglas did not hold strong feelings about slavery either way. On this, at least, Burke and W.H. could agree. Perhaps, wanting to keep the peace on the day before Mary Cowper's wedding, Burke had even overagreed.

"You'll get no argument from me on Douglas's motives," Burke said as the carriage pulled within sight of the Cassville railroad station. "The senator himself says he prefers 'to leave the future of slavery up to the laws of climate, production, and physical geography.' "

"No matter," W.H. said confidently. "The South can make use of Douglas's willingness to *act* wisely. Let him leave it up to the weather, I couldn't care less. Just so that infernal Missouri Compromise is gone. Material forces will win out. I predict a close, close vote, but the South's prayers will be answered, Burke. Senator Douglas's popular sovereignty bill will squeak by in the House later this month, thanks to Secretary of War Jeff Davis, who used his skills to win over our lackadaisical President Pierce."

Burke hated the idea of slavery, but at the moment he was very willing to drop the subject. In fact, he made a direct point of changing to another topic, an even more risky topic, but too important, he felt, to ignore.

"I hope I don't sound presumptuous, sir," he said, slowing the team near the train platform, already beginning to collect a few people waiting too for the train from Macon, "but I suppose Mr. Low and Mary Cowper will have some time together this evening. Natalie tells me they don't know each other too well yet."

Burke was looking straight ahead but could feel W.H.'s eyes on him. "They know each other well enough, I'm sure," the older man said a bit sharply. "Your charming wife has exaggerated this entire thing all out of proportion, you know. Of course, the bridal couple will be alone all evening if that's their desire. The basic principles of this marriage are sound. Every newly married couple learn through the years to know each other. Why do you ask?"

"I–I just happen to care a lot about Mary Cowper."

"Of course you do," W.H. said, noncommittally. "I don't believe Lib has planned anything beyond supper. You and Natalie are invited, naturally."

"So Natalie told me, but I'm afraid she begged off for us both. The Stileses should be together on such an important evening."

"Thoughtful of Natalie," W.H. said, jumping down from the carriage to peer along the empty track.

"No sign of her yet?" Burke called, getting down, too, in order to hitch the team at a nearby post.

"None." As Burke walked toward W.H., he saw the older man tilt back his top hat and look away as though deciding something. "I say,

Burke, would it be rude of me to want to ride back in the carriage seats with our two distinguished visitors? I have a strong feeling I've bored you with my Southern talk. Perhaps Low and Green and I tend to agree more."

"You didn't bore me at all, sir," Burke laughed, "but I insist you ride in the carriage with them. After all, you three not only see eye to eye politically, but by this time tomorrow, Andrew Low will be your son-in-law."

"I take your point. Look here, Burke, you don't need to be careful with me on the subject of my precious daughter's–arranged marriage. Lib and I know too well what you and Natalie think." When Burke said nothing, he went on a bit lamely, "We know we appear to you and Natalie as insensitive, but we do what's best for our child. Mary C. and Andrew Low have been dinner partners twice in Savannah. She's always known who he is. The man's respected all over Chatham County and far beyond."

"I'm aware of that, sir. And I want you and Miss Lib to know that, to the extent that I can, I'll do my best to keep Natalie out of your family affairs."

"Ridiculous, Burke!"

"No, it isn't. Natalie loves your daughter very, very much. It's hard for her to see . . ."

"Hard to see Mary Cowper marry an older man who's a veritable stranger to the girl?"

"Something like that."

"I assure you, everything will work out most favorably. Mary Cowper and Andrew Low have a lifetime to get to know each other. Her mother and I can always count on our daughter to do her graceful best under all circumstances. You and Natalie remember that, Burke."

SIXTEEN

*M*ary Cowper sat at the family dining table in a
state of blank confusion, wanting desperately to do the right thing, but
as desperately realizing that she had no idea what the right thing might
be. First Papa and Mr. Charles Green, Mr. Low's groomsman, left the
table for brandy and cigars in Papa's office off the parlor. Then her
brothers, Henry and Robert, excused themselves to check their fish
traps down in the river. This left Mary Cowper—Mr. Low still seated
beside her—and Mama way down at the far end of the otherwise empty
table. Whatever possessed Papa to do such a thing? Even Henry and
Bobby should know she needed them there. What is it, she thought
wildly, that Mama and I are supposed to do now—here alone with Mr.
Low? He and Mama are both older. Shouldn't one of them say something? The normal thing for Mama to do right now would be to walk to
Natalie's house as an excuse for leaving me alone with Mr. Low. Poor
Mama . . . poor, trapped Mama! She no longer felt welcome at Natalie's cottage, in spite of the fact that the Brownings were there, too.

I must find a way to help Mama, she thought frantically, the old half-
sick feeling of responsibility to her parents surging over her. Neither
brother ever seemed to feel personally responsible for making Mama
and Papa happy. Why should I? There was no answer to that.

She *did* feel responsible, and as she glanced at Andrew Low's heavily bearded face, the actual *feel* of Stuart's smooth cheek and strong, young mouth caused her to grow faint. *None of this was happening and surely nothing that had taken place this evening at supper was real.* It was not the evening before her wedding to the heavy-shouldered, formal, older stranger beside her at the familiar table. A week or a month ago—whenever it was that she had come back from Savannah—sitting alone on the front steps, she had promised herself that she would work hard at learning how to live in two worlds at once. In one world would be the memory of Stuart, staying with her, helping her, comforting her the same as always. He would no longer be shattered or on the verge of anger or tears. Her champion, he would be quiet and strong and close and dear, as only Stuart could ever be. Her other world would be the new, scary, but necessary adventure of learning how to be Mrs. Andrew Low, wife of the bearded stranger who would make her mistress of a fine Savannah house and give her all the security that meant so much to Mama and Papa, so that for all the years of her life she would never have to think about there being enough money. With all her heart, Mary Cowper longed for a child, for children. Not once until now, when things were whipped into rigid finality, had she thought of anyone else's child but Stuart's. She still dreamed only of Stuart's children. Quickly, she forced away the thought that the man nearly Papa's age sitting in the awkward silence beside her would, before she could bear a child, have to touch her, make some kind of fateful love to her. It was fairly easy stopping the thought right there, because nowhere in her was the strength to pursue it. Stuart would have to take over and he would, oh, he would!

"Mr. Low, I'm sure you'll excuse me," Mama was saying. "I must consult with the servants about tomorrow's food preparation." In spite of her years spent entertaining even royalty in Vienna, Mama sounded so nervous, her laugh was almost gauche. "Anyway, I know you two want to be alone for a good, easy talk."

Mr. Low was standing because Mama was and in his low, rumbling voice was murmuring something gentlemanly and proper about his plan to go for a pleasant walk by the river with Mary Cowper before the sun fell from sight behind the magnificent hills of the Etowah Valley.

After another mundane remark, Mama was gone and Mr. Low, still standing beside her, reached for Mary Cowper's hand. His fingers felt warm and big and thick. He'd only been there a few hours, but, in an easy, familiar way, he led her straight for the hall tree and gallantly laid her cloak around her shoulders.

"Even at the table," he said, "I felt a draft. Your evenings do grow cool up here, don't they, my dear?"

They were crossing the veranda when she said as politely as possible, "Yes, sir, they do. Mama feels ever so much better in our upcountry air. I know she misses Savannah. She grew up there, you know, but I don't believe she misses the dreadful summer heat and she actually seems to enjoy our snow up here. It's her family she misses—my grandmother Mackay and Uncle William and Aunt Sarah and Aunt Kate." He knew all this, of course. She was rattling like a silly child, a quite silly child, as though she must fill up the time stretching endlessly ahead—as though lots and lots of empty-headed chatter could prevent something.

His heavy, muscular arm was hooked in hers as they strolled out to the river road and began walking in the direction of Papa's stables and the quarters. Walking, thank heaven, away from Natalie's cottage. Did he know that too already? Had Mr. Low heard about Natalie's strong opposition to their marriage? Mary Cowper realized and accepted easily at that moment the fact that she might never know what Mr. Low had heard or what he had not heard. By now, such a thought was simple to accept; she had accepted so, so much during the past few months. And she had done it. She needn't doubt her ability to accept—not ever. It was all right not being informed about Mr. Low's knowledge of anything that had to do with her. She would be a good wife to him. She'd promised Mama, and Mama had told Papa of the solemn promise, which she certainly intended to keep. "There will be so many glorious times as Mrs. Andrew Low, darling," Mama had said. "You'll see places you'd never see otherwise and meet continental society and Mr. Low is known far and wide for his generosity. You'll never, never want for anything!"

Walking along in the evening sounds above the river, its current chortling past beneath where they walked, she remembered the tinge of envy in her mother's voice. Poor Mama and Papa had found it difficult to keep up their standards with always limited means, with three children to educate properly, the new acreages Papa felt he needed to buy, such a huge house to pay for and furnish as a Stiles house had to be furnished. Plantation equipment cost a lot, too, she knew. If becoming Mrs. Andrew Low meant the easing of even a few of Papa's burdens, she would feel gratified. It would help her make all the still mysterious adjustments she'd have to make—without Stuart.

But I will not be without Stuart, she reminded herself quickly. *I've found a way to keep him beside me, giving me the strength and courage I've always believed he really has.*

It would help, too, never to have to defend Stuart Elliott again. No one would know—no one in the whole, wide world—that he was still close, so close in her thoughts, there would be no reason to defend him.

"We'll return to my Savannah home as soon as the wedding is over," Mr. Low was saying, as though he were laying out a business procedure. He had wasted no words with getting-acquainted talk. It was as though they'd been sharing his plans all along. "My two small daughters need us both there with them right now. I feel it wise for them to finish out the spring with their present tutor, then when you and I leave for England on a somewhat belated honeymoon, I can place them in a school I've found there near my home in Leamington. I'm sure you'll need to shop extensively in Savannah. Mr. Latimer told Charles Green and me on the carriage ride from Cassville that upcountry stores leave much to be desired."

"They're—they're awfully nice people running our stores up here, though," she said irrelevantly, a touch defensively, perhaps, then decided to laugh at herself. "Just because the clerks are pleasant doesn't, of course, improve selections much. There's nothing anywhere in the upcountry to compare with Low's Emporium, I'm sure." She giggled, then checked herself. "I'm chattering again, sir, forgive me."

The heavy arm squeezed hers, held her against him so hard, she could feel him tremble. "Don't apologize for chattering, my dear. I'm a man who knows what he wants. I want a young, spirited, beautiful wife— exactly like you. I need a good wife. My life lacks nothing else. Once we're on that train heading south to the coast, I will be a man fulfilled."

Frowning, she wondered helplessly what to say. His manner of speaking made response difficult because he seemed to lay one firm declaration after another, leaving no space for her. He hadn't yet asked one question that required her opinion.

"I know from your father's articles written from abroad when he was chargé d'affaires in Austria that your family traveled some, but you'll find me a superb tour conductor, familiar with the truly luxurious sites, the truly historic, the truly beautiful. In no time you'll lose your upcountry provinciality, have no fear."

"I'm not afraid of being upcountry provincial, Mr. Low," she said in a surprisingly calm, controlled voice.

He squeezed her arm again. "No, of course not. I weighed your fine spirit along with your beauty and youth, Mary Cowper."

"Thank you, Mr. Low," was all she could think of to say.

"My name is Andrew, as I'm sure you're aware." He had stopped walking and was looking down at her now, his beard thicker, redder somehow in the fading light. "Can't you bring yourself to call me Andrew yet?"

"Not yet, Mr. Low. Perhaps later." At least, he'd finally asked her a question, intended, she knew, to be flattering, but it could be a long, long time before he was anything to her but Mr. Low.

Still holding her arm, still looking down at her, he went on, "I've also learned that you're very good with little girls. My Amy is eight, my Harriet is six."

"I believe myself to be amenable with children. The Latimer child and I have always been good friends. Natalie's only child, Callie, named for Natalie's mother, Caroline Browning, is now almost ten. Will your daughters like me, do you think?"

"They will if they mean to please their father, who likes you very, very much—or he would not be making you his wife."

All she could think of to say was: "Thank you, Mr. Low."

"My dear, even your politeness is titillating."

Abruptly, almost roughly, he pulled her against him. She could feel his whole body trembling now and his grip on her was so urgent, she could only stand there and wait, longing for the moment when he might release her and let her go to her own room. Her familiar, safe room upstairs where she would be spending the last night snuggled down in her own comfortable bed alone. Mary Cowper would soon be twenty-one years old, a woman, but her heart pulled back toward her carefree girlhood at this moment so painfully she stifled a cry. She needn't have. Thick, hungry lips were covering her mouth. Covering it wholly, seeming almost to be devouring her. The beard surrounding the lips was disagreeable, wiry, it even *felt* dark red. "Old Redbeard Low" . . . Natalie kept saying in Savannah. Old, old, old . . . Papa's beard fringing his chin had always felt light and silky. Mr. Low was a few years younger than Papa, but he shook and grabbed like an insistent, old man.

Then, abruptly, he released her, stepped back, bowed from the waist, and smiled with such charm that his ruggedly handsome face looked almost poetic. It helped that his teeth were strong and even and white. "I'm sure you need some rest now, my dear," he said quite gently. "I'll take you to your room."

"Yes," she whispered. "And, Mr. Low, I promised my parents I'd do my level best to be a good, faithful wife to you. I now promise you that, too. Thank you for your kindness."

PART
II

February 1856–April 1857

SEVENTEEN

Wearing the shirred, rose-colored overblouse especially favored by Mr. Low and bought for her abroad last year, along with countless other daytime and formal clothes, Mary Cowper was alone in the master bedroom, which faced Abercorn Street. For a long time, she sat, elbows propped on the small writing desk, and stared out unseeing at the front garden, bordered by its wrought-iron fence. Before her on the desk lay the pages of a letter just written to her mother at Etowah Cliffs. Writing to Mama during the nearly two years she'd been married was a pleasant, but tedious duty and a careful rereading had come to be as essential as the writing itself.

6 February 1856

My dear Mama and Papa,

   Today is Wednesday and although Friday is my usual day for reporting to you on the week just past, I will have little or no time this Friday since the famous man of letters Mr. William Makepeace Thackeray is due by boat early Friday afternoon. Mr. Low is most excited by his arrival because he so enjoyed his company when Mr. Thackeray stayed in this house four years ago during his first lecture series in Savannah. My husband is quite proud that he was able to rescue him then from what Mr. Thackeray called "the bedbugged hotel" and looks forward again to being his host. I am glad Mr. Low has a wife this time and I will certainly do all I can to make the great man's stay with us pleasant. I know Mr. Low will relish long conversations with him, in part because they are both British subjects, but also because Mr. Low finds him excellent and, at times, quite humorous company. Of course, being a popular author, he is a master storyteller and, as Mr. Low says, always knows just when to embroider and when to stop. I pray our little one, Catherine Mackay, will not disturb our guest, even though her room is just off his. Mr. Thackeray is devoted to children, and vows he makes these hard, exhausting foreign tours only for the sake of earning money for the future security of his own two daughters, near the ages of my stepdaughters, Amy and Harriet. In your latest letter you asked how I am faring with my stepdaughters. Splendidly, both when they are here in Savannah and by letter from school in England. We became friends, I feel, during my time abroad with their father in my first year of married life. We still thank God that we were all away from Savannah during the ghastly yellow-fever epidemic. All around us still we see grief and hardship in town, especially among the poorer folk who could not get away. I write regularly to Amy and Harriet at their English school and for little girls aged ten and eight, they are also quite faithful.

I feel I have made you both happy and that is my main concern. Papa, you are, even way up there in Cass, still a popular man in Savannah. Items keep appearing in our newspapers of Chatham's pride in you for having been elected Speaker of the Georgia Assembly on the first ballot. And I know how enthusiastic you are to be back in the thick of politics. One of my main joys is that you have, in my home on Lafayette Square, a bona fide Savannah residence, since your views and talents are so appreciated here. Mr. Low's pride in you pleases me, too. He never fails to show me every mention of you in the *Georgian*. My parents form a good bond for my husband and me. I know that your happiness in me will only continue as long as I am a success in my marriage and my determination to remain so is as strong as ever. Though busy and often preoccupied with his many business affairs, Mr. Low is kind, and I can only say that my life here affords me everything a wife could sensibly desire.

Mary Cowper stopped reading and looked out the window onto Andrew Low's formal garden, the boxwood planted in unique hourglass designs. Had she lied to her parents when she declared herself to have "everything a wife could sensibly desire"? No. There had been nothing sensible in her love for Stuart, who could never have showered her, as Mr. Low did, with expensive gowns and jewelry. Had she married

Stuart, she would undoubtedly live now in one cramped side of a Savannah row house. Kisses and love would have had to replace luxury travel and diamond necklaces and famous guests in the house. She never lacked for praise from Mr. Low either—praise for her grace as a hostess, for her beauty and taste.

Abruptly, she got up from the writing desk and went to her dressing table to look at herself. The loose overblouse worn above a dark green cotton skirt became her, of course. Anyone with dark eyes and hair would look well in such a daytime costume. She leaned closer to the looking glass. I have the good features of both Mama and Papa, she thought, but who can take credit for that? Any woman was pleased when her husband praised her beauty, but didn't he ever really see her eyes? Didn't he notice that even her smile was a mask? Probably not. Mr. Low *was* preoccupied—seemingly even when he made his urgent, passionate, almost nightly love to her. It was as though he were driven to mount her so swiftly, so often, and yet so silently, not a moment must be needlessly spent in leading into the act.

She had almost found a way to respond to his ardor so that, even inside her own thoughts, she seldom compared his driving vigor with Stuart's gentle ways. At first, she had tried to manage by substituting Stuart—what she imagined Stuart might be like beside her in a bed alone. Doing so had only made her rigid in her body and in her heart. She had prayed each night, during the moments when Mr. Low was taking her, *not* to think of Stuart. In time her prayers had been answered, so that now she could honestly say that Mr. Low no longer seemed old, only intensely and hastily insistent.

These days she called up the sharp pain- and joy-filled memory of Stuart's kisses only when she was alone—as now. Or between chapters of a book she was reading or as her needle was busy with the numberless tiny stitches of petit point she worked. At times Stuart was still overwhelmingly close, but more and more of her hours were spent now in meeting the challenge of the enormously complicated public duties of being Mrs. Andrew Low, wife of Her Majesty's official representative in Savannah, the town's wealthiest, most revered merchant. She had learned to converse with the mighty during the years when Papa was chargé d'affaires in Vienna. There wasn't much difference between the royal Viennese and the prominent Savannahians or foreign visitors important to her husband's mercantile business.

Mary Cowper especially liked Mr. Low's business partner, Mr. Charles Green, also a British subject, who had come to Savannah at age seventeen. Mr. Green was a few years older than Mr. Low, but with the now familiar wry smile and sophisticated manner, Mr. Green went wisely on treating his partner with enormous deference. Andrew Low expected deference, seemed almost to crumple without it or at least to pout. The subject never came up, but her woman's instinct told Mary Cowper that Charles Green at times almost despised her husband, but with a man as sure of himself as Charles Green, the odd relationship could flourish. Her husband did indeed seem to lord it over Green. Mr. Low was a Scottish-born commoner, but he did a lot of lording with many people. She now knew that his self-esteem required it. He had been highly pleased when Charles Green had named a son Andrew Low Green, but she sniffed in it an act of Green's diplomacy, since her husband was wealthier and had been more firmly established for a longer period of time. In fact, Charles Green had once been a clerk in the firm of Andrew Low and Company, but Green's quick mind and courtly manners had evidently served him well. Andrew Low *was* a brilliant businessman and would never have made Green a partner had he not deserved it. While utterly fair, Mr. Low granted no unmerited favors.

Mary Cowper was always sorry when the Green family went to Virginia for the summer, and was relieved that Mr. Low had announced last night that the Lows, when her stepdaughters came home, would probably leave Savannah for Newport next summer. Mrs. Green, the third wife, was a Virginian and her husband had invested heavily in property there, although Charles Green's real pride was the elegant mansion he had been building since 1850 on the west side of Madison Square, close by the new St. John's Episcopal Church. After six years, the house still was far from finished.

She had no doubt the Greens would be her guests often during the stay of Mr. Thackeray—the Greens and the family of Francis Sorrel, whose own splendid house was on the northwest corner of Madison Square near the incomplete Green mansion. In spite of Mrs. Sorrel's strange behavior when a fit of depression struck, Mary Cowper liked the Sorrels, too, especially Lucinda, the daughter, a few years her senior, but such good company, it had not been easy keeping the solitary secret of her love for Stuart Elliott from Lucy. She could trust Lucy Sorrel totally and, of course, Lucy knew, as had so many in social circles of both coastal Georgia and South Carolina, that Mary Cowper had once been engaged to Stuart. If Lucy suspected that Mary C. still cared for him, she never mentioned it. Stuart had remained in town, and

Lucy, unmarried in her late twenties, saw him occasionally at parties. That Mary Cowper had not glimpsed him once was of itself a miracle. She had thought one morning during the long months she carried Catherine Mackay that Stuart had crossed Bull Street just ahead of her, but she'd looked the other way and now would never know for sure. She trusted her own determination to make a success of her marriage to Andrew Low in every way except for the risk of a face-to-face encounter with Stuart, who was, according to Lucy Sorrel, still working as an assistant teller at the Bank of the State of Georgia. "No one expected him to stay on at the bank after you broke the engagement," Lucy had told her early last year. "They say he does drink quite a lot these days. He's gambling again, too, so I'm sure he needs to keep earning even that paltry salary they pay him at the bank." Lucy had asked no questions about the broken engagement or Mary Cowper's marriage to Mr. Low. A lady wouldn't meddle to that extent, even with a good friend. When Lucy did mention Stuart, it was casually, as though, along with everyone else, she believed that for Mary Cowper it was all over long ago.

Hurriedly, since it was almost time for Mr. Low to return from his countinghouse for dinner, she scanned the last page of her parents' letter, in which she sketched their social calendar through the ten days William Makepeace Thackeray would be a guest in their home, mentioned the gist of his lectures—mostly on the British Georges—and wrote down some planned menus.

Mr. Low preferred her to dress for dinner even when they were to dine alone. She folded and sealed the letter and only then did she notice that her gown had been laid out on the bed. The big house was chilly in spite of roaring fires in every room, so she'd asked her personal maid, Bertha, for a wool challis gown of a fine black print design on pale green. She adored the now fashionable hoopskirt and the newly stylish silk hairnets women were wearing. Her net today would be spangled with jets, to appeal to Mr. Low's pride in her almost jet-black hair.

Thursday, tomorrow, they had invited the Brownings and the Mackays for dinner, so this would be their last meal alone before Mr. Thackeray arrived on Friday. Being comfortable with Mr. Low was always easier with dinner guests.

EIGHTEEN

*O*n *Friday,* February 8, after a three-hour meal of clear soup, a course of gigantic oysters, venison, four vegetables, chicken, paper-thin slices of baked ham and biscuits, a dessert of sylla-bub and fruit, Andrew Low led his guest, William Thackeray, into the back parlor for cigars and claret. Once again, he was proud of his young wife—proud of her epicurean meal, her bright conversation at table, her extreme beauty and charm. His own waistline feeling tight, he smiled to himself in utter gratification as he watched the tall, amply built, travel-worn Thackeray make his way across the hospitable room to the largest brocade chair, where he literally sank down, heaving an unmistakably satisfied sigh.

"Forgive me, dear Low, for having dropped my overstuffed frame into what is undoubtedly your favorite chair," Thackeray said, short of breath from overindulgence.

"If the truth be known," Low said, taking the leather chair opposite, "I'm partial to both these pieces of furniture, sir. My wife thoughtfully had them moved nearer the fire, so take your ease. Claret will be here directly. You'll find cigars in that humidor beside you. Mine are right here. If I know my wife, there will be one or two already clipped and ready to light. Sulfur matches in that mother-of-pearl box."

Both men lit up, and then Thackeray, exhaling an enormous plume of smoke, mused, "My previous stay in this superb house, sir, was a highlight of my 1852 American tour, thanks to your kind generosity, but what a magnificent difference this time! You were alone here then—both little daughters at school in England, I believe—and now, although they're still abroad becoming educated to be superior creatures, here you are in a new, veritable heaven, a paradise. Not only a beautiful wife, but a fine baby daughter has been added to your blissful state. Tell me, Low, where on this foul earth did you ever find such an angelic young lady?"

Andrew Low smiled through his own layer of smoke. "Right here in Savannah. Fine family, too. Her father's a Stiles, son of the late Joseph, a wealthy planter over in our Yamacraw section; her maternal grandfather, John McQueen, was a special emissary for President George Washington to Lafayette during the unpleasantness with Her Majesty's government. Her paternal grandfather, Robert Mackay, had in his line not only a successful father who was an Indian trader; his mother was descended from the Malbones of Newport."

"Indeed."

"Indeed," Andrew echoed.

"Not for the snob value, I must insist, but I, too, revel in the solid continuity of good family. Mrs. Low, though, could stand alone on her own pretty feet. How long have you enjoyed such bliss?"

"It will be two years in May—May seventeenth, in fact." He wanted to speak further of Mary Cowper, but as always, more than his usual reserve made him change the subject. Mary Cowper appeared to be contented, but he despised uncertainty, especially when it in any way applied to his own worth, and he was still hard at work convincing himself that she shared his total fulfillment in their marriage. "So you came here from Augusta, eh, Thackeray?"

"New York to Charleston to Augusta, and what a queer little rustic city, Augusta! A great, broad street two miles long, old, quaint-looking shops, houses with galleries, warehouses, trees, cows, and Negroes, of course, strolling about the sidewalks, plank roads—everywhere a happy, dirty tranquillity. But then, I'm sure you know Augusta, Georgia, surrounded by endless plains of quite unattractive swampy pinelands. New York, of course, was New York—bustling, also dirty, clamorous, noisy— magnifique. And Charleston, as before, older-looking than Savannah, but quite as elegant and even more snobbish. I do find Savannahians extremely pleasant. Still genial, slow of movement, and as I remember from before, seemingly too lazy to laugh or respond much to my erudite lectures."

Andrew remembered Thackeray as being always dependable in his humor. One could count on the man to smooth off any edge of criticism with the fine sandpaper of a joke, however pointed. He envied the man that skill. He did not envy him the never-ending task of finding the proper diplomacy in his exchanges with Americans, though.

"These tours, sir," Thackeray went on, "are an eternal round of 'Mr. Thackeray, may I present Mrs. Jones-Smith,' and Mrs. Jones-Smith responds with 'Oh, Mr. Thackeray, what do you think of America?' After which Mrs. Jones-Smith presents me to Mr. Blank-Blank, who assails me with 'My dear, sir, what is your impression of our fair country?' And so on and on ad nauseam. But I've no desire to do anything but try to bind our two countries together, so I assure you that, in the main, I mention nothing that I cannot honestly set forth somewhat in the manner of a compliment."

Well, no need for that now that he and I, both British subjects, are alone, Low thought, and said as much to his ebullient guest.

"And what a relief, Low. A gigantic relief," Thackeray said. "And now that you've reminded me of that singular freedom here in this serene room, alone with only another Englishman, I find I think of nothing at this moment to criticize. I do not exaggerate when I tell you that the letters I write back from Savannah to my beloved daughters, Annie and Minnie, I shall be writing from the most comfortable quarters I have ever had in the United States!" He chuckled. "Of course, I *am* free to speak as I please to you. Others in Southern and Northern cities have shown me much kindness, but their hackles would surely rise were I to speak my true feelings about the enchanting city of Savannah." It's as though he's still lecturing, Low thought, amused. "A tranquil old city," Thackeray went on, "wide-streeted, tree-planted, with a few placid cows and handsome carriages toiling through the sandy roads, a few happy Negroes sauntering here and there, a red river with a tranquil little fleet of merchantmen taking in cargo to be stored in tranquil warehouses barricaded with packs of cotton—no rows, no tearing Northern bustle, no ceaseless hotel racket, no crowds drinking at the bars—well, at least not large crowds—and," he took a deep, luxurious breath—"all because of the gracious hospitality of my friend and benefactor, Andrew Low of the great house of A. Low and Company, cotton dealers, brokers, merchants—uh, what's the word?"

Andrew laughed a little. "Merchant will do, sir."

"And now, the added charm of a pretty wife and a new little daughter—an infant daughter crowing happily in the nursery adjoining my spacious room."

"I'm afraid little Catherine doesn't always 'crow happily,' Thackeray," Andrew apologized. "You'll just have to find out tonight how much she can, at one year of age, disturb a grown man's sleep. My wife has trained a young Negro girl, Midgie, to care for the baby, though. The girl sleeps right in the nursery with Catherine. We'll hope Midgie's control over all but 'happy crowing' is in effect tonight and every night of your visit." While he had an opening, Low went on, "As for our tranquil city, you'd have thought differently had you been unfortunate enough to visit in the fall of 1854. Of our eighteen thousand folk, all but six thousand fled a fearful yellow-fever epidemic. Twelve hundred died in one day. And while that raged, a terrible storm struck, drowning a still undetermined number of hapless people—blacks and poor whites mainly. Of course, we were abroad and our friends fled the city." He recalled Mary Cowper's agony of worry during their time in England— fearful, he secretly suspected, that her old lover, penniless Stuart Elliott, might be ill or dead. Well, he was neither, Low now knew, and forced himself to dismiss the thought.

A servant brought in their claret and glasses on an ornate silver tray, and when Andrew had poured two drinks, Thackeray raised his wine in a toast: "To the altogether lovely and discriminating Mrs. Low, who, if my insight serves me, is unusually skillful at handling her—your slaves."

Joining him in the drink, Andrew said, "My wife is excellent with servants. She grew up with Negroes, of course, but seems to have a special understanding of them."

"I was charmed that she'd even allow that black child into her elegant dining room, to say nothing of permitting him to handle her Sèvres porcelain. Is that unusual? Or was she giving the boy a chance to show off for me?"

Andrew laughed. "Oh, you mean little Midnight. He's just turned five, but I thought he did rather well. He's always been one of Mrs. Low's favorites."

Thackeray leaned forward. "The boy's name is—Midnight?"

"That's typical of slaves—of Negroes. As I recall, Midnight was only a year or so old at the time of your previous visit. Still living on the other side of town with his family. At any rate, he was born after my first wife died, I'm sure, and at midnight. Bertha, his mother, my wife's personal maid, chose his name. Typical. My work keeps me too busy for much contact, but I have learned something of the picturesque ways of slaves. Odd, to say the least."

"I'll make use in a book or essay or lecture of Midnight's name, naturally, but evidently I was misinformed in New York on another Southern custom."

"And what was that?"

"Twice now, you've called your Negroes 'slaves.' I was told on what I considered good authority in New York that Southerners dodged the use of the word 'slave.' That you always called your human properties your 'people.' "

"Oh, you weren't misinformed at all. True, my mercantile business centers in the South and I love the city of Savannah, but I'm not a typical Southerner. Native Southerners do call their slaves their 'people.' Mary Cowper is forever correcting me, a thing she seldom does, but she's been trained to avoid the word. Evidently, they consider it ugly, in spite of their dogged defense of the peculiar institution of slavery. I doubt that it has much import, though, whatever servants are called. Negroes *are* property, except for the free persons of color, of which there are few."

"My Northern informant seemed to feel it most revealing of a secret guilt for Southerners to avoid using the word 'slave.' "

"Perhaps," Andrew said casually. "To me, it's of little relevance." He took another slow, appreciative sip of wine. "Tell me, Mr. Thackeray, who was your Northern informant?"

"The most respected newspaper publisher in America, I'd think. Mr. Horace Greeley. I spent an entire afternoon with him at his famous *Tribune* office."

Andrew frowned. "Greeley is a highly opinionated, wrongheaded gentleman!"

"But famous worldwide these days. His *Tribune* is more widely read than any other American newspaper."

"To the detriment of not only business itself but the working class dependent upon the success of business." Low frowned. "Horace Greeley's a gentleman of extreme views."

"He assured me he was never an abolitionist."

"But a Northern Whig, even so, highly opposed to slavery. Also highly sympathetic to the ideas of the utopian French socialists who followed François Fourier and the defunct English Chartists. Greeley fancies himself a champion of the working class. He even employs that incendiary communist revolutionist Karl Marx, now expelled by France to our beloved England, as his British correspondent!" Low could feel his own anger flush his face. "Marx's goal in life is to overthrow capitalism. To him, to Greeley and their kind, *I'm an exploiter,* my heel firmly on the neck of those whose very livelihood depends upon *my* wages paid to them. If you depend upon Greeley as your informant on the current state of American politics, sir, you are depending upon a dangerous man!"

Low saw Thackeray squirm a bit in his big chair, tap a thick, long ash from his cigar, and then wreathe his full, pleasant face in a warm smile. "It is not my intention, dear Low, to rouse your ire on this, my first night under your roof. I simply needed to be caught up, as it were, on current events in this country after four years away, and Greeley, who does write and print the news, seemed a fortunate choice. I know the content of his editorials. I wanted to know the *news.* He explained rather lucidly the Kansas-Nebraska Act, which has brought about such bloodshed and trouble in the Kansas territory. He gave me verse and chapter on—"

"Greeley strongly opposed the Kansas-Nebraska Act and it is a good piece of legislation!"

"Because it favors the South?"

"Because it follows the American way of permitting the people of this land to decide for themselves—popular sovereignty."

"By showing with their votes who can win the race to populate Kansas," Thackeray said firmly. "Both anti-slavery and pro-slavery factions are rushing settlers west, aren't they? And aren't they killing each other once there? Isn't Kansas being called 'bloody Kansas'? Doesn't it now have two legislatures—one slave and one free? What of the so-called border ruffians who make life wretched out there for those who have free-soil beliefs?"

"I'm still a British citizen," Low said, "but that very fact reinforces my faith in a free America where the people decide! The people elected President Pierce and he favors the South in this whole hideous affair. President Pierce favors the Kansas legislature supporting slavery *if* a man needs to own slaves."

"Aren't Northerners who oppose slavery to be reckoned with as well?" Thackeray asked.

Loathing the idea that he and his honored guest might oppose one another during Thackeray's entire visit to Savannah, Low cast about for a peaceable response that would still support his own strong pro-South beliefs. "The people of the North, the hotheads called abolitionists, must not be allowed to take control."

"That's exactly what Horace Greeley said to me! I have it straight, thanks to him, that all anti-slavery Northerners are *not* abolitionists. Greeley certainly isn't. Until now, he's always been a Whig. The abolitionists actually consider Greeley a conservative! Tell me, what do you know about the new movement some are calling the Republican Party, Low?"

"Only that it is made up mainly of those who feel it is their holy duty to oppose the South's cotton economy."

"But it's a new authentic American political party. You know, of course, that the first Republican National Convention will be held this June. Greeley plans to attend. He's dropped his Whig loyalties—even his close contacts with William H. Seward of New York, a longtime friend and political ally. He sees the potential of a new national dimension for the working class in the Republican Party."

"It is, as I see it, no concern of Northerners of any stripe what the people do down here," Low said more forcefully than he intended. "Greeley may claim not to be an abolitionist, but I'm convinced he means to use his considerable press power to force the South to give up its economic security—to *abolish* slavery. The industrial revolution has swept the North, but down here we're still dependent upon cotton and sugarcane and that's our business!"

"Oh, yes, the South celebrated, I understand," Thackeray went on quietly, "when Senator Stephen A. Douglas drove his Kansas-Nebraska bill through the Senate and the House, although there was bloodshed in the House, I'm told. But even though the South believed passage and the President's signature meant victory for them, it could be short-lived, according to Greeley."

"According to what Greeley *hopes,* sir."

"Well, he told me of an exchange during the Senate debate. In fact, he got out an 1854 copy of the *Tribune* and read it to me." Rummaging in his pocket, Thackeray explained he'd asked for a clipping. "Ah, here it is."

Low could not help smiling at his clever guest. "Knowing full well that you and I would be in just such a conversation as this sooner or later?"

"Perhaps," Thackeray said noncommittally as he smoothed out the somewhat crumpled news clipping. "Listen to this exchange on the Senate floor between Senator George Badger of North Carolina and

Senator Benjamin Wade of Ohio. I find it most telling. Badger: 'If some Southern gentleman wishes to take the old woman that nursed him in childhood and whom he called Mammy into one of these new Territories for the betterment of the fortunes of the whole family, why, in the name of God, should anybody prevent it?' "

"I agree thoroughly," Andrew said, knowing full well that Thackeray had an ace up his sleeve.

"So," Thackeray said calmly, still holding the clipping, "that tells you what Senator Badger of the South had to say."

"And it is altogether reasonable and humane."

"I agree. But, in fairness, listen to the response of a Northerner, Senator Benjamin Wade of Ohio: 'We have not the least objection to Senator Badger's migrating to Kansas and taking his old Mammy along with him. We only insist that he shall not be empowered to *sell her* after taking her there.' " Thackeray peered at Andrew over his spectacles. "I would not even consider using that senatorial exchange publicly, Mr. Low. I endure the vicissitudes of these foreign tours solely for the purpose of raising funds for the care of my two dear daughters after I'm dead, but I have no dueling interests now. The clipping is incendiary, but, I have to admit, not without merit on both sides."

"I'm relieved that you found Southern Senator Badger's question to be of merit," Andrew said, still wishing he could surmise accurately how much Thackeray had been influenced on the slavery issue by Horace Greeley. Why not ask? He did and waited for his guest to reply, which, after fortifying himself with a sizable sip of claret, he proceeded to do.

"You observed, I'm sure, Low, that on my first American tour, I held no particular brief for or against slavery. I noted that there was a strong sign that the Negro race might be intellectually inferior, proven to my casual satisfaction then by the fact that four British servants could do the work of twelve in the American South. I also noted that the Southern argument in favor of slavery had merit—that the poor worker in Britain was worse off and more miserable than the American Negro slave. I felt sincerely that Britain should do something about her own shame before meddling in the affairs of another country. I did not feel that Blacky was my brother, though God forbid that I should own him or flog him, or part him from his wife and children. I saw also that if it rained, the black servants were kept home and dry—not necessarily from compassion, but because they were susceptible to colds and the doctor charged the owner a dollar a visit. Through the South, plantation owners urged me to visit their slave quarters and see for myself that, unlike British workmen, once their working days ended, Southern black slaves were cared for in their old age."

"That troublesome novel *Uncle Tom's Cabin* had just been published shortly before your first visit here, as I recall, so I'm sure you had difficulty holding civilized converse with all Americans."

"I did, although I had not yet read the dreadfully written book, and so I managed by trying to come down somewhere *between* the warring factions—I tried, boring task, to be objective. To be fair."

Thackeray, Low knew, was doing just that now with him. He knew, too, that Thackeray's need for money from his tour made judicious talk necessary. In a smaller way, Thackeray, like Andrew Low, needed the goodwill of the American South because he needed good offerings at his lectures, as Low needed Southern planters whose slaves made cotton plentiful for the Liverpool market. Low lit another cigar, and waited for Thackeray to get to the point about what he now, in 1856, thought about slavery and the bloody turmoil it was causing among Americans of opposing views.

"I ramble," Thackeray said, exhaling mightily, "but I must choose my words carefully. I can tell you, sir, that on this second American journey North and South, I have tried diligently to keep my mouth shut, since I'm interested to see that my shame for the poor treatment of the British working class has enormously increased."

"To the extent that you have no compunctions at all over slavery here? Dare I hope that?"

"Oh, I wouldn't go that far. I find I was merely making a kind of casual comparison back in 1852. Now, I see my sympathies have swung drastically toward our own British poor. Take the great, hulking English footmen with their padded calves—shameful, hot, plush—hair plastered in bear's grease and flour, and only the prospect of a segregated work-house when their usefulness is over. They are the people I pity! For them, I can cry, 'There but for the grace of God go I . . .' "

"You're a clever gentleman, sir," Andrew said with a smile. "I can see you're not going to express yourself on the South's peculiar institu-tion. I also see that, if not on the subject of slavery, Horace Greeley has indeed influenced your thinking about the common man. But let's face it, a man fares in this life according to his intellect, his talents, his industry, and his choice of work. The common workingman carries none of the burdens and responsibilities of his employer. He's free of such things. He pays for that freedom by a lower standard of living, of course. As for slavery, most owners here in Savannah treat their slaves very well. Actually, only one man of real prominence is not a slave owner. A gentleman by the name of Mark Browning, came down in his youth from Philadelphia, and still holding to his anti-slavery notions—foolishly, but firmly."

"He must be a lonely fellow!"

"I hadn't thought about that, but while we all know Browning's abolitionist leanings, he does manage to keep his peace on the subject." Low smiled. "I suppose he's had good training in his own home. You see, Browning's wife is a rather large slaveholder. She owns a plantation out on the Savannah River. By the way, Thackeray, would you like to talk with Browning?"

"I think not, thank you." With a twinkle, he added, "I find it difficult enough to remain a peacemaker in the troubled United States. I certainly have no intention of positioning myself between a warring man and wife."

"The Brownings are a most charming couple. Browning has learned to control his distorted view of the South's economic need for slave labor."

"Surely you, as a British subject, can see that this so-called economic need for slavery is absurd."

Andrew frowned. "I must say I don't follow that, sir."

"Come now, Low, the ridiculous economics of the peculiar institution will eventually abolish slavery by its very nature—far sooner than the abolitionists can do away with it. Keeping slaves is a waste of money in the long run. When white workers are willing to compete for the Negro's jobs, you'll see I'm right. As I told a group of English ladies after my first U.S. tour, they waste their tears weeping for the American cruelty to slaves as they sob their way through Mrs. Stowe's powerful novel about her Uncle Tom. At least no American slave starves in old age." Cigars tamped out, both men rose to retire. "Of course, the ladies felt the cruelty of the occasional lash across the back. I've found, though, that a brand of kindness is usually the rule among slave owners. I must say, I contend that slavery itself is wrong, wrong, *wrong*, but the American who sees the cruelty of starving an English laborer, of driving an English child into a dark, dangerous coal mine, sees an equal wrong!"

At the foot of the stair that would lead them to their rooms on the second floor, the men stopped while Low lit a candle. "We'll have gaslight soon," he said. "Have a restful night, sir."

His surprisingly small hand on Low's shoulder, Thackeray smiled broadly. "I will, I will, thank you." His mischievous eyes twinkled in the candlelight. "I managed rather well this evening, I thought, to tread the delicate, taut tightrope without stirring the wrath of North or South—or the wrath of the esteemed merchant Andrew Low. Do you agree?"

At the door of the spacious bedroom prepared for Thackeray on the left front of the house, Low said, "The hour is too late to disagree, sir. And, truthfully, I commend you. I'm sure you'll find all you need in your room. Take your ease in the morning—breakfast at your pleasure. In fact, the entire weekend is free unless you'd care to attend church or meet the Brownings. They were dinner guests yesterday and their latchstring is out to you."

Grinning like a sleepy bear, Thackeray said, "Kind of them, but so far as I'm able, I mean to avoid divided households."

"Then, good night. I hope my infant daughter causes you no distress. Your time until your first lecture Tuesday evening is your own, sir."

NINETEEN

The following Wednesday morning, after Mr. Thackeray's second lecture at St. Andrew's Hall, Mary Cowper took advantage of the sunny February day to walk the two blocks along Harris Street to the Sorrel house in Madison Square. She seldom called in the mornings, but this visit to her friend Lucy Sorrel was not a social call. She had heard at the Thackeray lecture last night that Lucy's mother was again suffering one of her dark depressions and hoped she might help in some way. When Lucy was nowhere to be found in the gathering at St. Andrew's Hall last night, she suspected trouble. Miss Eliza Mackay, who had felt up to attending that one lecture, whispered the bad news about her longtime friend Matilda Sorrel. "My heart goes out to your friend Lucy," Miss Eliza had said. "I just wish there was something we could do for her—for her dear mother. But what?"

I can at least run by the house, Mary Cowper thought as soon as her eyes opened today, and while there was certainly nothing anyone could do when poor Mrs. Sorrel seemed to turn into another person right under the noses of her own family, Lucy would at least know she cared. "Sarah Gordon told me yesterday," Miss Eliza had said, "that this time Matilda just sits on the side of her bed and weeps. The last bad bout she had was even harder on poor Lucy, because then her mother walked the streets alone, sobbing. People talked something terrible for weeks after she came back to herself."

Seated a few minutes later in the Sorrel parlor, across from Lucinda, Mary Cowper floundered, as she knew she would, when she tried to comfort her friend without actually telling her that she knew of her mother's condition.

"I awoke this morning feeling you might need me," she said lamely. "Is there anything I can do?"

Lucy's eyes brimmed with quick tears. "No. There's nothing anyone can do and you've already proven your friendship by–by coming."

"I don't see how just sitting here helps, but–"

"It confirms that the tongues are wagging. Mama hasn't gone into the streets this time, but somehow they find out. I can't stop the tongues, but it does help that I know they're talking. At least it puts me on my guard."

On impulse, Mary Cowper crossed the room and hugged Lucy. "I'm so sorry. Please promise you'll send one of the servants to my house if there's anything at all I can do to help!"

"There won't be anything. You've enough on your hands as it is, entertaining Mr. Thackeray. I'm sure your husband would not approve any laxness on your part. I'll be all right. Please don't worry. You have that crowd of people coming to your house after the last lecture tomorrow night and–"

Both friends jumped when someone gave the loud front doorbell a hard twist.

"Oh, dear," Lucy asked, nervously getting up, "who could that be at this hour?"

"I must go," Mary Cowper said. "I do have a lot to do yet this morning and that could be your mother's doctor at the door."

"Papa hasn't even called Dr. Daniell yet. There's nothing he can do. And Dr. Daniell gets so cross with her. He does give her laudanum the minute my back is turned if she's slipping out of the house, but–"

"They's a Mr. Stuart Elliott to see you, Miss Lucinda," Zechariah, the Sorrels' portly butler announced from the open sliding doors to the entrance hall. "I told him you had company. He said if you could just step to the front door for *one* minute."

Mary Cowper stood rooted in the middle of the parlor floor, her dark eyes wide with fear. In all this time, she had somehow avoided meeting him. Not once had she confided to Lucinda Sorrel her inner-most feelings for Stuart, so she went on standing there, wondering wildly what to say, to do. She could escape through the kitchen, out the back door, but that would tell Lucy everything!

"What on earth does he want?" Lucy muttered, as though asking herself the question. For a long moment, she studied Mary Cowper's stricken face, then spoke to the butler quietly. "Tell Mr. Elliott I'll be right there, Zechariah. Ask him to wait in the hall." Then she turned to Mary Cowper. "I—I know more than you think I know and it's all right. I can't tell you how I know, but I do. The very best thing for you to do this minute is to stay right here in the parlor. I'll send him away just as soon as possible, then come back. Please wait and don't even cough or clear your throat, do you hear?"

Mary Cowper only nodded her head, steadying herself on the arm of a big easy chair.

Stuart stood, top hat in hand, just inside the wide front door and watched the slim, not unattractive Lucinda Sorrel come toward him along the spacious entrance hall, her usually pleasant face strained, troubled, but, as always, calm and intelligent.

"A dreadful hour to call," he said amiably, coming toward her. "Forgive me?"

Quickening her step, Lucinda held out her hand, allowed him to kiss it formally, and asked, "Is there a special reason you're here, Mr. Elliott?"

"There is indeed," he answered. "Will you be attending the Thackeray lecture tonight, Lucy?"

"I wasn't aware that we knew each other well enough for first names, but no, I'm sorry to say I won't be. My—my mother is not well. Why do you ask?"

"Because I'd hoped rather earnestly that I might escort you to St. Andrew's Hall. I hear Thackeray is highly entertaining. I'm sure my education is incomplete unless I expose my mind to him at least once. Tomorrow is his last lecture, you know."

"Yes, I do know. Thank you, but I can't leave Mother. In fact, I need to go to her now—if you'll excuse me?"

"Of course, but—I—uh, I believe your butler said you also have company this morning. Should your hands be too full, I would consider it an honor if you'd allow me to help out in any way. This is my day off at the bank."

Stuart had seen Mary Cowper enter the house, had by chance been taking his daily constitutional on the other side of Madison Square. Hidden behind a tall hedge opposite the Sorrel house, he'd watched Lucy herself admit Mary Cowper, welcome her. Obviously they were friends. Then he found himself crossing the square, heading up the Sorrel steps, with no idea what he might use as an excuse for the impromptu call. From somewhere, the Thackeray plan burst into his mind.

"I'm deeply disappointed, Lucinda," he said. "I've had you on my mind for a long time." Taking her hand again, he smiled warmly. "It requires quite a lot of courage, you know, for a mere assistant teller to ask a favor of the daughter of Frances Sorrel, but I've asked now and don't be surprised if I ask again at some more opportune time."

"I—I can't give that any thought today," Lucy said. To Stuart she looked still more troubled, more distracted. "I must beg you to excuse me. Under the circumstances, I simply cannot invite you in. Good day, Mr. Elliott."

"Good day, Lucinda," he called as she hurried along the wide hall and out of sight into the parlor, closing the sliding doors behind her.

Mary Cowper was still standing where Lucinda had left her. Neither spoke for a long time, then Lucy said, "He's gone. I'd give him a few minutes, if I were you, though, before you also leave." When Mary Cowper said nothing, Lucy added, "He—Mr. Elliott invited me to the Thackeray lecture. He's an odd one all right."

"My husband is very fond of Mr. Thackeray, though," Mary Cowper said.

Lucy knew perfectly well that her friend was purposely misinterpreting her words. She'd heard Mr. Thackeray was somewhat eccentric. She decided to let it go. "I can't attend the lecture at all, because of Mother."

In an almost magic transformation, Mary Cowper had regained her poise as Mrs. Andrew Low. "Of course. I'm sorry you'll miss the final performance. I've seldom seen my husband in a better mood than these last few days with the celebrated man as a guest in our home. Even little Catherine Mackay screams in protest when I remove her from Mr. Thackeray's lap at her bedtime. He's wonderful with children." She held out her hand to Lucy, who took it affectionately. "I must go, dear friend. There's really no reason for me to wait until Mr. Elliott is out of sight. It —it can't matter at all—now."

Lucy watched her turn her back and busy herself with her reticule, but she made no move toward the hall.

"Mary Cowper?" She saw the slender back jerk, fitfully, every fiber in her young body straining for control. "Mary Cowper!"

For a long time, Lucy held her friend in her arms, soothing the convulsive shoulders, feeling strongly that nothing she might say could possibly help.

Finally, her hat tied firmly in place, Lucy's guest moved deliberately toward the sliding doors, opening them herself, as though the very act showed strength. "Thank you, Lucinda," Mary Cowper said at the front door. "Thank you for not trying to speak any comforting words. There —are none. I'm grateful for what dignity you managed to preserve for me. The wife of Andrew Low lives her life striving of necessity to find *enough* dignity."

TWENTY

*H*is lecture series over, Thackeray, walking stick in hand, mind and heart vastly free, sauntered forth on a windless Monday morning for his customary walk before dinner would be served in the mansion of his hospitable friend Andrew Low. It had required almost no persuasion on Low's part to gain Thackeray's agreement to stay through Monday for a much-needed rest. Philadelphia was up ahead, and if the ghastly experience of his last lecture series in Philadelphia might be repeated, he was in no hurry to reach the thriving Northern city. Two years ago in Philadelphia, almost no one, it seemed by the newspaper accounts, had understood his talks, or his humor. Blessedly, he could not remember the exact words, but of one of his lectures on the royal Georges, a Philadelphia paper had vouchsafed that "Thackeray would never dare repeat it in his own country!"

On this uniquely pleasant winter morning, he would put behind him all thoughts of returning to Philadelphia. A man could, he firmly believed, choose to live in the moment and he meant to do just that.

Wandering into one of the walking paths of Savannah's old brick-walled cemetery, he glanced about at the ancient, weathered markers, recalling that, according to Low, the wall had been donated by the so-called Father of the United States, President George Washington. Generous gesture, he mused, and turned his mind to his own two daughters across the sea in England, scowling that, once more, even thoughts of his beloved girls invariably brought up the pitifully small offerings he'd received in Savannah. Oh, he had surely been entertained impressively by Low and his lovely wife, a lady of inestimable dignity for one so young, but the crowds had never exceeded three to four hundred and he would be carrying precious little money with him when he took a steamer north on tomorrow afternoon.

He stopped to gaze at a monument to Button Gwinnett, a signer of the American Declaration of Independence. The name Button tickled his fancy and his mood lightened. Then, a glance away from old Button's tomb brought the happy sight of a dancing child, a little girl of perhaps six or seven years, busily executing a strange-appearing dance in which her little feet—two stomps to each foot—pounded out a slow, but intricate rhythm first on one foot and then another.

"Halloo, little miss," he called as the child turned to smile up at the older gentleman with her, then waved at Thackeray himself, who promptly waved back.

"Good morning, Mr. Thackeray," the handsome, slender, graying, older man greeted him warmly. "What an unexpected and pleasant surprise to meet you on such a fine morning."

The girl, having stopped her peculiar dance, said brightly, "Good morning, sir. My name is Willow Browning. This is my grandfather! We take walks together every day."

The older gentleman, in his sixties, Thackeray surmised, held out his hand. "I'm Mark Browning, Mr. Thackeray. My family and I certainly enjoyed your lectures. Savannah will be sorry to see you go."

After a handshake, Thackeray nodded appreciation, then turned to the little girl. "How old are you, my pretty miss?"

"I'm nearly seven," she piped.

Laughing proudly, her grandfather said, "At times, I think her correct age to be seven going on sixteen, sir. She's an unusually bright child."

"Spoken like a true grandfather," Thackeray said, already sorry that he had been so stupid as to refuse Low's offer of an evening with Savannah's only abolitionist, Mark Browning. "Your name, Mr. Browning, is not unfamiliar to me. I've—I've heard of you from my host, Andrew Low."

He thought Browning's smile was a touch sardonic. "Yes, I expect you have. Mr. Low is married to the daughter of a longtime friend, Mrs.

W. H. Stiles. Her husband, once my attorney, is now Speaker of the Georgia Assembly."

"Interesting," Thackeray said. "But of far more interest to me is your courage in remaining an abolitionist in the heart of pro-slavery Savannah, Georgia!"

"Low told you that, too, I'm sure. But I'm not really an abolitionist. I could simply never live with my conscience if I owned another human being, and as I'm sure you know, true abolitionists generally act upon their convictions."

"And you don't?"

"Only in that I cannot own a slave."

"My grandmother is a slave owner, sir," the girl offered brightly.

Down on one knee so that he could look into her face, Thackeray said, "Well, you are a bright girl. And I'd also heard your grandmother owns slaves."

"Did Grandmother Caroline tell you she owns lots and lots of people at her Knightsford plantation?"

"No, she didn't tell me. I haven't had the pleasure of meeting your grandmother."

"Would you like to see me dance again? I'm part Cherokee Indian and my mama, who is half Cherokee, is teaching me some tribal dances."

With no urging, the child began again to stomp twice, then three times on each foot, swaying her little body to a rhythm she seemed actually to be hearing. Thackeray was enchanted and watched in silence for a time before he turned to Browning to ask, "And you and your wife have no social problems here in Savannah because—because—"

Browning smiled. "Because my son married a half-Cherokee girl? At first we did. This may sound vain of me, but somehow, having listened to all your lectures, I feel you'll know exactly what I mean when I say I'm fortunate enough to be rather well-off financially, so that we don't often *hear* about the town's problems with us."

"My grandfather can buy me anything my little heart desires," the child said innocently.

"Her mother, my excellent daughter-in-law, is teaching her soundly, though, the value of money," Browning said. "Willow isn't spoiled."

"Indeed I do know what you mean by being wealthy enough to silence tongues, Browning, and I'm quite annoyed for having allowed my social schedule to be filled right up to my sailing tomorrow, so that we can't talk. I can see I was remiss. Perhaps I could learn more from you, who live in a city hostile to your deepest beliefs about slavery, than

I learned from Horace Greeley, Emerson, Hawthorne, and Melville rolled together!"

"You flatter me, sir, and I, too, wish we had more time. Perhaps when you come again for still another lecture series. That is, if I'm still in the land of the living. After sixty, a man doesn't know."

Thackeray rubbed his forehead. "Dear Mr. Browning, after forty-five, especially if one is poor enough to be forced to travel and lecture, a man knows still less about when his end might come. One thing I do know, though: I won't be back in America again. Except for the generosity of Andrew Low, this, my second American tour, has not been particularly rewarding." He took out his thin gold watch. "Oh, I must head back toward Lafayette Square, but tell me, do I remember correctly that you settled in Savannah from Philadelphia?"

"That's right. Many years ago, in my early twenties. I was already in love with Savannah even before I saw her. I still am. Some here are my friends, others close acquaintances, but the old city has a soul of her own and we"—he laughed a bit shyly—"we, Savannah and I, go on belonging to each other, no matter what."

"Fascinating! I was dreading a return to Philadelphia, where, four years ago, many lampooned my lectures. I shall hold my head high now, just knowing that such a sensitive, warmhearted gentleman was born there! Tell me, Browning, did you find Philadelphia *not* to your liking? Is that why you left it to settle here?"

"No, I can't say that at all. I have only happy memories of my boyhood with my Aunt Nassie, who reared me." He laughed softly. "And undoubtedly instilled in me respect for the dignity of all human beings, black and white. You see, Aunt Nassie, far back in the early part of the century, *was* a convinced abolitionist. She'd be out lecturing and rousing both ire and admiration, I have no doubt, were she alive today."

Thackeray gave him a serious look. "And would she be troubled at the growing rancor between North and South?"

"She would be, certainly. Aunt Nassie remembered the American Revolution clearly. She revered the Union's Constitution."

"Ah, yes, the American Constitution, which bargained away freedom for dark-skinned people while proclaiming its own freedom from the Crown."

"I'm afraid that's correct."

"And you're sure you're not an abolitionist, Browning? Real abolitionists denounce the constitutional compromise over slavery, don't they?"

"Yes, sir, they do. My aunt did. Perhaps I lack her courage, but I seem, probably because I love Savannah with my heart over my brain, to be willing to wait for a political solution to the strife."

"You don't deny there is—in the near future—a dangerous chance for real trouble, even bloodshed?"

"No, sir, I don't. I fear it night and day."

"And what will you do if the South secedes from the union of all the states?"

"What is secedes?" Willow wanted to know.

Browning laid his hand on her bright blue bonnet. "Oh, darling, that would take a long time to explain, but I'll try someday. Can you wait?"

She was beaming her sunny smile now, doing a bit of the stomping again, turning slowly in her tracks. "If you want me to wait, Grandpa, I will. I love you!"

Thackeray was relieved, touched, and deeply grateful when Browning merely held out his hand to him. Time *was* running out. He was due back at the Low place now. There weren't any more words to be said, actually. He and Browning had simply experienced a profound meeting of minds. They would wisely leave it at that.

TWENTY-ONE

*T*he *May morning* was mild, the sky enfolding his beloved Savannah clear and spring blue, as Mark picked up a copy of the *Georgian,* just off the presses, on his way for an early visit with Miss Eliza Mackay. Midmorning was usually his time with Willow, but she had a sniffle today and Caroline and Mary felt she should stay in bed.

"It's nothing serious, Mark," Caroline had said, laughing. "Stop frowning! Children do have colds now and then. Why not visit Miss Eliza early instead? Then come home to me once you've made certain that Jonathan is perfectly able to handle the countinghouse without you." When Mark only gave her a half-smile, she went on, "Something's been bothering you lately. Something political, no doubt, or you'd have told me. I'm never jealous when you feel freer to confide in Miss Eliza." Her smile was amused, as though directed at a child Willow's age. "After all, except that we can't discuss politics, we do have a perfect marriage."

Today's *Georgian* for May 26 still tucked under his arm, Mark was headed for East Broughton Street and Miss Eliza. Caroline, as usual, was right. He had been more than bothered, but when, as this morning, she could mention their difference over slavery and remain calm, he felt thankful through and through. Theirs *was* a perfect marriage except for her continuing unlikely stubbornness on the subject of owning slaves. In Caroline such an attitude did seem unlikely. For all the thirty-six years of their married life, only Mark's tendency to spoil Natalie had ever raised a barrier between them—beyond Caroline's pathetic inability to understand how he could so love Savannah and still go on insisting that slavery was somehow sinful. He knew Caroline honestly felt he was judging *her*. He had long ago accepted that, but was helpless against it. With all his heart, he loved this loyal, devoted, altogether honest woman, had loved her for so long, he had trouble remembering life without her beside him. She had even relented against her own better judgment again and again where Natalie's headstrong behavior had brought them to the verge of trouble.

Did he dare hope today that the years of mutual devotion had finally opened Caroline's mind to his equally honest convictions on the subject of owning another human being? He would ask Miss Eliza's opinion, he decided, as he rounded the corner of Abercorn onto East Broughton, in sight now of the big old frame house where he'd always found a welcome with Eliza Mackay. Aging Miss Eliza owned slaves, too, but she understood him. He no longer expected Caroline ever to agree with him, but with the chaos and confusion and downright bitterness sweeping the land, he longed more than ever for her understanding.

He half hoped not to find Colonel Robert Lee's eldest son, Custis Lee, at the Mackay house. The young, handsome, much-beloved Custis had, since his graduation from West Point, made it his home while stationed as assistant engineer overseeing the work at Fort Pulaski and Fort Jackson near Savannah. Mark liked Custis, but he needed to be with Miss Eliza today. He hoped to find her alone—perhaps Kate and Sarah out marketing, Custis at his office in the Oglethorpe Army Barracks.

When he reached the familiar brick walkway that led to Miss Eliza's front porch, unaccountably he stopped and glanced down at the front page of the *Georgian*. Near the center of the page, a headline stunned him: SENATOR CHARLES SUMNER CANED AND SERIOUSLY INJURED.

He folded the paper quickly and hurried up the front steps, hoping that even William would not be at home. For that he felt ashamed, because, in spite of William's strong sympathies with the South, he and Mark had always been able to talk without rancor. Mark's fear had begun to grow with the passage of the incendiary Kansas-Nebraska Act, but the headline about the violence against Senator Sumner sharpened it, so that his hand trembled as he tapped the old brass knocker and waited for Miss Eliza. How would he handle fear of any kind after his beloved friend was gone? As he'd always done, he quashed the thought. Just being with Eliza Mackay had calmed him for most of the years of his life, even yesterday, when they'd shared the troubling story of what was being called the Sack of Lawrence, Kansas: Pro-slavery border ruffians had galloped into free Lawrence, bent on attacking abolitionist leaders. None were to be found, so the frustrated invaders had thrown printing presses into the river and bombarded the Free State Hotel into a pile of rubble.

Miss Eliza had helped calm his agitation over that story, but because Kansas was so far away, it had not struck him as hard as had the caning of Massachusetts's Senator Charles Sumner. Mark had long admired the arresting Bostonian, Harvard-educated, intimate friend of Channing, Longfellow, and Emerson. He had cheered silently when he read Sumner's denunciation of the Kansas-Nebraska bill, which had indeed fanned the flames both North and South.

He had never met Senator Sumner, but the fact that such a powerful man, well over six feet tall, large of frame, who could castigate slavery with more skill than anyone left in Congress, had actually been beaten, filled him with fear to the marrow of his bones. What had happened to civility in the Senate of the United States? Sumner himself had recently shouted in the chamber that "truly—truly—this is a godless place!" To Mark, standing on the Mackay porch, it had become just that. Senators were no longer able to argue vehemently, then leave the chamber arms entwined. Now they were beating each other over the head with canes!

The door opened and there stood William.

"Mark, old man," William said warmly, "come in, come in! Sorry to keep you waiting, but I was upstairs writing a letter and I thought sure one of the servants would hear the knock."

"No matter. I didn't mind waiting," he said, struggling to regain composure, embarrassed not to be glad to see the quiet, thoughtful man.

"Something wrong, Mark?" William led the way to the old parlor, still more like home than Mark's own elegant family drawing room. "Nothing's happened to your family, I hope. I thought this time of day you'd be out cavorting with little Willow. Sit down."

"Willow's got a case of sniffles today. Caroline and her mother thought she'd better stay in bed." He tried to laugh. "That is, if she can be kept there. Your mother's not here?"

"No, and she'll be sorry to miss you, especially if this early visit means you won't be back this afternoon. When she's at all up to it, Mama still pays that visit to Mrs. Sarah Gordon in the mornings. She formed the habit way back more than twenty years ago when W. W. Gordon, Sr., first died. She seemed to feel pretty pert today."

"Good," Mark said absently. "Doesn't seem possible that young Willie Gordon's old enough to be getting married already, does it?"

"No, sir, it doesn't, but it just goes to prove that I'd as soon not think about ages." William sighed. "I wish I felt as chipper in my early fifties as you seem to in your sixties."

Mark felt anything but chipper, but let it go. "I wonder how young Willie's bride will like our old city, coming as she does from the wilds of bustling Chicago." Mark added, "I hear she's a rather unusual young lady. What's her name?"

William laughed aloud, something Mark seldom knew him to do. "Nellie Kinzie. And from what I hear, she's more than unusual. Fine Chicago family, but they say she's a catbird! Likes to shock people."

Trying to appear interested, Mark said listlessly, "Well, you can't always believe Savannah rumors. When's the wedding?"

"December of next year, I think it is," William said, studying Mark's face quizzically. "You sure nothing's wrong, Mark? Is that today's paper?"

"Yes. I picked up a copy at the *Georgian* office." Without saying anything more, he handed it to William, suddenly anxious.

William read silently for a few seconds, then said, "Well! What do you think of this? Old stuffed-shirt Sumner got himself whacked good right on the Senate floor! Did you see that? Big headline. You read it yet?"

"Only the headline," Mark said stiffly. "Why don't you read it aloud."

Pushing his spectacles up into place, William scanned the article, then said, "Well, all right, if you like."

Mark listened intently, as William read: " 'The blast of bitter controversy blowing across the nation North and South, East and West, roared onto the floor of the Senate chamber itself on 22 May, as the vindictive Massachusetts lawmaker, Senator Charles Sumner, literally felt his own brand of vituperation descend upon his head. His carefully planned attacks on the South, in which he accused our people of moral wickedness and supreme sinfulness, were returned to the senator in a few moments of sweet vengeance.' "

"Sweet vengeance?" Mark gasped.

William grinned. "Don't forget I'm reading a *Savannah* paper. Your friend Sumner's no hero down here. Should I finish it?"

"By all means."

" 'In many of Sumner's provocative speeches,' " William read, " 'in

particular the one titled "The Crime Against Kansas," he had called the
revered state of Virginia, for example, a place "where human beings are
bred as cattle for the shambles." As with many Northern abolitionist
lawmakers, Sumner's oratory has been studded with offensive personal
attacks on the South. Sumner had charged not only Senator Douglas
hotly, he also charged South Carolina's Senator Butler as having chosen
a mistress who, "though ugly to others, is always lovely to him . . .
the harlot, Slavery." ' " As always, William's voice remained calm.
" 'From all over the Senate chamber, shouts of anger rang amidst cheers
for the pedagogical, irate Sumner, once described by his abolitionist
friend, the poet Longfellow, as speaking "like a cannoneer ramming
down cartridges!" On the day of 22 May, thirty-six-year-old Representative Preston Brooks of South Carolina, a Mexican War veteran considered amenable and moderate, heard some of Sumner's caustic remarks
and insults to Brooks's admired uncle, Senator Butler of South Carolina,
and took decided action. Brooks has said he would not challenge Sumner
to a duel, because that would imply that the Massachusetts man was his
social equal. He would simply thrash him, as he would any other inferior
being guilty of dire wrongdoing. Young Brooks waited gallantly until
some ladies had departed the Senate lobby, strode up to Sumner's desk,
and rained thirty or forty blows down upon Sumner's head with a gold-
knobbed gutta-percha cane. Bystanders had to drag Brooks away, and
Sumner, almost senseless, his head covered with blood, was carried from
the Senate chamber. For Northerners, Senator Sumner was beaten into a
state of not only pain but abolitionist martyrdom. In the South, though
no one rejoices in shed blood, vengeance will as surely be only sweet.' "

Without adding a word, William ended the account, refolded the
paper, and laid it on a nearby table. For a long time, Mark also said
nothing. There was no sound in the old parlor beyond the soft ticking of
Miss Eliza's mantel clock. From down the street a sudden ruckus—the
yelps, scuffle, and snarls of a dogfight—seemed almost a relief.

"Those sparrin' dogs sound about like our nation, don't they?"
William asked quietly.

"I—I guess so. *Yes.*" Mark jumped to his feet. "Yes! Dear God,
William, yes, they do!"

"Only one good sign on the horizon that I see," William went on in
his reserved way, "and that's the economic boom. The boom seems to
keep on roaring right through the decade, satisfying needs and greeds
and raising hopes. Maybe the raised hopes and expectations are the sad
part. If worse comes to worst, high hopes have farther to fall."

William, Mark thought, his own agitation rising, seems at a time like this only to be observing—sitting in a corner.

"We need a leader, William!"

"There we certainly agree."

"But we've lost the three men—all in such a short time—who really cared, even when they disagreed, about keeping the Union together."

William thought a moment, then said, "Calhoun, Webster, and Clay."

"In their different ways, they all tried to protect the Union!" Pacing the floor now, Mark groaned, "Oh, William, William, you and I don't see eye to eye on slavery, but we *can* still discuss it—sanely—in the same room together!"

"We're friends, Mark."

His mind still on the nakedness of the country without true leadership, Mark, though never in agreement with the South Carolinian, declared, "Even old Calhoun saw the need for staying together." Sinking back in his chair, he added helplessly, "Of course, he did despair as long ago as 1850 of the probability of holding the Union. What was it Calhoun said just before he died?"

"Don't recall his exact words," William said, "but he died doubting that two peoples so different and so hostile *could* exist together in one Union. I did agree most of the time with Calhoun, but I pray now he was wrong about that."

"Where is a leader coming from, William? We have mostly hotheads —North and South."

"And slavery's not the only thing stirring trouble. Neither major party gets along among its own members. I think the Know-Nothing or American Party is on its last legs, but Democrats fight among themselves and the Whigs—"

"The Whig Party is on its last legs for sure," Mark said.

"Do you think anything will come of the new so-called Republican Party when they meet in June?"

"What we don't need, it seems to me," Mark said, "is still another party, unless—unless . . ." He broke off and looked at William.

His friend's dry smile told Mark that he needn't finish the sentence. "Unless the Republicans can perform a miracle by keeping the Union together and abolishing slavery at the same time?"

Mark smiled, too, now, but with little mirth. "I know a miracle would be required for that. After all, Republicans are scarce as hen's teeth in the South."

"I'd say 'scarce' would be an exaggeration," William mused. "You've never been much of a party loyalist, Mark, but it could be you'll turn out to be the only Republican south of Washington City."

"I'm just watching now. The New York and Philadelphia papers do carry a lot about the ideas of the Republicans, but I'm weighing the thought of any kind of party loyalty. You're right, I've been only a sort of Whig, I guess, at times."

"What exactly do the Republicans stand for?" William asked. "I suppose they want to put a quick end to our slave economy."

"No, as I understand it, they want to stop the expansion of slavery."

William chuckled. "Then Mama could be a Republican, eh?"

"On that point, yes," Mark agreed. "Don't forget, the Kansas-Nebraska Act is the law of the land now, at least until a new administration comes to power. It says let the people out there in the territories decide. Oh, William, William, you know as well as I that to publicize Kansas as a utopia for homesteaders and planters alike and then to legislate that the people who go will decide peaceably over a red-hot issue like slavery is –is . . ."

"Is like putting two fighting cocks together in an empty rain barrel?" William finished for him.

"Something like that." Mark took a deep, helpless breath. "We just can't predict anymore, can we? As long as most of the country was east of the Mississippi, as long as we had real leaders, a man could at least wager on how things might be solved. The center of so much is moving west now! Look at Chicago. Back in 1850, just six short years ago, no railroads at all there. Now Chicago's like a distillation of the whole country–crisscrossed by railroads. Its economy is booming between the town's huge grain elevators and McCormick's reaper factory. The city itself is teeming with Irish and Germans. One part of Illinois thinks North, the other part South. Not only Chicago, but the whole state of Illinois can be ignored only at our peril. Look at the capital in Springfield!"

"Springfield's still a pretty rough place, though," William said. "At least I read somewhere it is."

The Exchange clock struck eleven. It was time to go. He got to his feet and shook William's hand. "I confess I came here this morning, old friend, hoping to find your mother alone. I–I felt almost unaccountably upset. I needed Miss Eliza." He smiled warmly. "But you've helped."

"I make no pretense of ever taking Mama's place."

"In a way you did, though. I'm not quite as hopeless since our talk.

When two men who disagree on something as tormenting as slavery can still reach each other with words, it gives me hope. But then, we've always been able to talk together, haven't we?"

William nodded. "I don't have to agree with you to be your friend. We are friends. Always have been. I try to keep my mind open to you. You always do the same for me." With a big smile—at least a big smile for William—he added, "Maybe we oughta run for something, do you suppose?"

Mark gave William a bear hug, then preceded him onto the front porch. "Say, Caroline tells me little Mary Cowper Low is going to have another baby in the fall."

"According to Mama, yes. She's got her work cut out for her in more ways than one, being married to Andrew the Great."

"I'm sure Eliza Anne's happy about the news of another grandchild," Mark said, as William walked with him out to the street.

"I'm sure she is. Say, Mark, I ran into Stuart Elliott last week. The boy's gambling again, and unless I missed my guess, he'd had quite a few drinks, too. I had such high hopes for that boy."

"So did I, I think," Mark said, unlatching the gate. "Well, you and I did all we could to help out."

"Time will tell."

"Remember me to Miss Eliza."

"Oh, I will, I surely will. We'll look for you tomorrow. Hope little Willow stops sniffling. Tell her old William loves her."

From the street, Mark called back. "Willow's always been partial to you, but then, so has her grandfather." Shaking his head, he added, "And that little girl's smack in the center of her grandfather's life! Sometimes I wonder how I managed before Willow came along."

Talking with William had helped calm him, but as he quickened his steps along Abercorn, fully intending to cut across Reynolds Square to his office on Commerce Row, Mark found himself hurrying as fast as his stiffening knees would allow up his own front steps on Bryan Street. William's concern for Willow's sniffles had suddenly blotted out the need to check the latest cotton prices from Liverpool. Using his own key, he opened the wide front door and stopped to listen. For what? What was he expecting to hear? And then he knew.

From upstairs, the subdued, worried voices of Caroline and their daughter-in-law, Mary, were almost drowned by the sudden, loud pounding of his own heart. Willow! Then he heard the child's cough—hard, tight, desperate. The word "desperate" had never crossed his mind with Willow. From birth, the child had been healthy, active, and so full of cheer, any thought of her had lifted him, whether they were together or not.

Heavy footfalls came from the direction of the kitchen and Gerta, growing stout and finding it more and more difficult to climb the stairs to the second floor, appeared bearing a steaming pan, her broad, flushed Teutonic face a mask of distress.

"Gerta," he gasped. "Gerta, what's wrong? Is it Willow?"

Without slowing her labored steps or even turning to look at him, the German woman began to plod up the stairway. "Yes, sir, Mr. Browning. The little thing's tightened up in her chest. What we were so sure was just the sniffles gets worse and worse!" Over her shoulder, she called, "But don't worry. The missus told me to tell you not to worry. I think she knew you'd come home soon."

Still rooted in the entrance hall, he stared after the climbing, cumbersome Gerta. "But, Gerta!" His whisper was nearly a shout. "Has anyone gone for Dr. Daniell? Shall I go? Gerta! *I have to do something!*"

From the top of the stairs, puffing mightily now, Gerta called, "What you can do is stop worrying! Miss Caroline wants you to wait downstairs. She and Miss Mary and I have work to do!"

Mark had already recognized the smell of onions. Obviously, Gerta had cooked onions for a poultice for Willow's congested chest. Dear God, he breathed, I can't just stand here and do nothing!

His own stiff knees forgotten, he went as fast as he could up the stairs and into the room where he'd seen Gerta disappear. Willow's own bedroom was on the third floor in the children's quarters. She'd always been so proud to sleep in the same bed Aunt Natalie slept in when she was a child. In the doorway of Mary and Jonathan's big room at the top of the stair landing, he could only stand silently, his heart crying out to know why the child had been moved from her own little bed.

Caroline and Mary, both seemingly calm and in control, bent above Willow's tossing, cough-wracked body—Mary bathing her forehead, Caroline quickly spooning out hot onions onto a length of white flannel. With one deft movement, she folded the dry side of the cloth against the soft poultice filler and tucked it gently under Willow's nightgown, pressing it high against the tender throat and against her heaving chest. For a few moments, Willow stopped coughing. Her eyes were frightened as she looked up at her mother and grandmother, then across the room at Mark. He took one, two steps toward her, his own gaze fixed on her flushed, pretty face.

"Is that you, Mark?" Caroline asked, not looking up, still holding the hot poultice in place as though if she let go, it might fly off.

"I'm here, Caroline," he whispered hoarsely. "I had no idea how sick she was!"

Now, Mary looked up at him. "Willow very sick, Papa Mark," she said, her much-improved English lapsing into the long-ago familiar way she used to speak when she was still Cherokee Mary McDonald. Fear, sometimes even laughter, he remembered irrelevantly, could cause her to lapse. "Very sick," Mary repeated, "but she be well and healthy soon. You see."

He looked from Mary's stricken face back to Willow. "I'll go for Dr. Daniell, Caroline. My girl needs a doctor . . ."

"We think not," Mary said.

"Not yet, at least," Caroline whispered, her voice breaking. Then she gained control and added, "After all, Willow only has a very, very bad cold. Dr. Daniell would tell us to do exactly what we're doing. Thank you, Gerta, for the onions. They will help, I'm sure. In just an hour or so, Willow, you're going to feel much better."

"I'm hot," Willow murmured, pulling at the quilt covering her.

"Yes. The onions make you hot, darling," Caroline soothed. "I know you're too warm, but Gerta had to cook the onions, you know."

"Does she have a fever, Caroline?"

Caroline gave him a quick frown that said don't mention a fever where the child can hear you, but Gerta was nodding her head yes.

"Should I—go back downstairs, Caroline?" he asked helplessly.

"Yes, Mark, please."

"No! Stay here with me, Grandpa. Just don't get in the way."

Willow had the talent for making him want to smile, even at a time like this. "All right, darling girl, I'll–I'll wait outside in the hall. Remember now, I'll be upstairs, close by, just on the other side of the door–" He heard his own voice crack and swiftly tried to control it. "On the other side of the door–waiting until *you* tell me to come back."

Mark saw Willow close her eyes. "I'll–let you know–soon," she whispered, then opened her eyes and did her best to smile at him.

Dr. Daniell came to see Willow morning and evening, only to tell them what they already knew: "The little girl is very ill, Browning. She's quite feverish now and if her complaints of a bad headache are true, I'm worried." Dr. Daniell started for the stairs. "I'm worried and, I fear, quite helpless. I don't like the sound of that headache one bit."

Mark stared at him, catching his coat sleeve to detain him. "Do you mean you think she might be—making up a headache? If Willow says her head hurts, it hurts, Doctor!"

"Take it easy, Browning. It's just that sometimes children confuse their symptoms."

"She's seven years old and far too smart for that!"

"I know how deep your distress must be, but your granddaughter could have meningitis and if she has—there's nothing on God's earth any doctor can do. There are times when a man simply has to face things as they are. No amount of sympathy from me can help her one iota."

Mark looked after the slightly built, jaunty figure as Dr. William Coffee Daniell went quickly down the stairs. The man was highly respected as a physician in town—one of the best, but not known for his tact.

"Please, sir," Mark called down, "don't repeat to my wife what you've just told me. Let it stop with us, I beg you!"

The door to Willow's room opened and Caroline stood there, her face white. "What, Mark? I heard you. *What* is to stop with you and Dr. Daniell?"

There had never been anything but honesty between them. Sick as it made him, he would have to be truthful now. "Our—granddaughter may have—meningitis," he whispered, and when she began to weep softly, took her in his arms.

Caroline pulled away, looked straight up at him and said, her voice firm. "Mary deserves to know."

"Oh, darling—can't we wait until tomorrow? Willow could be better!"

"Take my word for it, women need to be told the truth, the straight truth. We do far better with—shattered hearts than with—not knowing. I'm sure you meant only to be protecting her. Me, too, for that matter. But Mary is strong. I'm going to tell her now. And, Mark?"

"What is it?"

"I believe you should go to your countinghouse and tell Jonathan. Is that too hard for you to do?"

He pressed his fingers against both temples. "Yes. Yes, it's—far too hard, but you're right, of course. I'll go. Will you tell Mary now?"

She nodded. "I'll call her downstairs where she and I can be alone.

Mark, would you sit here on the hall bench and rest for a few minutes first? I'd feel better about you if you did."

"All right, darling, I will."

After Caroline and Mary had gone out of sight down the graceful curving stairs, Mark sat alone in the upstairs hall, his thoughts leaping back to another day he'd waited in this very hall for Miss Eliza to bring the perfect, flame-haired, newly born Natalie for him to see, to hold, instantly to adore. There had been no fine hall bench where he could rest that long-ago day. He'd stood petrified, for what seemed hours, on still unfinished floorboards, carpenter's tools strewn the length of the hallway because Caroline had insisted that their first child be born in the new house Mark was building for her. The barest smile tipped one corner of his mouth as he remembered that Natalie's greeting to him had been a rebellious, lusty, complaining scream which had been stopped only when a mighty clap of thunder split the dark noon sky. Willow, he remembered, had given Mary little trouble being born. Willow had always only given joy to everyone.

He'd stalled long enough. If Mary had a right to know about Willow, so did Willow's father, Jonathan. The walk to his countinghouse was longer, harder, more painful than any he had ever made.

Alone in Jonathan's office with his gentle, broad-shouldered son, Mark finished his sorrowful news by saying, "I'd rather die myself than tell you what I've just told you. Your mother and I felt you deserved to know."

Jonathan's back was turned as he stood by the tall window that overlooked the bustling port of Savannah. Mark knew he was not seeing the high stacks of cotton bales, loaded drays, cases of linens and silks, stacks of rawhides, crates of cabbages. Jonathan was merely protecting himself even from his father. Finally, he turned around. For an instant, Jonathan, to Mark's eyes, was a boy again: a boy of eleven or twelve, much as he had been during the agonizing days when Natalie had been shipwrecked and Mark had leaned heavily upon his young son for support. The support had been there. Jonathan's broad, sturdy shoulders became a symbol of strength to Mark, even as the boy's own heart was aching at the thought that his only sister might be dead. Those same shoulders were now silhouetted against the morning light outside the office window. Mark drew courage from the sight of them, in spite of the tears which filled Jonathan's eyes, then spilled down onto his smoothly shaven cheeks.

"I–I don't know what I'll do, Papa–if my little Willow dies! What will I do?"

"Oh, son–what will we all do?"

"She's–so young, so–cheerful–so full of life! Why, just yesterday morning, she was doing her little Cherokee dance for me at breakfast . . . I–thought then how blessed we are that she's such a healthy child." A spasm of anger contorted Jonathan's open, even-featured face. His hand clenched into a hard fist which he crashed brutally down onto the desk. A surge of the same anger struck Mark, so that he steadied himself with both his own hands on the other side of the oaken desk, his head bowed in the hope that Jonathan didn't notice.

When Mark looked at the boy again, he was no longer the young Jonathan, spunkily trying to cheer his father. Mark stared into the frightened, pain-filled face of a man suddenly older than his thirty years. The strong shoulders were slumped. Jonathan seemed to sway as though he, too, were ill. Then, scarcely able to believe what he saw, Mark felt the old, familiar rise in his own spirit as the smile that had always been described only as "the Jonathan smile" slowly lighted his son's face. The smile for which Mark had waited and inevitably found when his own heart was breaking years ago at the thought that Natalie might never come home again after the shipwreck.

"Your heart is as heavy as mine, Papa," Jonathan said, his voice quiet, though thick with sorrow. "You don't need me to–act like this. Mama will need me to–help, too. And–Mary! Oh, Papa–*Mary!*" Tears welled again in the boy's eyes. "Papa, I'm–so sorry! I made it all–worse."

"Son, no . . ."

"Don't try to make me feel better. Nothing could. Save your breath." Absently, Jonathan rubbed his knuckles, turning red now from the blow against the desk. "I'm angry. I've never been so angry in my whole life, but–" The smile almost came again, then vanished. "There is one thing I can do, though. I was furious because I felt so helpless. A man needs to–help his only little girl!"

"I know, son–dear God in heaven, I know. I still feel that way about your sister *and* little Willow!"

As though he hadn't heard Mark at all, Jonathan, staring above his father's head at the closed door across the office, began to put his newly forming plan into words: "Mary will be needing me in a whole new way now. We all have to pray and pray that Willow will get well, I know, but

I don't have much hope of that. It's like something inside is telling me to expect the worst. But Mary is going to be my—salvation—again."

Mark longed to ask how this would be, but felt restrained, felt he must let the boy talk.

"Mary has always been my salvation. Taking care of her, looking after her, trying to—protect her. All that makes me able to do a lot of things I'd otherwise never be able to do. Papa, I'm not—able to—lose my little girl. But I'll find a way through it because Mary will need me. Don't you see, Papa? Don't you see how plain it is?"

Mark saw nothing up ahead but black sorrow—sorrow, loneliness, missing, silence, lack of laughter, empty mornings forever because he had become so accustomed to the daily adventure outside with the grandchild he all but worshipped. Better not to say anything to Jonathan now. Let the boy draw what at least seemed to be courage from—Mary's need.

"Don't you see, Papa?" Jonathan repeated. "In the name of God, man, don't you see how much Mary will need me?"

Without leaving anyone in charge at the countinghouse, father and son hurried home as fast as Mark's weak, aching knees allowed. Inside the front hall, they stood and watched, transfixed, as Mary came slowly down the stairs alone.

"Mary?" Jonathan whispered, taking no step toward her, just watching her come down one step after another.

"Mary?" Mark echoed. "Where's Mama Caroline? How's—Willow?"

At the foot of the stairway, she stopped some distance from where they both stood. "Willow," she said almost in a whisper, "is—very sick. She—cries with her head that aches so much. It is hard to turn her head on the pillow. Her neck is—so stiff. I rub it. I rub it softly." Mary shook her head. "I—not help her."

Mark noticed again that Mary, in her fear, had reverted to the flawed Cherokee speech. Crazy thoughts kept coming into his mind. Crazy, useless thoughts such as wondering if Jonathan even noticed.

"I see you hurry up outside," Mary went on, really addressing neither of them. Just mouthing words. "I come down to tell you what I—will do—if Willow, like Ben, die, too."

Jonathan took a long step toward her, then another, and in a moment was holding her. "What, Mary? Tell me what you'll do. Tell me! I'll take care of you. I'll always take care of you, but—tell me, Mary, please!"

With a gentle gesture, she touched Jonathan's face as she stepped back. "If—God needs Willow—with Him—I will go to upcountry—to Natalie. You will have to be all right here, Jonathan, because I—go to Natalie."

"To—Natalie, Mary?" Mark whispered.

"To Natalie. We are friends. I will go to her for help. If God needs Willow, I take her to my home country. I bury her beside Natalie's—son."

Mark's impulse was to grab Mary's shoulders and give her a good shake. Jonathan, too. Both of them had given up! Both were—expecting Willow—to die! Surely, he could think of something to say to change that. Hope mattered. He meant to cling to hope. He struggled in the empty silence for words. None came.

"Oh, Mary," Jonathan said, "I'll—go with you. And—I know Natalie—can—will help us both."

"Yes," Mary whispered, then turned back toward the stairs. "I go with or without you, Jonathan. Now, I can think only that—Natalie can help—and that Willow need me upstairs."

By midafternoon Caroline knew Willow was dying. The child had vomited hard for over two hours. Julia Scarbrough, Sr., had once told her about losing a child of hers with meningitis. What Dr. Daniell had said would happen was all coming true. Before Caroline had left Willow's bedside only a minute or so ago to see to Mark, she had noticed the purplish rash on her little neck and shoulders. "A purplish rash," Daniell had said matter-of-factly, "then she may hallucinate some—say some nonsensical things—then a coma and then—"

Giving in to her own weariness—she hadn't slept all night—Caroline decided to look for Mark in their room before going all the way downstairs. He was standing by the window that overlooked Reynolds Square, his back to her when she opened the door.

"She's still alive, Mark."

"Thank God," he breathed, but did not turn to face her.

"Can I do—anything for you, my darling?" she asked.

After a long, heavy silence, he said, "No. No, thank you."

"I'll go back to—be with Mary and Jonathan, then," she whispered.

"Yes. Yes, you do that, Caroline."

When she let herself into the room where the child lay thrashing about on the huge bed, rumpled in spite of Mary's diligent efforts to keep it smoothed out, she stood listening to the first, mumbled words

Willow had spoken since last night. Mary and Jonathan bent closer to the tiny, flushed face covered now with the ugly, predicted purplish rash. Both parents were straining to hear whatever Willow might be trying to say.

When Jonathan grabbed Mary, Caroline rushed to the bed.

"Mary," her son gasped. "Mary, look—she's smiling!"

Mary only nodded, smiling a little, too, struggling, Caroline knew, for one tiny shred of hope.

Willow's weak scraps of laughter—as though delighted by something no one else could see—brought all three of them still closer.

"Mama," Willow said, a hint of her bright little voice in the one word. "Mama, look! Look at me."

"Willow, oh, Green Willow's grandchild, I'm—I'm looking!" Mary choked out the words, trying to make her own voice cheerful. "What are—you—doing, dear Willow? What?"

Under the patchwork quilt, the child's legs moved rhythmically, one, two—one, two, three . . . the smile on the sweet, rash-covered face brightened and Willow began to try to talk again. "I'm—dancing, Mama." The words were barely discernible, but they all understood. She was, in her delirium, doing the Cherokee dance, even turning slowly in her hallucinating mind, Caroline was sure, proud to have mastered it because each time she performed the dance perfectly it made her mother so happy.

When Mary swept the still-smiling child up into her arms, neither Jonathan nor Caroline made a move to stop her. Willow was Jonathan's child, too, but uniquely, as any mother knew, at that moment she was—Mary's child—too heavy at seven for Mary actually to pick up and hold, but, sitting on the bed, Mary was holding her anyway, rocking her, rocking her.

Unable to help herself, Caroline went to where Jonathan stood, took him, *her* child, into her arms and began to rock him too . . .

Jonathan saw it first when Willow's arms fell limply from Mary's neck, her slender body crumpling back onto the bed. Almost roughly, he pushed Caroline away and rushed to his wife and daughter.

Willow lay motionless, the smile gone, her perfect lips parted, eyes closed. Jonathan whirled to face his mother. "Mama! The—coma? Is that—the coma Dr. Daniell said would happen?"

Before Caroline could find her voice to answer, her son had rushed from the room, and when she heard his footfalls pounding down the stairs, she knew he was running for the doctor.

Mary, holding Willow's limp hand, lifted her own still lightly scarred face and said, "She–still breathes, Mama Caroline."

"Yes, yes, I see," Caroline said helplessly, flooded with a sickening, now irrelevant remorse that once, so long ago, she had resented Mary's Indianness, had even feared it.

Mary was dear to her now and her own courage rose a bit as Mary said, "We–wait, Mama Caroline. Dr. Daniell can do–nothing for Willow. We can, you and I. We can wait–with her, can't we?"

"Yes, Mary. We can–and we will. Oh, we will."

TWENTY-TWO

*R*iding *beside* steady William Mackay on the high driver's seat of William's new carriage on their way to the Central of Georgia to purchase tickets for the trip tomorrow to Cass, Mark was grateful for his friend's silence.

When William did speak as he reined the team at the station, it was comfortable, familiar talk, having nothing whatever to do with Willow's death last night just after ten o'clock.

"Glad you didn't mind," William said, "riding up here on this driver's perch beside me. Didn't see any reason why you should ride back there by yourself, no matter how hard this seat is. And I love to drive my team. Well, here we are, Mark. Think I'll pull in right over there by that baggage cart where you won't have so far to walk."

Both William and his mother knew how to be with someone with a broken heart, knew when to talk, when not to talk. Mark and Miss Eliza had sat together for nearly an hour this morning just after dawn; just sat together in the old Mackay parlor while she sustained him in his fresh, numbing grief, and when he'd left her, she made no effort to try to perk him up by saying that someday Mary and Jonathan would give him another grandchild. Enough well-meaning, bumbling people had already tried that utterly futile exercise.

He would never again take a walk with Willow skipping along

beside him, clutching his hand, would never again see her dance or hear her peals of laughter at one of his jokes. Miss Eliza knew all that, and so, an hour ago, as they said goodbye for the last time until the Brownings returned from the upcountry, she had done the one right thing—she had promised her prayers for them all.

"Wouldn't surprise me," Mark said woodenly as he stepped down from the high driver's seat, "to see you go right on driving for yourself, William. Why not?"

"Only one reason why not," William said while they walked toward the station. "If I keep getting any fatter, I won't be able to climb up there anymore." He patted his now ample paunch. "Can't get used to this bulge hanging on to the front of me. Doc Daniell says every pound I put on whittles a year off my life. Let's see," William mused, "we'll need four tickets and . . ."

"And whatever the Central of Georgia charges to take—my granddaughter's little sealed iron casket," Mark said brokenly. "Nothing would do Mary but that we—bury the child beside Natalie's son—my other grandchild."

"That earth up there belongs to Mary in a special way still," William said, his dry, powdery voice poorly concealing his own grief. "And Mary's right about Natalie being able to help her now. Just before I went to sleep finally last night, I thought how maybe Burke will be mighty good for Jonathan, too. He'll know exactly how a father feels at a time like this. A man doesn't forget those things."

At the entrance to the station, Mark stopped to place a hand on William's arm. "How in the name of God did you—bear losing your whole family at one time, William?"

"I don't look to live a long time," William said at last, "but if I live to be a hundred, I won't have an answer to that."

Willow had sickened and died in such a short time—barely two days— there had been no chance to let Natalie and Burke or the Stileses know they were coming. Over and over, as the train rolled through the long, dull stretches of pinelands, in an effort to keep control of his own emotions, Mark reminded himself how fortunate they were that one could now hire a carriage or a wagon at the Cassville station for the last few miles of the sorrowful way to Etowah Cliffs. There had been no need to make sure someone met the train.

Beside him, on the scratchy train seat, Caroline appeared to be resting. At least, her eyes were closed, her head against the high seat back. Jonathan and Mary had sat across the narrow wooden aisle until the last stop to take on more wood, when Mary insisted—begged, to be allowed to ride in the baggage car with Willow. Their seat was empty now, both young parents sitting cramped up on crates when Mark last saw them, one on each side of the small molded cast-iron coffin.

Mark was sixty-four years old. He felt ninety, yet some deep part of him was no older than the nervous young man he'd been when, in the happy, enthusiastic company of Miss Eliza's husband, Robert Mackay, he'd first seen Savannah. He felt even more helpless now than then, when all of life held promise and his first sight of the enchanting old city had been like falling in love. If anything could have swollen the misery of this already pain-filled journey away from Savannah, the mere act of being drawn away with every creaking turn of the train wheels could— and did. He liked Etowah Cliffs. With all his heart, he wanted Mary and Jonathan to receive what comfort Natalie and Burke might give them because they had both been through the particular agony of losing a child—in both cases, the first child. Selfishly, though, for the smallest ease for his own heart, Mark would have given almost anything for an hour's walk around his beloved city under its embracing sky. He had mentioned it to no one, but some small solace might have come to him, at least, knowing Willow rested in the earth of Savannah.

He found himself hoping everyone was well at Etowah Cliffs. Heaven knew it would be shock enough to have them all arrive without warning on such a tragic mission. Miss Eliza had promised to pray for Natalie and Burke, too. And for Callie, who, except for the loss of one of the Stileses' Negro children, would be experiencing death for the first time in her short twelve years of life.

"I certainly hope nothing's wrong in Cass with any of our family there," Caroline said, showing him that she had not been sleeping. "It will be hard enough, goodness knows, having us drop in like this with no warning."

His weary smile was one of continuing satisfaction. It was certainly nothing new that he and Caroline had just had almost the exact same thought.

"I'm not surprised you said that, darling," he said, reaching for her hand.

"I suppose you've been thinking the same thing." Her voice showed no surprise whatever. "We're close, aren't we? Do you suppose there's another couple anywhere as close as you and I?"

His heart was filled with so much, it choked off any thought of responding. He could only cling to her hand.

On the third day after the burial service in the little grove of trees just beyond the Stiles mansion, Caroline found herself turning surprisingly to Miss Lorah Plemmons for comfort. Surprisingly because although she'd always respected the wise lady and felt only gratitude for all she'd done to bring Natalie out of her own depression when her son had been born dead, she had to admit that a social barrier had stood almost unnoticed between her and Miss Lorah.

For an hour or more, while Mark and Burke and Jonathan went for a boat ride on the Etowah River, Natalie and Mary for a walk in the Park, she and Miss Lorah had talked together, just the two of them seated at Lorah Plemmons's kitchen table.

"Could I get you another glass of tea, Mrs. Browning?"

"No, Mrs. Plemmons. No, thank you."

"Some more of my apple pie maybe? At times like this, a body needs to eat."

"I couldn't, but the pie was delicious. I think it tasted better to me than anything I've tried to eat since—since—" She stopped, frowning.

"Don't bottle it up, ma'am," Miss Lorah said firmly. "Like I just told you, until the day I broke out of my shell and begun to talk about—losing my Luke and little Sarah, I sunk down deeper and deeper in self-pity."

"Self-pity," Caroline repeated.

Miss Lorah chuckled. "That word 'self-pity' used to make your daughter, Missy, as mad as a wet hen."

"It does happen, though. I think I feel sorry for myself. For all of us. My dear, kind husband in particular. We're at the age now when it seems to me that life should be smoothing out, growing more peaceful. Jonathan is entirely capable of conducting the family business. His father and I should be free to travel—to enjoy all those years of hard work." She surprised herself by reaching for Miss Lorah's strong, gnarled hand. "You're right, of course. With that long, self-pitying complaint, I just dug my own hole deeper, didn't I?"

Smiling, Miss Lorah said only, "I expect so."

"Tell me," Caroline said, straightening in the wooden chair, leaning toward Lorah Plemmons, "do you really think Natalie can help poor little Mary?"

"First off, I'd say it might be a good idea if you'd try to stop thinkin' of Mary as *poor*. Oh, I know her pain. I've had it. Still do at times so bad I think I might smother. Wouldn't help much for an old woman my age to tell Mary I know how she's feelin', though, but Natalie's a different story. They're closer to the same age. Wouldn't help even if I was to remind Mary that I was about her age when my husband and baby got drowned, either. I'm just too old *now*. When you're still in your twenties like Mary, you can't jump ahead to age sixty-some. Oh, Mary'd listen to me, but she wouldn't hear."

Caroline felt a rush of warmth toward Lorah Plemmons. For the first time in nearly a week, she almost felt like smiling when it dawned on her that Miss Lorah never quite told her exact age. She could understand that. Being past sixty herself was something she'd just as soon ignore in private or in public. She wondered if Miss Lorah knew exactly how old she was and didn't want to admit that either. Well, she thought, what possible difference does it make? This woman knows herself. She also knows me. She knows all of us, I'd think, better than we know ourselves.

After a visit to the tiny graves of both their dead children, Little Burke's grave sunken and covered over with the grass Natalie and Burke had planted so long ago and Willow's freshly mounded, still ringed with vases and jugs of fresh spring flowers and a big bouquet, cut only this morning, of Miss Lib's yellow roses, Mary and Natalie walked through the Park until they found a good, fairly dry fallen log. It had showered all through the funeral service for little Willow, and off and on for two days a misty rain had kept falling. The sun was bright today, though, and early June sun always dried out the woods fast.

For several minutes, after they'd ensconced themselves on the log, Mary sat bent over so she could dig up handfuls of upcountry woods dirt. One after another, her fingers grubbed the soil, as she'd always loved to do. Then she let the rich, black loam slide out of her hand, her eyes seeming to follow each clump, the fragrant remnant of each decaying leaf.

Natalie had sense enough to be quiet. She remembered too well how furious it made her, how it had hurt, when people insisted upon trying to make her talk or brighten up during the black weeks after she lost Little Burke. She was not going to do any of that with Mary. Natalie still felt strong, proud, certainly honored that Mary had announced even before Willow died that the one thing she meant to do was go to Natalie. "She let it be known right off," Jonathan had told his sister the first night they got there, "that whether I came along or not, she was coming up here to let you help her." Her heart squeezed for Jonathan. More than at any time in her life, Natalie wanted to help someone else. In her own grief, she had been so sure that only Burke could help. Then it turned out that because of Burke's own sorrow, it was Miss Lorah who had given Natalie the will to try life again.

Still sifting the black woods dirt, Mary said, "Talk to me, Natalie. Tell me."

Panic gripped Natalie as she cast helplessly about in her mind for words—any words that might help even a little. Miss Lorah had finally pulled her out of her black place by telling Natalie in detail about the deaths by drowning of her own little girl, Sarah, and her husband, Luke. There was no point in telling Mary about how Little Burke had been born dead because it was Mary who had—with her own hand—brought out the tiny, discolored, dead body. Well, she thought, I don't have to copy Miss Lorah. Maybe Mary is the one who needs to tell me about how Willow sickened and died—all in two short days!

"Mary, I want to say something—you don't know how much I want to—but maybe it would help you even more if you told *me* all about what happened. I don't know much about it, remember? It was all so fast. Wouldn't you like to tell me—everything?"

Still scratching up and then slowly dropping handfuls of dark woods dirt, Mary began to talk. First about the sniffles, so that Mary and Natalie's mother put her to bed and wouldn't let her take her usual morning walk with Grandpa Browning, then about the onion poultice Gerta made to loosen the tight little chest, then the dreadful coughing and high fever. Not once did Mary forget Jonathan, so that Natalie knew almost exactly when her father had told her brother, when the two hurried home, how Mary's heart ached for their helplessness—and for her own. The woods dirt was loosened all around Mary's feet by the time she got to Willow's headaches, so bad they made her cry, and the stiff neck—every change following almost exactly what Dr. Daniell said would happen.

"I don't like old Dr. Daniell," Natalie interrupted, "but I guess he is one of Savannah's best doctors. He's just so—stuffy and kind of brusque."

"Brusque means—cold?" Mary asked.

"Worse than cold. They say he has a terrible temper. Didn't you know he's called Doc Capsicum because he gives so much pepper tea for bilious fever?" She touched Mary's arm. "I'm sorry. I don't know what made me light into a perfectly fine doctor that way except that he is not very kind."

"Oh, he was kind enough. He wanted to help Willow. He just—couldn't. God wanted her too much."

"Hm," Natalie said, and wondered what she herself meant by it.

"Dr. Daniell is a good doctor," Mary went on. "The vomiting came, too, then, as he said. And—and it hurt me so! She had nothing in her little stomach to—vomit. Then, the purplish rash. Mama Caroline saw it first. Dr. Daniell said it would come."

When Natalie heard her begin to sob, out of control, she slipped her arm round Mary's shoulders and tried to comfort her. Not with words. Words, she well knew, could be awful. She just held her and hoped Mary would finally let go and cry all she needed to. Just about the time a squirrel started a loud barking in the tree right over where they sat, Mary's sobbing began to flood the woods with a wail so elemental, so shrill, so filled with primal pain that Natalie felt suddenly afraid and jerked her arm away.

Mary seemed not to notice. Bending her body up and down almost as though she were bowing, Mary filled the woods with such grief and anguish Natalie was ashamed even to tell Burke later that all she could think of was how much she wanted to run!

She didn't run, though, but made herself sit there, not touching Mary, not speaking. Then, nearly as abruptly as the keening had begun, it stopped, and Mary slumped against Natalie. In a moment, almost as though she hadn't wept, Mary picked up the thread of her story at the point where she'd grabbed and held Willow when she began to talk about dancing.

"Dancing?" Natalie asked incredulously. "Was she delirious?"

Mary nodded. "And I—held her close to me. Her little feet and legs were jerking under the covers. She was—dancing." For the first time, Mary looked straight at Natalie, smiling proudly. "I was teaching her every Cherokee dance I could remember—and she was learning so fast! Papa Mark said she danced for a famous man named William Thackeray they met on one of their morning walks and Mr. Thackeray was—charmed by Willow. Oh, Natalie, she could really dance. Enough Cherokee blood coursed through her veins so that she was learning—fast!"

Natalie was holding Mary again when she told her how Willow suddenly went limp and into the final coma from which she never roused. Mary spoke softly, even to giving her the exact time—ten minutes after ten o'clock that night—when Willow died. For what to

Natalie seemed a very long time, they just sat there, the loosened black woods dirt piled around their feet.

Then Mary jumped up. "I find Jonathan now. You help me so much. All the way here, Jonathan tried so hard to help me. He begged me to let him, but—I was—dead, too. I find him now and let him do what he must do to bear the burden of his—own grief. Do you mind if I run ahead, Natalie? Because of you, Jonathan can now—help me all he needs."

TWENTY-THREE

The grieving Brownings had been at Etowah Cliffs for over a week when, on June 17, W.H. returned finally from his inspection visit to Calhoun, north of Cartersville. Eliza Anne literally fell into his arms when he dismounted at their veranda and turned his horse over to Ezra, the new groom bought last year in Savannah.

"Why on earth did you ride all the way back here, darling?" she demanded, clinging to him. "Now someone will have to go for your trunk. Couldn't you hire a carriage? I don't know why you took a whole trunk anyway. Didn't you spend the past ten days just riding around Mr. Peters's plantation? Oh, W.H., I've missed you so!"

He held her away from him, a warm, excited smile on his face. "What a peculiar greeting, Lib," he laughed. "What a peculiar—fussing greeting. I thought you missed me."

"I did, I did, that's just the trouble. Something dreadful has happened and there hasn't been time to let you know and—oh, I thought you'd never come home!"

"But the new ideas I collected from Peters's experiments with sorghum could make us rich! What on earth happened here?"

In another tumble of words, half tearful, half desperate, and annoyed because she'd had to face it all without him, she told W.H. of the quick heartbreaking death of little Willow Browning and that only yesterday she'd had a letter from Mary Cowper with the news that she was, sometime this fall, going to have another child, that Natalie and Burke had been wonderful with the Browning family—all of whom were still there—that Miss Lorah, as usual, rose to the emergency, that she, Lib, had been most inadequate because learning of the impending birth of another child to Mary Cowper had somehow caused her to panic over the sudden, ghastly way a disease could attack a healthy child and kill it, that she hadn't slept a wink last night worrying about what might lie ahead for Mary Cowper. She was about to launch into a long, obviously nervous justification of Mary Cowper's marriage to Andrew Low when W.H. firmly, but tenderly, laid one hand over her mouth. Then, his face anguished, he led her up the walk and into the house. There he replaced his hand with his own lips and was still kissing her when Little Sinai waddled in to inform them that the reason the people had not been out to welcome W.H. home was because they'd all gathered at Natalie's cottage to comfort Jonathan and Mary Browning in their terrible loss with a song.

Fat Little Sinai finished her speech, giggled because she had caught her master and mistress kissing, and vanished.

"I'm glad they weren't around when I rode up," W.H. said, heading for the stairs. "I like being met only by my beautiful wife. How about something to eat? I'm starved."

"I'll see to it right away," Eliza Anne called up to him from the bottom of the steps. "Then, I think we'd both better walk over to the Latimers' so you can pay your respects to—poor Mark and Caroline, to Jonathan and Mary. Oh, W.H., we're so blessed that our children lived to be adults!"

He turned to look down at her. "Lib, I'm blessed that I still have you. Poor Mr. Peters's wife died five years ago. The man is trying to redeem it by all this experimental work he's doing. The results of his labor—new breeds of cattle, hogs, sheep, goats—will help our whole community, but he spoke of almost nothing in the evenings but his black loneliness. I want to wash up and change my shirt. Have some warm water brought up, please. I—I also need a few minutes to absorb the blow of the dreadful thing that happened to poor Jonathan and Mary."

"I know, I know. But do hurry. And please thank God that our three children are well. We had a letter from Henry in Savannah, too. He's deliriously happy that he and his Cliffie have set their wedding date."

"I don't suppose he said when he might be home to help his poor old work-worn father?"

"No, but don't you want to know the wedding date? And have you noticed at all, sir, that your wife *did* miss you? That she can't even leave you alone long enough for you to clean up? Can you tell how happy I am to see you?"

"I've noticed," he called down, out of her sight now, around the sharp turn in the steep stairs. "It's all right to be happy, Lib. There's quite enough to cry about."

Jonathan appreciated the sympathy call from the Stileses. He felt their being there had especially comforted Papa, who'd known them both for so long. After they had left to walk the senior Brownings as far as Miss Lorah's cottage, where they slept, and after Callie and Natalie and Mary went to bed, he felt somehow relieved that Burke seemed inclined to sit with him a while.

The night was warm enough for them to stay on the front porch. A full moon in a cloudless, star-strewn sky made the lamp Natalie had brought useless. Burke lifted off the globe, turned down the wick, and blew out the flame.

For a moment or two, the men sat in silence, listening to the night sounds Jonathan had tried so hard to call up in Savannah. Oh, the city had its own night sounds—an occasional horse trotting by, now and then a carriage, barking dogs, wheeling swallows chirping at twilight, bursts of laughter or a shout in the streets. But up here in the foothills of the Georgia mountains, the night world was as different as the look of the land. He understood better each time they visited the upcountry why Mary felt unprotected in Savannah, why she missed the sheltering hills, the somehow equally sheltering riverbanks. His native coastal marshes and salt creeks left her feeling, she said, as flat as the flat land.

Mary. Since his first sight of her up here in her Cherokee country, his life had centered on protecting her, making her happy. He frowned in the half-darkness now, at the comparison between that long-ago desire just to look after her and the drive he now felt literally to—*live* for her. A man needs a reason for living. Willow had given them both that reason. There could be no substitute for their child, but there could be— there had to be a reason left for them both to go on living. There was. Jonathan laid his head against the high-backed rocker and sighed heavily. For the first time since Willow stopped laughing and dancing, he felt an undercurrent of hope.

"I'm familiar with heartbroken sighs like that, Jonathan," Burke said softly.

"Thanks, Brother. I should tell you, though, that, strange as this must sound, there was relief in it. Sitting here in the quiet like this somehow made me realize that as long as Mary and I both live, we do have something fine to live for. I know as sure as I'm sitting here that she loves me with all her good heart. God knows, I love her. We have that. I—I guess I'm trying to concentrate on just how good that is. To give thanks by—by taking even better care of Mary's heart."

After a time, Burke asked, "Jonathan, do you have any idea how I feel about you and Mary?"

"I know you've cared about Mary for a long, long time. From way back when you first found her and her brother, Ben, living in that cave." He shuddered. "I wish I could tell you how I do battle sometimes when I even try to imagine how hard her life was in those days. I think of my Mary being driven out of her home by those brutes they called the Georgia Guard. I think of it at the craziest times—at night beside her when she's sound asleep. Sometimes at the office in the middle of reading the latest cotton prices, I think of those ugly, filthy men storming right into the little cabin, grabbing Mary up from the table where the family was doing nothing worse than having a meal together, and I get so—so ashamed of being a white man, too!"

"Hold it, hold it. You know that's a waste. They hadn't begun to call it by the high-and-mighty name of Manifest Destiny yet, but those men who drove the Cherokees out of their homeland didn't do it only because they were white. They did it out of greed for the fertile Cherokee land. You're not like that, Jonathan. I thank God I'm not either. At least, I guess I'm not."

"Oh, Burke, no, you're *not*."

"Sometimes I've wondered. I didn't drive anybody off their land, but the minute I could buy a piece of it, I did. I don't think all the whites who moved into the old Cherokee Nation were brutes, probably because if I thought that, I'd have to feel like one, too. I have to think that a lot of the settlers back then just plain fell in love with the country up here, the way I did. The way I think W. H. Stiles did."

"I guess it's best that God is our judge," Jonathan said.

It was good to sit here like this with Burke. Maybe it wouldn't seem as good with anyone else anywhere. A man could exchange honest talk with another honest man. Burke Latimer was nothing if not honest.

"We're a great country, I think," Burke said. "We're certainly growing, the economy is booming. We see it up here. I have more houses and stores and churches to build right now than I could ever handle. I love the country, I make no bones about loving it. But—" He seemed deliberately to have stopped what he was about to say.

"But—what, Burke?"

"I'd never dare tell Natalie this, but there are times, when I'm all by myself riding to or from a job, working alone on a roof somewhere, when I—I feel almost thankful that—my infant son doesn't have to grow up to be a man in it. Little Burke, as Natalie still calls him, would be fourteen now, old enough in a few years to fight in a war. There could easily be one, you know. Many people up here are strong Unionists, but hotheads live everywhere. North and South."

Jonathan rubbed at the dull ache in his forehead which he'd had ever since the service in Miss Lib's little grove. "I—I remember I was getting pretty worried, too, about all that before—before we—lost Willow. Seems like a long time ago."

"Time is tricky, isn't it? Tragedy drags it out, being happy makes it fly."

"I was just trying to remember. Didn't I read—probably not too long ago—that this new anti-slavery Republican Party is holding a convention soon?"

"This week, I'm sure, in your father's birthplace, Philadelphia. Wait a minute. This is June 17. I'm sure the first Republican National Convention started today!"

"Papa says there won't be a Southern delegate in it anywhere. That could help divide the country even more," Jonathan said.

Laughing softly, Burke said, "Your poor, isolated father might be the one exception. If he were in Philadelphia, I think he'd be a Republican. He's a courageous gentleman, living as a Northern anti-slavery man in Savannah, Georgia. I guess you know that."

"I do know it," Jonathan answered thoughtfully, "and I often wonder what Papa would do if all the secession talk at the Southern Convention in Savannah this past December really turned out to be prophetic. Papa's too old to fight, but—"

"You wouldn't be, if things erupt as soon as I think they could, Jonathan."

"That's right, I wouldn't be."

"Respecting your father as you do–the two of you as close as you are–what would you do?"

For a long time, Jonathan said nothing, his thoughts abruptly mangled by the ugly idea that he might have to leave Mary to go to war. How could he carry out the one plan that offered any hope for either of them? How could he double his efforts to look after her, to protect and shield her, if he were away fighting other Americans?

Burke waited, then said, "I'm sorry, Jonathan, I have no business even bringing up such a thing at a time like this. The South hasn't seceded yet. Forgive me?"

"Nothing to forgive. The old cliché applies here. Life has to go on. Maybe what I need is to work at getting my mind back on what's happening in the world–outside the one that just shattered for me."

"Your parents' world just shattered, too."

"Oh, yes. My little girl *filled* Papa's world! You know how he always adored Natalie. That will go on, but Mama and I felt that maybe having a granddaughter right in the house would help him sort of stay level where worrying about Natalie was concerned."

"Don't tell me he still worries about her!"

"I guess not too much anymore. Sister has really grown up. I wish I knew what she said to Mary. Whatever it was, Mary was–more like herself when she came down to the river hunting me after we went out in your boat the other day. Up to that point, Mary had seemed numb all over. Almost like she–was dead, too. Like she couldn't even find a way to be with me."

"She's better already?"

"I think she is."

"Mary's tough in the good sense. She's always been. You can count on her trying to let her heart heal, Jonathan. Mary's heart has had to heal many, many times, you know."

"And mine hasn't. I'm no expert at–recovery. I never had to learn. My life's been easy until now." He made a little snorting sound. "And here I am vowing to be the one to–help Mary!"

"Thanks to Miss Lorah, Natalie was the one who pulled me out of my grief when our son was born dead. I bluffed my way along until Miss Lorah finally got to Natalie, but once she came out of her shadows, she lifted me out, too."

Jonathan got up, went to the porch railing, and looked out over the yard, its moonlit path leading out to the river road. "Does—does a man—ever come all the way out of the shadows, Burke?"

"Yes. It doesn't seem as though you're going to, but you will. Unless a person does what poor Ben did, life moves on. No one who meant anything to you ever died—until now. Isn't that true?"

"Yes."

"Well, I can promise you one thing. Except to lose Mary, nothing will ever be harder on you. You'll make your way out of this, and when you do, only losing Mary will ever be so hard again."

"Not even losing my parents?"

"I lost both of mine when I was only a boy. But bad as that is, it's somehow—different. Different enough so that you'll manage. Try to keep it in mind during the worst times. Once you get through this, things will begin to look up."

Jonathan turned back to face Burke. "Something terrible just struck me, Burke!"

"Wanta tell me what it is?"

"Sure. It just dawned on me how many broken hearts there would be should the North go to war against us!"

Burke got up, too, now and went to perch on the railing beside Jonathan. "Thousands and thousands and thousands! Nothing easy about losing a little girl who didn't have a chance to grow into a young lady—or losing a son before he'd even had a chance to learn anything—but with my Callie heading for her thirteenth birthday next year, I *know* parents only love their offspring more as they get older. I guess that's some-thing of what I meant when I said I find some solace now and then knowing my little boy can't grow up to be a fighting man."

"Will you fight for the South if there is a war, Burke?"

"Dear God in heaven, don't ask me that! I hate slavery. I also hate the Yankee tariffs against us. I believe in the Union. I love my land here. I might bear arms against anybody trying to take it over, but I honestly can't answer that tonight, son."

"It sounds funny for you to call me son, Burke."

"It does? What are you—about thirty?

"I'll be thirty-one my next birthday." He held out his hand. "Any-way, thanks for this talk. And don't be surprised if I write you a letter now and then once we're back in Savannah. You're good to talk to. You're all right out there in plain sight."

"I was never much of a letter writer, but I'd be honored if you did let me hear now and then. Natalie and I do care."

"I know you do. Mary still swears by Mr. Burke. And I—I need you to be my friend. My father needs you, too. You two see eye to eye, even on politics. And right now, Papa needs a friend."

TWENTY-FOUR

The next morning, Burke rode alone into Cartersville for the mail. He'd thought of asking his father-in-law to ride along with him, but he'd gallop faster alone and Natalie needed extra flour in order to make Mr. Browning his favorite Lady Baltimore cake that afternoon.

The morning was cloudy. It looked like rain, so he headed out the river road on Dolly, his new dappled gray mare, a little after seven. By noon, he was back, a sizable stack of mail in Dolly's saddlebags—mail for the Stileses, one letter from a man in Macon wanting Burke to go all the way down there to build a house, and two letters for Mr. Browning, both from Savannah.

He reined Dolly first at his own cottage. By now, the Brownings would be there and Browning's mail might be important. He knew, as soon as he'd dismounted and hitched Dolly to his new double hitching post, that Callie was certainly at home. He could hear her banging away on the new pianoforte. His own steps across the porch stopped the music, if it could honestly be called music, and his daughter hurried out to give him a big hug and a shouted greeting.

"You here by yourself, honey?" Burke asked.

"No, Grandpa and Grandma are here, too—I'm giving them a recital. Mama took her sugar and butter over to Miss Lib's so Little Sinai would blend it for her."

"My wife will go to almost any lengths to get out of blending sugar and butter," Burke said, laughing, as he greeted the Brownings.

"Sometimes I wonder how much our daughter has really changed," Mrs. Browning said pleasantly. "Except that *we are* friends now. She's made that clear. She surprised me, actually. I'd rather taken it for granted."

"Let our girl take advantage of all the help she can wangle, I say," Burke's father-in-law said with a smile. "After all, she's baking that fancy cake just for me. The rest of you will share in it only because of my generosity."

"I'm going to spread the custard between the layers," Callie said, still almost shouting.

"Darling Callie," her grandmother chided, "we're all in the same room in the same cottage. Do you have to shout?"

"I like to, Grandma."

"But you were so quiet and ladylike when you were visiting us in Savannah before Mary Cowper's wedding. How did that happen?"

"Oh, I can be ladylike if I have to be. Up here, where *my* parents live, I'm free! I don't have to do anything I don't feel like doing, do I, Grandpa?"

Her grandfather laughed. "I think I'll just leave that alone. Any mail for us, Burke?"

"Yes, sir, you got two letters."

"Did you bring me a present, Papa?"

"Not this time, honey," Burke said, "I was in a hurry to get this flour back to your mother. I promise to bring two presents next time."

"That really isn't necessary," Callie said. "I may shout, but I'm not spoiled."

"Correct," her grandfather said, "you're not."

Burke handed his father-in-law the letters and excused himself to ride on over to the Stileses with theirs.

"I'm going to ride behind you, Papa!"

"Sure thing, but"–he tweaked one of her light brown braids–"I think you're shouting again."

"I am, but I'm up here by the river, don't forget."

"There's no mail for Jonathan," Burke said, "but–is he around with Mary somewhere? I thought I might take them for a short boat ride before dinner."

"Come on, Papa," Callie urged, pulling at him. "I want to go and get back so I can play some more for Grandpa and Grandma."

Laughing as he headed for the door, Burke said, "I'm not exactly sure my daughter's going to grow up to be a concert pianist, are you?"

"Callie is so beautiful, she will probably be a model for some world-famous artist," Mark boasted.

"Mark," his wife scolded, "shame on you! I doubt that could be called a ladylike profession."

"I expect you'll find Mary and Jonathan out walking along the river, Burke," Mark called. "We didn't ask where they were going. They need time alone now."

"It's very awkward not having a servant, isn't it?" Caroline asked when Callie and Burke were gone and she had managed to make tea for herself and Mark in Natalie's kitchen. "I'm too old ever to get used to it. I hope this is all right, darling," she said, handing him a cup. "Does your mail look interesting? Is it business?"

"One, yes, but there's a letter here for both of us from the Mackays." He broke the seal and found the signature on the final page. "From Kate. I'll read it to you. Let's see, Kate wrote on June 13. She must not have posted it for a day or two, since this is June 18. She begins: 'Dear Mark and Caroline, and of course, Mary and Jonathan . . . My heart is heavy for all of you and now for us because of William.' William?" Mark interrupted himself. "I hope nothing's wrong with—"

"Darling, please read on!"

" 'On the day after you left the city, William had what Dr. Daniell is calling a slight stroke.' Oh, no, Caroline," Mark gasped, "what next? 'He did not become unconscious, but his speech is still somewhat slurred and he does not have full movement on his left side. Mama is being strong and calm and so cheerful with William, who seems annoyed with himself for, as he says, "pulling a trick like that." ' "

Caroline set down her cup and went to him. "Drink your tea, Mark. I know how much William means to you, but it sounds as though he's not about to die."

Mark made a move toward his untouched tea. "I don't know what I'd do—without William. He's just always—been there. I can always count on William."

"You still can, darling. You can still count on him."

"I wonder if we should go home," he said, thinking aloud. "I know Miss Eliza needs us."

"We'll be able to leave soon, I'm sure, but we do have to think of

Mary and Jonathan. They both go every day to Willow's little grave. Just being up here in the old Cherokee Nation seems somehow to help Mary." She took the letter and began to read the remainder of it aloud. " 'William still has a fairly good appetite and, of course, Hannah and Emphie make all his favorite dishes. Last night, he ate three bowls of egg custard and a good-sized helping of fried pork and gravy with rice.' "

"That's what's wrong with William," Mark interrupted. "The man must have put on thirty or forty pounds over the last year or so. He's always been thin. I tried to tell him he shouldn't eat quite so much."

"William has so little in his life to–to give him joy," Caroline said. "And since he opened his own factoring office, he's also been working too hard. He's so proud of that sign: *William Mackay, Factor.* Miss Eliza told me it is ten at night sometimes when he gets home."

"Go on, Caroline. What else does Kate have to say? Maybe there's something that can give us an idea what we should do."

" 'Everyone knows I've always loved the ground my one remaining brother walks on, but I think what troubles me most right now is Sarah. It's like William had his stroke just to spite Sister, and this is awfully hard on Mama and me. Oh, she's good about doing her part in nursing him, but it's as though poor William had no right to get sick. Mama keeps telling me Sarah acts the way she does because she doesn't know how to deal with the ugly way she's always treated William, that she's battling within herself because they have sniped at each other all these years, that she's just now realizing how much she really cares about him and doesn't know what to do but keep on sniping.' "

"Miss Eliza is right, I'm sure," Mark said. "She's always right. Does Kate say anything else about how her mother is?"

Scanning the few remaining lines of the letter, Caroline said, "No, she evidently wrote in a hurry. She says to tell Eliza Anne and beg her forgiveness because there was no time for another letter and they all send love to all of us and prayers and that we are not to worry about William since Dr. Daniell says he should improve daily from now on unless he has another stroke. She tells us not to let this cause us to come back sooner than we should."

Mark got slowly to his feet and went to the small front window of Natalie's cottage. "Caroline–what on earth will we do when we no longer have–Miss Eliza?"

"Oh, darling, I don't know!"

"I'm sure she needs us now," he repeated.

"Shall I talk it over with Mary and Jonathan? Mary's so honest, I'm sure she'll tell me if leaving early would be too hard for her."

"Leaving that little mound of earth is going to be too hard for them both, no matter when we go. Going back into our empty house will be like losing Willow all over again . . ."

"Oh, Mark, Mark, come here and hold me."

He crossed the room and took her in his arms. "We still have each other," he said at last, his voice husky. "One thing I *couldn't* bear would be losing you!"

"I'm here. And as long as you want me, I'll be here, Mark, I promise. I promise."

For the first time since Willow died, he began to sob. Caroline was holding him now, holding him and giving him a chance to rid himself of some of the weight in his heart over the grandchild he so adored and over his best friend, William. Finally, she lifted his chin to look straight into his wet, deep-set gray eyes.

"Don't you feel a little ashamed that you haven't promised me anything?"

"What? What should I promise, dear one?"

"Oh, I'll settle for the same promise I just made to you." She was smiling now, the smile that had always lifted his heart.

"That I won't leave you as long as you need me?"

"Neither of us can guarantee such a ludicrous promise, but we can make it, Mark!"

He tried hard to return her smile. "I—promise, ma'am." She kissed him, then let him go. "Where did you say Mary and Jonathan went?"

"I guessed they're out walking together, needing to be alone."

He turned away abruptly. "At the grave in the little grove, I've no doubt."

From the back yard, they heard Callie, Natalie, and Burke talking and laughing softly.

"We have a lot to be thankful for," she said. "Callie's parents are almost as happy as you and I, aren't they?"

Natalie's voice reached them now from outside the house. "I'll go tell Mama and Papa where they are," she was saying. "They'll both be glad."

"What's this we'll be glad about?" Caroline asked as Natalie and Callie hurried into the parlor.

"Jonathan and Mary," Callie said. "Mama thought you'd like to know they've gone to town together."

"To Cartersville?" Mark asked. "Jonathan and Mary?"

"Well, at least for a long drive," Natalie said as cheerfully as possible. "Burke and I thought you'd be overjoyed. Burke talked them into going in his new carriage. They'll be back in time for dinner at Miss Lib's house. They haven't been farther away from Willow's grave, you know, than to sleep at night in our cottage, except for that one meal at Miss Lib's."

"We are glad, so glad," Caroline said. "And Mark, I promise to talk to them just as soon as they're back this afternoon."

"Talk to them about what?" Natalie wanted to know.

"William is not at all well, darling," Mark said. "He—he had a slight stroke." When he saw Natalie's stricken face, he added, "Don't worry too much. I know how fond you are of old William, but Kate wrote that he is improving."

"I love Uncle William Mackay, too," Callie whispered.

"We all do, dear," Caroline said. "We all—depend on him."

Natalie's light blue eyes were swimming with tears. "Poor Miss Eliza! Oh, Mama—Papa, too many people are dying! Far too many people die, don't they? I hate it. I hate it!"

***

When her mother decided they should all go over early for dinner since Eliza Anne didn't yet know that her brother, William, was ill, Natalie left a note at her cottage for Jonathan and Mary telling them to ride on to the Stileses'. The light noon shower was ended, so that they enjoyed the walk along the river road, although Natalie hoped no one would comment on her silence. There had been no letter for Miss Lib from Mary Cowper when Burke rode for the mail today and it would be up to her to keep the conversation going at dinner, since Miss Lib clammed up each time she didn't get Mary C.'s weekly letter. Of course, she'd be worried about William, too, and at times Natalie felt the weight of always having to be the one to keep the chatter going. At least it seemed to be up to her. Oh, Callie was a big help, but with Henry still in Savannah, where he could be close to Cliffie Gordon, and no other children around, even Callie couldn't always be depended upon. Being the only youngster did guarantee her a place at the table with the adults, though, and it was obvious how she loved that. Bobby Stiles would be there, she supposed, unless he was out fishing again, and he was a talker, but except for politics, no one could count on Uncle W.H. helping much. Miss Lib just seemed to sit there like a bump on a log. When she did say something these days, it was so socially proper and dull, Natalie wanted to shake her. She had wanted to shake Miss Lib for a long time, then throw her arms around her and beg her to come back.

Wanting to shake someone didn't mean you'd stopped loving. Natalie seldom mentioned Mary C.'s name, but she still felt heartbroken over Miss Lib. She'd promised Burke to stay out of the Stileses' family affairs and she'd kept her promise, but that didn't mean she'd stopped missing the closeness they'd always known. She missed Mary Cowper something terrible. The two friends had not exchanged one letter since Mary Cowper's marriage to old Andrew Low. What was the point? Of course, she knew Mary Cowper was going to have another child. Miss Lib had told her that, and no matter how delighted Miss Lib had seemed, Natalie knew, down in her heart, that her now icy onetime friend knew she'd forced her daughter to do the wrong thing.

It had been a long time since Natalie had even mentioned Mary Cowper to Burke, and her parents had said little or nothing beyond the fact that the Lows had entertained William Makepeace Thackeray in such an elaborate way last winter that the whole town still talked about it. Why wouldn't they entertain him royally? Andrew Low needed a wife mainly to inflate his already fat pride in his mansion and his wealth!

Even Papa and Burke had fallen silent as they neared Miss Lib's veranda walk. Mama and Callie had lagged a little behind to pick some laurel for Miss Lib, but they were catching up now.

"You're awfully quiet, Natalie," her mother said. "You will try to help with dinner conversation, won't you, darling? And to help us reassure Eliza Anne about poor William?"

Her sigh was exaggerated. "Yes, Mama. I'll be a perfect angel, but I doubt–with all that's going on in everyone's mind today–that anyone but Callie will be saying what she really means. I know poor Mary and Jonathan have to work hard to say all the socially acceptable things."

"It doesn't help a bit, dear, to resent Eliza Anne."

"Well, I do!"

"Everything Mama does that might not be right," Callie said, "is because she knows Mary Cowper married the wrong man!"

"Callie!" Natalie's mother stopped walking and looked at the girl almost pityingly. "You must *not* say such things, darling."

"Callie knows she's free to say whatever is true and honest," Natalie corrected her mother. "But for the sake of Jonathan and Mary, Callie, we'll both try to be on our best behavior at dinner. Agreed?"

The child, growing more appealing and more beautiful every day she lived, beamed up at Natalie. "Agreed, Mama."

TWENTY-FIVE

Jonathan and Mary arrived at the Stiles house just as Little Sinai, who had all but taken over the kitchen, announced that if they didn't sit down right now, her corn soufflé would fall flat as a flitter. When the meal was over, W.H. excused Jonathan from brandy and cigars with him and Burke and Mark.

"You made that easy for the boy, W.H., and I'm grateful," Mark said as the men left the ladies at the table and moved to W.H.'s study to smoke. "Jonathan is rather one-tracked these days, you know. He seems to be able to cope with his own grief only by spending every waking moment with Mary."

"Mary appears to be holding up well," W.H. said. "I see no sign of anything but perfectly normal grief." He busied himself pouring small splashes of brandy into initialed crystal snifters brought back from Vienna. "Burke, I'm sure you know how difficult this could all be for Jonathan were Mary any less courageous."

For an instant, Mark thought Burke might flare at the discreet, but quite direct reference to the long, dark months required for Natalie to come out of her depression following the death of her first baby, but Burke rallied.

"Yes, Mr. Stiles, I do know. It took me a while, too, if I remember rightly."

Throughout dinner, Mark thought they'd all done rather well in holding the conversation to reasonably safe subjects. He felt especially proud of Callie, who had drawn Mary irresistibly into their talk by "testing" herself out loud to show how well she'd learned Mary's lesson on how to build a Cherokee fish trap out of stones in the shallow part of the river. When Mary had instructed his granddaughter, Mark had no idea. So far as he knew, Mary and Jonathan had been together every minute, but Callie sounded eager to pass on her new art of fish trap building to Bobby Stiles if he got back from his own fishing expedition before dark.

For a few minutes, while Eliza Anne had delved at some length into the Lows' hospitality to the famous British author William Thackeray, Mark had watched Natalie closely. Any mention of Mary Cowper's arranged marriage could still incense his daughter, but the talk had moved to W.H.'s plans for the next Georgia Assembly now that he was Speaker. Political talk could turn ugly these days, too, and as he clipped and lighted one of W.H.'s good Havana cigars, he hoped fervently that he and Burke would be able to steer their after-dinner conversation around the prickly topic that had so divided the country.

He tried to catch Burke's eye, but failed, because, having refused a cigar, his son-in-law was busily lighting his pipe. Mark still hoped for some time alone with Burke. Once back in Savannah, there would be no one, not one single person except Miss Eliza, with whom he could express himself freely and safely. In spite of their basic disagreement on slavery, he could discuss politics with William, but Kate's letter had said that even his speech was somewhat impaired now. William. As a topic for conversation, he would bring up William's stroke. Both Burke and W.H. were partial to William and Mark needed to talk about him. Sad though it was, William's health would be a safe subject. W.H.'s dislike— disdain—for anti-slavery Northerners ran so deep, Mark dreaded the thought that the out-and-out massacre which had just taken place in Lawrence, Kansas, might even be mentioned. No one needed to tell him what W.H. thought about the strange, violent abolitionist, John Brown. Certainly not W.H.

He felt, though, that he could count on Burke to help. After all, W.H. was their respected host. Mark took a bigger drink of brandy than he intended. It was a sorry thing when three good friends had to walk as though on eggshells to keep out of trouble.

"Say, I'm certainly sorry about William Mackay, Mr. Browning," Burke said, as though he'd been reading Mark's thoughts. "My respects to you, too, sir." He looked at W.H. "I know it's going to be hard on Miss Lib being so far away up here."

"It is indeed," W.H. said. "She appeared as though she might faint when you told her, Mark. We'd heard, of course, about how heavy William was getting," W.H. said. "Too bad. I know most of us have to watch our waistlines, but my wife's brother is the last man I'd have guessed would ever put on a pound."

"William always did eat well," Mark said. "I guess age does more damage than we care to admit. Miss Eliza always said she was sure William had a tapeworm when he was young, because he almost ate them out of house and home and still stayed thin as a sapling."

W.H. sipped his brandy. "I'd wager worry had a lot to do with his illness. William's always been a strong Union man. As am I. In fact," he went on, leaning quite self-assuredly back in his chair, "I believe myself to be Speaker right now because of one speech I delivered in Milledge-ville in which I expressed my deep hope—even my prayer—that North-erners could be somehow persuaded to relent, to mind their own busi-ness, to leave us alone down here. There isn't one Southern gentleman who doesn't believe with all his heart in the Constitution of the *United* States of America. With William's background, his strong Revolution-ary ancestry, I feel sure his fears for the very survival of our nation helped bring on his illness. He's always kept his own counsel too closely. Bottles up his fears, holds his griefs inside. Not good for a man. I find I can feel quite ill before I rise to my feet to speak. Afterwards, once I've had my say, vented my spleen at the very evil that motivates this new Republican Party, I am all but well again! Poor, reserved William." He shook his head. "I wonder if I should go back to Savannah with you out of a sense of regard for my wife's only remaining brother. Might help to have someone of his own kind."

Mark glanced at Burke, who looked back at him and then once more struck a sulfur match and worried with his pipe. Mark could not fiddle with his own cigar. Cigars didn't go out. He simply sat there and said nothing.

"He's so fond of you, it's too bad you can't share William's sense of right, Browning," W.H. added.

Mark didn't risk glancing at Burke this time. "I do believe the weight aggravated William's problems, W.H.," he said lamely. "I also remember that Miss Eliza said he had been working too hard, putting in ten and eleven hours a day at his new office."

"All Southerners—planters and factors alike—have to work long hours, Mark. Your Northern colleagues leave us no choice. Or hadn't you heard about increasing railroad tariffs?"

"I think some people just tend toward strokes and heart trouble," Burke said. Mark knew the younger man was also trying to keep the talk neutral. "I know my own father died of heart trouble in his thirties. He wasn't fat. The doctor said my mother's grief over him killed her. Hemorrhage in her head, and she was two years younger than my father."

"Heaven knows," Mark said, "William's had enough grief to–to make anyone ill."

"We've all known grief," W.H. said. "Perhaps nothing to compare with the grief nationwide should bad come to worse. Has either one of you thought about the grief–the tragedy–in the families of those five fine men hacked to death out in Lawrence, Kansas, a short time ago?"

Mark had indeed lain awake nights thinking of the bloody horror inflicted in far-off Kansas by John Brown and a tiny band of what Brown called his Liberty Guards. Willow's swift illness and death had wiped all thought of it from his mind until the past day or so when he'd begun to long for a talk alone with Burke. What did Burke really think of abolitionist John Brown? Mark's son-in-law hated slavery, too, but what did he really think of the angry man, Brown, who had committed such an atrocity with the help of his own sons? Evidently, according to a letter from Mark's Philadelphia attorney, Leroy Knight, which had come just before he'd lost Willow, Brown had been on his way with his band of marauders to Lawrence, having heard of the sack of Lawrence by pro-slavery border ruffians. Leroy Knight's opinion was that the lack of resistance shown by the leaders and citizens of free Lawrence had so infuriated Brown that he and his men had resolved to take revenge. And as Brown cried, "Fight fire with fire!" he led his own ruffians to the homes of four pro-slavery men in town and, mistakenly, two others who opposed slavery. While wives and children watched, Brown's fanatics hacked five men to death with cutlasses.

"I know both your viewpoints on our peculiar institution," W.H. was saying. "You are, of course, entitled to those opinions, as I am to mine. But I also know you both to be intelligent gentlemen and, in all other areas, fair-minded. Can you possibly embrace the fiendish conduct of such a beast as John Brown?"

Burke jumped to his feet, angered. "I believe you already know the answer to that, sir!"

"Sit down, Burke, please." Mark spoke as calmly as he could. "W.H. knows you and I don't hold with a violent act like that."

Burke took his chair again, almost broke his pipe knocking out the burnt tobacco on the hearth, then took a long time to refill and light up again.

"More brandy, gentleman?" W.H. asked with pronounced courtesy.

Mark didn't want more, but hoping for at least a small respite, held out his glass. "Yes, please."

W.H. poured the amber liquid into Mark's glass, then turned to Burke, who laid his broad hand across his own snifter.

"I'm sure I've ruffled your feathers, Latimer. You, too, Mark, I have no doubt, and as your host, I apologize, but can either of you honestly tell me you understand the demon John Brown?"

"Whether we understand or not is beside the point," Burke said tersely. "But have you thought that an already fanatical man might have been incensed at the caning given a United States senator by a Southern member of the Congress? Do you grieve for the worried wife of Senator Charles Sumner—still seriously injured?"

Mark waited because again he could think of nothing pacifying to say. He honestly did not know what he thought of John Brown except that he was violent—violently anti-slavery, certainly a fanatical moralist, who as a boy had seen a young slave beaten half to death with a shovel by his master. Everyone knew Brown was a stern Calvinist who had obviously dedicated his life to a merciless effort to do away with slavery. Mark had even wondered at times if perhaps John Brown was simply a murdering lunatic from a family of lunatics.

Again, as though he had read Mark's thoughts, Burke said, "I'm not at all in favor of any of John Brown's actions, Mr. Stiles. He may be a real lunatic for all I know, but *do* you favor the actions of South Carolina's Representative Preston Brooks, who might have beaten Massachusetts's Senator Sumner to death if his fellow lawmakers hadn't jerked him bodily away?"

"Congressman Brooks was at least a gentleman," W.H. said stiffly. "He did wait until the ladies had left the chamber. I realize that the truly gentlemanly way might have been to challenge Sumner to a duel for his heinous insults to Brooks's admired uncle, Senator Butler of South Carolina, but . . ."

Burke finished for him. "But he couldn't do that since it might appear that, heaven forbid, he considered Senator Sumner a social equal!"

"That's correct, Latimer," W.H. snapped. "I must make it clear, however, that I am against dueling as well."

"You're—you're really not in favor of what young Brooks did to Sumner, are you, W.H.?" Mark dared to ask because if he could get W.H. to say that he did *not* approve of Brooks's act either, perhaps this whole thing could be ended. For now anyway.

"What do you say, Mr. Stiles?" Burke pressed the question.

"In truth, I despise violence in any form. A man's honor must at all times be taken into consideration, of course, but . . ." W.H. picked up the cut-glass brandy decanter and held it out toward Burke. "Are you sure, Burke, my man, you don't need just a small touch of something to part on?"

"I'm very sure, sir," Burke said. Then he smiled halfheartedly. "You and my father-in-law and I should know better than to discuss the peculiar institution from any angle. We are all three agreed, though, that all the states—slave and free—must stay in the Union."

Mark watched the slow smile that began to break on W.H.'s sensitive, still handsome face. "A gigantic revolution would have to take place in my thinking, Burke, for me ever to favor dissolution of the Union. You're right. On that we're all agreed."

"Indeed so," Mark said, relieved that some of the sharp edge had been smoothed away. "I'd say there's another place we're all agreed—the so-called American Party or Know-Nothings." He was smiling, too, now. "There isn't a Know-Nothing in the room!"

"For that," W.H. declared, "we can all give thanks. I'm not only opposed to the American Party; it *is* made up of true 'know-nothings.' And I'm pleased to find that you both see it, in spite of the party's anti-slavery bias. There's no room for the American Party's bigotry against either foreigners or Catholics. Our great Constitution forbids such bigotry. You gentlemen might be interested in the fact that, after long hours of work, my speech slated for July 4, the opening day of our State Democratic Convention, is taking shape. I intend it to be a strong defense of the domestic institutions of the South, the rights of the states, the preservation of the national Constitution as it was, as it is, and as it must remain."

Mark stood up. The seeds of another argument lay in what W.H. had just said. After all, the Constitution did uphold the ugly fact that slaves were considered the property of slaveholders. W.H. was well known, was greatly admired for his golden oratory, but he did tend to go on at length, and Mark's mind had by now flown back to his own grief for

Willow, his deep concern for Jonathan and Mary, for Caroline, for William. Perhaps such a political conversation had helped some, but he was growing anxious now to rejoin his family. Mary and Jonathan, he was fairly sure, were making their late-afternoon visit to the fresh grave of their dead child.

"I expect the ladies are on the veranda," W.H. said as they all three got to their feet. "We can continue our talk at a later time, I hope. Few have any doubt but that the Know-Nothings will ratify the nomination of Millard Fillmore for President. Whatever influence I have in my own Democratic Party, I certainly mean to throw to James Buchanan if, as I suspect, Pierce doesn't make it. Even if he is a Pennsylvanian, Buchanan at least believes in the rights of Southern moderates such as myself. He will go on holding with popular sovereignty in the territories, I have no doubt. All the South has ever asked, you know, is that the people *in the territories* be allowed to decide."

Mark was glad Burke did not respond. They both expressed their gratitude for the Stileses' hospitality and followed W.H. out onto the veranda just in time to hear Natalie say, her voice sharp, but, Mark could tell, on the verge of tears, "We're *not* going to agree *ever*, Miss Lib, so why don't I just go on home? Mama and Callie will wonder where I am."

"You're being ridiculous now, Natalie, but by all means, run along home if you like."

The three men saw Natalie flounce down the low steps and head for her cottage.

"What on earth's wrong with Natalie?" W.H. asked.

"She—she sounded as though she might—cry," Mark said. "Were you two arguing over Mary Cowper again, Eliza Anne?"

"As usual, yes. And I wish I wouldn't go on letting her trap me into such useless talk! Burke, can't you do something about your stubborn wife?"

Burke stood for a moment looking after Natalie as she pounded along the river road. Then, smiling a bit sadly, he repeated his gratitude for the hospitality to Eliza Anne, bid Mark and W.H. a quick good evening, and loped off after Natalie.

"Burke will know how to handle her, Lib," W.H. said casually, easing himself into a veranda rocker. "You'll join us, won't you, Mark? You and I've never had much trouble over politics." He chuckled lightly. "And I think you'll have to say I was admirable in my restraint before Burke just now. We all converged around our disapproval of the Know-Noth-ings, but I want Lib to hear straight from you that I did not even mention the dangerous, doomed new Republican Party. I was admirable, Lib—admirable."

"I'm the last person who needs to be convinced of that, my love, but —tell me the truth, now—did you spoil our lovely dinner party by arguing politics?"

"We did find a point or two of disagreement, Eliza Anne," Mark said, casting about in his mind for a logical reason to get back to his own family. "Our discussion ended on a peaceable note, though."

"Good," she said, her tone short, not really much interested in whether or not they'd argued, Mark thought. "Whatever you and Burke do tonight," she went on, "don't bring up the ugly subject before Caroline, Mark."

He laughed softly, with very little mirth. "If you don't think I've learned *that* by now, my dear Eliza Anne, you're not thinking with your usual clarity."

"According to your headstrong daughter, I *can't* think clearly. My mother, at this point, would scold me: 'Eliza Anne, not one more word to Mark on the subject of Natalie. He's like a member of our own family and so on and on and on.' That's true. We're close, Mark, but if we're to stay close, you're going to have to control Natalie! W.H. and I need no help whatever with our own children. If you still can't handle Natalie, I suggest you urge Burke to control her."

"Natalie is thirty-four years old," Mark said helplessly. "What is it you want me to do?"

"Keep her beautiful nose out of our family affairs! Kate, at least, is happy over Mary Cowper's marriage to Mr. Low. Mama, as usual, keeps her own counsel, as does poor William. Caroline realizes it's *our* affair and ours only. What you think, Mark, only you know, but—"

"I know how happy Kate Mackay is that the Lows named their first child Catherine Mackay. And I'm so fond of Kate, that makes me happy, too," he said. "I quite agree that things seem to be working out well for the Lows and that none of it—none of it is any affair of the Brownings or the Latimers. Natalie is a grown woman now, though, and even if I had been able to handle her when she was young, I certainly respect her too much to try now." He felt quick, hot tears sting his eyes. "Eliza Anne, my—my own heart is too broken over little Willow to—to—"

She got quickly to her feet and went to him. "Mark, forgive me! Can you? I don't want to be—the way Natalie swears I am—flinty and insensitive!"

"She accused you of that, Lib?" W.H. asked, a deep frown creasing his high forehead.

"Yes. She accuses me of it on a regular basis, but I just consider that it *is* Natalie making such outlandish accusations and try to let it go." A hand on Mark's arm, she went on, "But your grief over your adored grandchild is a different matter, Mark. Can you forgive me for jumping on you about Natalie?"

"I was insensitive, too, Lib, to have brought up a sore political issue with Mark tonight. We aren't getting–getting . . . ?"

"No, W.H.! We're *not* getting hard and insensitive. We simply know what's best for our own daughter and I'm just going to begin praying that someday Natalie will see we're right!"

Still searching for a valid reason to make his escape, Mark waited through the moment that followed Eliza Anne's outburst. Finally, W.H. broke the silence.

"Mark, do you ever see that Elliott boy in Savannah?"

"W.H., hush!" Eliza Anne's voice was like a whipcrack.

Mark decided to answer W.H.'s question. "No. I understand he's still at the bank, though. It's strange that I don't run into him. I happen to do most of my business these days at the Planter's Bank. Dr. Daniell did mention Elliott once at my house, as I was seeing him to the door after a call on–on little Willow."

W.H. seemed stunned by this. "Dr. William Coffee Daniell mentioned a ne'er-do-well like Elliott?"

"By chance, as I remember," Mark said. "His son, Tom Daniell, plays some poker with young Elliott. I gathered Dr. Daniell is not too pleased about it."

"You see, Mark?" Eliza Anne demanded. "W.H. and I saw young Elliott for what he really is!"

"Why doesn't Dr. Daniell forbid his son to see Elliott?" W.H. wanted to know.

"Oh, I didn't think that he disapproved of Elliott as much as that he was sick and tired of paying off his son's gambling debts. And anyway, Tom Daniell is not a child. By his father's own admission, the young man's as stubborn as the good doctor himself." Mark got up. "I must be going." Shaking W.H.'s hand, bowing over Eliza Anne's, he thanked them once more and added, "Caroline needs me, I'm sure. I was the one to spoil our blessed little Willow, but she was the apple of her grandmother's eye, too."

He turned in at Natalie's path just in time to hear Caroline almost scream: "Mary, I can't bear one more moment of this! Please—*please* stop crying. I want her back, too. God knows, I want Willow back with us, but what can we do? What can any of us do?"

Mark stopped to listen. Mary's sobs—out of control—tore at his heart. The girl had tried so hard to be brave for all of them, for Jonathan especially. Caroline had no right to lose her temper like that. No right at all. Unless—unless she felt that an unfamiliar outburst might bring Mary out of her hysterical weeping. Caroline almost never, never lost control of her temper. This was so unlike her, it could—it just could be intended as a splash of cold water.

He could hear Jonathan's low voice trying to comfort Mary, then Mary's sobbing lessened. Primitive people dare to give vent to their emotions, he thought irrelevantly. "Mary's mother, Green Willow, walked from sunup to high noon alone in the woods," Jonathan had once told him, "when Mary's father died, and with every step, she wailed her grief. When Green Willow came back to the cabin at noon, she was dry-eyed and ready to learn widowhood." To Mark, such conduct had seemed so unlike Mary, he had dismissed it from his mind until this minute as he listened to the pitiful struggle his daughter-in-law was making to stop weeping over her dead child.

"Oh, Mary, Mary," he heard Caroline plead from inside the open parlor window. "Mary, I'm sorry! Go on and cry. All those tears have to —go someplace." And then a moan escaped Caroline's throat and her pain-filled heart: "I need to get rid of my tears, too! Cry, Mary! Cry . . . I'd give anything if only I could!"

Longing to rush inside, but unable to think of one word to say, Mark just stood on the path staring at the open window, its cheerful print curtains moving in a soft breeze off the river. In a moment, Mary appeared there—quiet, no longer sobbing, her eyes seeming to see something in the distance—far in the distance, far beyond where Mark stood, beyond the river road and the river and the thick green bank on the other side.

Then, she smiled. He could see her smile plainly. She had only a little sight left in one eye from Natalie's runaway-horse accident years ago. How could it be that both eyes lit up when Mary smiled? They did. Her whole scarred, but lovely face was bathed in light even though she stood inside the room untouched by the red-gold slants of the lowering sun. She had seen Mark, and when she waved her hand, he waved back.

"We can now go home to Savannah, Papa Mark," she called, her voice still thick with weeping, but as steady as a waterfall. "Willow is safe up here in her people's good, tender land. When you say the word, we can go home. You and I will help Mama Caroline and we will also help Jonathan—to live again."

TWENTY-SIX

*B**ack in Savannah* by the end of June, Mark was relieved to find William much improved. "I was struck by his pallor, his slightly halting speech," he told Miss Eliza when he made his daily visit to the Mackays, "but he's still William."

"You can't know how much better he is, Mark," Miss Eliza assured him. "I missed you terribly, but I'm ever so glad you were away when it first happened. I honestly don't know what I would have done without dear Custis Lee in the house. When the only man left in our family is ill, it's hard. But Custis was here and he's young and strong, and except for the time he just had to spend in his barracks office and one or two inspection trips to Fort Pulaski, he never left William's bedside. When I'd try to thank him, he kept reminding me how much his father loves us all. Not once did he make us feel we were imposing. His superior officer, Captain Gilmer, gave us every consideration possible, too. I know he cleared the way for Custis to spend so much time with William."

Mark, seated beside her on the Mackay porch, reached to pat her hand. "We're going to be all right, Miss Eliza," he said. "Custis was able to stay until the day before we got back. Between Jonathan and me, you'll go right on having a man to help. I know you'll miss young Lee, but Jonathan can be at your service. The boy needs to be needed now. Mary actually seems to be doing far better than Jonathan."

"Oh, Mark," she said, giving his hand a squeeze. "How empty and quiet your beautiful home must be!"

"If you don't mind, dear friend, I–I still can't talk about it. It's worse now that we're home again. As long as we were in Cass, we were at least near her little grave." He got up. "I must go back up to William. I'm sure Dr. Daniell is through examining him by now. Daniell is a man of so few words, I mean to remind him before he comes downstairs to give you a full report. He's a fine doctor, but I wish he'd melt a little just once in a while."

"It's all right. As long as he takes good care of William, I can't complain. The doctor may feel a lot down inside. The man's just all business. Do go to William now. Your visit is the bright spot of his entire day."

When Mark peered around the half-open door of William's room a few minutes later, William smiled at him and raised his left hand a few inches above the covers to show how improved he was.

"Even old Doc Capsicum had to admit I'm better," he said as Mark pulled a rocker nearer the bed.

"One thing I know, you're certainly talking more like yourself. Do you realize you made a whole sentence without stopping once or even hesitating?"

William nodded against the pillows. "Felt good, too. Don't–don't expect it to–to–uh, to hold up, though. I'll start–fumbling for words. Your–family? Little Mary? Is she–holding up? Jonathan? Caroline? You– holding up?"

Never mind, Mark told himself, that William seemed stuck again on one phrase. "Holding up" was the right one anyway. "Yes," he said, "they're all holding up fine. Sometimes I think Mary's the strongest one of the lot."

"She's–she's had more–more–" The helpless, deep frown creased William's forehead. The frown Mark knew he'd have to learn to expect while William was still struggling for a word that just wouldn't come. "Mary's bound to be–strong," William tried again. "She's had more– more–"

"Practice?" Mark suggested.

"Practice!" William took a moment to savor his small triumph. Then, moving both hands in gestures that must have felt helpful in his effort to find the right words, he blurted: "You voting for—that rascal Frémont, Mark?"

"Say," Mark exclaimed, laughing, "you *are* better! Do you realize that's the first word you've said to me about politics since I've been back in town?"

William only nodded, but his eyes went on questioning.

"You're a rascal, too, my friend," Mark teased. "That was a very neatly laid trap if I ever heard one."

"Your own Whigs—have all but—disappeared. Or so it seemed before I—got this frazzlin'—stroke. Catch me up, Mark. I—may not look it, but I—am back in the land of the living."

"I can certainly see that and your mind is just as astute as ever. That's right. The days of the old Whig Party are, at least, numbered. But you know, William, I've always voted for the man, not the party. I'm definitely not voting for Fillmore and the Know-Nothings. They're working too hard to build a following out of fear and bigotry. I never had anything against Catholics or immigrants and . . ."

"And anyway, the Know-Nothings are—mostly on the side of slavery." He tried to flip his partially paralyzed hand in a careless gesture. "Never had much use for—Fillmore either."

"W.H. is supporting James Buchanan, of course. He claims, and he's right, I think, that those left in the old Whig Party are living on nostalgia. They also seem unwilling to face the fact that in all domestic politics there's a real *revolution*. I've always respected Democrat Senator Benton from Missouri and Frémont is his son-in-law. I hear Benton is strongly opposing him for President."

Mark saw a slow, crafty smile come to William's face. "You're going —all around the—barn to keep away from—a word."

"A word?"

"I know the word. I got it—right on the tip of my tongue. Always liked—the word, too. Just sounds—sacrilegious hooked to—a political party."

Mark laughed. "You're better, all right. So you think I'm dodging even mentioning the *Republican* Party, eh? Well, I'm not. I just don't feel inclined to support Frémont. The man may be a great adventurer, but I don't see him as President."

"A rascal," William scoffed. "The whole new party's full of—rascals."

"No matter what Dr. Daniell reports to Miss Eliza, *I* can tell her you're improving by the minute!" He laughed again, and when William made a sound very similar to his own familiar dry laugh, Mark stood and held out his hand. "We're laughing together again, man, and it's like a tonic to me. I hope you know how much I value you, William. I know it more now than ever. And I do need you."

The warm, reasonably firm handclasp felt good. "I'd better get back to the office," Mark said. "After I've said one more thing that should leave you in a good state of mind. This November, I plan to vote Democratic–for Buchanan. I think the Southern Democrats made a wise compromise when they ratified his nomination. Now, does that make you feel better?"

"Fine as a fiddle." William turned his head to look out the window. "Georgia–matters, Mark. We're–prospering, we've got–almost a million people, we cover such a big area–Georgia matters to the whole South."

✳

Throughout the steaming Savannah summer and into early fall, Mark pored over his Northern newspapers, which, because of his growing concern for the country, seemed slower than ever arriving. Jonathan was a little more like himself, almost cheerful at times, but still too distracted by his own grief, his determination to strengthen Mary, to give much thought to what was happening anywhere in the world outside. Now and then, he and Mark could discuss the furious political combat going on in the North among fiery orators and politicians locked in battle for the White House–Frémont's Republican-North Americans, Buchanan's Democrats, and Fillmore's Know-Nothings, containing most of what was left of the Whigs. By comparison, Mark fully expected the South to remain in relative quiet, since the Democrats were so strong.

He devoured every letter from his Philadelphia attorney, Leroy Knight, who evidently felt himself a committee of one to support Mark in his lonely isolation in the pro-slavery Savannah business community.

Mark had tried once to explain to Leroy Knight that he was not absolutely alone, that he felt sure his son, Jonathan, would not own a slave and that there was one Southern lady, Miss Eliza Mackay, who, while a slaveholder by circumstance, despised the thought of expanding slavery into the new territories. Knight had never acknowledged the mention of Miss Eliza. What women thought didn't count. Nor had Knight responded in any way to Mark's letter in which he'd concentrated on the irrefutable fact that his friend W. H. Stiles, along with a majority of other vehement Southern Democrats, believed so strongly in the Union that they willingly chose the moderate Pennsylvanian,

James Buchanan, as their nominee. Leroy Knight was a rabid abolitionist —as extreme in his anti-slavery views as any pro-slavery Southern fire-eater. Of course, he was now an enthusiastic Republican and was throwing his full and considerable support behind John Charles Frémont.

"We Republicans," Knight had written in May, "are attempting to offset the hordes of jobholders and the other thousands of Democrats who can't forget the glory days of Jackson and Van Buren by enlisting the country's literati. A small group of neighbors," Knight wrote, "knowing he has never meddled in politics, called at Ralph Waldo Emerson's house to urge the great man to join the Massachusetts delegation at the Republican National Convention. Emerson was away, but Mrs. Emerson gave the party enormous hope by saying at once that her husband would put aside everything to help out in this moment of crisis. How I wish you could make a visit up here, at least by early fall, Browning. It would lift your soul to experience Republican enthusiasm. Our own state of Pennsylvania will be a swing state."

By careful attention to the wording of each of his responses to Knight, Mark managed not to mention the fact that he honestly felt that Buchanan, the Democrat, would simply be the better-balanced President. On the whole, writing to Knight had not been difficult, since they could agree on other, less major issues which divided the country. By mail, they discussed temperance, keeping the Sabbath, women's rights, prison reform, free land, tariffs, schools, banks, foreign policy—all topics men argued and against which some women dissented. In fact, so many Northern women joined members of the clergy to preach and speak and write pamphlets for women's rights and against slavery that Democrats North and South attempted to dismiss both preachers and women as "Pulpit and Petticoats."

Even Mary had laughed at the Pulpit and Petticoats remark, which he felt safe to mention at dinner before Caroline. Mary was laughing again, at times spontaneously, Mark thought, and now and then allowed himself to wonder if and when his son and daughter-in-law, because of their deep love, might give him another grandchild.

"That is something you and I must leave unmentioned," Caroline said as they sat together in the back garden of their Reynolds Square home one soft autumn afternoon. "I know we've all reached a plateau in our grieving over Willow. Perhaps we'll never really learn to live in such an empty house until there's another child to fill it. But only Mary and Jonathan must decide about that. We've gotten through the summer and part of the fall. We must leave well enough alone."

He had no intention of doing otherwise, but he also knew of Caroline's old fear that another child of Mary's could easily *look* Indian. The subject was never mentioned, though, and long ago he'd learned the wisdom of giving his wife free rein in the areas she feared. It had seemed too good to be true that Willow had inherited no Indian features beyond the native rhythm born in her for Cherokee dances. Caroline had been only amused by that. Rhythm didn't show.

Using her pearl-handled folding fan now and then in the unusual heat of early November, Caroline told him the news from her visit to the Low house that morning. Mary Cowper's time was almost at hand. Tomorrow was presidential election day. The new Low baby was due to be born sometime soon after. At least, Eliza Anne was coming to Savannah to be with her daughter on November 5, the earliest possible moment, because W.H. would only return from campaigning for Buchanan the day before Eliza Anne was to take the train south.

"Does Mary Cowper seem to want her mother here?" Mark asked.

"Of course she does! Why wouldn't she? It's not only customary; a mother's care is needed at a time like that, Mark. I forget sometimes how much you men are alike."

He only smiled, not wanting to risk upsetting her, since the bitter mood in the country had sometimes seeped into their own home. Oh, little or nothing was ever said about the North-South trouble. He and Caroline were too divided on it to risk discussion, but a shadow hung over the city and in it moved the specter of a nameless danger. Nameless because to have given it a name was too terrifying. Daily, he heard more and more loose talk of secession *unless* Buchanan and the Democrats won.

Mark never heard whether or not Ralph Waldo Emerson took an active part in the Republican convention, but within three days after the election, everyone knew the decision had not hung on Massachusetts or any other New England state. They had all gone Republican, while the swing states, his own birth state of Pennsylvania, Indiana, and Illinois, joined the Solid South, so that James Buchanan, for better or worse, would be the next President of the embattled United States.

Mark's first letter from Leroy Knight after the election results were known had a ring of triumph, though. His disappointment had been tempered by near exaltation over the 1.3 million Republican popular votes. "We suffered a glorious defeat," Knight declared, still assuming that Mark's heart was with the Republicans. "And out of the battle," Knight went on, "may have arisen a strange, countrified, oddly reserved potential leader for our side. His name is Abraham Lincoln, and although he felt John Charles Frémont was not cautious or conservative enough, I am told that Lincoln is now, due to his strong anti-slavery stand, fully enlisted in the Republican cause. We can also rejoice, Browning, in the humiliating defeat of the Know-Nothings. Our Republican Party is now the only *major opposition party*."

Mark had heard of Abraham Lincoln, a gaunt, bearded country lawyer, who, while considering himself a Whig, if anything, was being spoken of as an abolitionist. Still others called him a Know-Nothing. Lincoln in no way thought of himself as an active abolitionist, but he was steadfastly opposed to the Know-Nothings. He opposed the extension of slavery, but declared that he could never be called a Know-Nothing because he failed to see how anyone claiming to oppose the oppression of Negroes could be in favor of degrading certain classes of white people! A portion of a speech Lincoln had made stayed in Mark's mind: "As a nation, we began by declaring that *'all men are equal.'* We now practically read it," Lincoln had said, " 'all men are created equal, *except Negroes.'* Should the Know-Nothings ever get control, it will read 'all men are created equal, except Negroes, *and foreigners and Catholics.'* " The lawyer from Illinois had then added that he would prefer to emigrate to some country like Russia, "where they make no pretense of loving liberty."

Even William Mackay chuckled when Mark told him what Lincoln had said. Miss Eliza, who also disliked the Know-Nothing Party, had cheered and clapped her hands in delight.

"Better not applaud, Mama," William had said. "That Lincoln fellow has a way with words all right, but there's a sharp hook in what he said—for the South anyway. I'd say the man bears watching."

The South had been so elated over the Democratic victory that news of the establishment of the Western Union Company, which, by telegraph, would help tie the country together, was taken by many in Savannah as a further good omen. Secession talk was still to be heard, but all across the city there had been a sigh of relief. Buchanan would be reasonable. Immediate trouble had been avoided. The South had in Buchanan more than a fighting chance of keeping its influence in Washington.

Andrew Low called unexpectedly at Mark's countinghouse the day the election results reached Savannah and, smoking one of Mark's Cuban cigars, rejoiced not only for the Democrats but in the birth yesterday of a son. He was discoursing at length to Mark about the South's extreme good fortune when Ezra, his butler, breathless after a run all the way to Commerce Row from Lafayette Square, was ushered in by Jonathan.

"What on earth are you doing here in Mr. Browning's private office, Ezra?" Low demanded.

"Sorry to interrupt, sir," Jonathan said, frowning, "but Ezra has some—bad news."

Haltingly, tears streaming down his brown face, the servant informed Low that the new baby had died less than an hour ago.

After walking Andrew Low in near silence to the entrance of Browning and Son, Jonathan and Mark admitted to each other they had never before felt real pity for the man.

TWENTY-SEVEN

*W*hen any event took place in the life of a man as prominent as Andrew Low, word spread like windblown fire through the city. Stuart Elliott had learned of the birth of Mary Cowper's second child before he left the Bank of the State of Georgia yesterday. In the same kind of helpless desperation he'd known at the birth of her first child last year, sick with worry over Mary C. herself, he had drunk most of the night away. Only this morning, Thursday, just before dawn did he fall into restless, tortured sleep. Late for work, he had been told by his immediate superior just before noon that Mary Cowper's infant son had died. Everywhere in the bank, employees talked of nothing but the tragic death of Andrew Low's first son.

Eyes red and swollen from hard spells of weeping through the long, drunken night, with a pain so sharp in his head, he was certainly not able to work, although he tried through the noon hour and into the early afternoon. There was no one to blame but himself that his head, his whole body, throbbed from drink and exhaustion, but there would have been no sleepless night, no drinking, if Mary Cowper had been beside *him*. He tried to shut out the gossip around his small desk, but only head-high partitions separated him from the other tellers, and their sickening expressions of sympathy for old Andrew Low—as though the dead infant hadn't been *her* child, too—drove him by half past two to run from the lobby of the bank on Bryan Street all the way to Lafayette Square.

He was in sight of the big, impressive, hated Low mansion where she lived before he gave one single thought to what he meant to do. He knew only that he had to be near her, at least near enough to learn something perhaps of what was happening to *her*. The infant, he'd heard a dozen times at the bank, was to be buried late this afternoon, at Laurel Grove Cemetery, bought by the city and opened four years or so ago on a part of Springfield plantation, land once owned by Mary Cowper's grandfather, the late Joseph Stiles.

Rounding the corner of Abercorn, Stuart tried to stroll sedately for a few steps along Charlton to where he would have a full view of the south side of the Low mansion. He stopped before a high brick wall, more like Charleston than Savannah, that surrounded the lush garden of William Battersby. Stuart had been in the enclosed garden once, only weeks after the enormous brick house was built back about 1849. His late stepfather and Battersby knew each other, and although Battersby was now a close friend and associate of Andrew Low, he had always been kind and tolerant toward Stuart. If there had been a gate to the garden from the street, it would have made a perfect hiding place—in full side view of the Low entrance. But the wall was both high and solid. The only entrance to the garden was from inside, by an enclosed side-porch doorway flush with the street.

There was nothing to do but sit down on Battersby's steps. What he meant to do if, by some miracle, she might be able to attend the burial of her baby, he had no idea.

His aching head pounded as he eased himself down on the topmost of the four stone steps which led up to the Battersby mansion. He felt dizzy, exhausted after the long run, but he would be able to hear voices from across the narrow street, even to see, when family and friends came out of the house. Then he would get to his feet and pretend again just to be passing by. He felt so desperate over what had happened to her that he might, should he even glimpse her, step into the middle of Charlton and give her a chance to notice, at least, that he was there, willing and eager somehow to help.

For a full fifteen minutes, until the Exchange clock struck a quarter past three, he waited. The thought of food still nauseated him, but it had been so long since he'd eaten, he could hear his stomach growl even above the abrupt, earsplitting screech of a blue jay in the top of one of Battersby's tea olives inside the high wall.

Then, without warning, he heard the heavy Battersby front door swing open and a man's voice called to someone inside that he would undoubtedly not be home until he'd paid his respects again at the Low house following the burial.

As though rooted to the top step, Stuart could only turn his head to look at the elegantly dressed Battersby as he came out onto the small stoop. The prosperous, middle-aged gentleman was dressed in a black cutaway coat with pearl-gray trousers, a handsome top hat in hand.

Startled at the sight of Stuart sitting on his front step, Battersby demanded, "Young man, who are you?"

"How do you do, Mr. Battersby," Stuart said, looking up at him. "I–I hope you don't mind my using your steps as a–as a–"

"As a what? What are you doing here?"

"Perhaps you've forgotten me. I'm Stuart Elliott. I believe you knew my late stepfather, James Stephens Bulloch, of Roswell."

If possible, Battersby looked even more startled. "Why, I certainly did know Bulloch. But look here, are you feeling quite well? How did you happen to stop on my front steps?"

"I'm hoping for a glimpse of the burial party soon to leave the Andrew Low house across the street."

Top hat still in hand, Battersby frowned. "Then why not go over with me? I'm heading that way myself."

"I–I wouldn't be at all welcome, sir."

"I see. Haven't I noticed you in town, young man? Don't you work at one of the banks?"

"Yes, sir. The Bank of the State of Georgia and you're on the board of directors."

Battersby brushed off a bit of lint from his top hat, then settled it on his head. "Well, we do have each other identified at last, but the question of why you're sitting here on my steps remains unanswered. No matter, I suppose, and I'm due at poor Andrew Low's house. Are you sure you're quite well?"

In spite of his throbbing head and frantic heart, Stuart got to his feet and smiled wryly. "The truth is, sir, I feel like the devil!"

"You look as though you might," Battersby said, still not unkindly. "Those bloodshot eyes come from one of two causes, as a rule–bitter weeping or too much drink. Which is it with you, Elliott?"

"Both."

"I see. Tell me, young man, are you a friend of Mr. and Mrs. Low?"

Having decided in favor of a change of subject rather than a direct answer to Battersby's question, Stuart simply studied the darkening sky, which would surely soon bring one of Savannah's late-afternoon thunderstorms. "Wouldn't it be too bad, harder on everyone in the family, if they had to bury the infant in a rainstorm?" he asked.

"It would indeed and I must hurry on over. You're welcome to go into my house and rest if you're really ill, Elliott. Are you?"

"Not in the literal sense, but thank you."

"You're sure?"

Bowing, Stuart said, "Mr. Battersby, what I need—no man could give me. Not even a gentleman as kind as you."

As Battersby hurried across Charlton Street, he turned to give Stuart one more puzzled look, then walked quickly up the flagstone walk that led to the entrance of the Low mansion. Stuart was standing in the middle of Charlton Street now, plainly there for anyone to see. He watched two elegantly dressed gentlemen, Francis Sorrel and Charles Green, carry the tiny white casket through the open door, down the steps, and out to a black hearse drawn by a jet-black span of four which had pulled up in front of the mansion.

Andrew Low himself followed with five women—only two of whom Stuart knew. One was Lucinda Sorrel, the young woman he was trying desperately to care about, a friend of Mary Cowper's. He also knew the woman beside her—the older woman in stark black with a wide-brimmed hat tied beneath her chin. Mary Cowper's mother, Mrs. W. H. Stiles. He despised her. Behind the silent, grieving mourners, the door still stood open, but no one else came through it.

Dear God, he thought—as he turned and ran in the opposite direction along Abercorn—Mary Cowper is too ill or too heartbroken to leave her bed! He swore—not under his breath—he cried the oath at the top of his voice, *up, up* into the roiling, sullen sky.

His head still bursting, legs weak from running, Stuart reeled along some minutes later, across Bay Street and aimlessly onto Factor's Walk. His one true friend and drinking partner, Robert Hutchinson, worked as a clerk in a cotton factor's office out there by the river. He needed a friend, and anyway, it was almost quitting time, so he quickened his steps and found Bob Hutchinson just closing the office windows for the night.

"What in the name of all that's good and holy are you doing here in my office?" Bob asked, grinning as he sized up Stuart's bleary eyes and drawn face. "In need of a snifter, old boy?"

"In need of—a reason to go on living. How about a trip to Europe?"

Robert Hutchinson whirled to face him, smiled broadly, and repeated, "Europe? Did you say—*Europe?*"

"You've heard of it," Stuart said. "On the other side of the Atlantic Ocean from Savannah—a continent extending west from Asia?"

"Are you out of your mind? What about our jobs? What do we use for money?"

"I won at blackjack last week, don't forget. To make a good appearance at the bank, I've been saving a little each week. Surely you could come up with a couple of hundred. We'd take our chances from there. What do you say? Don't answer that. Let me tell *you*. We're going. I have to get out of this town and you're the best friend I have, so you have to go with me. Next week all right?"

Bob Hutchinson was sitting on a desk now, stunned. "You've literally knocked me off my feet! I admit I've always wanted to see Europe, but—*next week?*"

"Say one week from today. That gives us six nights at the Gentleman's Club to stack up more winnings. Tom Daniell's doctor father is good for his debts. I can always outplay him. I'll get our travel papers tomorrow before noon."

"What about the day's work you have to do tomorrow?"

"I walked out of the bank today."

"You quit?"

"Not in so many words. I just walked out. If I've ever been sure of anything, I'm sure I have no job to worry about tomorrow or the day after or the day after that. What do you say, Bob?"

Bob was evidently beginning to take Stuart seriously. His face grew solemn, then sympathetic. "It's Mary Cowper still, isn't it?"

Stuart sank heavily into the empty chair behind the desk where Bob was perched, both hands out. "Everything—everything is—because of what happened to her, idiot!" And not caring a whit if others still in the factor's office might hear, Stuart wept and wept and wept helplessly.

The office door burst open and a strange young man Stuart had never seen yelled, "Somebody sick in here? Anything wrong?"

"Nothing that I can't handle," Bob answered, embarrassed. "Thanks, Jim, but go on—get out, will you?"

"Sure, gladly," the young man said, and slammed the door behind him.

The intrusion shocked Stuart into some control over his weeping, and wiping his face with a handkerchief, he looked up at Bob. "I've tried, old boy. I've really tried. Her new baby died yesterday. I know Mary Cowper's grieving, but she might be sick unto death herself and—and I can't even go near her! Don't you see? I've *got* to get as far away as possible. I've got to get so far away from her that I can't get near where she lives! Help me, Bob. Help me get away!"

"Will your mother give you any money for travel abroad?"

"She's no longer in Roswell, you know that," Stuart said. "She's up North in Philadelphia with my stepsister. Yes, the old darling always gives me money, but I can't wait long enough to get letters back and forth."

"You can send a telegram or can't we stop and see her in Philadelphia on our way?"

Good old Bob was going to go abroad with him, that was plain, and for now he'd agree to anything just so they got out of Savannah in a hurry. "Say, friend, that's a splendid idea." He stood up and they shook hands. "Does that mean you're going to help me, Bob?"

"You knew I would, you hound dog. A man doesn't find a friend like Stuart Elliott but once in a lifetime."

Walking idly along Factor's Walk toward a bridge that would take them to Bay Street, Bob asked, "You think we'll miss this old city when we're on the other side of the world?"

"The city? Never."

"What about Lucinda Sorrel, Stuart? You two seem a likely match. I think she's in love with you." Bob stopped walking. "Say, she's giving a birthday party for you later this month! What are you going to do about that?"

Stuart shrugged. "Nothing. Nothing I can do. By November 20, we'll be on the high seas." He gave Bob his devilish smile. "Lucy will just have to find someone else to squire her around. She's the understanding sort of girl almost any man desires, you know."

"Almost any man but Stuart Elliott, eh?"

"Almost any man but Stuart Elliott."

TWENTY-
EIGHT

*T*he week before Christmas, Mary Cowper allowed her mother and Lucinda Sorrel to persuade her to go with them for a visit to Grandmother Mackay—her first venture out of the house since the sudden death of the baby who had not lived long enough to be named.

The December day was sunny, and inside the new, comfortable carriage Mr. Low had ordered—carefully designed, Mary C. knew, just to please her—she would be warm enough. The cold wave which had gripped Savannah for two days was gone, the wind laid. She had recovered from the birth. Except for her empty heart, there seemed no plausible excuse to keep to her house. Sooner or later, she would have to face Savannah friends, would have to endure their well-meant expressions of sympathy.

Mr. Low had treated her with great gentility and kindness. He had even agreed to her request that she be allowed to sleep alone for a time in the master bedroom. There were no house guests except Mama and he would be quite comfortable in the spacious room across the upstairs hall. The endless evening hours while he sat faithfully beside her bed, reading to himself or now and then aloud to her, ended eventually. The blessed solitude after he left for the guest room had come to be her reward for having managed to live through another long day, containing the two separate pockets of grief inside her. With Stuart in Europe, she felt somehow safer in venturing out into the streets of the city. Mama and Lucinda would both be firm in protecting her from unnecessary encounters.

"We'll drive straight to Mama's house," her mother had promised. "It's like your second home, darling. And you know you won't have to struggle to be either cheerful or brave with your grandmother."

"That's right," Lucinda had agreed. "Everyone in town knows how understanding Miss Eliza is."

Just before noon, Bertha finished fixing her dark curls and was ready to settle a new velvet hat in place. Mary Cowper felt a little apprehensive because the new hat and matching velvet dress were dark blue and not black. Someone would surely criticize her for wearing a color when her baby had died only a little over six weeks ago, but it had become her habit to please Mr. Low and he had himself selected the gown's pattern and ordered it made by the head seamstress at Low's Emporium. Mama had assured her at breakfast that they'd see no one but Grandmother Mackay and, unless they were out calling, her aunts, Kate and Sarah.

She stood up from her dressing table to inspect herself in the pier glass. The image she saw was thin, her face so wan, the dark, shadowed eyes startled her. She was feeling stronger, though, and just seeing herself lift her chin gave courage. She was Mrs. Andrew Low and nothing would ever change that. He was a gentleman through and through and generous with her to a fault. Her first-born, Catherine Mackay, was a lively, healthy child, soon to be toddling on her own.

It helped, oh, she could not even explain to herself how much it helped that Lucinda Sorrel was going along, too, this morning. Lucinda, because she knew Stuart, went on somehow being a safe, dependable tie to him. Now and then, Mary Cowper seemed to sense Lucy's deep understanding of the young man who was the real Stuart Elliott. Lucy often made jokes about his impetuous nature, his gambling, the selfish way he'd suddenly decided to sail off to Europe just before she was to give him a birthday dinner, but Mary Cowper believed her friend knew Stuart's worth, too. Of course, she would never, never ask. At least, Lucinda seemed fond of him, would surely know and tell Mary Cowper the minute he got back from abroad. Without doubt, Lucy had been her main comfort in the loss of her child. For a childless woman, her sensitivity was steady and dependable. Lucy was steady and dependable.

Descending the stairs to the front door where her mother and Lucinda waited, she felt so trembly, so dreaded facing even her grandmother, she found Lucy's support even more important.

When they were all seated in the warm, familiar Mackay parlor, the easy talk about how handsome Mr. Low's carriage was, the kind white lies about how well Mary Cowper looked, even her grandmother's special way of sharing the still fresh grief, lessened Mary Cowper's nervousness. Grandmother Mackay did know and she did understand how difficult this first call was and the tea was hot and comforting. Even Mama didn't spew at all over Mr. Low's enormous generosity. She didn't even mention that he'd already begun to plan for a trip to England in the spring, maybe even before her brother Henry and Cliffie Gordon were married at the Gordon house in April. Mary Cowper hated the thought of missing Henry's wedding, but if Mr. Low's business meant they'd have to leave, so be it. "So be it" was working quite well, actually. There seemed, at times, to be much solace in her secret, growing belief in fatalism. Without Stuart, she would always live only a half-life, but "so be it." Convincing herself that marriage to Andrew Low was meant to be had not been easy. God knew that, but He had allowed it to happen. And her small, happy-natured daughter made it seem bearable, especially when the child smiled up at her as she did every time Mary Cowper spoke her name.

"You'll never know what you did for your Aunt Kate by naming your first-born for her, Mary Cowper," Grandmother Mackay was saying. "It's as though Kate's life now has captured something that's always been missing. She'll be sick to have missed your visit today."

"But Kate knows we'll be back," Mama said, trying so hard to be cheerful, Mary C. felt sorry for her. "We'll be back soon and often and we won't stay but a few minutes this time. We know you pay your regular visit to Sarah Gordon in the late mornings, Mama. How is she? I hope there's time to get by to see her before I go back to Cass day after tomorrow."

"Oh, Eliza Anne," Grandmother said, "Sarah knows why you're in town! She, of all people, knows you've been needed every minute." She gave Mary Cowper a warm, encouraging smile, not too sympathetic. The kind of strengthening smile only Grandmother Mackay knew to give.

"I'm sure there's already high excitement at the Gordon house," Lucy said, as usual knowing just when to move to another subject. "You'll come back for your son's wedding, won't you, Mrs. Stiles?"

"Henry would never forgive me if I didn't," Mary Cowper's mother laughed. "You know Henry proposed to Cliffie Gordon when they were both still children. His father and I are so happy for the boy. There's no joy quite like a parent's joy when a child chooses to marry well and–" She stopped abruptly, then fixed her eyes on her teacup.

Poor Mama. Poor Mama, Mary Cowper thought, but said nothing.

Grandmother Mackay came to the rescue. "With Henry married, that leaves only Robert, but he seems to be determined to share his handsome self among several more privileged young ladies before he settles down to married life."

"He does seem rather taken with Margaret Wylly Couper," Mary C.'s mother said, "but who knows–who ever knows about Robert?"

"I suppose your husband is pleased with the election results, Mrs. Stiles," Lucinda said. "I know my father certainly is."

"Oh, yes, Lucy." She laughed. "That is, when he isn't fretting over his new brick press. There are times when I wish my talented husband would decide permanently whether to be a gentleman farmer, a successful politician, or a manufacturer of bricks. But he's just as nearly perfect as a husband could be."

Mary Cowper avoided her mother's eyes and wondered why Mama even brought up Papa's failed venture in brickmaking. It was certainly no secret to her grandmother that Papa owed Mr. Low nearly $19,000 in borrowed money, but she hoped, at least, that Lucinda didn't know it.

Mama must have regretted her thoughtless remark, too, because very soon she suggested that Grandmother Mackay should be getting ready for her visit to Sarah Gordon. At the front door, their cloaks and hats on, Grandmother promised Mama she would try to get firsthand information through Sarah Gordon on the condition of Washington City in general. "I promise to tell you in a letter, just as soon as Sarah gets her monthly letter from her uncle, Judge Wayne."

"W.H. still misses the capital," Mama said as they walked out onto the porch. "I admit I don't miss it often," she added with a short laugh. "I am forever rooted in the upcountry and"–she touched Mary Cowper's arm affectionately–"if my daughter can do without me, I'll be so glad to get back again."

"We don't live in the same place anymore, Mama," Mary Cowper said in a firm, mature voice that surprised her. "I now live in Savannah and you and Papa in Cass. I've had to learn how to do without you."

Mary Cowper hadn't looked at her mother when she spoke. Now she did glance at Grandmother Mackay and Lucy Sorrel. They both smiled, but nothing more was said beyond pleasant goodbyes.

TWENTY-NINE

*C*hristmas in Savannah at the end of 1856 had not been so festive for years, in spite of the prosperous decade moving, it seemed to Eliza Mackay, far too swiftly to a close.

"Sarah Gordon, can you believe tomorrow will be 1857?" she asked her friend during her New Year's Eve visit to the Gordon mansion on Bull Street.

"Do you realize I'll be fifty-one years old this time next year?"

"Don't try to impress me with fifty-one," Eliza laughed. "I'll soon be seventy-nine, and that's just one year away from eighty! Your coffee is delicious today. If Hannah or Emphie could learn to make coffee like this, I'd prefer it to tea, I do believe. Oh, Sarah, I promised Eliza Anne I'd let her know all the latest news from Washington City as soon as you heard again from your uncle, Judge Wayne. Has he written?"

Crossing the room to a tall, narrow writing desk, Sarah Gordon picked up a thick sheaf of pages. "I got my monthly Washington report from dear Uncle James just yesterday. He's so in demand in the capital. You know how charming he is. Washington hostesses feel no party's a success without him." She returned to her chair, flipped briefly past the family news in the lengthy letter, and mused as she searched for an interesting passage to read aloud, "Uncle James is still so handsome, even though he's nearing seventy. That graying hair is still long and curly, his kind eyes still captivate." She'd found the page for which she was looking and laid aside the rest. "Here. Eliza Anne and W.H. will be most interested, I think, in what my uncle has to say about the city itself, not only what it looks like these days but what people are thinking about all that's been happening across our troubled land."

"Do read some of it to me," Eliza urged. "The nation is so blessed to have your wise, steady uncle as a Justice on the Supreme Court, but you and I are doubly blessed with his letters. However would we learn the really important things without him?"

Sarah looked proud and began: " 'The country has been stormy, my dear Sarah, with bloody violence continuing in Kansas, veritable mob scenes in Boston, and everywhere so much hatred, yet the quiet eye of the storm seems to be right here in our nation's capital. I would have to say that the city is quite calm since James Buchanan became our President-elect. At his inauguration ceremonies in March, he will attempt to exert a still more quieting effect by appearing on that great day in a plain suit of rural homespun, which fact will, I daresay, calm and satisfy some, but stun and upset high society. It will still be an untidy city for another presidential swearing-in ceremony, an unfinished city through which the new President and retiring President Pierce will ride on their way to the White House. Oh, the Capitol building itself is imposing, some say noble, though two enormous wings will be incomplete for the swearing-in ceremonies. Huge marble blocks are scattered about the Hill among standing pendant cranes which, I presume, will just be left standing. The base of the Washington Monument is awe-inspiring, but funds have run out and a still unfinished shaft protrudes some 150 feet into the air and stops. There are grand plans for a Mall, but now its area resembles a cow pasture, as magnificent avenues and monuments intermingle with shanties and swill in the street and slops in the alleys. Dare I say it is an unfinished city harboring a still unfinished government? I mind where I say it, but some days our government resembles a collection of fragments—military and diplomatic—a presidency and a Congress often furious with each other, even a Supreme Court not yet solid in the fullness of its authority.' "

"Now, what do you think the Judge means by that?" Eliza asked.

"I'm sure I don't know all he means, but while Uncle James disapproves of slavery on a moral basis as much as you do—more than I—more than the majority of Southerners—he does believe the Constitution confirms it, guarantees it, actually protects slavery. After all, it *was* a compromise between free and slave states. Doesn't our national Constitution protect slavery by calling our people—our property?"

Eliza thought a moment. "Yes, yes, I guess it does. Oh, Sarah, do you think the calm he writes about in Washington will ever stretch across our poor land? Do you really think that once Mr. Buchanan is in office, the—the darkness might lift?"

"Oh, my dear, I know the President-elect is a Northerner, but a rational Northerner. He will insist, Uncle James thinks, upon keeping things as they are. That can bring calm, can't it?"

"I hope so, I pray so."

"Somewhere in his letter, Uncle James says he believes firmly that Buchanan will use all his power as the new President to plead for sanity with those hotheaded abolitionists and our hotheads down here. The splendid Kansas-Nebraska Act is law now. Our local politicians firmly believe, according to my son, Willie, that popular sovereignty will work. Things will quiet down if the nation will only allow the people out there in the territories to decide on being free or slave, and where slavery already exists, just keep hands off and leave well enough alone."

"I envy you your certainty, Sarah. I truly do."

"Didn't young Custis Lee feel that Senator Douglas's Kansas-Nebraska Act will help?"

Eliza laughed softly. "Young Custis Lee is, in many ways, exactly like his dear father, Robert. Not at all involved in politics. Did I tell you Custis is on his way to San Francisco now to take up a new post out there?"

"My, my, those poor Army boys are sent so, so far from home, aren't they?"

With a short laugh, Eliza pulled herself slowly to her feet. "The way I get up out of a chair these days, you'd think I'm already eighty! But I must be going. Dear Mark Browning is giving me a ride home in his carriage. I expect he's waiting out front." As though she'd just remembered her friend's comment on "poor Army boys," she added, "Soldiers are being sent farther and farther from home, Sarah, because our nation is growing faster than chickweed after a soaking rain."

The friends embraced. "Happy New Year, Sarah! God give you a healthy, happy, calm, and peaceful year. God grant us all—calm and peace."

*B*eyond the mouth of the Savannah River, the steamer from New York, her stacks spewing black smoke, had eased past Tybee Island, plying the muddy water carefully as she seemed only to inch her way toward the city wharf. To Stuart Elliott and Bob Hutchinson, out on deck at the ship's railing in spite of a drizzle of rain, the distance was endless. Their impulsive journey abroad had been an almost complete disaster. Neither had warm enough clothing and their precious, minuscule purse was further diminished by having to buy heavy coats and caps in London the first week.

Without looking at Bob, eyes fixed on the green strip that was Long Island, Stuart said, "You're a real friend. Have I said thank you?"

"For what?" Bob asked. "You seem just as moody as the day we steamed out of Savannah."

"If it had been summer, seeing more of the sights might have helped."

"You really think so, Stuart?"

"We should have stayed in the Tower of London. I felt freer inside those gloomy stone walls than I'll feel back here in town."

"We did it, though. You needed to get away and we managed to eat most of the time and . . ." Bob threw an arm around Stuart's hunched shoulders. "We found out a man can sleep on a stone bench if he's had enough to drink."

"Do I owe you an apology?" Stuart asked, slipping out from under Bob's arm to look at him squarely. "If I do–this is it. I'm sorry to have put you through so much." He turned abruptly to stare again out over the river and surrounding marshes. "Aw, you wouldn't tell me if there's a need for an apology. You're too good a friend."

For over an hour, as the steamer eased upriver, they said almost nothing to each other. Finally, in sight of old Fort Jackson, Bob exclaimed, "Look! The Department of Engineers must have worked a little while we were gone. They actually finished the brick barracks, the magazine–*and* the parapet. I know some military men in this town who thought there'd never be a brick anything to replace those old wooden structures."

"I never paid much attention to Fort Jackson," Stuart said. "Anything about the military is far too confining for me."

Bob laughed. "That explains a lot."

"What do you mean by that?"

"Every young gentleman accepted in Savannah society or its world of commerce joins an outfit of some kind. My father would have skinned me alive if I hadn't agreed to get into the De Kalb Rifles." He peered at Stuart. "How did you get out of joining? Or are you a halfhearted member of a Roswell company?"

"I'm just halfhearted. I'll always be." Still looking out over the water, he asked, "Do you suppose she's–still grieving, Bob?"

"Oh, Stuart, old boy, are you thinking about *her?*"

Stuart gave him a quick, hopeless look. "You have to admit I haven't once mentioned her name."

"You don't need to."

"That's right. I don't need to–ever again." He took Bob's arm and urged him to a brisk walk around the deck. "We're already soggy wet, old boy. Maybe if we get some exercise, my brain will begin to work again. You'll go back to your job on Factor's Row. I don't have a job and we don't own three dollars between us. I'll owe a ton of room rent. But at least my good, new sack-coated suit will still be hanging there. If my landlady lets me in the room, I can get myself presentable enough to lay hands on some money at the Gentleman's Club tonight."

Robert chuckled. "Your mind's working all right. In the same old rut."

"I won enough from that hothead Tom Daniell to keep us for nearly a month, along with two tickets to Europe, didn't I? If I'd played old Tom one more night, we wouldn't have had to work our passage back from Liverpool. I aim to surprise Thomas Daniell this very night. Make life a bit easier for him—relieve him of some of the weight of his father's money."

For a long time, they just strolled along the deck. Then Bob asked, "Do you aim to see Lucinda Sorrel soon? I'll never forget the look on her face when our steamer moved away from the Savannah wharf last November. If ever I saw a woman fighting tears, she was that woman."

His flip manner gone, Stuart said, "Yes. Yes, I'd better see Lucy—soon."

"Because she's good for you or because she might tell you something about Mary Cowper? Which is it, do you think?"

Stuart stopped walking to look straight at Bob again. "Both. I get along a lot easier if I just—don't think. But I *do* think a lot. I think about how I need a kind, steady woman—and I also think about *her*."

Stuart's landlady, under his melting charm and heartfelt promise to pay up the rent due within a week, not only allowed him to reoccupy his old room but insisted that he eat his dinner at her bountiful boardinghouse table as a welcome-home gesture.

By a little before seven o'clock that first evening back in town, he had dined, bathed, dressed in his new winter-gray sack-coated suit, and was about to run up the front steps of the Gentleman's Club as William Mackay's driver stopped the Mackay carriage in front.

"Well," Mackay called, his hand out. "Glad to see you, Elliott. When did you get back in town?"

"Nice to know I was even missed, Mr. Mackay," he said, returning the handshake. "I'm surprised you even knew I was gone. And I must say, sir, you're looking well again. You were quite ill for a time, I hear."

Mackay had put on pounds and pounds, but his smile was still as dry and as pleasant as ever. "I had a slight stroke, but as my father always said, you can't keep a cork under water. You just got back?"

"Only this afternoon."

"Haven't been to London for quite some time," Mackay said. "How's the old place faring?"

Stuart knew Mackay was always interested in anything political, so he said, "Faring rather well, I'd say. My best friend, Bob, and I heard a lot of talk, though, about the new President-elect. A lot of worried talk, especially among businessmen in the taverns, about how, unless Buchanan brings off a miracle, the United States is going to start fighting itself North and South." He laughed as they entered the lobby of the club. "I mostly kept my mouth shut."

"Because you didn't know what to say or because you don't care one way or another?"

Stuart hung up his coat. "You still don't think too highly of me, do you, sir? I was born in Liberty County. I've lived my whole life in Georgia." He stood very straight, chin up. "I care about the South as much as anyone too poor to own a single slave."

When Mackay smiled approvingly, Stuart was relieved. He'd said the right thing, but after all, Mackay did own slaves, was prosperous from his own cotton factorage. He'd felt pretty sure of his ground.

"I guess we just have to pray for that miracle the businessmen mentioned," Mackay said, wasting no words. Stuart remembered that about him. "Most believe James Buchanan reasonable where the South is concerned. I'm not sure how strong my own faith is, but most are now trying to believe the North might come to its senses. When Buchanan's inaugurated next month, he may be taking on the hardest job a man's ever had. He does seem to want to keep things as they are, though."

He helped Mackay out of his heavy overcoat and hung it for him on a hall tree.

"Thank you, son," the older man said. "I know you didn't come here on your first night home just to talk to an old man like me."

"Oh, it was a pleasure seeing you, sir."

"Go on about your business now, Elliott. And be a little careful upstairs?"

His last sight of Mackay was from the wide landing on the stairs leading to the gambling rooms on the upper floor. The old gentleman was just standing there in the lobby, evidently deep in thought–but still alone. For some reason, Stuart turned and looked down at the portly man, remembering that Mackay had, many years ago, lost his whole family at sea. He had lived on, had prospered, but Stuart felt a surge of pity for him. He must be really lonely, he thought. Then, to dispel his depression, he took the remainder of the steps two at a time and entered the familiar, smoke-filled gaming rooms.

For more than an hour, he had played the most rewarding hands ever drawn by man. That this was going to be his lucky night, he now hadn't the slightest doubt, since at the very moment he'd walked into the room, Tom Daniell was swearing a blue streak because the fellow who'd promised to be there for the poker game had not come. When Stuart had offered himself as a substitute, Tom Daniell stopped swearing and began to smile.

Daniell was a fairly handsome young man—tall, lean, arrogant, now sporting a fashionable thin line of dark beard from ear to ear, thick ringlets in his black hair above each ear—but the smile did not soften his face. He said not one word, but, deep-set eyes bright with even the thought that he might get revenge for the huge pot Stuart had won from him late last year, he gestured dramatically for Stuart to join the game.

"Five players do indeed make the best poker game," Stuart said as he sat down. His voice sounded as condescending as he'd intended.

For that first tense hour, Stuart either called or raised so systematically that, at one point, Daniell demanded a reshuffle.

"Gladly, sir," Stuart said, cocking his eyebrow, flashing his devilish smile across the table. "This is once more my night, Tom, old fellow. No matter who shuffles or reshuffles, the pot is mine already. You'll see."

Swearing again under his breath, Tom Daniell cut and recut the cards, then dealt.

As each of the five men sat examining his hand, Daniell did not change expression at what he saw in his. Nor did Stuart. Both bluffed well. Three of the other players made moves—two folded, one called—and then Stuart showed his hand: a royal flush. With one triumphant, sweeping motion, he scooped the pot—one hundred and fifty dollars—into a pile beside him.

No sound came from Tom Daniell. The others at the table groaned.

Then Daniell leaped to his feet, dashed his whiskey into Stuart's face, and struck him with a hard fist in the mouth. The blow addled Stuart so that he reeled back and upended over a chair. Fighting was the last thing he wanted. He wanted only Daniell's father's money, so he got up and struck back only halfheartedly, his head still reeling from Tom's blow.

Blood spurted from Stuart's nose as fellow gamblers pulled Daniell away and held his long arms pinned to his side. Then someone grabbed Stuart, who jerked free, yelling, "I don't wanta fight Daniell or anyone else. I just want my winnings!"

The royal flush had done it. For an instant, Stuart almost wished he had drawn only three or four of a kind instead, then he began to laugh at

Tom Daniell, still struggling to free himself from his companions' grip. When he failed to do so, fury rising, Daniell shouted: "What's your goal, Elliott? To cheat enough to make yourself richer than old Andrew Low? Is that the way you hope to get your little upcountry piece back? Aren't you rich enough for her? Is that why she threw you out for a randy old man like Low?"

Stuart's face turned dark with anger. An insult such as that could not be ignored. Could not be ignored or satisfied except by a total apology spoken in the presence of others, or–recourse to the dueling ground across the river in South Carolina!

Stuart wanted no more than a complete apology. He begged Daniell to apologize now and be done with it. "We're gentlemen, Tom," he called across the room where other players were still restraining Daniell. "I'll settle gladly for even a reasonable apology. Go on, ask your friends what they think you should do."

When all of Tom Daniell's friends urged him to apologize, Stuart felt enormous relief. He disliked Tom Daniell intensely, but he had no desire whatever to kill him. He couldn't help a small grin when he heard one of Daniell's compatriots remind Tom that Stuart Elliott was the best shot in Savannah, but he concealed the smile in a faked cough. He wanted the apology *now*—even a halfhearted one.

"Wouldn't you rather be a bit embarrassed than dead, Tom?" one friend shouted. "Elliott can kill you before you get a trigger pulled!"

"Nonsense," Daniell growled. "No Daniell has ever been afraid of another rifleman!"

"Your father is," someone yelled. "He'd rather mow a man down with words than bullets. But then, old Doc Capsicum is smarter than his son!"

"You refuse a reasonable apology, Tom?" Stuart asked once more. "I refuse, sir!"

"Then I have no choice. We'll meet at nine sharp on Monday morning, February 16, at Screven's Ferry in South Carolina. Rifles."

"I accept!"

The fistfight and ensuing scuffle could be plainly heard from downstairs and William Mackay went up to watch from the door of the gaming room on the second floor.

When Stuart, his winnings stuffed in the pocket of his coat, strode out of the room and started for the stairway, William stopped him.

"Elliott," he called, catching him by the coat sleeve. "I want to talk just a minute, if you have time, son."

"Certainly, Mr. Mackay. I suppose you saw and heard what just took place."

"I did and I'm just as sorry as I can be."

"I tried to settle it amicably," Stuart said.

"I said I heard. You did try. I've never known a Daniell to back down from a challenge, though. Even I, with the same basic political opinions as Tom's father, have had it hot and heavy with him a time or two. They don't call his father Doc Capsicum only because he prescribes red pepper tea for whatever ails a patient. The Daniells have hot heads, too. I hope you know what you're doing."

Calmly, Stuart said, "I'm the best shot in town, sir. I hope Tom Daniell knows what *he's* doing. Obviously, he doesn't."

"I hope this doesn't get too talked about over Sunday," William said.

Stuart looked at him questioningly, his stricken eyes asking far more than his words. "You—you hope Mrs. Low won't learn that I'll be fighting a duel, sir?"

William shook his head. "Yes, with all my heart, I hope she won't. I also hope there isn't too much talk, because dueling is frowned on now in Savannah. I keep hoping you'll find your way, I guess. Giving folks reason to talk never helps set just the right reputation in town."

With a slight bow of deference—to his age, William supposed—Stuart said, "I'm grateful to you, Mr. Mackay, but you know as well as I that it's too late for me in Savannah. Maybe it's too late for me—anywhere."

THIRTY-
ONE

*A*ndrew Low sat alone at his countinghouse desk on Monday morning, his mind for once not on his work. He was sure that his wife had been, by his own protection, kept from hearing even a hint of gossip about what might happen before noon today. He and Mary Cowper had taken dinner after church with the Brownings yesterday, then had paid a call on his partner, Charles Green, and his family. They had learned at the Brownings' of Miss Eliza Mackay's severe cold, so Andrew found it easy to persuade his wife to stop at the Mackay house in the late afternoon. The old lady was up, bundled in woolen shawls, but upstairs in her room, so that Andrew had talked briefly with William Mackay in the parlor while Mary Cowper visited with her grandmother.

He had no doubt that Mackay knew what was to take place this morning at Screven's Ferry, on the South Carolina side of the river, where dueling was still legal. He'd always suspected that Mackay knew far more than he about the young scoundrel Elliott, but the subject was not mentioned until Andrew had heard his wife's voice in the upstairs hallway and knew she was about to rejoin him for the carriage ride home. Only then did he ask, "Will you be among the bloodthirsty group waiting at the waterfront tomorrow for the return of the two heroes from Screven's Ferry, Mackay?"

Mackay had given him an enigmatic look, and had said only that he would be there all right. "I'm a friend of Doc Daniell's. I find the man as prickly as the next person finds him, but he loves his son, Tom. I thought I'd be on hand out of respect."

What Mackay had said told him nothing at all. He had gleaned not one hint of what Mackay really thought.

Mary Cowper had given her husband no reason whatever to be suspicious of her feelings about young Elliott. At least, no outward reason. Still, inexplicably and to his own annoyance, he had gone on doing battle with a phantom. Did he dare hope that maybe—just maybe— after this morning, that battle might be over? Even if the handsome young whippersnapper survived the duel, his wife had obviously committed herself to being Mrs. Andrew Low. All strength was on his side, and perhaps with still more self-control, he could learn how to remain gentle with her during their most intimate times, to cease doing battle. That she responded to gentleness was so obvious, he grew impatient with himself that the tenderness he was able to show her during the day seemed to desert him entirely once she was in his arms.

He strode across his office to peer out over the waterfront, plainly visible from the window. There was no sight of rowboats returning with or without a corpse or a badly wounded man. The knot of people waiting for the same reason he waited had grown a little. He could see Dr. William Daniell, two friends beside him. He could also see William Mackay, standing to one side of the small crowd, his heavy coat collar up against the sharp February wind off the river. A glance at his watch told him it was far too early to be neglecting his work, far too early to be standing there nervous as a cat. The duel, he'd heard, was to take place at 9 A.M. It was now only ten o'clock.

He'd heard from a member of the Savannah Gentleman's Club that Elliott had literally pleaded with young Daniell to apologize, not to go through with a duel. Typical, he thought. He's not only a worthless scoundrel, he's a coward. Only God knew what might be going on this minute at Screven's Ferry. Young Elliott could be pleading still for an apology, terrified of the bullet that could stop his heart.

———✦———

Stuart had borrowed the rowboat which he and his second, Bob Hutchinson, used to get them across the Savannah River to the South Carolina side. Bob, of course, did the rowing, and in their boat, as in the other larger skiff, rested a folded canvas litter with two long handles. In Tom

Daniell's boat were the oarsmen and two friends, plus his second. Each boat also carried a doctor, black medical bag at hand. The skiffs made their way across the sun-bright water through the cut and over the back river in a little over half an hour, so that his watch told Stuart when the boats scraped against the sandy bank that only forty-five minutes remained until nine o'clock. Plenty of time to walk to wherever it is we'll go, to select a spot. Everyone would have to be agreed.

His breathing was quick and shallow as the little procession walked steadily from the ferry landing along the old dirt-covered corduroy road through the Carolina lowlands, brown and dead now in February. In the rice fields on either side, he sensed more than actually saw Negroes working on the dikes and ditches in preparation for spring planting. The Negroes stopped to watch the tiny procession, probably grinning, Stuart thought, because they'd seen other white men plod along the same old road for the same ugly reason. They'll stand there not working a lick, he thought irrelevantly, waiting for the crack of our rifles.

No one spoke. There was no human sound beyond the crunch of their boots along the corduroy road. The morning was so quiet and windless, even the unmindful, whistling redwings in the brush seemed to make music. Dear God, he thought, as he moved his heavy feet along, life is sweet! Even without *her*, on a morning like this life is sweet. I don't want to lose mine and—I don't, I *don't* want to take Tom's!

"Your honor is at stake, Stuart." His friend Bob's words had sounded hollow last night. They seemed downright silly this morning. What honor?

The spot agreed upon was not far from the river. All too soon the distance had been covered. They were there, standing on a broad, flat embankment. Arrangements could proceed.

Each man and a doctor and friends grouped themselves together for last-minute discussion. It was customary, Stuart knew, for the seconds to make one more formal effort to settle the problem peacefully. His rifle in the hand which hung at his side, Stuart felt fresh revulsion.

He grabbed Bob's arm and said urgently, "I don't want to kill Tom Daniell! I've never liked the fellow—but *I don't want to kill him.*" When Bob only stared back at him, Stuart said, "I'm willing—more than willing to accept any reasonable agenda!"

Without a word, Bob turned and strode toward Daniell's group to deliver the message. The two groups of men stood close enough together so that Stuart could hear almost every word. He had no trouble at all hearing Daniell's angry retort: "Indeed not! Just as I thought, Elliott's afraid. Tell him, Hutchinson, it's too late for fear."

Then a thought—a last resort—struck Stuart so quickly that by the time Bob had walked the few paces back to him, he had already laid down his rifle, picked up a clod, and was tying a piece of string from his pocket around it.

"What on earth are you doing, Stuart?" Bob gasped.

He held out the clod and twine. "Tie this to that bay tree over there —then watch!"

Rifle in hand again, with little or no aim, Stuart fired, and at a distance much greater than the paces to be counted off between the two men, he cut the twine. The clod dropped to earth.

For a time, no one moved or spoke. "If I fire at him, Bob, I'll—kill him," Stuart breathed.

He and Bob stood facing Tom Daniell and his second, waiting. In a moment, Tom's second, on an order from Tom, walked to where they stood. "What's Daniell's reply?" Stuart asked.

There was fear on the second's face, but his voice was firm: "Tom said, 'Damn it, Elliott's got to fight!' "

The sight of the severed string, waving now in a rising breeze, had evidently only angered hotheaded, reckless Tom Daniell, as though the string itself were an insult, not a warning.

"All right," Stuart said. "Don't say I didn't warn him."

Stepping off twenty-five paces took only a moment—a mere seventy-five feet over which the bullets would speed. Then the inevitable pause came, but because it was expected, the seconds once more inquired if some settlement might be reached.

"You know it's too late for that," Stuart whispered. "Tom's seen to it."

"I know," Bob mumbled, and Stuart saw tears in his friend's eyes. "I know, Stuart—but don't just hit him in the leg—you have to shoot to kill or he'll kill you. And—old friend, I can't lose you!"

"Don't worry, Bob. I'll kill him."

One of the doctors flipped a coin and it fell Bob's lot to give the signal. If Stuart hadn't seen the toss, he wouldn't have recognized Bob's voice as he called out: "Are you ready, gentlemen?" Both principals took aim and Bob cried, *"Fire!"*

The crack of two rifles was like one shot. Tom Daniell sprang a foot in the air, his gun on the ground, his body pitched back beside it. Then he lay twitching on the sandy earth.

By the time both doctors pronounced Tom dead—shot through the heart—by the time they carried the still bleeding body back to the boat, by the time they crossed the river again, it would be after eleven. What difference did that make? Old Doc Capsicum would be there to receive his dead son, but except for those who would gather at the East Broad Street dock to be able to boast that they had been eyewitnesses, no one would be there who cared how Stuart came back—alive or dead.

As Stuart retraced his steps along the corduroy road on the way to the rough, rudely built dock at Screven's Ferry, his mind went to William Mackay, who said he'd be on hand to show his respects to Dr. Daniell. Up ahead, Tom Daniell's two friends and his second carried the litter that bore the bleeding corpse.

I killed a man. Stuart seemed to hear, not think, the hideous words. I just killed a man. I just—murdered Tom Daniell.

For every possible reason, he dreaded the landing at the East Broad Street dock in Savannah. He was accustomed to being thought irresponsible. At this moment, he saw no way he could ever grow accustomed to being thought of as a murderer. Mostly, though, and he found it hard to understand, he dreaded the thought of meeting William Mackay's kind, oddly tragic eyes.

By the time the two skiffs approached the East Broad Street landing, William, still standing to one side by himself, had seen Andrew Low watching from the tall riverfront window of his office. Low's question yesterday, while Mary Cowper was upstairs with Mama, William thought, meant a lot more than the words he used. He looked away from Low's silhouette in the window at the end of Commerce Row, back to the boats moving now into the dock.

Out of the cluster of curious bystanders, Dr. William Daniell moved slowly to the edge of the overhanging wharf, shielding his eyes against the bright sun off the water, trying, William knew, to pick out his son, Tom. William could tell the instant Doc Daniell discovered that one body lay under a tarpaulin in the bottom of one boat. The doctor had taken two steps forward, then stopped, his tall, lean body slumped. William saw him turn his head, hat in hand now, shielding his eyes with it. In the second boat, which docked a minute later, stood young Elliott—alive. Dr. Daniell lunged one step forward when he saw Stuart, then turned and began to walk slowly, as though even now following his son's coffin, toward where the first boat had already been tied up to a piling.

In the second boat, still seated until an oarsman had tossed a rope to someone on shore, one of Dr. Daniell's compatriots, his medical bag on his lap, reached a hand to steady young Elliott.

The second boat moored securely a few feet away, William watched Stuart climb slowly onto the dock. The boy was not bleeding, evidently hadn't even been nicked, but he moved as though he were in a trance, looking at no one, his young, drawn face a mask. Dr. William Daniell appeared not to see Stuart; at least, he showed no sign of it as he stood watching four litter bearers lift his son's body up onto the dock and, as they slowly carried it away, he walked woodenly beside it, one hand on the tarpaulin.

Maybe Doc Daniell had noticed that he was there, William thought, maybe not. Either way, it was all right. He'd been there and would go to the funeral and to Laurel Grove Cemetery. The respected doctor and William had never been close, but knowing Daniell, he felt sure the man never once thought his son wouldn't come out the victor. He was sure Daniell knew the duel was going to take place; most other folks did. But the outcome must have been a shock, since young Daniell had fought a previous duel a few years back. Fought over some local politics, as William remembered. Two shots had been fired. Both missed. They had then reached an amicable settlement of their differences. Poor old Doc Daniell hadn't been so fortunate this time. His beloved, hot-tempered son was dead.

William looked around for Stuart. The attention of the crowd had followed the litter and Dr. Daniell. Only Stuart's best friend, Bob Hutchinson, stood beside him on the dock. Both young men, backs turned, stared out over the river.

With no hesitation, William walked up to them. "Stuart? Bob? I'm glad to see you're back."

"Thank you, Mr. Mackay," Bob said, his face also drawn and pale. "I —I know Stuart's glad you're here. He—he's pretty shaken."

"I can certainly understand that," William said. "And I don't have any mind to make either one of you talk. I just wanted Stuart to know I was here." When Stuart still did not look at him, William added, "Tell him he knows where to find me if he needs to talk. I'm in my office most days."

As William turned to walk away, he heard Stuart say, "Wait, Mr.

Mackay, please?" Still staring out over the water, never once meeting William's gaze, he asked, "Does—*she* know?"

William thought a minute. "Not that I'm aware, Stuart. Would you like for me to be the one to tell Mary Cowper when I can talk to her alone?"

The young man only nodded his head yes and William turned and headed slowly back to his office.

Sometime later, about halfway between his rooming house on St. Julian and the Sorrels' four blocks away, a veritable cloudburst struck the city and by the time Stuart twisted the brass bell at the Sorrels', he was drenched.

Lucinda herself opened the door and stood staring as though she'd just heard that he, not Tom Daniell, had been killed. "Stuart! Oh, Stuart—come in. Come inside out of that terrible rain. You're soaked through."

Rain water dripping from the brim of his hat, from his nose and chin, he stepped inside, seemingly unaware that he was so wet. "Lucinda," he whispered, "I have to know something!"

"What, Stuart? Don't worry about anyone hearing. I'm alone, except for servants." Impulsively, she threw both arms around him. "Oh, thank God—you're not dead! I didn't even know you were back in town until I heard that—"

"I killed a man?"

"No, did you? I only heard about the duel early Sunday. I was told at church."

"I always thought people went to church to gossip!"

"The way you look right now, church might help you some," she said gently, no hint of criticism in her voice.

He nodded agreement. "I know you're right, Lucy. God knows I need something. I—did kill a man. What am I going to do?"

His helpless question was not fair and he knew it, but he had no one else to turn to but Lucy. Poor old Bob was as shaken as he after the shooting. In his room, after he and Bob had left each other following his brief talk with Mr. Mackay, Stuart had even tried to pray. A remote, indifferent God had not heard. The horror of what he'd done had only seemed to grow, to fall like a blanket of suffocating darkness around him there in his tiny room on his knees by the lumpy bed—so black, so thick, he hadn't noticed the stormy sky when he rushed out into the street and fled to Lucy for help.

On the way, he realized that the first thing he had to know only Lucy could tell him. "I *do* have to know one thing!"

"What, Stuart?" she asked, leading him by the arm toward the parlor. "I'll tell you anything I can."

"Does—does *she* know what I did? Does Mary Cowper know I killed a man today? Have you—seen her since—it happened?"

"No. Mama's Eunice is sick today. I helped Mama get dressed. But Mary Cowper must have known about the duel, unless Mr. Low managed to keep her from finding out yesterday. I know they were out calling most of the day."

The mention of Low's name froze Stuart's heart. "Why would he want to keep it from her?"

"I've avoided telling you, but I can see—I can sense his jealousy of you," she said too calmly.

"You—what?"

"Mary Cowper is an honorable person. Women have honor, too. We just don't fight duels to uphold it. We endure instead. Mary Cowper is determined to be an honorable, suitable wife to Andrew Low. She's committed to him. In a very real way, Stuart, her honor is at stake. She may or may not still—love you. She never mentions that even to me. She told me once that until her marriage she really confided only in Natalie Latimer. She no longer feels free to do that because Natalie disapproves of her marriage. I'm sure Mary Cowper talks to no one about her true feelings anymore. I'm also sure that's best, so I never pry. But Mr. Low goes out of his way to be so good to her, I sometimes know, as surely as though he told me himself, that he worries terribly that, in her secret heart, it's *you* she loves." They were both still standing in the middle of the parlor. "Isn't this rather silly, Stuart? Shouldn't we sit down? You must be exhausted."

He was so tired, so bone-tired, he sank into a nearby chair without even waiting for her to be seated first. Lucy sat ramrod straight on the edge of a couch where she could look at his every change of expression. He was more than aware not only that Lucy possessed a kind of sixth sense about some people but that she cared intensely about him. She was watching him now, even though he kept his eyes on the carpet. She watched him too much for comfort. She always had, and yet, so few really felt any concern for him, her scrutiny helped more than it irked. He tried to laugh. The sound was ugly, hard, out of place.

"Was that a laugh?" she asked.

"It was supposed to be."

"Would it help to tell me why you laughed?"

"I doubt it, but I just realized that no one gives a damn about me or how I feel tonight after what I did, except good old Bob Hutchinson and you. Don't you think that's funny?"

"No, and I doubt if it's true. You yourself have told me many times that your mother, Martha, cares deeply about you."

He tossed that off with a careless gesture. "Oh, mothers care, yes. But my mother lives in the North now with my proper stepsister, Mittie, and her proper husband, Mr. Roosevelt. Mama doesn't know what I did—today."

"She would still care, though."

He glanced at her, then back at the carpet. "Sometimes I think Mr. William Mackay cares a little. I know it doesn't make any sense at all, but he's been—well, he's kind of gone out of his way a time or two to see me. He was there at the dock today."

"Mr. Mackay was there when you came back from Screven's Ferry?"

"He said to pay his respects to Tom's father. But he didn't say a word to Dr. Daniell. He was good enough to talk to me." He looked up at her now, humiliating tears burning his eyes. "He even promised me he'd do his best to be the one to tell—*her*."

"I see."

Lucy looked so hurt, he demanded, *"What* do you see? Why are you giving me—that look?"

She smiled weakly. "There, is that better?"

"Some."

"Maybe Mr. Mackay has told Mary Cowper by now." Lucy began to twist her lovely hands in her lap. "I know almost nothing can help," she went on, "but does it—lighten your burden even a little bit if Mr. Mackay has told her? And, Stuart, if it does make you feel any better, *why* does it?"

He jumped to his feet, suddenly out of control. "I don't know, Lucinda! *I don't know.* I don't know—anything that makes sense. Can't you see that? I thought you might, but I can tell you don't." He ran into the front hall and headed for the door.

"Stuart, wait!" She was beside him in an instant, clutching his arm. "Don't go, please don't go! You need to talk to someone and I'm here. I know I don't matter a lot, but I'm here. I'll listen. Even if you want to go over every terrible thing that happened this morning, I'll listen and I promise not to say a word."

He pushed her away, grabbed his hat, which he'd thrown on a hall table, and jerked open the door. "Good evening, Lucinda. Thanks for—trying!"

When he'd slammed the door behind him, he stood as though rooted on the front stoop—longing to be comforted. God knew he needed help from someone, but what did God care? The thought of his empty, drab room terrified him. All night, he knew, he would relive that hideous moment when he'd seen Tom Daniell leap into the air and then fall like a sack of grain to the ground. He would never forget the young body twitching, twitching, because he had put a bullet straight through Tom's heart. Where in God's name could he go this minute to try to find a little peace, a little solace? Once, twice, he reached back toward the brass doorbell, then jerked his hand away. Lucy would let him in again. She'd listen and listen and listen. He'd known for a long time that Lucinda Sorrel cared. Knowing had only made him feel more of a scoundrel, more guilty for being alive in a world so impossible to get along in. Her kindness just now increased his suffering. He'd better get away fast.

The night was so quiet, he was startled to notice that the hard downpour had stopped. So much rain had chased people off the streets, and there was no sound except the drip, drip from the thick magnolia tree in the Sorrels' front yard down onto fallen, dead leaves on the ground.

He fully intended to go. He dared not trouble Lucinda again, but he did need to talk, and since there was no one to hear, he spoke to himself in a whisper: "I can't go back to that room. Poor old Bob has had enough agony for one day. *Where in God's name can I go?*"

The Exchange clock struck seven times.

Seven o'clock isn't too late, he thought. He could go to the Mackay house! William Mackay's mother was quite old, and might be in bed, but Mackay would be up at seven o'clock in the evening. It was at least worth a try. He could walk there in five minutes.

As he forced himself, purely on the strength the tiny hope of help from Mackay had brought, to straighten up and walk down the front steps, he heard Lucinda's voice. Evidently she was still just inside the door—crying out to herself.

"Stuart, Stuart, I love you enough to—live the remainder of my life in second place! Dear God, please give me even second place in Stuart's heart!"

That she'd been just on the other side of the door for all the time he'd been standing there desperately wondering where to go, only added to his humiliation. He had to get away from her. Lucinda's lonely cry had decided him. He was going to the Mackay house, because if he didn't find some kindness that didn't make him feel even more guilt, he now realized that another bullet could also stop his own heart.

THIRTY-
TWO

*W*ith *William* and the girls gone to the two-piano
concert at Masonic Hall, Eliza Mackay decided to enjoy the quiet
evening in her parlor alone. Kate and Sarah had made her promise not to
wait up for them if she grew too weary. As usual, William had only
grinned his approval of whatever she felt like doing. More and more
dear William was her comfort in her old age and he seemed to be himself
again after his stroke. God had spared him, she was sure, because God
alone knew she could not make it through the increasingly weakening
days of her own last years without William. How could William be fifty-
three? At times like tonight, in her thoughts, she still pictured him as he
was during the first, black days of grief after the loss of his beloved
Virginia and both babies at sea. If she closed her eyes now, she could see
him—young, thin as a rail, face white and stricken—stepping out to join
her in the sorrowful parade the city gave in memory of all those
Savannah loved ones drowned when the fine steamship *Pulaski* blew up
back in June of 1838.

William didn't much resemble that tragic young man now. His once
spare figure was quite fleshy and rounded, but he was still William and,
between them, the bond of understanding held. He knew that she knew
perfectly well he was making a sacrifice to escort his sisters to the
concert this evening. William had never cared much for one piano, let

alone two! But he'd gone, giving her a wink that said volumes as Sarah once more poked fun at his somewhat bulging stomach under his vest. Sarah had always made life hard for William, but Eliza knew that, in a pinch, they'd defend each other. Three times she'd caught Sarah sobbing while William was so sick some months ago.

Eliza didn't feel too smart these days, but she hoped it was true about mothers having a special insight into all their children. The kind of gift from God that gave them enough of a glimpse down into their offsprings' hearts to understand, as she felt she understood William tonight in the minute or two they'd had together before the girls came downstairs dressed to go. Not only had she seen into William's heart, her own had taken on the weight of her son's concern for young Stuart Elliott, whom Eliza had met only once. Oh, dear, she thought, it must be these long winter evenings that keep my mind so restive.

The memory of William's startling news about what Stuart had done that morning seemed to rush back, almost as though, until this minute, she'd forgotten the whole tragedy. She knew, of course, that her tender granddaughter, Mary Cowper, had been in love with Stuart, that her daughter Eliza Anne had forbidden the child to marry him. Mark and Natalie and William still couldn't figure Eliza Anne. Natalie had grown up, but she needed a spanking for turning against poor Mary Cowper, too, just because the child chose to obey her parents. Eliza Anne wasn't the only problem. Mary Cowper's father, W.H., had been almost as determined that she marry Andrew Low. Eliza Anne had even admitted that W.H. already owed Mr. Low nearly twenty thousand dollars, borrowed to finance his harebrained brickmaking scheme.

Eliza Mackay had stayed out of the whole affair, but she had hoped Mary Cowper's parents might have given the girl a little more time.

Still, Andrew Low needed a wife and a mother for his girls and she had to admit that she'd never heard much good or honorable about Stuart beyond his fine family. Now, he'd killed a man! Eliza shuddered. Would this have happened if he'd been married to Mary Cowper? Would it have happened if her parents had only allowed her to delay her decision?

As always, Eliza turned to God for wisdom and advice. She turned to Him now for Stuart. Most likely, she'd never again lay eyes on the boy, but God loved him, was concerned over him this very night in spite of what he'd done—more to the point, *because* of what he'd done this morning.

In the short time she and William had spoken of the death of Dr.

Daniell's son, she sensed William's worry over Stuart. If William cared so deeply, God certainly did.

"He broke a commandment, Mama," William had said. "He killed a man. The fact that dueling is still going on, that some believe it's a fair way to settle a dispute, doesn't change the fact that Stuart still broke a commandment. Tom Daniell is as dead as if he'd been murdered at that card table down at the club."

What William didn't have time to say, she knew perfectly well, was that Stuart needed help fast. She couldn't quite remember whether or not William had actually told her that Stuart's guilt showed in his face, that he hadn't wanted to go through with the duel, had tried everything he knew to get Tom Daniell to apologize, but it was all in the way William had looked at her. She sighed. Honestly, she thought, sometimes I think I hear things and sometimes I hear things I only think!

There was no doubt she heard slow, heavy footsteps cross her porch now, though. A prickle of fear ran through her. Except for Hannah and Emphie in their rooms over the carriage house out back, she was alone. Who would be coming to her door at this time of night?

She pulled herself up out of her rocker. "I'll soon find out, I guess," she muttered to herself. "It's these long evenings—it gets dark so early in February."

It was too late by the time she remembered she had promised William always to ask who was there before opening the door. A young man, his face ashen in the glare of the new gas hall light William had left burning brightly, stood there unsteadily, and for an awkward time, wordlessly—looking at her with eyes so full of pain, she forgot her manners and stood staring back at him.

"I'd like to see Mr. William Mackay, please, ma'am," he said at last. "My name is Stuart Elliott. I've got to see Mr. Mackay!"

"I'm sorry, sir, my son isn't home. He won't be before nine-thirty or ten, I'm afraid."

"You're—*afraid?*" he asked, his dark, tragic eyes glinting in the hall lamplight.

Her heart was thumping harder than usual, she could feel it in the vein in her neck on the left side. It made a whistle more than a thump, when she gave it any thought. Her heart was whistling now. The stricken young man named Stuart Elliott had killed another human being just this morning.

"Am I afraid?" she repeated the question. "For just a second, yes, I was. I—I couldn't think who was coming up on my porch." Then she heard herself say, "Won't you come inside, Mr. Elliott?" The words were no sooner out of her mouth than she felt a rush of strength—of calm. "I'm by myself this evening. My children have gone to a concert at the Masonic Hall. I'd welcome some company."

He did manage a small bow, but, without another word, walked past her and stopped there in the front hall, his eyes riveted on her worn carpet.

"I—killed a man this morning, Mrs. Mackay," he said at last.

"Yes, I know. William told me."

"What do you think I should do next?"

She linked her arm in his and led him into the parlor. "I think you should sit down and let me get you a cup of good, hot tea."

"No, ma'am. I couldn't swallow anything. I will sit down, though, if you aren't afraid to—sit down with me in the room."

Immediately, she took her rocker, then smiled up at him. "I'm less afraid now with a strong young man in the house, Stuart."

"You called me Stuart."

"I think I'm old enough to use your first name, don't you?"

"I didn't want to kill him," he said. "I tried, right up to the end to—get him to apologize."

"So my son, William, told me."

"He did?"

"Yes. William told me as much as he knew, but if you need to tell me about the whole terrible ordeal, I'm here to listen."

Eliza didn't notice what time it was when he began, but he stopped talking only when her mantel clock chimed half past eight. He not only recounted everything he could remember from the boat trip across the Savannah River to the boat trip back to town—when the dead body of Tom Daniell lay motionless on the bottom of his father's skiff—he also included the awful sight of Tom's body as it twitched his life away on the South Carolina earth.

"I may never be able to live the way any other man lives—after what I did," he said, "and it's no consolation at all that had I not been a better shot than Tom Daniell, I wouldn't be here talking to you now, Mrs. Mackay." He leaned forward, his hands out as though beseeching her. "Would it be best for me to work my way somewhere on a ship and never come back to my own country again? It would be best, wouldn't it? Best all around. I—never cared what most people thought of me. I do care now, suddenly! Why? Why, after I—killed a man, do I begin to care? Could *you* ever treat me—think of me as just another struggling young buck trying to put the pieces of his life back together? Or will you always think of me as the murderer, Stuart Elliott, who blew a man's heart open?" He was on his feet now, pacing back and forth in front of Eliza. "I—I almost became your grandson-in-law, Mrs. Mackay! Surely, you know that?"

"Yes, Stuart, I know it. I know more than I feel free to tell you. I have no proof, of course. They're just things I—know."

He stopped pacing and looked down at her. "You're her grand-mother. Does—she know what I did? Has Mr. Mackay told her yet? He promised me he'd try to get to her before anyone else could, but there he sits at a concert!"

"I believe Mary Cowper and her husband are there, too," she said carefully. "Perhaps William will find a moment alone with her tonight."

The look Eliza Anne had described to her mother as devil-may-care, cynical, crossed his face. Then he laughed. "I won't count on Mr. Mackay finding her alone." He started toward the door, then turned back. "Maybe, maybe—just for tonight, if you told me you could ever forgive me, even if you can't forget what I did, I could—rest some."

"Oh, Stuart, my forgiveness doesn't count. But you do. You count with me and you most certainly count with God."

"Ha!"

"You do count with Him. This minute, standing there just as you are, you have God's full attention!"

A deep, puzzled frown creased his forehead. "He has a funny way of showing it. God has never heard a thing I've said to Him. I don't expect Him to start—today!"

"Did you pray as a child—with your mother at night?"

He tried to smile. The smile failed. "Oh, yes. Every child does that if he's born into a respectable Christian family!"

"Do you know what praying is?"

"No."

"It's simple, as simple as what you're doing now with me. Prayer is—talking to God. You evidently just had to talk to someone this evening." When he remained silent, she added, "For an hour and a half you talked to me, a perfect stranger. I'd like to make you a promise, Stuart."

His impishly handsome face seemed about to light up. "You would?"

"Yes. You're a frightened child inside. You broke one of God's commandments. You're truly sorry, even I know that."

"Do you?"

"I do, and so does God. And I can promise you some real rest if you'll go home now and tell Him you believe He knows in His heart how you really feel in yours—about what you did this morning."

He just stood there looking down at her as though his very life depended upon what she would say next.

"You are repentant in your heart, aren't you?"

"If you mean I'd give anything if I hadn't been forced to pull that trigger on my rifle, yes!"

"That's close, but not close enough. Real repentance means not only that we're deeply and truly sorry for what we did but that you ask for forgiveness—with no excuses for having done it. Of your own volition, son, you were in that poker game gambling with Tom Daniell. Tom didn't force you to be there, did he?"

In one long step, he returned to his chair and collapsed into it, the taut muscles and nerves of his young body loosening now. She could almost see them. Eliza waited and waited and waited.

Finally, he looked at her in genuine astonishment. "You mean—I'm not really a—victim in all this?"

"We never are," she said softly.

Mary Cowper had once told her when she was so openly and happily in love with Stuart that he was the gentlest of young men. At this moment, she knew it was true. Spoiled, impulsive, headstrong, the black sheep of a fine family, but no one could ever convince her that Stuart Elliott, even though he'd killed a man, was not—gentle.

"When we're truly victimized, son, we turn to God for comfort. When we sin, we turn to Him for forgiveness. I still have so much to learn, but I've been forced to learn quite a lot about repentance. True repentance means we promise God that we won't do that harmful thing again—ever. We won't *be* that destructive way again. When God's Son was just about your age, you know, He hung on a cross to make true repentance and forgiveness possible. It cost Him quite a lot—His life. But even though we don't understand how, He somehow took care of your sin a long, long time ago. Even then, He knew this day was coming for you."

"Mrs. Mackay, could I ask a question before I leave?"

"If you'll promise me you'll discuss all this with God before you go to sleep tonight."

"Yes, ma'am, I promise. Although, I'm not used to people believing my promises."

"Well, after you finish your talk with Him back in your room, you'll just have to get used to it, because eventually people will believe you. I believe you now, in fact." She gave her own hand a slap. "Oh, dear, there I go, letting my mind wander again. You said you wanted to ask me a question."

"Yes, if I can be forgiven, after killing a man in cold blood—do men in battle have to ask forgiveness when they kill other men?"

"Oh, my goodness, Stuart, that's a question I can't answer! My son Jack was a soldier. Colonel Robert Lee, as dear as a son, killed other men in the war with Mexico. His son Custis is a soldier, too. I—I don't have an answer to your question. The older I get, the fewer answers I seem to have—except that I do know about God's forgiveness."

When she began to pull herself unsteadily to her feet, he rushed to help her. "Thank you, son. I am tired now. You must be, too. And when you get back to wherever you live, you'll find God waiting for you."

She hooked her arm in his again and walked with him to the front door. "Lean over here a minute." She kissed him tenderly on the forehead. "Good night, Stuart. Now, scoot!"

THIRTY-
THREE

*O*ne early March morning, Eliza Mackay was still reading her Bible upstairs in her room when Mark sounded his familiar rat-a-tat-tat on the front door knocker. Oh, dear, she thought, hurriedly closing the book—so hurriedly, in fact, that a sheaf of things she was keeping fell to the floor—two pressed flowers cherished for all the years since she'd sold the old Mackay plantation, the Grange; some verses clipped from the newspapers, yellow and old with age; her last letter from Jack; her husband's obituary. As she stopped to pick up her treasures, she fussed aloud to herself.

"Why is it so hard for me to keep track of the time anymore? It seems as though we just finished breakfast. I didn't think I'd been reading more than ten minutes—and there's dear Mark come to take me to Sarah Gordon's house!"

She gathered the mementos and stuffed them back into her Bible, then saw still another, which had drifted to one side under her rocker. "Oh, dear, Tom Daniell's death notice!" The brief, terse announcement, so recent it hadn't begun to yellow, still startled her: FATAL DUEL, the headline read, then the story, if it could be called a story. Even the newspapers were hesitant to write about such a tragic, barbaric thing! She must get downstairs for Mark's sake, but she took a minute to glance at the piece she'd torn from the Savannah *Daily Morning News* to keep in her Bible to remind her to pray for Stuart:

> A hostile meeting took place yesterday at Screven's Ferry on the Carolina side of the river, between D. Stuart Elliott, Esq., and Thomas S. Daniell, Esq. The weapons used were rifles—distance twenty-five paces. On the first round Daniell was killed.

And that was it, not one word more. Nothing else in the paper at all. William, when he'd gone out to select a plot for their family at Laurel Grove Cemetery last week, had just accidentally discovered that even the notation in the cemetery record book was startlingly brief. It read only that buried in the Daniell plot was "Thomas S. Daniell, aged 30 years, February 16, 1857; buried February 17. Brought dead from South Carolina."

She tucked the clipping quickly back into the old, worn book and laid the Bible on its small table. So much on her mind this morning—the need to get downstairs, the hope that she could be of some help to Sarah with Cliffie Gordon's wedding plans, a half-prayer still moving in her mind for Stuart Elliott. The body of Tom Daniell "brought dead from South Carolina" because Stuart had killed him. . . .

At the parlor door, her daughter Sarah appeared, bustling as always, wanting to know if she needed any help. "Mark's carriage is out front, Mama!"

"I'm coming, I'm coming. Hand me my heavy cape, please."

"You'll need it. It's chilly and it could rain. You know how easily you catch cold," Sarah warned. "It does look to me like Mrs. Gordon could visit you more often. She's a lot younger and you just shouldn't be going out in all this cold wind. Half a shutter just blew off the back of the house!"

"Our old house is creaking at its seams, too, just like me," Eliza said. "But we're both still here and I have no intention of sitting in my chair till I turn to stone!"

Snug in her warm cape beside Mark in his comfortable carriage, she wished with all her heart that he had more time, that they could talk for an hour at least. He and William were busy for the remainder of the day with some kind of railroad stock purchase they were making together. Oh, he'd be back by the Gordon house to take her home after a while, but she longed to know what Mark was thinking about all that was going on in Washington City, when or if he and Caroline were still making the trip up to Newport this summer. Lately, it seemed they'd all been so preoccupied with poor Mary Cowper's continuing grief over losing her second child, with discussing what might happen to Stuart Elliott, who was still in town. So much, so much, and so little time.

"I have news for you," Mark said, holding her gloved hand in his, as he always did when they rode side by side. "News I think will make you happy—at least give you some hope for Stuart."

"Tell me, tell me! I've had that boy so much on my mind this morning."

"He's working at the bank again. They took him back after a long, serious interview. Same position as before. Assistant teller."

"Thank the good Lord! You know what that means, don't you?"

Mark gave her a quizzical look. "I know it's a step in the right direction."

"Yes, yes, but if Stuart was able to convince his employer that he was going to straighten up, it has to mean that he—feels forgiven. I've had to hang on to hope by my fingernails since I sent him off that night to ask God to forgive him."

"And I don't think he's been even courteous not to have let you know he's working again. I guess, most of the time, I don't understand young people at all. None of them seems actually rude, but the way they conduct themselves, Natalie included, keeps me confused."

They were already turning into Bull Street, their time together almost over. "Oh, dear—is anything wrong for Natalie?"

"No, nothing's wrong. She just writes so seldom! It's almost as though she forgets her mother and I are down here wondering." He laughed a little. "Actually, Callie does better than her mother with letters. She has a pet pig now—a boy pig, as she says—named Cinderella. I think Callie also has a wide streak of her mother in her. She has informed us that no matter that her father bought Cinderella for fresh pork, he is not going to be allowed to butcher him when the time comes!"

At that, Eliza laughed, too. "Did she use the word 'allow' in her letter?"

"She did." He sighed. "Of course, Caroline and I should be used to being 'allowed' by Natalie after all these years."

"But not by Jonathan."

"No. Our son is far from submissive, though. He does not like the idea that William and I are buying so heavily into the new stock issue at the Central of Georgia. He makes no bones about disapproving, but if I make a firm decision against his judgment, Jonathan is at least philosophic."

"He's always been a peacemaker. Oh, Mark, we need time to talk! Our poor, torn-up country needs a peacemaker!"

"And we don't have one. I guess we'll know a bit more about where it's all heading once the Supreme Court hands down a decision on that Negro, Dred Scott."

"Except to be so proud that Sarah Gordon's uncle, James Moore Wayne, is a Supreme Court Justice, I guess I don't pay enough attention to what the Court does, but the Dred Scott problem could put an end to all the efforts toward peace, couldn't it? Am I right to believe either way it's decided could bring things to a climax?"

"I'm afraid you are," he said, as his driver, Jupiter Taylor, pulled the team up in front of the Gordon mansion. "Whether or not the Court declares that having been taken into a free state by his owner makes Dred Scott a free Negro, the effect in the country could be more trouble than we've even thought about."

"If the Court says he's free, the South will rise up. If the Court declares him still his owner's property, the North will."

"Yes," he said, one hand still holding hers, the other on the carriage door handle. "We'll talk more about it when I come back to take you home." He kissed her hand and held it for a few seconds against his cheek. "Do you know even William and I can't discuss the national trouble as freely as you and I, Miss Eliza? What would I ever do without you?"

She patted his hand. "That's one thing you don't need to know, dear boy. I'm still here and I intend to stay a while. Now, help me out and up Sarah's steep, steep steps. We still have a lot of history to live through together, Mark. Big history that has to do with things over which you and I have so little control and—all-important family history. Right now, I am going to let you go or William will fidget waiting for you and anyway I need to get inside and help Sarah with her guest list for Cliffie's wedding."

He lifted her frail body down from the high carriage step, and as they climbed slowly up to the Gordon entrance, Mark whispered, "Try to find out from Mrs. Gordon, if you can without provoking her Southern loyalty, what she's heard from Justice Wayne about the Dred Scott affair. The decision should be handed down almost any day now, I'd think."

After Mark twisted the bell, as they waited she whispered back, "Don't worry, I'll find out all I dare." Then abruptly the idea struck her as funny. "I know it's no laughing matter, Mark, but you and I talk about things as though I'm not Southern at all. The truth is, you know, I am. And in your heart, you're still a Northerner."

"I think the truth is that we're both trying to be reasonable people," he said, giving her arm a brief hug. "Reasonable people who love their country. You keep me reasonable, dear friend, more surely than you seem to know."

"Could it be, Mark, that with you sixty-five, and with me pushing eighty, we've finally learned how to love?"

Over a cup of tea, Eliza and Sarah Gordon spoke first of the guest list for the big wedding to take place next month on April 16. As Eliza suspected, Sarah was still troubled over Lucinda Sorrel's invitation.

"It's your decision to make, Sarah," Eliza said, "but since your family and the Sorrels have been friends for so many years, I see no kind way to exclude poor Lucinda."

"Oh, dear, I suppose," Sarah mused, "that I could just send a blanket announcement to the entire family and hope that Lucy is sensitive enough not to bring that young man. Mrs. Mackay, she's Mary Cowper's best friend these days. Lucy knows Mary Cowper will attend her own brother's wedding! Surely, she wouldn't dream of asking Stuart Elliott to escort her. Lucinda is nearly thirty years old and she is discreet, don't you think?"

"Indeed I do and sometimes we just have to ask God to handle these difficult things," Eliza said. "He knows you're only trying to avoid hurt and embarrassment. I shudder to think how awkward it would be for Mary Cowper to have to face Stuart for the first time in the company of Mr. Low! For that matter, it would be dreadful for Stuart himself."

"You actually seem to care about that scoundrel, Mrs. Mackay, but that's certainly none of my affair."

It wasn't, Eliza agreed silently, but knew too well that Sarah Gordon, usually so charitable, was far from alone in her low opinion of Stuart. "I do care about young Mr. Elliott. I knew his mother, Martha, in the old days before she married Mr. Bulloch and moved to her lovely Bulloch Hall in Roswell. The boy's from a fine family. I think your idea of a blanket invitation to the whole family is best, Sarah. Poor Mrs.

Sorrel could be unwell in her mind again by then, so that Lucinda can't come at all."

Through all the years in which Eliza had made her morning calls on Sarah Gordon, she'd found it easy to turn the conversation to Sarah's famous uncle, Judge James Moore Wayne. Today, when she'd promised Mark to find out anything she could about the touchy Dred Scott case before the Supreme Court this very week, she felt a strange hesitation. A kinder, more cultivated, more Christian woman didn't exist than Sarah Gordon, but the last time the subject of slavery had come up between them, Sarah had flared as though Eliza had struck a match and ignited her. It was a tragic thing when old friends had to be so careful! She didn't intend her heavy sigh to be audible, but Sarah had heard it.

"Is something wrong, Mrs. Mackay? Are you not feeling well?"

"Oh, yes, yes, I'm feeling the same as usual. Now and then when one is old, sighs seem to escape all on their own. You'll find out someday, Sarah." Deciding to plunge right in, she said as casually as possible, "I suppose your dear uncle is feverishly busy these days on the Court. Such a difficult decision for those poor men to have to make!"

Sarah replaced her empty cup in its saucer with a nervous rattle. Even the mention of the current Court case had riled her. As Sarah reached for Eliza's cup to refill it, her hand trembled noticeably.

"I've upset you and I'm sorry," Eliza said. "You've quite enough on your mind with all these wedding plans. I really came only to help. It's just that I so value your exchange of letters with your uncle. Our papers are so lax in reporting on the Court. Does Judge Wayne still believe a Supreme Court decision against the Negro, Dred Scott, can settle the dreadful issue once and for all?"

Anyone could see how distraught Sarah had become. Absently, she was brushing crumbs from their muffins right onto the carpet!

"I don't mean to be rude, Mrs. Mackay. We're both Southerners, both slaveholders." She held out her hands. "How do you stay so calm when our whole way of life is being threatened? If Uncle James and the others on the Court don't rule against this arrogant Negro, the South could—*will secede!*"

"Arrogant, Sarah? The Court has been arguing this since early last year. Surely there are Justices who believe the poor man has a right to have his case heard!"

Sarah asked, as though addressing a child, "A Negro has a right? Everyone knows they're an inferior race! Fine legal minds like Uncle James's have declared that our Founding Fathers never meant for the

Negro people to be fully franchised citizens. They're the legally purchased *property* of Southern men and women and the Constitution
protects personal property! I no longer speak of our peculiar institution
as being for the common good. I suppose it may end, may even wear
itself out someday. Heaven knows, keeping our people is expensive and
difficult, but I so respect my uncle's opinion that I can never be convinced that those haughty New Englanders—all those bigoted abolitionists up there—have any constitutional right to attack us as they do!"

Instead of a response of any kind, Eliza rose painfully out of her
chair and hobbled across the room toward the front window.

"Forgive me, Mrs. Mackay," Sarah begged, quickly jumping up and
taking her arm. "I just sat there in my fury and let you get up all by
yourself! Is it time for Mr. Browning already?"

At the window, Eliza looked out. Mark's carriage was nowhere in
sight. "I guess not," she said. She knew it wasn't time yet for Mark, but
her labored journey across the room had at least broken some of the
tension.

Seated again, the two ladies exchanged warm smiles. "I am so
sorry," Sarah said. "These are days when the whole country snaps and
stabs at one another, my son, Willie, says. He's been in Chicago, you
know, visiting his fiancée's family, the Kinzies. All of Chicago—most of
Illinois, I guess, except the southern part—is agog over those fiery
Republicans. Willie even heard that someone named Lincoln, I think it is
—a veritable country man, ill kempt, gross—is likely to run as a Republican against Senator Stephen Douglas, whose splendid Kansas-Nebraska
Act is keeping what peace we have."

"Oh, my, Sarah," Eliza said, surprised. "Do you know what date it is?
March fourth. A new President is being inaugurated in Washington
today! We must *pray* for Mr. Buchanan." She heard herself sigh again.
"Goodness knows, the slavery issue would be more than enough all by
itself, but there's the fight for women's rights, the dreadful Mormon
trouble out there in Utah, and—"

"What I'll never understand is how a woman as intelligent as Susan
B. Anthony could act in such a giddy manner. What on earth do women
know about handling serious problems that would ever give them a
right to vote? Southern ladies would never think of such a thing!"

Eliza paused, then decided just to come right out with it: "I believe
myself to be a Southern lady, Sarah, and I'd give almost anything to be
able to vote!"

She had no trouble at all picturing the battle going on inside her dear friend Sarah Gordon. As her hostess, Sarah would never dream of challenging what Eliza had just said. She herself had, of course, over-stepped the bounds of common courtesy by exploding such a bomb-shell, but she felt better for it and decided to give Sarah a chance to brush it aside by raising the matter of Dred Scott again. "Does your dear uncle feel the Court will reach a decision soon on Dred Scott's case?"

Her friend reacted perfectly to the little trap Eliza had laid. "Yes," she said at once. "Yes, I believe he expects a final decision to be announced this week. And he feels certain that he and the other cooler heads on the Court will prevail. Uncle James does not want to promote more slavery per se, he just feels that any sudden action to end it would devastate not only the country, the slaveholder, but the Negro himself. He feels it should come about gradually. I'd think Chief Justice Taney should be reading the final decision most any day now."

"So that Dred Scott will then know whether or not he can ever be free."

"I must say that's a very odd way of putting it."

"But it is one way. Once that decision comes down against Dred Scott, it will, if I understand it, mean that no act of Congress can deprive a slaveholder of his human property, *ever.*" Eliza felt rather relieved when Sarah said nothing. By now, she felt quite sorry that she'd upset her. "Such a decision would also prove the old Missouri Compro-mise unconstitutional," she went on, "and, Sarah, had you thought that the decision, if it's against the Scott Negro, will also make Senator Douglas's popular sovereignty Kansas-Nebraska Act null and void? That there will be nothing even to slow the spread of slavery into the territories?"

Sarah frowned. "I hadn't thought of that, but it's true. No matter, though. Senator Douglas's act won't be needed if the Court does the right thing. The whole terrible problem will be over! I suppose the abolitionists will rant and rave, but they'll just have to calm down."

In the silence that followed, Eliza heard the squeak and rattle of Mark's carriage out front. She must struggle up out of that chair again. Accepting Sarah's arm in the effort, she thanked her for her gracious hospitality, offered her daughters' help with the wedding plans if needed, and said almost sadly at the parlor door, "Dred Scott felt he was entitled to be free because he accompanied his master, a military man, into the free state of Illinois and the free territory of Wisconsin, then was taken back to pro-slavery Missouri. I don't know what the final decision will be, but I'm afraid I do understand why the man might have believed he had a right to be a free citizen. I'm sure we can't know what it must have been like breathing free air, even for a short time. I guess it made him–feel like a full-fledged citizen."

"I suppose so," Sarah said, barely controlling herself, Eliza knew, because they were saying goodbye. "I feel very safe in Uncle James's belief, though, that this Dred Scott will find out once and for all that he isn't and will never be a true citizen. The United States was founded as a free *white man's* nation, Mrs. Mackay. The American Constitution was written so as to *keep* it that way. I'm perfectly willing to let them do as they like up North. They should afford us the same courtesy."

Mark asked Eliza no questions as he helped her down Sarah Gordon's front steps, but inside the carriage she told him everything, even the way she'd egged poor Sarah on.

When she finished, he was quiet for a long time, then said, "Well, if the decision is against Dred Scott, it will end all hope for a solution under the law for those who oppose slavery. It will also guarantee something to the Negroes."

"To the Negroes, Mark?"

"Permanent servitude."

THIRTY-
FOUR

*W*ithin a week, word reached Savannah that Chief Justice Taney had read the final Supreme Court decision in the case of *Dred Scott* vs. *John F. A. Sanford:* The Negro, Dred Scott, was denied his claim to freedom on the grounds that a slave is property, that a property right is protected, except through the due process of law under the Constitution. No such due process occurred in the Dred Scott case. There were a few dissenting opinions, but the majority of Justices agreed, even added to the opinion (which becomes the law of the land) that *no act of Congress can constitutionally deprive a slavemaster of his property*—in either a state or a territory.

Mark read the decision in the *Daily Morning News* on March 9 with a heavy heart, a heart heavy with disappointment, alarm, and heightened dread. The Supreme Court decision had declared slavery to be constitutional! In the year past, as tempers flared and bitterness between North and South heated to a boiling point, he had subscribed to Horace Greeley's New York *Tribune* in order to keep abreast of what people in the North were thinking. His *Tribune* report of the Dred Scott decision had not yet reached him in Savannah, but Mark knew without reading it that this decision had made even the old Missouri Compromise of 1820 unconstitutional, that Senator Douglas's popular sovereignty had become invalid, and that the Kansas-Nebraska Act, which permitted the people in the territories to decide whether they would be slave or free, was gone. There was simply no more statutory relief for any free-soil advocate anywhere!

He read the Savannah newspaper account alone in his office. Of course, it was written with a triumphant pen, with a spirited assurance to all Southerners that the South had *won*. The piece ended with an exultation: "Southern opinion upon the subject of Southern slavery is now THE SUPREME LAW OF THE LAND. Any opposition to Southern opinion upon this subject is now outright opposition to the Constitution and morally treason against the Government."

He would wait to read his Northern paper before he expressed his deepest concerns either to Miss Eliza or to William. He longed as never before to be able to talk about it with Caroline. A sad, hopeless smile crossed his face. Impossible, of course. They had never been able to talk about the contentious subject with the good, close confidence they shared in everything else—absolutely everything else. In this moment of panic and fear at the ugly consequences which would surely fall upon them all from the Supreme Court decision, he realized that he had never loved or needed Caroline so much.

He scanned the *Daily Morning News* report once more, felt the growing isolation because of his own beliefs, and yet was overwhelmed again with love for the city which, through the long years he'd lived there, had become such a part of his own identity. Mark Browning, he knew, would not have recognized himself apart from Savannah, Georgia. Nor would he want to.

A familiar light knock at his office door meant that Jonathan had also seen the morning newspaper.

"What do you think, Papa?" the young man asked, perched on the corner of Mark's desk. "How will they take the Dred Scott decision up North?"

"Not lying down, son. What do you make of it?"

The open, honest, always disarming smile lit Jonathan's young, sensitive face. My son is no longer a boy, Mark thought, as he watched the now lightly bearded face, plainly showing his desire to say the encouraging thing to his father.

"Mr. James Clack was just in my office," Jonathan said carefully. "It was no surprise to hear him declare the Southern triumph. Clack's a real hothead, a fire-eater."

"And a South Carolinian at heart. I'll bet he quoted old John C. Calhoun, didn't he?"

Jonathan grinned. "He did indeed. He even went back to Calhoun's response to President Jackson's famous toast."

"Ah, yes, I remember," Mark said, turning in his chair to stare out over the river. "Jackson's toast: 'To our Federal Union—*it must be preserved.*'"

"Will it be, Papa?"

"Right now, I don't see how. What old Calhoun said in his counter-toast to President Jackson is still the credo of the elite of South Carolinians: 'The Union—*next to our liberty the most dear.*'"

"I'm not sure," Jonathan said, "that I understand at all what South Carolinians mean by liberty. Do you?"

"I lived through the period of Calhoun's enormous power, I felt the impact on the country of his intellect. He was a political giant. But it always seemed to me that his definition of liberty meant that each man had a right to individual freedom, to unlimited use of his skills and talents—only if he agreed with Calhoun. Honestly, son, it almost seemed at times that the man wanted two presidencies! One for his kind and one for the rest of us, each having veto power over the other."

Jonathan said nothing for a time, then he spoke one word: "Secession."

Mark frowned. "Not yet. But so many people down here scream that what they want is liberty, and if I live to be ninety, I will never know what they mean by it."

"Liberty for everyone except slaves and women?" Jonathan asked, his face solemn. "Does it ever seem just plain stupid that Mama and Miss Eliza and Mary have no right to vote only because they're women?"

Mark looked at his son, wondering if this might be the time to ask the central question point-blank. He'd put it off for reasons even he didn't quite comprehend. "Jonathan," he said finally, "I need to know something. Would you like to see the South freed from slavery?"

Without a second's hesitation, the boy said, "Yes, sir, I would, but I guess I'd never admit it to Mama."

"Did you say that because of my influence on your thinking?"

"Probably, because I don't believe friends my age give freeing their slaves any thought. They've just always lived with it. Wherever I got the idea, it's mine now. But I don't think the United States will go very far as a nation unless it really is united. Threats and violent talk tear down even the good in us. In our copy of the new *Atlantic Monthly*, I read about a chemistry professor in North Carolina who said last year that if any Republicans had been on the ticket down here, he'd have voted Republican."

Mark laughed a little. "A brave man. What happened?"

"A public uproar, naturally. The Raleigh *Standard* called for his kind to be silenced or driven out! Chapel Hill students burned him in effigy and he was hounded out of the university. As you said, down here they seem to want two countries, two presidents, and two sets of laws. I guess it's no wonder Congressman Brooks felt it his right to beat Senator Sumner to a pulp."

"Brooks is even from the same district in South Carolina as Calhoun. The streak of independence runs deep," Mark said. "In all fairness, though, our compatriot James Clack is not altogether a typical South Carolina elitist. He's just a real hothead. There are no more cultivated, better-educated gentlemen anywhere than in Charleston–Columbia, too, for that matter." He took a deep breath. "Oh, son, it's confusing, isn't it? So much to like about so many people–so much to deplore."

Jonathan was smiling. "But you and I have each other, Papa. However it turns out, we're in the middle of all this conflict together."

For the next weeks, until mid-April, when Eliza Mackay's grandson Henry would be married to Sarah Gordon's only daughter, Cliffie, the family's collective mind was on the wedding. Feeling, as he did, a part of the Mackay-Stiles family, in spite of an increased work load Mark entered into the excitement of the romantic event which had been at the center of young Henry's life for so many years. Business hours were longer and the work more nerve-wracking because Mark saw definite signs of a possible financial panic in the country.

"It already looks as though William and I may have bought too heavily into that railroad stock," he confided to Miss Eliza two days before the wedding as they sat together on her porch. "I guess we'll both be all right in the end. These business slumps do right themselves eventually, but William and I have all but admitted to each other that we probably should have waited."

"Oh, Mark, so much depends on what happens in our poor country! It must be very hard for businessmen like you and William to predict anything about the future these days," she said. "And it seems to me that you've been quite silent, even with me, about that Supreme Court decision. The women of Savannah are still rattling on about the South's great triumph. I listen to them, but I don't forget that the North is in the

Union, too. It isn't like you to keep so quiet with me, and if you're protecting me because of my advanced age, just stop it. I'm not one day older than I've always been compared with you. You have been reading your New York *Tribune,* haven't you? And your Philadelphia papers? There *is* a storm of protest going on up there and I know it. Now, if you won't tell me about it yourself because I'm doddering, bring the papers here and let me read them! I can still read, you know."

The best Mark could do was force a laugh. Actually, he had found his dear friend's outburst funny—funny and frighteningly accurate.

"I'm glad you find me so amusing," she said drily.

"Miss Eliza, I haven't been trying to protect you. I've just been trying to sort it all out first. You know I've been poring over all my Northern papers. There *is* a fire storm raging up there and not only in the papers—in the pulpits, too."

She sighed almost in disgust. "Poor God!"

"Yes. Both factions, it seems, have placed Him firmly on their side. In the North, God wants the abolition of slavery, and down here, He offers His full power to slaveholders."

"There's only one God and He does not contradict Himself!" she said tersely. "Are you going to tell me exactly what they're saying and writing up there? Or aren't you, Mark?"

He fumbled in his suit-coat pocket, pulled out a sheaf of news clippings, and held them out to her with a sly grin. "To prove to you that I've had you on my mind all the time, I've been collecting these—clipped them for easier reading, but if you prefer I'll even read a few aloud."

"All right, so I misjudged you—some," she said, teasing. "And you know I prefer you to read to me. So, read."

"First, this is from the New York *Tribune.* It says: 'The uprising in the North can no longer be called a mere protest. The horrendous decision handed down by the Supreme Court of the United States carried as much moral weight as the judgment of a majority of those congregated in any Washington barroom!' "

"I thought so."

"Greeley's journalist goes on: 'We point for proof to the chicanery among the Democratic Court, the Democratic administration, and the Democratic House and Senate. In fact, we of the North smell a plot. Did not Buchanan and Chief Justice Taney hold a whispered conversation during a pause in the inaugural ceremonies? Are not the new President and at least two of the other Justices as thick as a gang of thieves? And

did not President Buchanan say in his inaugural address that the Supreme Court would soon hand down a decision on the entire issue of
slavery and that "to their decision, in common with all good citizens, I
shall cheerfully submit, whatever this decision may be"? The hypocrite!
Buchanan knew at that moment how the Court would rule. Not only
that the Constitution protects the human property of slaveholders but
that no Negro may ever be considered a citizen!' "

She sat for a moment, letting all that soak in, then asked, "And do
you agree with the *Tribune* journalist, Mark?"

"I can say only that I am in no position to know."

"That's not an answer!"

"You and I both believe in the coequal power of the three branches
of government, Miss Eliza."

"So did the Founding Fathers!"

"But the Supreme Court does strike me as having usurped the
power of the other branches—the elected branches. I'm inclined to
believe, in spite of the fact that he's freed his own slaves, Chief Justice
Taney probably holds a deep-seated prejudice against the anti-slavery
men."

"He *is* from Maryland. Tobacco farmers up there need lots of field
hands."

"Justice Taney, like most Southerners, hates Northern capitalism
and the hypocritical reformers it seems to breed because Yankee indus-
trialists pay wages to their workers. There's no question in my mind but
that Southern power is massed in the federal government."

"And your—Republicans would change all that?"

"*My* Republicans, Miss Eliza?"

"Come now, dear boy, don't you think I've known for a year or
more that if any Republican managed to run down here, you'd vote for
him?"

He smiled at her. "It's amazing how safe I always feel with you."

"Not amazing, dear boy, in any way. You simply know my heart. We
can discuss any quarrelsome, fractious subject and remain friends because you do know my heart. And anyway, I can't vote!" Her sly smile
vanished. "The answer to the question which I know perfectly well is
whirling around in your mind this minute is: No, Mark, I don't think *I*
could vote Republican, even if women were allowed to vote. I might be
tempted if I knew more about what they believe, but at my age I have
no notion of disturbing the eternal peace of my Democratic ancestors.
Women will get the vote someday after I'm gone. For me, now, it's far

better to believe that women are equally needed—to stay unceasingly in prayer."

"In view of things as they are," Mark mused, "prayer may be even more important."

She rocked in silence for a time, her dim eyes on her bloom-laden azaleas. "I expect you're right, dear boy, because only God knows what's up ahead. But sometimes I *do* wish He'd tell us!"

THIRTY-
FIVE

Eliza Mackay thought the wedding of her grandson took place without a hitch. Sarah Gordon had skillfully supervised her people in lavishly decorating the impressive house. Cliffie Gordon's bridal gown was a creation of beauty—a sheer lace veil, ivory satin dress embroidered with what looked like a million pearls. Henry was, she honestly believed, the handsomest groom she'd ever seen, his father's son, without doubt—strong, but almost poetic features, broad of shoulders, taller and far more muscular than W.H. Both Eliza Anne and W.H. were on hand, of course, and many guests remarked to Eliza that they rivaled the wedding couple in elegance. That Eliza Anne was her most beautiful daughter, she'd long known, and in middle age she certainly carried her years with grace and inordinate charm.

At the festive home reception Sarah had planned and was now executing to perfection down to the last detail, Eliza sat in a chair of honor, enjoying her special role as the groom's only living grandparent. During the ceremony, she'd strained to find out if Lucinda Sorrel had come, but couldn't see well enough. She felt relief as she saw Lucinda now, moving toward her across Sarah's front parlor alone. Evidently, her mother had not come and, thanks be to God, Stuart Elliott was nowhere in sight.

"Lucinda, my dear," she said warmly, extending her hand. "Did you have to come alone? I'd hoped to see your dear mother."

"She planned to be here," Lucy Sorrel said. "Wouldn't you know she'd wake up today of all days with a dreadful headache? Papa is with her." She glanced around the room. "My brother, Gilbert, rebelling at being so dressed up in the daytime, *is* here somewhere."

Enough chitchat, Eliza thought, and decided that the best way to find out about Stuart was to come right out and ask. "I was so hoping for a few words with you, Lucinda," she said. "Have you seen Stuart Elliott lately?"

Lucinda looked startled. "Why, yes, I've seen him."

"I feel as though I know him better than I do, I'm sure. I know I care about him. Is he—is he glad to be back at the bank?"

"He seems to be." Lucinda stopped looking around the crowded room to study Eliza's face. "That isn't what you really want to know, is it? I know you're not a gossip, Miss Eliza. Mama has always said you hate gossip as much as she does." She took a deep breath. "I—asked Stuart to escort me to the wedding today. I knew he would refuse and he did. Oh, I wish we could talk in privacy!" Her intelligent face was now plainly disturbed and Lucinda didn't try to hide it.

"We can, my dear. Anytime you need to talk, just come by my house. I'd be honored."

An almost shy smile came to the troubled face now. "Until this minute, I hadn't thought of talking to anyone else. Mary Cowper and I have grown so close, she's been all the friend I needed, but . . ."

"But there are certain things you can't confide in her."

"Yes! Oh, she's a marvelous help to me when I get so worried and confused over Mother, but—yes. Mary Cowper has quite enough to handle. There are some things I can't talk about to her. Thank you. I just may come by some day." Lucinda turned to leave, then added, seeming to surprise even herself, "I—I love Stuart Elliott, too. And he wants me to marry him."

On impulse, Eliza reached for the girl's hand. "Oh, my dear!"

"I know," Lucinda said, trying to smile a little. "One would think that with Mother's spells and Papa being so restless since he retired from business, I already had enough trouble."

"Perhaps, but Stuart Elliott is—somehow lovable," Eliza said. "I'll expect you tomorrow afternoon, if you're free to come, Lucinda."

By three the next day, Eliza was dressed for a caller. They had eaten an early dinner because her spinster daughters and Eliza Anne and Mary Cowper were calling on old friends. Eliza was relieved. It was important for her to be alone when Lucinda Sorrel arrived. Her grandson, Henry Stiles, and his new bride were already on the boat for New York, en route to Newport for their honeymoon. She had warned Sarah Gordon that there would be no call at her house today because Sarah, of all people, needed to be alone and rest.

Eliza waited now, breathing a wordless prayer. What she meant to say to the young woman, only God knew, but she was in the parlor waiting for her knock.

When she heard it, her heart caught. It was not the formal knock of an acquaintance, and Lucinda Sorrel was only that; it was the familiar quick tap-tap Eliza Anne always used, followed by the sound of the door flying open.

"Mama," her daughter called from the front hall. "It's just me—Eliza Anne!"

"What on earth are you doing here, child?"

"I begged off from the first call because Kate and Sarah and Mary Cowper were going by the Sorrels'. I saw Lucinda at the wedding, and anyway, I needed to talk to you alone." Pulling up another small rocker, she sat down. "We have to get back to Cass tomorrow and I can't seem to find any time alone with my own mother in this house!"

"Oh, pooh!"

"You don't seem very glad I'm here."

"Nonsense, of course I am. I just hope Matilda Sorrel is up to having callers. She wasn't well enough to attend Henry's wedding yesterday."

Eliza Anne dismissed this with "Maybe she'll be better today. Mama, what do you *really* think about Mary Cowper's marriage? Do you see her enough alone, away from Mr. Low, to know whether or not she's happy?"

This was the last question she'd expected from her own daughter. "That seems a very odd question, Eliza Anne," was all she could think of to say offhand. "Can't *you* tell about your own daughter?"

"Only that if she isn't happy, she's expecting far too much from life. That girl has everything any woman's heart could possibly desire, Mama! W.H. and I have been married for all these years and we've never managed to have enough money, at times, even for our needs. If she isn't happy, I've failed somewhere as her mother."

"Is there a reason why you think she might not be?"

Eliza Anne jumped up and began to walk around the parlor. "Mama, all through her childhood, I never had to worry about Mary Cowper, but Henry and Robert, even though they're men, haven't puzzled me the way she—began to puzzle me when she—when she . . ."

"When she met Stuart Elliott?"

Her daughter sat down again abruptly. "I might have known you'd go straight to the heart of the matter. I think I *despise* that young man and God just may strike me dead for it."

For a moment, Eliza Mackay struggled with her mother heart. Any mother longs to ease a troubled child's pain. Eliza Anne was in pain over Mary Cowper, but middle-aged "children" were supposed to have learned enough to work their own ways out of the traps they contrived for themselves. She was her daughter's staunch friend, but it was far too late for correction or discipline. Eliza Anne would always try to have her own way. "God won't strike you dead for anything," she said at last. "And everyone in town considers Mary Cowper's marriage a huge success, I'm sure."

"I'm sure, too," Eliza Anne said. "But what about my daughter's *heart?* Does a mother ever stop worrying about things like that?"

"No, not ever."

"Mr. Low is so good and generous with her. He obviously adores the ground under her feet, but, Mama, do you feel he's—just a bit domineering?"

"My dear, when I see Mary Cowper, she's here alone visiting me. Except at rare social occasions such as yesterday, I almost never see the two of them together."

"What do you and Mary Cowper talk about when she's here?"

"Her little girl, Catherine Mackay, mostly. And Kate is so proud still that the child is named for her. She and Sarah are almost always with us."

"I should have known that."

"The last time Mary C. came," Eliza said, "we spoke at length, as I remember, about the long stay in England she and Mr. Low plan for later this year. They may be over there well into next year, as I understand it. His business interests are so enormous and so unpredictable, you know."

"And wouldn't you think she'd be ecstatic just knowing that she has not only the Low mansion here but a huge, lavishly furnished country house in England, too? In each home a full staff of servants, the advantage of so much extensive travel. They spent two whole months at Newport last year."

"Yes, Eliza Anne, I know."

"Mama, sometimes I think you still like to pin me against the wall like a butterfly!"

"What a peculiar thing to say."

"I'm sorry. I know I'm almost forty-nine years old, but now and then I still want to run to Mama for answers. You've always made me do my own thinking and I know that's right, but I felt ten or eleven again when I suddenly slipped away from the girls just now and ran to you."

"As far as I know, Eliza Anne, Mary Cowper is making a success of her marriage. Outsiders can't always tell about things between a husband and wife, but the child certainly obeyed you and W.H. Her little heart seems peaceful in that. Andrew Low is a respected man, a fair man, and, as you say, with her, a most generous man. And in her grandmother's biased opinion, a most fortunate man." She paused. "No marriage is perfect, you know. None succeeds unless both people work at it. Mary Cowper is doing her level best."

"Yes, yes, she is." Eliza Anne glanced at the mantel clock. "And I must go. I promised to meet her and my sisters at the Minises at three-thirty."

"If Matilda Sorrel feels worse today, they could be there waiting for you by now," Eliza said. "Give the Minises my best."

Eliza Anne stood to go. "You're all dressed for callers. And I know you weren't expecting me, Mama. Who is coming?"

"Lucinda Sorrel."

Eliza Anne stared at her. "Does she call on you often?"

"No. But she asked yesterday to see me."

"Oh."

"I told Hannah to open a jar of your good, tart wild-blackberry preserves. I'll offer her tea. Emphie's baking bread."

Just as soon as the Mackay sisters and Mary Cowper left, Lucinda Sorrel hurried into a shawl and bonnet and walked rapidly to the Mackay house on East Broughton. She felt uneasy about leaving, but thought her mother had made a fairly successful effort with their callers, who, happily, could not stay long. The talk had moved smoothly around the Gordon-Stiles wedding yesterday and in spite of her headache Mama had entered in some. The sinking, terrifying, but now too familiar old fear had almost engulfed Lucy when at one point Mama, seeming suddenly quite disoriented, had called Sarah Mackay, Eliza Anne. Her mother's bewildered face when she realized what she'd done was so pathetic.

It's as though Mama divides into two people, she thought, turning the corner of Abercorn into Broughton. One person knows perfectly well that she's mixed up and tries so hard to get straight. The other person inside her barges right ahead being dead wrong and confused. It's her distress I can't bear!

Not altogether sure why she was hurrying to Mrs. Mackay's house, she nevertheless walked straight up to the front door and knocked. After what seemed a long time, Eliza Mackay herself opened the door.

Seated near Mrs. Mackay's small rocker in the parlor, Lucinda refused her kind offer of tea, explaining that she could stay only a short while because of her mother's headache.

"Then, why don't we get right to the reason you're here, Lucy."

Something in the old woman's gentle, still pretty face made her blurt: "I know he still loves Mary Cowper, Miss Eliza. Much of the time, although she never mentions him unless I do, I believe Mary C. loves Stuart. She's married, though. The mother of a dear little girl. Am I a fool even to consider marrying him? Could I possibly be enough for him after the kind of love he and Mary Cowper shared?"

"Oh, dear Lucy, you have asked a difficult question!"

"I know. And I have no right to place you in such a position. I—just have no one else. My mother doesn't even know that I love Mr. Elliott. She—she can't think clearly much of the time now anyway. She did seem almost strangely pleased when I told her you'd invited me today, though. That alone means a lot to me." Twisting her gloves into a tight cord as she spoke, Lucinda's words tumbled out. "Miss Eliza, I'm going to be thirty next year! Oh, that isn't the reason I'm so eager to marry Stuart. But it is the reason I'm embarrassed to be placing you in such a difficult predicament this minute. I'm old enough to know my own mind."

"I'm eighty, Lucinda, and at times I seem unable even to *find* mine."

Not amused, Lucinda said somberly, "If you lived day in and day out with someone searching for her mind, truly searching for it as Mama has to do, you wouldn't joke."

"I wasn't joking," Eliza said evenly. "I seem to remember like yesterday things that happened in my life fifty or sixty years ago, why I did this or that, why I thought this or that, then I forget what happened or what I did this morning!"

"I just feel I'm old enough to know more than I know," Lucinda went on. "I do know that if I marry Stuart, I'll always, always be in second place in his heart. He does love me, in a way. Maybe that's enough. He vows he needs me more than he's ever needed anyone."

"I expect he does. I don't know Stuart well at all, but when I saw him the one time we've spoken together, he was in dreadful need."

Lucinda nodded. "He told me he came to see you the night after he—killed Tom Daniell."

"Stuart told you?"

"He tells me a lot of things. Important things. He clings to me, actually. You see, he swears he will never get over what he did. He didn't *want* to kill Tom! He really tried to stop the duel. He failed. He feels a failure in everything. He's so sure I can help him succeed in *something.*"

"Lucy, did he tell you he promised me he'd ask God to forgive him for what he did?"

"Yes. He did ask forgiveness that very night. He stayed on his knees begging God to forgive him for most of the night."

"But he doesn't feel forgiven."

"That's right. And if God can't cause him to feel forgiven, I can't! I wish I could. I can't." Lucinda was on her feet. "I dare not stay any longer. Mama could be having one of her bad spells by now. And maybe it's better if you don't even try to give me an answer." She bent down to kiss the older woman's forehead because she herself needed to feel close to her. "Forgive such a rushed, inconsiderate visit, please?"

"Oh, Lucy," the old woman said, reaching up her arms to hold her a moment. "I'm honored that you came. You're so—alone. I can sense that, and please come again anytime. I won't try to give you an answer. I wouldn't dare. But I will pray that you'll have God's wisdom in this. You must pray for that, too. And for your dear, ill mother. And for Stuart. We'll make a pact. We'll team up, you and I, and pray for them both. And oh, my dear, I will remember *you.* I have a lot of time on my hands now. You can count on me."

PART
III

May 1857–December 1859

THIRTY-
SIX

*A*t *the end* of May 1857, William was visiting in Cass County, this time as a house guest of the Latimers. Eliza Anne, of course, wanted him at her much larger home and it was the expected thing to stay there, but Natalie insisted and he secretly preferred her cottage. Not only because it was so homey but because William, when possible, had always tried to steer clear of family problems. Sleeping at the Stiles mansion would mean his sister could pump him to a fare-thee-well about her daughter's marriage to Andrew Low. Mary Cowper hadn't once mentioned any kind of secret turmoil to him.

Before he left Savannah, William admitted only to himself, not even to Mama, that he studied Eliza Anne's lengthy letters at home in his room at night. He had spotted his sister's unease, due mainly, he supposed, to the fact that Stuart Elliott was still in Savannah. It had taken Eliza Anne a long time even to hint at her concern that perhaps she and W.H. had pushed their daughter too hard. Even now, her hints were veiled. Of course, Eliza Anne had always had trouble admitting she might have been wrong about anything. Not long ago, William had gone so far as to ask Mary Cowper outright about her marriage. Her only response had been that grief over the death of their second child had given her and Andrew Low a shared bond. Not one word about how much they might have needed that bond.

Shaving on Natalie's back porch on the third morning of his up-country visit, he mulled over his relief that he and Eliza Anne had not yet had any time alone and that his one talk with W.H. had let him know that his brother-in-law, while stronger than ever in his support of the South, was *not* for secession. W.H. was bearing down these days, he had told William at length, in his various speeches and articles, on what, to him, was the irrevocable fact that the one hope of the South lay in its full support of the Democratic Party. W.H., though, was still a Unionist.

No one wanted to see the South win out over Northern slander more than William, but common sense told him that, as usual, W.H. was taking an extreme position. Oh, he'd never call his brother-in-law a firebrand, but in spite of the Dred Scott decision in favor of the South, bleeding Kansas was still bleeding Kansas. The success or failure of the Union still hung on exactly what was happening in Kansas and all future problems over expansion. Everyone, North and South, had been bitten by the expansion bug and the lines were being drawn tighter and tighter every day.

William rinsed and dried his razor, splashed the remaining blobs of lather from his face in Natalie's ample washbowl, and picked up a dry, clean towel Callie had laid out for him in her most grown-up manner. He glanced at his face in a looking glass propped against the porch railing and caught himself smiling a little wryly. He'd put on so much weight the past couple of years, even he couldn't get used to looking at those chins. He'd shaved off his sideburns and whiskers, hoping that might keep him from resembling a pig. It hadn't helped.

The word "pig" had no sooner crossed his mind than Callie's Poland China hog, Cinderella, came lunging and grunting across the back yard, Callie in hot pursuit. The thirteen-year-old girl still limped, but she seemed not to notice it, and William controlled his sadness over her crippled foot by reminding himself that she was not only pretty as any picture but adept now at keeping other people's minds off her handicap.

"Catch him, Uncle William!" Callie was shouting as she ran. "Catch Cinderella for me before he runs into the woods!"

Chuckling as he lumbered along, William still thought it funny for a male pig to be named Cinderella. "I got him, Callie!" he called back to her, grabbing the animal. "Cinderella's as fat as I am. He's so fat, he can't outrun me anymore. No wonder your father wants to butcher him!"

"Well, Papa's *not* going to butcher him. Mama and I have decided that long ago." Both her arms were around the hog and her pretty face was pressed against the huge neck. "Mama says you're an immortal pig,

Cinderella," she said, smoothing the ample side with one sun-browned hand. "But you've just got to stop running away from me, do you hear?"

Looking down at her with an amused smile, William asked, "What did Cinderella say? Did he hear you, Callie?"

"Of course he did, Uncle William. Pigs can hear perfectly well and they're smart, too. Much smarter than horses. The only trouble Cinderella ever gives me is when he insists upon wallowing in the mud. Do you know I've had to give him a bath three times this week?"

"You—bathe Cinderella?" William gave her an incredulous look.

"I most certainly do when he rolls in the mud! Uncle William, would you please hand me that rope hanging on the woodpile?"

William gave her the length of rope, stood watching her loop it around Cinderella's neck. Then leading the pig with one hand, she slipped the other into William's hand and headed him down the backyard path that led into the woods.

"I need to have a talk with you. And with Papa on his way to Cartersville to work and Mama at Miss Lorah's cottage, this is our chance."

Delighted to be with the girl whom he loved as he had always loved Natalie, William went along gladly, his normally hard to arouse curiosity definitely a spur. "Cinderella walks right along on that rope, doesn't he? Looks as though he's forgotten all about his plan to run away."

"Oh, he wasn't really running away. Before Mama went over to Miss Lorah's place, she and I had been busy doing my lessons. Cinderella just felt neglected. He knows he'll always get my full attention if he breaks out running."

"Smart hog."

"If you don't mind, I wish you wouldn't call him a hog."

"He's big enough."

"Maybe, but Mama and I prefer that he be called a pig. We don't like the word 'hog,' " she explained, stopping by a slab of rock plenty large enough for them both to sit down. "This is my favorite place. Please be seated, Uncle William."

"Thank you, I will," he said, forcing his somewhat stiff knees to accommodate themselves to the foot-high rock. "Can Cinderella be trusted not to run away or do you have to hang on to that rope?"

"What I have to talk about is serious, so I think I'll just hitch him to this scrub pine."

Settled beside William, Callie, chin cupped in her hands, said, "It's about Mary Cowper."

Uh-oh, William thought, and here I was avoiding a talk alone with Sister for fear she'd get on the same subject. "What about Mary Cowper?" he asked.

"I love her just as much as I did all those years ago when she was my tutor, Uncle William. Even though I haven't seen her since she got married. And that was ages ago."

William, trying to keep things light, chuckled. "That was all of three years back."

"There's something kind of mysterious going on," Callie continued, "and I need you to tell me, since you live right in Savannah, what it is. I know Mama is still heartbroken that Miss Lib and Uncle W.H. made Mary Cowper marry that old man when she was only in love with Stuart Elliott. In fact, I know Mama still won't write to Mary Cowper and I know why. A lot of times at night, when they think I'm asleep in my room, I can hear Mama and Papa talk about the whole thing. Papa thinks Mama is wrong. He thinks she shouldn't act as though she holds a grudge against Mary Cowper because she knuckled under to her own parents, but I think Mama's right."

"You do? Why?"

"No, I shouldn't have said that. I *don't* think she's right and that's why I had to talk to you. You see, I do love Mary Cowper. She's the most beautiful person in the whole wide world! But if Mama thinks *she* has a broken heart because Mary Cowper had to marry a horrid old man, hers is nothing compared to mine!"

"Is that a fact? Your little heart's broken over Mary Cowper, Callie?" He was trying to tread softly, feeling his way with the sensitive, troubled girl. "And do you know for a fact that Mary Cowper isn't happy with Mr. Low? I know she lost her second baby, but her sun rises and sets in little Catherine Mackay Low. Why is your heart broken?"

Cinderella was wallowing in the woods dirt, but Callie ignored him. "I–I just know I still feel sad when I think about Mary Cowper. Papa says I once had a schoolgirl crush on her and that when I'm a year or so older and go away to school, I'll get over it and that I'll also stop feeling bad because I can tell Mama misses her, too."

"Well, that makes a lot of sense to me. Your father generally does make sense, don't you think?"

Callie sighed heavily, still cupping her chin in both hands. "Papa's sweet," she said, "and I don't ever bring up the subject with Mama anymore because her eyes get all full of tears when anyone even mentions Mary Cowper and I can't bear that."

William gave her a little hug. "Callie, I'm ever so sorry about all this, and I wish I could say something that would let you know Mary Cowper seems to be doing just fine. I'll bet if you could see little Catherine Mackay, you'd stop being heartbroken."

She reached her hand up to take William's and squeezed it tenderly, but firmly. Callie, he thought, was certainly both tender and firm in her very spirit, the spirit which had helped her grow into a fine, independent young lady without ever once turning into a crybaby because she was born crippled.

"Is there going to be a war, Uncle William?"

Her question startled him, but he tried to keep his voice casual. "A war? You mean in our own country?"

"Certainly! Papa and I talk a lot about it. I try very hard to help him, because if there is a war, he's going to have a terribly difficult time."

"I guess we all will, honey, but why your father especially?"

She turned abruptly to face him. "Uncle William, you must know Papa doesn't approve of slavery! He's already worried about what he'll do if there's a war. He really has Northern sympathies in a lot of ways. Of course, it infuriates Mama."

"Because he has some Northern sympathies? Because he doesn't own any slaves?"

"Oh, Mama doesn't care about any of that one way or another. My grandfather Mark is against slavery, too. Mama grew up in a house where her parents disagreed on all that. It isn't slavery, but she gets absolutely furious if Papa even mentions that he might have trouble knowing whether he could fight for the South."

"Can you tell me why your mother gets furious?"

"I'd think it wouldn't be hard to guess, Uncle William, since she's so terribly in love with Papa. Mama really gets all red in the face and fumes if he even mentions fighting for anybody! She forbids him to fight on either side."

"Poor Burke!"

"Could you explain what you mean by that, please?"

William took a deep breath. "You'll know what I mean by and by, when you're a little older."

"I get so sick hearing that."

"I expect you do. Forgive me?"

Callie's outburst was short-lived. She was holding William's hand now in both of hers.

"Oh, yes, Uncle William. I forgive you. I'll always forgive you because you're my favorite gentleman."

He could feel himself flush with pleasure, but he said nothing.

"All men called gentlemen are not–*gentle men,* are they?"

"I wouldn't know about that, honey."

"I think you know exactly what I mean. You should know, since you are a *gentle man.* My papa is one, too."

"Your father's true blue, no matter what you call him. He and I don't see eye to eye on some things," William said, "but Burke Latimer and I go back a long way together. All the way back to when your Aunt Mary Browning's people were run out of their homeland up here in the old Cherokee Nation. Little Mary and her brother were mighty good to me. As was your father."

"Do you think Uncle Jonathan Browning did a good or a bad thing when he married a half-Cherokee?"

"He did the best thing a man could do for Mary and for himself."

"I'm so sorry they lost their little girl. Mama and I take flowers to her grave often. We keep weeds back on Willow's grave and my baby brother's."

"Callie, I know it must worry you that your mother and Mary Cowper don't write to each other anymore, but once, a long time ago, your mother wasn't too close to Mary Browning either."

"I know about that."

"You do?"

"Mama tells me a lot. Especially now that I'm older. She likes her fine now. Back then, she didn't like her because Aunt Mary was in love with Papa. I understand all that."

William gave a short laugh. "You are a wise one, aren't you?"

"What you're saying, I guess, is that if Mama could get to like Aunt Mary, she may also be friends again someday with Mary Cowper."

"You're already smarter than the rest of us, Callie."

"I think I must be pretty smart," she said, deep in thought, "but I wish I didn't have to go away to school."

"Now, listen to me, you're going to get along just fine with those other girls at Montpelier down in Macon. And you'll not only be among the smartest, you'll definitely be the prettiest."

"Oh, I'm not worried about any of that, Uncle William." She swept her arm in a wide gesture about the woods. "It's leaving here that will be so awful!"

William could understand that, but she must also be fearful of social life in Macon, where one of the main things a girl thought about was attending balls. He'd be careful of what he said next. "You do put some stock in what I tell you, don't you, Callie?"

"Oh, yes, or I wouldn't be talking to you like this. Whatever you say, I believe."

"Then take my word for it that the good Lord has given you so many talents, such a pretty face and figure, He's more than made up for any old dance."

"Poor Uncle William!"

"What?"

"I should have known you'd think that was the reason I don't want to go away to school. It isn't. I settled that long ago. If I find a young man to fall in love with, and I'm sure I will, he'll be the kind of man who won't mind that I can't dance. We can just walk around the dance floor together and talk. The reason I don't want to go is because I love it here so much! Did you know Mary Cowper taught me how to shoot before she went away? She's a much better shot than either Henry or Robert and she said I am, too. And I can swim the river as many times as Bobby. I make expert fish traps. I really like being a country girl. Papa's proud of that. So is Mama. Mama says anyone with my intelligence can be an elegant country girl and that's what I intend to be. I'm one now and I plan to stay that way."

Callie had always charmed him, but never as much as this minute. He was more than charmed, he was impressed and found himself wishing he'd live a long time just to know how Callie's life turned out.

The clatter of Burke's old wagon reached them from the river road and William got slowly to his feet. "You think that's Sam with the mail from Cartersville, Callie?"

"I'm sure it is," she said, unhitching Cinderella. "And I know how men are. You're hoping for mail and a newspaper from Savannah."

Plodding along beside her, William said, "You and I don't need to bother to talk to each other. You already know what I'm thinking."

THIRTY-
SEVEN

There was no mail for William, not even a Savannah newspaper. He should have extracted the promise from Kate to keep the newspapers coming. But lately, he'd felt that Sarah, after all the years of fussing, was making a little effort to smooth things out between them, so he'd agreed to count on her keeping him abreast of the trouble in Kansas.

Walking now along the river road at sundown from the Stiles house, where he'd gone for dinner and a good, long visit with W.H., he almost felt sorry for his brother-in-law. Poor W.H., always the politician, was hanging on for dear life to his belief that the Democratic Party in the South, if it stayed solid, could save the Union. William certainly hoped something could, but he put little stock in W.H.'s theory this time. Almost as clear as if he were way out west in Kansas this minute, he somehow knew that the trouble there was the key, not only to the strength of the Democratic Party but to that of President Buchanan, Congress, the South, the North—the nation itself. W.H. had been enthusiastic that Georgia was offering free railroad fares west to all pro-slavery families who wanted to move to Kansas. Well, Northern states had been sending free-state people out there for years. And now it looked as though Buchanan had maneuvered himself into a real trap by appointing Robert J. Walker governor of the Kansas territory. Buchanan's predicament was due to the fact that Governor Walker had promised that the White House would support a full vote by Kansans themselves on which constitution would be accepted, and there *would* likely be two. There was already the prickly fact of what you might call two capitals, one in Topeka, where the free-staters held out, and one in Lecompton, where the citizens were strongly pro-slavery. Lecompton was apt to submit its constitution first. They'd do it this fall no doubt, and there was no doubt in William's mind that it would be rigged in favor of slavery. The free-staters would be bound to erupt.

Turning in at the pine-straw walk that led to the Latimer cottage, William hoped Natalie and Callie might be busy at something, so he and Burke could have a talk. In a way, they were on opposite sides, but Burke was a reasonable man and he loved his country. A reasonable man in a box of his own making. Anti-slavery in his beliefs, he was also a Georgian by choice.

"My choice of Georgia was made," Burke said as he and William walked along the river cliffs in the blue-gray twilight, "because I loved this land up here, Mr. Mackay. I'd searched my own state of Maryland over, I'd taken a good look at most of Florida, even Virginia and both the Carolinas. Still can't put my reason into words, but just before I found Mary and Ben McDonald hiding in that cave near New Echota, I knew this part of Georgia was going to be my home. I only learned the ins and outs of Georgia's politics after I settled here."

"I know all that, Burke," William said, stopping to catch his breath and to feast his eyes on the shadowy, tree-banked curve of the Etowah River. "Always thought the Etowah looked like an Indian river," he mused. "You take our marsh rivers and creeks down on the coast and they're somehow ours. Belong to the white man. Rivers up here, though, with all those brush- and tree-filled banks, make me think of Cherokees. I can picture them hiding and gliding around these cliffs, can you?"

Burke laughed softly. "I suppose I can. I had my heart set on the land up here, but not on what white men were doing to the Cherokees. I guess, for me, it's a good thing men in these parts are mainly Union loyalists. They don't want to give in to the North, but neither do they want to break up the Union. If there is a war, it wouldn't surprise me to see a bunch of my neighbors join up with the Northern forces. I fit in up here far better than I would on the coast. We're an independent lot in north Georgia."

Burke had noticed that his old friend couldn't walk at quite the clip he once did, so on the pretext of pointing out the grace and soaring beauty of the flight of two high-sailing buzzards making a last daylight hunt for food, he stopped walking. "Buzzards are so handsome and rhythmic in flight, so doggone ugly on the ground," Burke mused.

"Like some politicians' speeches, maybe?" William asked. "Flowery, graceful rhetoric when they're before a crowd, but clumsy and red-wattled up close once they're in office. Say, Burke. Do you think President Buchanan is a big enough man to shape our history or do you think he might end up being a victim of all that's going on?"

"He'll have to be a model of consistency and conciliation and I'm not sure he's man enough," Burke said. "I certainly hope so. I voted for him, even though I admit I like the Republicans. The thing that worries me most about Buchanan is that he seems to try to evade the slavery issue."

"And quite neatly, as I see it," William said. "He walked around the problem while he was minister to Great Britain, all through his campaign he either avoided or straddled it, and certainly he evaded it in his inaugural address. I don't see how he's going to keep on doing it, though, after appointing Senator Robert J. Walker to govern the Kansas territory. From what I hear, Walker's a man of his word and he means to let the people of Kansas vote fair and square on the pro-slavery constitution they're drawing up in Lecompton."

"Everybody knows in spite of all the South's effort to populate Kansas, there are still more free-soilers out there," Burke said. "And they'll rise up for sure if the pro-slavery folks try to ram through their constitution."

"Before I left Savannah, I read how one Kansan put it in a nutshell. He said, 'We'll end up voting this arsenic with bread and butter or without bread and butter.'"

They turned back toward the cottage, Burke somehow sure that in spite of their difference of opinion on the ugly issue, he and William Mackay were of one mind on their love of the Union.

"Good to be with you again, Burke," William said as they reached the Latimer front yard. "Before we go in the house, let me ask, do you ever hear Eliza Anne say anything much about Mary Cowper and Mr. Low?"

Burke gave William a guarded look. "I'm not exactly sure what you mean by that, sir."

"She seems worried about her daughter, whether or not she's happy with Low. I can tell from her letters home. She veils it, but she just strikes me as more and more anxious."

"I was afraid that's what you meant," Burke said, not wanting at all to get involved in such a personal family matter. "Of course, Natalie notices, but Miss Lib and I don't talk much alone anymore. Not like when I was building the Stiles house."

The evasion made William grin. "You'd make a pretty good diplomat, Burke."

"Miss Lib knows better than to mention Mary Cowper outright around Natalie."

"Ah," William sighed. "And that's sad, isn't it?"

"To me, it is. They need each other a lot. Always have."

"I doubt Natalie would admit that. She's never really needed anyone but you."

"I manage, too, without a close friend up here aside from Natalie. My world revolves around her and Callie."

"But now and then, you feel the need for a man friend you can open up to?"

"I guess I do, but I don't have one." On the porch, Burke turned to William and said in all honesty, "You're the best friend I've had since Ben died, Mr. Mackay. I wish I were better with words, sir."

"Me, too, Burke. Me, too."

It rained too hard for three days for anyone to ride to Cartersville for mail. Sam went on the fourth day, and by the time he got back, it was well after dinner, which they all took at the Stileses'. Everyone gave Sam a warm hurrah when he rode up at last, the horse's legs caked with mud.

"You even have mud on your face, Sam," Callie yelled at the skinny, still shy young man who had come over the mountains from Ellijay with Miss Lorah almost fifteen years ago. "I thought only Cinderella could get that muddy!"

Everyone but Miss Lorah, back in her cottage making jelly, had run out to the river road, sure that after three days there would be a lot of mail for everyone.

"Miss Lorah don't expect none," Sam said, still in the saddle. "All her friends and family live right here."

"Glad to see you feeling so chipper, Sam, after that long, hard ride," William called up to him. "Don't see you smile too often."

"No, sir," Sam said, and ducked his head to fish around in the burlap bag hanging from the saddle. "Got a pile of all kinds of stuff." He handed the lot down to William.

William thought Sam must feel a little embarrassed since he couldn't read enough to sort such a bundle. Deliberately, he leafed through the letters and papers himself. "Looks like two bills for you, Burke, from your lumberyard and the mill. And, let me see, four letters for W.H." He handed those to Eliza Anne, who had just joined the group as Sam rode up. "Here's one for you, Natalie, and I bet it's from your mother. I got one from Mama and these forwarded from my office—and, good, here are three newspapers! We can catch up a little, Burke, finally."

"What about me, William?" Eliza Anne asked. "None for me?"

"Sure enough, Sister. It was hiding in between two of my papers. Here you are, the very letter you wanted. It's from Mary Cowper. Her handwriting looks just like it did when your family all lived in Vienna."

Eliza Anne almost jerked the letter from William's hand, mumbled her thanks, and hurried without another word to her big house.

"She always does that," Natalie said. "Miss Lib never shares a single letter from Mary Cowper with anybody!"

"Mama, do you mean she doesn't even let Uncle W.H. read them?" Callie wanted to know.

"You know better than that, dear," Natalie said. "That question did not sound like someone going to be fourteen!"

"She was teasing," Burke said.

"Burke, I know she was!"

As Sam rode off down the road toward the stable, William studied Natalie's face briefly. She wasn't actually angry, he thought. More hurt and taking it out a little on Callie. Well, he supposed Natalie knew, if anybody did, that Callie would pay her no mind.

"I wish we could sit right down and read those newspapers, Mr. Mackay," Burke said as they walked toward his cottage, "but I have to do some repairs on the Stileses' stable door before dark."

"Sam tries to help Papa," Callie explained to William, "but he's all thumbs. Even Miss Lorah says he is. She takes good care of Sam, though. She loves him as though he were her real son."

At the Latimer porch, Burke hurried around back, calling over his shoulder to William, "I'll get right at that stable door just as soon as I get my toolbox, Mr. Mackay. Be home soon, then you can give me the gist of what's in the papers."

"There will be no war talk and no talk of politics tonight," Natalie announced. "Callie and I have planned a musicale. I forgot to invite Miss Lib and Uncle W.H., so, Callie, you'll have to run back and invite them yourself."

"A real musicale, Natalie?" William asked, amused.

"The best, William. Callie's been practicing four new pieces on her pianoforte and everyone is going to listen to every note. Sit down right now and read those papers, because this evening we want your full attention, please."

William had no sooner settled himself on the narrow, vine-shaded porch, reading spectacles polished up and in place, than he saw his sister Eliza Anne coming slowly along the river road, head down. Funny sight, he thought. Eliza Anne almost never strolls, she cuts along at a good clip, nose in the air.

He took advantage of the time it would take his sister to reach Natalie's cottage to glance at the headline on the latest edition of the Savannah *Daily Morning News* and his eyes widened in disbelief: VICTORY, the headline proclaimed, PRESIDENT PUBLICLY ENDORSES LECOMPTON PRO-SLAV-ERY PLAN.

Of course, William was glad. Anything that helped the South in its fight with the North was good, but his smile was not a gloating smile. He knew too well that old Buchanan had been trapped into endorsing the pro-slavery Lecompton Constitution. Never mind that he'd appointed Robert Walker governor of the Kansas territory. Never mind also that Walker had vowed to give the people out there a fair chance to vote on any new constitution. Politicians are politicians, and that's why William smiled. He felt sorry for Buchanan. By endorsing the Lecompton Constitution, Buchanan would surely splinter his own Democratic Party into bits and pieces. Still, most of the Southern leaders demanded it and the President was dependent on Southerners. After all, most of his electoral votes had come from the South. He would surely need Southern support if he ran again in 1860. Without the Southerners in Congress, Buchanan had no hope of getting his bills passed. But more than anything else, anybody knew that if the President did not endorse the pro-slavery constitution, making slavery the law in Kansas, the South would secede from the Union! Pro-slavery firebrands were now making almost daily threats. Old Buchanan must be trembling in his boots.

"William!" Eliza Anne called, quickening her steps up the pine-straw walk, obviously upset about something. "I need to talk to you, so get your nose out of that newspaper! You should have stayed at our house, you know. It's foolish for me to have to hike all the way over here every time I need my brother."

"Sorry, Sister," he said, in his usual noncommittal way. "Come on up on the porch and take a seat. I'm available."

"Put down that paper, please!" She took a rocker. "I want you to read Mary Cowper's letter."

His own spectacles still in place, William took the single page and began to read: " 'Dear Mama and Papa. This will not be long because Mr. Low is waiting downstairs to take it to the post office on his way to work and he hates waiting. Anyway, there is only one thing to tell you and with all my heart I pray it will ease both your hearts for all time. On Monday evening, June 1 of next year, my close friend Lucinda Sorrel will marry Stuart Elliott. Because I care deeply that they both be happy in whatever circumstances they find themselves, I wish them God's very best. Your loving daughter, Mary Cowper Low.' "

William looked from the letter to his sister's face, studying her.

"Don't just stare at me, Brother! What do you make of it? Even with Mr. Low waiting, wouldn't you think she'd at least have sent her love to you and the others by name?"

"No, I hadn't even thought of that," William said, still holding the letter in his hands. "So, Lucy Sorrel and Stuart are going to get married. I knew they were courting. At least, most people in town knew they saw a lot of each other, but somehow I just didn't dream they'd make up their minds so fast."

Eliza Anne grabbed the letter. "You can be absolutely infuriating! Whether Lucy Sorrel and Mr. Elliott surprised people or not is beside the point. What I want to know is—is . . ."

Looking straight at her, William asked, "Is what, Sister?"

She slumped back in her chair. "Why did Mary Cowper feel it might —ease her parents' hearts to know about that utterly foolish and danger-ous engagement?"

"One thing you're not, Eliza Anne, is stupid. I think you came over here to get me to tell you I have no idea why the girl felt you'd be relieved to know Stuart Elliott is finally going to be out of reach for her, but I'm not saying anything of the sort. Mary C.'s dead right. Now that he's going to marry her best friend, you can rest your hearts, you and W.H., even about her most private thoughts of Stuart. What in the world were you worried about anyway?"

"Who said we were worried?"

"Nobody. I just know you both. If ever a wife tried to make a good marriage, Mary Cowper is doing it, but even you and W.H. know neither one of you has any control over her private thoughts."

She jumped to her feet. "I suppose *you* can read her mind!"

"Of course not, but it's good she wrote what she did. Got it right out on the table that she's known all along that, with Stuart still a bachelor, you'd both go on stewing."

"When have we stewed?"

"I don't have times and dates on that, but whenever any of us can get something out in the open, it helps. We both learned that long ago from Mama. Right now, I'd say you should be proud of Mary Cowper."

"Proud?"

"Proud, because she's proving she inherited a big, wide streak of her grandmother Mackay's honesty. She didn't palaver. Not one wasted line in that letter."

"There certainly isn't!"

"That's like Mama, too. Get it said, get it out in the open, and from then on, everybody can feel more comfortable."

"I know what you're trying to say, Brother, but I don't feel at all comfortable."

"Well, maybe I used the wrong word. With any abrupt airing of facts, somebody's going to feel uncomfortable for a time, but in the long run, all parties concerned know where they are." He handed back the letter.

Eliza Anne took it almost hesitantly. "William, why do I feel uneasy about my daughter? She has everything her heart could desire!"

"Only you can know that, but you will. In time, you'll know."

That night, after supper, Natalie joined Burke and William in her parlor once Callie was in bed, worn out from her vigorous performance at the musicale.

"Do you think I'm spoiling her because I still tuck her in the way I've always done, William?" Natalie asked her casual question as she sat down beside Burke on the sofa. "We still say our prayers together before I put out her lamp."

Burke gave her a hug. "I'd say you should keep on. Otherwise you might forget to say *your* prayers, Missy."

Natalie punched his arm. "No one asked you, sir."

"Without a doubt, I agree with Burke, Natalie," William said, and Natalie stuck out her tongue at him.

"You always agree with Burke."

"That's just not true," William said. "Your husband and I disagree about several national issues. Just so happens we're friends. We can disagree and not get riled up."

In her most commanding voice, Natalie said, "No, no, *no!* I can smell politics seeping right into the room, and once it's here, war can't be far behind, so silence, both of you!"

Still teasing her, Burke suggested, "You could go to bed, Mrs. Latimer."

"And lie in there fuming while you and William elect a whole Congress and fight a dumb old war? You know I'm not going, so hush."

Natalie had had enough teasing. The slightest mention of war, even when she was the one to bring it up, paralyzed her with fear. "William," she pleaded, all command gone from her voice, "tell Burke that even if there is a stupid decision made up there in Washington that the North is going to fight the South, he still doesn't have to do anything about it! Tell him he and Callie and I can just go right on here in our cottage–together, being us. Being–happy!" Her voice choked with tears. Then, losing control, she burst into long pent-up sobs and clung to Burke for dear life.

His big arms were around her, his strong hand smoothing her back– Burke's safe arms that always brought comfort. They brought none now because of what he was saying to William. He was talking over her head as though she were younger than Callie!

"For the life of me," Burke was saying, "I don't know what's going to happen, but it's plain that Buchanan's cooked his own goose for 1860."

She literally jumped out of his arms. "Who cares about 1860, Burke? Didn't I say *no politics?* Didn't I say that, William?"

"I believe so," William answered in his slow, quiet, maddening way. "But you brought it up."

She stood in the middle of the floor glaring at William.

For a long moment, no one spoke. Then Burke said, "She's scared. Natalie gets more scared at what's going on in the country than anyone guesses."

She stamped her foot. "Don't apologize for me!"

"I'm not."

"Then don't explain me as though I'm a nitwit, just because I care more about you than politics or who's President! I love you and I don't want you shot at and killed!"

"Keep your voice down, darling. Callie will hear you." The last thing Natalie wanted was for Callie to sense her terror. "You're right. I—I get too afraid to think straight. I get so scared when I even think of you going off to war to be killed. You're so tall and big, no one could miss you, and neither you nor William can call me crazy for saying that. You'd be sure to be shot, Burke!"

She had lowered her voice some, but it was too late. Callie, in her nightgown, stood in the doorway.

"Mama doesn't like to be talked to as though she's a child," Callie said, sounding, Natalie knew, exactly like her, "and neither do I!"

There was a long silence in the room. Then Burke said, "It's your bedtime, Callie."

"I know it is," the girl said, limping to her mother's side. "But I do have one thing to say. I think we ought to wait and hope there won't be a war."

"There's no war tonight anyway," Burke said. "You're right, honey. It's best to wait before we get all riled up."

Desperately, Natalie looked at William, her eyes pleading. "Tell her, William. Callie believes you. Tell her I always make mountains out of molehills."

"Who knows that for sure, Natalie?"

"Thank you, Uncle William," Callie said solemnly. "Nobody knows anything for sure and Miss Lorah says *hope* never hurt anybody!"

THIRTY-
EIGHT

The newlyweds, young Henry Stiles and his bride, Cliffie, spent the summer at Etowah Cliffs, and William, who waited to ride the train back to Savannah with them in October, got a head start on other Savannahians where Nellie Kinzie was concerned. Cliffie's brother, Willie, named for his late father, W. W. Gordon, was due to marry Nellie in Chicago on December 21, and as Cliffie told William on the train home: "Anyone needs a little preparation for Nellie! She was one of my best friends at the North in Madam Canda's School and she made it all so much fun, was such a cultivated tomboy and thrived so on upsetting us all, the last person I ever expected her to marry was my sedate, reserved brother, Willie."

The train trip south from Cassville actually didn't seem long, William so enjoyed Cliffie's tales about Nellie Kinzie. They helped pass the time. He felt he couldn't wait to tell his mother and sisters about the twenty-two-year-old hoyden from Chicago who was evidently *not* born to become a proper Savannah Gordon.

"Nellie's future mother-in-law, Sarah, has a perpetual surprise in store," he told them on the first night back. "I'm not good enough with words to begin to repeat all Cliffie's stories about Nellie Kinzie, but she's going to liven up the old town for sure."

His family seemed glad to have him home, William thought, and he was pleased to be there, although he'd enjoyed the summer in Cass.

"You'll never guess, Mama," he said, "what Nellie Kinzie's opinion of Willie Gordon was the first night she met him during a visit she and Cliffie made to Yale College."

"Well, tell us," Kate demanded.

With a sly look at his sister Sarah, who usually complained that William sat like a bump on a log, he went on, "When Nellie came back upstairs to where she and Cliffie roomed, Cliffie wanted to know what she thought of her brother, since, in spite of being fairly handsome, he'd never exactly shone socially. Besides, that night poor Willie even had to hold his neck stiff because he had a big boil on it."

"Brother, you either don't say a word or you talk too much," Sarah scolded. "Get to the point. What did Nellie say about poor Willie?"

"She scandalized a roomful of schoolmates by declaring that he looked like nothing so much as a Methodist parson!"

When they all seemed to enjoy that, feeling encouraged, William went on to tell them that the next morning, when Willie took Nellie and Cliffie to see the Yale Library on the Old Campus, they somehow got separated from Willie and ended up at the top of a long stairway by themselves. Well, it seems temptation got the best of Nellie and she slid down the banister smack into Willie's arms!"

Even Sarah laughed and laughed and Mama had to take off her spectacles to dry her eyes.

"The best part is that Willie swears now that it was at that moment, when she landed in his arms, he fell in love!"

"And they've been in love ever since!" Kate sighed. "How romantic, William! How utterly romantic!"

"Obviously," Sarah put in, "she changed her mind about Willie Gordon looking like a Methodist parson."

"Entirely," William said. "They've been engaged for three years and you know how much time Willie's spent in Chicago. Nellie's mother must be some lady, too. She's writing a book about her life among the Seneca Indians on the frontier before Chicago turned into such a bustling town. I guess Willie even got to like sleigh rides up there."

"I wonder how his Nellie will like living in our old, sometimes quite proper city," Mama wondered aloud. "For that matter, I think we'd all better start praying that Sarah Gordon will cotton to Nellie."

"Cliffie says Nellie swears like a sailor," William said, enjoying the fact that he'd saved his most startling announcement until last.

"*What?*" Kate gasped.

"You're making that up, William!"

"I am not, Sarah. Ask Cliffie tomorrow if you don't believe me."

"Sarah Gordon won't—won't think that a bit ladylike," Kate ventured. "Do you think she will, Mama?"

"I've already decided to hold my opinions until I've had a chance to meet Willie's bride-to-be face to face," Mama said. "William's so much more cheerful since he spent the summer in Cass, he just might be joshing some to make us all laugh."

"Mama, I'm telling the absolute truth. Nellie Kinzie swears. Of course, Cliffie vows she never takes the name of the Lord in vain except when mighty angry, so considers it isn't really swearing." He chuckled. "Cliffie also says Nellie's improved with the years, because now she can swear in French."

William liked most the fact that his cantankerous sister, Sarah, seemed to spark to his tales of Nellie Kinzie. Only when Mama brought it up did he even mention his growing desire for him and Sarah to find a way to build some sort of bridge. After all, they weren't getting any younger and he had been pretty sick for a time after his stroke. He was trying not to eat so much these days, but he knew his added weight could bring on another stroke, and although it would be hard to admit even to Mama, he longed in a new way for his younger sister's approval. The interest she seemed to show in Nellie Kinzie somehow encouraged him, if only because he happened to be the one telling about her.

"I certainly want to read Nellie's mother's book," Sarah said. "What's it called, William?"

"Indian name, *Wau-Bun*," he said. "Means Dawn or Early Day. She writes about the time she lived among the Seneca Indians on the frontier in Wisconsin, too, I guess. And the Fort Dearborn Massacre. She also tells about her own mother. Seems the Senecas called her mother a name that meant Little Ship in Full Sail."

"Well, I must say it sounds to me like that describes the young lady Willie Gordon's going to marry," Mama said.

"I predict she'll make some waves in Savannah all right."

"You've gotten to be quite a good conversationalist, William!" Sarah acted genuinely surprised and almost pleased with him. "Maybe you find life here as dull as Sister and I sometimes find it."

"Sarah," Kate scolded, "that might hurt Mama's feelings! She didn't mean anything by what she said, Mama."

William was happy to be back where he could hear his mother's laugh again. Even at her age, it still sounded like bells and still made everyone who heard it feel good.

"I'm sure it does get monotonous," Mama said, "living here day in and day out with an old woman, but I'll know when I become poor company. Somehow I don't feel I am quite yet. William, do you think Willie Gordon's bride will find it troublesome living in the South? The Gordons do own their people. Did Cliffie say anything about that at all?"

"Yes, Mama, she did. At first, it seems Willie and Nellie had it around the barn on slavery. She does *not* approve of it." He grinned. "Mark will no doubt be glad to have Nellie Kinzie Gordon around to talk to. She and Willie disagreed on slavery and the church. You know Willie's a dyed-in-the-wool Presbyterian and she's a strong Episcopalian. Cliffie thinks they've made a good compromise, though."

"What?" Kate asked.

"She's agreed to keep still about the slavery issue and Willie's going to be married in her church in Chicago. They'll attend Christ Church once they're here, too."

"Sounds to me as though Nellie got the big end of the stick. All she has to do is keep quiet about slavery. She doesn't have to change her mind on it. Poor Willie has to change his religion."

"Not his God, though," Mama said.

"I'll be hoping to learn something from the future Mrs. Willie Gordon myself," William said. "She'll know about this Illinois politician Abraham Lincoln. Mark's taken with him."

"But that Lincoln man's a *Republican*, William!" Sarah exclaimed. "I know how Mark feels about owning people, but he's too loyal to all of us to show real interest in a terrible man like Lincoln!"

"How well do you know Mr. Lincoln, Sarah?" their mother asked calmly. "Well enough to know he's terrible?"

"Well enough to know he's a Black Republican, Mama!"

"You're right, Sister," Kate said, frowning. "And he is from the same state as Nellie Kinzie, isn't he? I agree, she sounds fascinating, but oh, my. Do you suppose poor Willie Gordon's bitten off more than he can chew?"

THIRTY-NINE

At the end of February of the new year, 1858, Mark stopped by William's small office on Factor's Walk, and as was the case all over the city, they talked first of the weather. After a warm, rainy beginning to the month, today's newspaper carried the surprising weather story that snow had actually fallen on the Central of Georgia tracks not twenty miles away.

"Sarah got out my woolen sweater late yesterday," William said, gesturing toward the dark blue sweater stretched across his ample stomach. "I thought that was good of her."

Mark, sitting on a straight chair to one side of William's neatly kept desk, laughed. "It sounds to me as though you and Sarah might be a little closer these days. I know that makes Miss Eliza happy. She's worried some through the years that you two went on sparring."

"Oh, we still spar. Habit's a hard thing to break." He reached for the New York *Tribune* Mark had laid on the desk. "Speaking of sparring, I take it there's something in this Yankee paper you want me to see?"

"There is. The day after Buchanan recommended that Kansas become a state under the Lecompton Constitution, Senator Douglas made a speech that condemns Lecompton as a violation of his popular sovereignty policy. It was such a strong speech, I thought you'd like to read it for yourself and not take my opinion of it."

Scanning the speech, William mused, "Hm! This won't be printed in our papers, I can tell you that! I thought Douglas had ambitions for the White House next time round. He can't manage that without Southern Democrats. This will lose us all in a body!"

"I agree," Mark said. "And if Douglas means to return to the Senate this year from Illinois, he'll have the Republicans to fight."

"Unless he turns Republican himself," William said.

"Stephen A. Douglas? I hadn't thought of that."

"Neither had I till this minute, but nothing a politician might do surprises me anymore. You had a chance to talk to young W. W. Gordon's new wife since they got back from their Niagara Falls honeymoon, Mark?"

"Only with too many Gordons and Brownings present. I hope to find out what she thinks of that Springfield lawyer Abraham Lincoln."

William chuckled. "Even Sarah's calling him a Black Republican. Poor man."

"Why on earth would you say 'poor man' about Lincoln?"

"He's barely come out as a Republican. I don't like anything I know about him politically, but he must be at least cautious. I surely would like to know, Mark, why he interests you so much."

"His ideas, I guess. He seems able to—think," Mark said. "We just so desperately need a leader in this country, and while Lincoln is against only the spread of slavery, he seems, as you say, a thoughtful, cautious man."

"What little I've read," William said, "he's a sloppy fellow in his appearance, likes to tell stories, a smart lawyer, and rough as a cob in a lot of ways."

Neither spoke for a time, then William asked, "What are you hearing from the businessmen who pass through your office these days?"

Mark sighed. "I wish you hadn't asked that. Just this morning, James Clack came by. I tried my best, as usual, to stay off the troubling subject, but as he was leaving, he turned around and said as though he were threatening me personally, 'Whatever takes place in Washington or in the congressional elections this fall, Browning, a war can only be deferred. There's going to be one and the longer it's put off, the bloodier it's going to be.' "

"And you're thinking about Jonathan."

"Jonathan and Burke and Willie Gordon and Stuart Elliott and young Henry and Robert Stiles . . . Oh, William, I'm thinking about every single one of us, North and South!"

The weather stayed too cold through the first weeks of March for Eliza Mackay to venture out, and so, when she finally did get William to agree to drive her to the Gordons' on the last day of the month, Sarah Gordon was not at home.

"I should have let you know I was coming," she explained to Willie's new wife, Nellie, when they sat down together in the back parlor, "but I'm plenty old enough to blame my forgetfulness on my age."

Nellie's laugh delighted her. Eliza had liked the Chicago girl on sight, a few days after Nellie and Willie returned from their honeymoon. She was straightforward, vivacious, and on that first meeting at the Brownings' for dinner, had not uttered one swear word either in English or in French.

"I think I'll just come right out and say, Mrs. Gordon, that although I long to see your dear mother-in-law after all this time shut up in my own house, I'm quite glad to find you here alone."

"Good for you," Nellie said quickly. "I'm also glad. I'm shut up here, too, you know. With Willie at work at his new position as junior partner at Tyson and Gordon, I languish. My proper mother-in-law, as I'm sure you know, can't imagine anyone languishing in the Gordon mansion, but I do take her word about *you!* I'm ever so glad you're here. Tea will arrive any minute."

"That will be lovely," Eliza said, "but what is Sarah Gordon's 'word' about me, my dear?"

"That one can say anything at all to you and be certain of full understanding. Oh, Mrs. Mackay, Chicago is such an exciting place to live! There's so much to do all day long. My mother's a most successful author now and all the literary greats who venture that far west call at our house. Savannah is a beautiful, old, picturesque city, but I'm growing old, too, in it!" Nellie cocked her dark head and asked, "Now, did you understand that? Or are you about to preach a sermon to me on how grateful I should be to have captured the most eligible wellborn young man in town?"

Eliza laughed easily. "We're going to get along just fine, Mrs. Gordon," she said.

"Not if you don't begin at once to call me Nellie!"

"All right, Nellie. And my close friends call me Miss Eliza."

"Not my mother-in-law!"

"I know. Dear Sarah is permanently fixed on calling me Mrs. Mac-kay. I answer to either. I'm sure you do miss your family—perhaps your mother especially—and Chicago's social life. I'm sure you and young W.W. are blissfully happy together, though. Even you couldn't convince me I'm wrong about that. I've seen you with him, don't forget."

"I adore him! I didn't at first, you know." The merry laughter came again. "I thought, in fact, he was quite like a Methodist parson. He isn't. He's simply a Savannahian *and* his mother's son. Actually, he's rather like my mother, too. Isn't my husband the kindest, wisest man you've ever met?"

"He's always been. Even as a child."

"He's like Mother in that he's so kind and attentive, but equally hard to fool. Brides like to be spoiled, but Willie, while he also adores me, shows no signs at all of spoiling me. He even declares he wants children!"

This did stun Eliza, but she tried not to show it. "And you don't, my dear?"

"I hate children! I wrote that to Mother last month and whew! what a letter I got in return." When a servant brought tea, she suspended her story long enough to receive it, dismiss the servant, and begin to pour. "Now, where were we? Oh, yes. Mother's hard at work on a novel now, but that certainly didn't stop her from penning a long, firm reply to my loathing the idea of having children." She passed cream and sugar to Eliza, took some for her own tea, and smiled devilishly. "Tell me, my dear lady, do you understand my eccentricity about children?"

"I—accept it and I'm quite aware that you're testing me, so I'll go along. I don't understand it. Bearing children is in God's plan for married women. I know you love God."

"And how do you know that?"

"Would *you* understand if I said that I just know?"

"*Touché,*" Nellie laughed. "My esteemed mother-in-law has gone up a notch in my estimation. You *are* a wise and understanding lady. What a relief!"

"Did you really write to your mother that you—hate children?"

"Oh, yes. I thought I'd forestall a sermon, but it worked just the opposite way. It isn't that I literally hate them, I just don't want the bother or the trouble they inevitably cause. I married Willie because I love him with all my heart and he's more than enough for me."

"And here I thought you said you were restless, shut away here, feeling deprived."

"The thought of caring for a child is an out-and-out personal affront to me!"

"Nellie, are you going to have a baby?"

A look crossed the young woman's face like a thunder cloud. "Mrs. Gordon said you're hard to fool. Yes, in the very first year of my marriage, I'm facing that–this fall! And don't tell me what my own life might have been like had my darling mother felt the way I feel. Don't tell me that, because she's already told me at length. Miss Eliza, I don't *want* to be a mother!"

For a long, tense moment, Eliza could only try to compose her own emotions. Then she surprised herself by saying quietly, "Unless I miss my guess, Nellie, you're *not* a selfish person. You just have strong opinions of what you want your married life to be like. You miss the social life in Chicago. You think what little fun you've had here so far will end with the coming of a baby. Right now, there doesn't seem room for little ones. Oh, my dear, you have a happy surprise up ahead."

Nellie sat almost glaring at her, but also beseeching her. "I need you to–help me!"

"Can you think of a better way to show your love for Willie than to move through what seems to you a dreadful ordeal with colors flying?"

After a pause, Nellie said, "No. No, I can't think of a better way and I've tried and tried and tried!"

"Giving him a child will doubly prove your love for him. Isn't it even greater proof when a strongly opinionated woman like you changes right before his eyes?"

The girl's expression changed with the challenge. "Now, that does give me something to work on. And I will, I promise. If my twenty-two years have taught me anything, they have taught me that no matter what gets in the way, there is always some means of getting around it."

"Or *through* it," Eliza said.

"My mother-in-law would give me her sweet, genteel look if she heard me being so forward, but I *do* like you, Miss Eliza. I like you very much!"

"And I like you."

With an abrupt display of her contagious vitality, Nellie changed the subject. "That nice Mr. Mark Browning tells me even those of us who strongly disapprove of slavery can feel free to discuss the ugly subject with you. I didn't believe him. I do now."

"I hadn't realized there'd been time for you and Mark Browning to talk alone."

"There wasn't time, really. You were there at his home, too, the only time I've seen him. I'm afraid I stole a moment as we were all saying goodbye. You see, I'm trying so hard not to put my foot in it here among Savannah slaveholders, but Willie had told me of Mr. Browning's refusal to own his servants. What an admirable gentleman!" Not bothering to hide her curiosity, Nellie went on, "Actually, you may be even more admirable, though. After all, you are a slave owner and Mr. Browning whispered that both you and your son, William, can discuss the matter without a hint of rancor. How does that happen?"

Eliza smiled. "We're not all alike down here in the South, Nellie. I'm sure you'll discover that for yourself."

"But I need to be careful, don't I? I know marrying into the Gordon family gives me the benefit of most doubts, but will you keep an eye on me? I do love my husband with my whole heart, but I stay safely clear of the subject with him, believe me. I can't be anything but what I am, you know. Still, I don't want to blunder into unnecessary trouble. I won't lie about what I think, but adoring Willie as I do, I won't want to give offense." Without waiting for Eliza to respond, she asked, "How is it that you, as a born and bred Southerner, are so approachable on the forbidden subject, Miss Eliza? You do agree that I need to be careful, don't you?"

"Yes, and there will be times when you will walk a fine line. You are safe, though, with my son, William, and with me. And of course with dear Mark Browning." She set down her cup. "As for my being approachable, I hope I am, but if I am, it doesn't mean I have any special wisdom on the subject; it's just that our country is only a little older than I. We declared our independence two years before I was born. I literally grew up with the Union. I have always done my level best to take care of my people and I confess that most of the time I haven't thought one way or the other about owning them. I *have* always thought about the Union, though. I revere it. Being a part of the United States of America is like being a part of my own family." She sighed and smiled a bit sadly. "I'm not sure these days that either the country or I have learned much in all those years, but both still full of faults, we have tried to grow up together."

Nellie Gordon had been perched attentively on the edge of her chair. Now she sank back into it. "Oh, thank you," she said. "Do you suppose I'll ever grow up? Do you think I even want to? Do you *feel* marvelously mature and wise? At twenty-two, I do. Does that mean I'm not wise at all?"

Eliza laughed softly. "At the risk of sounding as though I'm about to launch into a sermon, I just have to say that only God is wise enough to trust fully no matter what the problem."

"That didn't sound at all like a sermon! I agree. I pray a lot. Sometimes on the run, but I do pray and I do try to pay attention to God's word. That's the problem, really. I've grown up believing that God loves us all the same."

"Including Negroes."

"Exactly!" She jumped up to give Eliza a hug. "What a wonderful lady you are! I honestly believe you might even be able to help me learn how not to give the appearance of taking over my mother-in-law's house."

"*If possible*, dear boy," Eliza Mackay said to Mark when he came for his daily visit on a sweltering early morning, "our times together mean more than ever. I go on getting blinder and blinder, but I also go on seeming to care more and more about what's happening in our land. Have you read the paper yet today?"

"I have," he said, taking a nearby rocker on the front porch, where at least a semblance of breeze stirred. "And the Kansas territory is still the Kansas territory, not a state."

"Good," she said, and clapped her hands lightly. "The people of Kansas must have voted down the Lecompton Constitution. That's an answer to prayer, isn't it?"

"It's proof, I'd say, that the earlier so-called vote they took out there was rigged. This time, on August 2, they voted the Lecompton Constitution down by an almost eleven-to-one margin. Now they have to wait to become a state until the population reaches more than ninety-three thousand. Abraham Lincoln's launched his Republican campaign to unseat Senator Douglas, too. I'm afraid none of this is very good news to Andrew Low. He stopped by my office early today and said he pitied me because I had no one with whom to celebrate." Mark laughed. "His pity didn't sound convincing. Actually, he was furious. That man's as much a Southern sympathizer as though he'd been born here."

"I'm surprised Mr. Low even came to see you. Isn't he a strange man, Mark? He does seem at times to be reaching out for your friendship."

"I agree. I do my best. He's difficult for me, though. He always has been. But he does take good care of Mary Cowper. Low asked me to tell you how sorry he is not to have taken her out of Savannah sooner."

"Thank heaven, the yellow-fever epidemic this summer isn't as bad as before. Too many have died, goodness knows, but nothing like the last time. Sarah Gordon went to New Jersey to be with Julie, her youngest, Cliffie and Henry went to Etowah Cliffs." She smiled. "You and Caroline and I must be fever-proof by now."

"Jonathan wanted Mary to go with Cliffie and Henry. Of course, she wouldn't hear of leaving him." Mark reached for her hand. "Keeping my family here proves I grow more selfish by the day, doesn't it?"

"It does not. You just love Savannah more by the day. Anyway, Mrs. Minis told me yesterday the word is that the epidemic is almost over." They rocked in silence for a time, then she mused, "I wish Mr. Low felt free to come by to tell me himself when he has a message for me. I wonder why he doesn't."

"This town is all ears and tongues," Mark said. "My theory is that Low's heard somehow that you're fond of Stuart Elliott."

"I am fond of Stuart and of his new wife, Lucinda. They were here just yesterday, in fact. Lucy's pathetically happy. If her dear mother stays reasonably well, Lucinda just may have a good life with Stuart."

"What about Elliott? They're living at the Sorrels'. Do you think that can work out?"

"Mark, Stuart is all right. I'm sure he is. I can't say he's actually happy, but he and Lucinda married each other with their eyes open. They have honesty to build on. He is truly grateful to Lucy for marrying him, it seems to me."

"You'll miss Mary Cowper when the Lows leave next week for England. Caroline will visit you more often, she says, although she certainly knows she isn't Mary Cowper."

"That's right. No one else is Mary Cowper. No one else in all the world is Caroline either. Is she well today?"

"Seemed to be when I left early this morning."

"Your household is such a happy one, Mark. Your 'cup runneth over.' "

Words where his devotion to Eliza Mackay was concerned were far beyond him. He only gave her hand a hard, loving squeeze.

"Because your cup runneth over, dear boy, so does mine." Again, they shared an easy, familiar silence, then Eliza said, "Wouldn't Jack be bubbling over with joy that the city finally has a harbor beacon light out on Bay Street? How that boy did get irked at the slowness of government action. I miss Jack so much of the time."

"So do I," Mark said. "But William seems just like his old self, don't you think?"

"Well, I can't get used to all that excess weight, but he certainly does seem well. Oh, Mark, we couldn't get along at all without William!"

When Nellie Gordon's celebrated mother, Juliette Kinzie, scoffing at the danger of a yellow-fever epidemic, made the long journey from Chicago to be with Nellie at the birth of her first child, due the last week of September, Eliza Mackay made a point of inviting her to tea. She accepted for the Saturday afternoon of August 21.

The weather was so hot, cold lemonade was served and, with a tray of Emphie's benne-seed cookies on a table between them, they sat together on the Mackay porch, both women obviously enjoying each other.

"My daughter tells me you are a lady of infinite wisdom, Mrs. Mackay," Juliette Kinzie said, fanning herself. "She assures me that she is perfectly free to hold an intelligent discussion with you, a born Southerner, even on slavery. I find that amazing!"

"And did Nellie also tell you why that is?"

"Something about how much you love the Union?"

"It has everything to do with my love of our entire country."

"Then you should visit Illinois at once! Is your health good enough for such a trip? You'd be most welcome to visit in my home, and Nellie is bringing her new child when it arrives, just as soon as they're both strong enough for the train ride. You could come with her."

Eliza studied the woman's quite handsome face, the intelligent deep-set eyes. "That's most kind of you, Mrs. Kinzie, but I'm past eighty and just the thought of such a trip tires me. I'm sure Nellie will be happy to be back in Chicago for a good, rousing time with her many friends there."

"I see you have my daughter figured out and that takes some doing. The main reason I'd love you to come, though, is to expose you to a rather homely, but highly intellectual man named Lincoln."

"Oh, yes, he's running for the Senate on the Republican ticket.

Lincoln's going to hold debates with Senator Douglas. I believe seven in all. I've always been a Democrat, you know."

"I'm sure you have been, but then, many Republicans were. My dear husband and I are quite active in the party, and this man, Abraham Lincoln, has a way with words that should make even Douglas tremble in his boots. I do believe the first debate will take place today in Ottawa, Illinois. I'd give almost anything I own to hear it! Lincoln's rise in the party after such a hesitant start is breaking precedent, you know."

"Yes, I do know. When the Illinois Republicans nominated him at their convention in June, it was the first time a state convention had ever done such a thing."

Juliette Kinzie finished her lemonade and set down the glass. "Are you sure, wonderful Mrs. Mackay, you're not equal to a train ride to Chicago? You'd find the whole political atmosphere charged with excitement. And what a coup it would be for me to bring to town such an astoundingly open-minded Southern woman!"

Eliza laughed. "I expect it would cause some talk. Thank you again, but my place is here for all reasons."

"I'm so thankful to the dear Lord, Mrs. Mackay, that Nellie has you. The poor child is being smothered in Savannah. She can't even speak freely to her own husband, you know. Mrs. Sarah Gordon was already away, of course, when I arrived in town, but I hear she's ramrod stiff in her views."

"Sarah is a close friend," Eliza said carefully, "but we try to stay on safe subjects."

"You do amaze me! Tell me, have you heard of the stunning speech Mr. Lincoln delivered at the June convention, the one they're calling the House Divided speech?"

"Mark Browning read it to me from his copy of the New York *Tribune.* A few phrases still ring in my ears and, I'm afraid, in my heart."

"And why are you afraid, Mrs. Mackay?"

"Because Mr. Lincoln just may be right. 'A house divided against itself cannot stand.' "

Juliette Kinzie's gaze moved across the shaded side yard. "Lincoln believes," she said, "that 'this government cannot endure permanently half slave and half free . . .' "

"Do you believe that, Mrs. Kinzie?"

"Yes. I also believe Mr. Lincoln is far more than just another ambitious politician. He's no demigod, he's wealthy now, of course, and he *is* ambitious, but he *sees.* He sees that 'it will become all one thing, or all the other . . .' "

"I pray not," Eliza said. "I've always been against the *spread* of slavery."

"Then, you're against your own South!"

At one and the same moment, Eliza felt admiration, pity, and sorrow for her guest. Admiration because Juliette Kinzie quite evidently thought deeply, felt sincerely that it was wrong owning people. She felt pity for her because there seemed to be no way to get across to her Eliza's own heart-deep concern for the Union. Her sorrow was for them all, North and South. She also felt a hollow kind of helplessness and so said nothing.

"Aren't you against your own South to be against spreading slavery, Mrs. Mackay? Don't all Southerners demand that they be permitted to take their poor benighted slaves with them when they move west?"

Eliza forced a smile and took advantage of her advanced age by remaining silent.

"I must say that was quite a sad smile, Mrs. Mackay, almost as though you've moved suddenly to a faraway place."

"That's a coincidence, Mrs. Kinzie," Eliza said, hearing the age in her own voice–age and the hollow helplessness. "I was just a bit over-whelmed at the surprising distance I suddenly felt between us." Quickly, she added, "In spite of the warm, pleasant way we're able to talk together. You see, we're not all lords of the lash down here. We're not all alike. There are hotheads and coolheads. Perhaps fewer coolheads now, but does everyone in Chicago agree with you and your husband about our peculiar institution?"

"No, of course not, but I thought–"

"Maybe now you won't think," Eliza interrupted, "that our beloved country is as sharply divided as too many believe it to be. There are thousands of Southerners who love the Union as I do, as you do. As you say your Mr. Lincoln does."

"But a divisive issue is a divisive issue," her guest said, with convic-tion. "We do use words, all of us, to express what we believe. I loathe the whole idea of slavery and I want it abolished. You own slaves, my dear lady. If I didn't keep the simplicity of knowing I'm on one side and you in the South are on the other, it could become dreadfully confusing."

"Life is confusing. Oh, my friend, *life is confusing.* The older I get, the more clearly I see how confusing . . ."

Juliette Kinzie was smiling. "And 'God is not the author of confusion.' "

"That's right. Mrs. Kinzie, will you promise me when you're back in Chicago, you'll try now and then to remember that down here we're not all poured out of one mold? We're caught, as our whole quaking country is caught, in an *emotional* tug-of-war and emotions don't easily succumb to reason."

FORTY- ONE

The first thing Burke wrote at the new desk he paid Sam to build for his just finished office at the back of his original property at Etowah Cliffs was a letter to William Mackay.

Alone in the tiny, compactly constructed building, he had sat for some minutes trying to decide whether he would write to his father-in-law or to William. True, he felt free to express himself to either man, but if he wrote to Mr. Browning, it just could turn out that he'd be stirring conflict, because Burke was writing this letter out of his own deepening need to confide all that he was pondering and worrying about. There would be much in the letter Mark Browning wouldn't dare let his wife read and undoubtedly he would feel he had to share any letter from Burke. Best, he decided, to write to Mackay, who could decide about letting Mr. Browning read it.

Settling his big body in the good chair—Sam was improving when it came to building furniture—he dipped the steel nib of a new pen in the inkwell and began with the date, November 1, 1858:

My dear Mr. Mackay,

I warned you when you were up here last summer that I might actually write a letter sometime and here it is. You'll be interested to learn, I think, that I'm writing from the privacy of my own new office. Natalie, I'm glad to report, is at her very best, even with Callie away in Macon at school. I worried some that Natalie might fret, but she reminds me that she doesn't intend ever to be a hovering mother. Callie hasn't mentioned her concern over Mary Cowper lately, either because the Lows are abroad or because school occupies her mind now. The Stileses are all well, but I confess W.H. may be the main reason I'm writing. I worry these days because I can see him growing more and more pessimistic about the nation and leaning more and more toward what he once hated: secession. The man actually seems bitter. The other night, he vowed that he no longer called the Compromise of 1850 a compromise, but a capitulation to the North. When Stephen Douglas and Lincoln were holding their big debates, I didn't dare bring up the subject. He considers a man like Republican A. Lincoln to be the Antichrist on earth. When I try to tell him that on the whole some good things have happened this year, like the first message actually sent on the new transatlantic cable, Minnesota admitted as a new state back in the spring, the Mormons some quieter now in Utah, he scoffs. What does he care about Minnesota when it joins the free-state column? Natalie even gave her Uncle W.H. a piece of her mind when he all but ignored the fact that the W. W. Gordons' new baby, Eleanor, was born in September, a strong and healthy little girl. "Your own son Henry is married to Willie Gordon's sister," Natalie scolded. "What kind of family loyalty is that? If you'd ever lost a child," she went on, "you'd think twice about sluffing off such good news!" I still find Natalie sitting beside the two little graves in Miss Lib's grove. We go on, but parents never forget the death of a child. I know I don't need to tell you that, old man.

I write, I guess, out of a kind of shut-off aloneness up here. Natalie still can't stand it when I worry aloud over the growing bitterness in the land. Mr. Stiles is so focused on the fact that the only real problem now is slavery, I can't discuss any other national issues with him. Whatever he stands for, Miss Lib is with him all the way. I thought sure he might be excited last month when the big news hit the papers that the first mail and overland stagecoach service—all the way from San Francisco to St. Louis—took place in only 24 days and 18 hours. He was too angry at Lincoln daring to debate a Democrat for a seat in the U.S. Senate to pay much mind. Tomorrow is election day in Illinois, and if the Democrats don't take control so that Douglas is sent back to the Senate, W.H. might explode, although he isn't keen on Stephen Douglas right now. It's just that the alternative is a red flag to W.H., a dangerous red flag in the person of that tall, (to me) peculiarly wise country lawyer, A. Lincoln. Natalie and I hope for an improvement in the Stiles disposition soon, though, because since John E. Ward of Chatham County, the presiding officer of the Georgia Senate, is resigning to take a diplomatic post in China, it looks almost certain that Gov. Brown will call a special election and that W.H. will win it. The man needs to be in active politics for sure.

Whatever happens, the often pro-Union lawyers up here in Cassville—Fred

Bentley, in particular—contend that, on a purely intellectual level, Lincoln won the debates. With Douglas sticking to his popular sovereignty, "let the people decide," and Lincoln declaring that a "house divided against itself cannot stand," it seems to me they've painted each other into corners. Mr. Mackay, I hope you are still favoring the preservation of the Union. I know we don't see eye to eye on slavery, but I'm thankful so many of our small farmers up here are strong Unionists. Please feel free to share this letter with your mother, and, if you think wise, with Browning. I just felt the need to write to you, because friendship is really proven in disagreement and we are friends. I am not a big praying man, but I do pray that should the time come when I might have to choose to fight for or against the South, I will know my own mind. It could be I'll be too old, so can avoid a decision. My regards to all there, and by the way, do you ever hear anything more about old John Brown? I wonder what he's doing these days. I'm building a new church in Cartersville and am doing well enough to have bought 200 acres of good land only a quarter of a mile from the piece I own. W. H. Stiles will farm it for me, thereby, in time, repaying five thousand dollars he owes me. I'm certainly not a farmer. I hope to die with a hammer in my hand and the good old Stars and Stripes flying over my head. I sincerely hope you are well. I value you.

Yr friend, Burke Latimer

William, as soon as he read Burke's good letter, decided to give in to the way he felt and go home. He wouldn't have to lie to his mother about not feeling well with Burke's letter to share. He could read it to her, then go to his room and rest a while. His head had been swimming some ever since he woke up this morning, but Doc Daniell was undoubtedly right that pork chops and gravy and biscuits were no help to a man William's size—especially for breakfast. Somehow, it always seemed to him that when his head swam, a little food helped. This time, it didn't.

He was just rounding the corner onto Broughton, taking his time, when from down the street he heard a man call his name. As soon as the man got close enough for William to recognize without his spectacles, he greeted Stuart Elliott warmly.

"I have good news, Mr. Mackay," Stuart said. "Lucinda just told me at breakfast that I'm going to become a father!"

Into William's mind right off came the question: How would Mary Cowper feel about this? He quickly dismissed it. She was not only abroad with Andrew Low and their children; she and Stuart were married to other people and it couldn't concern her.

"Congratulations, Stuart," he said, pumping the young man's hand.

"I can tell you it's a good moment becoming a father for the first time. For every other time, too, but the first is special. I know Lucinda's happy."

"Oh, yes, sir, she's walking on air." He laughed his still slightly wicked, self-deprecating laugh. "At least, she's as happy as an heiress married to an *assistant* teller could be."

"Money's good to have, Stuart, but it isn't the only thing that makes for happiness. On a day like this, though, you don't need a sermon from me on values. How's Lucinda's mother these days? Maybe the baby coming will help her some."

The smile vanished from Stuart's face. "Lucinda manages to stay reasonably contented in spite of her mother and the fact that we still live at the Sorrel house."

"I'd think Lucy might worry more than ever if you moved out."

"I vow that's the only reason I've agreed to stay. Poor Lucy doesn't deserve her mother—or me. This very morning when we went to Mrs. Sorrel's room to tell her the good news, she just sat there staring up at both of us as though she'd never heard of a baby!"

"Pathetic soul. My mother saw her not long ago and thought she seemed better."

"She does some days. No one ever knows how she'll wake up in the mornings, though. Will you give my regards to your mother?"

"I will. Heading home now." He stuck out his hand again. "You've found your way, haven't you, son?"

Gripping William's hand warmly, Stuart said, "As much as I suppose I'll ever find it, sir. In part, thanks to you."

William's head felt dizzy. "Nonsense," he said, needing to move along. "You and Lucinda did it together."

"You were my friend when I needed one. You and Mrs. Mackay. Please tell her my good news."

In the parlor at home, in spite of the dizziness, William managed to read Burke's letter to his mother and tell her Stuart's news. Relieved that his sisters were both out, he said, "I thought I'd go right up to my room, Mama, and answer Burke. The boy needs someone to understand how troubled and lonely he feels a lot of the time up there."

"But it's so near time for dinner, son," she said, peering at him closely. "Do you feel all right?"

"Sure," he lied. "I just ate too much breakfast to want any dinner today. Has Mark been here yet?"

"Not yet, but he'll surely come any minute. Can't you wait for him? I know he'll want to know about poor W.H.'s bitterness."

"Send him up if he does. Looks like all the trouble would calm down some for Thanksgiving and Christmas, doesn't it?" He got unsteadily to his feet and did his best to walk firmly to the parlor door, nervously aware that he was *not* fooling her. Burke's letter had upset her, but she was more upset by William.

"Maybe things will quiet down for a time," she said anxiously. "I'll tell Mark you heard from Burke."

"I'd as soon you didn't," he snapped. "Burke's really troubled down in his soul about what he'd do if worse comes to worst. I'd like to answer his letter without—a Yankee's influence."

"William!"

He had really shocked her, he knew, and regretted it. Why take it out on Mama just because his own head was swimming so fast that it made him cross and snappish? "I'm sorry, Mama," he said from the front hall. "I guess I just let things pile up inside me too much."

"Burke doesn't have to make any big decisions right now," she called as William began to plod up the stairs. "William? Can I send something to eat up to you?"

"Oh, maybe a little applesauce, if there's some left," he said, and tried to hurry up the stairs to escape any more questions.

Eliza told Mark Stuart Elliott's good news, but not a word about Burke's letter. To keep such an interesting letter from Mark made no sense to her whatever, but it was surely no time to upset William. He had not fooled her one bit. The boy was not feeling at all well or he wouldn't be home at this hour and surely he wouldn't leave for his room with Mark on his way over.

When Mark plunged almost at once into his own story of the way Caroline had acted at breakfast today, she understood his reason for asking so few questions about why William had gone to his room in the middle of a workday.

"It was almost like the night Colonel Robert Lee was here," Mark said, his face troubled. "Oh, she didn't weep the way she did that night, but she was terrified. Miss Eliza, Caroline has begun to listen to the women of the town who are sure we're about to have a Negro uprising!"

"Oh, Mark, no!"

"Caroline's hackles go up in defense of slavery, but so help me, sometimes I think she's just plain afraid of black people."

"Is there any special reason? Has there been trouble out at Knightsford plantation?"

"Not that we know of. The new overseer from Atlanta seems to have everything moving along smoothly. Caroline went to a meeting of the Widow's Help Committee yesterday and Mrs. James Clack was there stirring them all up."

"I fail to see how gossip about a nonexistent slave uprising is going to help widows and orphans," Eliza snapped. "That Clack woman tries my Christianity. Everyone who prattles without anything to base the prattle on tries my Christianity!"

"I like it now and then when you get all fired up," he said, smiling.

"Well, I fire, all right. Too often, I'm afraid. Was there any foundation at all for what those rattle-tongues were saying that so upset Caroline?"

"Nothing beyond rumors of what old John Brown might be up to. It seems they were rehashing the raid Brown led from Kansas into Missouri late last year. You remember, when he freed ten or eleven slaves and murdered a white man in the process."

She sighed heavily. "Do you know I sometimes wonder what it must be like to be John Brown's mother?"

Mark smiled again. "Only you would think of her, Miss Eliza."

"I don't even know whether she's alive or not, but what if William were a firebrand like John Brown? Brown is somebody's son, you know."

"Even in a good cause, a certain kind of person can act like a maniac. I wish we knew more about John Brown, but he must be a driven fellow, bent on freeing all slaves single-handedly."

"If we make room for a violent man like him, we have to make room for dear Caroline's terror," she said. "Heaven knows, not often, but Negroes *have* attacked their white owners. I well remember what Nat Turner did—like John Brown—all in the name of God."

She felt Mark's eyes on her. "Miss Eliza, I know there's more danger of an uprising on plantations than here in town, but do you ever fear what Caroline fears?"

"I think about it now and then, but I can't live with fear. No one can. Where is Brown now, do you know?"

"The New York papers say he's taking the slaves he freed to Canada, but he and his sons and the others in his band will be back in this country speaking up North, raising funds, bent, I'm sure, on freeing more Negroes, inciting them to rebellion where possible. The man's whole radical heart is in his cause. I guess he's a hero to many abolitionists by now."

Eliza sighed. "We both know poor Caroline, so levelheaded and serene most of the time, is helpless against her imagined terror. Still, the people on our plantations *do* hear about what Brown's doing. Most can't read, but as William says, they have a grapevine. Oh, Mark, insurrection of every kind has always been contagious. Tell me, did something trigger Caroline's outburst this morning?"

"I simply asked if she wouldn't enjoy spending a week or so out at Knightsford since the weather's so nice. I'll never forget how she looked!" Abruptly he stood to leave. "Her face still haunts me. The panic may seem imagined to us, Miss Eliza, but to her it is real!"

FORTY-TWO

Whatever caused William's dizziness, it appeared gone by Thanksgiving. William was acting almost like William again, working regularly and too hard. Everyone seemed happy that W.H. had won the special election to the Georgia Senate by an overwhelming majority of Chatham County voters. A pleasant Christmas and New Year's holiday, with far less wild talk in town, seemed, Mark thought, even to help Caroline. So that as they shared the morning paper at the start of the second week in January 1859, it was she who finally brought up the traumatic scene she'd caused before the holidays, brought it up of her own accord—rather abruptly.

"Have you wondered, darling, if I'd *ever* ask forgiveness for my outburst back last fall?"

She didn't need to refresh his memory. Her near hysteria that her own people at Knightsford might rise up and murder them all in cold blood should they visit, was still sharp in his memory. "There's certainly no need for my forgiveness," he said, reaching to take her hand. "You couldn't help it."

"I know," she said in her usual direct way. "I was—afraid. I'm still afraid, but I've had time to get hold of myself. I've decided *you* don't deserve an hysterical wife!"

"I don't have one."

"Where *my slaves* are concerned, you do."

He'd never, in all the years they'd been married, heard her use the expression "my slaves." As with most died-in-the-wool slave owners, Caroline avoided it like the plague. Mark had long since stopped trying to understand why. As always, he said nothing, but waited for her to take the conversation in whatever direction helped her most.

"I must seem a bundle of contradictions to you," she went on. "I do see myself as being an understanding wife—except when this issue comes up—and I have also seen you, dear Mark, through the long years, struggle to avoid it when possible."

He started to object, but she stopped him.

"Don't do that this time. I've prayed—dear Lord, how I've prayed—all over the holidays to find the courage to talk to you honestly about the whole thing! I think I can do that today. Not, I'm afraid, out of my own courage, but because that Lincoln man lost the election to the Senate in Illinois." Her smile poked a bit of fun at herself as she handed him the section of the *Daily Morning News* she'd been reading.

"Lincoln lost?" he asked, as noncommittally as possible.

"The Illinois legislature voted Douglas in. At least now, the South still has a powerful senator who firmly believes in letting the people decide. Your idol, Abraham Lincoln, failed because he would have fomented even more trouble. He's an out-and-out abolitionist."

Mark waited again, pondering his response. "What makes you think Lincoln's my idol?"

"Not this time," she said firmly. "You're not going to change the subject so easily, sir. I need to let you know I've made up my mind to control my fears. I may still have them, but they aren't going to upset *you* again. As for your idol, Mr. Lincoln, I consider him a dangerous man, but you are free to admire him and go right on with your own—political ideas." She laughed a little, again at herself. "There. Isn't that progress?"

Mark did not laugh, nor did he smile. He sat looking at her with more love than he'd ever felt. "I've—never said Lincoln is my idol. He isn't. I find him interesting, maybe even promising. He's certainly no John Brown abolitionist. Enough of Lincoln. I—I've never loved you as much as I do right now." He felt tears in his eyes and blinked them back. "Your husband is an incurable romantic. Married to you, he has no choice."

She got up abruptly and went to him. "His wife has no choice either," she whispered. "Oh, Mark, maybe it's just as well we have that one thorny issue to come between us now and then. What we have might be too perfect otherwise."

He stood, too, and took her in his arms. "You're perfect," he said, holding her close to him. Then, as he jumped back to avoid her offending hoopskirt, they both laughed. "You're perfect, that is, except for that infernal new style!"

"Aren't they dreadful? But give me a little more time. That's why I'm practicing so early in the day. I'm learning how to manage hoops. Not as fast as Mary, maybe, but I'm learning." She clung to him. "Oh, Mark, I'm trying *hard* to learn—how to deal with—everything! What if I didn't have you? And what if you were any different from—*you?* What if you were like other men?"

By spring, the Oregon territory had been admitted as a state, trouble raged again in Utah between Federal troops and armed Mormons, and a Southern Commercial Convention was meeting in Vicksburg, Mississippi. It was, William knew, labeled a commercial convention and there were commercial problems galore for the South, but to him, they all seemed to hinge on the trouble up North over slavery. On the whole, the newspapers mostly irritated William. He let off steam with his mother, for example, about the word from the National Women's Rights Convention held May 12 in New York.

"Read this, Mama," he said, handing the May 15 *Daily Morning News* to her as they sat together on her front porch, vainly hoping for a breeze.

She shoved the paper back at him. "You know I didn't bring my spectacles out here with me. You read it."

"Yankee *men* aren't the only crazy people up North. The women are crazy, too," he grumbled. "Listen to this petition Susan B. Anthony's hoopskirts just signed! They have the brass to demand that the word 'male' be eliminated in state constitutions, so that they legislate for all citizens, women included."

"*This* hoopskirt quite agrees, William," his mother said in her pert voice. "But read their petition to me, please."

"They seem only to pose a question, which sounds just like a woman," he grumbled. "But here it is: 'Where, under the Declaration of Independence, does the white Saxon man get his power to deprive all women and Negroes of their inalienable rights?' *What* inalienable rights?" William demanded. "I can read! The Declaration plainly states that all *men* are created equal!"

"Except black men, son?"

"Except black men, Mama." He gave her one of his rare smiles. "Do you have any idea how glad I am that you're my mama? And that if I thought at all that it was the thing to do, I'd give you the right to vote?"

"Thank you, William," she said tersely, but she was smiling, too, now. "Oh, mostly I thank you for feeling better! My old heart just about stopped when you seemed as though you might get sick again last fall. I wake up every morning thanking God you're all right. Our poor country isn't all right, but what's left of my family is, and, William, you're my sheltering rock. My fine, steady shelter."

"Even when you and Mark don't agree with me about women and Negroes?"

She nodded. "Even then. I thought Mark would be here by now, didn't you? He might have found something in one of his papers about the convention in Vicksburg. Oh, dear, William, are there any cool heads at that convention?"

"Sure," he said, a bit defensively. "And they are all good Southern men."

"Yes, son, I know they are."

William thought her voice gave a hint that it was time to change the subject. "I wonder how long it will take for the rest of the country to benefit from that oil well they're boring up there in Pennsylvania? It says here in the paper they expect to find petroleum that could replace whale oil, but I suppose they'll do their best to keep it up there away from us."

"Poor William. I wish you didn't always have to jab at Northerners." She sighed. "I suppose you do, though."

"Afraid so, Mama. But I try. Honestly, I try. It's—like a rage builds up inside me."

"I know," she said.

"That maniac John Brown, it says here, is back in this country making speeches and raising funds for more murderous attacks."

"Does it say he plans more murders?"

"Not in plain words, but you know he does."

"I do not know that. He could, of course, but I refuse to let myself fall into the panic that seems to grip other Savannah women—even your sisters. Just this morning, I forbade them both ever to say one more word about being afraid our Negroes will murder us in our sleep!"

By the end of May everyone in Savannah knew that the Southern Commercial Convention had advocated what to Mark was an appalling thing: *"All laws, state or Federal, prohibiting the African slave trade ought to be repealed."*

As Mark read the provocative words in the *Daily Morning News,* he felt a new dread. Why? he asked himself as he reached for his hat on the office rack to head for the Mackay house. Why would such a decision strike so much new dread in *him?* Was he falling into the trap of mounting hysteria that seemed lately to be spreading like fever across the city? Did the Southern Convention's advocating such a drastic measure mask something far darker?

Walking steadily toward Miss Eliza's house, he seemed to hear her voice from that dreadful night a decade ago—the night Colonel Robert Lee had dined with them all at the Mackays' and Caroline had lost control so completely over Lee's anti-slavery views that Miss Eliza urged Mark to take her home and hold her. What he heard again so plainly as he hurried along Abercorn now was Miss Eliza's voice on the porch that night right after he had told her that, even way back then, *he,* Mark, was truly afraid: "So am I, dear boy," she had said. "We have reason to be, because—without light in every heart, such a darkness could fall over this land that no one of us alive now may ever be able to see things whole again . . . "

Was that darkness now beginning to fall?

Heavy rain yesterday, the still damp air today, caused both his knees to hurt when he walked, but he quickened his stride because he had to be with the frail, aging beloved friend who could always turn up the light for him, at least a little.

"That Southern Convention statement is enough to plunge you into the darkness I spoke of that evening so long ago, Mark," Miss Eliza said when he joined her in their favorite porch rockers. "But look out there at all those bright, new green leaves. My azalea blossoms are about gone —I found only one or two early this morning—but there's even more promise in all that new green on the bushes. Flowers go fast, leaves hold their promise for a long time. Azalea leaves will be doing their best to keep us feeling cool all summer, just as the live oaks will. The Lord Himself is behind every new leaf."

Mark took the glass of lemonade she handed him and returned her smile.

"I meant to walk past Forsyth Park on my way," he said, almost sheepishly, "to admire our handsome new fountain. I confess I let that article about the Southern Convention blot it right out of my mind. I can't explain why it shook me. I just know it did. Would you like me to take you to Forsyth Park later this afternoon? Jupiter can drive us and we can watch the new fountain together."

"Another day, dear boy," she said, "if that's all right with you. William wants me to look over some papers. I—I'm afraid it's—his will."

Mark grinned. "You're afraid? Any wise man has a will made far ahead of when it might be needed."

"I know that, but as careful and wise as William's always been, this is his first will." She set down her glass and gave him a long, loving look. "Don't worry about William. I'm not going to. I just feel I want to be here when he comes home." She reached to touch Mark's hand resting on the arm of his chair. "I know you were expecting me to lift your spirits, dear boy. With all my heart, I wish I knew how."

He smiled at her. "It's past time I began to find a way to lift yours. Old habits are hard to break, I guess. When I worry, I—run to you. But I do feel better just being here and, Miss Eliza, by some means we do have to stay on top of everything that's happening, don't we?"

She straightened her stooped shoulders. "Yes, Mark, and we will, we will. All the way on top!"

FORTY-THREE

*E*arly on an overcast, damp July morning, the sun already beating down through low-hanging coastal clouds, Mary Browning slipped out of the house while Caroline attended a meeting of the Widow's Help Committee and hurried to the Low mansion. She wasn't actually slipping out. Mary had told a surprised Gerta that she was going out to make a call.

If her mission had not been so deadly serious, she might have laughed at Gerta's gaping surprise. Mary had been Mrs. Jonathan Browning of Savannah for fourteen years and until today she had made not one social call alone. A few years ago, Miss Eliza had actually asked why Mary never visited anyone without her mother-in-law or Jonathan in tow. "You're Mrs. Jonathan Browning now, Mary, and if people still prattle about you now and then, they certainly keep it to themselves. I don't think they do. Why don't you venture out on your own?"

Dear Miss Eliza had seemed to understand when Mary replied, "If I get bitten because I rouse a sleeping dog, it is my fault."

Today was different. Even Jonathan didn't know yet that she was all but certain they were going to have another child early in the next year, 1860. Mary was both happy and frightened. Happy because maybe this time she would give Jonathan a son, but in the pit of her stomach she still felt the dread that another child could bring fresh heartbreak.

Willow, so full of health and life, had sickened and died in two short days! She was hurrying to ask a friend she trusted, who had also lost a child and now, just home from across the ocean, had recently given birth to still another. Mary Cowper's new infant daughter, little Jessie Low, on July 29, had just been baptized at Christ Church in Savannah. Mary and Jonathan and Mama and Papa Browning had been there.

I know I acted strange all through the ceremony, Mary thought, as she climbed the steep front steps of the Low house. I did, or Jonathan would not have asked so many questions last night. There was no reason for me to cry at the baptism except that *I am afraid*, she thought, as she gave a few timid knocks at the great front door.

Her young friend Mary Cowper was glad to see her, and within minutes after they sat down together in the grand front parlor of the Low mansion, she was pouring out her fears.

"Jonathan deserves to know that I am going to give him another child," she said, "but I am so afraid! I am afraid for me and I am also afraid for Jonathan."

"Oh, Mary, Mary," her friend said, "of course you're afraid."

"Jonathan and I still cry tears for Willow. Do you and Mr. Low still cry for your baby who lived but one day?"

Mary Cowper fell silent. With one hand, she fingered the braid on her costly silk morning dress. Her friend, Mary thought, looked like a fashionable European lady must look and yet, on her pretty face, there was sadness as heavy as a rain cloud.

"Do we cry—together? No. Mr. Low and I have a most luxurious life, a good life, but I–I do my crying alone, Mary. For the one day my baby lived, I was almost too ill to know much of what was happening. I barely remember what he looked like, but I still miss him. Mr. Low so wanted a son. To this day, he longs for a son, an heir."

"You are still in love with Stuart Elliott, Mary Cowper?"

She might as well have slapped her young friend across the face. For an instant, Mary thought she'd angered her and began to beg forgiveness. "I do not gossip," Mary said in her direct way. "I have been gossiped about too much."

"Yes, of course you have. And I'm not accusing you," Mary Cowper said softly. "You just took me by surprise."

"It is none of my business," Mary whispered.

"Maybe it is and maybe it isn't," the grand lady of the fine house said in a small voice that sounded for all the world exactly the way Mary Cowper used to sound as a little girl at Etowah Cliffs.

"Do not answer my wrong question, please! I am sorry."

"I–hadn't planned to answer it."

"You hadn't?" Mary asked.

"No. As for your giving Jonathan another baby, by all means, be happy! And oh, Mary, be happy that you and Jonathan are–lovers." Mary Cowper's great, dark eyes searched hers. "You do still love him with all your heart, don't you?"

"With more than my heart," Mary said simply. "With all of my body and mind and soul. Without Jonathan I die." She laughed a little nervously. "I mean–without Jonathan I *would* die!"

"You're speaking so well these days, truly," Mary Cowper said. "Mary?"

"I am listening."

"All of life is a risk. You do risk more sadness when you have another child. I was terribly nervous, but it's–all right. Look at me. Can you look straight into my eyes and see that something good, often exciting and pleasant usually replaces what we've lost or walked away from? Can you see that, Mary?"

At that moment, Mary would have given almost anything if her command of English had been good enough to let her friend know that indeed she did see. That not only the two living children but even her privileged life with Mr. Low had somehow replaced loving Stuart. She would never find the words for all that, so what she said was: "Thank you for not making me feel ashamed that I mentioned Stuart or that I ran to you with my–fear."

"Surely, you've told Jonathan!"

Mary shook her head no. "But I tell him–I *will* tell him this very night!"

"Good. And will you please pray that the next time, I–can give Mr. Low a son?"

Mary blurted out what came to her guileless mind before she realized how cruel it was: "Lucinda gave a son to Stuart!" She could have bitten off her tongue.

"Please don't look so stricken, Mary," her friend begged after a long silence. "We've been friends long enough for me to know you don't have a hint of malice or ill will anywhere in your heart. I think I even know–why you said that. Will you come again after you've told Jonathan the wonderful news?"

The next day, July 31, there was such a hard storm that a store on Montgomery Street was struck by lightning and burned. Whitaker Street, from Liberty down to Broughton, was flooded.

Even William stayed home from his office and, because his mother had a bad headache, was pestered half the day by Sarah, of all people, trying to do nice things for him.

The fourth time she barged into his room, first with tea, then a cup of soup, then cookies and milk, he yelled, "Sarah, what now? I'm just about to lock that door from the inside! Can't you see I'm trying to get some of this paperwork done? A man can't get to his office through that downpour out there, but it does look like he might get a chance to do a little work in his own house."

"This isn't your house, William Mackay, it's Mama's house."

William leaned his straight chair back on two legs and grinned. "I reckon habit's a hard thing to change with us both, Sister," he said. "I bawl you out and you snipe back. Come on in and take a load off your feet."

"You're right. I do snipe and we have picked on each other for more years than either one of us wants to admit. Could I talk to you just a few minutes without being smacked down with condescension?"

William gave her a quizzical look. "Why don't you try me?"

"I'm scared half out of my wits every night when I go to bed!"

"Why on earth?"

"Aren't you scared at all that our nigras might turn on us?"

"Well, now, let me think about that."

"Do not, do *not* tease!"

William rubbed his chin thoughtfully.

"There's old Hannah—I'm fifty-five, she must be close to eighty. She does scare me some. And there's Emphie, who's got to be nearly seventy-five and must weigh at least ninety pounds. And out in the yard doin' his odd jobs, there's old Solomon and he's—"

Sarah's face contorted with what William saw was real fear. "Stop it!" She wailed and broke into such hard, wracking sobs that the only thing he could think of doing was to go to her and put his arms around her.

He held her until she calmed down enough to gasp, "At night, William—what's to stop even—an *old* nigra from—cleaving our heads open while we sleep?"

He was so unused to showing affection or tenderness to Sarah, the only thing that came to him to say was: "There, there, there."

It didn't help, because his sister was sobbing again as though she might choke. "I–I love Mama so much–and I–love Kate–and *you*, Brother–I love you, too! And–I don't want to–be murdered–and taken away from any of you!"

"Well, now, that's comforting," he said, attempting again to tease since nothing else had worked. "All these years I've wondered if you held one shred of affection in your heart for your old brother. How many times have I tried to make a bridge to you only to get repulsed?"

With a strength he didn't know she had, Sarah pulled free, flounced to the door, and jerked it open. "What do you think *you* just did?" she demanded.

After she'd banged shut the door, William stood there trying to take it in that his sister must really be terrified of their faithful, old family servants. God in heaven, he thought, what is coming over us all? The whole town's full of crazy people!

From the hall outside his room, he could now hear both sisters talking in low voices. He put his ear against the door and listened.

"From now on, Kate Mackay, I'm *not* one bit afraid," Sarah announced.

"Why, whatever did William say to you to turn you around?" Kate asked.

"I don't know what he said to me, but as always, he made me so angry, I'm cured. I'm not scared of one single thing on this old earth!"

The next morning, Jonathan awakened Mary by kissing her nose, her forehead, her scarred cheek, and when she opened her eyes, he closed them both again with kisses. "This is the day, beautiful Mary," he whispered. "We kept our bright secret just the way you wanted, all day yesterday through the storm. We can tell Mama and Papa this morning at breakfast, can't we?"

Her arms circled his neck. "Oh, yes, dear Jonathan. Soon, as soon as we dress, we can tell them. Will they find a way to hold their joy, do you think?"

He laughed. "That will be their problem, not ours." When she bounded out of bed, he grabbed for her and missed, jumped up, ran after her, and took her again in his arms. "We managed to contain our joy, didn't we?" he asked, laughing down at her.

"What was it–Willow used to say? We did–'sort of.' "

"Oh, thank you," he breathed. "Do you know that's the first time you've made a happy little joke about something she said?"

"Yes, Jonathan, I know. I have thought other little jokes, but only now—oh, only now, can I speak them!"

FORTY-FOUR

*F*or *twenty-one* long years, the first thing every morning when William woke up, his mind and his prayers had gone to his
dead wife, Virginia, and his two dead children: "For this day, dear Lord,
please give them all my love!"

Still lying flat in his bed, today things seemed different. This morning, he felt no need to send his love—he felt no need to give them back to
God—a thing he'd struggled to do all this time. Instead, he sat up in bed
fully expecting to see all three of them, to hear Virginia's laughter, to
see his daughter, Delia, curl her fingers the way she did waving at him
when she was little. He almost mentioned to Virginia that infant William
was fussing and needed her attention.

Both bare feet on the floor, he shook his head, rubbed it. The
dizziness was back again! Bad this time, but under it a kind of quiet
peace that made him feel sure he could bathe and shave and dress and
get right on to work without too much trouble . . .

He slipped his nightshirt over his head and gave himself a pretty
good sponge bath, then lathered up his face to shave. He shaved every
morning of his life, but for some reason today it made him think of the
mornings he'd shaved on Natalie's back porch when Callie had made a
to-do about seeing that he had warm water and a clean towel. He should
write to Callie at school in Macon more often. They were fast friends

the last time he'd been up there to visit. And because his own little family *was* so close this morning, his heart moved in a great swell of love toward Natalie, who, all those years ago, had almost lost her own life trying to stay afloat in that big, mean ocean while she held on to his little son. He wondered about Burke, too. He hadn't heard from him in a while, but he would surely like to know if the matter of Burke's allegiance—North or South—still plagued the boy.

Right now, splashing off the blobs of lather from his face, the whole country, both North and South, the very idea of a war seemed so remote, he almost whistled. He did try, but couldn't make a sound. His lips felt numb.

He reached for a towel to dry off his face. Callie must have been there, or Virginia, because there was a clean white one hanging right where Virginia kept it for him every morning. He tested his ability to walk a straight line across the room to where his wardrobe stood. Made it fine. Then, all dressed for the office, he headed for the bedroom door.

I'm still dizzy, he thought, but I surely teased the fear right out of old Sarah yesterday. The thought brought a smile as he opened the door and moved, he believed, firmly and directly to the top of the steep stairs that would take him down to eat breakfast with Mama.

Eliza Mackay had just taken her place at the table and was beginning to cream her coffee when she heard the worst thump and racket she'd ever heard—right inside the house. It sounded like something heavy or somebody falling down the stairs—all the way down those steep stairs! It kept on coming, the racket, the thumping, and when it finally stopped, she sat there foolishly trying to remember how long it had lasted.

Then she screamed.

*B*efore *Mary* and Jonathan had quite finished sharing their own joy at the coming of another child, Mark, elated, kissed Caroline and Mary, hugged Jonathan, and grabbing his top hat, ran out the back door and across the garden shouting for Jupiter Taylor.

"Morning, Mr. Mark," Jupiter called, hurrying toward him from the open door of the carriage house. "What you doin' out so early, sir?"

"Saddle the King, Jupiter—and hurry! No, wait a minute. You need to know the happy news." A hand on his driver's shoulder, he made the glorious announcement that he and Caroline were going to have another grandchild!

"Lord be blessed," Jupiter cried. "If ever a man on this ol' earth needed a grandchild, it's you, Mr. Mark! An' I'm the happiest free nigger in Savannah—maybe in the whole state of Georgia! But you gonna try to *ride* King to the office today? You sure you're limber enough?"

"You bet. I'm in a hurry and it'll take too long to hitch up the carriage. Anyway, I'm not going to the office. I'm on my way by the fastest means to tell Miss Eliza Mackay!"

When, minutes later, Jupiter and the high-strung black riding horse appeared, Mark had already hauled a mounting stool into position, so that with a minimum of exertion for them both, Jupiter hoisted him into the saddle and with a surprised, glad snort from King and a shout of triumph from Mark, man and horse headed out the stable gate, in the direction of Broughton Street.

In his ears, as he galloped along in the almost cool breeze off the river, Mark could still hear Jupiter's parting words: "Don't you let that horse forget *you're* really the king today, Mr. Mark!"

He was. Mark Browning felt stronger and more powerful than *any* king and there would be time, once he'd told Miss Eliza the wonderful news, to thank God properly. "I am thankful, though," he said aloud, "but, Lord, isn't there some way You could get this horse to move a little faster?"

In sight now of the Mackay house, he hoped fervently that William hadn't left early for his office. Next to Miss Eliza, he needed to tell William. Good news such as this would surely cheer his old friend, who lately had struck Mark as being overworked, anxious, at times almost irritable. The bond with William had only strengthened with the years, even in the face of their disagreement about the troubled country. Mark tried, as he knew William tried, to keep their high regard for each other open and free. "Regard" was a flimsy word when he thought how he depended upon William. Aside from Jonathan, he was the only gentleman friend in town Mark really trusted. The only man who, even in opposition, shared Mark's own desperate longing that the country not be split apart.

He rode King up to the iron hitching post in front of the Mackay house, managed rather agilely, he thought, to dismount, and as he tied the reins around the familiar post, he smiled at himself because, in his excitement, he was all thumbs.

His heart, at least, took the front steps two at a time. Thankful that the door stood open and welcoming in the heat of the first day of August, he called Miss Eliza's name, then, without waiting, rushed into the shadowy entrance hall and stopped as though he'd been shot. There, sprawled on the floor at the foot of the stairs, lay William, blood on his face and shirt. Anyone could tell William was not ill again. *He was dead.*

Even so, when Miss Eliza's hollow voice spoke his name from the parlor, Mark was kneeling, fingers pressed against William's limp, still warm wrist.

"Miss Eliza—oh, Miss Eliza!"

"Come here, Mark, would you, please?" she called.

Inside the dear, familiar parlor, he stood looking down at her in her little rocker.

Dry-eyed, she looked up at him. Then both her arms lifted and he fell on his knees, his head in her lap.

"We didn't have anyone strong enough to help us get William up— off the floor," she said. "Old Solomon's not here."

"When—when did it—happen?" Mark whispered.

"Not half an hour ago. You—you came at just the—right time, dear boy."

Mark lifted his head and saw that tears were starting down her tender, wrinkled cheeks. He would have to think what to do next. It was up to him to do something.

"Where are the girls?" he asked.

"I don't know exactly. The last time I saw them, Kate was practically carrying Sarah upstairs." She shook her head. "Oh, Mark, poor, poor Sarah! This—will hit her very hard, won't it? No matter how she plagued William, she loved him."

"And William knows—*knew* that," Mark said uselessly. How long might it take for him to realize that William, so a part of all their lives, was gone? He *was* gone, and they couldn't leave his body lying there on the floor of the hall.

As though reading Mark's thoughts, Miss Eliza murmured, "I—need to ask—William what it is—we do next . . ."

"I know you do," he said hoarsely. "I need to ask him, too."

After hurrying to a neighbor's house for help with William's body, Mark sat for a time with Miss Eliza, then rode to the mortician's himself, promising her to return just as soon as he'd told his own family.

"God spaces things for our benefit, Mark," Miss Eliza said as he took her hand at the door. "You came here to tell me about the new life coming to Jonathan and Mary. William went away. There's a pattern in it somewhere, isn't there? One we can count on. Don't hurry too much, but—I'll be watching for you."

"Oh, Mark," Caroline gasped when he told her, "poor Miss Eliza! What will Miss Eliza do without William?"

"What will—I do without him?" Mark whispered. "William was— always there. In a hundred ways, day in and day out, everyone is going to miss William." Then, for the first time, he thought of Natalie and

Burke. He'd promised Miss Eliza he'd write to Eliza Anne, but until now, he hadn't been clear enough in his own mind to think of the deep bond William and Natalie had always shared . . . William and Burke, too.

"Caroline," he breathed. "This is going to devastate Natalie!" He rubbed his forehead. "I must get to the office—write both those letters from there—tell Jonathan. Get back to Miss Eliza. You remember, Caroline, how our son helped William way back when Jonathan was just a boy and William wouldn't come out of his room after the loss of his own family? Jonathan visited him every day. He's going to be crushed by this." Hands out in a helpless gesture, he half sobbed, "William wouldn't believe how crushed we all are! Don't you wish I could tell him?"

"Oh, darling," she said, taking both his hands in hers. "Yes, yes! Everyone needs William as a guide through all of this." A look of near panic swept her face. "What in the name of heaven will we do when we lose Miss Eliza? Mark, she's eighty-one!"

"*No!*" The sharp edge in his own voice startled him. "No, not today —not *today.*"

She had taken his hat from his limp hands. Now she let it drop to the floor and rushed to hold him. They were locked in a desperate, helpless embrace when Mary slipped out of the drawing room.

"I can help in any way?" she asked. "I could not help hearing. I loved Mr. William, too!"

"Of course you did, Mary," Caroline said, turning to look at her. "We all loved him. You once saved his life."

Mark felt a new, almost painful rush of love for Caroline that left him weak. She *had* overcome her fear of Mary's Indianness. It must be all gone. Mary and Indian Ben had indeed once saved William's life years ago after he'd been robbed in the upcountry. He felt grateful, relieved somehow, that Caroline was the one who remembered it.

"Ben loved him, too," Mary said.

"Yes, Mary. Your brother loved him." When Mary stooped to pick up the top hat, Caroline thanked her and added, "Papa Mark is going to the office now to tell Jonathan."

"I go for you, Papa Mark?"

"No, thank you, Mary," he said, still clinging to Caroline's arm. "I know you want to do something. Jonathan will, too, but . . ."

"But we cannot bring back Mr. William."

"That's right, dear," Caroline breathed. "Go, Mark. You know Jonathan always helps. I'm sure he can do something to help Miss Eliza, and

Kate and Sarah, too. The newspapers need to be notified. The funeral arrangements . . ."

"Yes," Mark said woodenly. "Jonathan will help. Sarah especially needs it. This is hitting her very hard."

"I've already made up my mind to talk to her," Caroline said firmly. "After all, I despised my own grandmother. Maybe I can say something that will give poor Sarah a little peace."

"You and Ethel Cameron had time to talk it out, though, before she died," Mark said hopelessly.

"Do we know that Sarah and William didn't?"

"No," he said. "I didn't get a chance to ask her. She–took to her bed."

"There's something else I mean to do, too," Caroline said, and Mark began to sense her new strength to a degree that he wondered if his own grief was causing him to imagine things. This strength flowing from Caroline did seem new, as though it had somehow begun to come over her as the three of them stood there in the hallway . . . as though she were changing before his very eyes. Or was she making a secret new resolve?

"I can help you, Mama Caroline?" Mary asked.

"No, thank you, Mary. I've just decided I will be the one to write to both Eliza Anne *and* Natalie before I go to the Mackays'. You've had enough to bear already today, Mark. Just go to Jonathan and for today, at least, leave everything else to me." When he tried to thank her, she stopped him. "I find I need to write those letters–especially the one to Natalie–for my own sake."

Only after Mark left for his countinghouse did either Caroline or Mary remember that between her Uncle William and Mary Cowper there had also been an affectionate bond. William, along with Mark, had done all in his power to help Natalie prevent the marriage to Andrew Low. Right or wrong, they had all three tried to give the girl a chance to make up her own mind. They had failed, and as far as Caroline knew, Mary Cowper seemed content now, but she deserved to know from someone close that William was gone.

"There *is* something you can do, Mary," she said, on her way upstairs to her writing desk. "You can walk over to the Low house and tell Mary Cowper. You two are friends. You'll tell her in just the right way."

Mary was so pleased to be trusted, she clapped her hands. "Thank you, Mama Caroline! Thank you. I will change my dress and go now."

From the graceful stair, Caroline turned back to her. "And, Mary—I'm truly happy that you and Jonathan will have another child."

Beaming up at her, Mary asked, "Even if my child–look Cherokee?"

Her question stabbed Caroline. Believing in honesty as she had since her own childhood, she wondered why Mary's honesty was so disarming. She looked away until she could return a genuine smile. "Yes, even if–that, Mary."

Compelled by the need to get right at the letters, Caroline went straight to her writing desk and wrote:

Savannah
1 August 1859

Abruptly, she stopped. The temptation to include the Stileses and the Latimers was strong. Writing one letter would make the difficult job far easier. If she knew they would all be sharing the same letter, she could at least postpone putting her new resolve down on paper to Natalie. The firm resolve made downstairs only minutes ago: to be truly open with Mark. Didn't she herself need time to get accustomed to the idea? The new resolve would have to last for the remainder of her life. Shouldn't this letter contain only the news of today's grief over William?

"I am simply trying to squirm out of telling Natalie that her mother has finally grown up!" she said aloud, and began again, her pen flying across the page:

My dear Natalie and Burke,

When I finish this letter, I will be writing to Eliza Anne and W.H. with the same tragic news that dear William Mackay died quite suddenly this morning at home. He was on his way downstairs, fully dressed for the office, fell all the way to the hall below, and Miss Eliza found him. We are all devastated, but there is also happy news that Mary and Jonathan will give us a new grandchild early next year. That sustains your father and me, because new life is even dearer in the face of death, but our grief over William is enormous. He had seemed fairly well for some time and the shock to everyone is great. Natalie, I beg you to write to Miss Eliza and Kate, and to poor Sarah, who mourns terribly, since she and William tended to rub each other the wrong way at times. I know you both held William in high esteem and our hearts go out to you, too. We will send more details soon.

Caroline laid down the pen and scanned what she had written. It seemed all right so far. Now the hard part began. She dipped the pen again and wrote:

If I address the following to Natalie, I ask Burke's indulgence, although he is more than welcome to read it. *Just this morning, my dear daughter, a permanent change has come over your mother.* Such a change that even I am not yet comfortable or even acquainted with it. With all my heart, I believe our friendship has grown over the past few years and perhaps if I am able to put into words the gist of my new resolve, you will find still more room in your private heart for your mother, who has struggled for so long with her own raging battle over the one area in me where your poor father has had to tread softly for all the years of our married life. I have accused him time and time again of spoiling you. He did spoil you, of course, but my accusations were, I now find, hateful and unjust, because as I held him in my arms late this morning in his grief over his beloved William, I, quite *unexpectedly,* saw how much added anxiety I, who only loved him, have caused the dear man. I find I am not at all sure what, if any, beliefs you hold, Natalie, where slavery is concerned. (I even hate writing the word!) I am not sure you feel strongly one way or another. No matter. What does matter is that, although I cannot change my own bitterness at the hated abolitionists who so flail us with false accusations, *I can do my level best to change* my own defensiveness with your gentle father. *I mean to do just that.* Any human being, especially such a superior one as Mark Browning, has a right to his own opinion in this land of liberty. For our entire life together, he has had to be careful, to walk as though treading on eggshells around his touchy wife anytime the detested subject came up. None of this means that I see our Knightsford people or any owner's people as worse off than the common laborer in the North who works a fourteen-hour day and at times prefers to stay on at the workplace rather than go home to hideous, airless, rat- and bug-infested lodgings. I have made myself stop writing here for a time because none of that is the issue in this letter! The issue here is your mother, Natalie, and she hereby promises you (and Burke) to find a way to give your blessed father more freedom. He will miss William and their talks for as long as he lives. Miss Eliza is going to leave us, too, one of these days. Of course, he has Jonathan and, I am sure, will now lean heavily on him, but ask Burke if it isn't important in a unique way that a man be able to speak freely, without fear of upsetting a touchy wife! Dear Natalie, there it is and I promise to do all in my power to change my ways.

I know you will both mourn William's passing. Everyone who knew him will miss the man. And will go on missing, because too many depended upon William Mackay for both large and small favors and for understanding. Even Sarah, who plagued him, once she's forgiven herself (and I mean to try to help her do that), will miss turning to her brother for all kinds of help. I find that even I regret not having made more over William, not favoring him more in various ways, but he was so reserved and so available, we all may have rather taken him for granted. When Callie learns of it, I want her to know her grandfather and I realize how much William's death will hurt her, too. He did and does love you very much, Callie, and we can all rejoice in the sure knowledge that William is, at long last, back with his little family.

I'm sure you'll hear from your father when he has had time to get his bearings. Next to Miss Eliza's, I feel somehow that Mark's grief may be the most painful of all. Sorry to have been the bearer of such tragic news. This letter, dear Natalie and Burke and Callie, has been written from my heart.

Yr loving mother,
Caroline Cameron Browning

FORTY-SIX

On a late August afternoon, unusually hot and muggy even for Savannah, Jonathan sat on the corner of his father's office desk reading aloud to him from the New York *Tribune.* For ten minutes or so, he'd been reading this and that, attempting to break through the cloud which had hung over Papa's mind since the day William died. Jonathan tried only briefly to interest his father in a "novelty piece" called *Pike's Peak, or The Search for Riches,* which had opened the season in New York at the Old Bowery Theater. The diversion didn't work, although, as always, Papa was politely tolerant.

I don't mind that he sits with his back to me looking out the window, Jonathan thought, but I know what he's staring at. It isn't the river or the ships. He's got that carefully clipped piece from the *Georgian* in his hands. I know as surely as if his back weren't turned that he's reading it again. Even Jonathan knew it by heart: "August 3, 1859. The funeral of Mr. William Mackay will take place this afternoon from the residence of Mrs. Mackay, on Broughton Street."

The brief clipping was nearly worn to shreds the last time Jonathan had seen it several days ago. His father was never without it. Maybe he's just trying to convince himself that it's true, that old William is really gone.

"Funny, son," his father said, turning around, "the old *Georgian* is gone right along with William."

"The newspaper's only suspended, Papa. Once the advertisements pick up again, it'll be back, I'm sure."

"I wonder how many times William and I have launched into one of our talks from something one of us found in the *Georgian*. The very last time, I think, had to do with the fact that our economy isn't suffering down here. That up North, while they're past the worst of the panic, its consequences go on causing trouble."

"You mean," Jonathan said almost too brightly, "the sniping and bad feeling among the people up there in spite of all their resources, machinery, droves of workers, the continuing flow of gold from California? It does seem strange that they don't have some kind of leveling out."

"Well," Papa said, "the farmers are still angry at the middlemen and the Eastern buyers. Workers are fuming with employers, depositors quarrel with their bankers . . . William knew all that. He kept telling me we're blessed. Our economy suffered only slightly for a short time. William loved to remind me that, indeed, Cotton is King!"

"What do *you* think, Papa?"

For a long time, his father just sat there. Jonathan, even in his eagerness to draw his father into a conversation, waited.

"The deepest scar left anywhere in the country from the brief financial panic is between North and South, son," he said at last. "If I'm able to think at all anymore, that's what I believe. Men down here, whether they grow cotton or tobacco, still blame what they call avaricious Yankee bankers, factors, and jobbers for robbing them of their profits."

"I thought things seemed to be lightening up a little. Have you heard quite as much hate talk around town lately?"

His father shook his head. "You know I don't discuss anything these days, except with you, son. William was the only man with Southern sympathies to whom I dared speak my mind."

"You do have me," Jonathan said. "Do I help at all?"

He saw tears well up in Papa's eyes. "Oh, son, of course you help!"

"Miss Eliza will be feeling well enough again soon to discuss the country with you. You can talk to her and not have to worry."

"I know, I know. She's still so affected by Sarah's dark moods, though, I hesitate to bring up anything that might add to her burdens."

"Mama said when she went to see Sarah the day before the funeral, she thought maybe Sarah understood that where William is now, he's already forgiven her for picking at him all those years."

"I hope so." Papa picked up a sheaf of market reports. "I'd better get through these. It's almost time for us to go home to dinner."

"I've already been through them, you won't need to. I made our clients' billings first thing this morning. Don't you want me to see what else is in the New York paper?"

"Not especially, thank you."

"Oh, but listen to this!" Jonathan turned a page, flattened the paper, and began to read: 'On August 25, Secretary of War John B. Floyd received an anonymous letter warning him that John Brown, also known as Osawatomie Brown, plans to enter the state of Virginia at Harpers Ferry on the upper Potomac to begin a slave insurrection. Little attention was paid to the report because it is not considered reliable.' There, what do you think of that?"

"I'd say we haven't heard the last of John Brown. The Federal troops in the North can't seem to catch up to him. He's lionized by the elite abolitionists *and* the literati. The man leads an enchanted life so far, but although I'd like to see an end to slavery, too, I *don't* like Brown's violence."

Not wanting to tire his father, Jonathan tossed aside the paper. "I hate the thought of any kind of killing," he said.

For a long moment, his father studied him. "And do you hate slavery as much as I do, Jonathan?"

"I've already told you I expect so. If I ever had to choose sides in a war, though, I don't know what I'd do."

After another pause, his father said, no longer looking at Jonathan, "William always believed since you're a native Savannahian, you'd fight for the South."

"He never told me that."

"He only told me once. William and I did not see eye to eye on many things, son, but he always knew when *not* to hurt me or push me too far." Papa sighed heavily. "Do you really think there's a bit less talk of secession in town now?"

"I haven't heard as much, honestly." Jonathan beamed his sunny smile. "That's one reason I don't waste time trying to decide what I'd do. If there's no secession, there won't be a war." Jonathan leaned across the desk to touch his father's slender, aging hand. "Even Mama doesn't seem so afraid of a Negro uprising. She hasn't said anything lately to you, has she?"

"You're right! I don't think she's mentioned it once since William went away. She's been only considerate of me."

"Which is what she always tries to be."

"Always, always. She's been trapped all her life by her need to defend slavery. Even a loving, loyal woman like your mother can't reach out to help someone else if she's caught in a trap."

FORTY-SEVEN

With breakfast over on the clear, bright morning of October 21, Andrew Low took Mary Cowper's arm to escort her to his splendid carriage waiting in front of the house. She was on her way to get Grandmother Mackay for a trip to Laurel Grove Cemetery to inspect the newly carved monument just set in place at William's grave. She smiled at him when he helped her up the steep carriage step.

"Thank you, Mr. Low," she said as he stood looking at her, his perfectly groomed red beard glistening in the sunlight. "Isn't it wonderful that the day is so beautiful for Grandmother's sake? Thank you for the use of your carriage, too, of course."

Low returned her smile a bit sadly, she thought, and said, "My dear Mary Cowper, this is your carriage, too. Must you always thank me for small comforts you, as my wife, so justly deserve? I wish you wouldn't. Could you promise me that?"

"I'll try to remember," she said. "You're most kind and always generous."

He laughed a little. "So you've said many times. But, my dear, dare I hope for a somewhat more personal word than 'kind' or 'generous'?"

Why, she wondered, carefully keeping her smile in place, did he always wait for some public place to ask a provocative question? "But you are both kind and generous, sir," she said, "and—quite dear."

Low bowed elaborately, reached up to touch her gloved hand, sent his warm regards to her grandmother and his continuing sympathy in her loss. Then he instructed Earl, his driver, and raised his arm in farewell as the carriage pulled away.

Mary Cowper waved twice, hoping to please him, and turned her thoughts at once to what she might say to Grandmother Mackay as they rode together on their sad mission. The tombstone would be of medium size, quite plain. She hoped it would be like Uncle William, who had loathed any sign of pretense but appreciated quality. She smiled a little as the carriage rocked through the ruts of the sandy street, because she had just remembered the day Uncle William had seen her elegantly furnished house for the first time and had stopped to run his hand over the back of a fine Chippendale dining chair. "Puts me in mind of Burke's work," he'd said. "That man can take a chunk of hill-country pine and turn it into a thing of beauty whether it's a chair or a table or a plain old footstool." Well, she thought, if something is well made, what's the difference whether it's made by a master craftsman in Philadelphia or in London or in her still beloved upcountry?

A thought such as that she could never share with Mr. Low, who seemed at all times to define himself by his rare and costly possessions. I'm one of those possessions, she thought, the truth no longer embarrassing her, just bringing a wave of girlish regret. Stuart belonged to her girlhood, but Mr. Low dominated her present as the respected father of her two little girls. More and more, she also felt the bond strengthening between her and her two stepdaughters. These days she wondered if she experienced no jealousy of their mother, Low's first wife, only because she felt only genuine gratitude and regard for their father.

This isn't preparing me for cheering Grandmother, she told herself as the carriage slowed before the Mackay house, then came to a stop. I'm sure Grandmother Mackay will be the one to cheer me anyway.

<hr />

The narrow dirt road that led into the huge acreage that was Laurel Grove Cemetery was rock hard from so much dry weather, its wagon-wheel ruts deep and jolting. Eliza Mackay hung on to Mary Cowper's arm for dear life and, since it was always better to laugh than cry out in pain from the rheumatism in her old back, chuckled at herself as the carriage made the wide turn toward the Mackay plot.

"You're a wonderful lady, Grandmother," Mary Cowper said. "And I know exactly what you're thinking—that Uncle William would smile, too, at these dreadful bumps. I hope I can be half the woman you are when I'm your age!"

"There's a time for weeping and a time for laughter," Eliza said. "The Scriptures back me up on that. I've cried my tears. I'm sure more will come, but if I gave in to the way my old back hurts right now *or* the way my heart hurts, you and I would be in a real fix."

"The Mackay plot is right over there, isn't it? In that empty space?"

"Yes, child. I remember exactly where it is. I thought the day we buried William that it's just as well he'd learned through the years how to be by himself. And, look—there's his new marker! Oh, I'm so glad it's in place. I fretted some that it took so long."

Mary Cowper instructed Earl to stop, and the carriage had only begun to slow when Eliza saw a lone man heading straight for the Mackay plot. A *young* man her dimming eyes saw as strangely familiar. "Who is that?" she asked. "Who's that young man, Mary Cowper?"

When her granddaughter, in stunned silence, sat bolt upright in the carriage seat, Eliza knew. The gentleman was familiar because he was Stuart Elliott! For an anxious moment, she just sat beside Mary Cowper, wondering what to do, what to say. It isn't too unusual for townspeople to visit new graves, especially if word was out that the local monument maker had just set a new one in place—she knew William had befriended the boy—but what would be the best way to bridge such an awkward, unexpected meeting? Had the two young people ever met face to face since they'd both married other mates? Eliza could honestly not remember.

"Earl! Earl," Mary Cowper shouted in some panic at the driver. "Earl, please pull up ahead just a short distance! Don't stop beside the Mackay plot. Up there—a little beyond that next plot, the one with three monuments."

"Whose plot do you think that one is?" Eliza asked uselessly, stalling for time.

All but scrooched down in the seat beside her, Mary Cowper did not look where her grandmother pointed but kept her eyes on the carriage floor. "I–I have no idea, Grandmother, but–I can't get out to look at Uncle William's stone! *I—can't!*"

"I know, dear, I know. Just tell Earl to take us on back to my house."

"No! You need to see it. You need to be sure it's carved correctly—all the right information. *No.*"

At that moment, Stuart strode up to the carriage, doffed his modest top hat, and bowed. "Good morning," he said in a reverential voice.

"May I help you down from the carriage, Mrs. Mackay? It would be an honor to walk with you to–his grave."

Eliza blinked. Stuart's strikingly handsome face was far more distinguished than she remembered. He'd grown a neat beard and his dark sideburns made her think of a portrait her husband once owned of the Scottish poet Robert Burns. Stuart had, up to now, addressed only her. Mary Cowper wasn't looking at him, but courtesy demanded that he bow in her direction, too. He did, but with no change of expression.

"If I'm intruding, I'll leave and come back later," he said to Eliza. "But I'd consider it a true honor to be allowed to escort you over the rough ground, Mrs. Mackay."

"Thank you, Stuart," Eliza said, her heart aching for both young people, her mind uncertain of what each might be thinking. And that's not age, she thought. It's just plain confusing! "I'd be pleased, Stuart, to have a strong arm to lean on."

Far better, Eliza thought, just to go right through with it. Mary Cowper still did not look up at him, which told her grandmother exactly what she had most feared. The poised wife of Andrew Low would normally have bluffed her way gracefully through any awkward social encounter. Mary Cowper sat in a pitiful, wretched heap on the carriage seat, as though attempting to hide even from her own true feelings.

He was lifting Eliza to the ground and she took his arm without a look back for fear of heightening her granddaughter's distress. Together, they began the short walk to the Mackay plot.

"I didn't plan this, Mrs. Mackay," Stuart said when he felt they were out of hearing. "I swear I didn't."

"I believe you, Stuart."

"Mr. Mackay was my friend. I was at the funeral, too, but I doubt you saw me. I stayed on your front porch. The windows were open. I could hear every word of praise the rector said about him. Not praise enough, but then, nothing could be."

They had reached the low picket fence that surrounded the plot of ground where Eliza and her daughters would someday lie.

"The monument was just set in place yesterday," she said.

"I know. I've been out here four or five times since your son died." Stuart spoke softly. "I valued Mr. Mackay. He showed me respect always."

She looked up at him. "You've come to visit William's grave four or five times, Stuart?"

"Yes, ma'am. As soon as my new son is old enough to understand, I'll be sure he knows about the kind of man he was."

"The kind of man he *is*," she corrected gently. "We can't see William anymore, but he's alive and he's somewhere with his little family and his brother, Jack, and his father and . . ."

"And God."

Her heart lifted. "Oh, yes, yes–and God. You and God are friends now, Stuart?"

"Thanks to you," he said simply. "The headstone is just right, isn't it? Shall I read the inscription to you?"

"If you please. I hope it's correct. William wouldn't want a lot of palaver, you know."

Stuart knelt inside the picket fence and read aloud from the simple, freshly carved marker: " 'William Mackay, born March 27, 1804, died August 1, 1859. Psalm 41:1.' Was that his favorite psalm?"

"That was the verse I thought best spoke of William's life."

"I don't know it, Mrs. Mackay. I wish I did."

" 'Blessed is he that considereth the poor: the Lord will deliver him in time of trouble.' William considered the poor, always. Trouble ran long and deep for him. He learned firsthand about that deliverance."

"One of my sisters and her two small children died in the *Pulaski* explosion," Stuart said.

"Oh, Stuart! That's right. William wasn't the only one who lost his dear ones."

Their recollections held them in a hushed silence until a wren called.

With a half-glance toward the waiting carriage, Stuart said, "I hope she can forgive me for being here. It's just a crazy coincidence, I swear."

Eliza hooked her arm back in his. "I said I believed you. I do. You'd have no way of knowing Mary Cowper and I were coming this morning. Stuart, visit me anytime, will you? I'd like to make something for your new child if my old eyes hold out."

"Do you mean that? Yes, you do," he answered his own question. "Mrs. Mackay–did Mr. Mackay think there's going to be a war?"

"Oh, dear!"

"I'm sorry. I didn't mean to upset you. I just thought maybe you'd read the paper this morning about the horrible thing that happened up in Virginia. Your friend Colonel Robert E. Lee was in the thick of it. He captured that maniac John Brown at Harpers Ferry, Virginia, just a few days ago."

"Robert did? Is–Robert all right?"

"He must be or the paper would have mentioned it. The whole thrust of what the *Daily Morning News* said was that if anything could fan the fires of war, another attempt at a slave insurrection would do it." She could see the gentleness had gone out of his eyes. They were smoldering now. "I'd hate going to war! I'd be scared half to death if I had to go, but how long can the South sit still in the face of all this Yankee viciousness? If that Black Republican Party ever got control of the country, we'd have to secede, and I say the sooner, the better!"

Her heart sank. She had felt pure panic at the first mention that John Brown had struck again. She breathed a prayer that Robert Lee might write all about it to her or to Eliza Anne. In her helplessness, all she could think to say was: "Oh, Stuart, Stuart, we both need William to talk to us. We both need him, don't we?"

"I know I do," he said, starting to lead her back toward the carriage. "I am sorry I—did this to her. And to you. It hasn't been easy for you either."

"Life is seldom easy. But I'll be all right with Mary Cowper on the ride home. I love her—too." Her hand flew to her mouth. "Oh, my! I had no right to say that."

"With me, you have every right dear, wise lady."

Seated beside her granddaughter again, Eliza only held her hand and said nothing.

The Low carriage had reached town and was almost to Broughton Street before Mary Cowper said, "I'm glad the marker is to your liking, Grandmother. I know you feel better about it. I'm—sorry about the rest of what took place."

"I'm not, my dear. Except for you, of course, and what went through your mind while Stuart and I were at William's grave is entirely your secret. The boy and I are friends. I thought we were. I know it now, so it's all right."

Mary Cowper turned abruptly to look at her. "You and Stuart are friends?" she gasped. "Oh, I'm so glad! Thank you, thank you!" She grabbed Eliza and kissed her. Then, when she leaned back in what appeared to be deep relief, she added, "We—we don't need to mention to anyone—what happened, do we, Grandmother?"

"We'd both be pretty stupid if we did, I'd say." After a moment, Eliza said, "You're doing a remarkable thing, Mary Cowper. I'm sure there's no one to tell you that. I felt I needed to let you know I'm proud of you." A glance at the young woman beside her somehow startled Eliza. Mary Cowper was looking straight ahead. Not a muscle flicked on her all but expressionless—still very beautiful, but suddenly almost—old face.

Dear Lord, Eliza breathed, this child needs a confidante! I wouldn't pry for anything, but this minute, she needs help in bringing herself back to the way things are for her *today*. Should she tell her that dear Robert Lee had actually captured John Brown somewhere in Virginia? Yes. It might distract the child. She did tell her, and although the telling brought more uneasiness to Eliza, Mary Cowper seemed to spring to life.

"Good for Colonel Lee," the girl exclaimed sharply. "But that doesn't mean we don't have to secede! We do, Grandmother. We can't just go on letting those arrogant Yankees kick us in the face forever! Mr. Low says the time is long past for conciliation. He thinks those rotten Black Republicans are going to destroy us down here one way or another. Because that monster John Brown has been captured won't stop them! All the elite up North are making a martyr of Brown and he's a vile, violent man! Just because Colonel Lee has stopped him doesn't mean Ralph Waldo Emerson and Thoreau and Longfellow and the other Black Republican abolitionists won't find more lunatics to incite our nigras against us. We have to get out of the Union or we could be murdered in our sleep!"

The carriage had pulled to a complete stop in front of her house, but Eliza Mackay sat staring at her usually gentle, sweet-tempered grand-daughter. She had come back to life all right, and at this moment Eliza could feel, could almost touch the bitterness filling the lovely, once tender girl. Why, at some quieter time, hadn't she had sense enough to find out where the child stood amid the flames of hatred that seemed to be spreading around them all?

Had the accidental meeting with Stuart so upset her or had it merely lanced a long-festering hatred?

On the Mackay porch, after the perfunctory goodbye kiss on Eliza's cheek, Mary Cowper said she had to hurry home. "I can't wait to tell Mr. Low at dinner about that fanatic John Brown," she said. "My husband is still a British subject, but love of the South's cause runs in him like his blood. Love of the South's cause and hatred of the North!"

Eliza hadn't meant to say it, but she heard herself gasp, "No, child, *no!*"

"Oh, yes, Grandmother. Oh, yes. The strongest bond Mr. Low and I have is our hatred of everything Yankee! His partner, Mr. Charles Green, goes on trying to be reasonable and diplomatic and I can see it coming between them. It can't come between us because my husband stands firm and loyal to my native Georgia! It's *our bond*. It will endure, too. I mean to see to it and with all my heart I cherish it. I pray every night that God will somehow, quickly, bring about secession before we —all perish down here!"

When Mary Cowper had run back down the front steps, Eliza moved woodenly through her front door, glad for once not to be met by either daughter, needing desperately to collect her thoughts.

She hung her dress bonnet on the hall rack, her shawl beside it, and made her way to the little parlor rocker which had, for years, cradled her aching back and spirits more restfully than any other chair.

"Whew!" she breathed as she sank carefully into the rocker. "I do need to think things through." She spoke aloud often these days, by herself. "Oh, how I wish for—William! He'd agree with Mary Cowper and Mr. Low, I suppose, all down the line, but he'd also take his time sorting things out. That's one thing he was so good at—sorting out. Your headstone looks quite nice, William. I'm glad I saw it. I know you're with your blessed family now, but—" A flood of fresh tears came and, alone in the house, except for Hannah and Emphie, who understood, she sobbed as loudly as she needed to because William seemed so far away from her.

ecause Burke and Lorah Plemmons's boy, Sam, were away from Etowah Cliffs for a week in order to finish a row of stores and shops in Cassville, W.H. himself prepared to ride to Cartersville for the mail on the fifth day of November.

"I'm hoping," he told Eliza Anne as he sat his horse, "to find a letter of confirmation that I'm to be at least an alternate delegate to the national convention next year."

She clung for a moment to his hand. "Of course you will be, darling," she insisted. "Now, do be careful on the way and I'll expect a smile on your face when you ride up this afternoon." She gave him an encouraging smile. "Not that I don't love you just as much when you scowl."

"Oh, Lib, Lib," he sighed, "there's reason for a man to scowl these days. Surely, I'll attend that convention even as an alternate. Someone has to be there who knows what might happen if the Southern Democrats don't stay solidly together. We're surrounded up here by Unionists. I'm still a Unionist, in fact, but not at the expense of *our kind* here in the South! Senator Douglas is a traitor to our cause and we dare not split to follow him. If we do, the Black Republicans will–"

"Dearest," she interrupted, "I know, I know. I hate you out of my sight and I'm sorry you have to go, but the sooner you go, the sooner you'll be back to me. Do try to learn some local reaction to that dreadful John Brown's latest madness, though, will you?"

"Brown's merely a crazed maniac, Lib. Why *can't* people use their brains? I fear the Republican revolution far more than I fear John Brown. I'm sick to my stomach at their babble about a Free Society!" He rubbed his forehead, the gesture she knew so well meant that rage was about to erupt. "The article I read last night and memorized to use, was right: 'What is a Free Society as the North envisions it but a conglomeration of greasy mechanics, filthy operatives, small-fisted farmers, and moon-struck theorists hardly fit for association with a Southern gentleman's body servant!' "

She kissed his hand. "You're *my* Southern gentleman, my darling, and I wouldn't change you for any other. Go now, please, and tonight, I guarantee you won't go to sleep thinking such disturbing thoughts."

He did manage a smile before he galloped off. "You're disturbed, too, dear wife, and don't try to convince me otherwise."

As she waved what she hoped was a cheerful farewell, she knew not only that W.H. was right but that he seemed far more ready for a breakup of the country than she might ever be.

She saw him out of sight and walked slowly back to the house, full of the heaviness that lately almost overwhelmed her because, isolated by the river as she was, there was no one else with whom she could talk. Last year when W.H. had failed to be sent again to Washington as a congressman, she'd worked so hard at cheering him, her own disap-pointment had been pushed somewhere down inside. Lately, because she was so sure more dastardly things were taking place in the land than they had any way of learning, the heaviness and anxiety were growing harder and harder to hide.

As she paused for a moment to look down the road toward Natalie's cottage, a sense of isolation almost choked her. Nothing new, of course, about not being able to discuss important matters with Natalie. She'd always been uninterested to a fault in politics, but Mary Cowper's marriage still loomed between them and Eliza Anne felt less and less able to accept the truth of how much she missed Natalie.

The ache which never left her now that dear, dependable William was gone sharpened some days to outright pain. There hadn't been time to go to Savannah for his funeral and the only letter so far from Mama had been as expected, strong and full of courage and faith. "Where is *my* *faith?*" she asked aloud as she climbed the veranda steps. "Don't I believe God has a hand in all this national trouble? Even in my loneliness today and my worry over W.H.'s frustrations, do I believe God cares or not?"

She went inside. There was no one there but the servants. She was alone and frightened. The house seemed enormous and unlived in. If only Robert Lee would write a firsthand account of how he captured that terrifying John Brown! A silly wish, she told herself, heading for her sewing room.

Isn't it enough that Robert captured the fiend? But what's to stop those Republicans from sending out more and more John Browns to stir up our people against us?

The abject loneliness turned to something akin to a pulsing panic she had never actually experienced in her fifty-one years . . . Only the house servants were nearby, but didn't they keep their secretive, primitive communications with W.H.'s dozens of brawny, often rebellious field hands? Negroes couldn't read newspapers, but she'd swear the word was being passed around that murderous slave insurrections were spreading in the South. And not in towns—in the solitude and isolation of remote plantations like Etowah Cliffs . . .

When W.H. returned just after noon, she ran out to greet him. There was no smile on his face; rather, he appeared more distraught and gave her only a cursory wave as he rode up.

"Mail, Lib," he said, his voice showing what seemed only impatience. "Here." He handed her a letter as soon as he dismounted. "You have a letter from Colonel Lee. If I'm not intruding on your privacy, I need to have you read it to me. The man can give us information we can get from nowhere else."

"You've seen every letter I've received from Colonel Lee since we've been married, W.H.!" Oh, dear, *now* is not the time to upset him, she told herself firmly. "Of course we'll read it together, darling. July's on his way for your horse. Come inside, please, and have some tea. You look as though you galloped every foot of the way home!"

"It was that—letter," he explained, catching his breath as they hurried inside. "Lee's letter could supply some valuable material for me to use at the convention in Milledgeville next month. By the way, I am at least an alternative."

"Sit down in your big chair and rest," she said. "I'll send for tea."

"Lib! I don't want any. I want to hear what Lee wrote!"

She gave him an indulgent look. "All right, darling, all right. I honestly marvel that he found time to write to me, of all people."

"He has always found time for you, Lib."

In spite of her own anxiety about what the letter might contain, the tinge of W.H.'s old, familiar jealousy pleased her. She broke the seal and, without even scanning the first page, began at once to read aloud to him:

> Harpers Ferry, Virginia
> October 25, 1859

My dear Eliza,

I hasten to write the facts concerning our capture of John Brown, not only to reassure you and your family in Savannah of my well-being but because, even back here for a second time and busy securing this place, I hear of the national ruckus old Osawatomie Brown is causing. Brown, undoubtedly, would be in high spirits if he knew in his jail cell that he is being praised at the North as hero/martyr.

On October 17, while struggling with accounts of expenditures on the still incomplete repairs at Arlington, my bright, clear morning was broken into by a surprise visit from my friend Jeb Stuart, who, judging from the sealed War Department message he handed me, was not there on a social call. Without taking time to change into my uniform, I rode with Stuart to the Washington office of John Floyd, Sec. of War. I was then ordered to take command of a detachment of Marines already assigned and a body of troops from Fort Monroe, in order to capture a man calling himself Isaac Smith, a prospector, at Harpers Ferry. His band had seized the U.S. Arsenal from its single watchman, had secured a number of hostages and taken over the sleeping village with the avowed purpose of freeing the slaves.

After much travel confusion, Stuart and I reached Sandy Hook, then I marched my troops a mile and a half to Harpers Ferry. During the day, hundreds of armed citizens and two companies of militia had reached the town. After a desultory exchange of fire and several casualties, Smith and his raiders and 13 hostages took refuge in the fire-engine house at the Armory. If the militia had had proper leadership, it would have been over by the time I could reach there. To make the story short, we stormed the engine house about seven the next morning. By then, 2,000 were looking on. The man who called himself Isaac Smith appeared at the crack in the door, his cocked carbine trained on Jeb Stuart, and reached for the paper Jeb held out. The man was, of course, old John Brown, who had given us so much trouble in Kansas. My terms were surrender. Our agreed signal was that if Brown refused, Stuart would wave his hat. Brown refused, and with guns firing, battering ram and sledgehammers, we moved in.

Three minutes after Jeb had waved his hat, the thing was over. Brown, bleeding profusely, was carried out. The mob demanded their revenge, but my orders were to protect Brown and his men. Cots were set up and a surgeon called to dress wounds. That afternoon, I saw Governor Wise of Va. calling on Brown, who made his riotous motives quite clear. He had but one purpose, he vowed, *to free all slaves.* Rumors abounded about the countryside—one family lay murdered by their Negroes, etc.—but when I had investigations made, only peace and tranquillity were found. I then returned to Washington City to make a full report. Brown's trial was set for October 25, a fact which has set the entire North afire at what many consider "undue speed." The Va. Gov. was flooded with abusive, threatening mail. I am told that the abolitionists who had encouraged and backed Brown began preparing the way, from pulpit, rostrum, and in the press, for his martyrdom.

Until she reached that part of Lee's letter, neither W.H. nor Eliza Anne had made one comment. Now W.H. jumped to his feet.

"Just today in Cassville, I heard that! I found it hard to believe, but now we know it's true, Lib."

"What? What did you hear?"

"That Bronson Alcott, Ellery Channing, and Henry David Thoreau met at the home of Ralph Waldo Emerson to unite in their evil plan to lionize that despicable, murdering fanatic Brown! Does Lee have any comment on their madness?"

Eliza Anne scanned the final page of the letter. "Not a word. That's so like him, though, to hold his counsel. He does say this much: 'The result proves that the plan was the attempt of a fanatic or a madman.' "

W.H. had been pacing the room. Now he sank into his chair again. "Yes, at a minimum," he said, "Brown's a madman." Hands trembling, he clipped and lighted a cigar. "Sorry, Lib," he murmured, blowing a huge billow of smoke. "I know you don't like me to smoke in here."

"You're nervous, dear," she said. "I wonder why Robert's back at Harpers Ferry."

"They were wondering that today, too, at the newspaper office. As soon as Brown was sentenced to be hanged, the—"

"*What?*"

"The man has already been found guilty of murder, criminal con-spiracy, and treason," W.H. said, as though she should have known it already.

"But why didn't Robert mention any of that?"

"How do I know? He's obviously telling you—and with undue modesty, I'd say—only of his own part in the horror. Actually, the trial wasn't over when Lee wrote to you. It lasted until November 2, and believe me, old Osawatomie Brown made a dramatic spectacle of it." W.H. reached into his coat pocket for a folded newspaper. "Listen to this insanity, Lib: 'I only intended to free slaves,' Brown told the court. 'If it is deemed necessary that I should forfeit my life for the furtherance of the ends of justice and mingle my blood further with the blood of my children and with the blood of millions in this slave country whose rights are disregarded by wicked, cruel, and unjust enactments, I say, let it be done.' " W.H. hurled the paper across the room. "And it will be done on the second of December, Lib. He will walk or be dragged kicking like a wild man to the gallows on the glorious day of the second of December and I, for one, shall revel!"

She'd seen W.H. angry before many times, but now his eyes burned with more fury than even he, the poised diplomat, seemed to know how to control. "Darling, *darling!*" she cried.

"Brown's one of those extreme Calvinists, you know," he went on, obviously trying to talk himself back to some semblance of calm. "They believe a lot of things about shedding blood. That nothing can be solved or purged but by the shedding of blood. The man's insane! Lee agrees with that, certainly," he said bitterly.

The look he gave her, she absolutely did not deserve. "Yes, W.H., he does." Her voice was cold.

"I'm relieved to know you offer me at least partial vindication because the great Lee believes Brown to be mad, too!"

Now she jumped to her feet and went to him where he sat. "Why in the name of heaven should you and I be talking to each other in this irrational way, dearest?"

"Because we are human," he almost shouted. "We're human and those revolutionaries at the North are beating us into a corner!"

"What corner?"

Now he did shout: "Secession, Lib! *Secession!*"

"No!"

They were both on their feet, in each other's arms. "Oh, Lib," he moaned. "Nothing can ever be the same for us again here, by our river . . ."

"It can be and it will, my darling," she murmured, not convincing herself. "You'll have a much better idea of what's really taking place when you reach the convention next month. We're so—shut away up here—so cut off from the whole wide world!"

He hugged her, then walked to a window. "That's the way it seems to you, isn't it? Did I make a terrible mistake dragging us all up here to the hill country? You feel as though you're married to a quixotic failure, don't you?"

"W.H., how can you even think such a thing?"

He turned back. "I don't, actually. I'm just spouting because I'm so— so helpless!"

"And you're still just a tiny bit jealous of Robert Lee?"

She saw him start to flare back at her, then a slow smile spread across his face. "If I didn't know that by *choice* your legal name is now Mrs. W. H. Stiles, I might be jealous of a far-off Army colonel. Your name *is* Mrs. Stiles, though, and you lie every night in *my* arms."

She stood some ten feet across the room from him, but her smile, she knew, said far more than she could have put into words.

"If I read that smile correctly, it is telling me, Mrs. Stiles, that I now sound more like your husband."

"W.H., could we sit down together, if you're not in a rush to do something else?"

He crossed the room in two or three long strides and led her to the somewhat worn brocade couch, then took her lightly in his arms. "I was about to tell you I also need just to be with you," he said. "The trip to Cartersville, that infernal letter about Brown—upset me strangely."

"I was upset the whole time you were gone."

For a moment, they sat side by side, touching hands, then he whispered, "I need to tell you something I can't tell anyone else, Lib. I'm ashamed of myself—a grown man talking like this, but—"

She sat up for a better look at his troubled face. "What? What, darling?"

One arm swept the room lined with bookcases. "Everyone who knows me," he said, "knows how much I love books, that I could, if I had the time, live in books. Lib, it sounds foolish and like a schoolboy, but I've—*lost so many idols!* Friends. All my adult reading life, I've almost worshipped at the shrine of Ralph Waldo Emerson. He and Ellery Channing both, undoubtedly to your sorrow, since you don't agree, deeply influenced my religious thinking."

She didn't agree. Emerson and Channing were Unitarians who rejected the deity of Christ, but this did not seem the moment to lecture W.H. on his somewhat irregular religious habits or lack of them. She said nothing, listening intently.

"I've read and reread them both. It was from them that I learned of the danger of an extreme Calvinist view of God." His hand clenched until the knuckles turned white. "The view that John Brown espouses which leads to all that violence and bloodshed."

"It–doesn't have to unless one's nature is extreme," she ventured, "but you're trying to say something else, aren't you?"

"Yes, yes, I am." He let his clenched hand fall free. "I–I am confessing that–these days, I *miss* Emerson and Channing and Henry David Thoreau and Longfellow! Lib, I even miss reading Margaret Fuller!"

She took his restless hand in both of hers. "Oh, W.H., dearest W.H., how–sad for you! I honestly hadn't thought of any of what you've just said. These authors were *all* old friends, weren't they? Can you forgive me?"

He made a disdainful little sound. "Nonsense, Lib! Why should a wife consider that her husband of over thirty years might be shedding tears over a group of Yankee abolitionists who happened to write books he's read and reread for much of his life? Those thinking men are now lionizing the maniac John Brown! They not only received him socially in recent months; they are the *leaders* of all those ill-begotten, abolitionist, Yankee literati who fan the fires of Northern hatred against you and me! Perhaps I deplore my own bad taste. I think I rather despise myself for missing them out of my own life!" He had turned so that he faced her now. He was almost crying out. "Lib, I–do miss them! It's as though a nameless, faceless monster is loose in the land, bent on devouring us all with hatred! How can I, in my deepest heart, ever learn to hate Emerson and Thoreau and Longfellow and Channing? How can I hate the Northern part of the country I was taught to love and revere?"

"Dearest, dearest," she soothed, "we don't have to hate. Although I–I think we do sometimes. I know I do."

"Do you, Lib? Do you?"

"Yes, but it makes me feel guilty."

He fell back on the couch. "Well, I don't feel guilty–I feel resentment . . . I only know I'm lonely and worried and in all ways–up against it."

"And when we're up against it, Mama says, we pray."

"Yes," he said.

"Next year, it can all be solved if the men at the convention will only listen to you, dear W.H. There is one hope. You've convinced me that if Southern Democrats–all Democrats–stay together, we'll be strong enough to–to carry the day."

"I'm assuming you mean election day, next fall."

"Don't you still believe that?"

He exhaled noisily, wearily. "Yes. Yes, of course, I believe it."

FORTY-NINE

*T*wo weeks before Christmas in 1859, Mark sat alone in his office, reading and rereading the last words of John Brown. Moments before he was hanged early in the month at Charles Town, Virginia, according to the *Tribune*'s account, Brown had handed his jailer the following statement: "I, John Brown, am now quite certain that the crimes of this guilty land will never be purged away, but by Blood." Was Brown crazy–or right?

John Brown had disturbed and fascinated Mark ever since he had appeared on the national scene leading acts of bloody violence against slaveholders. At this moment, Mark saw himself as a wrenching composite of both North and South. Along with most Northerners, he despised slavery, but as with most Southerners, he also despised the trail of terror and anger and violence that followed Brown to his grave. He did not agree with Southerners who believed that because of Brown there would surely be slave uprisings, but he was almost alone in not fearing it. The dark expectation hung even today over Savannah, and it was personified for him in his beloved wife, Caroline. In her, the dread was alive right in his own house. True, she had seemed less nervous lately, but he could take no risks, preferring, as always, to shield her from the trauma.

Mark did understand her reasons for feeling as she had all their married life and he respected them. Caroline was a slave owner and her lifelong loyalty to the culture of the South made her defensive when that culture was threatened in any way. John Brown's maniacal behavior, even in what to Mark was a worthy cause, surely lay behind much of Caroline's anxiety. Brown's violence lay also, if he were truthful, behind the anxiety Mark now felt in the stifling contradictory solitude of his own lonely beliefs.

At the window, as he looked out at Savannah's busy waterfront, his thoughts went, as they did so often, to William. Had William been alive, Mark would surely have hurried to his old friend's office. There would have been no plausible explanation for why he would have done that, since John Brown's final words would surely have fired William, too. Still, he and William, in spite of their differing beliefs, could have talked it out. "We just have to make room for each other, Mark," William would have said. "Giving each other room is pretty important in anything."

Mark had spent the long years of their married life trying to give Caroline room. He was weary of the effort. Today, for the first time, he could admit that he longed desperately for some sign that she might someday meet *him* halfway. Perhaps the weariness was due to his age or William's death, or both. If William and Miss Eliza could meet him, why had it always been impossible for Caroline?

Struggling to think back clearly over the months since William went away, he tried to be honest about his own reaction to what, at times lately, appeared to be an opening, at least, in Caroline's rigid bias. An opening in her bias itself or to him? Had there really been an opening or was he, out of wishful thinking, only imagining it? He did not expect her to change, to abandon her lifetime, almost religious-like love of the South and all it stood for. She had every right to that, as he had every right to his own hatred of owning another human being. Was he being honest with himself this minute when he felt that his beliefs had not in any way stood between them? Did her disagreement actually stand between them, or had he merely lacked the moral strength to find a way open and intelligent enough to stop shielding her?

He looked at his hands. They were trembling. Old men's hands trembled. He didn't feel like an old man. He just felt tired. Tired to the bone of being forced to tiptoe around his adored wife's Southern loyalties.

Miss Eliza would be at home. He could run to her as always, but it was Caroline he needed. Needed in a way he had never needed her before. Surely that was an exaggeration. They had been married too long for a sweeping generalization like that!

He got up again and began to pace his office. He missed Jonathan. His son was out of the countinghouse today and would not be back until the day after tomorrow. Normally, he would have protected himself in such a restless mood by calling Jonathan to him, but even Jonathan's reason for being away was troubling. Mark had tried to ignore it, but if he were truly honest, Jonathan's behavior lately had been more than troubling. The Chatham Artillery, to which they both belonged, had called special drills out of the city that would last two days. His son puzzled him lately because without saying one direct word, the boy was suddenly showing keen interest in exercising, in eating properly, in military drill itself. Jonathan had always attended regimental functions, but there was a difference now which Mark felt he could not share with anyone because he could not define it. He knew that Jonathan felt as he did about slavery and yet the boy had never said outright whether, should there be war with the North, he would or would not fight for Georgia. Mark had not pressed it. His son remained his buoyant, cheerful self, was still attentive to Mary, especially during her frequent morning-sickness spells, but it seemed to Mark at times that the young man was holding a close secret even from her.

The Exchange clock struck ten. Time to visit Miss Eliza, but for the first time, he even felt unsure about that. Did he intend to tell her John Brown's last disturbing statement? That today he was finally facing the new strangeness in Jonathan? That he had at last admitted to himself that he was no longer equal to guarding against Caroline's prickliness on the subject of slavery? The way he felt as he reached for his heavy coat and muffler, a visit to Miss Eliza now would lead to burden dumping and she didn't deserve that. At nearly eighty-two, how much more could she stand?

Settling his top hat against the sharp December wind, he left his countinghouse in the charge of the clerks, crossed the iron bridge that led to the Bay, and headed for his own house and Caroline.

"I'll be there directly, Mark," Caroline called from upstairs. "Just as soon as I make sure Mary has drunk all her peppermint tea. She's been quite sick this morning."

Back in the room Mary and Jonathan shared, Caroline smiled down at the pale, brave face of her daughter-in-law, trying hard, she knew, to return her smile. "Don't try so hard, Mary," she said softly.

"I know I am trouble, Mama Caroline," Mary said. "Tomorrow it might not be so bad. I–I miss Jonathan."

"Of course you miss him. And if you're sure you're all right, I'll run downstairs now to my husband."

"Papa Mark is here?"

"It's his usual time to visit Miss Eliza, but for some reason, he came home. I'll go down and find out why he's honored us with a midmorning visit."

Mark was rubbing both hands over his face almost roughly when Caroline hurried into the family drawing room where he waited.

"Is anything wrong, darling?" she asked. "You're not ill, are you?"

"No. I just needed to be with you."

Without a word, she led him to the love seat, sat down beside him, and pulled his head onto her shoulder.

After a time, he took a deep breath. "Thank you, Mrs. Browning. I do thank you."

"Oh, Mark, it's past time I let you know what's really happened to me."

He lifted his head to look at her. "Something–happened to you?"

"You don't know, do you? You haven't noticed it for yourself. You don't know and I don't know how to tell you! But, Mark, there's nothing left, nothing left anywhere for you to have to be wary about in me. Does that make any sense?"

He smiled weakly. "I must be dense."

"You need never be fearful again of talking to me about–anything!"

He frowned, struggling, she knew, to understand, still not daring to hope. As he'd always done when he felt unsure with her, he waited.

"You're waiting again, and, Mark, you *don't need to*. I've set you free with me in all ways. I even wrote to Natalie and Burke that I had."

He stared at her. "You–wrote to Natalie and Burke?"

"It was like throwing away the key to an airless room. Dearest, we need never go into that room again. We can both breathe now. *You* can breathe as freely as you want to when the–ugly subject comes up." She smoothed his hair back from his forehead. "Mark, it's true! We are never going to be trapped in that room again. We're not young anymore. It's past time for you to stop treading softly when the subject happens to come up. And it's going to–it's all people talk about these days. I know it will take time for you to believe me and I haven't changed my opinions one iota. I'm still a born Southerner and I'll always be, but I'm through torturing you with it. I didn't fall in love with a slave owner, I fell in love with you. We disagree wholly, but we'll never, never again be trapped in that airless room where neither of us can breathe!"

He gave her such a long, careful, cautious look, she felt herself waver. Had the barrier been there between them too long? "Mark," she whispered. "Oh, Mark . . . "

After a time, he got slowly to his feet and stood looking down at her. Then, in a voice almost devoid of expression, he said, "They hanged John Brown at Charles Town, Virginia, on December 2. Does that relieve you?"

He was testing her. Caroline stood, too, facing him. "That was justice," she said as evenly as she could. "John Brown deserved to be hanged. I know you need to find out, so I'll tell you that, yes, it does relieve me. It relieves me enormously, but—between us, Mark, even John Brown *alive* could raise no more walls. That's finished."

Instead of the embrace she expected, he stepped back a little and said simply, "If I were younger, I'd be on my knees to you in gratitude."

"No, I'm very late with all this. I couldn't bear you to do that." When he said nothing, she felt she had to go on. "Seeing your grief over losing William prodded me to it first, I think, but also—our son."

"Jonathan's been talking to you about it?"

"Not a word. It's the way he's been acting lately, as though he's preparing himself physically and mentally, even emotionally, for some dreadful event. You know he had a choice about attending his regiment's drills for two days. He didn't have to go. Oh, darling, I'm rushing you and that isn't fair, but you can *talk* to me about all of it now, Mark. You're worried about Jonathan, too, aren't you?"

He turned away. "Yes, I'm worried, although I'm not sure why. This stretch of duty was voluntary. He could have refused and it would have been all right with his commanding officer. Caroline?"

She rushed into his arms. "I know what you're going to ask and I need you to hold me." He grabbed her to him as though everything depended upon their being as close as possible. "I'll ask the question for you, Mark—the one we both need answered. Does our son think there's going to be a war? Is that why he's working so feverishly hard at—learning to be a soldier? Dear God, is that it?"

"I think so," he said, just above a whisper. "I've thought so since before William died." His arms tightened around her still more. "But there—isn't a war yet, darling."

"No. There isn't a single barrier left between us either." She reached up to take his face between her hands. "Look at me. No matter what happens, I'm here." She tried their familiar brand of humor. "From now on, I even want to read the papers with you. Even your rotten old Northern papers! Miss Eliza's been through so much—William's gone—you need someone to help you keep up with the news. Someone you can talk to—not handle with kid gloves!" He was returning her smile now, stroking her hair, holding her. "I'll even read your old *Atlantic Monthly* and the *Harper's Weekly* with you—oh, dearest, even Horace Greeley's lies in the *Tribune*! I may hate every word I read, but, Mark, I'll be here—all the way here."

They were both laughing now, holding, Mark pleading, "Don't make me love you more! Please, Mrs. Browning, don't make me love you any more . . . "

"How have you stood me, darling—all this time?"

"That's past," he said, holding her head against his shoulder. "And just watch me obey you. Every day a Northern paper reaches my office, home it comes in my hand—to read with you!"

She pulled away enough to look at him for a long time, then said, "I'm in awe of you."

"Of me?"

"What a truly—big person you are. The human thing would be for you to feel you deserve to punish me—just a little, anyway. You couldn't do that, could you?"

He shrugged. "What possible good would it do?"

"Mrs. Sarah Gordon was here earlier today," Caroline said, crossing to a tall front window. "She told me some of what President Buchanan said in his message to Congress. He believes there will be a war. He believes there's no way to avoid it. He believes we face an open war by the North to abolish—slavery. Sarah Gordon's uncle on the Supreme Court agrees. Four young Savannah men have already withdrawn from Yale and Harvard to come home, to get ready." When he said nothing, she whirled to face him. "Mark, don't!"

"What did I do?"

"Don't stand there—being careful of me. I said all I said calmly, didn't I? I didn't flare. Our son may be going to war—a war that will find his parents on opposite sides—but still together. Right now, I don't know *how*. I just know we will be. In the spring, we'll be grandparents again. Mary's baby could come into a country at war, but there will be new life in our house—in our hearts. No matter what else has happened by then, we'll have the child to be happy about and you'll have a wife who no longer flares—not even when she feels like doing it."

"Do you have any idea how much I love you?" he asked.

"Yes. And I am still in awe of you."

"What if Mary's baby looks—Indian, Caroline?"

Her breath caught in her throat. Then she smiled. "You are—testing me, aren't you? And I don't blame you one bit. What if Mary's baby looks Indian? I feel it will be all right—either way. We'll just have to wait and see. But, dearest Mark, we'll wait *together*. You're sure to have doubts about me, but you *won't* need to wait alone again—not ever."

PART
IV

May 1860–June 1864

FIFTY

*T*hroughout *the* long winter months of 1859 and into 1860, Mary tried, in spite of the talk of war, to think only beautiful thoughts for the sake of the infant she carried. Spring came with the back-yard garden hanging sweet with wisteria banners and the city alight with azalea blossoms. Talk of secession and war went on, but it was all so confusing, she tried hard not to hear.

"I try, Jonathan," she told him as he was ready to leave for work on a cloudy mid-May morning, "to worry about nothing, to think only beautiful thoughts for our child."

Smiling down at her as he brushed a fleck of dust from his coat sleeve, he asked, "Are you sure you're not sick this morning?"

"I'm sure." She returned his kiss eagerly. "Even my back does not hurt so much today."

"Good!"

"But tonight, will you tell me something I need to know?"

"Anything." He reached for his hat from the hall tree, handed it to her, then bent down so that she could settle it into place on his head as she had done for luck every morning of this year. "That is, I'll tell you anything I can. How do I look?"

She stepped back to inspect him. "Handsome! Handsome enough to be President of the United States."

"No, thank you," he laughed. "That's one job I would not want these days."

"It is bad to be President now?"

"It's *hard*, Mary. By the way, how a man looks has nothing to do with whether or not he'll be a good President. But I thank you, ma'am. If I'm handsome, it's only because you love me so much."

"Not right," she said. "You were handsome long ago before I knew I loved you. You would make a good President because you are gentle and full of love and not joining in all the anger." She was frowning and promptly made herself stop it. *Their* new child must not come from a frowning mother! "You will tell me tonight why the people hate and fear the man named Abraham Lincoln?"

He looked down at her. "You never stop trying to learn, do you?" he asked.

"Every new thing I learn brings me closer to where you are," she said simply.

"Then we have the right plans for this evening. My friend Charles Olmstead is an informed, intelligent gentleman. Especially to be so young. I think he's only twenty-two or three. Ask him about Abraham Lincoln when he and Mrs. Olmstead come to spend the evening with us. My parents will be attending the lecture at the Historical Society and . . ."

"And Mama Caroline will not have to be upset if we talk about—the trouble."

She saw him look away. "That's right, but I don't worry about Mama and the trouble the way I used to. I'm not sure just why. Do you?"

She beamed up at him. "I try not to worry about anything now. Our baby is sure to be here soon. When I ask you to teach me about the trouble and Mr. Lincoln and Mr. Douglas and all the conventions in different cities, I am not worried. I just want to understand."

"So do I," he said, resetting his top hat. "So do I."

"You hate and fear Mr. Lincoln as President, Jonathan?"

He took a long time to answer. "No. Papa thinks too highly of him for me to hate him. I guess I worry that he might be elected in the fall."

"That is bad?"

"I must get to work, darling," he said, glancing at the hall clock. "And just to be safe, don't bring any of this up at the dinner table. We'll talk more this evening when Mama and Papa are out."

She went to the door with him, holding fast to his arm. "Your new, close friend, Charles Olmstead, will like me? I cannot pull my corset strings very tight anymore."

"Charles will like you and so will his wife, Florie. They're good, young people, intelligent people, and almost as much in love with each other as we are."

"They were married only last year?"

"Yes. Uh—let me warn you, honey, that all of what Charlie Olmstead might say will be strictly from the Southern viewpoint."

"Well, he was born in Savannah."

"Right, but so was I."

"I know what we will do, Jonathan. We will listen to Charles Olmstead, and then when they are gone, I listen to you!"

He laughed, still holding the knob of the now open door. "Good luck," he said, teasing her. "There are times, you know, when your husband feels as though he might have been born—on the moon!"

She clapped her hands. "I like that! I think maybe you were born on a full moon or a shooting star!"

Throughout supper, which Mary had carefully planned with Irish Maureen, she ate little after the delicious crab bisque, but watched and felt glad that Jonathan and the Olmsteads seemed to relish the idea of a corn soufflé as the main dish, crisp bacon slices, and hot, hot rolls with Natalie's wild-blackberry jelly. They had all eaten their big meal in the early afternoon, so to Mary, brandied oranges sprinkled with coconut seemed enough for dessert.

"Whoever planned this meal," gentle, soft-spoken Charles Olmstead said, "has imagination. Thank you, Mrs. Browning. Everything is delicious."

When Florie Olmstead agreed warmly, Mary felt the glow she always felt when she knew Jonathan was proud. "We will go to the drawing room now?" she asked, failing to remember that Jonathan liked her to announce things *not* in the form of a question. He had told her that the night he explained the meaning of the word "tentative." "It sounds tentative, darling," he'd said, "and you are Mrs. Jonathan Browning now and don't need ever again to be tentative or unsure about anything."

She was unsure though, about so much, and the four had just settled themselves in the drawing room when she posed her first question to

Charles Olmstead. "You are so happily married, sir," she said, "surely you do not hate Mr. Abraham Lincoln?"

Mary caught the quick, dumbfounded look her guests exchanged, but when Mr. Olmstead began to answer her, he sounded pleasant.

"I would hope, Mrs. Browning, that I don't hate anyone anywhere. As a Christian gentleman, I would hope that."

Mary gave Jonathan a quizzical look, saw that he was merely smiling, not, she thought, at her, but at his friend's discomfort. She must have chosen the wrong word—hate.

"We hate no one up there. Florie and I are even taking a trip to the North this summer," he went on, "to visit relatives in New York and to see some of the sights of Montreal. I grant you, Mrs. Browning, that this could be a fateful summer for both North and South with the elections coming up this fall, but we do not hate. We disagree, of course, as does any true Southerner who loves and reveres his section of the country."

"To you it is good to own slaves?" Mary asked.

Olmstead thought for a second, then said, "I see it as neither good nor bad. It is simply a question as old as our nation. I realize you are half Cherokee, but you must know that once there were slaves in the North, too. Most were sold down here because the Northern climate and short growing seasons made owning workers unprofitable. Great numbers of European workers flooded into the country up there, too. They didn't like either our climate down here or competing with slave labor. The North, then, had an abundance of laborers, so turned to mills and factories. Some in the South may hate Lincoln, but some in the North also hate slaveholders. It must be remembered that our way of life represents a capitalization of some four thousand million dollars. If slavery were abolished, we could not survive that kind of loss, as I'm sure you know."

Mary looked from Charles Olmstead to Florie and then to Jonathan. "I—do not measure in thousands or millions," she said. "I measure only in good and bad."

"I see," Olmstead said, rubbing his already balding head.

"Your face is good," Mary said to him. Then, turning to Florie, she added, "You marry a good man, Mrs. Olmstead."

Florie Olmstead turned to give her young husband a loving glance. "Yes, Mrs. Browning. A *good* man." Then she looked at Mary. "Our husbands have grown so close in the First Volunteer Regiment, could you both not call us Florie and Charles? We would be honored, wouldn't we, Charles?"

The terrifying words "First Volunteer Regiment" had stuck in Mary's mind, so that she blurted: "Jonathan! What *is* the First Volunteer Regiment? And what does it have to do with *you?*"

"Oh, I'm sorry," Florie said quickly. "I assumed you knew, Mary. Our husbands are both members of the First Volunteer. My—my husband has just been made colonel."

"An excellent choice," Jonathan said. "Colonel Lawton recognized the right man in you, Charles." Then he forced a short laugh. "But now that I'm outranked by your illustrious husband, Florie, I feel I should call him Colonel Olmstead."

"You're doing it, Jonathan!" Mary said accusingly, perched as best she could manage, being so big with child, on the edge of the love seat beside him. "You are talking—beyond me again!"

"You didn't know your husband's Chatham Artillery—in fact, every regiment in town but the Hussars—now forms a part of the First Volunteer, Mary?" Colonel Olmstead asked.

"*I did not.* Jonathan?"

"Just as Colonel Olmstead said, darling, most of the city's military regiments are in the First Volunteer. Only Charles qualified for the adjutancy, though, since he was highly trained at the Institute at Milledgeville. Actually, that's where the two of you met, isn't it, Florie? You were a Milledgeville girl?"

Before Florie could answer, Mary said, "I know they meet—met—in Milledgeville, Jonathan. What I did not know was—" She broke off, then plunged ahead. "Does not *volunteer* mean you do a thing because you want to? Because you believe it is right?"

Colonel Olmstead chuckled pleasantly. "That's as apt a way of putting it as I could think of, Mary. If you could see your husband drill and work, you'd know he believes in what he's doing in the First Volunteers."

"I try to do whatever I undertake in that spirit, Charles," Jonathan said lamely.

"No!" Mary struggled awkwardly to get to her feet. "Jonathan, *no!*"

"No, what, darling?" He was up, too, now, holding her steady.

"Not once have you kept a secret like this from me! You hear me ask silly questions about hating Mr. Lincoln and Northerners and you let me go on not knowing you are willing to hate, too!"

"Oh, Mary," he said, pleading with her for understanding, "I'm *not* willing to hate."

"You are willing to fight!"

"I—I—" He stopped and drew her to him.

"We're all willing to fight, Mary," Olmstead said firmly, but without raising his voice. "Some of us simply mean to be ready, not only to fight the Yankees if need be, but to do it well—to win! If Mr. Lincoln is elected this fall, the South will secede and then one overt act against us by the North will—"

"Charles!" Until now, Florie Olmstead had spoken only gently. Now Mary turned to watch her face. "I know how you and Mr. Browning feel about the First Volunteers, Charles, but do we have to talk about war tonight just when we're having such a pleasant evening?"

Sensing a possible ally, Mary took a clumsy, uncertain step toward her. "You are right, Florie! But at least your husband did not keep the First Volunteers a secret from you." When she felt herself losing control, felt hot tears burn her eyes, Mary made a little half-curtsy, fled from the room and upstairs, leaving Jonathan to cover the rude thing she had done in spite of her best intentions.

Not wanting to make matters worse, Jonathan did not follow her. He watched Mary heavily climb the stairs, then returned to their guests and apologized.

"No need for an apology, old man," Colonel Olmstead said. "I'm afraid it was I who spoke out of turn. You see, I—we know your charming wife is half Cherokee. I was afraid she might not understand. She did ask me if I hated Lincoln. I felt that she deserved to know the truth about why no brave people in the history of the world could accept such treatment as we would receive at the hands of a Republican administration, a Republican Congress, and a Republican Supreme Court without defending themselves."

"You explained it quite clearly, Colonel," Jonathan said, wishing they would leave so he could go to Mary. "Our child is due any day. A little overdue, in fact. My wife isn't quite herself."

"Oh, I think she's herself all right," Florie said.

"You only met Mrs. Browning tonight, my dear," her husband scolded lightly.

"But she's a woman and so am I, Charles. Women hate the thought of their men going to war over anything! Besides, it's common knowledge in town that here in the Browning house there are no Negroes, except the driver, a free person of color. You saw a white woman serve our dinner tonight. How would Mary know which side she's supposed to be on in this dreadful trouble? You should have kept her informed, Mr. Browning!"

"I know," Jonathan said, "but you both need to realize that while I'm doing all I can to prepare myself for—a possible war—I'm still not sure I'd fight to preserve slavery."

As he spoke, Jonathan kept his eyes on Charles's slender, thoughtful face. Keeping the cool head Jonathan had come to expect of him, Colonel Olmstead stroked his dark beard and thought a moment before he spoke. "I—I like you, Browning," he said at last. "And you have my word that I will say nothing to Colonel Lawton or to any other man in the First Volunteers until you've made up your mind. Isn't that as you wish it?"

Without a moment's hesitation, Jonathan said, "Yes, sir. That's exactly as I wish it and my gratitude to you, Colonel."

At the front door, when Jonathan was seeing them out, Charles Olmstead repeated his promise. This time, he added what sounded very like a warning: "I trust you realize keeping that promise indicates my full and complete trust in *you*, Browning, and that I have every right as your superior officer to expect you to inform me when you have finally made your decision."

Jonathan found Mary undressed and in bed, but eyes wide open. As soon as he entered the dimly lit room, she held out her arms. For a long time, they held each other in the quiet.

"Mary," he said at last, "I'm truly sorry. Can you believe me?"

"I am not to be trusted?" she asked.

"My darling, of course I trust you! I—I didn't tell you because I haven't told anyone. Not even Papa. Surely, not my mother."

"Mama Caroline is stronger than either you or Papa Mark think."

"I know she's strong. So is Papa, but like the rest of the country, they're on opposite sides of the fence!"

"You hate Mr. Lincoln enough to kill men from the North who want him to be President?"

He sat up. "That's too simple a way to put it."

"I am simple. A sweet-gum leaf is simple in the spring when it is bright green. It is simple in the summer when it is dark green. It is also simple in the fall when it turns red. It remains a gum leaf even when it dies and twists to the ground in a high wind."

"I wish we were dealing only with gum leaves," he said.

"Why am I half *Cherokee*, Jonathan? Charles Olmstead said he knew I was half Cherokee. Why doesn't he know I'm half Scot from my father?"

"I can't explain that, except that a man or a woman who might only be one-eighth Negro or even one-sixteenth is a Negro, not mostly white."

"Our child will then be *Cherokee*."

"Oh, darling, don't keep on making this so hard for me! I'm struggling as it is—fighting myself night and day over this secession thing! I know I mean to be ready, but that's all I know."

"Secession is wrong?"

"To me, it is. To my father, it's treason! To Charles Olmstead, it's every state's right under the Constitution. To him, to Mr. Clack, to Uncle W.H., to Miss Lib, to Mary Cowper and Andrew Low—to most Southerners—secession is an inalienable right of every state whose interests are gravely imperiled. If Abraham Lincoln is elected, the South will feel gravely imperiled."

"With a bayonet, I became a Georgian. Mr. Lincoln gravely imperils me? I do not think so."

"Mary, dearest, you don't have to worry. You don't ever have to decide how to vote. You can't vote."

"And that is wrong, if liberty is right. Why can't I vote?"

"Now you sound like Miss Eliza."

"I like to sound like Miss Eliza."

"You're innately wise, the way she is. Miss Lorah Plemmons is also innately wise."

"Innately means what?"

"That you were born wise."

"Secession means what?"

He sighed. "Tempers are so high these days, it means that if the North commits the slightest act against us down here that the hotheads might interpret as an act of war, the South will break away from the United States. The country we all love now, and call one nation, will be two. The North will be a foreign country."

"I will never secede from you, Jonathan!"

He could only hug her.

"We cannot secede," she said. "We are committed."

He laughed softly. "You've really learned the meaning of that word 'committed,' haven't you?"

"Oh, yes. I live committed to you. Why cannot your nation live committed?"

"Don't you—don't you feel as though it's your nation, too, darling?"

In the shadowy dimness of one low-burning gas lamp he saw her shrug. It wasn't a careless shrug. It was simply a shrug that said sometimes she felt like a member of her mother's Cherokee Nation—or no nation.

"Mary? Do you ever feel you could have, if you weren't so tenderhearted, hated white men for what they did to your nation?"

She laughed. "Oh, Jonathan, and love a white man as I love you?" She pressed her cheek against his. "I would not love you as I do if you did not have white skin!"

"Is that the truth?"

"You would not be Jonathan if you looked dark like my brother, Ben."

"I—I guess not." He laid one hand gently on her swollen body. "Do you think we'll have another little girl? Or a son?"

She fell back against the pillows, her lovely, even features glowing now with anticipation and peace. Peace? Hadn't she just minutes ago fled the drawing room because she was so hurt that he had not told her he'd volunteered for the newly formed combined regiment? At this minute, even a glance at her happy face could drown a man in joy. "You're unpredictable, young lady. Did you know that?"

"I know 'unpredictable,' and I am not. Always, always, you know what I will do."

"I do not!"

"I will go on loving you beyond my death and yours, my Jonathan. I love you so much, I love you with so many mountain ranges of steadfastness, I could never, never change. With you, I am never unpredictable. I am steadfast."

"I know," he murmured. "I do know, Mary."

"If you know, why did you keep the secret of the volunteer regiment from me?"

"You've always known I'm a member of the Chatham Artillery. I—I just hadn't happened to mention that many of the town's regiments had combined in one volunteer band. I was trying to protect you."

"To protect me and our child from fear you will be killed in a secession war?"

Her love *was* predictable, he thought, but *she* was not. And she was—born wise. He had indeed kept the secret, with forethought. There was no happenstance about it anywhere. "Mary, can you believe that I kept quiet because I still honestly don't know what I'd do if—there is a war?"

"You didn't say that downstairs!"

"I did after you left the room."

"Then I was wrong to run from the room." Her abrupt laughter tinkled. "I did not run, did I? As Miss Lorah would say, I lumbered. Oh, Jonathan, I will be slim and pretty again soon when our child is out of me. You will be free to pick me up again and whirl me round and round. You will also be free to whirl our child soon!" After another long, tender embrace, she breathed, "It is strange, isn't it, Jonathan, that when our child secedes from me, we will know joy, but to many people, secession is ugly. The sound of the word 'secession' is beautiful to me. Except, I will never, never secede from you. Not even if I die. Not even if you—die."

" 'Secession'—is a beautiful word, Mary?" he asked incredulously.

"A beautiful sound it makes on my tongue. Soft and lovely, like the Etowah lapping against the stone sides of a fish trap."

FIFTY-
ONE

*A*s soon as the news reached Savannah on May 18 that after three ballots at the convention in Chicago, Lincoln had indeed been nominated, Mark hurried from his office straight to Miss Eliza. His mood was one of genuine perplexity—an almost hopeless mingling of elation and outright foreboding.

As though she had been warned, she was on her porch, waiting. They were so close, no words were wasted in either greeting or small talk about the weather. He felt absolutely free just to sink into a nearby rocker and bury his head in his hands.

"I trust that doesn't mean Mary isn't doing all right," she said. "Will the baby come today? Has Dr. Arnold been there yet this morning, Mark?"

"Yes, he was there a little after seven. Mary's quite miserable, I think, but evidently doing well otherwise. The baby's just so much later than we expected." He lifted his head to look at her. "Oh, Miss Eliza, I wish—I wish—"

She gave him a sad, understanding smile. "You wish I weren't so old so I could be there to help."

"I always feel better about everything when you're on hand."

"I'm a little surprised you're here, Mark, with Jonathan at home today, too, but I had a feeling you were on your way. You read the *Morning News,* didn't you? You know about Lincoln."

He nodded. "And I'm glad I don't have to try to explain it, but I never felt so–lost or so alone or muddled in my life. And on the very day Mary's child should get here! But, Miss Eliza . . ." He held out both hands in a helpless gesture. "How can we bear being cut off from the country we both love so much? If Lincoln wins, the South will secede. There could be war!"

For a long, thoughtful time, she looked out over her yard, then up at the low-hanging branches of the three moss-draped live oaks that flanked her azalea bed, new, verdant summer leaves in place as though waiting to learn what the summer might bring. If the May heat was any sign, surely a summer of suffocation and storms and short tempers . . . a summer of rising hatred against the North, of jostling emotions and fiery words spoken without thought or real concern. Hotheads loose in the already almost unbearable Savannah heat . . .

"I'm almost glad I can't vote," she said at last, "and I almost pity you because you'll have to, come fall."

"I value my right to vote too much not to use it," he said, his voice sounding old even to himself, "but right now, I feel like a man who lives nowhere on the face of the earth. I even feel cut off from my own roots in the North. I–I talked to the city on my way here, as I usually do." He stopped to give her a look that said thank you for not thinking me too unhinged.

"And what did Savannah say to you, Mark?"

He tried to smile. "What did Savannah say to me?" he repeated her question. "She said, 'No matter what happens, you and I will go on.' Even though I know the Scriptures say, 'Here we have no continuing city,' somehow I believe that's what she said to me."

After a moment, Miss Eliza spoke in a quiet voice. "You have every reason to believe, dear boy. As long as you live on this earth, Savannah will continue for you. Someday, when I go away, I plan to leave you in her hands. Few people ever find an earthly city with a living soul like Savannah. Whatever happens this summer to you, Mark, to any of us, Savannah will go on. As she's always done. You just think you picked her out, Mark. Savannah found *you.*"

"You never stop amazing me," he said simply. "A few minutes ago, I felt more than a little crazy. Just hearing you explain has made me feel almost sane again. Miss Eliza, I was feeling cut off–not only from my Northern roots; worse, from the roots I've put down for myself here."

He got up to stand by the porch railing. "Is it a good thing that God lets a man get cornered?"

"I expect so."

"You've taught me it forces us to turn to Him alone."

"But God doesn't mind if we turn to Him through a city or a person we love. Or—a new grandchild." She paused. "Or—a presidential candidate we can't even vote for . . ."

"You know me like a book."

"By now, better than a book, I'd hope. Mark, I know you feel helpless, but you can pray. Whoever is elected the next President of our poor country is going to need a lot of prayer!"

"I guess I'd better get back home. I'm helpless to do anything constructive, but I need to be there."

"Of course you do. I'm just going to sit here and pray that things will be all right at your house. And"—she reached to take his hand—"and, Mark, I'm going to pray not only that Caroline will stay strong and free with you when she finds out that Abraham Lincoln was nominated, but that the baby, for Caroline's sake, won't look—too Indian."

"Thank you, dear friend. Thank you. Caroline is so changed these days, though, I honestly think, in time, she might weather that, too."

When Mark climbed the steps at his house on Reynolds Square a few minutes later, his heart raced as it always did these days when he walked too fast. Fumbling for his key, since Caroline was surely upstairs with Dr. Arnold and Mary, he wondered what he would do once inside. Where was Jonathan? Upstairs near Mary, he was sure. Grandfathers had no special place at a time like this.

He could read something, but he wouldn't know what he was reading. He could sit down in the drawing room and try to think things through. He had fully intended to ask Miss Eliza if she thought any one of the candidates running for President from four parties could win decisively enough to govern once in office. He felt sure the final count would elect either Lincoln or Douglas, since Bell and Breckinridge, who was W.H.'s candidate, were too factional. Savannah papers were delivered now. Had there been time for Caroline to see the news of Lincoln's nomination?

At the foot of the stairs, his coat and hat on the hall tree, he listened, but heard nothing beyond the subdued voices of Dr. Arnold and the ladies. Undoubtedly, Maureen and Gerta were both helping out in

Mary's room. Jonathan was probably somewhere upstairs by himself. Should he go up to be with the boy? Mark, because of his stiff knees, avoided the steps when possible and, at a time like this, Jonathan might well be better off alone. He would feel he had to buoy Mark's spirits.

In the drawing room, he sank into an easy chair and wondered again what to do. A letter from W.H. lay on a lamp table across the room. He could reread that, but reading it once had caused his heart to sink. As anxious as he was about Mary and the baby, this was not the time to be more upset. W.H. was now a rabid secessionist, doing all he could to help elect Breckinridge, declaring that the South would surely secede if Lincoln were elected. The man's dislike of Lincoln had almost scorched the pages of his letter.

After a minute or two of such jumbled thoughts, Mark went again to the foot of the stairs to listen. This time he heard the lusty, robust cry of a baby whose lungs, male or female, had to be strong!

Halfway up the stairs, he turned and came back down. He'd only be in the way up there. He stood waiting, fidgeting, listening, but the low murmur of voices from upstairs was too quiet to be understood. At least, he thought, no one sounds awfully worried. He would just wait.

A door opened upstairs and, after what seemed an incredibly long time, Caroline appeared on the second-floor landing, a tiny, blue-blanketed bundle in her arms. His pulse raced. The stifling heat in the downstairs hall welled up around him like warm, heavy water. "Caroline?" he called. "Caroline?"

She was smiling, but the smile looked strained. A hint of the old barrier was on her face. His waiting habit of the years took over, so that he simply stood there looking up at her.

"It's a boy, Mark," she said, making her way carefully down the curving stairs. "You have a new grandson, sir."

"Is he—is he all right?"

"Didn't you hear him cry?"

He nodded and held out his arms as she reached the downstairs hall. Only a thick shock of black, black hair showed above the blanket, but when Mark, the infant in his arms, folded back a blue corner, he saw a baby as brown as a nut!

His eyes met Caroline's, then went back to the infant. "Hello, little fellow." Again, he looked at Caroline. She had stopped smiling so that he saw her true feelings, showing him that inside a dreadful battle was raging.

She said nothing, but as though the last ounce of strength had drained from her, leaned heavily against the newel post, looking at Mark. Her eyes told him she had no doubt but that he, too, needed time to absorb the fact that this dark-skinned baby was his new grandchild . . . was Jonathan's *son.*

The infant kicked in Mark's arms, both tiny, dark hands flailing the heavy air—a protest against the Savannah heat.

"Does he—need this blanket on a day like this?" Mark asked.

"Dr. Arnold wrapped him in it."

"Has Mary seen him? Is Mary all right?"

"Exhausted, but I think fine. Yes, she saw her baby. Oh, Mark, is there one single drop of Jonathan's blood in the child? One single drop of yours? Of mine? He looks like a full-blood Cherokee!"

Mark tried to sound reasonable. "But, darling, don't you remember how *red* Natalie was? She—she didn't stay red! Can one really tell about newborn babies?"

He could tell. She could tell. *The child in Mark's arms would grow up to be the image of Indian Ben.* No wonder Caroline had looked the way she did coming down the stairs. Only the sight of Willow, for all the world like Mary, pretty and not at all Cherokee in appearance, had erased Caroline's dread back then. Would this child turn her permanently back to when she seemed almost to resent Mary for being a half blood? It would be up to Mark to see that his wife found a way to get past her horror of Indianness. But how? How was he to do it?

"Does—does he have a name yet?" he asked.

"Yes," Caroline said weakly. "They named him as soon as Mary and Jonathan set eyes on him."

When she didn't elaborate, Mark looked at the child. "And what is your name, little fellow?"

"His name is—Ben." Her voice was as blank as her face now. "Bending Willow Browning. And yes, his father was right there. He agrees wholly. Mark, I may never understand, but our son loves his Cherokee wife—the way you—love me!" The infant made a quarrelsome noise, but Mark kept his eyes on Caroline's and he seemed to *feel* her composure returning even before it showed in her eyes. *"Therefore,"* she said, "therefore, you and I will—love this child and help care for him as though he were—like us, Mark. Maybe we'll love him even more because he's—unlike us. That *is* what you want, isn't it?"

He was staring at her now, so dumbfounded, he could think of nothing quite sensible to say except "Yes, oh, yes! We'll love him, dearest, we'll love him . . ."

Caroline squared her shoulders. "And we'll *dare* the Savannah tongues to wag."

Mark handed the squirming infant back to Caroline, then his arms went around them both and they stood there overwhelmed by awe and newfound gratitude. After a moment, he watched her climb the steps with the baby in her arms and called, "Tell the new parents how happy I am."

She turned to look back at him. "I'll try, but only I can possibly understand how happy I've finally *allowed* you to be, Mark. It's going to be–all right. Somehow, it's going to be all right."

All he could manage was: "Oh, Caroline, thank you!"

When Jonathan joined his father in the drawing room a few minutes later, he held out his hand first, then rushed into Mark's arms. "Mary wants to see you when you feel up to climbing the stairs, Papa," the boy said.

"Soon, soon. I–just felt so happy–your mother just made me so happy, I knew I'd act a fool if I went up too quickly. Son, more than the miracle of a healthy baby has happened in this house today!"

"I know," Jonathan said, beaming. "Mama's going to love the boy–just the way he is. And if you can bear up under still more good news, there's something else you might find hard to believe."

"Right now, I think I could believe almost anything."

"Lincoln was nominated at the Republican convention and Mama was the one who saw the headline in the morning paper!"

"You mean–she told you?"

"That's right."

Feeling weak all over, Mark sat down. "What on earth did she say?"

"Nothing."

"Nothing?"

"Not one extra word. She just told me, and tried, oh, how she tried to smile. Papa, you always taught me all that's really required in life is that we try. Mama *is trying*." The sunny smile flashed. "I think I have to shake your hand now, sir. That lady really loves you. Congratulations!"

FIFTY-TWO

*A*s the debilitating Savannah summer inched along through June and July, Mark found himself hoping, even praying for self-control. Each new day brought the fall election closer, and all over town only deaf and blind persons could fail to miss tempers flaring at the least provocation. It had been so long since any rain had fallen to break the heat's grip on the city, it was no wonder everyone felt apprehensive and tense, as though the slightest unintentional spark of talk might set off an explosion. Near-hysterical so-called patriotism underlay even business and banking transactions. Certainly, unless a man could join in the mounting anti-Lincoln fury, it was not safe to entertain through long evenings when the relentless heat pushed gentle-manliness to the breaking point.

On the stifling July day he and Caroline had reluctantly accepted a supper invitation to the Andrew Lows', Mark stood watching the sun lower out the southwest window of his office anteroom. He marveled that he could actually see the movement of heavy waves of heat between him and the glaring sun. Sunsets were no longer spectacular. This summer, the sun was shedding its fury on them all.

The likelihood that the Republican nominee, Abraham Lincoln of Illinois, would carry most of the free states had created a mood of despondency, even for Mark, who admired Lincoln more each time he studied his speeches in Horace Greeley's New York *Tribune*. He could not have convinced anyone in Savannah but he believed that Lincoln just might exert a moderating influence in the North, so that from his new appointments there could come men able to find a way to keep the South from seceding. Miss Eliza agreed, as did Jonathan, that should the South break away, war would inevitably follow. War would mean that Jonathan would have to fight. Each time the thought came, Mark's despondency deepened.

This afternoon, dreading an encounter with domineering, pro-South Andrew Low, he faced the disturbing realization that he, Mark Browning, nearing seventy, would not have been strong enough to endure this horror-filled summer without the steadying companionship of Miss Eliza Mackay. The intelligent, open-minded lady who had lived her life with slavery continued, through each of his daily visits, to understand and never to take offense at Mark's beliefs. Even as they shared Eliza Anne's letters, sounding more and more secessionist in their tone, she said only that she did wish W.H. could simmer down and use his good, educated reason. The man was again neglecting the Etowah Cliffs land, riding off every few days to make campaign speeches for the secessionist Democrat, John Breckinridge, and while she complained in letters of her husband's neglect of their plantation, Eliza Anne herself was showing the brand of defensive anger Mark had come to expect from almost everyone in Savannah these days. Oh, she and W.H. still insisted that they hoped the Union would be preserved, but at the same time deplored that there were so many "blind Unionists" among the small, non-slave-owning farmers and storekeepers in the upcountry. Only this morning during Mark's early visit, Miss Eliza had said she expected Lorah Plemmons had a hard time keeping peace up there among Burke, who admired Lincoln as Mark did, Natalie, who only cared that Burke *not* let himself get drawn into a war, the Stileses and their well-to-do planter neighbors, who, as Miss Eliza saw it, only *thought* they wanted to see the country stay together. At the always quieting thought of Miss Lorah, Mark smiled for the first time since he'd played with Ben at home earlier this afternoon. If only the heat would let up a little, he and Caroline could take Mary and their grandchild to visit at Etowah Cliffs.

He mopped his face and neck with an already damp handkerchief and noticed irritably that it was time for him to go home, bathe, and dress in clean, dry clothes for the compulsory supper at Low's. His dread of the event was lessened only by his deep caring for Mary Cowper, carrying still another of Low's children. She had lost one baby and the births of the others had been far from easy, but Mary Cowper's youngsters seemed to keep her steady and reasonably content with her life. "She will go right on trying," Caroline had said at breakfast today, "until she gives Andrew Low the son he longs for. I pray she has a boy this time, before Mr. Low completely exhausts her. There's nothing wrong at all with large families," she'd said, "but people are talking about Mr. Low, simply because Mary Cowper just isn't strong enough."

"She had her younger daughter only a year ago, didn't she?" Mark asked.

"Yes, and now there's another child on the way in the midst of this dreadful heat!"

When they had moved to the front drawing room following Mary Cowper's beautifully served light supper, Mark was pleased to see how gently and courteously Low treated his wife, who was truly in that heavy, awkward stage. Why, he wondered, as he escorted Caroline to a chair near a tall, open window, did they invite us so near her time? Only a genteel lady could have managed to conduct herself so gracefully in Mary Cowper's condition on such a stifling evening. Even the breeze that stirred the elegant glass curtains at the open window was hot.

"I'm truly sorry," Low said, seating Mary Cowper, "not to have been by to view your new grandchild. I'm sure it's made all the difference in the world having a child around again. How old is he now?"

"A little past three months," Caroline said. "And of course, we feel he's quite advanced for three months. We have no doubt at all that he recognizes his mother and I do believe the child is going to have Jonathan's disarming smile."

"That's splendid," Mary Cowper said. "I always adored Jonathan's smile."

"Well, our Ben's a cheerful, contented boy and very thoughtful," Mark said.

Low raised an eyebrow. "Thoughtful at three months, Browning?"

"He does spend long, contented periods," Caroline put in to fill the silence, "deep in what really appears to be thoughtful study of his own little hands, examining each finger one by one."

"And is he a handsome boy?" Low wanted to know. "Mary Cowper and I pray for our first son, don't we, my dear?"

"Yes, Mr. Low. Oh, yes."

"Handsome?" Mark echoed Low's question. "We think so."

When Caroline lost no time in declaring the baby to be the living image of Mary's brother, Ben, Mark could have hugged her.

"Of course, you'd never guess the baby is Jonathan's son," Caroline went on, as though anticipating whatever comment Low had in mind. She would say it first. "The boy looks like a full-blood Cherokee, although he's only a quarter Indian. And yes, he's quite handsome, Mr. Low. Even at only three months. There's a dignity about the little fellow."

"And—strength," Mark added.

Low laughed. "I can see, Mary Cowper, that we must have a son! This in no way demeans our daughters. It would just be a unique pleasure to feel the extravagant pride Browning evidently has in his grandson."

Everyone looked toward Mary Cowper. She smiled—a bit weakly, Mark thought—and said only that she was praying harder than anyone for a son this time.

A brief silence fell across the splendidly appointed room and, exchanging what he hoped was an unnoticed glance with Caroline, Mark felt growing curiosity as to the reason for their visit to the Lows', if indeed there was one.

"I assume you are as gratified as I, Browning, that Savannah's economy continues strong," Low said, breaking the silence. "I'm aware, of course, that your sympathies in the current problems leave much for your Savannah peers to desire, but as the nation hurtles toward what could well be a disaster at election time, is there any hope that either your continued success as a merchant or your oft declared love of our city might be changing your beliefs? It must be most evident to the North by now that indeed Cotton *is* King down here and, if need be, we can not only fare but prosper without them—without any of them."

Mark had never in memory, felt air so still and choking. He ran a finger under his wilting collar, sat forward, then leaned back in the comfortable armchair.

When too much time went by, he heard Mary Cowper clear her throat and say, only half timidly, "Mr. Low, dear, I'd so hoped we could have a pleasant, easy talk with these close friends. Is it asking too much to stay away from politics in this heat?"

Mark looked at Caroline, who was watching Low, as he all but withered Mary Cowper with a glance. "It's only your condition, my dear, that makes you nervous."

"I don't think so," Mary Cowper said—rather firmly, Mark thought.

"Mark doesn't agree with us—he doesn't even agree with his own wife—so must we even discuss politics?"

"I've been assigned the duty of attempting, at least, to move Mr. Browning closer to the position of the rest of the Savannah business community, Mary Cowper," he said, as though he addressed a student from a teacher's podium. "I'll be grateful for your support. It seems quite plausible for Browning and me to talk in the presence of our wives, since both you and Mrs. Browning wield considerable influence over your husbands."

Mark was more than surprised when Mary Cowper actually laughed at that comment from the man over whom no one wielded any visible influence and whom she had appeared to be trying so hard to please in every way.

"I fail to see anything humorous in what I said, wife." The look Low gave her was stern, obviously meant to silence.

"May I ask *who* assigned you to move me closer to the secessionist views of other Savannah businessmen, sir?"

Mark's blunt question hung in the humid air while Low studied him. "You may indeed ask, Browning," he said. "Recently elected Mayor Charles C. Jones for one, your own client James Clack, my associate Charles Green, Mercer, Habersham, W. W. Gordon. Does that list suffice?"

"Of course," Mark said, determined to keep himself under control. "And I trust, my friend, that it will suffice to tell you, to assure you, that, as I've always endeavored to do, I plan in the future to keep my opinions—whatever they may be—strictly to myself. I do love Savannah. That is a widely known fact. I would hope that my eagerness *not* to cause trouble is, by now, also widely known. It is true that my wife and I do not see alike on the trouble between North and South—on the subject of slavery itself. I would also hope that in this room tonight we can all remember that although they are seldom mentioned these days, there *are* other vital issues that not only affect us all but on which we might find agreement. Along with your charming wife, I hope we can keep this a pleasant, congenial visit, but there is another issue, stressed far more in the lower North than slavery. Actually, an economic issue—the homestead plank in the Midwest, for example, which . . ."

"Which," Low interrupted, "merely points up the North's viciousness over slavery. Would those homesteads be opened to Southerners with their constitutional right to bring along their personal human property?"

Mark decided to ignore that. "Well, there is also the tariff plank in the Republican Party platform, strong in Pennsylvania. There are the rivers and harbors and Pacific Railroad planks. Surely a cross-country railroad would benefit us all—North and South." As he spoke, Mark watched Low carefully. He seemed, at least, to be listening. "Actually, Mr. Low," he went on, "while I know it infuriates you and my other business associates that I read Northern newspapers, it is a known fact that Mr. Lincoln himself is quite moderate on the subject of slavery."

Low started as though Mark had struck him. "That's nonsense!"

"It is a fact," Mark went on, "that at a Republican rally in Lincoln's hometown of Springfield, Illinois, only two of twenty-seven banners even referred to slavery. Abraham Lincoln wants to stop the *spread* of slavery, but he is perfectly willing to leave it alone where it is already established."

"You are a guest in my home, Browning, and I shall reserve my true feelings on this entire matter, except to assure you that you and perhaps your loyal son, Jonathan, are quite alone in the city in believing that the party of Lincoln is not made up of rank, South-despising abolitionists!"

"You have, sir, been misinformed on that point. At best the relationship between Republicans and abolitionists is ambivalent. Many of what you call rank abolitionists denounce the Republicans as being, in Garrison's own words, 'a temporizing and cowardly party' because it is pledged only to restriction of the peculiar institution and not to its total destruction!"

"Mark, please," Caroline whispered.

"Yes," Low joined her slyly, "I beg you also to temporize a bit, Browning. I am aware of what the Northern propagandists say. I've even read that *your* Republicans are calling themselves 'The White Man's Party' because they want to reserve the territories for free white labor. Even your three-month-old grandson could see through that ploy! They are merely holding the more dangerous abolitionists at arm's length because association with the fanatics can lose votes for Lincoln!"

In the momentary silence that followed Low's outburst, Mary Cowper said weakly, "Mr. Low, sir, I'm sorry to say I'm not feeling well at all."

Quickly, Caroline stood up, the men also. "We must go, Mark," she said, her voice strained, but determinedly pleasant. "Mary Cowper must be wretched—so beautifully dressed in all this heat. It's been a lovely evening and we do thank you for inviting us."

Low stopped bending over Mary Cowper only long enough to see them to his front door, where he made a halfhearted apology for having brought up the prickly subject.

"It's quite all right, sir," Caroline said, and Mark marveled at how calm she seemed, how much in control of her emotions. "We do hope Mary Cowper only needs to change into more comfortable, cooler garments. Please thank her again for us—and good night."

Low bowed. "Good night, Mrs. Browning—Browning."

"Good night, sir," Mark said, taking Caroline's arm as they went outside into the damp, stuffy, airless twilight.

Jupiter was waiting in their carriage, and as they settled into the tufted seat together, she asked, "Now, do you really believe you never have to be careful with me again, dearest?"

He worked at pulling off her lace mitt so he could kiss her bare, fragrant hand. "Yes, yes," he breathed. "I believe it, with all my heart."

They rode along in silence for a time, then Caroline said, "Could I say something else?"

"Anything."

"I think I find my behavior harder to believe than you do. I haven't changed my mind at all, Mark. I still have to quell a kind of panic inside at even the mention of Lincoln's name. I'm terrified of the way the North is still singing the praises of that murdering fiend John Brown. How can I not be afraid? Some of the men I've always thought of as intellectuals up there praise him as though he were a saint. Those men are now Republicans. How do we know that if Lincoln is elected, dozens of John Browns won't be sent down here to murder us?" She stopped herself. Mark could feel her doing it by sheer will, heard her take a long, deep breath. "But, dearest Mark, you've been a slave to my beliefs too long. That's over. So help me, God, that's—over!"

FIFTY-THREE

*A*s soon as Stuart left for the bank on the August day after Mary Cowper's baby came, Lucinda Sorrel Elliott set out for the Low mansion. Her marriage to Stuart Elliott had all but ended the meetings with Mary Cowper, but her love and concern for her younger friend went on. Lucinda had faced and accepted the probability of the severed friendship when she married Stuart, if only because she cared too much for Mary Cowper to put her through any more discomfort over him.

I'm one of the few people in town who even suspects that she might still be in love with my husband, she thought as she held her parasol low over her head against the unyielding Savannah sun. I am still in second place with Stuart. There's no doubt about that, and I feel foolish at times, but the truth changes neither my gratitude that he married me nor my feelings for Mary Cowper. I just miss her. Maybe she won't even see me today. Maybe she's still too ill from the birth of her new son, but I have to try. If Mary Cowper still cares for my husband, as I'm sure she does, I just might be able to lift her spirits a little by letting her know that I not only care about her, I'm doing all in my power to make Stuart happy.

Wiping perspiration from her forehead as she climbed the steps of the Andrew Low mansion, Lucinda smiled a little because sometimes

her own unselfishness sickened her. Stuart despised goody-goody people, but he did seem as contented as Stuart would probably ever be.

When Andrew Low himself, his handsome face wreathed in smiles,
opened the door, her own spirits lifted. Mr. Low seldom looked anything but impressive. Mary Cowper must be all right. The new baby
must also be well or he wouldn't be smiling.

"Come in, Mrs. Elliott," he said, bowing over her hand. "My wife is
indeed quite up to seeing you. Not just anyone, but I'm sure you're an
exception. You may go right upstairs to her room if you like."

Low, she thought as she climbed the stairs to the second floor,
appeared not only happy but extremely proud. From the old days of
their intimate friendship, Lucinda knew that Mary Cowper's main goal
in life was to give her husband a son. One glance at her friend's face
when she entered the master bedroom told her that the goal had been
met entirely to everyone's satisfaction.

"I've done it, Lucy," Mary Cowper said. "And even though I don't
recommend giving birth in such a heat wave, I've given him a boy
child." She held out one pale hand. "You're ever so good to come. Had
you heard about my tiny, beautiful William Mackay, or are you here to
find out if I finally accomplished what my husband so desired?"

Lucinda smiled down at her and took the outstretched hand. "I'd
heard and I was just so happy for you, I had to come. But don't feel you
have to talk. I—dare not stay but a few minutes anyway. You've been
through too much to risk wearying you further."

"Oh, I want you to stay at least until Nurse has bathed Willy! No one
from outside has seen him yet, and, Lucy, he's so beautiful. Far more
beautiful than most girls at the age of one day. His hair is golden, his
eyes deep blue, he has all his little fingers and toes, and already I'm sure
he's going to be lithe and graceful when he's a little older."

"I hadn't planned to stay but five minutes."

"Nonsense. Nurse can't possibly be finished with his majesty's bath
in five minutes. She just took him before you came in. Please sit down—
please?"

Lucy sat tentatively on the edge of a straight chair beside the bed.
She would stay ten minutes by her watch, no longer. Stuart had begun
recently to come home for half an hour or so at midmorning. She'd told
no one that she was on her way to the Low house, but Stuart had surely
heard at the bank that, at long last, Andrew Low had a son. Morning was
no time for a social call anyway. Household servants needed space to
get their work done. "I really can't stay, but if it's all right, I'll come

back soon. I long to see the boy. I really do. Mostly today, though," she said in her straightforward manner, "I came to make sure you're all right, Mary Cowper. You see, I still miss you so much. I haven't made another close friend. Have you?"

Mary Cowper turned her head away. "No, Lucy, I haven't. I still concentrate on pleasing Mr. Low." She looked back at Lucy. "Do you have to get home so quickly for any special reason?"

After the merest pause, Lucy said, "Yes. Yes, I do. Stuart has taken to coming home for a short time in the mornings. He's evidently unable to stay away from his own son for more than two or three hours at a time."

"I'm glad you gave him a son," Mary C. said. "I'm—very glad."

"Men do long for an heir," Lucy said. Feeling the need to move the subject to safer ground, she added, "It's so wonderful that you gave Mr. Low a son right now, when I'm sure he's as upset as other gentlemen in town over that dreadful Lincoln. Have you thought how blessed you are, Mary Cowper, that Mr. Low isn't an American citizen and won't have to fight if there is a war?"

"Yes, I've thought about that. You're not so blessed."

Lucinda made herself smile. "But I am in other ways." The smile vanished. "Mary Cowper, before I go, I just have to tell you that, considering all things, I believe Stuart is contented."

For a long time, she seemed to be studying Lucy's face. For such a long time, in fact, that it made Lucy quite uncomfortable. Then Mary Cowper asked, "Does Stuart still despise himself for what he did? For killing Tom Daniell?"

That was the last thing Lucy had expected. More than a year had passed since Stuart had even mentioned the duel, but, by now, Lucy could read his thoughts on the ugly matter and sense his deep-seated guilt. A particular look now and then told her. There were other times when his dark moods were inscrutable. These, she knew, were the times when his thoughts shot like arrows to Mary Cowper herself. Mary Cowper's question still hung unanswered in the close heat of the room.

"I'm sure," Lucy said, "that Stuart believes God has forgiven him. Whether he's really forgiven himself, I honestly can't say."

As though she sensed that that answer had to suffice, Mary Cowper quickly changed the subject. "I suppose, like every other man in town, Stuart's fired up over secession. The South will secede, Lucy, if Lincoln is elected. My husband is convinced of that. Is Stuart?"

Lucy found it impossible to remember one other time when Mary Cowper had spoken so freely of Stuart. In the past, when she did mention him casually, she always called him "your friend Elliott," or after her marriage, "your husband." This morning, he was Stuart. Did Lucy dare hope that Mary Cowper's young love for him was fading? That maybe she had become genuinely attached to Andrew Low?

"Is Stuart convinced that the South will secede if the Republicans win the White House?" Lucy repeated the surprising question. "Yes, although he isn't particularly fired up to fight." She shuddered. "I think he loathes the thought of another gun in his hands, but he says all the men at the bank are voting for Breckinridge as the South's only hope." She tried a smile. "Stuart isn't very involved in politics, you know." Then, quickly, before Mary Cowper could detain her any longer with another difficult question, she kissed her friend's forehead, promised to come back soon, and left.

Andrew Low was downstairs to see her to the door, still all smiles and pleasantries until he asked abruptly, "Your husband is well, I hope? And in full favor of breaking up the Union in order to preserve Savannah's economy?"

She gave him a dumbfounded look. Low had never once mentioned Stuart in her presence, let alone politics. She managed a smile, because the awkward moment had suddenly struck her as ironic. "Your first son has indeed made you a happy man, Mr. Low. And yes, my husband is quite strongly in favor of secession."

"Good. Because it's as inevitable as that man Lincoln's election!"

On the early November day when the *Daily Morning News* published the election results, a kind of elated fury swept like a raging fire across Savannah because Abraham Lincoln had won. Breakfast at the Mackay house went almost uneaten, and the talk at table, Kate Mackay thought, sounded like gibberish.

"I don't know about you, Sister," Kate said, excusing herself after methodically folding her napkin and inserting it in its silver ring, "but I'm going calling. I can't just sit here like a bump on a log and hear absolutely nothing of what's taking place in town!"

"I'll go with you," Sarah said. "It's too cool for you to venture out, Mama, so please be all right. We'll be back in plenty of time for dinner."

When Eliza Mackay sat staring at the wall opposite her chair, Kate asked, "You do feel all right, don't you, Mama? You do understand why we just have to get out and—"

"Yes, yes, I feel all right and I understand," their mother said, her voice filled only with weariness and what certainly sounded to Kate like plain old dread.

"You don't have to dread anything, Mama. It isn't as though we have any men here young enough to be soldiers, even if there is some kind of military skirmish. Oh, I could weep for all the women in the city who do have sons and husbands." Her mind hopped immediately to another subject. "Sarah, we must call on Nellie Gordon! It's been nearly a week now since her new baby was born and we haven't even paid our respects or shown one shred of interest. Now that Mama isn't well enough to make her daily calls on Sarah Gordon, the least we can do is show some interest in the new little girl, Juliette."

"They're already calling her Daisy, I hear," Sarah said. "And you're right, Sister. I'll be ready to go just as soon as I fix my hair and tack that bow back on my good hat."

"Don't rush, girls," their mother scolded. "You both know it's too early to make calls, especially with a new baby in the house. It isn't nine o'clock yet!"

The sisters sat back down. "Of course, Mama," Kate said, reaching again for the newspaper. "Shall I read more of this dreadful news about that abolitionist Lincoln?"

"That would be nice," their mother said, "but Mr. Lincoln *isn't* an abolitionist. He only wants, as I want, not to spread slavery beyond where it is already."

"Mama, I declare," Sarah said, "Mark Browning has influenced you far more than I realized."

"I think for myself, Sarah, and I don't want to hear one word against Mark Browning and not another word about our not having any young men of fighting age. We not only have Bobby and Henry, we have dear Jonathan!"

"Oh, dear," Sarah breathed. "I hadn't thought that far."

"Neither had I," Kate said, subdued.

"Well, *think*. You need to fix your hair, too, Kate."

"All right, Mama. But won't it be strange—peculiar—not to be United States citizens anymore?"

"We are citizens of the United States yet this morning," Eliza said sternly, "and both of you mind your tongues while you're out. I'd imagine our old city is at the boiling point."

After the Mackay girls had exclaimed over little Daisy Gordon to their hearts' content, the baby's nurse took her upstairs and Nellie Gordon served tea.

"I didn't dream Savannah would ever again cool off enough for hot tea," she said, handing a cup to each caller.

"The weather's cooled," Sarah said, "but just walking over here, the talk we heard was hotter than August was! We don't want to upset you so soon after the baby's birth, Mrs. Gordon. We both know you're on the other side, but we're neighbors now and I hope it's not too upsetting that we both favor secession just as soon as possible."

"The sooner the South breaks away from the Union, the sooner things can get back to normal," Kate put in.

Nellie Gordon's short laugh was just plain careless, Sarah thought. Young, pert Nellie sounded as though she couldn't care less about what happened, even if she tried.

"I'm sure Willie's most riled up," Kate said after a sip of tea.

Nellie tossed her head in disgust. "Oh, my, yes! In his mind, he's already mounted on his white charger ready to do battle for the South's Noble Cause! This may upset the two of you, but I don't care a fig about what the South does and, although I wouldn't want my parents to hear this, the North either. I only care about my husband and my children. I don't want my husband shot at and killed. I happen to be madly in love with him, as stuffy as he can be at times."

"Stuffy?" Kate gasped. "I never thought of Willie Gordon as stuffy."

"Stuffy in the sense of perpetually choosing what he considers his Gordon Duty, seemingly without a thought for me or his daughters. Look here, dear ladies, I simply can't take sides. One way or the other, these stupid predicaments governments create get settled. They pass. They end. So will this. I'm sure joy reigns in my parents' home in Chicago today because that truly extraordinary Abraham Lincoln will be the new President. I can almost hear my mother caroling about the house. I'm pleased for them, for everyone everywhere who is happy with the election results, but truly, I just don't give a *d* about what either the North or the South decides to do!"

Sarah almost spilled her tea and Kate jumped as she demanded, "You don't give—a *what*, Nellie?"

The melodious, careless laughter came again. "In deference to you both, my dear Miss Mackay, I said only that I don't give a *d*. What I meant was—"

"We know," Kate gasped quickly. "We know what you meant!" She exchanged looks with her sister, and said in what she hoped was a composed manner, "If we're to make our other calls, Sister, I suppose, charming as this is, we should be going."

"Oh, dear," Nellie Gordon sighed, not sounding at all apologetic, "I've offended you, haven't I? But really, I can't go about town forever concerned over my naughty vocabulary. Now and then, I find only a swear word conveys my true meaning. You'll all learn eventually that whatever I'm not, I am honest about what I think. It was lovely of you both to come this morning and I hope you'll give my warmest regards to your remarkable mother. There's a lady even I cannot surprise."

"We know," Sarah said as they both stood to go. "Mama is far more poised than Sister or I, and at her age, too. Your new baby is so sweet. And I love her name, Juliette."

"My *Lincolnian* mother's name, you know."

"Well," Sarah said, not too tactfully, "people *are* already calling her Daisy."

Nellie laughed again. "I, too, have a quite remarkable mother, ladies. Even if she is a Republican."

FIFTY-
FOUR

*S*outh Carolina, its politicians fiery and impetuous as always, had rushed to secede from the Union five days before Christmas 1860. Savannahians received the news with violently mixed emotions—some shouted for joy and began to wonder when Georgia would follow suit, others urged caution, pled for time to think through the possible consequences. But as far as Jonathan had heard by January 2, the first working day in the new year of 1861, those who objected outright to withdrawing from the United States were few in number. He would swear, actually, to only two—his own father and Miss Eliza Mackay—and perhaps, because of his advanced age and thoughtful conservatism, Papa's respected acquaintance Judge William Law.

Jonathan had always felt that he agreed with Papa where the North-South trouble was concerned. His own life in Savannah had not been touched by slavery except for family visits to Knightsford, his mother's Savannah River plantation, and there the Negroes were simply familiar, friendly people he'd always known. He seldom thought of them as slaves. At his father's town house, there had been only hired white servants, Maureen and Gerta—now Gerta's niece, to help out with Jonathan's new son, Ben—and Jupiter Taylor, a free person of color. Papa certainly admired the President-elect, Abraham Lincoln, and for that reason, so did Jonathan, until the shocking talk began, a few weeks after

Lincoln's election, that Georgia, too, must seriously consider seceding from what had always been Jonathan's native land.

With all the determination he could muster, for Mary's sake, for the sake of his parents, Jonathan had tried to stay cheerful through the Christmas season. For once, he had not found it easy. Savannah seemed to be hurtling headlong into a kind of frenzy of patriotism that, to him, all but blotted out the true meaning of Christmas. Oh, he'd marched with the First Volunteers in two parades, listened to the rabidly secessionist oratory, tried to stay away from the subject at home, but found no answer to the struggle inside himself.

Still he could not deny that, as he stepped along with his fellow volunteers in the spirited parades while drums and bugles stirred his blood, he had found himself responding to an entirely new pride of Southern birth. In fact the occasional surge of exaltation he felt had almost frightened him. The exaltation had also caused him to be careful, maybe for the first time in his thirty-four years, in the company of his father.

Alone at his desk in his office in the firm of Browning and Son, he sat staring at nothing, his back to the window that looked out over the busy waterfront, the casement closed against the chill January morning. The din of shouts and whistles and bells and wagon wheels rattling over the cobblestones that now paved River Street seemed remote with the windows shut. Stevedores, even some hot-tempered merchants, were, he knew, shouting more than usual these days, some cursing, of course, but most excited. With the window closed, they were all remote, too. He rather liked the odd, unfamiliar sense of being alone in the world, but he also disliked it. Jonathan Browning felt at home usually with almost anyone, in any place. Today, he seemed to belong nowhere or perhaps everywhere and so felt a stranger even to himself.

He would hear his father's hesitant, slightly uneven step when he returned from his daily visit to Miss Eliza and, because Papa's rheumatism had so slowed his pace, would have plenty of time to slip back behind the mask he'd been wearing lately—forcing his usual smile, filling a greeting with a few proud words about his new son, Ben. Being with Papa, he thought, was what he needed now and he wished the steady, dependable man would return. But he no sooner wished for the reassurance of his father than he was on his own feet, hat in hand. Pulling on his overcoat, he headed toward the double front doors that led outside onto Commerce Row and Bay Street. With no idea why he was going, he turned right on Bay and strode past four or five buildings to the firm of

Brigham Kelly, where his close friend Colonel Charles Olmstead had just been made cashier. What he meant to say to Charles, he had no idea, but he had avoided his own father in order to hurry to his new friend, now adjutant of the First Georgia Volunteer Regiment, of which Savannah was so proud.

Brigham Kelly himself met Jonathan just inside the counting room and after a warm exchange of greetings said, "A strange thing happened, Browning. About an hour ago, Colonel Olmstead received a note from Colonel Lawton requiring his immediate presence in the colonel's office. He's still there, so far as I know, but you're welcome to wait in Olmstead's private office right across the hall."

Jonathan thanked Kelly and began the nervous wait. Half an hour he waited, pacing the floor, sitting for a minute or two at Charles's desk, pacing again, the minutes inching past so slowly, he began to worry that Papa would be anxious about him. They had both kept to a pact made when Jonathan first entered the business that, when at all possible, one of them would be there if the other happened to be away. His father was surely back by now. Then from the hallway he heard the soft but excited voice of Colonel Olmstead, who, almost at once, burst into the room beaming from ear to ear.

"Browning," he said, with more excitement than Jonathan had ever heard from the quiet-mannered Olmstead. "Browning, my friend, we're in business! We're in the real business of soldiering! Wait till you hear."

They faced each other across the small office as Charles Olmstead described what he'd found upon following Colonel Alexander Lawton's order to appear before him. With Lawton was none other than Governor Joseph Brown himself, on a secret mission to Savannah to order the immediate occupation of Fort Pulaski.

"But, Charles," Jonathan interrupted, "Georgia hasn't seceded yet and Fort Pulaski is the property of the United States!"

"It is," Olmstead said, "but the United States has already begun to strengthen Fort Sumter in Charleston, South Carolina. Who's to say we Southrens shouldn't be in possession of Pulaski before they have a chance to make capture by us impossible?"

Jonathan could imagine his father's troubled, puzzled face. "But, Charles," he argued, "we here in Georgia are still legally a part of the Union. Pulaski belongs to the Union!"

"Do you think I haven't thought of all that?" Olmstead asked. "Savannah's very safety is dependent upon Fort Pulaski! Where would we be if we left it defenseless once war is declared?"

"War hasn't been declared!" Jonathan was gripping the corner of Charles's desk so that his fingers ached.

"An ounce of prevention, friend. If war is declared, won't you be relieved to know your family is as safe as those thick Pulaski walls can make possible?"

"Yes, yes, but—"

"The Governor left quite soon," Olmstead went on. "Then, invited to stay, I was present when Captain John Anderson of the Blues, Captain John Screven of the Guards, your Captain Joseph Claghorn of the Chatham Artillery, and Captain Francis Bartow of the Oglethorpes all stood around talking in solemn, somber voices about the plans I was ordered to put in shape and distribute—which I mean to do before I sleep tonight." Olmstead smiled warmly and held out his hand. "And you, my friend, are to go with your Chathams, from now on, as a first lieutenant! Isn't it just the best thing possible that we'll be making this important move together?"

Jonathan grasped the slender, warm hand. "Yes, Colonel. Yes. If I'm ordered, of course, I'll go."

Olmstead took one step back. "You don't seem at all glad of the chance, Browning. Is it your father's—politics?"

"Not so much his politics as my father himself," Jonathan said, not sure what he really meant. "There's nothing much to taking over Pulaski, is there? Isn't there only a caretaker and maybe a guard on duty out there at the most?"

Olmstead grinned. "And both hold strong Southren feelings."

"What is this word 'Southren'? " Jonathan asked.

"You'll grow to love it. I expect it to be our own special identification from now on," Charles said. "It denotes a man or a woman who truly loves the South and is willing to fight for it—to die for it." Olmstead's young, sensitive face grew solemn, questioning. "You *are* willing, aren't you? You were born and raised in Savannah, Georgia, Jonathan. The South *has* to be in your very blood!"

Jonathan tried a smile that failed. "Yes. Yes, I was certainly born and bred in Savannah. I–I love the old city with all my heart."

For a few seconds, Olmstead studied Jonathan's face. Studied it so intently, Jonathan looked away—out the window.

"Nothing about soldiering is supposed to be easy, friend," Charles said at last. "And don't think I'll forget for one minute what this might cost you with your own father."

"My father has always wanted me to think for myself."

"Good! Now it's time for me to clean up my desk here at Brigham Kelly Company, hand over my books and papers, and work on distributing our new orders."

Olmstead spoke with such enthusiasm, such eagerness, that Jonathan could only think of how he used to feel on Christmas morning when he was a boy. "How will your wife, Florie, take the news that you'll be leaving for Pulaski?" Jonathan asked.

"Like the strong woman she is," Olmstead said, already opening and closing drawers, stacking papers on the desk. "Somehow, I feel your Mary will be brave, too," he went on, "in spite of how she stormed out of the room that night she found out you were in the regiment." He stopped pulling out papers and books long enough to glance at Jonathan. "And by the way, it's easier sometimes to accept something hard when there isn't much notice. We sail out to occupy Pulaski at eight tomorrow morning."

Dawn had barely begun to push darkness from the city the next morning when Eliza Mackay, bathed and dressed, made her way carefully down the stairs. Halfway down, she saw both her daughters in the hall below, standing together as though they were little girls, tentative, hopeful smiles on their faces.

"Well!" Eliza said, still coming down slow step by slow step. "I see I'm not the only one who couldn't sleep with all that drumming and tooting outside. Have you had breakfast yet?"

"Yes, Mama," Kate said. "We hope you don't mind, but it's such an exciting morning, so much going on out at the waterfront, we just had to get an early start."

"You do so well coming down those steep steps alone," Sarah said. "Emphie's made corn cakes—your favorite. And Hannah informed us that she'd opened the last jar of apple butter. You'll like that on your cakes. Are you sure you don't mind that we went ahead and ate, Mama?"

"Why should I mind? And if I don't know how to get down those old steps by now, I'll never learn. Corn cakes will be just fine." She had reached the hall now and her daughters' excited, beaming faces were so exactly the opposite of what she felt, corn cakes and apple butter seemed a welcome subject of conversation until they could get into their coats and hats and gloves and out of the house. "I'm sorry we're into the last of Hannah's apple butter. Did you both have some?"

"We did," Kate said, fidgeting only a little less than Sarah. "And there's nobody on earth can flavor apple butter like Hannah. Are you sure it's all right if we both go out to watch the soldiers board the *Ida* to sail out to seize Fort Pulaski?"

"Of course it's all right. If you can stand the sight of such a terrible thing, help yourselves. Hannah and Emphie and I will do fine here."

"Mark will be by, I'm sure," Kate said, her voice actually trembling with excitement. "They're supposed to set sail at eight, and he's almost always here by ten." An absolutely irrepressible smile lighted Kate's broad, aging face. "Oh, Mama, in all my life I've never felt so patriotic!"

"I can see that," Eliza said, knowing her voice dampened their high spirits, but a heavy heart meant a heavy voice and she was too worried to try to hide it.

"Come on, let us help you to the table," Sarah said, taking her mother's arm. "You really have a treat in store with those corn cakes and—"

"Most of the time, dear girls, I do very well keeping my mouth shut when you treat me as though I'm either senile or have one foot in my grave. Today, in spite of the way you both rejoice in the madness at Fort Pulaski, I'm too worried to tolerate being handled with kid gloves, so let me past and I'll go in the dining room for my coffee."

Both daughters stepped aside, allowing her to seat herself. "You do want Savannah to be safe, don't you, Mama?"

"Yes, I've loved Savannah a lot longer than either of you has been around to love it," she said, pouring her own coffee. "I also love the country. The United States and I are almost the same age, you know."

"We do know, Mama," Sarah said. "You've told us that for years."

"Well, it's been true for years and Fort Pulaski is the property of the government of the United States. Georgia hasn't seceded and I pray to God it never does! For Governor Brown to order Pulaski seized is an act of outright vandalism."

Her daughters still stood near the dining-room door, busting at the seams to go, she knew, but Eliza took a few appreciative sips of hot black coffee before she said as gently as she could, "Now scoot, both of you. I'm not an invalid and you're both about to die to get out there in the craziness at the waterfront, so scoot. Oh, and if you see Mark, tell him not to hurry. He'll be here eventually, and after all, his only son is sailing out with his regiment to do this dastardly thing and I don't want Mark to be under any more of a burden than he already is, just because of me."

"But, Mama," Kate said, "they're only going to hold Fort Pulaski until Georgia's had time to secede, until the State Convention is held."

"I know that. I know I'd like to eat in peace, too, so tell Hannah I'm waiting, please. And do be careful in all that wild, cheering, senseless crowd."

"But, Mama," Sarah said helplessly, "the Union has turned against us!"

"The Union is run, North and South, by men who all seem to have forgotten the meaning of leadership. Such goings-on as are taking place this morning are not the Federal government against us down here—the whole country is turning against itself!"

The air had been filled with martial music since dawn, so that just after seven the Brownings could hear it plainly at the breakfast table. Caroline sat at her usual place at the far end, taking an occasional sip of coffee, but merely moving around on her plate the food placed before her, eyes never off Mark's face.

"Move closer to me, darling," she said, breaking another tense silence. "You're so far away at your end of this long table. Are you finished eating?"

He threw down his napkin. "All I can swallow," he said as he picked up his own coffee cup and sank into the chair Jonathan had vacated more than an hour ago, just to her left.

"At least, now I can touch you." She laid her hand over his. "I wish my touching you—helped," she whispered.

"It helps. It has always helped. This whole thing with Fort Pulaski is just so—abrupt," he said. "Abrupt and crazy!"

Caroline took a deep breath. "I'm—trying, Mark. I'm really trying."

His faint smile eased her a little. "I know you are. Believe me, I know that, dearest. I can't imagine how—lost I'll feel if Georgia goes through with secession, but today, Fort Pulaski still belongs to the United States."

"Yes."

"Is that all you can say about it?" He almost grabbed her hand, as though needing even more of her attention. "What do you really think about the First Georgia Volunteer Regiment seizing United States property while the state is still part of the Union?"

"I don't know, Mark. I honestly don't know, except that Joseph Brown is our governor and he ordered it seized. With good reason, I'd say, if Washington has already begun to fortify Fort Sumter up at Charleston."

But South Carolina seceded before Christmas of last year!" Mark dropped her hand and picked up his cup, then, as though he couldn't swallow even coffee, set it down again. "I'm sorry. I know we went through this all night long. I–I just feel so helpless. Somehow I can't accept that–our son is out there a part of the command about to do this–violent act!"

"Well, Jonathan's there because his company is there. You're also a member of the Chatham Artillery." She was keeping her voice surprisingly calm. Adding to Mark's burden was the last thing she meant to do, but what she'd said was true. He'd always been so proud of the Chatham Artillery. There had never been a thought of Jonathan's signing up with any other in town. Mark Browning's son was, after all, Mark Browning's son. "Normally, you'd be right there in your own uniform, letting the world know he's yours. Does it help a little that, as of now, your son's a full lieutenant?"

"No. I expected that anyway. Only holding your hand helps today. We are close, aren't we? I mean, closer than ever before–still?"

"Have I lost control once through all this recent mess, Mark?"

"No, thank God. No, darling, you're wonderful."

"I'm just hard for you to believe after all the years you had to handle me with care."

"Maybe. I–I can't bear distance between us. Never could."

"Me either," she said, covering his hand with both of hers. "Even when I put the distance there, I couldn't bear it. That's why I made myself change."

Another smothering silence came, but she felt no distance between them, just helplessness.

"Will you go out to the wharf to see them off on the plucky little *Ida?*" she asked finally. "And do you want me to go with you?"

"Yes, oh, yes. Would you, please? I know Jonathan will be looking for us."

"Shouldn't Mary go, too?" she asked. "It's almost more than I can bear to think of her upstairs in their room without him. Evidently, from what Jonathan said when he came down to breakfast, they've said their goodbyes. He won't be home tonight, you know."

"I know. We don't have any idea *when* he might be home again. At least, for any length of time."

"The boy's going to be wretched in those miserably primitive quarters, but we can be thankful he's in no real danger. The Volunteers will just march in and settle in, I'm sure. I packed everything I could think of for him to take. Do you want me to go up to Mary? Ask if she'd like to be a part of this with us?"

"You decide, please. You know how a woman feels at a time like this."

Caroline shuddered. "No, Mark. I don't know. The Chatham Artillery has always only meant a smart parade for me, a ball. And you the handsomest man present. I have no idea how Mary must feel right now. I just know that I'm truly glad she has little Ben."

"You have changed, haven't you? Or is it just the real you with me now?"

"Do we need to know which it is? I hope not, because I honestly can't tell you." She tried a flash of their old humor. "Sometimes I'm so perfect, I almost hate myself!"

He didn't join her in the attempt this time. She knew he couldn't.

*A*t *a few* minutes past eight, Jonathan stood, with the others who made up the commands designated to seize Fort Pulaski, on the deck of the much admired little steamer *Ida*, dependable Captain Circoply at the helm. The men were at ease under the bright, climbing sun, at least as much at ease as any group of young men could be who were reveling in their own manhood and the golden chance to take possession of an important "enemy" fort.

Shouts and cheers from the *Ida*'s crowded deck mingled with even more shouts, music, and cheers echoing over the harbor all along the waterfront. As the *Ida* started down the river, Jonathan was sure he must be the only Savannahian not cheering, calling, singing, or whistling. He smiled in the direction of his friend Colonel Charles Olmstead, who was standing beside Colonel Lawton, proud to be his adjutant. When their eyes met in all the noise and confusion, Olmstead smiled back, but Jonathan's thoughts were riveted still on one room upstairs in his father's house on Reynolds Square where Mary, he knew, sat holding their tiny son, Ben, sound asleep, the black Indian eyes closed in his dark little face. Only babies, he felt sure, could sleep through such a din.

As the *Ida* made it to the middle of the river and was firmly on its way, she received whistles and salutes from all crafts afloat, while the balconies of the stores and countinghouses along Factor's Walk and

Commerce Row were crowded with people waving handkerchiefs and scarves and cheering at the top of their lungs. Still Jonathan could not shout, could not cheer. Then, as the *Ida* passed Commerce Row, he saw his parents out on the Browning and Son balcony and his heart both leaped and sank. He'd urged Mary not to come, but he realized at the sight of Mama and Papa that he'd really expected her. She was nowhere in sight.

His parents were waving, waving. For the first time, Jonathan waved back. He was torn apart over Mary's strange, perplexed silence when they'd said goodbye, but he longed for her to be there waving, too. The bright morning air felt good, invigorated him, in spite of the deep ache over Mary's lack of understanding of anything he was doing. He had tried last night before they went to bed and again in the middle of the night when they were both up with Ben. He had tried hard this morning before dawn to make her understand that he was going because he had been ordered to go, but Mary had only clung to him or looked at him from across the room or, dry-eyed, stared down at their son, then back at Jonathan—in almost total silence. If his life depended on it he could not, at this minute, remember anything she had said beyond "I love you forever, Jonathan. Do not worry over me. Ben will be here. Ben will take care of me always, as the other Ben, my brother, cared for me."

"I'm only going out to Cockspur Island, Mary," he'd tried to reason with her. "I'll be in no danger. I can come to the city often, I'm sure, and depending on what happens about secession, regiments will be changed at Pulaski. I won't be gone forever!"

Mary had only looked back at him, the scar on her cheek plainer than usual, her eyes—the good one and the half-sighted one—still dry. Even when he asked a question, she answered only, "I love you, Jonathan. No man was ever loved as I love you."

"Mary!" He heard his own voice cry out into the cheers and the laughter and the joking aboard the *Ida* as it moved almost out of sight now of Papa's balcony. No one heard his cry. He called out her name again, his heart squeezing with pain, his arms still waving in the direction of the Browning and Son balcony above their big warehouse on River Street. "Mary, *Mary* . . . *!*" No one aboard knew what he was shouting. He was sure no one cared. He was the only man there who wasn't entirely caught up in the fervor, the sheer exhilaration of the moment. Shouting, crying out helped . . . helped release some of the pain, the awful indecision, the not knowing how he really felt about

seizing Fort Pulaski, an act Papa said Miss Eliza was calling "vandalism" against their own country.

Jonathan didn't like the idea of slavery, but neither did he hate it as Papa did. The whole hullabaloo isn't about slavery anyway, he thought, and tried to shout "Huzzah!" with the rest of his soldier companions. "Huzzah" didn't come out right, nor did it help, so he shouted Mary's name again and wondered wildly if he were going to be sick, because just crying her name had let loose a new bitterness within him he didn't even know was there. He could shout anything he liked in the bedlam around him and no one would hear, so he cried at the top of his voice that he hated it because his only son had dark, Indian Ben skin! He had liked Mary's dead brother, Ben, and always he had loved and somehow cherished Mary's Cherokee blood, her enchanting Cherokee ways. "That's the truth," he yelled. "That's the God's truth! I love Mary exactly as she is, but I hate my son's Indianness! I hate it, I hate it, *I hate it!*"

He rubbed his hands over his face, and felt dizzy, as though he could topple overboard into the brown water over which the *Ida* plowed its inelegant, plodding path. He didn't fall overboard. His head cleared and, from somewhere down inside, a great weight shifted, shifted to an unexplainably more suitable place. His shoulders straightened with no effort. The dread of a single night away from Mary's warm body remained, but he would manage now by some means. He had cried out his hatred of his son's dark skin and, in the doing, had somehow been freed of it. Never again would he have to bite his tongue to keep from telling Papa—or Mary. Somehow, because he knew Mama fought her own loathing and fear of it, too, he hadn't thought of telling her—ever. Now, there was no need.

In sight of Cockspur Island, a whoop akin to what he thought a battle cry must sound like rose again on board the *Ida* as the men got up from sitting on their trunks or just squatting and began to shout and cheer, until Colonel Lawton himself ordered them to be silent. Too bad, Jonathan thought, since he was only now, for the first time, beginning to feel as though he were really a part of the little force, the tiny privileged force of fewer than two hundred men chosen to seize great Fort Pulaski, where Miss Eliza's friend the admired Colonel Robert E. Lee had worked as a young Army engineer, younger than Jonathan today.

When his fellow passengers on the *Ida* calmed down, he joined them by sitting on his own huge trunk of extra clothing, a place setting of family silver, everyday crystal, and china which Mama had insisted he bring along. So much baggage had embarrassed him at first, but one look at the luxuries of home the others had brought put a swift end to that. The fellows were on a lark, better than a picnic—more real than boyhood fantasy.

Captain Circoply was easing the *Ida* toward the fort's wharf now and they were all standing again, beating each other on the back and shoulders, trying not to cheer too loudly, but all so full of youth and patriotism and vigor and zest for action that the corps drummers struck up even before they touched land. The drums set off more cheers and even Colonel Alexander Lawton smiled.

The *Ida* docked at last and, on shouted orders, the little battalion was formed on the North Wharf. Then, with drums rolling, colors flying, every pulse began to pound and every heart to swell—Jonathan's included, for the first time without any dregs of confusion—as they marched over the drawbridge, under the portcullis, and into the massive fort. Would any one of them ever be able to forget that shining moment? Would Jonathan as an old man be able to shut his eyes and see again the proud step of officers and men, colors snapping in the stiff breeze from the ocean, then their sunlit parade as they emerged from the shadow of the archway? At the first sight of a big gun through an open casemate door, Jonathan's memory raced back to a long-ago day when, as a boy, Papa had taken him for an outing at Fort Pulaski on a Sunday afternoon. Was it possible that now, marching in on his own two feet, he was actually there as an officer of the garrison ordered to defend the fort against all enemies? Enemies . . .

Once there, he had found no time alone for anything resembling reflection until late that first night as he sat on a camp chair from home in his assigned quarters in a casemate, guards mounted outside, police squads detailed, cooking squads installed in the kitchens, the newly occupied fort nearly quiet at last. As though ordered by some inner command, he began a letter to his parents in which he told them what he'd had time to learn of the fort's armaments, just twenty 32-pounders, long naval guns mounted on cast-iron carriages and all in the casemates. On the ramparts, he had seen platforms for barbette guns but no guns were there. The 32-pounders were in bad shape, carriages and chassis stiff from rust and disuse, and only a small supply of powder in the magazines, a fairly good supply of solid shot, but no shells. He closed the letter by saying: "We have plenty of work to do. Colonel Olmstead agrees and sends his best to you both. Except for one or two old cadets from the Military Institute at Milledgeville, none of the officers or men are familiar with the routine duties of garrison life, but we will learn. Don't let all this talk of guns worry you, Mama. I knew Papa, as a fellow artilleryman, would want to know. I am surprisingly glad to be here, and wish I had words to explain why, because the change in my attitude has been sudden. A kind of release happened en route on the *Ida.* I see now that I fully agree with neither of you where slavery is concerned, but *I am a Southerner,* born and bred, and I will conduct myself as such. Colonel Olmstead says I may tell you that he and I will come into the city at the earliest possible time and, of course, I will write again soon. Yr loving son, Jonathan Browning."

His letter to Mary was far harder to compose. With all his heart, he longed to help her understand why he felt it right to be exactly where he was. He could not tell her, because the reason was so new to him. Even he did not fully understand or quite believe that he had, on the short river trip to Cockspur Island, become a true "Southrener."

And so, truly freed of hating Ben's Indianness, he wrote only that he loved her with his entire being, that he missed her, and then tried for the first time to put into words his gratitude for their son, Ben. "No matter where I am, I belong," he wrote, "to the two people with the most beautiful faces on earth: you, dear Mary, and our Little Ben. Kiss him for me. Tell him to kiss you. I kiss you, I kiss you, I kiss you . . . I kiss your scar and Ben's tiny, proud Indian nose . . ."

On Tuesday, January 8, Eliza Anne surprised everyone by arriving on the evening train from the upcountry. Even Mary C. and Andrew Low weren't expecting her.

"W.H. didn't object a bit," she told her mother on Wednesday morning as they settled, with Kate and Sarah, in the old Mackay parlor for a good visit. When her sisters and mother seemed full of questions about W.H., she explained in what she hoped was a casual way that, as usual, her husband was head over heels in the secession dispute. "I've given up trying to pigeonhole W.H.," she laughed. She knew the laugh was not very convincing. "As soon as I begin to see him thrive on his books and writing, or his work as a gentleman farmer, off he goes to Milledgeville to address the legislature on how Georgians must unite in the face of the common foe. He's there now and I must say the speech he wrote is magnificent."

"The common foe, I take it," her mother said in a firm, almost ironic tone, "is the government of the United States."

"The *new fact* of an abolitionist government of the United States after March, Mama," Sarah said sharply. "We all know that W.H. believes that Lincoln man and his ugly ilk will destroy us down here!"

"I asked my question of Eliza Anne, Sarah," their mother said.

Sarah only snorted.

"I can see you're not even of one opinion in this house." Eliza Anne spoke in what she still hoped was a casual manner. "I suppose that's true all over the state. I know the Unionists in Cass are fighting mad at the thought of separation. Of course, most of them are small farmers or laborers who own no people."

"Like Burke," Kate offered.

"Oh, Burke's as bad as Mark on the subject," Eliza Anne said, with an edge she knew showed her own turmoil. "Burke's no farmer and he's really quite successful as a builder. He's just self-righteous. So is Mark. He's never said much before W.H. or me, but we know he thinks slave owners evil."

"And *that* incenses me!" Sarah's outrage showed plainly. "Mark goes around being so kind and considerate and loving with all of us, but I know what he really thinks about us and sometimes I have to curb myself to keep from telling him what I think of him right to his face!"

"That's enough, Sarah," their mother said firmly. "Not another word against Mark! With W.H. in Milledgeville," she went on, "I think it's fine that you came down to see us, Eliza Anne. Will Robert and his new bride, Margaret, be coming by, too, on their way back to Etowah Cliffs?"

"They're not going to live up there, Mama," Eliza Anne said, both glad and sorry to have the subject changed. She had come on the spur of the moment for a reason—to seek her mother's counsel on the frightening subject of secession—but all the way down on the train, she'd worried about resisting that counsel in view of W.H.'s rapidly growing pro-secession views. "Bobby and Meg have decided to live down here. Her parents, the James Hamilton Coupers, are just down the coast, you know, at Hopeton near Brunswick. They're very happy, really, and I never believed Bobby's wandering eye would ever settle on one person. Evidently it has, but he would be even more restless up there surrounded by all that Union sentiment."

"Even with W.H.'s strong Southern beliefs?" Kate asked.

"Yes, Sister." Eliza Anne herself had turned the subject back to the troublesome topic and felt somehow relieved. After all, that was her reason for coming—to try to sort out her own thoughts concerning it. "W.H. is even more restless than Bobby, actually. You know," she explained carefully, "in spite of being asked to address the legislature before Georgia holds its secession vote, my husband is only an alternate delegate. He—he chafes under that. He always has. The poor darling wants so much to serve!"

"And along with serving the public," Sarah said, "I've always thought W.H. isn't happy unless he's in the center of things being looked up to for advice and leadership."

"I think I'll let that pass, Sister," Eliza Anne said testily, determined not to cause any more anxiety for her aging, frail-looking mother. "I know W.H. I know what he's really like down inside. He's my husband, not yours." From her reticule, she took out the letter she'd brought from Mary Lee, wife of their longtime cherished friend Colonel Robert Lee. "This is one of the main reasons I made the trip down to Savannah, Mama," she said abruptly. "It's a letter from Mary Lee. You know how I admire and respect her. I haven't even shown the letter to W.H. It disturbed me too much. Of course, I longed to see Mary Cowper and my precious grandchildren, but this is really the reason I came the very next day after Mary Lee's letter reached me."

"What on earth did she write?" both sisters chorused.

"I take it you mean to read it aloud to us," their mother said.

"I'd like to, if it won't tire you, Mama. I need to share it."

"I probably look tired every day," her mother said with a twinkle, "because I'm so old and wrinkled, but it's midmorning, Eliza Anne, and that's my very best time of all."

"The very best time of all," Kate echoed, already on the edge of her chair. "Read it, for heaven's sake!"

Eliza Anne unfolded the pages and got only as far as the date, January 5, then stopped. "Mama, isn't this about when Mark visits you every day? I don't want any outsiders here when I read Mary's letter."

"Mark's no outsider," her mother snapped, "and now that Jonathan's stationed out at Fort Pulaski, it's sometimes late in the afternoon before Mark makes it over here. Bless him, though. As busy as he must be without the boy to help out, he comes every day. No more outsider talk!"

"Mama, I know Mark's not an outsider, but do you really think it strange that when the hideous Northern trouble is the topic, I might feel he isn't as close to us all as before?"

"No, it isn't strange at all, dear," her mother said evenly. "Except that Mark, however you might resent it, has been perfectly consistent in his beliefs since the first day he set foot in our house back in 1812."

Eliza Anne frowned. "I know, I know. And you also know that Mark has always been very dear to me. It's just that . . ."

"Things are different these days," her mother finished for her.

"Yes. Anyone who admires that Lincoln monster is—beyond me!"

"Does Mark really admire the new President?" Kate asked.

"Very much," their mother said. "And that's Mark's prerogative. The letter from Mrs. Lee, Eliza Anne, please?"

She smoothed the pages from Mary Lee over her knee, took a deep breath, and began to read: " 'Your letter received, dear Eliza Anne, from which I learned of your earlier one that did not reach me. Therefore, I am so much obliged to you for thinking of me in these troublesome times with a second letter, tho' I have thought of you and yours often and had determined to write to know if you could approve of all these riotous proceedings in the land. Has all love and pride in their country died in the South? Are they willing to tear her in pieces and some even to expect to see her glorious flag trailing in the dust? It should rather have drawn tears from their eyes, as their actions do from mine! We have lived and fought and prospered under this flag for so many years and tho' the South has suffered much from the meddling of Northern fanatics, yet do they expect to fare better now?' "

"But only South Carolina has already broken away," their mother said.

"That's true—so far, Mama," Eliza Anne said, and went right back to Mary's letter: " 'Are there no rights and privileges to Americans but those of Negro slavery? You, Eliza Anne, by your situation are removed from any active interference, whereas we in the border states are so much annoyed. Our slaves have become almost useless. In our own family, we have lost numbers who have been decoyed off and after my father's death we were preserved from an outbreak excited by two abolitionists who were constantly over here (one of whom, I am happy to say, is now in the penitentiary for fourteen years). We were spared, I say, by the *special* Mercy of God. The *Tribune* and New York *Times* published the most villainous attacks upon my husband by *name* and upon my father's memory in language I would not pollute my lips to repeat, and yet after all these wrongs, I would lay down my life, could I save our *Union!* ' "

"Oh, my goodness," Kate gasped, "we did hear about those horrible attacks on dear Robert Lee! Of all the mean injustices to say a kind man like that, who isn't even in favor of slavery, could mistreat his own people!"

"I sincerely hope, Kate, that we might be quiet long enough to allow Eliza Anne to finish this sane, sensible, truly patriotic letter!"

"Yes, Mama."

Their mother sighed. "If it would do a nickel's worth of good, I'd lay down my life for the Union, too."

Eliza Anne stared at her. "You'd actually do that, wouldn't you?"

"I'm not in the habit of saying what I don't mean, daughter."

"I guess I knew you felt that way, Mama, even now, with other states of the South on the verge of secession."

"But only South Carolina has so far," her mother repeated. "Now, please read."

" 'What is the use,' Mary Lee writes, 'of a government combined as ours is of so many parts, the *Union* of which forms its very strength and power, if any *one part* has the right, for any wrong, real or imaginary, of withdrawing its aid and throwing the whole into confusion, as South Carolina, who has refused all overtures for peace and imagines the world will admire her independence. The truth is, they laugh at her folly, which is perfectly suicidal. You know, my dear Eliza Anne, that my feelings are all linked with the South, but you will bear with me in the expression of my opinion. While there are many Northern politicians who deserve no better fate than to be hung as high as Haman, believe me that those who have been *foremost* in this Revolution will deserve to meet with the reprobation of the world, North and South, for having destroyed the most glorious confederacy that ever existed—the United States of America! You and yours, who have lived abroad, will always be dear to my heart and I feel certain that all your sympathies cannot be confined to your *State* to the exclusion of our *Country*.' "

No one had interrupted. Eliza Anne simply stopped reading.

"And is that true of you?" her mother asked after a moment.

"I'll tell you what's true of *me*," Kate said. "I'm in total sympathy with the state of Georgia! I'm glad, glad, glad that Governor Brown ordered our soldiers to seize Fort Pulaski!"

"I know about you, Kate, and Sarah, too. I asked Eliza Anne."

"Yes, Mama, I know you asked me. The truth is, I'm—not sure. For years, W.H. and I have loved the Union. You and Papa taught us all to revere it. Now, with so much gone awry, such bitterness and hopelessness in my heart about the way the North is treating us, the dreadful things one knows about Lincoln, how can I possibly be—"

"Abraham Lincoln isn't even to be inaugurated until March," her mother broke in. "What dreadful things do you expect him to do to us down here? He *isn't* an abolitionist, you know."

"But he's an activist and only heaven knows what he and his ugly followers might do to the constitutional right to own slaves! Mama, don't remind me that all the trouble *isn't* over slavery. I know that. It's really over our power and States' Rights and no freedom-loving Southerner can sit still and submit to domination over our state from Washington!"

"Is that all of Mary Lee's letter?" Sarah asked.

"Just about, Sister. Let me see. She says that no matter what happens our family and hers will remain close, 'our association unbroken.' Then she adds, 'I only wish the other Southern states would leave Carolina *alone* and she will soon tire of her sovereignty. She has been teeming, anxious to show her independence for many years, and it would be well for her to have to try the experiment alone. Mr. Lee is in Texas, *deeply grieved at the state of things.*' "

"Is that all she says about dear Robert?"

"Yes, Mama. There's just a line or two about their grandchildren and this: 'The Almighty may intend to punish the United States and all of us for our national pride in the past. I pray now that He will preserve us from civil war. We can never boast again as a Nation unless all can be restored.' "

"Dear Robert Lee," their mother mused, almost to herself. "What a battle he'd have to wage within himself should Virginia ever secede from his beloved Union. I'm glad there's a diversity of opinion up in Virginia. At least, they don't seem on the verge of doing anything foolish right now."

Her face genuinely perplexed, Sarah asked, "But, Mama, you *do* believe Georgia will break away, don't you?"

"No, I hope Georgia will *not* secede. In fact, almost hourly, I pray she won't!"

FIFTY-SIX

*W*hen *Mark* learned that Mississippi voted on January 9 to secede from the Union, Florida on January 10, and Alabama on January 11, he left his office in the hands of his chief clerk and started for Miss Eliza's house before noon on Monday, January 14. Halfway there, he surprised himself by turning the corner and hurrying along as fast as his stiff knees would permit toward the home of Judge William Law, the venerable, wise, conservative old gentleman respected by every person in town, no matter his political beliefs.

Mark had not been able to bring himself to tell even Eliza Mackay the terrifying gist of Jonathan's first letter, written the evening of the very day he had, with the regiment of inexperienced local bucks, illegally seized Federal Fort Pulaski. When he and Caroline had read Jonathan's letter declaring himself now a Southern sympathizer, Caroline's proud smile had isolated Mark somehow, even from Miss Eliza. Oh, he had visited her every day but even she had no inkling of what Jonathan had written. In sight of Judge Law's house on York Street, Mark tried to understand his own retreat into himself. He could not. Jonathan had simply always been there, comforting his father, his mother, and certainly Mary. Mary . . .

Do I feel cut off from Mary, too? he asked himself, slowing his pace both from pain and from nervousness at facing erudite Judge Law in this cluttered, lost frame of mind. Surely Mary has said or done nothing to shut me out. Surely Mary is as lost as I am! There can be no other reason for her almost total silence. She speaks to Caroline and me only when we ask a question. With all her might, she tries to smile when either of us praises Ben, but no one could expect her to understand what Jonathan is doing in a military uniform, sleeping every night away from her way out at Fort Pulaski! Mary must be far more isolated than I. By the wildest stretch of no one's imagination could she be expected to feel any loyalty to the United States of America. Certainly not to the state of Georgia. While they were still living here, the Creeks and the Cherokees intermingled some, but they also fought some and she is a resident now in what was once Creek land!

That Mary was devoted to him and Caroline, Mark had not the slightest doubt, but her world had been *Jonathan* since the moment her brother Ben's body had been found at Etowah Cliffs with a self-inflicted bullet in his head. Savannah is not her city, the nation not her land. Mary has only her private world and that world *is* Jonathan. He sighed. If she feels as cut off from him as I feel, he thought, she's all but alone on the face of a strange earth. Not quite alone, of course. There is her son, Ben, little dark-skinned Cherokee Ben with the proud Indian nose. *Bending Willow Browning.*

He stopped in front of Judge William Law's three-storied brick house and pretended to look up and down the street as though watching for someone. Why? To catch his breath? No. Even he wasn't short of breath from having walked the last block so slowly.

I'm trying to right myself inside, he thought, and the thought startled him. What caused Little Ben to come to my mind now? Hadn't it always been Caroline who resisted Ben McDonald's Indianness? Mary's? None of that ever bothered me, he lied to himself, and was genuinely stunned by the realization that, somewhere deep in his mind, he had indeed been bothered. Was bothered now!

Judge Law was not expecting him. There was certainly no earthly reason why he had to mount those front steps. He took out his watch. Yes, there was a reason, because soon it would be too near dinnertime to count on Miss Eliza being alone and he did have to see her—alone. *After* he had spoken with Judge Law. But, he wondered, as he struck the Judge's ornate brass knocker, what was he expecting from his revered friend Law?

Seated in the small, orderly room the Judge used in his retirement as a home office, Mark waited for the old gentleman to appear. "It takes him a while," the light-skinned butler had said when he ushered Mark in, "but he'll be here dreckly, sir. This's a good time of day for him and he enjoys company."

Years ago, when W.H. was in Congress and then in Vienna, Mark had spoken to Judge William Law about taking over his own legal affairs, but Law was an active judge then and the matter didn't work out. Their easy friendship had been established, though, and there had been, through the years, many times when he'd received the Judge's legal counsel for friendship's sake. A fairer-minded man never lived, and as with so much else, for that friendship he had Miss Eliza Mackay to thank. Mark had always felt free to discuss his often awkward political position with her, but it was she who urged him to take counsel also from Judge William Law.

"I am a woman, Mark," she'd said one day, "and although I know you respect my opinion, there are so many things I don't know. You'll find Judge Law able and willing to give you sound advice. He's a devout Southerner, as I am, but he's a true conservative and a gold mine of wisdom, balanced wisdom." Again, Mark had found her to be right. Law had helped him understand that slavery was not the underlying differ-ence between North and South—it was the emotional trigger, but not the root cause. The root cause was power in Washington to guarantee States' Rights: the right of every state to decide for itself.

The high, paneled door of the office opened and aging Judge Wil-liam Law entered—thick white hair freshly clean, eyes still bright with interest and sharp enough so that the gold-rimmed spectacles were worn for the most part up on his forehead. He used an ebony cane to steady himself. Balance seemed to be the problem, but the old energy of mind was there. Mark shook his hand warmly.

"I've been expecting you, Browning," Judge Law said, sinking into the chair behind his handsome desk. "I was just thinking this very morning that you must be feeling quite alone. Is your fine son doing well as a soldier at Fort Pulaski? You must be proud of him." He chuckled. "But then, I've never known you not to be proud of young Jonathan."

Mark, seated, too, now, returned the smile. "You're right, as usual, Judge. On both counts. I'm proud of my boy and I'm—also more alone than I can ever remember. Of course, I came to you."

"I'm indeed honored. How old are you, Browning?"

"About to enter my seventieth year, sir. Certainly old enough to have learned how to keep my emotions under control."

"You learned to do that long ago, but you'd be ready for the coffin lid to be nailed down if you weren't experiencing inner turmoil today."

"Thank you."

"We all have to accept each other exactly where we are at the moment. You are on the opposite side of the issue that is tearing our city apart. Our state. You are there in all sincerity, even though it has cost you dearly through the years to hold to your beliefs so doggedly."

"Do you really think I've held to them *doggedly*, sir?"

"You've honored me by confiding that even your beloved wife disagrees with you, so, yes, doggedly. Courageously, too, I might add. Can't you give yourself a little credit for courage?"

"Today I don't have much. One of the reasons I'm here, I'm sure. But, you see, I haven't felt I had to *hold* to my beliefs, no matter how troublesome they've been here in Savannah. I *am* my beliefs. I have simply never felt it morally right to own another human being."

In a quiet, unruffled voice, Judge Law said, "Your abolitionist Aunt Nassie's influence from the days of your youth." It wasn't a question.

"Yes, I suppose so. But Aunt Nassie has never been a part of my life in Savannah. I chose Savannah myself."

"Could Savannah have chosen you?"

"Miss Eliza Mackay believes that."

"A wise, wise lady. You aren't alone in your beliefs, Browning. Every drop of blood in Eliza Mackay is Southern, but she is endowed with God's own wisdom and I've thought about her lately, too. It's quite possible, I think, that she is also in turmoil now. She loves our great nation."

An easy, almost agreeable silence fell between them, until Mark said just above a whisper, "This is a danger-filled day for Savannah, sir."

"You refer, I'm sure, to the so-called secession meeting scheduled for tonight. I was afraid that had occasioned this impromptu visit this morning, Browning. You've heard, of course, that I'm on the program as the final speaker." The old gentleman thought for a minute, rubbing the carved ebony knob of his cane. "Yes, I was afraid that was your reason for coming to see me."

"You were *afraid*, Judge Law?"

"You want to know what I'm going to say after Captain Francis Bartow, General Henry Jackson, Colonel Tom Foreman, and the others speak their pieces. We know already, both of us, what they'll say, don't we?"

"Yes, sir. They are all strong secessionists."

"And because they're honorable young men who love the South, they will be putting themselves in positions of backing up their fiery words with their very lives. I won't be doing that, *whatever* I decide to say when I mount the podium at Masonic Hall tonight."

Mark stared at him. "You–haven't decided your own position on secession yet, sir?"

"Not yet. I intend to spend the afternoon on my creaky knees and in deep searching. When my turn comes, I will know. But you're right, Browning, this is a danger-filled day for Savannah, for Georgia, for the nation. Ours, you know, is the first secession meeting to be held in the entire state. I assume you will be there."

"No, I think not," Mark said, making up his mind that very second. "Jonathan and Colonel Olmstead are hoping to make it into town, but I've just decided to spend the evening with Miss Eliza Mackay. Her daughters will want to be as near the meeting as the crowds outside will permit. I need to be with Miss Eliza."

"Undoubtedly, she needs you, too. Have you made your visit to her today?"

"Not yet and I've stayed too long with you to go there now. She won't worry about me this morning because she knows I have my business all to myself these days with Jonathan gone." He stood to go. "Forgive me for taking so much of your time, sir, and thank you."

"You picked a most opportune day to visit me, Browning. It is I who should thank you and I do."

"I can't see why."

The Judge smiled. "Shall we call it mind-clearing?"

Mark's characteristic little frown came, a sign that what the Judge had said puzzled him. He made himself smile. "I know better than to think I might have influenced your speech tonight in any way, Judge."

"That isn't what I implied. I simply always find it refreshing, mentally, to speak with you, Browning." He smiled, too. "You have a way of making me feel in my own seventies again–young, clear, like you!"

The Judge walked beside him to the front door. "I don't feel particularly clear today, sir," Mark said. "One might say I'm as scatterbrained as a young man in love."

"You are," Judge Law said, opening the wide outside door. "Your problem has always been that you're in love with Savannah, Browning.

If you weren't, you wouldn't have the horrendous problem of being in town at a troubled time like this."

That evening, with no chance to learn if Jonathan and Olmstead had been able to leave Fort Pulaski for the city's secession meeting and with Caroline's full assurance that she and Mary would be just fine alone, Mark headed for the Mackay house on foot. The cloudless, embracing Savannah sky was still lit softly by a lowering sun, but the streets were already swarming with people—even a few children had been allowed the privilege of joining the excited crowds. There were as many ladies as men passing in carriages, buggies, barouches, and gigs, many walking in clusters for safety because, inevitably, a citywide gathering brought out disreputable men from the Yamacraw section—foreign sailors as well as local ne'er-do-wells.

Caroline seemed to have no desire to be a part of the event and he had no reason to doubt that she meant it when she told him that Mary deserved at least one member of the family at home with her. Every sight of Mary's face tore at Mark's heart these days. How alone Mary must feel!

A sense of total loss engulfed him as he turned the corner onto Broughton Street. How lost must Mary feel! In a way that he hadn't been able to share even with Miss Eliza, he, too, was lost from his own son. His confidence, through all the years of Jonathan's life, that the two were one in their deepest beliefs had been so shaken that he despaired of ever righting himself again. Maybe, just maybe, Jonathan's tiny son would grow up in a city peaceful enough so that Mark's own love for Savannah and for human equality might become a part of Little Ben. That particular thought had never struck before and he felt a sense of almost foolish hope, because it had come to him—*tonight,* when the first such meeting in all of Georgia was being held, when Savannah's decision on secession was to be made known. To Mark, Georgia *was* Savannah. Of course, so was Natalie's home on the Etowah River, but his adored daughter had never seemed so far away as on this anxiety-filled evening. Would peace and dignity ever find their way back out of the madness loose in the streets this minute?

The sight of the familiar old Mackay house eased some of his terror, but what he felt was plainly terror.

When Eliza Mackay herself opened the front door to him, they embraced, but said nothing as Mark led her into the dear, comfortable parlor and to her favorite rocker. He took his own special place in Robert Mackay's big cracked-leather chair. Still neither spoke. He knew both the maiden sisters and Eliza Anne had already gone to the home of a family friend on Bull Street, as near the site of the secession meeting as possible, since women were not allowed to attend. Undoubtedly Mary Cowper was with them since Andrew Low would be inside the Masonic Hall, a prominent part of the growing madness. If Georgia did secede and other Southern states followed her, there would be war. Mark knew it. Miss Eliza knew it. After tonight, because of the strong influence of Georgia and the high optimism of most of her people, who believed that secession was going to cure everything, nothing would, in their lifetimes, ever be the same.

"I have only one slim hope," he said at last. "I dropped by Judge Law's house today."

"Oh, Mark," she said in a trembly voice, "I'm clinging to that man's calm, judicious mind, his deeply held love of our nation."

Mark sighed heavily. "Turning that clamorous mob around will test even Judge Law. And I might as well tell you that when I left him a little after noon, he was still weighing both sides of the issue in his own mind."

She appeared surprised. "But he's on the program tonight. He's to give us his opinion on those resolutions to secede!"

"I know, and whatever the old gentleman decides will seal it one way or another. Young Captain Francis Bartow is introducing him."

"And fine soldier, brave young man that Francis is, he's going to be expecting the Judge to—take us out of the Union."

"Even the Judge can't do that," Mark said, "but one thing we do know—his opinion will count for more than any other voice heard in the Masonic Hall this night."

From a distance, but so loud it caused Miss Eliza to lay both hands over her ears, a band started playing the tune that lately had begun to sweep the South. It was called "Dixie's Land" and was composed by a Northerner, but the South had taken it as its own and, down here, the rousing tune was called "Dixie." For a time, they just sat together listening, hearing the cheers mount as the band blared on, finishing "Dixie" and launching directly into the "Marseillaise," another rouser that always stirred Americans everywhere. The music grew in volume and they both knew a parade had formed, probably from the overflow crowd, too large already for the Masonic Hall.

Leaning toward Mark, Miss Eliza said, "Those people all believe themselves to be freedom-loving folk, Mark!"

"I know, I know. I believe them to be, too," he said.

"Secession from our native land won't bring the kind of freedom they believe in, though. It will bring bloodshed, dear boy. Bloodshed. I wish I thought I wouldn't live to see it." She shook her still pretty head. "I'm afraid I will, though. I'm afraid I will."

The impromptu parade had evidently turned back toward the corner of Bull and Broughton, where the meeting was surely underway. After the spirited strains of "Dixie" were repeated once more, the music stopped. Not the cheering, just the music, but at least they could hear each other now.

Taking advantage of the lull, Mark blurted: "I meant to tell you days ago, Miss Eliza, but the time didn't seem right or someone else was with us. Jonathan has turned, almost overnight—he says while he was on the *Ida* heading for the seizure of Pulaski—into a Southern Rebel!"

For a long moment, she just looked back at him, her hands clenched. Then she smiled. "Well, dear boy, Jonathan *is* a born Southerner. A born Savannahian. You've always urged him to think for himself, but oh, I am so sorry for you! How—alone you must feel. I'm against the spread of slavery. I'm against secession from the Union, but"—her shoulders straightened—"I'm a Southerner by birth and loyalty, too, Mark."

He had always known that. It was hearing her say it that pushed him deeper into his solitude. Hearing her say it *tonight*. He remained silent.

"I know what just happened inside you, Mark, when I said that. You felt as though you'd lost your last understanding friend. Well, you haven't. It may take you a while to believe me, but while my head and heart are doing battle over this whole mess, I need your friendship more than I've ever needed it." She reached toward him. "You've always been one of God's great gifts to me."

Holding her dear, heavily veined hand in both of his, he said hoarsely, "Outside of Caroline and the children, you are His greatest gift to me. Even if your loyalty makes you a—Rebel, don't leave me! Don't ever leave me. We may *feel* on different sides, but we still *see* the same way, don't we?"

In response, she squeezed his hands. After a moment in which they both could hear two long, ringing cheers from the crowd outside the Masonic Hall, she said, "I can't fight my loyalty as a Southerner, but neither can I change my loyalty to my native land. I've always loved the South, but I've also always believed that the strength of our nation is in the *union* of the states." Another distant, but resounding cheer went up. She waited for it to die down. "We both know what the results of the secession meeting will be. The girls will come home after a while and tell me, but I already know."

A second, even more raucous, much louder cheer reached them in the familiar old parlor. This time it didn't die down, but went on and on, as though a whole city of people were shouting defiance, challenge.

When the cheering subsided abruptly, Mark said, "Listen! The din has almost stopped. Could that mean that even that wild crowd is pausing to listen to Judge Law?"

"I expect you're right," she said. "But we already know the results and I'm afraid even Judge William Law won't try to change them. Then we'll be at war. I also know, dear boy, that for as long as I live, I'll be living on my own private battleground. I've never had to fight myself for long at a time before. I'm trying to get ready to fight myself now."

FIFTY-
SEVEN

*T*he *Exchange clock* was striking ten as Mark finally left his office that wild, fateful January night, unable even to face Caroline and Mary once he'd said goodbye to Miss Eliza a little after nine. For the first time he was not comforted by a visit with her. Eliza Mackay herself had been too torn, too distraught by her own private "battlefield," too honest even to attempt to encourage Mark. And so, he had fled to the one place where he knew he could be alone—his own office on Commerce Row. For nearly an hour, he sat motionless at his desk and grieved.

Outside, across the city where he had once felt so at home, the madness had not lessened. His head ached from the steady clangor—the shouts and whistles and bells and bursts of martial music—but his soul was in far more pain. No one had told him outright that Georgia was going to leave the Union he loved. No one needed to tell him. In spite of the fact that Mark Browning had belonged to Savannah for most of his long life, within days he could belong to—nothing.

Literally elbowing his way along the gaslit streets of what had once been his very own place to be, he longed to break into a run, but where could he run? His own home on the familiar square was no refuge tonight. There was a good chance that his son would be there. He had not seen Jonathan since the morning he left with the regiment to take part in what to Mark was a treasonous act against the nation, but he had read and reread the letter written from Pulaski that night in which Jonathan declared his firm allegiance to the tragic, reckless Cause of the South.

With all his heart, he longed to find a way to bring Jonathan back, to come back himself to a semblance of the firm, steady friendship they'd always known. At last, rounding the corner of Bryan into Reynolds Square, he felt the futility of his longing. He also felt old, full of hurt and dread.

When Caroline did not open the door to him as usual, he fumbled through his pockets for his key, doubting that he'd remembered to bring it. Unless she'd been watching at the front window, Caroline would have no way of knowing he was struggling up the steep steps. Even if she waited in the family drawing room, she couldn't have heard him above the noise. At the closed door to his own home, he vainly searched each pocket again, then sank down on the top step and buried his head in his hands.

He may have sat there for five or forty minutes. If the Exchange clock had struck the half hour, he hadn't heard it. The din had not lessened, nor the pain in his legs and his heart. He had not found his key, nor one small shelter from the chaos in his mind. Not one thought had managed to complete itself, although he kept trying. Minutes ago, the steps had seemed so steep. Now, to his cramped, rheumatic legs, they were too shallow. He could only sit in a wretched heap, both legs stretched down over the steps below, seeking a little relief. Stretching his legs caused his back to hurt.

"God," he breathed. "God in heaven, help us all–this minute, *now*. Help me at least to think!"

Then a low, almost tender voice called, "Papa!"

In the street below stood Jonathan–not moving, just looking up at him with alarm.

"Papa," the boy gasped, and ran up the steps. "Papa, what on earth's wrong? What are you doing out here by yourself?"

"I don't know," he murmured. "I forgot my key. Hello, son. Welcome–home."

At the moment Caroline swung open the door, he allowed Jonathan to help him to his feet, to lead him inside. As Caroline plumped pillows behind him on a low sofa where he could stretch out, Mark tried to smile up at her. He couldn't.

"I found Papa sitting outside on the top step," Jonathan said, his normally firm voice shaking. "He—lost his key."

"Oh, darling," Caroline whispered, "I'm so sorry, but with all this shouting and noise, I didn't hear you. You know I always hear you. Tonight, I swear I didn't."

Mark managed a smile. "Tonight is—different in all ways," he said, his own voice sounding far older than Judge Law had sounded earlier today. Earlier today seemed a lifetime ago.

"Savannah's alive the way I've never seen it in all the years I've been here," Jonathan exclaimed. The unfamiliar excitement Mark dreaded was in the boy's voice, and when he looked over at Jonathan standing in his uniform at the foot of the sofa, the same look was on the handsome, flushed, eager face. The same look Mark had seen on the face of every wildly cheering young man he'd met as he'd made his lonely way toward home.

"Were you at the meeting, Papa?" his son asked too brightly.

"You know perfectly well he wasn't," Caroline said. "Whatever happened at that meeting has broken your father's heart, Jonathan. We know you've—changed. We know you've realized and embraced the rightness of the Southern Cause, and I give thanks, but your father is distraught. If I can manage to reach toward him now when he so needs us—I, who have tormented him all these years with my hot Southern blood—you must try. You, of all people, must try, son!"

Mark looked at Jonathan, who in one swift, eager motion was on his knees beside Mark, both strong, young arms embracing him.

"Papa, oh, Papa, I'm so sorry! I am caught up in the spirit of the city tonight. But none of that changes the way I feel about you. Maybe I haven't really changed. Maybe I've only just come to realize that I— belong to Savannah, too."

"I'm glad you're trying, Jonathan," Caroline said sternly, "but don't forget your father—has belonged to Savannah far longer than you have."

The warmth of Caroline's defense of him flooded Mark's whole body. Eased his heart. It even eased the ache in his legs. She stood squarely with Jonathan, a part of the wildness in the city tonight, but she stood with *him,* too! Mark could only grab her hand and cling to it, hoping she would sense his gratitude.

For a long time no one spoke. Finally, getting to his feet, Jonathan said in a subdued, but familiarly affectionate voice, "Miss Eliza always told me that loving in diversity is more important than loving in agreement."

The mere mention of Eliza Mackay's name enabled Mark to say, "She's always right, son. Always pay attention to Miss Eliza. Your mother has proven her right tonight, hasn't she? I know she's proven it to me. Earlier—all evening, I've felt so—lost. I even felt lost with Miss Eliza, who, it seems, agrees with both sides of this ghastly mess."

"Papa?"

"What is it, Jonathan?"

"I think it's good for me to—to disappoint you as I have. I've had a lot more pride in being the person you always turned to than I realized."

Mark said nothing, and when Caroline took him in her arms, he buried his face in her fragrant neck and gave her the best hug he could.

"As soon as you're up to climbing the stairs," she said, "I'm taking you to bed. That hug told me how much I need to be close to you."

"I'm ready now," he said. "And, Jonathan, welcome home, son. Isn't it time to go up to Mary?"

The smile vanished from Jonathan's face. "Does she stay to herself all the time?" he asked.

"Yes," Caroline said. "Your father and I try so hard with her, but she doesn't understand. I doubt somehow that your father feels as truly— abandoned as Mary must. You can stay here tonight, can't you?"

Jonathan nodded yes. "But I'll be on the *Ida* with Colonel Olmstead at seven tomorrow morning."

"Go up to Mary, son," Mark said firmly. "She deserves all the help you can give her."

When Jonathan eased open the door of their room upstairs, she was sitting by the window in the rocker Burke had made for her as a wedding present, Little Ben in her arms. That she heard him unlatch the door, he had no doubt, but she did nothing but begin to rock rapidly and pull the edge of the blanket more securely over the baby's dark head. She didn't even look up.

Jonathan stood for a moment just inside the room, then closed the door softly and went to her. "Mary? Mary, I'm here."

Still rocking, still holding their child close, she said softly, "I know. But because I do not know what to say to you, I—say nothing. I long to talk. I—cannot."

The new excitement, the high sense of adventure which had possessed him drained away. He felt desperately that if he didn't find the right way to get her to put down the baby and lie beside him, he would die of need, body need, mind need, heart need . . .

"Mary, don't try to think of anything to say. I want you close to me. Can't you—put Ben in his cradle and—and hold me in your arms?"

She went on rocking, still silent.

"Can't you do that, Mary? Then I promise you it will be easy to talk to each other. I promise to explain everything to you—everything I've been doing since I went away and all that happened at the meeting tonight."

Little Ben didn't wake up when she laid him gently in the same cradle Jonathan, Natalie, and Willow had used as infants. "I had just changed him," Mary said. "He will sleep for a time."

Jonathan enfolded her and held her to him. Neither spoke until Mary whispered, "I can let you love me now, Jonathan. I need, too. You will be Jonathan again without that—uniform."

Undressing hurriedly, he made himself think of nothing but her words, "I need, too," and the kiss of them was still on his heart as he gratefully eased into the bed beside her and lost himself in the glorious contradiction that although he'd hated his tiny son's Indianness, he had never stopped adoring it in Mary.

"I need, too," she breathed again, lifting herself to him.

Fear or worry or passion often caused Mary to lapse back into her old way of speaking and, drawn by it as always, Jonathan ached and strove with his body and with his soul to pull Mary back to him again, as close as they'd been before he'd been ordered to leave her.

Their love this strange, desperate, celebratory night, with freedom-loving people outside still cheering and singing, was wild and sharp and sweet. "Sweet, yes, dear God, how sweet," he murmured, clinging helplessly. Once she had cried out when he shouted his own release, both safe from being overheard because of the raging celebration which seemed to be swinging the city almost out of orbit. The noise was still raging in the streets of the once quiet, sedate city where the Brownings, because of Papa, had lived their privileged lives. The beloved city, where Mary had never felt at home, but where she had strained with every fiber of her being to make a home for Jonathan. For these few rudderless moments in which his old, familiar simple life as son, husband, father had returned to haunt him in a way he had never expected to be haunted by anything having to do with the purity of Mary's love, there had been the old oneness, the dear oneness, but there had also been

—in Mary, from Mary—a heretofore unleashed primal grasp. There had been her first scream of pain or joy, but there had been more.

When he finally eased his body beside her, still kissing her hand and forearms, she asked, almost in full control of her voice, "I scare you, Jonathan?"

Up on his elbow, he tried to laugh at her. "Scare me? You—gave me what I needed. More than I knew I needed, but you didn't scare me." Abruptly, he jumped out of bed and turned up the gaslight slightly, ever so slightly. He *had* to see her face. It was suddenly important that she not be able to avoid his eyes as he struggled to explain the change in him . . . how he hoped Mary would at least try to grasp why it was he had to be ready to defend the land he had abruptly come to revere in a still unfamiliar, but compelling way.

"We have to talk now, dearest," he said, slipping back under the covers beside her.

She sighed softly. "I guess so. I will listen, though I cannot promise to understand. You will tell me poor Jonathan—again."

He pulled her onto his shoulder and began to try to tell her of the high excitement at the waterfront the day he had boarded the *Ida* with the regiment, of the cheering and drumming and waving from the deck of the *Ida* and from the balconies along Factor's Walk and Commerce Row as the little steamer moved out into the river and began the short voyage to Pulaski. At first, he wasn't going to mention how he'd looked and looked for her beside his parents when the boat passed the Browning office and warehouse, but he did tell her and in case she wanted to make even a small explanation of why she hadn't come, he waited. Mary said nothing, so he went on. As simply as he knew how, he told her of his own confusion and indecision over what he was doing. He'd done his best to make clear the night before he left that a member of a military organization had to obey orders. She hadn't understood then, so he moved past that now, made a few feeble jokes about the mountains of trunks and camp chairs and china and crystal and tableware the regiment took along. When she didn't find that amusing, he plowed ahead into the difficult part. Difficult since he was determined to tell her of the surprising, seemingly sudden resentment he'd felt because their son looked even more like a Cherokee than had her brother, Bending Willow.

"Can you begin to feel the agony I knew, Mary? I was torn between two strong loyalties on the trip out there. You know how I love my father. You know I'd always felt he and I agreed on the whole spectrum of political issues—slavery in particular. I still feel it's wrong for a man to own another man or woman. That hasn't changed, but something bigger than that began to take me over and it seemed to happen when I shocked myself by resenting the Indianness of our innocent little son. Mary? *Mary?*"

"I am here, Jonathan."

"I'm past all that now, I swear it. I was past it before we landed at Cockspur Island and occupied the fort. Do you believe me?"

She waited. "You did not hold Little Ben in your arms when you came to us tonight."

"I couldn't wait to hold his mother! You've got to believe that. I'm— I'm ashamed of myself, but Mary, Mary, I've missed you so and—and Ben was sleeping. I knew I'd be able to handle myself much better, explain what I'm trying to tell you far more clearly, if I loved you first. Surely you can understand that."

"I understand that, yes. I also need still more of you."

"Isn't it better that we try to *talk* together now?"

"No."

"No?"

"No. I do not yet know in my spirit that you are really here once more. Could you love me again, please? You may never come home again."

"But, darling," he said, unexpectedly wanting her again, too, *"I will be home* again and again. I'm just in training at the fort now. In no time at all—a matter of weeks anyway—other soldiers will take my place and I'll be—"

She was pulling him to her, caressing his shoulders and back, her whole body pleading for what he knew instinctively would be a new and different—and wilder kind of emotion than he and Mary had ever experienced. The passionate woman in his arms was Mary, his good Mary, the person in all the world he most wanted to shelter and protect, but through him a new, stormy spirit of adventure had begun to surge, so that even before he had reached the part of his explanation that had to do with why or how he, Jonathan, had become an eager, cocksure Southerner, fired with desire to charge to his death if need be to protect the honor and glory of the South he loved, he was actually seeing himself ride into battle astride a good horse, shouting for joy. With the men he'd already come to love riding hard beside him, together they raced with their battle flag, each impelled to keep it flying, snapping in the high wind of their zeal for victory.

After some immeasurable span of time he sank down beside her and said in a hoarse whisper, "Oh, Mary, there's no way a woman can understand how a man feels about joining his very life to a regiment of other men who thrive on courage and final triumph!"

He had been so caught up in the frenzy of both love and battle, he didn't notice that she was crying. When he took her in his arms again, she broke into hard sobs. There was no way for her to feel what he felt about his newfound bond with the men in the regiment. No way at all that Mary could feel as he did.

"Dearest," he murmured, sensing for the first time that the celebration in the streets outside was lessening. "Dearest Mary, I beg you to be with me in some of this—I beg you to talk to Colonel Olmstead's Florie! She hates the thought that we might have to go to war, too, but she's doing all she can to make things easier for Charles. She doesn't love him any more than you love me. It's just that men and women are—different. It's a good thing, too, isn't it? Someone has to protect home, family, loved ones. That's a man's work, but men do need women to understand."

The sobbing stopped. "I understand more than you think," she said. "I understand you—*will die and leave me*. I need you to understand me, too."

He took her in his arms again, kissing her tears. "Oh, beautiful Mary, I'm not going to die and leave you!"

"Once I believed you know everything. But *you die*. You never come back to me. I know that."

"Mary, listen, let me tell you about the absolutely memorable moment at the secession meeting tonight when young Captain Bartow introduced old Judge William Law to the cheering, shouting throng of people in the Masonic Hall—packed to the doors and spilling out onto the streets. I'm sure you've heard Papa say that several prominent military officers in the city would already have made their speeches in support of the resolutions to secede from the Union—"

"Papa Mark's heart is broken for love of the Union."

"I know it is, but let me tell you about tonight. Oh, if I thought I could be half the soldier Captain Francis Bartow is, I'd be happy. He's a splendid man, incredibly handsome, with his square face, small, neat mustache, broad shoulders—every inch a soldier. Courage and daring exude from his every movement, his every word. His introduction of the respected old gentleman was rousing, jubilant. During the other speeches, the people had not been able to silence their cheering and enthusiasm, but the moment Bartow spoke the name of Judge William Law, the entire room grew silent. Then the Judge walked feebly, but determinedly to the podium as though he knew that whatever he said Savannah should do, Savannah would surely do.

"Picture the moment, Mary. There stood the revered man, knowing that if he gave the word, the great city of Savannah would call upon the state of Georgia to leave the Union forever. Quietly and with no attempt at oratory, the Judge reviewed the entire political situation between North and South, enumerating the dangers that might come from secession, but also—and here he began to warm to his subject—he unflinchingly told us to take into full account the hideous wrongs and the loss of liberty we were suffering at the hands of the North now. Judge Law spoke but a few minutes and closed with a firm declaration that a free people cannot sit passively by while their rights are being trampled upon. There was a slow gathering of movement all over the crowd as he cried out: 'Therefore, I give to these resolutions my hearty endorsement!' "

Jonathan was so excited by now, he was sitting on the side of the bed, imitating the swing of Judge Law's arm as he'd made the pronouncement. "Oh, Mary, my darling, I wish you could have heard the pandemonium that broke out then! A wild roar went up from every throat in the hall and like an echo the roar came back from the overflow crowd in the streets. There seemed no end to the shouts of deep feeling from every corner of the city. Charles Olmstead and I looked at each other and admitted later that we both thought the cheering might go on forever! Men embraced each other, some with tears running down their faces. If I live to be older than Judge Law, I'll never, never forget that moment. I was caught up in it. I'm—I'm still caught up in it, Mary. Even here in our own room, with Little Ben asleep over there in his cradle, I'm still a part of it!"

He looked down at her. Mary's dear face told him nothing. "You are here with Ben and me, but you are not here," she said at last. "So, come to bed and sleep, beloved Jonathan. And do not try to explain more when you wake up in the morning."

"Did I tell you I have to go back to Pulaski at seven A.M.?"

"No, but you will go. I will not detain you ever again. I told you I understand far more than you believe."

FIFTY-EIGHT

Sitting alone in a coach of the Western and Atlantic train on the morning of January 19, Burke felt both foolish and desperate. Desperate in the face of the insanity sweeping the state as people waited to learn the results of the secession vote soon to be taken in Milledgeville, where delegates from every county were now meeting. He was heading for the thriving town of Marietta. He'd been there only twice to buy building supplies and to interview carpenters, but for the past few months he had learned a lot about Marietta because of his subscription to the *Southern Statesman,* to his mind the best Southern newspaper he'd yet found. He was going today, when he could ill afford to be away from the new hotel he was building in Cassville, because he felt such a strong need to meet and talk with the publisher, Mr. Robert McAlpin Goodman. Cass County was definitely divided on whether or not Georgia should leave the Union. Burke had found several average men in Cassville, in Cartersville, in Kingston—even Holder, the Stileses' overseer—who, like him, bitterly opposed secession. But Goodman was educated, plainly an intellectual; a thoughtful man with the courage of his pro-Union beliefs. In contrast, many young men in Cass were raring to sign up for military duty the minute the state seceded. Not that anyone really thought there would be a war. In fact, most laughed at the idea, sure the Yankees would turn tail the minute they faced even a threat of Southern might and determination. But like a fire raging in a wind that blew two ways at once, the county was in an uproar. He had convinced Natalie that his trip to see Goodman had nothing to do with what Natalie called "secret, men's plans about the stupid war people keep talking about."

The thought of Natalie made him smile, as it always did, with pure joy in her and with amusement that in spite of her keen mind the North-South trouble interested her only as it might affect Burke himself. She had no difficulty believing that he cared deeply about the Union. In fact, that was fine with her, so long as he didn't do anything "dumb," and dumb meant getting involved beyond caring. "I think it's honorable to love your country, Burke," she kept saying, "but there are more than enough politicians like Uncle W.H. blabbing high-blown phrases about patriotism and who is or isn't President and how many senators the South has and how many are from the North. We have each other—Callie will be home to stay in one more year, beautifully educated—so you mind only *our* business, do you hear?"

He looked up and down the swaying train coach and saw it was clear, so he stretched his long legs out into the aisle. The W. and A. was due in Marietta in two hours. He hoped he'd be lucky enough to find Robert Goodman in town. Presumptuous in a way, he supposed, to be making the trip without having made sure by letter that Goodman would even be there, let alone free to talk as much as Burke felt he needed. He longed to know the man personally, something that hadn't happened to him often since he'd settled in the upcountry. Heaven knew he couldn't have a real discussion with W.H. these days, because the older man was hurtling headlong toward becoming an out-and-out secessionist. Oh, Stiles still preached Union, but only among Southern states and in order to make their points with the Federal government.

Burke was fond of W. H. Stiles, certainly of Miss Lib, who would, he knew, end up being exactly where her husband was in all the trouble. Not that she didn't think for herself—she did—but her love for the brilliant, impetuous Stiles grew stronger daily. Busy as he stayed, Burke couldn't miss that.

He pulled his legs out of the aisle when he saw the conductor come into his car to pick up tickets from passengers who boarded at Acworth a ways back. On the empty side of his seat lay a copy of the *Southern Statesman*. A good time, he thought, to reread what Goodman had written in the issue which came yesterday. It took real courage to stick with a belief as long as Goodman had stuck with the Union. Burke had read it a dozen times already, but once more, knowing—hoping, at least—that within a couple of hours now he'd be sitting face to face with the man he'd grown to admire, Burke read Goodman's piece again on the secession convention now going on at the state capital: "Far more than just another convention of leading Georgians will take place in Milledgeville. The future welfare, even the lives of children at their mother's knee today, of young men ripe with the rush of life beginning can be deeply affected. The designated delegates at the convention will decide whether citizens of the United States of America, the land for which our forefathers fought and surrendered their lives, will endure."

Burke stopped reading for a time and looked out the train window at the rolling fields and hills of the good, rich land that *was* Burke Latimer's Georgia. He had seen the coast, he had visited the lower Piedmont, even the states of Florida, Virginia, and Kentucky. The Georgia upcountry had grabbed his attention and him. Out there was *his* Georgia, with more Union sympathizers than along the coast, where the planters owned slaves by the hundreds. Were they on the brink of tossing him, Burke Latimer, out of the Union he'd been reared to love? The Union he still loved as a nearly forty-seven-year-old man, loved because he *knew* that the strength of the nation lay in the union of all the states. This, of course, is what had attracted him to Goodman's mind. Robert McAlpin Goodman needed far more courage than Burke in order to hold to his loyalty to the Union. Goodman had to write and publish it for everyone to see. Goodman was surely attacked in print by other Rebel newspapers, probably enough times so that he had grown accustomed to it. But attacks in person would be worse. Burke imagined a face-to-face encounter on the streets of Marietta, perhaps in the busy square itself, where the *Southern Statesman*'s editorial office and press were located—Goodman being derided by a fellow citizen, perhaps even a friend or neighbor.

Burke looked at his watch. In an hour now, if Goodman was to be found in his office, he'd know the answers to many of his own questions. "What in the world *are* your questions for Mr. Goodman?" Natalie had wanted to know this morning before he rode off to catch the train. He couldn't tell her actually and now he wondered if perhaps he was making the trip for the express purpose of finding a friend who agreed with his own point of view. Those who were hot for secession were calling themselves Rebels. To him, they were. Burke had nothing against rebellion. Rebellion had won the liberty Americans were supposed to cherish—did cherish. Southern Rebels cherished it, too. To him, they were closing their minds to a real understanding of what liberty meant, though. He'd ask Goodman for his definition of liberty. It seemed to Burke that a definition might just hold the key. "The key to what, Burke?" Natalie would ask as sure as gun's iron, he thought, and smiled. Even when he was away from her, she still permeated his every thought. She and Miss Lorah were working together today on a gift for Miss Eliza Mackay, a handsome, colorful quilt for which they'd been saving "pieces" for over a year. The last letter from Miss Eliza to the Stiles family had shown that, for her advanced age of nearly eighty-three, she was in fairly good health. Burke was glad. The one time he remembered talking with the old lady alone had been surprisingly satisfying. Eliza Mackay not only had a level head, she had a deep heart, and he felt sure, now that he thought about it, that she, too, must be quite torn up inside by all the wild secession talk he knew was raging in Savannah. Eliza Mackay loved the Union. He would never doubt that.

Looking again at the paper folded in his lap, he found the place where he'd stopped reading: "In my younger days," Goodman wrote, "I worked for a newspaper called the *Constitutional Union* and as far back as 1840 there were Southern men looking with wistful eyes at what, to them, were the bright prospects of withdrawing from the Union. Other, more thoughtful Whigs and Democrats chuckled and poked fun at them, but the seed was planted. In the *Constitutional Union* I promptly quoted lines from the inaugural address of the one man all Democrats had to respect, Thomas Jefferson, who said: 'The state governments in all their rights form the best security for our domestic concerns and the general government in the whole constitutional vigor forms the sheet anchor of our peace at home and our safety abroad.' Those who agreed with me felt I had the agitators for disunion up a stump because what Democrat would dare argue with Jefferson? Whether I did or not, to this date, January of the year 1861, I still agree with Jefferson, who, were he alive and a Georgian, would be beseeching our delegates now in Milledgeville to hold firmly to our sister states through our protective Federal government in Washington as 'we reason together.' "

That word "reason," Burke thought, as he felt the screech of wheels beneath him when the engine began to slow for the station on the square in Marietta, is the key word. He felt pretty sure that phrase "reason together" came from the Bible. Waiting for the inevitable sharp jerks as the train finally stopped, he remembered that Miss Eliza had often said in her letters to Miss Lib, "Come now and let us reason together."

The final jolt came as iron grabbed iron below him, the engine gave off a long puff of steam, and Burke stood, taking down his hat from a wall peg. He had no luggage since he meant to catch the evening train home tonight.

I could easily be called crazy, he thought as he jumped to the ground in Marietta from the high coach step and stood looking about him at the busy, crowded, prosperous Marietta Square. Maybe only a crazy man would leave his own work on a wild-goose chase like this. Goodman's the best journalist around. Many journalists are in Milledgeville today reporting the results or scary consequences of the secession convention. But he strode purposefully past the station and across the street and learned from the first man he asked that the office of the *Southern Statesman* was just a short walk of a block and a half from where he stood. He set off as excited as though he were about to meet a celebrated person. To him, Robert McAlpin Goodman had become just that.

Inside the small front room of the newspaper office, a firm, but kindly man's voice called out as Burke closed the street door behind him: "Be with you in just a minute, if you can wait, please!"

Burke stood, hat in hand, looking around at framed copies of old newspapers hanging on every available wall space. In one frame, he saw the *Constitutional Union,* a name he already knew from having read so much of Goodman's writing. In other frames were copies of the *Augusta Constitutionalist,* bearing a date hard to read, but he could see that the year was 1844. Alongside the door of the room from where the voice had called hung a copy of another Marietta paper with which Goodman had been associated—the *Cherokee Advocate.* Burke liked a man who took genuine pride in his work. He certainly enjoyed showing people the buildings he put up. Had he been a news editor, he'd undoubtedly want to frame every copy!

"Sorry to keep you waiting, sir," a dark-haired, pleasant-looking, rather slightly built man said as he swung energetically through the open door from an inside office and came toward Burke with his hand out.

Returning the cordial handshake, Burke said, "If I'm lucky enough to learn that you're Robert McAlpin Goodman, I can only be pleased and relieved."

"Relieved?" the somewhat younger man asked. "Is there some kind of emergency, sir?"

"Well, in a way, I guess you could use that word," Burke said, giving his own name, place of residence, and business.

"You've had a fairly long ride, Mr. Latimer. I'm honored, whether you made the trip to see me or not. I am Robert Goodman. Wouldn't we be more comfortable in my private office? Please follow me."

"Thank you, sir," Burke said, entering the small, windowless inner office, every table, bench, chair, and the entire yellow oak desk stacked with books and papers except for the chair behind Goodman's desk where he'd obviously been working.

With a sweep of his hand, Goodman cleared off onto the floor a sheaf of newspapers on a scarred, straight-backed armchair and motioned for Burke to sit down. Robert Goodman then took the chair behind his desk and sat looking across at his visitor.

"You say I owe the pleasure of this visit to some sort of emergency, Latimer? Newshounds love emergencies, you know."

"I may have overstated it," Burke said, grinning a little. "I did make the trip here expressly to see you, but I can't honestly say that my reason is a real emergency."

"I'm the one who used that word," Goodman said, smiling.

The smile gone from his own face now, Burke said quite seriously, "In a way, I did have to come, Mr. Goodman. You see, I've been reading your articles on a subscription for nearly a year now, and although there are many loyal Unionists in Cass County, where my home is, I—I somehow don't feel too comfortable talking with most of them." He gave a half-laugh. "With others, I just don't dare. I'm sure you follow what I'm saying."

Goodman was smiling again. "If anyone can follow, I can. I am known as a fairly daring man, but with my neighbors and colleagues here in Marietta—with many of them, at least—I dare nothing more than erudite comments on the weather these days." Robert Goodman grew serious. "Latimer," he went on, leaning toward Burke, "with all my heart, I long not to fan the flames in our beloved South. I've been, as you know, pretty plainspoken in the paper lately. A man's convictions aren't worth warm spit if he can't stand up for them in public. If this trouble boils into a war between North and South—and in spite of what most of our dreaming Southern statesmen insist, it easily could—nothing but tragedy can come of it. One side or another always wins a war. One side always loses. There are few draws in warfare."

"I completely agree," Burke said. "And with their burgeoning industries up North, no matter how cocky or how courageous our Southern soldiers are, the odds are against us, wouldn't you say?"

"I've thought about that, actually, but there's no way of knowing now. Still, one side or the other is going to be decimated if we don't find sanity and grace enough to negotiate our way out of this trap we're in! Few seem to face facts. Toombs, one of our most flaming leaders down here, declares he'll drink every drop of blood that is spilt if such an impossible eventuality as war should come about. There isn't a braver or more arrogant man anywhere on the face of the earth than a dyed-in-the-wool Southerner, you know."

"I do know," Burke said, realizing that it wasn't that Goodman was so handsome or so convincing when he talked that drew him to the man, it was his genuine intelligence. The man's gray eyes didn't give the feeling that Goodman was looking right through him, they gave the certainty that a rare kind of discernment lay behind them which would help you see, if you would only open up and look thoughtfully, carefully. With all his heart, Burke wanted to see that way. "I do know what you mean about both the courage and the pride—all right, the arrogance of a Southerner who feels his own personal liberty is challenged. I'm not speaking only of slavery either."

"Splendid," Goodman said, slapping his hand on the desk. "I'm glad to hear you say that. Don't get me wrong. I've never felt comfortable with the peculiar institution. Although I own slaves myself, I see it eventually destroying our Southern economy. I understand that it will take time for slavery to die out of its own faulty accord, of course, and the smoldering fire underneath all this is being fanned by the madness to expand westward. Slave owners rightly believe their constitutional rights are taken away when they can't take along their slaves, their personal property. If they are not permitted to move west to find better land and opportunity, they're going to double up their fists and fight. Southerners believe with all their hearts that it is their States' Rights and only their States' Rights that are challenged."

"I've come to that conclusion, sir, on my own. Slavery is only a part of States' Rights. And in Georgia alone, there is a wide difference of opinion even about slavery. In fact, I know a sweet, deep-thinking, little old lady in Savannah who has always been a slave owner and who also hates the thought of spreading slavery beyond the current slave states."

"The problem may be, Latimer, that women can't vote."

"I agree there, too, sir. We do seem to have the meeting of minds I'd hoped for, Mr. Goodman. I also love the Union."

"Are you a Georgian by birth?"

"No, sir, Maryland."

"Are you a planter or do you call yourself a farmer since you live in the old Cherokee Nation?"

"Neither," Burke said. "I'm a building contractor–a carpenter. I work with my hands and I'm proud of it."

"Houses? There's a lot of building in your area right now."

"Houses, churches, banks, stores, a hotel in Cassville at present. I'm playing hooky from the job today. It may cost me some tearing out and rebuilding, but meeting you was something I had to do."

"The honor is mine, sir. Married?"

Burke laughed. "Oh, yes, *sir!* To the most beautiful woman I've ever seen."

"We all think that, don't we?"

"Only we can know for sure since we've done the looking, Mr. Goodman."

"I hope this isn't our last meeting. Could you call me Robert?"

"If you'll return the favor."

"Burke Latimer, is it?"

"That's right."

"Is your wife from north Georgia?"

"No, Savannah. Her father is Mark Browning, owner of the Browning and Son mercantile firm there. I guess he's the second-wealthiest gentleman in Savannah, next to a Mr. Andrew Low."

"You're acquainted with Andrew Low?"

"I've met him. He's married to the daughter of W. H. Stiles, my neighbor at Etowah Cliffs. I built Stiles's house." He grinned. "It was the first real mansion I tried."

For a moment, Goodman looked at him, his head cocked to one side. "How do you get along with W. H. Stiles, Burke? I hear he's become an out-and-out 'secesher,' as they're calling it now."

"I'm not in a position to say he's gone all the way. I get along fine with him, though, as long as we stay clear of politics. I wish that weren't the case. His wife and my wife are so close–or were for years–that they're like members of the same family. I'm afraid the Stileses are both leaning toward being seceshers, as you say."

"Is your wife with you in your belief in the Union?"

Burke laughed. "My beautiful wife is with me and that's the sum of it. I'm a blessed man."

A loud rapping on the front door interrupted and then the door burst open so fast it banged against the wall.

"What on earth?" Goodman gasped, jumping to his feet. "Who is it?" he called out.

"It's me, Mr. Goodman! Tom Burrick. Got a mighty important message on the telegraph for you. Georgia's done voted to git outa the frazzlin' Union! Whoopee! I'll just leave it on the table out here if you're busy."

"Yes, thank you, Tom. Thank you." Without leaving the inner office, Goodman sank back into his chair. When they heard the front door bang shut again, he said, "Well, it's happened, Burke."

"Oh, Lord," Burke moaned. "I was afraid it would."

"God help us all." Robert got slowly to his feet. "Wait here. I'll get the message. It will be good to have some sympathetic support when I learn the actual size of the vote." Burke stood up, too. Somehow he had to. His head whirled with too many contradictory, troubled thoughts for him to remain seated. Oddly, and he would be sure to tell Natalie this, the first person who flashed like lightning into his mind when the message had been called out was her father, Mark Browning. How alone he must be in Union-hating Savannah! And then he remembered Jonathan. At least, Mr. Browning would always have his son, Jonathan—levelheaded, sane. Jonathan would never be one to succumb to secession frenzy. He could no more imagine Jonathan turning against his own country than he could picture himself as a secesher!

Then Burke heard slow, almost dragging footsteps move across the bare wooden floor of the tiny front room back toward the inner office. In the doorway stood Robert Goodman, a blue slip of paper in his hand. "Even Burrick's chicken scratching can't hide the ugly truth, Burke," the younger man said, his voice shaking as though someone had died. "You and I are without a country. The final vote to secede was 208 to 89. You may take some comfort in the fact that your county—Cass—voted with the 89 men who wanted to stay with the Union." For a long moment, Goodman just stood by his desk staring down at the blue slip. Then he went to his chair and slumped into it. "Poor Benjamin Hill did his level best. He tried hard, at least, for cooperation. In the end, the message reads, Hill went with the majority. I know him. I know Hill. He loves Georgia, but I'd wager my last dollar that his heart is as broken as ours."

Burke still had said nothing. Finally, he spoke. "I guess I can take some comfort from those good old Union votes from Cass County." He laughed drily. "The county's named for a Northerner, you know. Lewis Cass of Michigan. If it all weren't so tragic, there'd be a funny side to that."

"We need all the humor we can muster from now on, Burke," Robert said, his voice steady now. "This secesh spirit spreads like wildfire, they tell me. It wouldn't surprise me a bit if even pro-Union Cass didn't try to change its name now that the country's been torn apart." For a time, Robert sat folding and unfolding the blue slip of paper, then he looked up at Burke. "How old are you, Burke Latimer?"

"Nearly forty-seven. How old are you?"

"Forty. At least, you're too old for conscription if it comes to war, but no one's too old to be responsible for an opinion. His own."

"That's right. And we'll have to hold it against all comers," Burke said. "More than an opinion, I'd say. A position. And we're both in what could turn out to be enemy territory."

"Maybe we're jumping the gun. Do you think so?"

"I'm not sure what I think yet except that I—feel like an orphan for the first time in my life, and I've been an orphan since the age of twelve." Standing now, Burke reached for his hat. "I'd better leave you to write your story. I know that's uppermost in your mind now. I'll never be able to thank you enough for talking to me, Robert."

"You're welcome to take dinner and spend the night at my place on Powder Springs Road if you don't want to make that train ride back to Cartersville tonight."

"Thanks, but I need quite desperately to get home to my wife. As it is, I'll have to sleep in Cartersville and ride home tomorrow early. I left my horse there." He smiled almost boyishly. "I always need to get back to her, but somehow this time more than ever before."

"I understand," Robert said. "You will come again, though?"

"As often as I can possibly manage," Burke said, his hand out.

Without another word, they shook hands, cementing their friendship, both visibly moved. Then Burke turned and walked silently out of the office, across the tiny outer room, and into the cold January air.

FIFTY-NINE

On February 4, 1861, a congress of representatives of all the Southern states which had seceded before that date met at Montgomery, Alabama. It adopted a provisional constitution and elected Jefferson Davis of Mississippi President of the Confederate States of America and Georgia's Alexander H. Stephens, Vice President. One month later, Abraham Lincoln was inaugurated as President of the United States. Burke still belonged in his heart and his mind to the United States, but he woke up beside Natalie now in their cottage by the Etowah River as a citizen of a newly formed foreign country called the Confederacy.

"You are still with *me* here, though," she reminded him almost daily through the month of March and into what she'd always called "enchantment time" when April came again to the hills and valleys of their beloved upcountry. "Look, Burke," she said at the kitchen window before he left for work in Cartersville on a misty, still cool morning during the second week of April. "Look out there. That isn't a foreign country! It's *our* country and we're together in our place. I know Papa's being as difficult for my poor mother these days as you are for me and you should both be ashamed. We all four have each other, and now and forever, that's all—absolutely all that matters! This stupid government palaver will end one day and there will *not* be a war."

Dressed in work clothes, a heavy jacket slung over his shoulder, he took her in his arms and held her so tightly she finally began to fidget. "You're really trying, aren't you, darling?" he asked, releasing her. "I'm trying, too. It's all just so insane!"

"But not everyone is insane," she declared. "You certainly did the right thing to make that trip to Marietta back in January to see Mr. Goodman. He's a sane, intelligent, levelheaded man or you wouldn't think he is, and now you know the two of you see this whole business alike. Doesn't that help? Just stay away from Miss Lib and Uncle W.H. and all their fiery talk!"

He laughed a little. "With them living almost next door to us?"

"The days are still pretty short," she argued. "You don't get home until after dark most evenings and by then it's time for us to be alone together. They know that after all these years." She helped him into his jacket and slipped both arms around his neck. "Can you get here a little earlier tonight, please, sir?"

"Any special reason?"

"Yes, *me.*"

After another embrace, he went to the door. "I'll do my best. It all depends on how the men get along today with their interior finishing on the hotel."

"It all depends on how soon you start home," she corrected.

"As soon as I possibly can," he promised and, after another kiss, left the cottage and headed for the stable out back. Because he wanted time to ride by the Cartersville post office for his copy of Goodman's paper before he went to the job, he'd already saddled his horse while Natalie cooked breakfast.

Goodman had covered the tragic story with remarkable objectivity so far, he thought. Doing so must have been tough work. Goodman's facts were, Burke knew, as accurate as was humanly possible. What he so admired in the unbiased writing was that underlying all the facts ran the thread of sadness he knew was in the warm, sensitive heart of the writer, who must be feeling as isolated as Burke felt these days.

Galloping along the road to Cartersville, he thought back on how much had taken place in such a short time. Earlier in April, the new Southern forces had already seized Forts Moultrie and Pinckney in Charleston Harbor because the Confederate Constitution declared that all United States properties in the South belonged now, by law, to the Confederacy. Burke found it hard to believe that just the day before yesterday, April 12, under Brigadier General Pierre Beauregard, the

South had even begun a bombardment against key Fort Sumter at Charleston. Both sides would surely now call up thousands of additional troops. War had begun. Needing more than ever to see what his trusted friend, Goodman, had written, he urged his horse to a faster gallop.

Still standing in the post office, Burke opened Goodman's *Southern Statesman* and scanned his friend's strong editorial in which he was "able to relate with shock and sadness that Fort Sumter in the harbor of Charleston, South Carolina, had fallen to the Confederate forces and because of my deep belief in the only source of strength for the once great United States of America, I must declare that this act means treason against all the wisdom and patriotism of the fathers of the Union of the states, to all hope of progressive civilization on this continent, and I will have none of it."

Burke folded the paper and thrust it deep into his jacket pocket. To write that *now* took more courage than even he knew Robert Goodman possessed.

As he rode toward the hotel he was about to finish, Burke's mind went again to his father-in-law in Savannah, who must feel sickeningly shut away in a private world of torment. Down there on the coast, a man couldn't even discuss what now would surely be a civil war, because, so far as Burke knew, Mark Browning still stood strong for the Union. He had heard that Justice James Moore Wayne was staying with the Union and would hold his seat on the Supreme Court. But if Burke remembered correctly, Wayne lived the year around in Washington. Even though his property and family were in Savannah, Mr. Browning would not see him.

Up here at least, a man is still fairly free to express himself, he thought, hitching his horse. I hate to get Natalie on the subject because I honestly don't think she's on either side, but I'm sure Mr. Browning is all by himself among those slave-owning planters down on the coast. He's alone and getting old, and Mrs. Browning's latest letter told us that even Jonathan had turned Rebel! The long-ago impulse to protect little Indian Mary stabbed him. Poor Mary, he mumbled aloud, picking up his tools. She'll never understand any of it. Poor, poor little Mary . . .

Eliza Anne tiptoed into W.H.'s office just off their parlor and stood looking at his slender, only slightly stooped shoulders as he sat hunched over his desk writing busily as always. All that was happening in the country—in both countries—had changed him. W.H. had long believed the South would have to secede, and now that it had happened, he was at once elated and driven. His dauntless patriotism had always been high among the traits she'd loved, but she'd never seen him as bent on plunging into still another new field of endeavor as now. She was still in the process of trying to accept the fact that at his age—in his early fifties —her husband was determined to raise a regiment and become an officer in the Confederate Army. W.H., her man of letters, author, diplomat, planter, a military man? Such daring, dangerous missions had, in her mind, always belonged to danger-seeking men like her late brother Jack and her beloved friend Robert Lee.

For an instant, her thoughts left W.H. and flew to Robert. Where was he today? In Mary Lee's last letter, received early in January, before Georgia's secession, Lee was still in Texas, "deeply grieved," Mary Lee had written, "at the state of things." Robert, Eliza Anne knew, revered the Union and had dedicated his life to the service of its army. Other Southerners in his position in the United States Army were resigning their commissions, coming home to the South to be made officers in the Confederate Army. She must write again to Mary Lee because, suddenly, she had to know about Robert. That he would be fighting his own war within himself, she had no doubt whatever.

W.H. was still writing, lost in concentration, obviously unaware that she had been standing just outside his office door. "Darling," she called softly. "May I come in?"

He jumped as though she'd hit him with a rock. "Oh, Lib. Hello, Lib. How long have you been standing there? I was so intent on this letter to Governor Brown, I didn't hear you."

"Is my handsome general still forming his army?" Teasing, she saw at once, was a mistake, but the words were out. His dear face was drawn in anger. She'd not only taken him by surprise in the midst of an earnest effort, she had stupidly touched his sore spot by calling him her "general."

"I'm quite aware that I lack military experience and expertise," he said sharply, the corners of his perfect mouth turning down, pouting. "But I've told you and I've declared it in a dozen speeches, Lib, that what I lack in military efficiency, I offset by military ardor equal to anyone!"

"I know, darling," she said, trying to cover her blunder. "I do know!"

"If I've said it once, I've said it a hundred times that I came by my military ardor visiting famous battlefields and witnessing actual battles when we lived in Europe," he went on. "No man estimates more highly the importance to the South of the cultivation of a true military spirit, not only as a means of defense against the enemy of our common country but as a means of protecting the peace and honor of the South!"

She remembered those exact words from the rehearsals of his latest speech delivered at newly formed Camp McDonald, now being built at Big Shanty outside Marietta. "I know how you feel and I quite agree!" She was almost pleading with him now to calm down. "I shouldn't have teased you and I'm truly sorry. Come to dinner, but do forgive me on the way, please?"

He got to his feet, the sheet of paper still in his hands. Frowning as he read, he scanned it again before he spoke. Then, after tossing aside the unfinished letter to Governor Brown, he followed her to the dining room.

"There's nothing to forgive, Lib," he said as he held her chair. "I just have too much on my mind these days. We are truly at war now and war is not only an engagement between two hostile armies, but in it is a contest of the military armament, wealth, resources, and productive energies of the nations involved. The South is justly at war with the North. Lincoln, as I knew he would, provoked us to it. Had we not fired on Sumter, after our Confederate ordinance decreed that all such installations within our boundaries now belong to the Confederacy, we would have been remiss in our duty! When we seceded, the United States became a foreign government and it would be intolerable that a fort built for the protection of the principal Southern seaport should be held by aliens. Northerners are aliens now, Lib!"

"I know, beloved, I know." She handed him a bowl of creamed potatoes. "Please eat something."

"How long would England submit to the domination of the lower Thames by a German fortification?" He was sitting at their table, serving himself far more potatoes than he'd ever eat, but she knew he felt as though he stood at a podium. "So long as alien Major Anderson and his enemy garrison held Fort Sumter, the city of Charleston was under his thumb and the vaunted freedom we have declared was a mockery! *We had no other choice.*"

"Of course not, W.H.," she said, in what she hoped was not a too placating tone of voice. "I do agree with you all the way, dear!"

"Let our action fire the Northern heart," he said between mouthfuls. "We had no other course of honor."

"Do eat something besides potatoes, darling."

"Oh, yes, yes," he said absently, reaching for the platter of fried chicken. "Yes. And first thing after I finish that letter to the Governor, in which I'm doing my best to use my influence in behalf of commissions for both our sons, I must ride to Cartersville. Those weapons I ordered for my regiment should be there today. If not tomorrow, I write another letter direct to the Governor himself."

"I know Governor Brown's often impetuous actions get on your nerves," she said carefully, "but there are times when I feel downright sorry for the man. He must be literally pelted with requests for all sorts of favors, all kinds of guns and supplies. Even shut away here by our river, one can't miss how busy most men are trying to raise regiments."

He laid down his fork. "At times, I have the distinct feeling that you include me among all those other busybodies begging favors from 'poor Governor Joseph Brown.' If that's true, Lib, have the courtesy and the kindness of heart not to tell me."

"You are never like anyone else, W.H.! Not *anyone* else."

He did his best to give her an affectionate smile. "And wouldn't it be splendid if I were to see my influence work in behalf of our boys?"

She frowned and hesitated. "Yes. If our sons have to go to war, I'd certainly want them to be officers at the outset. Both are superior enough to reap quick rewards, promotions. I–I *do* fear for them, though. I'm as spirited as you, W.H., believe me, but I'm also a mother." She sighed. "I give thanks every day that Mary Cowper's beautiful little Willy is still just a child. Too young to fight, if it comes to that."

W.H. wiped his mouth on a damask napkin, folded it, got to his feet. "My dear wife, it's already *come* to that. I'll wager that your Lieutenant Colonel Lee is now an officer in the glorious Army of the Confederacy! I hope you'll excuse me," he said, "I know you're not finished, but I really must ride to Cartersville. My new Etowah Cavalry is of the utmost importance right now."

"Do be careful, W.H." When he stooped to kiss her hair, she clung briefly to him. "Do always, always, be careful, darling."

"There's no doubt that my letter requesting arms from my old friend Adjutant General Henry Wayne went unanswered because the man's so upset that his own Southern-born father, the Justice, has turned his back on us down here."

"I doubt he's turned his back on us," she said. "Judge Wayne has always taken his seat on the Supreme Court as his solemn duty."

"But where does his solemn duty lie now? With the enemy?"

"I find it hard to accept, too, darling, but don't ignore me when I beg you to be careful. From now on, if you're actually in the Army, I'll be saying it often, I assure you. Wait, W.H., don't be in such a hurry. I want you to promise me you won't forget your many other talents for leadership *and* that there is definitely a movement to run you for governor!"

She had now touched the right chord, because he turned smiling from the doorway, hat in hand. "How could I forget that, my dear? And as I'm ready to serve our blessed Confederacy as an officer, I am also, of course, ready to take the helm of our dear state. Please do send my best regards to your godly mother when you write to her this afternoon."

"I will, I will. Try to be home by dark, please. Bobby's Meg wrote, don't forget, that both our sons and their wives could be here by the evening train from Marietta."

"I won't forget, Lib. And speaking of Marietta, I really must find out by some means if our sons can receive proper officer training there when Camp McDonald is completed."

With that, he left the house. Eliza Anne couldn't help thinking how often these days, with all his military flurry, their Etowah Cliffs property was being neglected. She was also thinking more often of her sons. Somehow they seemed older than their father.

Cass County
14 April 1861

Dearest Mother, Kate, and Sarah,

I fully intended to write yesterday as soon as W.H. rode off in high hopes of receiving his often requested shipment of arms, but other duties intervened, among them a somewhat difficult visit from Natalie, who seems actually offended that either the North or the South should have the audacity to interrupt her paradise by the river with a "stupid war." And dear God, *it is war,* isn't it? A war which undoubtedly will bring much suffering if Lincoln and his abolitionists have their way, but which will be short-lived if all predictions of victory for the South come true. A war which, so far as I can see, will affect Natalie very little, but you know Natalie. Burke is too old for conscription if it comes. I fear any service of his would have to be by conscription since he goes bullheadedly along loving the Union. As apparently does that once loyal and wise man Judge James Moore Wayne. It is more than W.H. and I can conceive that the Judge, always so strong in his love of liberty, could turn against us as he has. Burke, vainly trying to conceal his own delight in the way the Northern press is praising Judge Wayne, sees to it that we are informed—if not directly, then through Natalie. She declares the New York *Tribune* praises "this pure-minded and deservedly distinguished judge from Savannah, Georgia." Our splendid Atlanta paper, the *Southern Confederacy*, responded, we thought, with careful, though grim restraint: "Judge Wayne is not a citizen of Georgia. He once was; but his residence has been in Washington for a number of years past. Georgia does not claim him, and he is no more of us." My heart goes out to poor Sarah Gordon, who always held her uncle in such high esteem. W.H. marvels that the Judge could turn on members of his own family, his long-held Southern way of life, and even his own noble son, Henry, who now serves the Confederacy.

I am troubled, of course, for Robert Lee. So many of his fellow officers have resigned and are now in our glorious Confederacy. Has he written to you, Mother? He so respects you and knows of W.H.'s loyalty to the South, so it is far more likely that you will hear from him than I, once he has determined his course of action. Naturally, our sons are in all ways fired to battle with their beloved father. I fear for them, but then, without my firm faith in the right of our great Cause, I would fear for us all. I hear from the Hugers in South Carolina that Judge Wayne even blithely attends gay social functions in Lincoln's White House! The old gentleman has surely taken leave of his senses. I will write again as soon as there is further news.

> Yr. affectionate daughter and sister,
> Eliza Anne Stiles

Eliza Mackay read her daughter's letter aloud to Mark on April 20, the day after Lincoln ordered a total blockade of all Southern ports. Mark listened to the end without comment. Then, slumped in the old leather easy chair in her parlor, he looked across at her and said simply, "I need you now more than ever, Miss Eliza."

The pain on his dear, aging face cut her deeply. He hadn't missed one day visiting her through all this, and although they talked of little else but the danger ahead, of Jonathan's abrupt transformation into a fiery Rebel, of Mary's silent anguish, of Caroline's still miraculous tolerance of Mark's beliefs, until today she had somehow not seen total despair in Mark's eyes. It was there now, and her own personal battle—her love of Georgia, as deep and rocklike as her love of the Union—raged so within her, she felt suddenly too weak to reach toward Mark in his pain. Her hand could reach, though, and as she touched his, quickly held out to her, through her mind ran, like a soft, soothing rain, the words: "Thanks be to God who giveth us the victory through Christ Jesus our Lord."

She had heard herself quote that Scripture so often, but with all she and Mark had weathered together through the years, there had never been anything as hard as this. Today she did not quote the comforting words to Mark, although she couldn't have explained why. They had come to her, and for now, that would be enough.

"I need you, too, Mark," she said. "You don't have much to turn to in me this morning. But we both have God. People are torn to pieces all over the South. All over our blessed country, I have no doubt. I think so often these days of poor Judge Wayne way off in Washington. The folks around him up there accuse us down here of treason. The folks down here accuse him of it. He doesn't deserve the kind of suffering he must be enduring, this very day." She managed a weak half-laugh. "Right now, I'm tempted to think that *we* don't deserve what we're suffering either!"

He was leaning forward in his chair now, still holding on to her hand. "I might have known you'd bring up that word, deserving. I've been haunted by whether or not I deserve what I'm going through. Does any of it have to do with anyone *deserving* this kind of torment?"

"I honestly doubt it. I pray, oh, how I pray for an end to it before things have gotten any worse, but I don't pray for God to save us from war as though God sends war. To my dying day, I vow He doesn't. When we heard the prayers for the victory of the South in church on Sunday, I wondered if you were thinking the same thing I was thinking. Women just like me—no better than I, no worse—at the North are praying for victory for their side. Who am I to question their Christianity? Jesus said that His followers would be recognized *only* by the way they love each other. Not a word about whether their side won or lost a war, was right or wrong."

Neither spoke for a long time, then Mark said, "Lincoln's blockade will be in effect soon. We're a port city. No amount of money will buy food and the other things we need if nothing is coming in because ships can't get through."

"We're also told to take one day at a time, Mark. Don't borrow trouble. We'll find a way to eat. You'll always find a way to feed Little Ben."

He took a deep breath. "I've been putting this off," he said, "and I can't do it any longer. It seems superficial, downright silly to me now in the face of what could lie ahead. But I've never been able to keep my faults to myself with you. It's about Ben."

"Ben?"

"I swear I didn't know it. At least, I certainly hadn't faced it, but I had quite a struggle with myself recently concerning the baby's Indianness." He held out both hands in a helpless gesture. "How in the name of common sense can a man sort out even his own feelings about bloodshed and war and a shattered country when he can't even comprehend the way he feels about his own innocent little grandson's dark skin and hair?"

"But have you straightened it out now? Are you all right now about Little Ben?"

He nodded yes. "I'm all right now. Especially since I've confessed it to you. Did you have any problem with it at first?"

"No, but I'm not surprised that you did. What about Caroline?"

"That's what made me feel so infernally guilty! She was stunned when she first looked at him, but whatever has taken over in her that makes her able to be so understanding of my dogged love of the Union, has moved her past any disappointment she must have had over the way Ben looks. Miss Eliza, I hate being superficial! I've always defended Mary's Cherokee blood, but I was so noble about that because she looks like us!"

She was smiling at him now. "Excuse me if I quote a little Scripture, dear boy. We're also told to give thanks in *everything*. That includes Ben." She rocked for a moment. "But do you suppose either of us will ever learn to give thanks in the midst of this national trouble? I think it would help."

"You mean to give thanks because going through it can show us so much about what's been wrong inside ourselves? Can show us faults, sins we didn't know we had?"

"That's right. That's exactly right."

He leaned back in his chair. "As usual, almost as though you didn't mean to be doing it, you've cleared away more of my gloom. If I can keep on learning in my old age, if I even think there's a chance for that, I guess I feel hopeful."

"We *can* feel hopeful," she said. "Not the kind of cocksure palaver most of the young bucks in the military are spouting now—that the South can bring the North quickly to its knees—but, Mark, as long as there are wise and good men like Robert Lee on the scene, God has channels through which He can help. I don't know how, because I don't understand so much." She started to pull herself out of her chair. "Oh, I *do* know I'm getting old and dotty and forgetful! I fully intended to read another letter to you the minute I finished Eliza Anne's, and off I went talking in all directions."

On his feet, he asked what she needed. "Let me get it for you."

"Thank you, dear boy. Over there in that little table. In the right-hand corner of the drawer. A letter from blessed Custis Lee—only a note, really, but he copied and enclosed a part of his latest letter from his father, and I must read it to you!"

Mark handed her the letter and sat back down in his chair as she looked for the part she wanted to read. "No point in reading Custis's little note, but it's sweet and I am so grateful that he bothered to send me this paragraph from his father's very latest from Texas. Robert's commanding Union Fort Mason there now, out in the wilderness, Custis says, and his father likes that much better than being in town. Here's what Robert wrote: 'The proceedings of the Southern states in seques-tering the public property within their reach or, as it is pompously termed, *"capturing"* the U.S. forts, arsenals, etc., etc., when there are plainly no Union forces to defend them, I fear will never calm the angry feelings in the country. Except in self-defense, I think such action is unnecessary.' "

"That's exactly what Jonathan's regiment did at Fort Pulaski," Mark murmured.

Eliza Mackay merely nodded, then went on reading: " 'If the bond of the Union can only be maintained by the sword and bayonet, instead of by brotherly love and friendship, and if strife and civil war are to take the place of mutual aid and commerce (North and South), the Union's existence loses all interest for me. Surely, no one can doubt my love of the Union or my hatred of slavery. I can, however, do nothing but trust in the wisdom and patriotism of the nation as a whole and to the overruling providence of a merciful God. I am particularly anxious that Virginia should keep right, should not secede, as she was chiefly instru-mental in the formation and inauguration of the Constitution. So, with all my heart, I can only wish that our state might be able to maintain her national loyalty in order to help save the Union . . .' "

"Oh, Miss Eliza," he interrupted. "Lee is—suffering now, isn't he? His whole life has been devoted to the Army of the United States! Virginia is expected to secede within a few days. What will Lee do?"

"I was struck," she said sadly, "with his having written that if the bond of the Union isn't strong enough to keep us all together, it could cause him to lose interest in it. His first loyalty, or I'm vastly mistaken, is to Virginia. Robert was taught that way, to believe that his first loyalty must be to his state."

She saw Mark's little, quick frown come and go and knew he was deep in thought.

"When did Colonel Lee write that?" he asked.

"Oh, early this year, before Texas seceded, surely. Dear Custis forgot to tell me the date of his father's letter, but Robert was still in Texas on duty when he wrote it. He's had to leave, return to Washington, I'm sure, since the state of Texas has now seceded. Mark, Mark," she groaned, "how can it be? How *can* it be? Our beloved old Union . . ."

"Since we're being honest with each other, I might as well tell you that I have about given up ever really understanding why men would go to war because of their love of one state or another. I still love my native state of Pennsylvania, but not to the exclusion of the nation as a whole! I *chose* to become a Georgian. I've lived my life here, contributed what I could to the community with my whole heart. But I don't love Georgia more than I love the Union. As much as I live by my devotion to Savannah, I would never have moved here had Georgia not been a part of the United States. At least, I don't think I would have. Although I can't imagine life anywhere but in Savannah now."

"You didn't become a Georgian, dear boy. You became *yourself in Savannah*. Savannah helped you—find yourself. *Savannah is still holding you.*" She fell silent for a moment. "Promise me you'll never forget, Mark, that even though she is noisy and belligerent and wrongheaded today, through all the years of your life, Savannah has held you."

"I'll try," he said. "But do *you* really understand States' Rights taking precedence over the nation?"

After a long pause, she answered him in a quiet voice, "Yes, dear boy, I understand that. I don't wholly agree with it, but I understand it. If I didn't, I'd be in despair over all three of my own daughters, my grandchildren. Some things have to be understood with the heart. And right now, I'm thankful for that, because my head would never understand turning against our Union. All of that causes such pain for Robert Lee, I know. He nearly worships the memory of George Washington. It's been a long time since I've had a letter from Robert, way back in the late 1850s, I guess, but the trouble was mounting then, and he wrote one sentence about Washington I'll never let slip my mind."

"Can you tell me what Lee wrote?"

"He said he'd written the same thing to his wife, Mary. I always felt honored that he shared it with me. What he said was: 'How Washington's spirit would be grieved to see the impending wreck of his mighty labors!' "

A week later, Eliza Mackay sat reading the newspaper alone in her parlor, trying to take in the barrage of facts and figures and military actions—all terrifying—jumbling together in her mind, her heart doing little to help her sort them out. The Federal arsenal at Harpers Ferry had been seized by the Confederates, and the Federal navy yard at Norfolk, Virginia, was taken, with a vast quantity of war material and supplies. If she could have made herself hope or pray for either side, things might not be so hard to figure out, but how did one pray for victory or success in a family quarrel? Through her many years she had often been torn by grief or worry or pain for a loved one's suffering. This time she felt as though her own heart was being torn, as strongly one way as another. It seemed the North had superior material resources, but the U.S. Regular Army of officers and men had, under President Buchanan, been sent to distant parts of the country and quantities of arms and ammunition lately moved from Northern to Southern arsenals. Most of the ships of the U.S. Navy were at foreign stations. These disadvantages were being cheered all over Savannah.

Eliza could only grieve for both armies. And because, in a very real way, especially since Jack's death, Robert Lee had become like a son to her, she grieved for what must surely be his agony of soul. How in the name of heaven would Robert resolve the ugly, ugly battle that had to be raging within him?

"I'd write to the boy myself, busy and troubled as he must be," she said aloud, "if I knew where he's stationed now. The last thing he needs, though, is a nosy letter from an old woman who has no power at all to help him!" She'd been talking to herself so much lately, she rather enjoyed it. "His beloved Virginia has jumped off the deep end, too, now," she mused. "Robert is as dedicated to the United States Army as Jack ever was, no matter how they both grumbled. But he once told me that Virginia's very air and the feel of her soil under his feet brought him a comfort he could find nowhere else. What Robert decides to do can sway so many others. I wonder why he made no apparent effort to keep Virginia from seceding? Poor, poor boy! Has he fought this out all alone, within himself? And if he has, what has he decided to do?"

She scanned the remainder of the news article, hoping to see his name. It was not there.

Sarah brought the mail to her right after dinner. There was, of course, no letter from Lee, but addressed to Eliza Mackay herself was one from his sister, Ann Marshall, who had never before written to her or to anyone else in the family, as far as she knew. Her hands trembled as she broke the seal and began to read the first of two pages: "My dear Mrs. Mackay," she read silently, even though both daughters stood in the middle of the floor all ears. "I am writing this at the urgent request of my dear brother, Robert, who is now too occupied with frenzied duties to handle his personal correspondence. I'm sure you have read in the papers that he regretfully resigned his commission with the United States Army and is now in command of the army of Virginia for the Confederacy."

Eliza's involuntary gasp sent both daughters scurrying to lean over her shoulder and peer at what she had just read.

"What is it, Mama?" Kate demanded.

"Can't you at least read it aloud to us?" Sarah wanted to know.

After a moment in which she tried to collect herself, Eliza handed the page to Sarah. "Here, you read it."

"Who's it from?" Kate asked.

"Robert Lee's sister, poor Ann Marshall," Eliza said.

"Well, for heaven's sakes, read it, Sister!"

" 'My dear Mrs. Mackay,' " Sarah began. "Oh, my Lord!" she interrupted herself. "Colonel Lee's resigned his commission!"

"What?"

"You heard me, Kate. He's resigned his commission in the U.S. Army and is now in command of the entire army of the state of Virginia! Listen to what his sister writes: 'I am now to be tortured for all the months the war lasts, because my devotion to Robert is total, as is my devotion to my husband and son, both of whom are strong Union men. I will have to find a way to appear to agree with them, to encourage them, while within me I will know only torment, since I know in my heart that they can't whip Robert! At Robert's insistence, Mrs. Mackay, I am copying for you a portion of his letter to me once this fateful decision had been reached. His high regard for you and yours never wavers and he wanted you to hear from me—in his words—"all that he knows as to his reasons for doing what he did." How he could have done it, believing as he did, and does, in the efficacy of the Union, only Robert knows. This is what he wrote to me.' "

Kate still stood in the middle of the floor. Eliza sat motionless in her rocker, hands clasped together.

" 'Now that we are in a state of revolution, into which Virginia after a long struggle has been drawn, though I recognize no necessity for this state of things and would have forborne and pleaded to the end for redress of grievances . . .' "

"Colonel Lee sees no necessity for the state of things? He sees no necessity for us to stand firm down here for our liberty?" Kate asked in a choked voice.

"Are you going to let me finish or aren't you?"

"I'm sorry. Please go on, Sister."

" '. . . and would have forborne and pleaded to the end for redress of grievances (real or supposed), yet in my own person I had to meet the question whether I should take part against my native state. With all the devotion to the Union and the feeling of loyalty and duty of an American citizen, I have not been able to make up my mind to raise my hand against my relatives, my children, my home . . . I know you will blame me, dear Ann, but you must think as kindly of me as you can and believe that I have endeavored to do what I thought right. Much of the fighting, if indeed it comes to that, will take place in my beloved Virginia and probably in the immediate vicinity of Arlington, where my heart is . . .'

" 'Now I have done my brother's bidding,' " Ann goes on, " 'and be assured that had he not been so busy in his advisory capacity to President Davis in Richmond he would have written to you himself. I must tell you that Robert expects the war, if it comes to that, to last for years. He does not see the North as a "nation of craven shopkeepers" as do the fanatics in the South. He sees the North as a "nation of shopkeepers able to turn out cannon, small arms, munitions, ships, clothing, blankets, and drugs." He, as well as I, asks for the prayers of all of you. Most sincerely, Ann Marshall.' "

For a moment, no one said a word. Then Kate breathed: "Mama?"

"Don't ask me to say anything," Eliza said weakly. "There isn't anything to say."

SIXTY

Since the capture of Fort Pulaski and through the spring of 1861, Jonathan worked in the hot sun along with his fellow officers and men at cleaning rust from the guns, oiling and refurbishing them. His hands were callused for the first time in his life, his muscles hardened, and he had never felt so ready for anything as for active duty —and Virginia was where the need lay.

"Governor Brown is a man we all have to try to understand," Charles Olmstead said as he and Jonathan stood on the *Ida*'s deck in mid-May heading for town, both men eager for the three-day leave which could be their last. "It will be our last if the Governor can see his way clear to trust the protection of Savannah to the newly formed local regiment. They're able, I'm sure, and I fully understand why our regiment is so high-strung, so eager to get to Virginia for some action. I also try to keep the Governor's loyalty to Savannah and the coast in mind."

"You try too hard, Colonel," Jonathan said. "It's time we got a crack at those Yankees! We've earned it. Captain Francis Bartow is my only hope. He's a man after my own heart and I'd follow him anywhere."

Charles Olmstead studied his friend's face. "You really would, wouldn't you? So would I, if we could only get permission to leave, but a soldier has no right to select his place of duty. I'm not sure Bartow can restrain himself, though."

"Do you suppose Governor Brown cares more about Georgia than the Confederacy and President Davis?"

"I wouldn't go that far." The cautious Olmstead laughed. "The law *is* now passed so that President Davis can accept independent commands smaller than regiments. Captain Bartow won't waste any time. Maybe if his Oglethorpes can go, so can we."

"Aw, you're going to be given command of Fort Pulaski," Jonathan teased. "Just watch. Colonel Lawton means to get into the thick of it, too, and you deserve the command. You've spent enough nights on those lonely vigils of guard duty in command of tame Tybee Island. It's your time, old man."

Olmstead punched him on the arm. "Do you know how much it pleases me when you call me old man? I'm afraid I stay conscious of how much younger I am than you, Browning."

"You can't feel any younger this minute," Jonathan said, his sunny smile beaming. "A man of any age feels young when he's free to go home to a beautiful wife. We're both mere boys today. Mary and Florie will see to that."

"Is Mary any more understanding of what we're doing?" Charles asked as the little steamer moved in toward the Savannah waterfront.

Jonathan frowned. "At least she manages to act cheerful. There's a–a quiet, even silent side to my Mary I've never been able to penetrate. I doubt I ever will. I suppose it's the Cherokee in her. At least she doesn't cry anymore when I go home on leave. She tries–God in heaven, how she tries!"

"I've been meaning to ask about how your father's faring in all this. Is it hard for you to talk with him these days?"

Jonathan didn't answer at once. "Not really, I guess. Papa's kind. He cares about me with all his heart. We talk about everything else as long as possible. The subject invariably comes up, though. He falls almost as silent as Mary. But my mother is with us all the way. She's a magnificent lady! I've never felt so free with her, and the odd thing is that she has finally learned, after all these years, to let my father feel free, too." He turned to look straight at his friend. "Disagreement, I now know, needn't get in the way of real love, Charles. Mama and I stand alone for the Confederacy at our house, but in spite of that, we don't stand against Papa and Mary. Nor they against us." He grinned at young Colonel Olmstead. "When you're put in command of Pulaski, and if the Governor still hasn't agreed to let me go to Virginia, I hope I'll be right there with you."

That very night the Oglethorpes met in Savannah amid a storm of enthusiasm and excitement and unanimously offered their services to the Confederate States. President Davis immediately accepted Captain Francis Bartow's offer, and when Governor Joseph Brown issued an order prohibiting any company from taking equipment beyond the state's borders, even the *Republican* attacked him, declaring that "he had picked a most unfortunate time to stand on such punctilio. It is high time this business is brought to a close. From the beginning a misunderstanding seems to have existed between our Governor and the Confederate authorities."

W.H.'s longtime friend and former Savannah law partner, Judge Levi D'Lyon, wrote to Etowah Cliffs that "the Governor has grown entirely too large for his breeches! Brown has always been a picayune of a man."

"You've been right about Governor Brown all along, W.H.," Eliza Anne said at breakfast when D'Lyon's letter reached Cass in late May. "You, my husband, are a brilliant and perceptive gentleman."

"Perhaps," W.H. said glumly. "But frustrated at the moment. Do you realize it's been weeks since Brown has acknowledged even my request to learn what kind of uniforms my regiment will be supplied?"

Wanting, if possible, to prevent another of his despondent moods, Eliza Anne tried to focus his attention back on Judge D'Lyon's letter, which W.H. had laid beside him on the table. "Does Judge D'Lyon have any more news of what's happening in Savannah, darling?"

"Oh-oh, perhaps I haven't read it all." He picked up the pages. "Let's see, he says, 'To the anger of Governor Brown, his stupid edict was ignored by Captain Francis Bartow, who wrote the Governor on May 21 that he, Bartow, was leaving with the Oglethorpe Light Infantry for Virginia, under the orders of the President of the Confederacy, and that he hoped the blessings and commendation of everyone in Georgia would follow him.' Good for Bartow, I say," W.H. exclaimed, slapping his hand on the table. "And listen to what else young Bartow wrote His Highness, the Governor: 'I go, sir, to illustrate, if I can, my native state. At all events, to be true to her interests and her character.' Oh, I like that, Lib! Bartow got off a tremendously powerful line!" He leaned back in his chair. "That's exactly what I long to do with my Etowah Cavalry, my dear. No more, no less—I long to 'illustrate my state.'"

"I know, W.H. I do know that's true."

"Here, let me read the rest of what the Judge wrote: 'An immense multitude turned out to see Bartow off. The other military companies, among them the fine son of your Union friend, Mark Browning, who marched with his Chatham Artillery to the Central Railroad depot while bands played "Bold Soldier Boy." A flag made by some of the ladies in town was presented to Bartow, who accepted it with a few apt remarks: "I have not led these brave boys to this fight. They have led me, and I pledge to you that should we fail to bring back this flag, it will be because there is not one arm left among them to bear it aloft." I fear though,' D'Lyon wrote, 'that the malice of the Governor followed Bartow to Virginia. The mightily transformed Lieutenant Jonathan Browning told me that his Colonel Olmstead had heard from Bartow, now a colonel, and that in Bartow's letter he copied some of Brown's scorching words: "You have carried away from Savannah, Colonel Bartow, some of the city's bravest and best young men. Should the city be attacked or destroyed in your absence, I fear you would not receive the commendation of these mothers and sisters, whose sons and brothers you took from that city to fill places in Virginia which thousands of others would gladly have occupied." ' "

"How did Governor Brown *dare* write in that insulting manner to so brave a young officer as Francis Bartow?" Eliza Anne demanded.

W.H. gave her a look of personal triumph. "You'll learn that your husband has the knack of sizing up a man, be he governor or not, Lib."

Deciding to leave that alone, she urged him to read more. "Did he tell you what Colonel Bartow said in reply to such insolence?"

"He did. 'Colonel Bartow's response, written en route to Manassas, was brief: "I assure you, sir, that I shall never think it necessary to obtain *your* consent to enter the service of my country. God forbid that I should fall so low!" ' There," W.H. said gloatingly, "is a man after my own heart. I can all but hear Brown fume!"

SIXTY-ONE

"*I'd give anything,*" Natalie said one morning at the end of June, while Miss Lorah cleaned up their breakfast dishes, "if Burke and I didn't have to make that carriage trip to Cass Station to meet Mary Cowper today. It does look as though Uncle W.H. could have postponed his silly regimental business until his own daughter and grandchildren got here." When Lorah Plemmons went steadily on with her work in her maddening silence, Natalie heaved an enormous sigh. "You do know how to irritate me, don't you?"

Miss Lorah gave her an impish smile. "I don't reckon I make you any way, Missy. You're the one decides about that. I didn't say one word."

"That's what goads me and you know it. Can you imagine Burke leaving something as important as Callie's return from school up to a mere neighbor?"

"I been here long enough to know that the Latimers and the Stileses are closer than just neighbors."

She sighed again. "We were once. Who knows about anyone these days? Oh, Miss Lorah, I do know about *you*. You make me furious at times with your silences—especially when I need an answer—but *we're* close, aren't we? The older I get, the closer we are. Do you feel that way about us—you and Burke and me?"

"We're blessed that way. But even the Lord can't bless folks unless they stop trying to change each other."

"Oh, I know what's coming. But I'll never understand how Miss Lib and Uncle W.H. can go around fanning the fires of this terrible war and feeling patriotic about it." She sighed. "I know I don't have to understand. I'd give almost anything if I could, but I don't have to. So don't tell me I'm judging. I already know it."

"Wasn't aimin' to. They've got their ideas, you've got yours."

Gathering up her cup and saucer, Natalie went to Miss Lorah's dishpan on the dry sink and dunked them in the hot, soapy water. "I have to ask you something," she said, taking the dishcloth from the older woman's hands. "And I want a straight answer. Not a smart, preachy answer, a straight one. Are you on the side of the Union or the Confederacy, Miss Lorah?"

"I never did like flying off the handle. Never trusted the outcome of it. Seems to me like the states that broke with the Union flew off their handles."

"Then you agree with Burke."

"Looks like it. I wonder sometimes if the folks that happen to be born in South Carolina, Alabama, Louisiana, Georgia, Texas, now my own state of North Carolina and Virginia—all of 'em—I just wonder if at night, in the quiet and the dark, any of those folks ever thinks about President Jefferson, Washington—or either one of the Adamses."

"You think a lot, don't you?"

"I try." She smiled impishly. "Much as a woman with few brains and no education can think, I guess."

"You may not have much schooling," Natalie flared, "but don't insult God by making fun of your mind!"

Lorah Plemmons chuckled. "Miss Eliza Mackay told me that very same thing once. What time do you and the Mister have to leave?"

"In about an hour, I think. Burke will be back from whatever charity he's performing on the Stiles smokehouse in plenty of time. Oh, Miss Lorah, isn't Burke good? You know they never get caught up paying him for all he does to keep their place repaired."

"Burke's a good neighbor. He doesn't mind helping them out. The fact that they're so fired up about the Rebel side don't bother him. He let's people be."

"All right," Natalie said, making a face. "I catch on. *I* don't leave people alone. I know I don't, and even if I thought it a good idea not to make clear what I think about things, I don't know how *not* to do it!

Take my mother, for example. If she hadn't come to her senses and begun acting with Papa the way she should always have acted, I'd be compelled to set her straight now that this stupid, dangerous war has started."

"That just shows what a fine woman your mother is, though, that she can feel so strong about the Southern Cause and still not take it out on your father."

"You know, I suppose, that I dread going to Cass Station to meet Mary Cowper only because I know we'll argue."

Miss Lorah nodded yes, that she did know that. "But I'm not sure you will argue much, Missy, because I'm not sure you know exactly why you favor the Union—or even if you do."

"Of course I do!"

"When did you make up your mind to that?"

"I don't know! I still care most that Burke not get involved in any of it on either side. Don't pin me down on this. Loving my father, who loves the Union with all his heart, would be enough for me to love it, too, wouldn't it? I could never understand why my mother was so bullheaded about slavery. None of it is that important. Nothing like politics is enough to cause problems between people who truly love!"

"You've never wavered once from that in all the years of your life, have you, Missy?"

"How could I? No other woman ever had a husband like Burke, and now that he's older, he's even handsomer and dearer and more to my liking than ever, and he *is*, outside his new friend Mr. Goodman, the Marietta newspaperman, probably the most loyal Union man anywhere around these parts. Oh, a lot of men talk like they are, but do you know what I heard when I went to the post office with Burke the other day? There are even some around here who want to change the name of Cass County just because Lewis Cass—born in Michigan—is now the enemy."

Miss Lorah laughed. "And what are they going to change it to?"

"Oh, I don't know. I doubt if they do." She thought a minute. "How am I going to bear to be with Mary Cowper as much as we'll surely see each other this summer? She and the children are staying up here with Miss Lib, you know, all summer."

"You'll get along fine if you just remember how you've always cared about the poor girl. How sweet and good and kind she's always been."

"She turned her back on real love!"

"I know that's something you can't quite get past, Missy, but what's done is done. She's married now to an important, powerful man who is as strong for the Confederacy as though he'd been born in Savannah, Georgia, and not way off in England somewhere."

Natalie thought a while. "I suppose Stuart Elliott's as big a Southern fire-eater as Uncle W.H."

"I wouldn't know about that poor boy. I expect he's got his hands full comforting Lucinda after her mother jumped out the window and killed herself. That was so sad. Did you know the woman?"

"Not very well. Oh, I knew who she was when I was young. The Sorrels are prominent Savannahians. Mama says Matilda Sorrel always had bad times when she acted very strangely. I'd give almost anything to know if Mary Cowper and Lucinda Sorrel still go on pretending they're close friends."

"You're not much of a gossip, not nosy as a rule," Miss Lorah teased.

"And I'm not now! There's just no possible way Mary Cowper could really be friends with the woman who married the one man she will ever love."

"Bless your heart, you'll never let go of that, will you?"

"No, I won't, because I don't live in a dream world!"

"And Mary Cowper does, being contented to be married to her Mr. Low?"

Natalie shuddered. "A nightmare world would be more like it."

———◆———

Mary Cowper and her children were at Etowah Cliffs three whole days before she and Natalie were alone long enough to talk.

If I'm truthful, Mary C. thought as they took their first walk together along the river road, *I haven't tried very hard to be alone with Natalie, nor she with me.*

"Your children are beautiful," Natalie said, grabbing off a still pinkish, young branch of sassafras as they passed by. "I don't think I ever saw a prettier little boy than Willy. Does Miss Eliza Mackay spoil him rotten?"

"Absolutely not. I doubt that Grandma ever spoiled any child." She laughed a little. "I can't say as much for Mama, though. Oh, she's good to both my little girls, but she's smitten with Willy. It's probably just as well she lives up here. I don't think I've ever seen her so happy to have us visit her, have you?"

"Probably not. If anything can make her really happy these days with this dumb war and Uncle W.H. racing around raising regiments."

For a while, they walked in silence. "You're pro-Union along with Burke, aren't you?" Mary Cowper asked.

"Yes. Because I'm more in love with him than ever. I don't get over real love."

Mary Cowper had long ago learned to ride with Natalie's sarcasm, much the way she knew how to ride with a horse whose quirks were familiar to her. "I'm side by side with my husband, too," she said. "Except for his Scottish accent, I find myself forgetting that Mr. Low wasn't also born right on the good soil of Georgia. He is utterly dedicated to the Southern Cause. A true Confederate patriot."

"In his business, why wouldn't he be?"

Mary C. made herself keep still.

"Burke's construction business can't shake *his* beliefs," Natalie boasted. "He lost a big job just last week with a man in Kingston who declared himself to be strong for the Union until that foolishness at Sumter. Now he's canceled Burke off the store he was going to build, because overnight he's a Southrener! Burke warned me we could be quite poor again, because if this trouble isn't over soon, there won't be much building. All he could do to earn a living would be to begin making barrels for the Confederate Army and Burke has too much respect for our forefathers ever to do that!"

"I don't want to argue, Natalie," Mary Cowper said, "but I fail to see what our forefathers have to do with any of this."

Natalie stopped walking to look at her. "You were once so sweet and good and kind and *smart*. Now look at you—listen to you. You've become a Savannah socialite! Which means you've stopped thinking at all."

Another moment of silence fell around them, so that the song of a summer tanager in a treetop some distance down the riverbank came clear and lilting. "Are the trees ever quite as green as now, in June?" Mary Cowper asked, changing the subject. "Isn't autumn hard to believe today?"

She hoped fervently that she had switched Natalie's thoughts to safer ground, until Natalie accosted her with "How is Lucinda Elliott getting along after her mother took her own life, Mary? Did you see her before you left Savannah? Do you still try to be—friends?"

"We are friends and, yes, I saw Lucy the day before we took the train up here. She's a very brave woman. Her poor mother is better off and her new little daughter is such an adorable child. Lucy named her Matilda Moxley, after both her mother and her favorite brother."

Natalie made no comment on that. Instead, she asked, "Where's Stuart now? Has he enlisted in the Rebel Cause?"

Mary Cowper had tried to stay on guard, but she hadn't expected so blunt a question as that. "Of course he enlisted. Lucinda's husband is in Captain Charles DuBignon's Company, Phillips's Legion, Georgia Volunteers. When I left Savannah, he was stationed on the Isle of Hope."

"You certainly know all the details about him, don't you?"

"Lucy and I *are* friends, Natalie."

"Is Stuart an officer?"

"He's a private."

"I'm relieved to hear that."

"Why?"

"I don't know. I just am. Living as close as Burke and I live to Uncle W.H., we both get a little nauseated at the way some sons of privilege pull every possible string to start out at least at lieutenant colonel, even if they know nothing whatever about the military. Uncle W.H., your handsome father, is a prime example."

That remark somehow upset Mary Cowper even more than what Natalie had said about Stuart. Hold your tongue, she warned herself. Just be quiet and keep on walking.

"I'm sorry," Natalie said quickly. "Mary Cowper, I'm truly sorry. I didn't really mean what I said about Uncle W.H. At least, I didn't mean it to sound so downright nasty. I'm thirty-eight. It's time I learned not to blurt out every single thing I happen to think. Can you forget it, please?"

"All right."

"That doesn't sound very wholehearted to me."

"I've never attacked you because your father believes as he does, Natalie."

"That's right, you haven't." Natalie stopped walking again and took Mary Cowper's arm. "Can you look me in the eye and tell me you're happy with Mr. Low? Can you?"

Mary C. felt her eyes fill with quick tears, so she looked out over the river. "I–I can't look you in the eye and say it, but I *can* say it, Natalie. I'm happy with Mr. Low. Our wholehearted dedication to the South has given us an even stronger bond."

SIXTY-
TWO

Word reached Savannah by telegraph on Monday, July 22, that the bloody, daylong battle fought near Manassas, Virginia, on Sunday had ended in "a glorious victory for the Confederacy." President Jefferson Davis had himself gone to the encounter, and although he arrived as the Yankees were fleeing Manassas, many Virginians who didn't discover this until later greeted Davis's return to the capital in Richmond as a hero.

In the early evening Andrew Low sat alone in his back parlor reading the newspaper account of the costly battle. True, he thought, the Confederate forces did soundly whip the Yankees, but at enormous cost in men killed and wounded. No other single section of the South had been harder hit at Manassas than Savannah. Of the seventy-eight members of the Oglethorpes, all young, valiant, fearless men—"Bartow's Beardless Boys," people had called them the day they entrained for Virginia—six were killed and forty-nine wounded. All tragedies for the families involved, Low thought, but the greatest loss of all to the South's Cause was the death of Francis Bartow himself, already brevetted a general. "Although not wholly free from minor defects," the editor had written, "Bartow's name is now immortal and will be ranked in future years among the purest of patriots and most chivalrous men who ever served in council, or commanded in the field." That very afternoon, Mayor Jones had told Low of his own deep admiration for young Bartow. "None ever for a moment doubted his bravery," Jones had said, shaking his head. "Not only had he been promoted immediately upon arriving in Virginia, he has left to our army and to his country a signal illustration of true Southern valor."

Mary Cowper and Bartow's widow knew each other, Low remembered. I must write to my wife at once. I need contact with her anyway. She doesn't even know that Charles Green has left my firm, or that he is now in Liverpool on Confederate business.

For a long time, he sat sipping one, then two, then three glasses of fine port, the vintage he always saved for drinking alone. Odd, he thought, that I never think to confide in her where business matters go when she's at home.

He admitted freely now, port in hand, that informing her on business affairs made writing somehow easier. With Mary Cowper in his arms, alone in their room, he could *show* his love and adoration. He had drunk just enough port now to be able to admit to himself that the trouble lay always in putting his feelings into words.

He poured another glass from the nearly empty bottle, tossed it off far too quickly for such superb wine, and went to his writing desk in the far corner of the back parlor, needing, dear God, truly *needing* to pour out his thoughts to her, to tell her of the ache in his body and his arms and his heart because he had never yet been altogether sure that he had truly touched a hidden part of this beautiful young woman he loved with all his being . . .

Savannah, Georgia
22 July 1861

My dear Wife,

I find the house very empty tonight without you and the happy chatter of our little ones.

To give an idea of how swiftly events happen in these times—your friend Charles Green not only left the firm of Andrew Low and Company, he left the country, too, at the behest of Confederate Secretary of War Leroy Pope Walker. Green is in Liverpool, I believe, in an effort to assist Savannah's Edward C. Anderson, now Major Anderson, in the purchase of arms and supplies for our Cause. There was no more ill will than usual between Charles Green and me when he left. In fact, our relationship seems to have been strengthened by our mutual war efforts with the British. Green is flourishing in his own right and severance of our partnership is a mere legal formality, which I will handle.

Major Edward Anderson, as you know, is not only a fine-appearing gentleman but an ardent Southern patriot, for whom I've always possessed a liking. That, too, is strengthened by the power of our shared Cause. Anderson, it seems, is having great difficulty buying munitions and arms abroad, so I could be further involved and will be should my services appear needed.

There is also, my dear, glorious news of the first Southern triumph at Manassas in Virginia. Surely, by the time you receive this letter, you will have heard that young Colonel Francis Bartow was killed. He was knocked by a bullet from his horse, remounted, and hit a second time by the fatal ball. So Savannah is in deep mourning, not an easy emotion to blend with the equally deep joy in the victory of our Cause in this, the first key battle of what, many now realize, will be a blessedly short conflict.

The city steams with heat tonight and I rejoice that you and the children are up there by the cool river, with the hills as shelter.

He laid aside his pen and reached for the port decanter. "No!" He spoke aloud, admonishing himself. "It is too hot for more port. You will only feel more keenly the pain of missing her if you allow yourself to lose control of your emotions. Finish the letter off and climb up to that lonely bed."

Pen in hand, he sat for a long time, not writing. "I'm a helpless, powerless man," he groaned. "Undoubtedly, I will be able to help Major Anderson buy guns . . . but I can't tell my wife how I really feel about her! So, finish the letter, Low, finish—the letter."

The sound of his own slurred speech pulled the knot more tightly inside him, so that he could write only:

> Yr affectionate husband,
> Andrew Low

Mary Cowper read his letter aloud to her mother as soon as Miss Lorah's Sam brought their mail from Cartersville on Wednesday.

"Now I'll go help Little Sinai cut out those dresses for the quarters children and you'll have time alone to read your personal pages in Mr. Low's letter," her mother said.

"There is no personal letter to me," Mary Cowper said in a quiet, remote voice that seemed directed at no one. "Mr. Low and I have an understanding about such things. But do go ahead with whatever it is you have to do, Mama. I promised to take the children to see Natalie anyway."

She saw the frown on her mother's face and wasn't at all surprised when she said, "Well, all right, darling. Just don't allow Natalie to preach Yankee doctrine to you—and if I were you, I'd never, never tell her that Mr. Low didn't include the usual personal note in your letter."

Mary C. smiled. "I'm a grown woman, Mama. Is it so hard for you to remember that?"

Two days later her father was home again, bouncing his year-old grandson, Willy, on his knee, when Mary Cowper came in with the mail Sam had just brought. To everyone's surprise, there was another letter from Mr. Low.

"I'm glad you're here, Papa," she said, stooping to kiss the baby's blond head. "Now I can read Mr. Low's letter to you, too. And this one feels much longer. I'm sure he's still happy over our wonderful victory at Manassas. Is Willy dry?"

"Yes," Eliza Anne said, "I just changed him. Do sit down, dear, and let's find out why Mr. Low has written again so soon."

"Hold your horses, Mama," Mary Cowper said. "I'm going to read every word as soon as I can get it unsealed. If Willy wiggles too much, Papa, let Mama hold him."

"Have no fear," Papa said, hoisting the boy high over his head. "My grandson and I are doing just fine, aren't we, little fellow? Don't you both think he's the picture of his grandfather Stiles?"

"Stop playing, W.H., so that Mary C. can read her letter!"

"I'm ready, Mama. It's dated Monday, July 29. He must have gotten it on the train first thing in the morning. Today is only Thursday. 'My dear wife,' he writes. 'My heart is, as with every heart in town, battling within itself for both joy and sadness. The glorious victory at Manassas Junction has been celebrated since last Sunday when our superior forces made a mockery of the North, but there is also citywide grief. The loss of six Savannah heroes was accentuated yesterday when the body of brave General Francis Bartow was returned for burial in the land he so loved and for which he gave his promising life. One week to the day after his tragic death last Sunday, Savannah paid her highest respects. Four gray horses drew the hearse which bore the coffin. All the military turned out and an immense concourse of citizens thronged the Bay. I wish I had time to give you details, my dear, but I don't because I must get this off at the earliest possible moment due to my own immediate plans. I was at the funeral, of course, and while I must wait to give you more particulars, I felt certain that your parents would want to know, as will you yourself, that your grandmother, Mrs. Mackay, made the effort to attend, too. I felt concern for her under that blazing sun, but, as usual, she was supported fully by her close friend Mark Browning and his wife, along with the two Mackay daughters. The eulogies were long, but the old woman stayed to the end. Perhaps I should mention that young Jonathan Browning also attended from Tybee Island, where he is now stationed, under the command of his friend Colonel Charles Olmstead. With young Browning was his Cherokee wife, but without their infant son, undoubtedly due to the brutal heat. Young Mrs. Browning appeared stoic and unfeeling, but that is the way of Indians, I'm sure. One could not rightly expect a half-savage young woman, pretty as she is, to grasp the heroic drive within her husband to defend his native land, even against his own father's treasonable beliefs.' "

"Jonathan's loyalty to our Cause serves Mark Browning right," Papa broke into the reading, his voice tight, almost angry. "Whatever brought the boy to his senses, I commend him. And I'm sure his good mother is proud."

"W.H., do you think that's quite fair?" Mama asked, a little uncertainly. "You were once Mark's attorney, his friend. Heaven knows I don't agree with his condescending Northern views, but he's entitled to them, isn't he?"

"Oh, I don't believe what I'm reading," Mary Cowper blurted, actually feeling the color drain from her face. "Mama, this will come as a blow to you, too!"

"What? What on earth?" Her mother had jumped to her feet.

"I couldn't help scanning ahead in Mr. Low's letter," she said. "He'll be here tomorrow!"

Almost shouting, Mama echoed: "*Tomorrow?* Oh, not tomorrow, Mary Cowper! There's no way I can be ready to entertain him so soon."

Papa hurried to where her mother stood and almost dumped the baby into her arms. "What's happened, Mary Cowper?" he asked. "Were you expecting Andrew to visit us so soon?"

"I wasn't expecting him at all, Papa! If you'll both just listen, I'll read more of what he wrote.

'Aware that this is going to rush you, my dear, it is, nevertheless, of the utmost importance. I have been urgently requested, through a letter from the Secretary of War in Richmond, to join my ex-partner, Charles

Green, and Major Anderson in Liverpool as quickly as I can work out passage. Of course, since we will be spending time with my daughters at school in Brighton, you will come with me. My mission to England is of such secrecy and importance that I can say no more. Only that you are to be ready to leave by train for Nashville with me no later than July 31. I will be at the Cass Station R.R. depot on Friday. Honor me by giving my love to your family, to our three little ones, and your true-spirited self. Yr affectionate husband, Andrew Low.' "

"Well, did you ever," Mama gasped, testing the baby's diapered bottom. "Oh, Willy!" She rushed from the room to make the needed change. From the doorway, she called back, "Get busy, Mary Cowper! Concentrate on your wardrobe. I'll see to Willy and be back directly."

"So, Low is going to England to buy guns for us," Papa said proudly. Then, his eyes burning with zeal, he gave her a penetrating look. "You're married to a highly important gentleman, Mary Cowper. If there's one need overshadowing all others for our beloved South, it is —armament and ammunition."

"Yes, Papa. I know he's important and I'm sure you're right."

"Now then," he went on as though this sudden, inconvenient, disrupting trip abroad were no more than a trifling incident, "I must call for my horse and ride quickly to Cassville to the courthouse. Once my mission is complete there, I will be home to write immediately to Governor Joseph Brown. There's not a minute to lose!"

"But Mr. Low said his European trip was strictly secret, Papa!"

"My mission to the courthouse is another matter entirely, daughter. Actually the brilliant thought struck my mind as you were reading what Low wrote about the burial of General Francis Bartow."

She frowned. "Papa—what *are* you talking about? What does poor General Bartow's funeral have to do with—"

"It has to do with the very land on which our home stands here in what must no longer be called Cass County! There's already unrest over the fact that our beloved county bears the name of a Northerner who is at this very minute undoubtedly up there in enemy territory still donating his own personal property in order to sustain a wicked war against our people. *Against us,* Mary Cowper! I intend to take advantage of that unrest and push through the renaming of the county to Bartow!" He gestured dramatically. "I can see it now—W. H. Stiles, Esquire, of *Bartow County!* Doesn't that make the bells ring for you, daughter? General Bartow's name will ring through all history—and doesn't the sound of Bartow County have a definite tone?"

SIXTY-THREE

Eliza Anne, beside W.H. on the worn seat of their once elegant carriage, rode toward home from the Kingston W. and A. train station, where they had just delivered Mr. Low and Mary Cowper. She rode in silence for as long as she could stand it.

"Don't you have anything to say in the face of what is up ahead for *me,* W.H.?" she demanded at last.

"For you, my dear Lib?" He seemed distracted, preoccupied. She felt like shaking him.

"The responsibility of caring for three small children now falls entirely on me," she snapped. "Or hadn't that occurred to you at all?"

"Oh, yes, yes, of course. I look forward to the prospects of having the grandchildren with us for the remainder of the summer, though. And once you've calmed down from the flurry you put yourself through just preparing for Andrew Low to be in our house for one night, you'll enjoy them, too."

"Sometimes I wonder if you even remember you're married to me! You must know that our only daughter is in the direst danger and will be every hour she is away on this peculiarly hurried journey. You must also know how long it's been since our children were young. I'm out of practice!"

He patted her hand. "Lib, Lib, calm yourself, my dear. Do try to calm yourself. You're merely exhausted."

"I am exhausted and it's not 'merely' either! Are you so bent on getting into battle with your precious regiment that you find it easy to ignore even Mary Cowper's danger? Why, after Nashville, even Mr. Low wasn't sure how two Southerners could manage safely to make it through the North to Canada! They'll have to sail from Canada, you know, because of that monster Lincoln's blockade."

"I do know and I also know Andrew is a seasoned world traveler. Our little girl is in the best hands possible."

"You didn't try at all to help me dissuade them from going!"

"No. I'm doing all in my power to help the Confederacy, Lib, not hinder it."

"Hush!"

"Could I politely recommend the same, my dear?"

"You could, but I wouldn't try, if I were you. It's been so long since I've cared for small children, how on earth will I do it alone?"

"You won't be alone. There are our house servants and Natalie and Miss Lorah. They'll all be at your service."

On impulse, she threw both arms around him, unmindful of the fact that July could see them plainly, if he happened to look down from his driver's seat into the open cab of the carriage. "Oh, W.H., I die a million deaths every time I think of you actually in this terrible war, but you're so distracted, sometimes I think you'd be far better off—I know you'd be far happier—if you were already on your white charger in full-dress uniform, heading into battle. I do wish Governor Brown would stop blocking you at every turn. Why isn't your regiment already accepted into the Confederate Army? Can you tell me that? You've been oddly quiet about it all month, you know."

He moved out of her embrace and sat very straight against the carriage seat. "Yes, Lib, I know I've been silent. With reason. The Etowah Cavalry became a Confederate regiment three weeks ago."

"What?"

"Without me, though."

"W.H., I don't understand!"

"I wasn't elected its colonel by the men who seemed to want to serve."

"Well, are they serving now?"

"Yes, confound it, but without me!"

Sensing that his pride had been dreadfully injured, she said nothing until she'd had time to think. "Did—did the men in the regiment resent the movement among our politicians to make you governor? Did they learn of how hard Levi D'Lyon and the others down in Chatham County had been working in your behalf? Military men often resent politicians, but didn't Judge D'Lyon insist that a term in the Army would be of help in going after the governorship? Still, I suppose fighting men don't understand these things."

He laid his hand over hers. "Don't worry your beautiful head about any of it, Mrs. Stiles. Give your full expertise to those adorable grandchildren of ours this summer. Your old husband has a splendid new plan."

"You have?" she asked.

"It will undoubtedly take me to the Capitol in Richmond soon, but there isn't the slightest need to fret. We're a part of history, Lib. With all my heart, I want to be a useful part of it."

As always, his scattered motivations, which at times sprayed in all directions like buckshot, were invariably focused for her in his young-boy desire to perform some act of merit. "You're good, W.H., you're such a good, thoughtful man. You try so hard and . . ."

"And sometimes you're sorry for me when I fail, as I did by not being elected by the very men I longed to lead in the Etowah Cavalry."

"No! No, no, no! I'm never sorry for you. I respect you too much, I'm too aware of your brilliance, your influence in the state, your . . ."

"My love for you, Lib? Please, always be aware of that. I'm—I'm also trying to remember to pray every night before I drop off to sleep."

"Because you know that would please me?"

"If I'm honest, yes."

"I was afraid of that. But I love you for trying to remember. Forgive me for complaining about the care of our precious grandbabies this summer and for my own lack of faith that God will look after Mary Cowper and Mr. Low. You know I'm a worrywart, and only God knows what that Lincoln might do against us next!"

SIXTY-FOUR

Seeing her every day, as Mark had done for so long, kept him from realizing Eliza Mackay's growing frailty, but when Caroline called on her one morning in the late summer, she sent for her daughter-in-law the minute she came home.

"I was so stunned by the way Miss Eliza looked, Mary," she said as soon as Mary came leading Little Ben into her room, "I simply had to talk to you about her. Mark has said so little lately. He's free with me these days, so don't you think he'd have mentioned how thin and pale Miss Eliza looks? How weak?"

Ben broke away from his mother and toddled on his fat brown legs to Caroline, both arms out. "Grandmother Caroline is busy, Ben," Mary said, taking the child's arm. "She'll hold you on her lap in just a minute." Ben let out a stream of chatter, then laughed. Taking him in her arms, Mary turned back to Caroline. "How long since you saw Miss Eliza, Mama Caroline?"

"Oh, ten days, maybe two weeks."

"At her age, weakness can come in such a short time."

"I suppose," Caroline said. "I haven't seen her since General Bartow's funeral, actually. A little more than two weeks. Don't you think I should warn Mark that she struck me as being really ill?"

"He knows Miss Eliza is old," Mary said, kissing Ben's thick black hair.

"But he won't even discuss it. Oh, Mary, I'm trying so hard to give my husband room, to stand by him through all this ghastly war business. I don't think he goes about wishing ill to the South. I know he doesn't. He simply feels lost and alone in Savannah these days—and torn! He can't face the thought that Miss Eliza is so frail. Inside, my dear husband is torn to pieces. He loves Savannah so much, it seems almost to cloud his mind."

"Papa Mark worries about *our* safety in Savannah?"

"Of course he does! And if all the talk in town is true, we are in real danger. Jonathan backs up all we read in our papers about how poorly we're defended. He told his father and me last week when he was here from Tybee that Colonel Olmstead had heard from General Robert Lee that Savannah is the hardest place to defend anywhere! We have so many rivers and creeks. At times I actually feel sorry for Governor Brown. By one side he's criticized for keeping too many Georgians here to defend us; by the other he's scolded for not defending us strongly enough, for what Jonathan says is our pathetic lack of arms."

"Guns are bad!"

Mary had told Caroline long ago that for most of her life guns had been merely the means of killing food for the table, but since a gun in her brother Ben's own hand had blown out his brains, she feared and hated even the look of a firearm. "Oh, Mary," Caroline whispered, going to her, "it's what men do with them that is bad."

Tears filled Mary's eyes and her voice broke as she said, "Guns make Jonathan a stranger—even to me."

"No, my dear! Don't say that. I know it's true, but don't say it. A part of me can never associate gentle Jonathan with killing either, but he's obliged to do what he's doing, Mary. Can't you accept that?"

"No." Her cheeks were wet now; the tears had spilled over.

Caroline held out her arms for Ben. "Let me have him, please. You try to compose yourself." Holding her grandchild in her arms, Caroline asked, "How do you manage not to say these things to Jonathan when he comes home for a night or two?"

"I—say nothing. I just love him."

"He loves you just as much—you and Ben. You believe that, don't you?"

Mary nodded quickly. "I try so hard to give Jonathan one more child."

"Don't try too hard, my dear. Only God knows when it is time for another child."

As though standing were too difficult, Mary sat down abruptly and turned her face away. "I am selfish, too," she said almost fervently. "I try to give Jonathan another child to look like him—not Cherokee, as Little Ben looks. I long for Jonathan to—die happy and proud, with one white child."

Still holding Ben, Caroline sank into another chair. "Mary! Jonathan —die? Do you realize what you just said?"

"I tell him."

"You've said that to Jonathan?"

"When he first become a soldier."

Caroline sat holding Ben so close, he began to fuss and fidget. If Jonathan did—get killed in the fighting, she thought, Ben *would* be all she had left of her son! Over her horror at what Mary had just said, a kind of love she'd never before experienced rushed through her. A new, desperate kind of love for the Indian child in her arms . . .

"We all might die, Mama Caroline. Savannah is in danger, Lee says. He is now a general and Jonathan knows that generals are high and— wise."

"Not all of them."

"But Miss Eliza knows General Robert Lee is better than all other generals."

"Have you seen Miss Eliza lately, Mary?"

Mary only nodded.

"When did you see her?"

"Ben and I—yesterday, when I took him for a walk."

"And did you think she looked terribly frail?"

"More heartbroken. Miss Eliza Mackay love this—Union. She love the thing Jonathan tries to destroy. Miss Eliza sees into Papa Mark's heart on everything. It is all crazy!"

Ben had fallen asleep in her arms. Caroline began to stroke his straight black hair. "We must pray, Mary. We must pray that Eliza Mackay lives until the war is over. With his son and me unable to believe as he believes, my husband couldn't endure losing her!"

One particular day when Mark made his daily visit to the Mackay house early in September, he and Miss Eliza and her two daughters spoke about Commodore Josiah Tatnall's pathetic "Mosquito Fleet." Both sisters defended it. Both argued, until their mother shushed them, that old Josiah Tatnall, who had left his high post in the United States Navy to take command of Savannah's danger-filled water defenses, was not helpless and foolish, in spite of the feeble size of his Confederate "fleet" composed of a river steamer and four tugs mounted with such guns as could be found.

"We don't know how much our Navy is helping," Kate insisted. "None of us here in town has any idea what's going on out there around us on the ocean or the rivers!"

"Commodore Tatnall wouldn't have given his fleet such imposing names if he didn't know they were successfully plying the waters from Port Royal up in South Carolina down this way, aiding British vessels trying to bring us supplies." To Mark, Sarah's voice sounded desperate, but then most voices in Savannah were either desperate with fear of an impending attack by the Union forces or high-pitched with anger or both.

"Enough, daughters," Eliza Mackay said firmly. "If the Union Navy decides to attack Tybee Island or even Fort Pulaski—or Savannah itself—I'm not going to count on Josiah Tatnall and his pitiful little mosquitoes, which the poor fellow dares to call *Savannah, Lady Davis* after the Confederate President's wife, *Resolute,* and *Samson!* I do wish you girls would try to help yourselves by finding a little humor in all this."

Miss Eliza certainly hasn't lost her sense of humor, Mark thought, and that good mind is as sharp as ever. With all his heart, he wished the well-intentioned, but at times dense sisters would leave him alone with her. Surely they needed to be doing something else.

"Since both you girls are such loyal patriots," Miss Eliza said, her thoughts matching Mark's as always, "how is it you can sit idly in the parlor without your laps full of knitting needles or at least a soldier's shirt to hem? Shouldn't you both be busy with your needlework? Isn't today your day to take those finished socks and shirts to the Women's Aid meeting?"

The daughters got up. "Keep your chair, Mark," Kate said. "There's no need to drop a brick on our heads, Mama. We're going."

"And we'd better," Sarah grumbled, heading for the door. "Things are in a pretty pass when members of the same family can't speak together without sniping at one another!"

He returned Miss Eliza's telling smile when the "girls," as she still called them, left the parlor. "Sarah's right, you know," he said. "Will we ever go to sleep or wake up again without the—terrible nervousness?"

"You will, Mark. I'm not sure I'll make it to the end. Did you have something in particular to tell me this morning?"

"You always know, don't you?"

"I try. Any news of Jonathan since yesterday?"

"Nothing beyond the fact that Colonel Olmstead is awaiting orders to take command of Fort Pulaski."

"Not Fort Jackson?"

"No, Pulaski, and that's an enormous assignment for a young man. Charles Olmstead's only twenty-five. Jonathan will go with him, of course."

"My grandson Henry Stiles is at Skidaway. I was rather hoping he and Jonathan could be together." She took a long trembling breath. "What we hope is no longer important, I guess. I suppose now that his father finally has his own regiment outfitted and accepted by President Davis, W.H. will use his influence to have Henry transferred to his command. My other dear grandson, Bobby, is still with the coastal survey." She shook her head. "Oh, Mark, Mark, W. H. Stiles is no more a military man than I am!"

"He's full of Rebel fire, though."

"So is Eliza Anne." She paused. "I opened my eyes just today with such a heavy heart for Robert Lee, Mark. I do wish I knew about him, beyond the fact that he's now a full-fledged general. He seems to be stuck in Richmond advising President Davis. For his sake, I hope he's well past it now, but I know a little of how he suffered when he felt he had to resign from the U.S. Army. That must have been like draining out his own blood!"

"Jonathan said they heard rumors that Lee might be coming to Savannah to inspect Fort Pulaski's defenses. If the Northern forces take over Tybee Island, which they'll surely do, Pulaski has to be next."

"But Port Royal up in South Carolina stands between Pulaski and the North, Mark."

He gave her a proud smile. "Few men in town know as much as you about all this," he said. "How do you manage to keep up?"

"I read the papers and I'm the mother of as loyal an officer as the United States ever had in my blessed Jack. Maybe I have an instinct."

He studied her lined, but still sweet features, his smile gone. "Are you telling me the truth when you keep saying you feel fairly well?" he asked.

"Not my peppiest today," she said, "but for an old lady, I'm holding up. You and I both have to hold up, you know."

Some weeks later, when Mark walked through the still surprising heat of mid-October to spend a little time with Miss Eliza, he had an added spring in his step because in his coat pocket he carried a letter for his old friend from Eliza Anne. No one needed to tell him how Miss Eliza had worried throughout the months of August and September because no word had come from Mary Cowper or Andrew Low, still, so far as anyone knew, in England. One early letter Eliza Anne had received from Mary Cowper was from the Canadian side of Niagara Falls, a glowing account of how much she was looking forward to the water voyage from Quebec through the Gulf of St. Lawrence. Due to Lincoln's blockade, there had been no other route to Liverpool. Train connections from Georgia to the North had evidently been dreadful. Low's influence had eventually gotten them to England, but for more than a month now, there had been only one letter to her parents from Liverpool, in which Mary Cowper described the convenient London residence of Savannah's Major Edward Anderson. They had spent a few days there while Low and Anderson held solemn negotiations in Anderson's office, a private room off his living quarters, with closets built into its walls where specimen rifles and arms were kept while Major Anderson, Low, and others examined them and either accepted or rejected them for use by the Confederate forces. In Liverpool, they had often been in the company of another Savannahian, Captain James Bulloch of the Confederate Navy. "My husband is showing himself to be of the utmost importance to our beloved country," Mary Cowper had written in that one letter from abroad. "By adding his name, funds, and connections over here to the purchase of a much-needed ship, he may be the key to saving Savannah from starvation due to the hated Lincoln blockade. We found Major Anderson in fine spirits over our glorious victory at Manassas. His hopes, as ours, are high indeed for an end to the madness in the very near future. I know my children cause you work and worry, Mama, but do try to write more often. I have received only one letter from you and that sent on from Quebec."

This, Mark knew, worried both Miss Eliza and Eliza Anne almost as much as the long silence they endured. Eliza Anne had written to her daughter almost every day!

Now, slightly winded, Mark climbed the Mackay front steps and gave his usual merry tap on Miss Eliza's door.

When they had taken their familiar places in the old parlor, Mark took out the letter at once. "You look tired, Miss Eliza, maybe this will lift your spirits. A letter from Eliza Anne."

"I am tired. I'm tired all the way through this morning. But do read it to me. It seems for the past few days, just wearing my spectacles makes me feel dizzy. But I'm so eager to know how Eliza Anne's getting along with the grandchildren there. And if she's had one other word from Mary Cowper." She laid the back of one hand against her forehead, as though to stop its whirling. "My old brain can't quite take it in, it seems, that the President of the United States allows no letters to pass through up there from us—down here. I do get confused at times, but of course, when I get my bearings, I understand that he can't. We're—we're at war—with ourselves."

Mark responded by pulling himself up out of Robert Mackay's old leather chair and dragging up a smaller one so as to be near enough to take one of her hands.

"That's nice, Mark," she whispered. "I need you close by. Your hand feels good on mine, but you'll need it to open the letter. Please do it now."

"Are you sure you're up to hearing it? It's fairly long."

"I'm sure. Don't pamper."

"It's dated October 12, 1861—*Bartow* County, Georgia!" He looked up at her. "Did you hear that? I hadn't known the name of Cass County had been officially changed to Bartow, had you?"

Miss Eliza gave a careless toss of her hand. "Oh, Sarah's been blabbing about the name being changed. She heard it from the ladies in her Aid Society. I don't think it's official yet. Eliza Anne tends to be dramatic, you know. I guess no one can stop her from heading a letter 'Bartow County.' Before W.H. left with his famous regiment for duty here at Skidaway Island, he's supposed to have pushed through the name change. At least so he told me when he came for dinner last week. What does Eliza Anne say, Mark, please? I know I'm chattering. Don't let me get fuzzy!"

He tried to smile at her. He was too worried at the way she looked and acted. He began to read: " 'My Dearest Mother and Sisters, I will not have long to write, because the children are due to wake up from their naps and will need to be bathed. Little Sinai adores bathing them, but since the trouble began, all our people are defiant except our groom, July, who goes on treating us as though we are all still friends. Being alone, as I am, time for letters is at a premium. Servants seem more trouble than they're worth these days. We are also short on writing paper, so I will tell you at once that I have finally heard from Mary Cowper! The most dreadful thing has happened. They dared not take passage home on *Fingal,* the newly purchased British steamer, since in order to reach Savannah with arms and gunpowder, etc., Lincoln's blockade had to be run. Mr. Low would not risk that, so they took the *North Briton,* Mary Cowper concealing in her heavy, long curls duplicates of dispatches to be hand-delivered to Robert Lee upon their return to our shores. I am nervous even about mentioning such a thing to you in a letter, so great is the bitterness and danger now. Still, when they reached Quebec, they learned that the other duplicate set of dispatches, by great fortune, had been safely delivered, and so Mr. Low destroyed those Mary C. carried. They determined to come back here through Cincinnati and Kentucky, but were detained in Cincinnati trying to get permission from a Union general named William Tecumseh Sherman to pass through the lines, so Mr. Low got tickets to come by way of Baltimore instead. As they waited through the weekend, Mary Cowper left Mr. Low unwell at the hotel while she attended church. Imagine her horror and shock when she returned to find several rough men in their chamber with her husband, and all their trunks open and their contents strewn about the room! Most dreadful of all, Mr. Low was under arrest, and showing that the U.S. has set aside all law, the poor man was sent to prison at Fort Warren, leaving Mary Cowper to find her own way back to Georgia through enemy country.' "

Mark stopped reading and rushed to Miss Eliza, who had slumped in her chair, her face as white as a sheet. "I'm sorry. I'm so, so sorry, dear friend," he whispered, rubbing her hands, slapping her pale cheeks lightly. "Miss Eliza!"

She opened her eyes. "I'm—all right, Mark. You'll have to admit that's —a blow."

"Shall I put the letter away?" he asked helplessly.

"Of course not! Hand me a little of that water in the pitcher there, will you?"

When she'd sipped the water, she made herself sit straight up in her little rocker and demanded that he finish reading.

" 'The U.S. marshal who arrested Mr. Low allowed Mary Cowper to ride with them as far as Harrisburg, Pennsylvania, where she had to leave her husband to complete his journey to prison in Boston. She continued on her own to Baltimore, where fortunately she found kind friends who cared for her. A Mrs. Glenn, whose husband was also in prison, took her in. Weeks passed in which we all waited—poor Mr. Low knowing nothing of her whereabouts and without any word of his precious children. I now, at least, know where Mary Cowper is, although her letter from Baltimore was over a month reaching me. I suspect it was actually smuggled to Cartersville. That, dear ones, is where we are now–still separated by this ghastly war and waiting, Mr. Low in prison at Fort Warren, although someone kindly got word to him that his wife and children were doing as well as possible. I am sorry to write such gloomy news, but feel relieved that I have done it. We hear almost daily of the danger you are in there in Savannah and so my heart breaks in every direction for all I love. Do try to be safe. Mama, I would give years off my life were you able to write to me of conditions as they actually are there. My sisters try, but I long for your appraisal. I long to see you. Eliza Anne Stiles.' "

The letter finished, Mark laid it on a table. In a moment, he asked helplessly, "Miss Eliza–what next? I'm–I'm not at all sure I know how to weather one more blow."

"We–your family and mine–haven't really weathered a severe blow yet, Mark. I believe you spoke before you thought, didn't you? No one dear to us has been killed–yet. We can't buy as much sugar or coffee as we'd like, Mr. Low is in prison, but we're all–all right."

"Yes, we're all–all right so far."

"You're thinking about Jonathan stationed now at Fort Pulaski, aren't you? The Yankees will undoubtedly try to recapture it. It won't be as easy or exciting as the day Jonathan and Charles Olmstead and the other boys steamed out there on the little *Ida* and marched joyfully in under their snapping flags. But they haven't attacked Pulaski yet. How many times have you heard me say we have to take one day at a time?" She made a small sound something like a laugh. "My problem is that I've never quite learned how to take my own advice."

When Mark went to the Mackays' the next day, Sarah met him at the door. "Mama's not feeling well enough to get out of bed this morning," she whispered, "but she wants you to go upstairs to her room, Mark."

Desperately, he tried to hurry up the once easy stairs to the second floor of the old frame house where he had been young so long ago. It seemed to take him forever and in the upstairs hall he had to stop. His heart pounded, and not only from the exertion of the steps. It pounded from fear because Miss Eliza was ill.

When the door to her room opened and Kate stepped out with her finger to her lips, he felt as though he might faint. Kate's smile calmed him a little. "She's not at all well this morning, Mark, but she wants you to come in—just you. Sarah and I will be right downstairs in the parlor if you need us. We're writing a quick note to Eliza Anne, asking her to come."

Mark stared at Kate. "Is she that—ill?"

"Maybe not. Mama's just old and weary and so, so worried about— everyone and everything. Our note to Eliza Anne is just a precaution. Go to her. She—she loves you so much. Mama needs you now."

"Mark? Is that you out there in the hall?"

He went inside her room at once when he heard the attempt at cheer in her voice.

On his lame knees beside her bed, he grasped her chilly, folded hands in both of his. "Forgive me," he murmured, "I grabbed your hands like an eager schoolboy. Well, I am, Miss Eliza! Where you're concerned, I'm no more than that. I'm so sorry you're not feeling well today."

"It's only temporary," she said. "But I won't talk long."

"I'll go anytime you say. I can leave now and come back."

"No, dear boy, no. But since I have a big favor to ask, I'll get right to it, if it's all right."

"Anything!"

"Take Caroline and Mary and Little Ben and get on the train for Cass. Eliza Anne is longing for firsthand news of—all that's going on here and she *can't* come. She told me how anxious she is about Savannah in a letter not long ago."

"I know. I read it to you."

"Of course. Don't let me get so fuzzy! And don't tell me I don't get fuzzy, because I do. But will you do that for me, Mark? Will you try to think back to a long-ago day when you knocked me off my feet by begging me out of the blue to—go up there with you to see about Natalie before her first child came? Can you remember that far back? I can. I can remember everything from long ago. It's what happened this morning I don't seem to recall."

"I remember. You felt like smacking me, but you said yes. You went with me back then."

"I'm sure you feel like smacking me now and undoubtedly I deserve it, but will you go? Mary always loves going up to the old Cherokee Nation. Little Ben's roots are there, although he's never seen the dear old woods or the river. Somehow I feel Caroline will be glad to oblige an old woman." She gripped his hand with surprising strength. "Caro-

line's open to us now. She doesn't agree with us, but she includes us."
She smiled weakly. "This is the old lady who wasn't going to talk long.
Can you see your way clear to—humor her one more time?"

His mind raced to Jonathan and the imminent danger of an attack on
Fort Pulaski. "There isn't anything I wouldn't do for you, dear friend,"
he said after a moment's uncertainty. "Yes. We'll go up to Cass, just as
soon as it's humanly possible for me to arrange it."

T̖oward the end of the first week in November, Eliza Mackay was well enough again to come down to breakfast. She not only felt stronger but had obviously been doing a lot of thinking. "I know everyone doesn't like Governor Joseph Brown," she told her daughters as soon as she'd creamed her coffee, "but he certainly does his best for the coast. Just before the Brownings left for Cass yesterday, Mark told me that the Governor ordered ten thousand more troops to protect us here in Savannah."

"Well, they're not here yet," Sarah fussed, "and we're all probably doomed anyway, because W.H. leaves Skidaway today for Port Royal with almost five hundred of the soldiers we did have. Mama, there's no possible way W. H. Stiles can know how to command a regiment!"

"I hear the men under him, in what they're now calling the Sixtieth Georgia, stay in an uproar because W.H. wangled permission from Jefferson Davis himself to have the officers appointed, not elected by the men. He just did that so he could be sure *he'd* be the colonel!"

"You're right, Sister," Sarah agreed warmly. "How well could those men fight when they're constantly upset by the self-importance of their colonel?"

"That is more than enough!" Eliza scolded. "I don't want to hear one more word of criticism of W.H., is that clear?"

"Oh, we like him fine as a relative," Kate insisted.

"And he's a charming dinner partner, but that doesn't mean he can lead a regiment of men who aren't too fond of him in the first place!"

"I meant it," Eliza said, eyes snapping. "There will be no more such talk at this table—now or ever! The Yankee Navy is supposed to be on its way to take over Port Royal and that's just a hop, skip, and a jump from here!"

"Twenty-five miles on a map," Kate said, a bit subdued.

"Farther by water," Sarah put in.

"We are not in a discussion about the distance to Port Royal or any other place," Eliza pronounced. "We are all in God's hands, and W.H. will always do his best. You are both supposed to be so loyal to Jefferson Davis and he's the one who gave W.H. special permission to head his Sixtieth Georgia as an appointed colonel. So why don't you girls *think* for a change?"

Kate clapped her hands. "Oh, Mama, you're really better, aren't you?"

"Yes, Mama," Sarah chimed, "you're not only down to breakfast, you're scolding us. Thank God!"

"I hope you've really thanked Him, daughter," Eliza said, with a slightly shamefaced grin. "I did spout off, didn't I? I guess I'm sorry, but I mean it when I say no more criticism of your sister's husband. If something happened to W.H. at Port Royal or wherever he's going, you'd both be—"

"I think he's to command his troops while they improve earthworks at Fort Walker at the tip of Hilton Head. He's just in command of a shovel brigade, the mother of one of his men said at Women's Aid yesterday."

"The ladies seemed to know a lot about that whole business up there in South Carolina," Kate said. "The Yankees are going to be the only ones surprised. Word got to our command here that they're headed for Port Royal and we're going to be more than ready for them! And if we don't destroy their forces—bombard their nasty warships to smithereens —everyone will know it's the fault of General Thomas Drayton!"

"What in the world makes you say a thing like that?" Eliza asked. Mark told me Confederate General Thomas Drayton is in command of Hilton Head Island."

"Aha," Sarah said triumphantly, "that's the rub! His own Charleston-born brother, Percival Drayton, commands the USS *Pocahontas,* one of the enemy's main attack vessels. If we don't whip them soundly, it will be because there's chicanery between those two brothers!"

Eliza Mackay finished her coffee and set the cup down hard. "This dreadful war business is turning you both into a pair of mean gossips and I don't appreciate it in either one of you."

"We're not mean, Mama, we're loyal Confederates!" Sarah's eyes blazed. "We're in the midst of a real war. We have to keep our faith that God is on our side, but at a time like this, being kind and Christian can go only so far, then it turns to treason!"

"That's blasphemy, Sarah," Eliza said with great solemnity, "and that's all I'm going to say."

"Sister didn't mean it the way it sounded, Mama!"

"There *is* a war going on, daughters, and my own faith is shaky day in and day out, but the mean spirit of this war will be kept out of our house—at least, as long as the Lord lets me live!"

November 7 was the day when Commodore Josiah Tatnall, his tiny Mosquito Fleet, and the Army forces expected the Northern attack on Port Royal.

"It is such a beautiful Indian summer day," W.H. wrote in his journal as he waited at Fort Walker with his confused, grumbling troops. Their hard manual labor was almost completed, but their spirits showed, at least to their excited colonel, "an unwillingness to bury their own pride and willfulness in the blood-tingling Cause of their native land. In fact, they even accuse *me* of—vanity. If only they could look inside my heart, which beats only for love of my family and of my beloved South!"

November 7 was a day of waiting for Jonathan, too, at Fort Pulaski, heartsick that his short leave in Savannah had been canceled when word came that Yankee forces were heading for Port Royal, only a few miles north in South Carolina. Heartsick because somehow he had felt so certain that this time Mary would end her long, perplexing silence. Fort Pulaski's commander, Charles Olmstead, always returned from time with Florie looking and acting like a new man. Did Mary hate fighting more than Charles's loyal wife?

"I'm sure not," Charles had told him often. "My Florie despises my chosen profession and, although she's proud of me, that isn't enough to change her woman heart. There are many women, Jonathan, who just don't believe war gains anything in the long run. If soldiers gave that too much thought, they'd be unable to fight. Then where would the world be?"

On this glorious Indian summer day, Jonathan admitted to himself, as he sat alone in his quarters idly reading to pass the time, that he had no answer to that. There was no answer to where the world would be and no answer to anything else. Certainly not to Mary's silence, which seemed lately to be confusing him more, because her love had so obviously remained as strong as ever. She responded each time he was with her, not only with her yielding body but, as long as they were in each other's arms, with an outpouring of love words that had kept him going through all the tension-filled, waiting days. But not one word that she was even beginning to understand his part in the war.

He tried to return to the new book his mother had given him—George Eliot's *The Mill on the Floss*—but it was no use. He closed it and strode outside, hoping he might find Colonel Olmstead in his headquarters office. He had just started across the parade ground when the first broadside sounded from the north—far away, but plainly audible—followed by another and another and another, until, running toward Olmstead's office, Jonathan felt the earth shake under him. The Yankees were attacking Port Royal, only twenty-five miles away.

When the bombardment began, Eliza Mackay was alone in her house except for the aging Emphie and Hannah, and although she felt pretty well today, she sat gripping the sides of her little parlor rocker until her fingers ached.

"Lord, have mercy on us," she prayed, and was still praying when Hannah steamed into the parlor, with thin, birdlike Emphie hiding behind her ample girth.

Both servants fell to their knees beside Eliza's rocker and began to moan and cry out to the God who had declared that He came to bring peace.

"Peace, Lord Jesus," Hannah groaned. "Where the peace today? Can you hear us, Lord, over them guns? Can you hear us?"

Eliza tried to think of something to say that might calm her faithful servants, but when she saw Hannah take a rough swipe at poor, cringing Emphie with the back of her hand, she lost her train of thought.

"Why on earth did you hit Emphie?" she demanded of the big, gray-haired, trembling woman kneeling beside her.

"She's crowdin' me," Hannah said, and quickly went back to pleading with the Lord to bring peace to the house, to the city, to the world!

"Both of you, get up and bring chairs over for yourselves," Eliza ordered. "I know you're not comfortable sitting down in the parlor, but do it anyway. Do you hear me, Emphie? Hannah?" They were standing now, staring down at her, not sure just what to do. "I said bring chairs and sit with me. I need you with me until that dreadful firing ends!" After another brief hesitation, Emphie scurried for a straight chair and began dragging it across the carpet, but Hannah still stood there repeating "Peace, peace, Lord, peace . . ."

"You—really want I should sit down, Miss Eliza?" Emphie asked, holding on to the back of the chair.

"I do, Emphie, and you, too, Hannah—this minute! You've both been so good to me for so long, it's time we acted as though we're all three friends. I need you to be my friends—now! The girls won't be back for over an hour. Dear Lord, what are they doing through all this? I need you both to sit down with me. We need each other, don't we? Don't we, Hannah? Don't you need me, too?"

Hannah's mumbling at God stopped. Her mouth sagged for a few seconds, then her wide, almost toothless smile seemed to light up the shadowy room. Without another word, she picked up a small armchair and carried it lightly to where Eliza sat.

"I know I'm not making much sense, Hannah, but if those arms are too close together for you to fit, please take my husband's big leather chair."

The three women in the Mackay parlor did not leave their chairs until some four hours later, when the distant, but thunderous roar began to fade.

Finally, Hannah broke the silence. "Be Miss Eliza Anne's fine man up there in the battle, ma'am?"

Eliza had sat all that time with her forehead resting on the tips of the fingers of one hand. Now, massaging her aching head, she said, "Yes, Hannah, W.H. is up there and so is my grandson Henry. I pray they're both still alive."

"I pray our side won!"

Emphie's high-pitched utterance so surprised Eliza that she jerked her head up now and gave the rail-thin woman a weary half-smile. "And which side is—your side, Emphie?"

Emphie's small, dim eyes looked steadily back at her. "My side be Mr. Stiles's side an' Mr. Henry's, too. An' Lootenant Lee's side!"

"I see," Eliza said. "Lieutenant Lee's a general now."

"Emphie ain't too smart, miss." Hannah's deep voice was firm. "None too smart, but we do be friends, don't we?"

"Oh, yes, indeed, Hannah!" Eliza leaned her head against the chair back. "It's just that I'm not sure—if I'm on either side in this hideous war. But we *are* friends and I'd be ever so grateful if one of you could bring me a cup of good hot tea now."

When Emphie hurried off toward the kitchen, Hannah lingered, standing mountainous and solid in the middle of the room. "Did you want to say something more, Hannah?"

"Yes, ma'am. Miss 'Liza, if the North win out, what'm I gonna do? You send Emphie and me away?"

"Oh, Hannah, Hannah, no! You'll both be free to go if you want to, but you have a home with me for as long as I'm here."

"There are those among us who may try to put a good face on Port Royal, Jonathan," Olmstead said as, near dawn the next day, he and Jonathan finally headed for their quarters, "but it was a rout of our men, or all my reports are in error."

"And that's not likely," Jonathan said. "I wonder if the Federal ships were as majestic a spectacle as that first tired, scared boatload that docked here claimed. I guess old Tatnall did well, though, considering his tiny, helpless, dog-eared boats."

For a time, they walked wearily in silence, their boots scraping in the now quiet night.

"I hope what some said about General Drayton isn't true. I guess maybe for personal reasons, I hope and pray what they're saying about Colonel W. H. Stiles is also dead wrong! I'm sure you know Colonel Stiles used to be my father's attorney, that he and his wife and children— the whole Stiles family—are close to mine."

"I do know all that, Jonathan," his commanding officer said sorrowfully, "but it will be hard to refute the Mayor's word for Stiles's behavior. After all, Mayor Jones is a member of your own Chatham Artillery and he's a man of honor."

Jonathan stopped walking, his hand on Olmstead's arm. "What is Mayor Jones supposed to have said?"

"I thought you'd heard. The Mayor says that all the talk about Stiles having two horses shot from under him is simple nonsense. Evidently— and I'm saddened to report this—Colonel Stiles's men were so scared, they ran like rabbits to get away from the overpowering gunfire. They scurried off so fast, in fact, they were unable to return to camp for their blankets and knapsacks. This is only hearsay, but I'm inclined to think it's true, that Colonel Stiles himself was quite comical."

They walked on. "If it weren't so tragic," Jonathan said, "it could be funny, I guess. W. H. Stiles has always been a gentleman, though, and very kind to me."

"None of the tales we've heard from that first boatload of men can be counted on," Olmstead said comfortingly. "After all, they ran away, too—evidently faster than the Stiles troops since they returned first! Savannahians are always quick to criticize, don't forget."

"Yes," Jonathan said. "They certainly are. God knows, they've criticized my poor father while accepting his generosity and gifts to the city through almost every day of his long life here."

"That's true. And the man still loves the city more in his way than most of his critics, I'd say."

"Thanks, Colonel," Jonathan said simply. "My father and I no longer see eye to eye on our great Cause, but he hasn't allowed the change in me to make any difference in the way we love and respect each other."

Another wordless time passed, then Colonel Olmstead said in a strained voice, "With Federal troops in possession at Port Royal–Tybee, then Pulaski could well be next on their list."

"I was just thinking that. Oh, Colonel, *how* would our families endure hearing a bombardment from right here on Cockspur Island? It must have been bad enough for those back in the city yesterday, hearing it from up in South Carolina with no idea what was really happening!"

"I know I felt my skin prickle the whole time we all listened," Olmstead admitted in his direct, quiet way. "If they attack us here, at least you and I will be in the thick of it. We'll *know* what's happening. When you look at it from the point of view of those left behind, a man begins to understand a little of why our women don't understand."

"I know," Jonathan said. "I pray your Florie and the children weren't too frightened. I admit I'm relieved Mary and my parents were too far away to hear the shelling. They're all visiting my sister in the upcountry. I thought a lot about Miss Eliza Mackay, though, and her daughters. Everybody in Savannah must have been nervous, so scared for their loved ones who went up to Port Royal. Even if we were soundly licked, I hope we didn't lose too many lives." He made a half-embarrassed, scornful sound. "What in the name of common sense do I mean by 'too many'? One life is too many. Somebody back here or

somewhere in the South loves every fellow who was sent up there!"
Neither spoke until they reached their officer's quarters. Then Jonathan
said, "I guess the whole thing is just beginning to sink in on me, Colonel.
I'm sure you thought it all through even while you were still at the
Military Institute in Milledgeville."

"Now that it could be coming soon to us here at Pulaski, I don't
think I did. I'm sure no one anywhere, in any war, ever finds a way to do
that, Lieutenant Browning."

The two friends saluted, shook hands, and headed for their quarters.

*B*ecause of Miss Lib's differences with Burke's father-in-law over the war, it was agreed quickly that the senior Brownings would stay with him and Natalie, although it meant that Burke and Natalie had to sleep in Callie's tiny room.

"It just shows you how stupid this war is," Natalie declared at breakfast after her parents and Mary had been there for a week. "Not only does it cause rifts in families, it destroys common courtesy! If it weren't for the war, Miss Lib, stubborn as she is, would never think of allowing my parents to stay here in our cottage when she has all those extra rooms at Etowah Cliffs."

"Eliza Anne welcomed having us, Natalie," her mother said. "You're the one who insisted we stay here."

"Oh, I know you and Miss Lib could manage just fine, Mama. You could both sit and wave Confederate flags at each other, but you're *my* parents and I didn't intend to see Papa made uncomfortable by Miss Lib's fiery Rebel talk. Isn't that right, Burke?"

"On the mark, honey," he laughed. "But stop fretting about it. We've done the right thing." He turned to Mark, who had said nothing all through Natalie's delicious breakfast. "You and I haven't had this much time to talk ever, have we?"

"I'm enjoying it, Burke, and we only plan to stay another week or so. Callie doesn't seem to mind sleeping over at the Stileses'. She's a wonder, isn't she, with those children of Mary Cowper's? Somehow I have a feeling Eliza Anne is relieved to have Callie there. However much she and I disagree on the war, my heart goes out to her, not even knowing where Mary Cowper is these days."

"Only that she's back in this country—in Baltimore—and that Mr. Low is in prison," Caroline said with a worried look. "I honestly don't see how Eliza Anne makes it through her days."

"I guess the nights must be even worse," Burke said.

"The fault of the war again," Natalie said triumphantly. "If the South hadn't seceded, everyone would be at home where they belong."

"Darling, that's an oversimplification," her mother said. "There is a war. We're all disrupted by it. I doubt I'll ever learn how to drink coffee without sugar." Caroline smiled shamefacedly. "I'm sorry, that was a superficial, spoiled-child remark if I ever heard one!"

Burke studied his mother-in-law's still attractive face. The woman had certainly changed, although he had always noticed that no matter how much she rebelled in the past, Caroline Browning usually came through with an honest admission of where she'd failed or been mistaken. Natalie seemed no longer particularly interested in correcting her mother either. They were friends now. He was more than glad for that.

"I think everything's fine with us here," he said. "Mary and Little Ben like being at the Stiles house with Callie." Smiling, he added, "I noticed young Ben follows Miss Lib's granddaughter Katie around as though he loves the ground she walks on."

"And Katie adores it," Natalie said. "I think it helps take her mind off her absent parents. She's old enough now to realize that something is dreadfully wrong, because they're both gone out of her sight. And six is plenty old enough to notice her grandmother never stops frowning." She began to clear the table. "Miss Lorah needs to get these dishes washed. Mama, Papa—did either of you ever in all your lives see a young woman as beautiful as Callie is now? I'm being perfectly honest about saying she's prettier than I ever thought about being!"

Burke liked his mother-in-law for her good laugh at that remark. He liked her even more when she said, "Well, that's got to be the ultimate, Natalie."

To him, it was. No one, not even Callie, who had all the love his father's heart could focus on her, would ever be more beautiful than

Natalie. Even busy at the simple task of stacking dishes, she still put every other woman on earth to shame.

"I'm riding to Cartersville for the mail today, Mr. Browning. Are you up to riding with me?" Burke asked. "If not, we can take my carriage."

"I vote for the carriage," Mrs. Browning said. "My husband prefers comfort to exercise these days."

"Miss Lib is so cross, I could shake her most of the time," Natalie said, heading for the kitchen with a load of china, "but either way, go on, Burke. I know she's holding her breath for the mail. Sooner or later someone will be coming this way so a letter can be smuggled through from Mary Cowper."

Sitting together in the cab of Burke's carriage on the ride into Cartersville, Mark and Burke made full use of their time alone.

"I'm not used to being driven, sir," Burke said after he'd tucked a cushion under his father-in-law's knees for added comfort during their journey. "In fact, I like driving my team myself, but July drives well and I thought you and I deserved time for a good talk."

"I certainly welcome it," Mark answered, settling in the seat.

"I guess that was a real rout at Port Royal just after you left, sir. They could hear most of the Federal bombardment all the way down the coast in Savannah. My friend Robert Goodman reports that although there's a period of uneasy quiet right now, the Southern command at Savannah has already evacuated Tybee Island."

His father-in-law gave him a quick, worried look. "I've been hoping to find out what's really going on down there. Every day I've hoped for a letter from Jonathan. He's stationed at Fort Pulaski now, you know."

"Yes, I do know, and I want you to know how much I feel for you in his sudden turn away from you in all this."

Mr. Browning didn't answer at once. Then he said, as though still convincing himself, "Jonathan found he had to defend his birthplace, Burke, but the boy hasn't turned away from me. What I've discovered since he became a convinced Rebel is that until lately, as much as I thought I cared about every single thing that went on in the country, it is nothing compared to my anxiety now that Jonathan's in danger."

"I see worrying about him hasn't influenced your thinking, though. We've already talked enough for me to see that."

"You're right. I still agree with President Lincoln. 'A house divided against itself cannot stand.' Our strength lay in union with each other. Intellectually, I think I understand the doctrine of States' Rights, but only intellectually. I don't really grasp it, and God knows, I don't believe in it! What we're suffering now is still, to me, a ghastly family feud. We're fighting among ourselves."

"Did it surprise you when Lee resigned from the U.S. Army and joined up with the South?"

"Knowing how he felt about the slavery issue, how he revered the Union, it nearly knocked the breath out of me! Miss Eliza Mackay helped me accept it when she reminded me that Lee knew, as an expert military man, that much of the fighting would be right at his Virginia plantation. I'm still troubled by what he did, but most of the time I feel I understand why he did it."

"Except for the way I love the upcountry of Georgia, I never knew a man to care about a place more than you care about Savannah, sir. Would you and I have done what Lee felt forced to do?"

The older man smiled sadly. "I guess I don't see either of us doing it, but a man can't know really until he faces what Lee faced."

"General Lee could well be in Savannah now, you know," Burke said. "He's on an inspection tour down the coast."

"I hope he's there for Miss Eliza's sake. I can't think of anything that would perk her up more than a visit with General Lee."

"Sorry to learn the old lady's not well these days. Miss Lib has worry over her mother to add to all her other burdens. Even I, who have not been with her much, would hate to see Miss Eliza leave us."

"Oh, Burke, Burke, don't even mention that! I still have the members of my family, who mean most to me—Caroline, Jonathan, Mary, Ben, Natalie, you, and, of course, Callie. I try to count my blessings, but if I lost Miss Eliza—I honestly don't know what I'd do!"

Wanting so much to be helpful, Burke could only think to say, "It must be some comfort to you, sir, that Jonathan is still stationed at Fort Pulaski."

"Yes, and I'll feel a bit better after General Lee has inspected it and pronounced it as solid a fortification as the rest of Savannah seems to believe. Maybe there will be some letters today with definite word of Lee's visit. I find I'm counting on his coming more than I have any sensible reason to!"

"I tell you," Kate fumed at dinner a week later, "it's more than I can take in that those fiendish Yankees are now close enough to shell *us!*"

"Hush, Sister," Sarah scolded. "They're not about to shell Savannah. Our boys did have to leave Tybee, and I know the whole town is complaining that our defenses are all awry, that no one in our forces knows what's going on, but we'll be able to talk right to General Robert Lee when he gets here and then we'll know the whole truth! So hush. Don't upset Mama, do you hear me?"

"She's not upsetting me, Sarah," their mother said firmly. "I, too, am waiting for Robert to come. He'll know and he'll tell us the truth."

"I'm still so angry that some are calling him Granny Lee just because he wasn't properly equipped to win in western Virginia," Sarah fussed. "The very idea of calling a superior gentleman like General Lee a nasty name is beyond me! He simply refuses to take chances with the lives of his men. Do you know what they're saying Lee's comment was after the rout at Port Royal? They're saying he wouldn't have fired a single shot, because our forces were poorly prepared, and I say he's undoubtedly right. If Robert Lee had been in charge, poor W.H. wouldn't have had to endure the kind of ribbing he's still getting in town because he did—whatever he did up there."

"They say it's what W.H. didn't know to do because he's a world statesman and a politician and not a soldier," Kate declared.

"Whatever *they're* saying, we ignore it," Mama ordered, sounding, both girls thought, a lot more like herself. "I read the paper today. It's criminal what's being written about our Savannah soldiers." She picked up the paper. "Listen to what that critical *Republican* editor wrote: 'Do we intend to wait until the Hessians march up Bull Street before we repel them? Will the gallant Savannah boys permit the invasion of Tybee to pass without making an effort to dislodge the vandals?' One man dared to say that, with Tybee gone, Fort Pulaski is surely next. We are simply not going to believe that!"

"No, Mama, we can't! Dear Jonathan is there."

"That's right. And a lot of other dear boys, so enough talk."

"They're even calling our coastal defenses 'jackleg' experiments." Kate spoke rapidly so as to get out one more piece of gossip before Mama shushed her utterly.

"We have *stopped gossiping*, Kate. We are now about to oversee cleaning this first floor and, just in case he might be able to stay over, I want Robert Lee's old room in shipshape order!"

Mark urged Burke to tell July to hurry over as much as he could along the rough road home from the post office in Cartersville. They were bringing a letter from Mary Cowper to her mother, the first she'd had in over two months. All Eliza Anne knew was that Mary Cowper was being cared for in the home of friends named Glenn in Baltimore and that in spite of the fact that he was a strong Union sympathizer, a kind, Christian gentleman was attempting to get her to Fortress Mason. There she might be fortunate enough to board a flag-of-truce boat and eventually make her way home to Etowah Cliffs.

"Miss Lib is going to be so relieved at getting a letter from Mary Cowper," Burke said with a smile, "she might even welcome two Union men like us, Mr. Browning."

"Eliza Anne isn't herself," Mark said. "She's had more than even one strong woman can endure. I know how worried she is not to be able to go personally to check on her mother's condition. We've tried to reassure her that Miss Eliza, while feeble now, seemed well enough, or we'd never have left her. I don't think it helped much."

They both laughed when Burke said, "Miss Lib finds it hard to receive help from anyone but a Rebel."

"I guess we should feel a little guilty laughing," Mark said.

"A man can break in two mighty fast if he doesn't relieve the pressure somehow, Mr. Browning. I'm glad you opened your note from Jonathan right there in the post office. He didn't tell us much, but at least you know he was in good health three days ago and that General Lee is at Fort Pulaski now giving orders exactly how to secure it."

"I had to open it." Mark laughed a little. "I'm too old and feeble myself to pretend courage I don't have. Had I waited to let Caroline read it, as I might have done once, I'd deserve to be knighted."

"It's good to see you laugh, Mr. Browning."

"Thanks. I do wish we knew for certain that Lee will have time to visit Miss Eliza, though, before he goes on down the coast to inspect St. Simons Island."

When Burke and his father-in-law pulled up before the Stiles house, they could tell by the way the servants were hurrying about in the yard, some carrying bedding, others a wooden bed frame, that something had happened.

"Miss Liza Anne say Massa Stiles is comin' home," July shouted as he ran back to the carriage after inquiring of the three men carrying the bed frame. "He's comin' home sick from Savannah! Miss Liza Anne, she 'bout crazy with worry, I guess. You better go on inside. She need a letter bad!"

"Come on in with me, Mr. Browning," Burke said, all but lifting his father-in-law down from the carriage. "Your wife and mine will both be here at the Stileses' waiting for mail."

"Eliza Anne will need time alone, though," Mark said, standing on the veranda, where Burke had gently led him. "I'm not really as helpless as you seem to think, young man. My old legs are pretty limber today."

"We'll go in just for a minute so you can show your wife Jonathan's note. Maybe we can find out more about Stiles."

Inside the lavish, though now somewhat worn drawing room of the Stiles mansion, Eliza Anne grabbed her letter and headed for the stairs to the second floor. Abruptly, she stopped, turned gracefully, and excused herself like the lady she would always be, Burke thought. He admired the distraught woman in spite of their disagreements. His heart reached out to her now as she mounted the stairs sedately, clutching the long-awaited letter to her breast.

No one had dared ask her about her husband and she had volunteered nothing.

"We have a note—very brief, from Jonathan," Mr. Browning said to his wife. "Where's Natalie? And Callie and Mary? I'm afraid Jonathan wrote to all of us in this one short note."

"They've gone with Miss Lorah to hunt hickory nuts. She reached for the thin letter. "Oh, Mark, at least he's all right—for now!"

"Yes, darling. And General Lee will do what needs to be done to make Pulaski safe."

Burke saw her shoulders sag. "I hope so. I pray so. Lee will surely visit Miss Eliza, won't he?"

"If he has any time at all," Browning said. "How does Mary seem today? I'm surprised she went with the others, she's been so anxious for word from Jonathan."

"She took Little Ben along," Mrs. Browning explained. "I really had to persuade her to go, but as soon as I mentioned that Ben had never even been out in the Park under those huge nut trees, she decided to take him."

"Wanting Ben to walk on old Cherokee land," Burke's father-in-law said, not as a question, but as a statement which they all knew was true.

As Burke was trying to think of a plausible reason to excuse himself, to leave the Brownings alone with their anxiety over Jonathan, Miss Lib hurried down the stairs, her face an odd mixture of hope and torment.

"Listen to this," she called from the landing, then hurried down into the drawing room and began at once to read Mary Cowper's letter aloud. " 'My dear Mama, I am skimming the horrible ordeals I've been through because I have no way of being sure you will ever read this. After several trips from Baltimore to Washington and to Old Point, where we stayed in a most hideous hotel, I am back again in Baltimore with my kind friends the Glenns, awaiting a ship with a flag of truce on which I might be allowed by the vile Northern government to head toward home. I have just learned that through the kindness of his Yankee, but evidently Christian jailer, my poor husband and I can exchange letters and I am vastly relieved. He knows, at last, that though exhausted from my struggles to get back to you at Etowah Cliffs, I am not ill and that his children are safe with you. Mr. Low occupies a small room at Fort Warren with seven other gentlemen and must daily make up his own bed! He is not even allowed to walk on the ramparts or to look at the sea, but he is holding up nobly. I have little hope that a letter from you might reach me here, but do write and tell me what you know of Savannah, which we hear is in dire danger of attack. My heart aches for my blessed grandmother and all we love there and I would be obliged to know any news of Lucinda Elliott, her children"—Miss Lib stopped, took a deep breath—"and her husband, who is in Confederate service. I am sure he is throwing his whole Rebel spirit into all he does. I will write again if at all possible, but cannot say when since I still hope daily to find a way home. If you are not allowed a letter from me until next year, my thoughts and my heart will be with all of you at the coming Christmas season. Your loving daughter, Mary Cowper Low.' "

Burke, still standing with the others in the spacious room, looked from one troubled face to another. "At least she's well. When was the letter written, Miss Lib?"

"Two weeks ago," Eliza Anne said woodenly. "Poor Mary Cowper . . . poor Mr. Low!" Her voice broke. "My poor, *poor* husband!"

"Can you tell us anything at all about W.H.?" Browning asked.

Burke was in the act of helping Miss Lib to a chair when they heard the rattle of a wagon outside. He sprang to the front door and raced out to see a ramshackle contraption, pulled by one swaybacked horse. In the sloping wagon bed lay the Honorable W. H. Stiles on a heap of rumpled quilts. Running down the path to the road, Burke leaned in over the prostrate form, but at first said nothing for fear of saying the wrong thing to the pale, drawn, distraught man lying there.

"Welcome home, Mr. Stiles," Burke said at last. "You look as though you had a hard trip."

W.H. opened his eyes and, with enormous effort, whispered, "I well may be going—to die, Burke. In the name of God, get my wife!"

SIXTY-
SEVEN

So that Miss Lib could sit by Uncle W.H.'s bedside, Natalie agreed for Callie to spend the days, too, at the Stiles house with Mary Cowper's children. Walking along now with Burke and her parents, Natalie could think only of the agony on Miss Lib's face at the way Uncle W.H. looked lying in that wagon bed like an old, ill man. No matter how stubborn Miss Lib was, she did love Uncle W.H. and that Natalie could understand.

Autumn breezes fell about them with cool softness as they neared the pine-straw path that led to her cottage, but the evening failed to calm Natalie. Beauty seemed incongruous in the midst of all that was wrong in the world. Except for her mother's remark on the loveliness of the sunset, they walked in near silence along the river road. Uncle W.H. was plainly quite ill, but he had explained nothing. Even now she could discuss none of it with her own family. No one seemed able to tell anyone anything!

When they reached the path, Natalie stopped, hands on hips. "How can the three of you just stroll along as though Uncle W.H. hasn't done a terrible thing to Miss Lib—to all of us?" she demanded. "I know Miss Lib can be difficult, but she doesn't deserve this."

Her mother looked surprised. "Natalie," she said, "the poor man is ill! I'm sure Eliza Anne is relieved to the marrow of her bones that he came home to her. As I see it, he's given his wife a wonderful gift."

"Gift, my foot," Natalie scoffed. "He shouldn't have gone to war in the first place! Of course Miss Lib's glad to have him back—she loves him. But he didn't have to go. He did it to himself, Mama. Burke has sense enough to be here, where he belongs!"

"Think a little, darling, about what you're saying," Burke admonished gently.

"Natalie, my dear," Papa said carefully, "no man in his right mind makes himself sick."

"I agree, Papa, but I don't know of anyone outside of you and Burke who's *in* his right mind these days." She grabbed Burke's arm and began to pull him past the pine-straw path back the way they'd just come up the river road. "We're not going in the house yet, Burke. I might fly apart if we do."

"We'll go on inside, then, Natalie," her mother called after them. "I'm sure your father's weary. You two stay out under this beautiful sky as long as you like."

"We won't be long," Burke called back, walking fast to keep up with Natalie. "I have to get up early in the morning."

"Why?" Natalie wanted to know as soon as they were far enough away to be out of her parents' hearing. "Why do you have to get up any earlier than usual? You don't have any work, or did you get that new store in Kingston today and forget to tell me in all the fuss Uncle W.H. caused?"

"No, I didn't get the new store in Kingston," he said. "There isn't going to be a new store. We don't have any fighting up here yet, but the war's here just the same, in our economy. Businessmen are buying Confederate bonds with their money now." When Natalie began to walk still faster, Burke stopped her. "Hey, pretty lady, you can't change things by running from them."

"Do you think I don't know that?"

"Mind telling me where we're going?" he asked.

"To Little Burke's grave."

"I thought so," he said, his arm tightening around her. "I also think I know why."

"You should. With the whole world going crazy around us, including my once sensible brother, it's time *we* acted like sane Christian people!"

"Sane Christians, Natalie?"

"Sane Christians! I want us to go to his little grave and thank God that our baby son is safe in heaven." She stopped abruptly and threw both arms around him. "Oh, Burke, Callie's almost eighteen. Do you realize that Little Burke would be exactly the right age to become cannon fodder–for nothing?"

For a long time, while the setting sun stained the river with copper and rose beyond their bedroom window, Eliza Anne sat beside W.H., waiting for him to regain enough strength to try to explain what had happened. The last thing she wanted was to push him to talk if he weren't up to it, but after an hour or so, she could endure it no longer.

"Were you ill very long before you left Savannah, darling?" she whispered at last. "Can you tell me that much?"

"Actually, I felt well enough to visit your family the night before I left," he said weakly. He grabbed her hand. "Oh, Lib, I tried so hard not to give in to it–I tried so hard!"

"You always try hard, beloved, always. And I do appreciate your visit to Mama. I know it was an effort for you. Did she send any message?"

"Only that you are not to worry about her. That your place is here with the grandchildren."

"As soon as you can, please tell me the truth about Mother, W.H. Kate and Sarah write, but one time they beg me to go down there, the next time they say that Mama is much better. I can't go. Not with our darling Mary Cowper trying so hard to get through enemy country back here. Now–you! I do worry about Mama. I'm trying to be strong, but I'm so, so worried!"

"Your mother is going through what the elderly do, Lib. One week she can come downstairs for the entire day. The next, she stays in her bed. Of course, William's man, Magill, from Causton's Bluff, carries her back upstairs in the evenings."

Encouraged by the fluency of his speech, she said, "It took old Magill long enough to decide to leave William's old plantation, didn't it?"

"His devotion to your brother goes on," W.H. said, raising himself now in the bed. "Magill seems to give your mother extra care as a tribute to his dead master."

"You're so sensitive, darling," she said, kissing his forehead. "And I believe feeling a little better. Are you?"

He frowned. "I can't answer that, Lib. I honestly don't know how I feel. Better because I'm back here with you, but like a slacker for leaving my regiment."

"Nonsense. Can you tell me—was it dreadful at Hilton Head?"

He shuddered. "Ghastly! I–I guess I had no idea."

The look of innocent bewilderment on his dear face gave her the flash of insight for which she'd been groping. War *was* ghastly, and her poor, unwary W.H. had now experienced its horror—had been an actual part of it at Camp Walker on Hilton Head Island. For months he had been so fired with spirit and patriotism as he struggled to organize his own regiment that he had totally deluded himself into believing that he was prepared for such an ordeal. His utter helplessness while the Yankee bombardment from the waters of Port Royal Sound blew apart bodies of the men in his own regiment had shattered W.H. himself. W.H., her gentleman farmer, skillful politician, writer, diplomat, was now suffering real physical illness from the shock of actual battle! And why not? Dear God, why not?

Clutching her hand, he cried out, "I had no idea, Lib, and I–I was struck numb by fear–fear and cowardice!"

"Stop it, stop it!" Her voice was so sharp, she felt ashamed. What he needed was soothing, bolstering up, help in believing in himself again. He certainly did not need a wifely scolding. As he went on clinging to her, his whole body trembling, she managed to say, with a feeble attempt at their old kind of humor, "I'm surprised at you, sir. A man of your intellect must know that–a fish can't breathe out of water! You were a–fish out of water at Camp Walker, W.H. You weren't at all in *your* element."

He turned his head away. "I have no more brains than a fish!"

"I forbid you to say such a thing! Every year of your long, fruitful gentleman's life, you've proven yourself to be superior in all ways—in all ways because you've stayed within the vast sphere of your many and diversified talents. God has given you so many gifts, so many paths of service to your fellow man, but even you cannot believe yourself to be . . ."

"To be clever and brave enough to command a regiment?"

"That is not what I said!"

"You didn't need to say it, Lib. I already know it. What our blessed Confederacy needs now are men with the courage and proven skills of your General Lee. The South has no need for literary giants or men of taste!"

He sounded so bitter, so envious of Robert Lee, now in command of

Southern forces in South Carolina, Georgia, and Florida, she could have wept.

"W.H., it's *you* I love! And the Confederacy desperately needs statesmen of your caliber. You know Robert Lee has spent his entire life training to be a soldier. Why wouldn't he be superb at it? I'd like to see him handle a European revolution in the diplomatic best interests of his country as you did during our time in Vienna! I'd like to see General Lee or my late brother, Jack, stand before a legislature and spellbind every gentleman in the audience." Smoothing his brow now, she pleaded, "Oh, my handsome, brilliant W.H., please do what you alone do best!"

"I know you've always tried to dissuade me from the military," he said meekly. "I didn't listen. But what else can I do? Where can I be of service? I'm no longer in the running for governor."

"You can rest, then eat your supper and get strong again. You will be all right, I'm sure, once you make peace with yourself. Once you begin to–be your real self."

"And expect my fine sons to fight on in this terrible war without me? Lib, *I have to go back to my regiment.* I have to try again. I'll make it this time–if you believe in me!"

"You don't have to go back to your regiment tonight. And whatever you decide, with all my heart I believe in you," she said.

He sank back onto the pillows. "Mary Cowper will be home soon, won't she, Lib? I think my heartbreak at all she must be going through is part of the reason I'm not well. My sons are extensions of what self-respect I have left, but Mary Cowper is my heart."

"And mine, darling."

"I think about poor Low, too," he went on. "The man's loyalty to our Cause puts me to shame. He's suffering prison for our sake! And look at me . . ."

"I am looking at you, dearest. It's an impressive sight!"

"I–was quite ill, Lib. You believe that, don't you?"

"Of course I believe it."

"I promise not to be extra trouble for you. You already have your hands full with the grandchildren."

"But Callie is an enormous help now that she's home from school for good. W.H., she's a remarkable girl. Blessedly, a composite of the best traits from both her parents. She has Burke's good sense and Natalie's startling honesty and beauty. Callie will do worlds for your spirits, too."

"I suppose she still limps."

"Oh, yes, that's permanent, but it affects only her foot. The girl herself seems never to lack for spirit. Not even when her beau went to enlist. Callie sent him off with a big smile."

"Did he head for Camp McDonald at Big Shanty?"

"No," she said with a troubled frown. "Burke took him to the Tennessee border, loaned him the money to buy a horse. His name's Perry Clay. He began to work for Burke as a skilled carpenter sometime last year, I think. That's how he met Callie. The boy's plans were to ride up through Tennessee to Kentucky."

W.H. sat bolt upright. "To—Kentucky?"

"I might as well tell you—Callie's Perry is in the Union Army by now."

When he fell back on his pillows, his face was so horror-stricken, she loathed herself for telling him. "That hateful Lincoln has done a terrible thing to us all," she said bitterly. "The whole world has gone crazy because of him!"

For a long time, W.H. lay there staring at the ceiling. Finally, he said, "Lib, your kind mother is as attentive to the Southern soldiers in Savannah as any great lady could be. When she's able at all, she rides out in Mark's carriage or William's old one with your sisters, just to greet the soldiers, to hand out cookies. But sometimes I wonder what Eliza Mackay is really thinking."

"Did—did Robert Lee have time to visit her?"

"Not during his first stop at Fort Pulaski. He was totally occupied with the dreadful state of Savannah's defenses. But your mother assured me he'll come as soon as he gets back from a short inspection trip to St. Simons Island. I fully expect he'll see our son Bobby on St. Simons."

"Did—did you see General Lee, W.H.?"

"Briefly. Of course, he sends regards to you. It was he, as a matter of fact, who obtained my leave to come home. By the way, Lee has a gray beard now."

Early in December, about eight o'clock one morning, Eliza Mackay made her way downstairs without help to spend her day. She had bathed and dressed alone and, as she placed one foot carefully ahead of the other while descending the wide Mackay staircase, she breathed a prayer of thanks.

"Actually," she said as Kate led her to the chair at the head of the table, "I woke up this morning feeling hungry as a bear."

She saw the concerned look her two daughters exchanged and knew exactly what it meant.

"That's wonderful, Mama," Sarah said in the parental voice Eliza had grown so tired of hearing. "A good appetite is the best sign ever that you're much better."

"Emphie will be so glad to hear that," Kate said, with ludicrous enthusiasm. "She's made your favorite, griddle cakes!"

"Griddle cakes *used* to be my favorite," Eliza said, biting off her words. "Of course, I'll thank Emphie, but I do wish you girls would stop treating me as though I'm one of my own great-grandchildren! Isn't it hard enough to get along on griddle cakes with no syrup or preserves day in and day out without pretending it's not?"

"But, Mama, you taught us to stay cheerful when things go wrong."

"There's a difference between cheerfulness, Kate, and pretense. Wouldn't we all do better if you allowed me to shoulder my part of the load? Can't you just laugh at the monotony of our food or voice a few honest complaints without cajoling me into saying griddle cakes are a treat? I know I'm forgetful these days, but I'm not senile and I'm eighty-three, going on eighty-four, *not* three or four years old! Have you both eaten?"

"Yes," Sarah said. "Don't you remember this is our Women's Aid day? We've got twenty-four boxes to fill for Virginia before the day is over. Of course, we try to send as much food as we can, but bread needs salt. We send all the meat we can scare up, but how long will it stay edible without enough salt?"

"I guess I'm relieved you told us it's all right to complain, Mama," Kate put in, "because I heard yesterday that the people in the upcountry are scraping the floors of their smokehouses, too, trying to salvage the salt that dropped from their once plentiful supplies of home-cured meat! We're not the only Georgians going without. I guess being on the water keeps us reminded of that brutal blockade, but they're suffering up there, too!"

"What worries me," Eliza said, sipping sugarless coffee with a wry grimace, "is what the papers say about the high price of yarn. A dollar and a half for a single skein retail! And how long can we even afford to have Emphie's griddle cakes when corn is eighty-five cents a bushel?"

"You're amazing, Mama," Sarah marveled. "You certainly keep up far better than either one of us!"

"Well, I have to do something. The good Lord knows it's little enough to stay abreast as best I can." She chewed and swallowed a big bite of corn cake, then laid down her fork with a smile. "Maybe it's good for us to have to learn all over again how really good the taste of corn is without cane syrup all over it."

"Is that all you're eating, Mama?"

"For now. I didn't say I relished the taste of plain griddle cakes. I just said it's probably good for us to try."

A brisk knock at their front door sent Kate scurrying.

"Now, who could that be so early in the morning?" Sarah asked.

"It has to be somebody. Our door knocker doesn't knock all by itself," Eliza said.

Giving her a hug, Sarah chirped, "Oh, you do feel better today, Mama."

"Yes, I do," she said, patting her daughter's graying hair. "And I want you both to get on your things and go right to your Aid meeting. I'll be fine. I'll finish this bitter brew, try to give thanks that at least we still have rancid coffee beans, then I'll read my Bible and the paper, and by that time Mark will most likely be here for his visit."

At that instant, Kate burst back into the dining room, eyes as big as saucers. "Mama, Sister, it's—it's General Lee! General Robert Lee himself is in the parlor! He has a beard along with his mustache now and, without a doubt, he's the handsomest—"

"We know, Kate," Eliza said. "We all know how Robert looks. Did you just leave him all by himself in the parlor? Why didn't you bring him in so I can give him a cup of coffee?"

"I didn't even think about inviting a full general in here to see our paltry breakfast table, Mama," Kate blustered. "But if you insist, I'll go get him. He—he seems just as gentle and kind and—like himself as ever!"

Getting up from the table, Eliza shushed them both. "No. I'll go to him. And I don't want any help getting there either. Robert's got enough on his mind these days without having to fret about how old and feeble I'm getting to be."

"Don't apologize for not having time to visit us before you left for St. Simons," Eliza said when she and Lee were settled in her parlor. "We all knew how busy you were out at Fort Pulaski. And I've already had a letter from my grandson Bobby Stiles from St. Simons telling me he saw you there."

When she began to chuckle, Lee asked, "Now what on earth so amuses you, dear friend? I did indeed see Lieutenant Stiles on St.

Simons, but I don't recall anything funny. I only know that that lovely island, like Savannah, is in danger, that its people have already started to leave for refuge on the mainland."

Her smile gone, she said, "So Bobby told me in his letter and my heart breaks for them. A lot of women and children are leaving here, too. But as distressed as I am over everything, Robert, I do have to tell you what Bobby wrote about you. It gave us all a good laugh."

"That's good medicine," he said. "Tell me what young Stiles wrote."

"Better still," she said, pointing to her small letter table, "hand me his letter, if you please. Bobby said it far better than I can recall at my age. You'll find it right on top of a stack of letters just inside the drawer."

Handing her Bobby's letter, Lee stooped to kiss her white curly hair. "Except for that beautiful silver hair of yours, I'd never guess you weren't as young as when I first saw you a thousand years ago."

"You always did spread it on with the women," she said, hunting for the passage she wanted to read. "Oh, yes, here it is. Bobby wrote: 'I wish you could have seen the soldiers' eyes bug at the sight of General Robert E. Lee. Of course, it meant more to me than he'll ever know that I got a chance to see him again, but I wish he knew how he impressed us all–especially the privates, who stood gawking. You see, we were visited the same day by Generals Lawton and Mercer and a good many other little puffs. Of course, General Lee was dressed plainly, as always, but his inferiors swashed and buckled around him, dressed within an inch of their lives!' "

Lee grinned. "What we have in the Confederate Army, I'm afraid, is more than a handful of generals who love their fancy uniforms above all else."

She was not smiling now. "You do stand out, no matter what you're wearing, Robert. You always will. Because of what you are."

"You honor me, dear Mrs. Mackay," he said simply. "I have hope for our chivalrous Confederate officers, though, in spite of the quite unrealistic way they still view this war, especially the volunteer officers who have pulled every string to be able to wear those uniforms. Most of them feel 'born to command' at once, but they dislike hard work intensely. My longtime friend Jeb Stuart says they need to *reduce the ranks*. Most of the South Carolina and Georgia gentry who volunteered to be immediate officers still see little reason to dig trenches and erect earthworks, but they'll find out by and by."

For a time, they just sat together in the peace and silence of her parlor. Then Lee mused, "If the war goes on as long as I fear it will, everyone will learn that real camp life is a great leveler. Yeomen and gentry alike share plagues, you know—measles, fever, dysentery. They share a lack of tents and blankets and too soon, I fear, in spite of all everyone back home is trying to do, a lack of food."

"Oh, Robert," she said, her brow deeply knit, "are we in real danger here?"

He was quiet for a few seconds, as though weighing just how much to tell her.

"Don't try to spare me," she said firmly. "I'm old, and some days I don't leave my bed, but being old also means that my spine has had added years to stiffen. Tell me the truth, please."

"All right, I will. Jack always said you handled the truth better than anyone on earth."

"Dear Jack," she breathed.

"Yes, dear, dear Jack. I still miss him. I need him now more than ever." Lee took a deep breath. "The naked truth is that in all my long years in the Army I've never inspected a place as hard to defend as Savannah. The city is so riddled with rivers and streams—so many points where attack is possible—and defense next to impossible. I'm sure you heard that before I dipped down to St. Simons and Jekyll, I inspected Fort Pulaski. It needs almost everything! I informed the young officer in command, Colonel Olmstead, that with Union forces already dug in on Tybee, they could easily make it warm for him at Pulaski. Tybee Island is only seventeen hundred yards away. Olmstead blanched at the amount of work I ordered, but at least I could assure him that enemy shells *cannot* breach the fort's walls from that distance. I'm afraid I ordered a lot of ditches dug along with heavy blindages of ranging timber around the entire circuit of the fort to guard the casemate doors from shell fragments. Ditches and pits have to be dug in the parade to stop rolling projectiles. Mounds of earth must be piled upon the parapet to check a flanking fire. A veritable mountain of work for a small garrison of men, but I trust young Colonel Olmstead."

"I suppose you know my dear friend Mark Browning's son, Jonathan, is at Fort Pulaski now."

He nodded. "I spoke briefly with young Browning last week. I also remember vividly the dinner here at your house now well over a decade ago," he said. "The young man struck me then as being unusually thoughtful. Are you free to tell me, Mrs. Mackay, how his pro-Union father is taking his son's loyalty to the South?" Lee smiled wryly. "I'm sure his mother is well pleased."

"Oh, Robert, Robert, the Brownings are another divided family, except for the love they still hold for one another. Mark? Well, could I just say that he and I need each other more than ever now?"

"Yes, of course," Lee said, showing nothing, she thought, of what he was really feeling about her. "And I'm glad you and Browning have each other. With both his wife and son against his convictions, I'm sure he needs you." Lee seemed to be studying her. "Is it—terribly hard being old in the midst of a war?" he asked at last.

"Yes. It's unbearable to feel useless. And I am."

Stroking his well-trimmed beard, Lee looked at her again for a long time, then said, "No one is useless who can still pray, Miss Eliza. I know you pray day and night for us all."

"I do. I pray for every one of you, Robert, on both sides of the trouble. You don't object, do you, that I pray for—them, too?"

Tears filled his deep-set eyes. "You knew me first as a young officer in *their* army, my friend. Resigning to defend my home was like cutting off an arm."

"I felt it was," she said gently. "I prayed then, I still pray that you made the right choice. Oh, Robert, I just don't know about—war. I just don't know about it at all."

Lee stood up, went to where she sat, and took her hand. "It will soon be Christmas. God alone knows where I may be by then, but wherever I am, count on my thoughts of you—of all of you. I hear Eliza Anne's husband, Colonel Stiles, will be rejoining his regiment here any day now. They won't be together for Christmas either. I suppose you know that Colonel Stiles and his son Captain Henry Stiles will undoubtedly be sent to Virginia."

With Lee standing there holding on to her hand, she felt one of her fading spells coming on—"spells of dotage," she called them. Times when she felt hazy and sat staring at nothing, lacking the energy even to attempt to pull away the veil of languidness which seemed to drift down over her.

"I must go," he said in the gentlest voice she'd heard since William went away. "I wish I didn't have to leave you, but I'll come again. Christmas will be the Lord's birthday. He did come to earth to be one of us, didn't He?"

Her thoughts clearing for a moment, she looked up at Robert Lee and whispered, "Yes, He came and got into everything with us." Trying with all her might to grip his hand good and hard, she added, "And He's–still here–right with us in the whole ugly mess!"

SIXTY-EIGHT

On the day after the saddest, most difficult Christmas Mark had ever spent, his longtime friend and former attorney, W. H. Stiles, appeared at the door of his office.

"I was surprised to find your door closed," W.H. said as they greeted each other a bit stiffly. "Your countinghouse, like almost every other up and down the waterfront, is rather devoid of both people and business. Closed your door from habit, eh?"

Motioning W.H. to sit down, Mark sank back into his own chair behind an empty, clear desk. "That's right," he said. "I do most things these days from habit, I guess. I keep coming here every day as though I had my usual load of work to do. I take it you're feeling much better since we saw you last at Etowah Cliffs." Mark studied his guarded face. "We left so soon after you arrived in the upcountry, I hadn't yet heard of the stories about you in the papers here. I guess they began to come out while we were still in Cass."

"*Bartow*," W.H. corrected him.

"Of course. Saying Cass County is a longtime habit, too, I guess. It's going to take me a while to learn to use the new name, Bartow."

So far, ignoring Mark's mention of the news stories, W.H. said, "I'm honored to have spearheaded the drive for the change. Since early this month, Cass's name has been changed *by law* to Bartow County."

"So I've heard," Mark said, "and I do apologize. I'm sure it's a touchy subject with you, W.H."

"Think no more about it," his friend said coolly. "I would imagine you and I, our long relationship notwithstanding, may in future have far more prickly subjects to bridge. I did not, I assure you, come here today to disagree any more than we have to," W.H. went on. "I came to tell you the truth about the ugly rumors Major Duncan L. Clinch seems to have circulated about me." He raised his hand to keep Mark silent. "I'd appreciate your permitting me to speak my piece first, if you don't mind."

"Not at all. Anyway, W.H., it would take a lot more than newspaper gossip about something said in a little Georgia town like Waynesville to shake my personal regard for you."

W.H. bowed in acknowledgment. "Gossip from a small town is right. I do not in any way impugn the integrity of Major Clinch, but the story he is purported to have told—that I dismounted and begged him at Hilton Head to take over command of my men—is an outright lie! My horse was shot from under me in that disastrous battle. While my brain cleared—a matter of only a few minutes—I asked the major to assume command until I could return to my rightful duty." For just an instant, as W.H. smiled a little and rubbed his forehead, Mark thought he might be going to act like his old self with him. Obviously Colonel Stiles thought better of it. His handsome face turned stony again. "The fact that I'm back with my regiment, ready to do my part when my men, including my son Henry, are sent into the thick of the fighting in Virginia, should prove that Major Clinch's report has been wildly distorted."

"I quite agree," Mark said. "We needn't mention it again, ever. Is that really why you came here today. W.H.?"

"That was certainly one reason. The other is that Lib begs me to ask you to assure her sisters and her poor mother that she will be down to Savannah as soon as it is at all possible for her to leave our three young grandchildren." He lifted a hand again. "Oh, I know they understand her predicament, but the woman is worried half sick at her mother's worsening condition. It would ease Lib's nerves at least a little, Mark, if she knew *you* had delivered her message. By the way, I called on Mrs. Mackay yesterday as soon as I returned to the city. She made an effort, but I fear she's dying."

Mark looked startled. "W.H., don't say that!"

"But she'll soon be eighty-four! Surely you can't miss the pallor of death on her. We have to face facts as they are, you know."

Mark slumped back in his chair. "Yes, I do know. I've had a fair amount of experience lately at—facing facts as they are."

"You mean Jonathan's admirable show of loyalty to his native land, I assume." When Mark said nothing, he added, "I thought as much. Well, you *chose* Savannah, Browning. Jonathan didn't ask to be born here in the glorious South."

"That's right, he didn't. Miss Eliza always says Savannah chose me." Now Mark raised his hand. "I know what you're thinking, W.H. If Savannah chose me, it must seem these days as though I'm—rejecting her. Hard as this is for you to understand, I *couldn't* reject the old city. I grieve for her. Almost every evening, I walk her streets alone, looking for *my* city in the throngs of soldiers and officers crowding her lovely old thoroughfares. I limp up and down Commerce Row and Factor's Walk grieving for her once busy waterfront. I miss her—I miss Savannah herself."

W.H. looked at Mark for a long time, then an unmistakably sardonic smile appeared on his face. "An impressive speech, Browning," he said, getting to his feet. "You may still love Savannah in a sentimental way, but evidently you're content to risk only your son's life for her." At the door, he turned back. "General Robert E. Lee will be returning, I hear, at the end of January and for one deplorable reason—Savannah's defenses are in such a sad condition, the general feels he must return and take charge. We're short of guns, armaments—funds. I don't want to have words either of us will regret, but quite rapidly, Mark Browning, you're turning into an emotional, useless old fool rather reveling in an assumed grief for a city who needs him and his money as she's never needed him before!"

Mark, standing, too, now, simply looked at his friend and wished with all his heart that W.H. would leave.

"By the way," Stiles said, his hand on the doorknob, "Lib, by some stroke of good fortune, has not yet heard of the scandalous lies printed about me in the Savannah *Daily Morning News*. I'd appreciate your doing all you can to prevent her ever finding out."

Surely his former friend would go now, Mark thought, gripping the edge of his desk.

"You see," W.H. went on, "I was made so ill by the whole libelous episode that a recovery time at home became a necessity. Lib jumped to the wifely conclusion that the bombardment at Port Royal Sound was just too much of a shock to me since, as she declared, I'm really a man of letters, a diplomat. Of course, I allowed her to think that, since I feel bereavement over her mother's imminent death lies ahead." He reached for his hat, which he had placed on the corner of Mark's desk, and gestured with it. "But you watch from now on. My regiment and I are headed for Virginia soon and there I intend to show my real mettle! *My* kind of devotion to Savannah."

The minute W.H. left, Mark lifted his heavy overcoat from the table over which he'd thrown it earlier and struggled into the thick, padded sleeves. On this chill winter day, his whole body craved the coat's warmth, while every aching muscle rebelled at its weight. What W.H. said about Miss Eliza had filled him with such panic, his own blood pounding in his head felt like hammerblows.

In a rush to see for himself how his friend felt today, he was still carrying his hat in his hand all the way down the empty hallway and out the front door onto the bridge that led to Bay Street. Outside, a hard wind off the river struck his bare head, whipped his thick, long, graying hair so that settling a hat into place was an effort. The tide had changed since he left home right after dawn. Savannahians always knew that the wind changed with the tide.

I'm a Savannahian, he reminded himself grimly. No matter what W.H. said, I *am* a Savannahian.

The old friend whom he had always respected, even in disagreement, had upset him to such an extent that he felt anger. How dare W.H. be so insensitive? Only *he,* Mark Browning, knew light was going out of the world if Eliza Mackay *was* dying! Only he knew the depth of his own love for Savannah! What right did W.H. have to lash out at him on those two most troubling subjects? Not two—*three.* He had gouged Mark also because Jonathan had swung totally away from the Union. Was W.H. so humiliated by whatever had happened to *him* at the Port Royal fiasco that he had no choice but to castigate Mark? Had W.H. mentioned Miss Eliza's death twice, labeled Mark's love for Savannah as the mere sentimental love of an old man, in order to compensate for his own humiliation?

Pushing his way along Bay Street against a northeast blow, he wondered if he'd ever reach the corner of Abercorn, where he could at least turn out of the wind. In the old days, making the familiar walk to Miss Eliza's, he had often strolled all the way around Reynolds Square, where his own handsome house stood. Lately, he'd begun to cut across the square to save his rheumatic legs a few steps. Today, he felt an almost irresistible longing to go straight home to the warmth of his own fires, to the welcome and warmth of Caroline's arms. No. Today, because of what W.H. had said about Miss Eliza, about *him*, he would force himself across Reynolds Square and along two more blocks to Broughton.

Seventy is old, he thought, but is it old enough for such a crowd of memories as he struggled against now? Nearly fifty long years ago, on his very first day in Savannah, he and buoyant Robert Mackay, Miss Eliza's husband, who was taking young Mark Browning home with him after their chance shipboard meeting, had walked these same streets. Trudging now across Congress, he realized that this was almost the exact spot where he had first seen Miss Eliza as a young woman, a child, Katie, in her arms, Eliza Anne and the two small boys, William and Jack, running ahead to embrace their father.

I loved her at that moment, he thought. I love her now. Not the way I thought I loved her then, but so much more that the need to keep her on the earth within hearing and speaking distance is as vital as breathing. I would have made a most inadequate husband for Eliza Mackay had she been foolish enough to take my boyish infatuation seriously back then, he thought, but I *have been* an adequate friend to her. And the rocklike support of her fidelity and counsel has made me a good husband to Caroline. These things I know, he reassured himself as he came in sight of the big old frame house which had needed a coat of paint long before William died.

Nearing the brick walkway that would take him still another time to her front door, he gave thanks that he possessed enough knowledge of his own heart to be sure a man could truly love two women. He loved Miss Eliza and at the same instant felt he could almost not wait to take Caroline in his arms.

Along Broughton Street, coming toward him, a bundled, bustling woman went a step or two out of her way to pass him at a distance. Mark tipped his hat and bowed. The look she gave him would have withered a stout, young vine. He turned briefly to see if she was looking back at him. She was. She had stopped walking and was glaring after him. It was Madam Casier, the energetic, courageous lady who, in June, would be opening the Bartow Hospital for wounded Confederate soldiers. So hot did the flame of her devotion to the Confederacy burn in her, its heat singed Mark. Many Savannahians, he knew, had treated him with courtesy only because he'd been careful through the years to keep his opinions to himself and because of his wealth and influence and generosity in town. That shelter had all but been blown away by the storm of war—the war laying waste daily to the only place on earth where he knew how to feel at home. The war which was hourly laying waste to his peace.

"I'm coming, Miss Eliza," he whispered, plodding up the steps to her front door. "Wait for me, I'm coming. I'll always be here sooner or later. Not because I'm good or faithful—because I can't manage my own days without you . . ."

Sarah answered his familiar knock and told him to go right upstairs. "Mama couldn't quite make it down today, but she's waiting for you."

When he entered Miss Eliza's room at the top of the stairs, Kate stood by the bed, her usual smile fading the moment she looked at Mark. On her pudgy face appeared a puzzled, worried expression. "What on earth's wrong, Mark? You look dreadful!"

Reaching her hand to him, Miss Eliza said, "Yes, dear boy, come over here where I can see you. Has something terrible happened?"

He stood looking down at her, holding her frail hand, trying to force a smile. "It's those—steps of yours," he said in a hoarse old man's voice which he heard but could not help. "Remember when I used to take them two at a time?"

"I remember—everything from back then, Mark. Are you sure nothing's wrong?"

"Nothing more than usual, except, well, W.H. paid a call at my countinghouse this morning. He seemed to think you didn't feel too well."

"Mama just likes to surprise us every day," Kate said in a pathetic attempt at cheer. "Day before yesterday, if you remember, she and I were heading outside for a carriage ride when you left. We took a long one, too. Magill drove us almost out to Causton's Bluff and Mama gave corn cakes to the soldiers along the way, told them all she prayed for them and loved them—even stood up in the carriage now and then to make her little bows to them. Today, she's just—tired. I'm sure she'll be much better now that you're here. Won't you, Mama?"

"That's enough, Kate dear," Miss Eliza said. "I'd *like* to feel well every day." She gave Mark her determined smile. "I'm still here, dear boy. Still thinking things through, although I seem to jump around a lot. All my life, it seems, I've prayed not to lose control of my mind the way old people tend to do." The smile vanished. "I'm thinking so much today about poor Mary Cowper. I don't seem to know how to pray for Eliza Anne anymore. All this time without knowing when or how her only daughter's going to get through the enemy North and back to Etowah Cliffs again." She patted the bed, inviting Mark to sit down. "I think so much about poor Mr. Low, too, up there in prison at Fort Warren. I don't know Mr. Low well, actually, but it's so unfair for a British citizen to be in prison for trying to help down here. I don't feel as though I really know Mary Cowper well anymore either. I don't think any of us—certainly not Eliza Anne—knows everything that's in Mary Cowper's little heart. Maybe Natalie sees inside her more clearly than any of us."

"*Natalie*, Mama?" Kate asked in surprise.

"Doesn't Sarah need you to help her with those soldiers' socks downstairs, Kate?"

"Oh—oh, yes, I'm sure she does. I'll go. We all defer to you and Mama, Mark," Kate added. "We always have. Please keep coming—every day!"

For a minute or so after Kate had closed the door behind her, they just sat there together in the old familiar way.

Finally, Miss Eliza smoothed his hand. "Now do you feel more at home, dear boy? You seemed so—lost when you came in."

"You never miss knowing about me, do you?"

"You don't need to explain anything, you know. You don't need to, but you're free to. Either way." She glanced toward the window. "It's a beautiful winter day outside in the city, isn't it?"

"The wind's cold, but—oh, Miss Eliza, you're right. I felt *lost* all the way over here. I now realize, and it stuns me, that I didn't even notice— Savannah. I'm sure in all the years I've been here, I've never once—not noticed her in some way. Can you believe I've lived here nearly fifty years?"

"I try to let time rush ahead without me these days, Mark. There's been so much of it. Now and then, I feel as though even I wasn't really here—in Savannah, before you found us all."

"But you *are* Savannah to me. You always have been!"

She had been looking at him intently. Now her eyes moved vacantly toward the far wall of her room. "It came to me this morning when I was praying for you and Caroline and Jonathan and Mary and Little Ben that if the truth be known, *you* gave me Savannah."

"*What?*"

"I'm sure I've told you," she went on as though he hadn't sounded so surprised, "I was born at the Grange, our old Savannah River plantation. Back then, of course, it belonged to my British uncle, Sir Basil Cowper. After a short time in South Carolina, and my schooling in England, we lived at the Grange until my dear father and the McQueen family moved here to Thunderbolt. When I met and married my happy Robert in the year 1800, I was considered a Savannahian, but the day he brought you home to this house, your special Savannah, in a very real way–became mine."

Once more, she was rescuing him out of lostness. Once more, she was reaching toward him, knowing exactly where to find him.

"Seeing you then, so young and eager and full of joy in our old city, somehow gave the city as a *living* thing to me, too. One can so easily take a beautiful place for granted. Not one day since your first day here has Savannah seemed a taken-for-granted place to me!"

He lifted her hand and kissed it. "Miss Eliza, if I thought that could possibly be true, I–I might not feel as though my world here had completely fallen apart."

"It hasn't! I don't ever want to hear you say that again. You must promise me never to feel–a stranger in Savannah." The dim eyes filled with tears. "Mark, I've lived–so long, but I can't die in peace if I can't leave you and Savannah–together."

"Don't even mention leaving me!"

"I'm *going* to die someday. We all are. I'm glad I'm not leaving today, though, because lately I've felt–almost like a stranger in town, too."

He tightened his fingers on hers. "You?"

She was looking straight at him again. "Kate made a pretty story of my bowing to those poor soldiers the day before yesterday, but I was really enduring that long carriage ride because I was–searching for Savannah. The old, familiar, quiet Savannah you and I love."

"And did you find her?"

"No. I got tired and had to come home first. But maybe she isn't actually in the buildings we love, the church spires, the waterfront, the squares. Maybe Savannah is right here between us, with a life of her very own. A life that nothing–*nothing*, not war or hatred or bitterness or even death, can snuff out."

Through the minutes of silence that followed, broken only by the muffled ticking of her old mantel clock, he sat praying for Savannah to come back to them both. Savannah as she'd always been, lovely and elusive but, like her sky, able to embrace everyone blessed enough to be near her. He prayed for Savannah to embrace and accept him and Miss

Eliza again, both of whom still loved the old Union . . . but also to embrace Caroline and Jonathan and the Lows and the Habershams and the Mercers and tender, withdrawn Indian Mary and her dark, sturdy Cherokee son.

Take us all back, he begged: All of *us* as well as every strutting Confederate officer and every green young Rebel private eager to lay down his life for what he sees as the noble Cause of the South, of which Savannah is surely a part.

"Mark Browning, you're turning into an emotional, useless old fool rather reveling in an assumed grief for a city who needs him and his money as she's never needed him before!"

W.H.'s mocking words were flat now, off-key. In Miss Eliza's presence, only truth could ring real. W.H. had been right that she would die someday, of course, but not today! Today he would believe the two of them had found Savannah again *together*.

"Is there anything I can do for you before I start home?" he asked. "Time still flies when we're together. Are you warm enough?"

"I'm fine," she said softly, eyes closed. "I just wish I didn't get so tired—doing nothing! But, I'm quite comfortable, so go home to Caroline." She withdrew her hand. "I'm quite comfortable now, really, but—" Her eyes flew open and she stared at the ceiling. "When the *great struggle* comes at the end, Mark, how will I bear it? What will it be like? I'm so unaccustomed to pain and long sickness that I'm not prepared for—my death. Not ready to leave. Will I be a stranger for sure then? I dread it very much!" She reached for his hand. "I've lived such a long time, it must come soon. Something else will be done, you know, to separate my soul from my body. I do dread that, but don't tell the girls."

Fear rushed back over him, too, but he could say nothing. He clung to her tender, frail hand.

"Sometimes, you know, I think I'll probably choke to death," she went on. "The girls can tell you—I guess you and Caroline already know that lately—I choke very easily. Sometimes even coughing doesn't help much . . ."

With all his heart, he longed to say something to help. In a way he meant never to relinquish, during the last few minutes *she had* given the essence of Savannah back to him. If he could give her the remaining years of his own life, he would do it gladly if doing so might relieve her terror of dying. "Miss Eliza," he heard himself say, "you've always trusted God with everything else. Wouldn't you tell me that He can be trusted with—choking, too? And how could *you* feel a stranger—with *Him?*"

Her eyes were still closed, but she smiled. "Yes, dear boy, I'm sure I would tell you exactly that."

Still holding her hand, he got to his feet and stood looking down at her. "Would you like me to come back this afternoon?"

"Oh, I'd like it," she said, eyes open now. "But I also enjoy thinking of you—with Caroline. You're right, of course. God will be very capable of handling my dying moments. My goodness, when I think of the miracle God's made in Caroline's understanding for you, I feel perfectly foolish to dread anything that might happen to me—at the end."

SIXTY-NINE

*T*hroughout the month of January 1862, Eliza Mackay vowed she felt "tolerable." That meant, her daughters knew, that mostly she simply felt old and weak from so much coughing. Her heart was congested, the doctor said, and she joked with him that "in such a dark time in the land, it had better be congested with love."

She still awakened in the night afraid, worried about *how* she would die, but she meant never to mention it again to anyone but God. She kept her promise and felt well enough to spend most days downstairs in her little parlor rocker, reading, as long as her eyes didn't blur, from the Scriptures and the newspapers. The one verse to which she turned so often that her old Bible would fall open at the place was I Corinthians 15:57: ". . . thanks be to God which giveth us the victory through our Lord Jesus Christ." She had known that verse by heart for most of her long life, but now that she knew that Savannah was in real danger, it helped more to read the words from her own Bible. The newspapers held accounts of battles raging in various parts of the blessed land for which her own dear father, John McQueen, had endured imprisonment during the American Revolution, and she grieved for the nation. When the reports grew too sorrowful for her to bear, she picked up the Bible and let it fall open to the words which daily became more a part of her:

". . . thanks be to God which giveth us the victory through our Lord Jesus Christ."

"Victory?" she asked into the empty old parlor. "Victory, Lord, over what? North over South? South over North? Whose victory? Brokenhearted mothers up there over brokenhearted mothers down here?"

Was God promising victory to President Lincoln and his Yankee generals or to her beloved boy, General Robert Lee? To her son-in-law, Colonel W. H. Stiles, and her own grandchild, young Henry Stiles, now a major? Both were leaving soon to fight other fathers and sons in far-off Virginia. Victory over what? For whom? Well, God had promised. Someday they'd all know.

A rapid knock at her front door brought Hannah's heavy footsteps hurrying—as much as poor old Hannah could still hurry—to answer the door, on orders from the girls, who forbade their mother to leave her chair until they got back from Women's Aid.

"Lord have mercy," Hannah boomed from the front hall, "Lootenant Lee! If it ain't Lootenant Lee come to see us again! Come in, sir, Miss Liza be so happy to clap eyes on you!"

"And I'm happy to clap eyes on you, too, Hannah," Lee said in his cheerful voice. "Is Mrs. Mackay in the parlor as usual?"

"Yes, sir, Lootenant Lee! Yes, sir! You just go on in. You done come to stay with us for a while, Lootenant Lee? Miss Liza and me, we done got your old room dusted and swept—your old bed made up with fresh sheets! You done come to stay a while?"

"Never mind, Hannah," Eliza called out from her rocker. "Bring General Lee in here. He and I will talk about that, thank you."

"Don't even think of getting up," Lee said as he strode toward her across the room, both arms out. "Someone told me you hadn't been too well. Someone lied outright. You're as beautiful as ever. And I fully intend to hug and kiss you, dear lady."

She returned his embrace and ordered him to stand back so she could get a good look at his still fuller beard. "My, Robert, but you even *look* like a general now that you've stopped trimming your beard. Does Mary like it?"

Taking a chair nearby, Lee laughed. "My poor wife sees me so seldom these days, she hasn't even, as Hannah says, 'clapped eyes' on it yet." He leaned toward her. "Now, what's this about your getting my old room ready? And don't I wish I could accept such kindness!"

Genuinely puzzled, she asked, "And why can't you? This has always been your Savannah home."

"I dare not. This beautiful city is now surrounded by the enemy. Should Savannah be attacked, it would go so hard for all of you if I were found living in your house, I'd never forgive myself! So I beg of you—I insist, in fact—that you not bring it up again."

When she caught her breath from the shock of what he'd just said, she laughed a broken little laugh. "Well, *General* Lee, I can suddenly picture you giving orders which you fully expect to be obeyed!"

Now Lee smiled slightly. "I am sorry, but unless I can find a way to get our officers and men here moving—some of them strike me as not even realizing we're at war—the city is in real danger."

She straightened her shoulders and looked him in the eye. "Robert— might they actually bombard our—lovely old city?"

"Oh, my dear friend, there are so many points of attack around this town and so little means to meet them on the water, I must find a way to throw up a line on land strong enough somehow to hold them back. I do plan to be here for a time. Work has lagged terribly. There's dire need for constant supervision."

"Robert, Robert, what a dreadful burden you bear!"

"Will you pray we'll be assigned more troops?"

More troops, she thought, will mean more killing and more grief. "I'll certainly pray for *you*, General. The Lord knows your—needs."

He stroked his full beard. "I don't believe you've ever called me— General before, have you?"

"The very old get mighty careless," she said. "Hannah and Emphie believe your first name is still Lootenant. Even if I do seem to go on calling you Robert, I'm truly proud of you. Proud of the strong, sensitive, wise man you are down inside."

At that moment, Mark's familiar knock came at the front door.

"That will be Mark Browning, Robert. You remember him."

"Indeed, yes," Lee said. "I remember them all well. Young Mrs. Browning, I believe, was a half-breed Cherokee. The Browning son asked some highly intelligent questions."

"Good, you do remember well. Robert, could I please ask a favor? Poor Mark suffers deeply these days because of his son, Jonathan—at Fort Pulaski now, a Confederate officer."

"And I've heard Browning still holds Northern sympathies. Don't worry, my friend, don't worry at all. I've always tried to be disputatious only on the battlefield."

She called out. "Mark, come in and see who's here!" Voice low, she said to Lee, "The dear man comes every day to visit me. He has his own knock—and his own key."

After the two gentlemen shook hands warmly, Lee remained standing. "I really must go, Miss Eliza. And, Browning, even your responsible son and his commanding officer, Colonel Olmstead, can't seem to keep those Pulaski men working fast enough. Although I must say Lieutenant Browning never shirks, never shows the usual gentry aversion to hard labor. I hope you're proud of him. The work yet to be done at Pulaski is gigantic. We need real men, real patriots."

"I am proud of Jonathan, sir," Mark said, then, to Eliza's relief, quickly changed the subject. "Is that splendid animal tethered to the Mackay hitching post outside yours, General Lee? The magnificent gray?"

She thought Lee seemed relieved, too. "Why, yes, he is. Can you come to the window, Miss Eliza? I so want you to have a look at Traveller!"

The general helped her across the room. "Oh, Robert, what a beautiful sight he is," she breathed. "Have you had him long? I always thought you preferred mares."

"I did," he laughed. "Traveller changed all that, though. It took me quite a while back in western Virginia to convince his owner to sell, but Traveller and I have been together now for some time. He has a short, high trot that just suits me and plenty of endurance for all the travel I have to do these days. We go from my current headquarters in South Carolina at Coosawhatchie, up to Charleston, down here to Savannah, still farther down the coast to Fernandina. Our daily forays through pine thickets and palmetto, over sand and sedge, only seem to firm our friendship. Actually, his name was Greenbrier when I found him. He earned the name Traveller. I love the animal."

"It's good to know you have each other," she said as Lee helped her back to her rocker. "You'll come again, won't you? And often?"

"As often as possible," he said, bowing over her hand.

"If I may ask," Mark said, "how do you get to Pulaski now that the Northern forces have it cut off by water?"

Lee turned solemn. "It isn't easy. I get there only now and then when we're lucky enough to slip through by small boat. I'm headquartered here in the city. Sadly, though, not with the Mackays this time."

"And we had your old room all ready for you," she said.

"I certainly have no intention of starting a discussion, Browning,"

Lee said, "but you should know, if you don't already, that Savannah is in danger of attack from the Union forces at almost any time. Were the city to be captured, all manner of reprisal might fall on this house if I were to be caught living in it."

When Lee had gone, Mark immediately handed Miss Eliza a letter from Eliza Anne.

"Oh, why didn't you give this to me while General Lee was still here? He and Eliza Anne have always been so close and I'm sure he knows that poor Mr. Low is in a Northern prison and that our Mary Cowper is still battling her way back to the South."

Mark frowned. "Few of us behave in the usual ways anymore," he said. "I like General Lee, but to him I do represent the enemy."

"Nonsense, dear boy. I'd trust the two of you to talk about anything!"

"I'll read your letter to you, but I know how worried you are, so I can tell you some of what's in it. Caroline and I heard from Eliza Anne by the same mail." He gave her a smile. "Miss Eliza, Mary Cowper is home! She reached Cartersville last Thursday, hired a buggy, and arrived at Etowah Cliffs that day—January twenty-third!"

Her head fell back against her rocker in relief and, as Mark took his familiar chair, neither spoke for a long time. Finally, she said, almost as to herself, "How grateful I am! Dear Lord, how grateful I am. Now I'll get to see my blessed granddaughter again. Mary Cowper will be here just as soon as she's had a chance to rest a few days. I don't know the child as I once did, but I do know she'll be here *soon*."

SEVENTY

Although Natalie, Callie, and Burke joined Miss Lib in rejoicing that Mary Cowper was finally at home, Natalie still felt estranged from her young friend. Even Miss Lorah failed to convince her that Mary Cowper needed Natalie in a special way now.

"Stop badgering me, Miss Lorah," Natalie said on a mild February morning. "You're not as wise as I've always believed if you think for one minute that I can just embrace her in her falsehood!"

Dish towel in hand, Lorah Plemmons stood in the kitchen and took one of her longest studying spells. Then she asked, "What falsehood is that, Missy?"

"Her whole life's a falsehood! Hand me that bowl of potatoes so I can peel while we get on each other's nerves. I don't care how loyal Mary Cowper's been to Mr. Low all these years, she still loves Stuart Elliott, so her whole life's a pretense!"

Miss Lorah pushed the crockery bowl of potatoes toward Natalie, handed her a paring knife, then went back to drying dishes. "Maybe so, maybe not," she said, "but it's none of our business either way. None of your business, Missy, though I know you mean well. Mary Cowper's a married woman, a mother. Stuart's a married man and a father. What on earth can be gained by stirring up trouble at this late date?" The dishes dried, she sat down with Natalie at the kitchen table and began to peel potatoes, too. "I reckon I'd give most anything I own to find a way to unhook you from your stubbornness about this whole thing. You're wasting your breath and mine."

"Mary Cowper has wasted her whole life!" Unable to sit there and be lectured a minute longer, Natalie tossed a half-peeled potato back into the big bowl, grabbed her cloak, and hurried outside to find Callie. What she meant to say to her eighteen-year-old daughter, once she found her, was not at all clear, but Burke agreed with Miss Lorah about Mary Cowper while Callie, like her mother, was a true romantic.

I wish Callie stayed at home more, she grumbled to herself, heading along the river road toward Miss Lib's house. I suppose I'll have to palaver and make dumb small talk with Miss Lib and Mary Cowper before I can get my own daughter alone when I need her. She's spending too much time with those Low children. Oh, they're harmless, but Miss Lib and Mary Cowper might influence her. I have no intention of allowing Callie to be swayed one little bit by the way those two look at what's important in life. Callie's truly in love with her Perry Clay. It doesn't seem to faze her belief in him one bit that he hasn't written since he left to join the Union Army. She loves him and I intend to see that her little heart stays free to go on loving him. Conditions have kept him from getting a letter through to her from the other side of the lines. Burke says Kentucky won't be all Union until some kind of battles have been won and even then old Lincoln makes it next to impossible to get letters through. Nearing the path that led off the river road to Miss Lib's veranda, she said aloud, "I'm sure I don't care which way Kentucky goes if Perry is safe and goes on loving Callie the way I'm convinced he does."

Halfway up the path, she stopped, then sighed with relief when Callie came limping briskly out the big front door, her face lit with the smile that was almost exactly like Burke's.

"Mama, Mama!" Callie called, hopping down the veranda steps. "Look! Sam brought a letter from Perry! He brought it *yesterday.*" She grabbed her mother's hand and began pulling her back toward the road and her father's river-watching bench, where they could talk. "I could clobber Miss Lib for not sending it to me when it came, but anyway, I've got it now." She gave her mother a bear hug.

"I'm as happy as you are, Callie," she said, "but you act as though Miss Lib isn't furious that Perry chose to fight with the Union."

"No war talk," Callie ordered as they sat down. "I've got the letter and that's what matters!"

"Have you had time to read it?" Natalie asked.

Callie's smile was devilish. "I'm your daughter, aren't I? You know perfectly well I read every line right there in Miss Lib's dining room while being stared at. I didn't tell either Mary Cowper or Miss Lib what Perry wrote either." She held the letter close to her heart. "I didn't need to tell them, though. They could see how happy I was. Oh, Mama, he's not only a man of courage, as Papa says, he's—he's a man of beauty, too! And he's not only signed up and active at Fort Henry under General Ulysses Grant, they've broken the Confederate defense Papa told us about and Kentucky is now all Union! But oh, best of all—the very best of all, Perry still *lives for me!*"

After giving her daughter a quick, hard hug, Natalie jumped up and did a little dance in the road. For the first time in months, she felt as young as Callie. "Darling, darling," she caroled, twirling until her full cotton skirt stood out, "it's happened to you, just as it happened to me! You've found the one man you'll ever love and you and Perry are going to be happy *together*, just like Papa and me, for the remainder of your lives." Abruptly, she sat back down. "Can't you see how right I've been all along? Can't you tell by all the time you're spending at Miss Lib's since poor, aging, miserable Mary Cowper came home that love is the one way—the only way for anyone to live? Hasn't Mary Cowper aged because of her duty-bound life with old Andrew Low?"

At that minute, her daughter's look was so much like Burke, Natalie could have smacked her. The girl was *not* going to agree with her! With his exact same tolerant grin, Callie said calmly, "Now, Mama, don't forget Mary Cowper has been through months and months of hard times and all kinds of torment up North. Maybe you're right that she pretends to be contented with Mr. Low, but the man *is* in prison and he *is* the father of those adorable children. I do think we have to consider all sides."

"I hear you, Burke Latimer," Natalie snapped. "I hear you. I don't agree, but I hear you, and now I want to hear Perry's letter, unless it's too personal. I'm really not like Miss Lib and your grandmother Caroline. I believe in *believing* in love. I know in my bones that if Mary Cowper would be honest just once—would admit just once that she still loves Stuart—she'd find a kind of freedom inside, she would be an even better wife to old Low because she'd shed that shell she lives in." She grinned at herself. "I'm through preaching. The letter—read the letter."

"I mean to read every word to you—Papa, too." Callie unfolded the pages, flicked her hand over the first one. "That's the part where he tells how they broke the Confederate defense and won Kentucky. Here. This is where it gets beautiful. Listen, just listen: 'This is a time of self-knowledge, lovely Callie. A time of finding out once and for all that I know myself well enough to be certain for all my life of two things. First, that I made the right decision in setting out on my wild-goose chase to find the Union forces, to become one of them, and second, that for as long as God permits me to live upon this earth, I belong heart and soul and body to Callie Latimer and to no other human being! My great-grandfather, who fought with George Washington in our nation's battle for freedom from the British, taught me that I am a God-blessed citizen of a country whose strength and greatness lie in being *united*. I love Macon, where I have lived my life so far, and now I may never be able to return to my home and live in peace because of the stand I have made to fight for my native country and not only my native state. Our beloved state of Georgia is only one part of our native land, my beloved, and you can be sure I will try my best someday to help mend the whole again. Right now, with paper so short, though, I must try, and probably fail, to explain to you that what I have learned about my country is only half of what I have learned of myself at age twenty-two. In fact, were I a Rebel, beloved Callie, I would still *belong to you*. The most admirable trait I own is that I had the taste and wisdom to fall in love with a woman whose courage will hold me in battle, whose laughter will cheer my dreams, whose beauty haunts me both night and day. It is frightening, Callie, to fight in a war. I have been afraid every minute of each of two battles so far, but the courage you have shown me bolsters mine. I have never known you to be afraid of anything and I mean to try to emulate your spirit, if that is at all possible. My paper is gone, but my love for you will go on throughout life on earth and beyond. Your loving Perry Clay.' "

For a long time, the two women sat looking at each other, their eyes brimming with tears of pure joy. Finally, Natalie asked, "Did you tell me once right after you and Perry met in Macon, while you were in school, that he hopes someday to be a writer?"

Callie beamed. "Yes! And—he is a writer already, isn't he, Mama? I'm *so* glad Papa took him to meet his friend Mr. Goodman in Marietta before Perry left for the war. Mr. Goodman really encouraged him."

"Robert McAlpin Goodman has his own kind of courage, too," Natalie said. "There's certainly nothing soft about Mr. Goodman, your papa says. Like him, Perry can become an important man of ideas, Callie. I predict he will be when this madness is over. The country will need calm, intelligent, fine writers more than ever. I'm sure Mr. Goodman will give him a job on his paper."

"For a while, maybe," Callie said, looking out over the river, dreams deepening her gray eyes. "But Perry means to write books. Books that matter, that make life clear to other people, the way it's clear and sensible—and beautiful—to him." She turned to look at Natalie. "He—Perry *will* be safe, won't he? Oh, if other men could see life as clearly as Perry sees it, there wouldn't be all this killing and crippling!"

Natalie thought for a long time, then said, "Everyone believed my brother, Jonathan, was the one who always saw things clearly. Everyone considered me the fly-by-night, the impetuous, thoughtless one of the Browning children. I'm not as devout as your Perry or Burke about the Union, but neither am I flying off in all directions like my brother!" With great resolution, she stood up, Callie beside her. "At least, I'm sensible enough to see that killing accomplishes nothing. My brother is down there at Fort Pulaski learning how to kill good men like your Perry. I guess it just proves that what keeps me on track is that I believe first and foremost in true love! If a person believes love matters more than anything else, a kind of sanity comes."

They were walking arm in arm now back toward home. "Mama, I don't mean to disagree, but Uncle Jonathan truly loves Mary. And Miss Lib truly loves Uncle W.H."

"I thought my brother loved Mary. But if he did, would he be putting her through what he's putting her through now? He's got himself in a dreadful predicament! Everyone at Fort Pulaski is cut off from the city. Jonathan hasn't been home in weeks and all they're doing out there is digging ditches and waiting to be killed by Northern forces. As for Miss Lib and Uncle W.H.—I always thought they loved each other. Maybe they do, but it can't be exactly the same way you love Perry. It can't be the way I love your father! They're both acting crazy these days. Why, Uncle W.H. could be killed, too, when they send him up to Virginia. And look how they both wrecked Mary Cowper's life!"

"Isn't that another subject altogether?"

Natalie gave her a wry smile. "Maybe it is."

"I'm just not sure all war is unavoidable," Callie said. "I know my Perry had to go because of what he believes. Of course, I believe the way he and Papa do, but you have to admit, Mama, that the Confederates couldn't fight a war by themselves. There are Union soldiers in it, too, causing grief and worry for the women who love them. I'm not sure

I totally agree with you that putting the person you love ahead of everything else is all that matters—it's just the right thing to do."

Natalie gave her a hug as they turned into their path. "Sometimes I could shake you, Callie, for thinking so deeply. I've always found it far easier to stay simple!"

"My crippled foot makes it impossible for me not to think, Mama," Callie said quietly. "I'm sure even you forget my foot sometimes. I don't love Perry with all my heart only because I believe in love. I love him because I love him and because I'm sure he loves me—in spite of my foot." At the bottom of the three steps that led up to the cottage porch, Callie added, "It seems to me people in love are all different. You and Papa are the way you are, thank goodness. Uncle W.H. and Miss Lib are still different—Uncle Jonathan Browning and Aunt Mary are different in another way. Perry and I are—well, we're just us."

Natalie embraced her again. "I have a sneaking feeling I've just received some very wise insights from my eighteen-year-old daughter, but you know something? I don't mind a bit. Are you aware that every day you prove yourself to be more your father's daughter? Now and then, I want to hit him, but never you, beloved Callie. Not really. Don't you dare tell on me, but with you, I just want to go on learning . . ."

SEVENTY-ONE

*A*fter *Mary Cowper* had been at Etowah Cliffs less than a month, her letter reached Lucinda Elliott with the happy news that she would arrive alone by train Sunday evening, February 23, intending to surprise all the Mackays.

"I just know Mama is well enough to go to church because Mary Cowper's coming tonight," Sarah said as she and Kate prepared to bathe their mother early that Sunday morning.

"Sister and Mary Cowper have no way of knowing how much Mama needs her long, monotonous days livened up. It makes such a difference in her. I'm so happy I can't wait to get to church and sing," Kate said, filling a large white pitcher with boiling water to temper the cold water Magill had already taken upstairs. "In fact, I may sing right now!"

"Don't you dare. We both sound better in a congregation." Sarah stood thoughtfully in the middle of the kitchen, a fresh stack of folded towels over one arm. "Do you think we made a mistake, Sister, telling Mama when Mary Cowper meant to surprise her?"

"I do not. Way off there in the upcountry, they have no way of knowing how Mama needs something to look forward to. I think only you and Mark and I know about that. Anyway, if Lucinda Elliott hadn't told you earlier that Mary Cowper was coming, we wouldn't have been at all prepared by today to have her stay right here with us. I think Lucy felt guilty about telling us, but oh, that poor girl is almost beside herself with worry over her husband."

"Do you suppose Stuart Elliott is really sick up at Camp McDonald?"

"Of course he's sick! Lucinda had a telegram from his commanding officer, Captain DuBignon, a month ago. Stuart must be in a makeshift Marietta hospital by now. The telegram said Stuart could be discharged as 'unfit to perform the duties of a soldier in consequence of pulmonary disease with repeated hemorrhages.' Doesn't that sound familiar—from poor Jack, Kate?"

"Oh, yes, yes, it certainly does. Should we tell Mary Cowper?"

"I've got the towels and soft cloths, so don't try to carry anything but that hot pitcher," Kate ordered. "As for telling Mary Cowper, it seems to me that Lucinda should decide that. *If* Mary Cowper asks about him. After what she's been through with Mr. Low and all, I doubt she thinks often about Stuart Elliott. Come on, we need to finish Mama's bath in plenty of time for her to rest before she goes out in that winter air."

During her first morning in Savannah, Mary Cowper talked and talked to her grandmother about the trip abroad to visit Mr. Low's daughters by his first marriage and thought the startlingly frail old lady acted most interested in all they did in Brighton with the girls. She seemed pleased that Mary Cowper continued to have such a close relationship with Amy and Harriet Low. Grandmother Mackay listened attentively to her description of Savannah's own Major Edward Anderson's quarters in London, the social events attended by the Lows, Anderson, and Andrew Low's former partner, Charles Green, now abroad. She had always shown interest in talk of Low's palatial home near Liverpool, but when Mary Cowper began to speak of the hard work they'd all done trying to buy guns and ammunition for the Confederacy, she felt her grandmother's attention wander. At the point when she told of the duplicate copies of secret war dispatches Mary Cowper agreed to bring back to General Lee, Grandmother Mackay's little hand went up to stop her.

"I want to know all that you went through, dearest girl," the old lady said, "but as little as possible, please, about the war."

"Grandmother, the South is desperate for guns and ammunition! If Mr. Low hadn't helped buy the *Fingal* and if she hadn't made it through the brutal Yankee blockade right into the Savannah port, you'd be even shorter of salt than you are now! I can hardly believe to this day that poor Sarah Gordon's uncle, Judge Wayne, cast the swing vote on the Supreme Court that put Lincoln's blockade into effect against the Judge's own home city. I shudder at the thought of his treatment of all of us down here. Is Sarah Gordon heartbroken?"

"Yes, she is," Grandmother Mackay said in a strangely quiet voice. "But then, there are heartbroken people all over the land."

Puzzled by what struck her as a confusing indifference on her grandmother's part, Mary Cowper said, "I certainly don't want to tire you. We can talk more later after I've visited Lucinda. I suppose I just felt so certain that you'd want to know how large a contribution Mr. Low is making to our Cause, what he's suffering now up there in a ghastly Northern prison."

"Oh, my dear girl, I do want to know about poor Mr. Low! I can't express how wrong and unfair I think it is that he's in prison. I–I just beg you to forgive an old lady, whose time on this earth is short, if she trembles at hearing about either side buying guns. Is that so hard for you to understand, Mary Cowper? Is it?"

Frowning deeply, Mary Cowper said, "I don't know how to answer that, I guess. I'm not sure I understand what you're really thinking. Surely your prayers have to be for the right to liberty for our side!"

When her grandmother finally spoke, she said, "I pray for liberty for every human being on earth, Mary Cowper."

"I think it's time you rested some now," Mary C. said, getting up from the chair she'd pulled near her grandmother's parlor rocker. "Can you take a nap right here? Or shall I call for Magill to help you up to your bed?"

"I'll be just fine. Mark will be here soon. I'll just sit here and wait for him. Are you stopping by the church later to sew with Kate and Sarah for our soldiers? Can't you wait before you go for Hannah to serve her paltry dinner?"

"No to both questions. I'll work harder tomorrow to make up for not going to the Aid meeting today and I'm having dinner with my old friend Lucinda."

"Take my greetings to her, please. And do tell her I'm praying many times a day for her sick husband. If the boy's ill enough to be discharged from the Army, he's mighty ill. I certainly remember how Jack suffered from those terrible coughing fits and hemorrhages."

Standing in the parlor, Mary Cowper felt the earth slip beneath her.

The old room seemed to rock like a ship on a rough sea as she tried desperately to appear unconcerned. There was no use! "Lucinda's— husband is—ill, Grandmother?" she gasped. "Stuart is—sick?"

Grandmother Mackay smothered her face in both hands. "Oh, dear! Why do I do things like that? My mind is clear as a bell most of the time. I knew I wasn't to tell you about dear Stuart! *I knew that.*"

The shock had brought tears to Mary Cowper's eyes. They flowed down her cheeks now as she saw the trembling old hands reach toward her, the thin, wrinkled mouth quiver as her grandmother struggled for something to say that might cover the blunder she'd just made.

Taking quick hold of herself had, for Mary Cowper, become second nature by now. The room stopped rocking. Abruptly she stood quite straight and poised as she said, "Don't worry, please. You didn't mean to tell me, and after all, why shouldn't I know? Lucy Elliott and I have been friends for years. I certainly intend to tell her all about the horror my poor husband is going through in that rat-infested Yankee prison!" Stooping, she gave the old lady a quick kiss. "You doze now until Mark comes. Tell him his family at Etowah Cliffs is fine. I must go. I promised to come early so Lucy and I will have time alone before we dine. Her brother, General Moxley Sorrel, is joining us for dinner. I'll be back by late afternoon and we'll talk again."

As she hurried from the room into the front hall, she could hear her grandmother talking to herself, her voice still filled with despair at what she'd done: "Oh, dear, oh, dear! My poor, poor, blessed Mary Cowper . . ."

The old mantel clock in the Mackay parlor downstairs had just struck eleven times when Mary Cowper gave up trying to control her over-powering need to write to Natalie. Shivering in the cold February night, she pulled on the cashmere dressing gown Mr. Low had bought for her in London and crept close to the still smoldering fire in the grate. Quietly, so as not to wake anyone, she added small pieces of wood and waited for the flames to spring up in the shadowy room lit by only one candle.

Outside, a steady rain fell on the house's tin roof and Mary Cowper remembered other nights spent at Grandmother Mackay's when such a rain would have soothed her quickly to sleep. She loved rain, but as with so much else in her life now, it was troubling. Only her three children gave her joy.

The visit today with Lucinda had left her afraid and utterly defenseless. "I'm trying hard, Mary Cowper," Lucinda had said, "to reconcile myself to the fact that I may never see Stuart again. He's so ill they've discharged him from the Army. He writes hopeful notes when he's able, but my heart tells me Stuart is—dying. That he'll never be well enough to come home to the children and me again. I felt you had a right to know."

Dry-eyed, Mary Cowper sat holding the pen which she had dipped and redipped in the old crystal inkwell. Writing to Natalie seemed her one hope now, because of all people on earth, only Natalie had never believed she had been contented as Mrs. Andrew Low of Lafayette Square. She had even convinced herself much of the time that she felt settled, at peace. How had Natalie stayed so sure she was not?

Her fingers trembling, blue with cold, she began to write words that belonged to a long-ago time, to the day she and Natalie had sat side by side on Termination Rock at Etowah Cliffs when Mary Cowper was home from school in Macon. Of everyone in her girlhood world that day, Natalie had seemed her closest friend, the one person to whom she could confide her love for Stuart Elliott.

Certainly, Natalie is the one person anywhere tonight. I may not send the letter, she thought, but even I can't carry this new agony around for the rest of my life without telling someone!

"My poor husband, Mr. Low, is surely suffering at this minute, up North in prison, and I've done my very best to be a good wife to him," she wrote. "In fact, Natalie, you are the first to know that, as a result of our last night together, in July or August of this year I will give him another child. With all my heart I intend to live my life to please Mr. Low, but I need you tonight, Natalie, if only by way of this pen scratch. I will be coming back to my children in a fortnight, so that Mama can visit Grandmother here, and I want to assure you that when I am back up there we won't have to mention this letter—ever. Somehow I will get past what is devastating me tonight. I will go on as before, but if you could find it possible to be friends with me again, I feel going on will not be quite so hard. I have kept so much inside me for so long, but I cannot keep this new tragedy. Lucinda told me today that Stuart is very ill in a Marietta hospital. She believes he is dying . . ."

Her hand trembled so, the letter looked as though an old woman had written it. Why not just stop? Tear up what you've written and go back to bed! Natalie knows that you still love him anyway. What possible good can it do to tell her on paper?

Abruptly, she got up from the writing desk and stood staring down at the half-finished letter.

"Am I losing my mind?" she whispered into the empty room. "Isn't eight years long enough to find out that I *can* trust myself to—live without Stuart? Why do I have to tell Natalie? To give her the chance to remind me that she warned me this would happen?"

Back at the small desk, pen in hand, she wrote: "I feel quite crazy for having told you and I am going to stop this minute, but not before I have begged you to help me! Please don't write to me here, and whatever you do, *say nothing about the child I'm expecting.* Everyone has more than enough to worry about. Just help me! When I return, if you can find a way to be your old self with me, I feel I can then manage to go on . . ."

*A*t *the end* of March, just before she was to return to Etowah Cliffs from her own visit to Savannah, Eliza Anne went to see the Brownings.

"That little grandson of yours is the living picture of Mary's brother, Ben!" she told Mark and Caroline. "I knew he was an Indian-looking baby, but at only two, he is already the image of Ben. I'm so, so sorry."

"Why are you sorry, Eliza Anne?" Caroline asked evenly.

"I think you know what she means, darling," Mark said. "Actually, Caroline has handled the boy's appearance better than I. I'm ashamed, but it's true."

"All of that seems irrelevant now," Caroline said. "Who can possibly know what Savannah people will be like if this war ever comes to an end?"

"Even war won't change Savannah society," Eliza Anne said. "But you're right, Caroline, I'm sure. The child's dark Indian hair and skin *are* irrelevant. At least, my darling mother has done her best to convince me." Quick tears stood in Eliza Anne's eyes. "Oh, Mark, didn't you think Mama looked worse this morning?"

"Excuse me, Eliza Anne," Caroline said firmly, "but Mark's already beside himself over your mother. *And* Jonathan trapped out there at Fort

Pulaski. Please don't make things worse. Do you realize we haven't seen Jonathan in weeks? I don't know how those boys stand that ghastly waiting, waiting to be attacked!"

"They stand it by working from morning till night," Mark said, his face grim. "Your General Lee left them with an impossible amount of slavish work to get done before the attack comes, Eliza Anne."

"Robert *is their* General Lee, Mark," she said in a curt voice. "Whatever he ordered done is for their protection. Has another letter gotten through from Jonathan?"

"No." Mark's voice was tight and flat. "Not a word. The last we heard was two weeks ago. Every man in the garrison works from early morning until nightfall at the hardest kind of physical labor. Officers included. No one excused except the sick and the guard. Some bring in timber, some dig ditches, others build runways for wheelbarrows to haul dirt to the traverses, still others are bricking up embrasures in the hope of keeping shells out of their ordnance room and magazines. Thank God, W.H. and his regiment managed to sink an out-of-commission Confederate ship in the river just above Pulaski to block the channel."

Eliza Anne smiled. "If I didn't know better, I'd assume you were on our side, Mark! I meant that in the best possible way. Believe me, with both W.H. and Henry en route to Virginia, I *know* how you worry about Jonathan." She bit her lip. "At least Jonathan's safe behind the thick walls of Fort Pulaski."

"Oh, Eliza Anne, just give thanks that you'll get away from Savannah early tomorrow," Caroline said. "Is Miss Eliza still considering going back with you?"

"You dare not let her make that long train ride!" Mark spoke sharply.

"I agree, and I don't know what she's considering or if she's even decided. My sisters have worked for three days helping the servants pack up her treasures. At least, I'll be taking most of them with me. I'd give anything if I thought she *could* stand the trip."

"But Savannah is her city—her home," Caroline said. "Miss Eliza loves visiting up there, she longs to see the Low children, but she also needs to be here in her own home."

"I know she wants—to die here," Eliza Anne said.

"Don't say that!" Mark got up and began to pace the floor. "I won't listen to any more talk of Miss Eliza dying!"

"Mark, she isn't as weak as I thought she'd be," Eliza Anne said uncertainly. "I fully expect to see her again. Hasn't she gone to church with me all three Sundays I've been here? I marvel at her! She seems to stay in constant, unbroken touch with God—day in and day out. We read and reread the Scriptures to her, the Antiquary, every stanza of all the hymns she loves. It's—it's as though she's just now truly getting to know God. I don't quite know what I mean by that, but—"

"I do," Mark said, standing with his back to the gently whispering fire. "She and I used to talk and talk politics, what's going on in the country. She spoke often of God, too, but now, what seems to please her most is when I read a hymn to her from the Lyra Germanica or a Psalm. I read Psalm 103 not long ago and she repeated every word right along with me." Tears standing in his eyes, Mark went on as though to help himself. "When she said, 'Bless the Lord, O my soul: and all that is within me . . .' I did bless Him! For that minute, all that is within me—blessed His holy name. Right then, I wasn't a bit afraid." He swiped at both cheeks. "I confess my burst of courage didn't last. I'm afraid again now—for her, for Savannah, for us all."

Eliza Anne stood. "I must go. I need every possible moment with Mama. I need to hear her remind me again to give 'thanks to God which giveth us the victory . . .'"

As Mark took her to the door, she smiled up at him. "I'm not at all sure, Mark, how you and I both can be given victory in this hideous war. But then, I'm sure Mama means far more than either of us knows about."

Standing beside Colonel Olmstead on a parapet that gave view through binoculars to Tybee Island, where enemy forces were dug in, Jonathan recalled another afternoon late last year when he and Charles had watched their own men successfully set fire to the old Tybee light and the nearby King house because both structures offered the Yankees a point of observation and a shelter from any shells that might be fired from Pulaski. Since then they had seen little or no sign of the enemy. Now, early in April, they could actually see movement. They had heard sounds of building and other work during the night hours, but this was broad daylight and both stared in horror and a kind of anger as three men in blue uniforms came boldly down to Kings Point and climbed up onto the ruins of the burned house.

"Colonel, look," Jonathan gasped. "Those three Yanks are thumbing their noses at us—noses and worse! They're making indecent gestures toward our fort! Right in plain sight."

"I know," the colonel said, his quiet voice grim. "I know, Lieutenant Browning, and I need them to stay right where they are. I've been wanting to test the elevation of our 32-pounders. The shot won't carry that far, but I can try it."

"You mean you're going to shoot at them?"

Running to the nearest gun emplacement, Olmstead gave the order to train a 32-pounder in the direction of the three men, then shouted, "Fire!"

"Colonel," Jonathan gasped as the smoke and dust began to clear over on Tybee. "Colonel Olmstead, did you mean to blow that man in the middle to pieces?"

Back beside Jonathan again, Olmstead was rubbing the bald part of his head in dismay. "No! I hadn't the slightest thought to do any more than scare them—test the elevation! I've just—killed a man!"

Field glasses tight against their eyes, both men watched as the two remaining Yankees crawled on hands and knees over to the body of the man who had been standing between them. Then the two ran as fast as their legs allowed back over a sand dune and out of sight.

Neither Jonathan nor Olmstead spoke. Finally, his voice flat, Olmstead said, "Our cannon couldn't hit that man again from this distance in a hundred years!"

Heart pounding, Jonathan could only stand there, field glasses at his side. "I know," Jonathan said. "General Lee said he was positive *they* couldn't penetrate our walls from over there."

Staring dazedly out over the water, Olmstead said, "Don't say anything more—it doesn't help . . ."

For a few endless days, Jonathan went on with the work at hand, trying hard to encourage himself, to encourage serious, conscientious Colonel Olmstead and the three hundred or so others trapped along with him at Fort Pulaski.

One April morning he and Olmstead even pitched in with two other officers and some enlisted men in the breakfast cleanup.

"Who's ever going to believe the pickle we're all in now?" Jonathan asked. "Who'd ever think the officer in command of this fort would be washing tin plates?"

"If old Commodore Tatnall and his Mosquito Fleet hadn't engaged the Yanks at Venus Point so our supply barge could sneak through, we wouldn't have no grub to dirty up these plates," a blue-eyed Irish private laughed as he scraped up a pile of scraps for the gulls. "If you boys would hurry up some, I'll favor ya with a rendition of 'The Cruikskeen Lawn' while we all wait to get blown to bits."

Almost everyone was trying to stay cheerful, to make jokes, for which Jonathan thanked God. Daily, though, he grew more and more haunted by thoughts of Mary's pleading, sad eyes, her masklike face turning again and again to him for some explanation that she might understand. Mary did *not* understand why he was here in such danger. To her there was no reason for his voluntary, useless rupture of their life together. Mary's Cherokee blood deprived her of even the solace of being on one side or the other in the war. He tossed through his nights in torment for the feel of her skin against his, for her yielding, reaching beauty—the only part of her she wasn't withholding. It had been over two months since their last touch, his last sight of her dear, puzzled face. During the black, waiting hours of last night, the image of Little Ben had haunted him as much as had Mary. Long past the moment of resentment that his only son looked like a full-blood Cherokee, an aura of noble beauty had begun to surround the boy now. He felt drawn to it. The haunting went on by daylight, even in the noise and hysterical laughter and joking and racket of the other waiting men. *Waiting for what?*

If he could believe there was even the slightest chance that his now thick packet of letters to Mary might be slipped through the Yankee blockade, he would fare far better than he was faring now. He kept writing, though, during any moment he could snatch alone, but daily his hope dwindled. A barge of Tatnall's bearing food did slip through occasionally to Pulaski. Mail from the garrison could, one day, he supposed, be delivered, but no one really hoped any longer. All their letters were written more to soothe themselves than their loved ones.

Early on the morning of April 10, 1862, Olmstead sent for Jonathan. The colonel stood behind his rough hewn desk, his sensitive, scholarly face solemn.

"Thank you for coming so quickly, Browning," he said, his thin lips barely visible beneath a now shaggy, full black beard. "A sentinel on the rampart just reported to me that a boat from Tybee is approaching our South Wharf. I've sent Captain Sims down to meet the Union officer bearing the white flag. He should be here momentarily with a formal document from the enemy. I—I wanted you with me when it comes."

Jonathan tried hard to return the brave smile Olmstead managed. "I'm here, sir," he said. "We all are."

"I'm sure it's a demand to avoid the effusion of blood that will surely follow their attack. I—I will, of course, refuse, to my dying moment, to surrender Fort Pulaski."

"I'm with you, Colonel," Jonathan said. "I just hope they give us enough time."

"I've ordered assembly beat. The men are already heading for their guns, ammunition is being served, the magazine squads are positioning themselves."

"I'm sure the surgeon and his helpers are making ready," Jonathan said in a tight voice.

"They are. I'm also sure we won't be given much time, but"—he held out his hand to Jonathan—"our Cause is worth dying for. I pray few will die, but we'll all—do our best."

"I intend to count on General Lee's assurance, sir, that from that distance, their shells *cannot* get through our walls."

Jonathan knew Olmstead's second attempt at a smile meant that he, too, was remembering that a Confederate shell from a 32-pounder blew a Yankee to pieces from that same distance.

Reading his thoughts, Olmstead said, "That was a freak, Lieutenant Browning."

"Yes, sir," Jonathan replied. "Yes, sir, I know."

They could see Captain Sims hurrying now toward headquarters, a document in his hand. "I pray, Browning, that we will be able to keep our minds right here—and not on our loved ones back in the city. The whole town will hear every round that's fired."

On that same bright, soft April morning, Mark left Caroline asleep, drank only a little weak coffee, and left by half past seven for his office.

Doing his best to step right along on his rheumatic legs, always stiff in the morning, he turned onto Abercorn and headed for the Bay, his thoughts, as usual these anxious days, on Jonathan. At least Natalie is safe in the upcountry. And thinking of Natalie sent his mind back to the long-ago day when he had run to the Reverend White's school to find his young son the moment news came that the *Pulaski* had blown up at sea; the *Pulaski,* that luxurious steamer on which sixteen-year-old Natalie was voyaging north with William Mackay's little family. He had run for Jonathan that day—in frantic need of the boy's strength even though his son was then only twelve. Age had never seemed relevant with Jonathan. Both Mark and Caroline had found leaning on the boy as natural as breathing. Caroline still did so; she and Jonathan were as close now as mother and son could be in their shared loyalty to the Confederacy. As close to Jonathan as Mark longed to be. While Caroline's cough last night kept him awake hour after hour, he had made what he now knew in the light of day would be his very last effort to switch his own allegiance from the Union which he had revered through his seventy years of life. If he could do that, he'd thought, he might again feel close to Jonathan. He could not. In the mild spring air, he shuddered. War could be only destructive! Nothing short of war could have separated him from Jonathan—in any way.

He could feel his heavy steps lag as he came in sight of Commerce Row. What difference did it make where he was? There was little to do in his own once prosperous office but endure the loneliness.

For the first time in the past nervous weeks, he and Caroline had made love last night. Her uninterrupted openness to him in all ways was his only comfort. His only comfort aside from the blessed fact that, frail as she was, Miss Eliza was still in her house and would, later today, be waiting for him. He should, because of the poignant oneness with Caroline last night, feel decidedly better than he felt, but all he could think of as he unlocked the double front door at Browning and Son was his cheerful, dependable son—trapped by another Pulaski.

Limping along through the shadowy hall of his countinghouse toward his private office, he was pained by the irony of the two Pulaskis. The ship and the fort named for the brave Polish soldier who had done so much in the American Revolution to make possible the Union that Mark still loved . . .

Coat, hat, and cane were hung on the rack inside his office. He unlatched and opened the casement window where he'd stood for years to look out over River Street at Savannah's waterfront. The Union blockade had all but emptied it, all but silenced the once noisy din of it. Blockade runners did get through, but mostly with high-profit, low-volume cargoes. Only small amounts of baled cotton stood below on his dock. Caroline's cotton from Knightsford and that from one or two other Savannah River plantations to the north had slipped through. He must order hands from Knightsford to move Caroline's bales into his nearly empty warehouse below. For days, it hadn't seemed to matter much one way or the other.

Only Jonathan mattered. And Jonathan was lost to him. So much time had passed since he'd even seen the boy, their once strong, steady bond seemed frayed—ready to snap. How, he asked himself for the hundredth time, could Jonathan allow his abrupt embrace of the South's Cause to torture little Mary, who loved him more than she loved her own life?

He and Caroline saw less of Mary at home now. He'd lost track of the last time she came down to breakfast with them. Hour after hour, she sat in the room once shared with Jonathan, and watched Little Ben at play. He could stack wooden blocks, and one of these days, Mark was sure, the chubby brown fingers would find the trick to shooting a marble—even at a little past two years. Mark was trying his best to teach him.

He turned away from the open window to listen more intently to what sounded like the double front doors opening. Yes. Unmistakably, they just closed softly. Who would be here at this hour of the morning? Tom, his one remaining clerk, wasn't due until eight-thirty. He shrugged, hearing nothing more. Maybe Tom had some early menial task planned. The young clerk, too crippled for acceptance in the Confederate Army, had taken to cleaning up since there was so little billing these days.

Staring again out the open window, Mark took a deep breath of clean spring air. A man had to keep breathing, try to keep on the move. He lifted both arms high above his head to ease their stiffness. Once, twice. Then another deep breath.

He just might go early to Miss Eliza's today. He could then take Little Ben out for a walk. The child seemed fascinated and would happily have stood for hours, he supposed, watching green Southern soldiers perform their awkward, uneven drills in Forsyth Park. But the sight depressed Mark too much. In his own troubled heart, he had no room for the pity he found welling up there every time he recognized a new young, eager face among the recruits. According to the papers that got through from the North, and in some parts of the South, the new military conscription was not being received as eagerly as these young Georgians seemed to embrace it. It just didn't suit Americans, no matter where they lived, to be forced into anything, even if normally they might have been willing. Once the beardless boys reached training in Savannah, though, they appeared bitten by the desire to fight for what they called "the glory of war."

At dinner last night, Mary had asked a rare question—a question neither he nor Caroline could answer: "Why do they—kill? My people fought other tribes, but it did no good. Many of them had not learned that Jesus said people would only know we are Christians by the way we love each other. Doesn't–Jonathan love Yankee soldiers? They would surely love him if they got close enough to know him. Why do they kill without being close enough to talk first? I do *not* understand!"

That Mary did not understand Mark knew. In her thirties now, she still remembered well being driven from her home in the old Cherokee Nation, being thrown with her brother, Ben, into a stockade by the white fathers of some of the young men fighting on both sides of this war. In the silence that hung around his own dinner table following Mary's question, he felt cut off from her, too.

Unable to bear the solitude of his office for another minute, he got up, reached for his hat, coat, and cane, and headed down the empty hallway.

He was passing Jonathan's office, the door to which stood open, when he heard Mary's voice: "Papa Mark? Oh, Papa Mark!"

Staring in at her, sunlight streaming across her shoulders and light, curly hair as she sat forlornly at Jonathan's desk, he could only ask what on earth she was doing there alone.

"I could get no closer to Jonathan than his desk," she murmured. "His hands touch the arms of this chair. I touch them, too."

"Little Ben?" he asked hoarsely.

"Mama Caroline is with him." After a moment, she looked up at him, her face a tragic mask. "Papa Mark–Jonathan die soon now."

"*Mary, no!*" he cried. "In the name of God, don't say that!"

"Sh! Be still–and listen." She spoke on a choked sob. "You shout over –what I hear!"

The sound of an explosion–loud, pervasive–echoed across the city, followed by another and another. Eyes locked, both motionless, he and Mary looked at each other, exchanging terrors, exchanging the sure knowledge that at long last Fort Pulaski–with Jonathan behind its walls– was being attacked.

Then, without a word, Mary rushed past him and out of the building –home to Ben, he knew.

As fast as he could, Mark followed, not bothering to lock the big double doors. He had made his way along Abercorn as far as Bryan, where he meant to turn into Reynolds Square and head for his own house, when he recognized William's old carriage and in it Kate Mackay holding up the slumped form of Miss Eliza.

At the top of his voice, he called Kate's name and saw Magill begin to slow for him to catch up with the carriage.

"Mark," Kate cried as he limped up. "Was that ghastly noise what we think? Are they attacking Fort Pulaski?"

"I don't know," he gasped. "I'm afraid so. How is she? Did Miss Eliza faint?"

"No. It just startled her, she's—she's only resting. Oh, Mark, Mark . . ."

"Hush, Kate," he heard Miss Eliza say. "And do get in with us, Mark. They could be attacking Savannah! We'd all better get home."

"Mark will want to be in his own house, Mama," Kate said, eyes wide with fear.

"Of course," Miss Eliza said. "Of course, Mark. Hurry home to Caroline and Mary and Little Ben! Go, go . . ."

He stepped back. "All right, but get her home as quickly as you safely can, Magill," he called to the old Negro in the driver's seat. "Miss Eliza needs to be inside her own house—whatever happens." Then, to Kate, he said, "I'll see to my family and be at your place as soon as I can."

Breathing rapidly and hard outside his own front door, he stood fumbling in all pockets for the key he evidently forgot again this morning. His legs ached unmercifully and he looked longingly at the top step, desperate to sit down. But at that moment the door opened, and Caroline, without a word, slipped her arm in his and led him inside.

Twilight was beginning to fall over the city, in which Mark felt a stranger to everything but the steady, gnawing fear which had not eased once all day because the firing had not eased. He opened his front door and stepped outside to listen.

Caroline, who was standing right behind him in the entrance hall, touched his shoulder.

"I—I think the bombardment has slackened some at last," he breathed. "I'd better have Jupiter drive me to Miss Eliza's house."

"Jupiter could go himself and find out about her. It would be much easier to write out a Free Negro pass for him in case the police stop him in the streets than to go yourself, dear."

"You know I have to see her for myself, Caroline. I can't wait any longer."

"Give all the Mackays my love, then. And Mary's."

"Where is Mary?"

"Upstairs with Ben, of course. I offered to stay with him, thinking maybe it might do her good to go with you to the Mackays'. She wouldn't hear of it. Shall I go, Mark?"

His body sagged against the iron railing. "Caroline, no, no! Stay here and be safe. After today—if Mary's right—we may only have each other left."

"I won't hear that again. Jonathan is safe, Mark. He's safe!"

"I promise not to stay long. Just long enough to be sure Miss Eliza's —all right."

The huge red ball of the sun was out of sight when Colonel Olmstead and his adjutant, Hopkins, risked inspecting the damage they feared had been done to the walls of the fort that General Robert E. Lee believed impenetrable. Olmstead more than feared. From the first sign that the Federal forces were firing *rifled* cannons at them, he had known Lee was wrong. One after another, Confederate guns had been blown from their mountings. In the first hour of firing, he had seen the bricks under one of the embrasures bulge inward from only one strike. He had been near one of his own 32-pounders when a shell came all the way through the embrasure and burst under the gun, letting it fall on the chassis like a heavy log. He had seen an especially hardworking private named Shaw, who was handling the sponge staff at the time, literally blown to pieces— and he was inside the supposedly impregnable wall.

Slogging through the debris of battle outside, he and Hopkins grew more and more overwhelmed at what they saw. The outer wall of the casemate at the Southeast Angle was entirely shot away, the interior exposed to the falling darkness. As they stood in silence staring at one of their eight-inch Columbiads with its muzzle shot off, they marveled that it still hung trembling above the moat.

The Yankee firing from Tybee had grown sporadic now. One blast every five minutes or so. "Just often enough to be sure we don't sleep tonight," Olmstead said to Adjutant Hopkins as they headed back to their quarters.

"Do you have any idea where Lieutenant Browning is, Colonel?" Hopkins asked.

"No, and I've been looking for him. I only pray he isn't under some of this rubble. We couldn't find him now with the dark coming on so fast."

"I keep thinking of our families in town," Hopkins said as they pushed open the half-splintered door of their sleeping quarters.

"So do I," Olmstead said heavily. "If—Jonathan Browning's still alive, so is he."

Mark came home just after night fell over the city, his anxious heart a little eased by the few minutes spent with Miss Eliza.

"I knew she would help you," Caroline said. "Did—she say anything that might—help me?"

Climbing wearily into bed, Mark repeated dully, " '. . . thanks be to God which giveth us the victory through our Lord Jesus Christ.' She never tires saying—that."

"Did that help you?"

He sighed. "I don't know, Caroline. I don't know. I only know Miss Eliza isn't talking about a victory in this terrible war. She seems to mean far, far more."

He felt Caroline's head slip onto his shoulder and he tightened his arm about her with what little strength he had left.

After a while, he asked, "Did Mary say it again before she went to bed? Did she tell you—again that our boy is going to die?"

He could sense her effort to sound hopeful as she said softly, "No, Mark. No, she didn't—say that again at all."

Long before sunrise the next morning, the roar of artillery and the crash of falling masonry began again and went on without interruption until late morning, when Colonel Olmstead stood to salute his friend Lieutenant Browning and then rushed to embrace him.

"Jonathan, Jonathan," Olmstead cried over the racket, "where have you been? I was worried sick!"

"I ended up, sir, as a surgeon's helper," Jonathan said. "Spent the night in his rickety shelter out where those rifled guns crashed through our Southeast Angle. I felt I could do more good there. As far as I could tell, Colonel, only one man was killed, but we lost count of the wounded."

Olmstead stepped back to give Jonathan a long, troubled look. "We have only three parapet guns still usable, Browning," he said. "And of these, only one bears upon the Yankee battery doing us the most harm. I don't like it. Adjutant Hopkins is doing an inspection of his own. Can you come with me to examine the extent of the breach from inside?"

Olmstead was walking a few steps ahead of Jonathan when a shell struck the cheek of an embrasure just behind them. When he whirled to check the damage, he saw Jonathan stumble wildly and fall in a barrage of flying bricks, powder, smoke, and mortar dust. "Browning," he cried. "My God, Browning!"

He knelt beside the crumpled form in the blasted gray uniform of the Confederacy and prayed, his hand on the torn and bleeding dark head. Then he felt movement under his hand and opened his eyes to see his friend's handsome, powder-blackened face.

"In the name of heaven, Lieutenant," Olmstead breathed, "can you— can you hear me? Do you know me, Browning?"

Too torn to smile, Jonathan's face twisted, but unmistakably imitating one Georgia cracker private's way of addressing the colonel, Jonathan whispered, "It's—the kunnel!"

And then Olmstead saw the bleeding head sag and knew his friend had fainted.

As best he could, for the remainder of the morning and into the early afternoon of the second day of unremitting attack, Olmstead continued to command the pitiful resistance, sending an aide every few minutes to report on Lieutenant Browning's condition. A fragment of brick had lodged in the right temple. Under battle conditions the surgeon had no way of removing it. Jonathan had not regained consciousness. Multiple wounds on his body had been cleaned and bandaged and he lay in his own seeping blood on a pallet spread on the rubble-strewn ground in the surgeon's quarters.

"The doc says he can't stop the bleeding, sir," the aide said a little before one o'clock that afternoon. "Lieutenant Browning needs a hospital bad. Our surgeon is ready to drop himself."

Olmstead thanked the aide and slumped at his desk. He was still there when, a few minutes later, a violent explosion sent bricks and mortar hurtling through the wall and into the room itself. Within minutes, the aide rushed back in to shout that a shell had blown up in the passageway to the Northwest Magazine, filling it with smoke and setting a roaring fire! From outside, the young colonel heard the ordnance men from the exploded magazine running in panic to the adjoining casemates.

When Adjutant Matt Hopkins answered Olmstead's summons, his

decision had been made. "We've reached the end," the colonel said. "We're isolated. There's no hope of help from the Confederate authorities anywhere. I cannot expose the garrison to more of this. Our main magazine can—blow up at any minute. Run up the white flag!"

SEVENTY-THREE

*O*n *the morning* of April 13, even though she had slept so little for two nights, Eliza Mackay was up and dressed and on her slow, uncertain way down the stairs a few minutes after seven, leaving Eliza Anne asleep.

"Oh, Mama," Sarah called from the downstairs hall, "wait! I'm coming up to help you."

"No! This is the day when I have to find strength I don't—have, daughter. Mark will be here soon. He'll bring a newspaper. He'll—need me. Let me prove to myself that I can make it on my own. Don't disturb your sister upstairs."

She could sip only a little coffee, the last they had, Kate said, but no one said anything else except that Sarah couldn't quite tell which was worse—the two-day bombardment at Pulaski or this blank, hollow silence with no one knowing anything about anyone out there at the fort, which the whole of Savannah had believed impregnable.

"Mark will be here," Eliza said again. "He'll have the newspaper. We —may know something then."

Settled, as much as anyone could feel settled on such a day, in her little rocker, she prayed for Mark. Jonathan *had* to be safe. Young Colonel Olmstead had surrendered Fort Pulaski yesterday, but that was about all anyone knew. What she needed desperately to find out now was the state of Mark's heart. How he had managed to endure the anxiety—the not knowing.

The clock struck nine times. Soon. Soon, he'll be here, just as soon as he can be sure the newspaper office has the paper ready. He'll bring it to read to me . . .

"You know I pray for Jonathan, too, Lord," she whispered into the sheltering old room. "And Caroline and little Mary—that child's so cut off these days, she can't even face a visit to me anymore."

Even my prayers are disjointed, she thought, as over and over she repeated Mark's name and Caroline's and Mary's and Jonathan's and Little Ben's . . .

"Read to me, dear boy," she said, only seconds after he shuffled into the parlor, his face pale and drawn. "Read what's there!"

"I—know most of what's there," he said brokenly.

"Read!"

" 'The fortification on which Savannahians have depended for protection through the years is now in enemy hands,' " he read in a monotone. "Miss Eliza"—he broke into his own reading—"I—I still can't take that in!"

"Even Robert Lee can be wrong, Mark."

"That isn't what I mean," he said. "What I can't—grasp is calling the United States the—enemy!"

"I know, I know."

"Lee wasn't altogether wrong. The walls of Fort Pulaski were thick enough to withstand any kind of shells we had! The Federal forces used a kind of almost untried rifle cannon against those poor boys out there . . ."

"Oh, Mark!"

"I guess no one in town really knows much yet, but it says here that according to the terms of surrender agreed upon, the 'Yankees promise to protect the belongings of the garrison and the sick and wounded are to be sent at once to Savannah hospitals or to their homes.' "

"And you still came to see me! You'd better get back to your house. I prayed all night that Jonathan wasn't wounded, but they could be bringing him home—*today.* If the Federals promised, they'll care for the wounded."

"Or," he said grimly, "he could be—a prisoner of war. That means he'll be sent North without a chance to contact us in any way!"

"I don't suppose it says where prisoners of war might be sent?" she asked.

"No, but my guess would be Governors Island, New York."

"Go, Mark. Please go now, dear boy. You know I need you here with me, but Caroline needs you far more. Caroline and Mary. Did you see Mary this morning?"

He shook his head. "She doesn't come down for breakfast. I should have gone to her room." Tears stood in his deep-set gray eyes. "I–I couldn't do it. I'm ashamed of myself, but I couldn't do it." He stood to go. "Caroline is with Mary. Miss Eliza, Caroline is–so strong. I'm in awe of her today."

She reached for his hand and sat holding it. "What strength we all have–comes from God. But it helps Caroline reach for her own strength –believing as she does that Jonathan is risking his young life for a noble Cause. You don't have that comfort, dear boy."

Two days later, on the steamer *Oriental*, Colonel Charles Olmstead, a Federal prisoner of war bound for New York, sat praying hour after hour for his Florie and their children back in Savannah in the little house where they had been so happy. There had been no chance for any contact with them. No chance for any contact whatever with the city before he left. His prayers seemed trapped against the low ceiling of the primitive ship's quarters, but he kept trying to pray for Jonathan Browning's perplexed, grief-stricken wife, Mary, for his baby son, for his father and mother–for everyone who loved the cheerful young man.

Inevitably, he prayed for the strength *not* to hate every enlisted man and every officer in blue. The prayer choked him. For the first time in his twenty-five years he found it easier to hate than to respect. And the heavy burden was all his–he had surrendered the fort. He, Charles Olmstead, had signed the mutual agreement that every wounded Southern soldier would be taken immediately from the shattered fort to Savannah–to their homes or to hospitals. The agreement had been broken already, thanks to Union general David Hunter, uncle to Confederate lieutenant Willie Gordon's wife, Nellie Kinzie Gordon of Savannah. The wounded were left, poorly tended, at Pulaski. For Olmstead, whose loyalty to Savannah was unbreachable, it was doubly hard not to hate General Hunter, who could show such brutality to wounded family friends. Especially friends as close as the Gordons and the Mackays and the Brownings.

Olmstead had been told a whole day before he and the other prisoners were herded onto the *Oriental* that Lieutenant Jonathan Browning had, after forty-eight hours, been allowed to die on a pallet in the rubble, "for lack of medical attention."

SEVENTY-FOUR

"Mr. Goodman was kind to let you stop work on his house long enough to come home to me, Burke," Natalie said as she poured another cup of the foul-tasting liquid they called breakfast coffee. "And I'm kind, too, I think, for letting Miss Lorah help Mary Cowper this morning. Mary Cowper's been a grand lady for so long, she's helpless with Miss Lib not home yet. I thought she'd be back by now. Do you think I'm really growing up? I'm certainly trying."

Burke sipped the drink and made a face. "I don't think this stuff is foul-tasting. It just tastes like nothing," he said. Then, replacing the cup in its saucer, he reached for her hand across the table. "You're growing up, I suppose," he said tenderly, "but whatever it's called, I like it. I—love you more than I've ever loved you, Natalie. To prove it, I'll help you wash our dishes after a while."

Ignoring his offer, she asked, "Why did Uncle W.H. try all the way from wherever he is in Virginia to forbid Miss Lib's going to Savannah? He knows her mother's not well. Is it so dangerous there now, really?"

"With the Yankees occupying Pulaski, I wouldn't doubt that the city itself could be attacked any day."

"Are Mama and Papa in real danger? Am I being unspeakably selfish that I haven't gone down, too? If I just didn't love you so much, I'm sure I might be a—more attentive daughter, but I do love you and you have to be at Mr. Goodman's place for such long periods now, I can't go to Savannah, Burke!" She clung to his hand. "Am I selfish? I don't feel this mixed up very often anymore—please help me!"

He got up from the table and went to take her in his arms.

"You'd better not hold me," she said, reaching for him. "I'll cry."

"Cry, Natalie. You loved Jonathan! Why don't you allow yourself to grieve for him?"

"Because too much else is wrong." She was crying now, in spite of her resolve. "I'm trying to be a—lifter, Burke. Like you. How can I be a lifter—if I'm grieving? There's just so much wrong for everyone else we know. What good would it do if I sat around weeping my heart out? Don't talk about Jonathan!"

He held her for a time, then said gently, "I wish you had some idea how much I've come to depend on you, darling."

"That isn't a very safe thing to do."

"Yes, it is. And I'm not the only one. I can tell Mary Cowper does, too. I'm really glad for that. She needs you and you need her. You've both needed each other all the years she's been married. This can be a lonely old world without close friends. I don't know what I'd have done without Robert Goodman."

"I hate it when you're gone working on his house, but I know you need him as a friend. Especially because he agrees with you on this messy war. I also know we need the money."

"We do, and I'm afraid Robert's had to borrow what he pays me, but we do need it. He's lined up another fair-sized job for me building a small shirt factory in Roswell for later. Roswell's even farther away than Marietta."

"I know," she said as Burke went back to his own place at the table. "I hate that, too, but at least I can be sure you're not going to be killed building a shirt factory. I'm so blessed that you're too old to fight."

"Did Callie hear from Perry while I was gone?"

"No, and things could be bad for him in Mississippi, but Callie's so brave and cheerful, she makes me want all the more to be a lifter." Tears trickled down her cheeks again. "Burke, why do you suppose I waited so long to begin to care about other people? To care about the trouble I caused even the people I love? Do—do you think I—worried Jonathan a lot?"

"Jonathan loved you exactly as you are. He understood you."

"How do you think Mama and Papa face getting up in that empty house now? How does Mary bear the thought of never seeing him again?

I couldn't! And how has Mary Cowper endured all these years without seeing Stuart? Compared to those two, Burke, I've almost never had anything to complain about and I spent my life complaining."

"But you heard what Miss Lorah said yesterday. You've stopped now and that's what matters."

"Burke, how could you not ask a single question when I said a minute ago that I didn't see how Mary Cowper lived without seeing Stuart? You don't know anything she and I've been talking about."

"I figured you'd tell me if you wanted to."

"I suppose that's called patience."

"Maybe."

"Miss Lorah says impatience is lack of love. I don't believe that, because I've been impatient sometimes with you."

"Do you need to tell me about Mary Cowper, honey? Is that why you brought it up again?"

"Yes! I've never kept a secret from you, not ever, till she wrote a surprising letter to me from Savannah about Stuart being terribly sick, *and* that she's going to have another baby. I kept that letter from you because I felt Mary Cowper deserved that I be honorable with her–at long last."

He grinned. "You are honorable and–adorable. Did she actually tell you she's loved Stuart Elliott all this time?"

"Not in that letter, but she's told me since she came back. Of course, I knew anyway and I still don't understand how she can go right on as she is now, but she's pigheaded. As determined as ever to be a good wife to Mr. Low if he ever gets out of prison."

"How sick is Stuart?"

"His wife says–dying. In a makeshift hospital in Marietta. With consumption–like Jack Mackay." She swiped at her eyes. "Burke, I had no choice but to be friends with Mary Cowper again after she told me that. Now that–Jonathan is gone, I understand even more about death than I did–when we lost Little Burke. I'm not sure I can–ever face my parents' grief! That *is* selfish, isn't it?"

"Not selfish, human. Is Elliott's wife in Marietta with him?"

"No. She can't go. She has a sick father and two small children. The hideous war again! Stuart would be at home with Lucinda if he hadn't decided the way Jonathan did that he could single-handedly save the Confederacy–whatever that means. Everything is because of the war and you and I can't do a thing about it!"

"When is Mary Cowper's new baby due?" Burke asked after a silence.

"In early June, I think. That might be the worst time of all. Even Mr. Low won't be here with her in all that agony. It's going to be so hard for Mary C., Burke, knowing that the one man she's ever loved is—dying."

"Would it help you, darling, to go down to Savannah for a visit? I know it won't be easy, but it might help. I may as well tell you that after next month when I finish Goodman's place, I'll be away in Roswell for most of the summer."

She jumped up as though he'd struck her. "We've never been apart that long—not ever!"

"I know, but if seeing your parents now might help some, you can surely go while I'm finishing up Goodman's place."

"And be away from you for an even longer time? At least you can come home some now from Marietta. When Miss Lib is back and you're in Roswell, I'll go. Not until."

"Will you take Callie along?"

"If she's sure Perry can't get leave to come back while we're down there, of course. Not unless, though." She sank back onto her chair. "I guess I have changed a lot, but not that much. I won't allow one single thing to keep Callie from seeing Perry at the first possible moment. I definitely don't believe in separating two people who love each other!"

<hr />

With Burke gone again the following week, Natalie and Mary Cowper went with the Stileses' driver to what had once been called Cass Station to meet Miss Lib, due back from Savannah. It would still be Cassville and Cass Station were it not for the war, she thought, riding along in near silence beside Mary Cowper. Cassville was now called Manassas because Francis Bartow, for whom the whole county had been renamed, had been killed at the battle of Manassas. She thought the whole thing was dumb! What difference did it make that Lewis Cass was a Northerner? Everything is changed for the worse, she thought, but knowing how deep Mary Cowper's Rebel feelings went, she said nothing that might mar their new, close companionship. Now that Natalie knew her friend still loved Stuart, she was more certain than ever that the only bond Mary Cowper and old Andrew Low shared beyond the children was their fiery Confederate sympathies.

Miss Lib looked and acted tired as the three climbed into the cab of Burke's carriage for the trip back to Etowah Cliffs. Natalie's heart went out to her in spite of the resentment she still felt because Miss Lib had engineered the marriage to Low. She understood, though, how ill Miss Eliza was and how desperately Miss Lib missed W.H. and both her sons, so she vowed, if possible, not to bring up the war or Jonathan's death. These days, with Miss Lib, even a tiny spark could cause a conflagration.

"Did your mother cry when you left, Miss Lib?" she asked.

"She did not. She smiled and told me she'd see me again the next time I could come to visit her. She went to church with me every Sunday except the last one. It's—it's as though she's found a new source of strength for your father's sake, Natalie."

"I'm almost afraid to ask about Mama and Papa."

"Your mother is absolutely amazing. She can't speak of Jonathan, of course, with dry eyes. She may not be able to do that for a long time, but it's Mark who distresses me. And for reasons that go far beyond his stubborn attitude toward our war for liberty from Northern tyranny. But I don't intend to get into that, Natalie, so don't worry. I'm aware that you're almost as odd as—that hated General Hunter's niece, Nellie Gordon. She could at least show some shame over her uncle's deeds. It was her uncle, the brutal general, you know, who let Jonathan die!"

"He *let my brother die?*"

"For want of proper medical care!" Miss Lib said bitterly. "General Hunter promised immediate medical attention for the Confederate wounded. There was none. How your broken father holds so stubbornly to his Union cause in the face of the unnecessary death of his son, I don't know."

"You knew about that, didn't you, Mary Cowper?" Natalie asked.

"Yes, Mama wrote to me. I—I thought it best for your parents to tell you. When they didn't say a word about it in their letters, I kept still."

Natalie felt her eyes burn with tears, but she vowed not to give Miss Lib the satisfaction of an outburst against him—if it was true that some Yankee general had been at fault. She was *going* to control herself. It wasn't Mama's fault or Papa's that they hadn't told her, she thought. It was the ghastly war! She'd give anything to know if her parents had been able to talk to each other about telling her. Papa did love the Union. Her mother hated it now. Had they quarreled over that in the midst of their terrible grief?

"I'm truly sorry, Natalie," Miss Lib was saying. "I am tired, exhausted. I shouldn't have said a thing about General Hunter. Your mother told me you didn't know. I blabbed when I should have been quiet. Your poor father just sits there when General Hunter's name comes up and stares into space. I—I do think I understand how Mark feels. He's an alien now in Savannah. He's uncomfortable with—everyone, it seems, but Mama."

A chill of plain old fear went through Natalie as she tried to imagine what might happen to her father should Miss Eliza Mackay die. Finally, in an uncharacteristically weak voice, she asked, "Does Papa feel—estranged from my mother, Miss Lib?"

"In most ways, no, but there is—the war. Dear God, there is the war—everywhere! That same hated General Hunter is now rumored to be about to free all the slaves in his military command—in South Carolina, Georgia, and Florida! What manner of trouble will that cause? How will your distraught father explain a *Union* general plunging ahead of his own revered President Lincoln?"

"I hadn't heard about that, Mama," Mary Cowper said, showing a flash of her own Rebel spirit for the first time. "Could it be only a rumor?"

"Who knows, Mary Cowper?" Miss Lib moaned. "Everything is so wrong everywhere because the war is everywhere!" Her voice breaking, she cried out, "Do you have any idea what I'd give just to see your father for a few minutes? Just to look at Henry—or Bobby? We don't even know exactly where they are! Bobby's somewhere in Florida, safer by far than either your father or brother up in Virginia, but—"

Natalie couldn't remember ever having seen Miss Lib break into sobs before, but she did now. Uncontrollable, hard, tearing sobs that caused Mary Cowper to sit ramrod straight in spite of her already distended stomach from the baby she carried, her face an expressionless mask.

"We—we get through these times, Mama," Mary Cowper said finally. "Would it help to try to tell Natalie and me about some of our other friends in Savannah? How is poor Mrs. Charles Olmstead faring with her husband in prison on Governors Island? Did you see Florie?"

"Yes, I saw her," Miss Lib said, regaining some control. "She's had two letters from Colonel Olmstead. He's well, I guess, but I'm sure faring no better than poor Mr. Low."

"I heard from Mr. Low yesterday," Mary Cowper announced, as though she merely mentioned that a good shower fell. "He's no longer in prison, but still in custody. Able now, though, to be held in the home of a New York friend. He's happy about the baby. Mr. Low was kind enough to send Colonel Olmstead and his fellow Fort Pulaski prisoners a fifteen-hundred-dollar draft for their personal needs."

The news of Andrew Low seemed to calm, even to brighten Miss Lib's mood some, Natalie thought. She resented it, although she did feel relieved that Low was no longer in a tiny prison cell with seven other men. "Miss Lib, I just have to know about Jonathan's Mary. Is she—is she able to sleep at all now? Will she—ever smile again, do you think?"

"I'm not sure about any of that, Natalie. I'm never sure about Mary, though. I rather marvel at the way she behaves with poor Mark. It's as though she's found at least—something to do with her own grief."

"What does she do, Mama?" Mary Cowper wanted to know. "How does Mary behave with Natalie's father?"

"She's quite attentive to him. Sees to his every need. The one time I was there for dinner, she kept reminding him that it wasn't as though they didn't know Jonathan—would die."

"*What?*" Natalie demanded.

"Oh, it seems that before Pulaski fell, Mary kept insisting that he was going to die, that Jonathan would never come home again. Caroline vows Mary was certain about it, as though she had battled her own will to accept the inevitable. It's strange. Eerie, in fact. Mary is bereft, of course. Her world was—Jonathan, but she is focused almost entirely now on Mark. Oh, I wonder how that man keeps from flying to pieces. I thought if I heard either Mary or my own mother say once more that we all had to take one day at a time, *I'd*—fly apart!"

For a time, they just sat there bumping along the rutted road, then Mary Cowper said, as though to herself, "That is the only way one gets through—bad times. One day at a time."

"Still there are moments," Miss Lib said, "when one is too deep in grief or anxiety to be told again and again, no matter how true."

"I don't think Miss Eliza could tell my father anything too often," Natalie said. "She's his—rock."

"Well, I'm not sure Mark needs Mary to keep telling him."

Tired of Miss Lib's talk and sure Mary Cowper was longing to know, Natalie asked bluntly, "Did you hear anything about poor Lucinda Sorrel Elliott, Miss Lib? I heard her husband is quite ill in a Marietta hospital. Did you by any chance see Lucinda?"

The look on Miss Lib's face was unreadable. "I never knew her well, Natalie. Of course, I knew her mother years ago. I do half remember hearing one of my sisters say Lucinda's husband is indeed in a hospital somewhere. He may be quite ill. I just don't recall the details."

That night, with Burke home again and beside her in their bed, Natalie asked, "Is the house where Mr. Goodman lives on Powder Springs Road very far from Marietta?"

"A little over two miles. Why?"

"Do you work from daylight to dark on his house repairs?"

"Not every day and I know what you're about to ask me to do. Of course I'll visit Stuart Elliott for Mary Cowper—and for you."

When she snuggled to him and began to cry softly, he pulled her still closer. "Are those tears of happiness because I'm such an accommodating husband, Mrs. Latimer?"

"I guess so," she sniffled. "But oh, Burke, even with this stupid war, you and I have—everything! When you get home the next time we'll be able to give Mary Cowper at least that little bit. A firsthand report of exactly how poor Stuart is."

SEVENTY-
FIVE

*A*t *a little after eight* on the morning of May 10,
Mark met a crew of slaves from Caroline's Knightsford plantation at his
wharf on the waterfront. Both Caroline and Miss Eliza had tried to
persuade him not to supervise the storing of the newly arrived Knightsford cotton in his warehouse, but it needed to be done. The women of
Savannah, even one so closed away as Miss Eliza, inevitably heard
rumors first and what had upset them so about this one, he knew, was far
from foolish. Since yesterday, word had been sweeping the city that
Union general David Hunter, who had signed the surrender of Fort
Pulaski, was now—without notification to President Lincoln—about to
issue his own proclamation, from his headquarters in Port Royal, that
would immediately free every slave in his military district—South Carolina, Georgia, and Florida!

Mark set aside the rumor and he did it for a reason. He was simply
unable to allow himself to believe the Confederate hate story still
circling the city that General Hunter had intended to break his agreement to give medical care to the Rebel wounded when Pulaski fell to the
Yankees. If he permitted himself to believe the worst of Hunter, it meant
the respected Union general had let Jonathan die! Mark believed only
that Jonathan had been killed in the war. He refused to blame Hunter,
not because of Union sympathies, but because he could bear no more

bitterness in his own heart. Hour after hour, he and Caroline had gone over and over the known facts surrounding how their son died. Even Caroline rejected such a cruel explanation as Hunter's intentional neglect.

"I already hate the Federals," she had said. "I dare not believe General Hunter broke an agreement that allowed Jonathan to die! If I did, Mark, my hatred would kill *me*."

Nellie Gordon, General Hunter's niece, liked to say that her uncle was far more an abolitionist than an Army general. Nellie Gordon herself baffled Mark. What she contended about her uncle baffled him still more, when he really thought about it. These days being heavy with grief, allowed little space for real thought, though, and so he suspended all judgment of Hunter's actions. The general was a respected Union officer, had even been chosen by Lincoln to accompany him from Illinois to Washington after the election back in 1860. The agreement to give medical aid had *not* been kept, but surely because Hunter's orders had somehow been misconstrued or disobeyed.

Standing at the open doors of his warehouse waiting for the Knightsford men to return with another load of cotton, it occurred to him that Nellie Gordon was, in all the confusion of the war, rather like Natalie. Mark liked Mrs. Gordon, knew she adored her husband, Confederate officer W. W. Gordon II, but in spite of her Northern abolitionist background, seemed as impervious to taking sides in the war as was his own daughter. As long as Nellie's husband was safe and her small children fed, she simply went about her business, caring not one whit what Savannahians thought of her. She had casually told Mark and Caroline that it wouldn't surprise her a bit to see Uncle David Hunter issue his own emancipation edict. The idea still seemed so preposterous to Mark, though, that he had not expected it to happen. What Caroline and Miss Eliza feared, of course, was for Mark's safety today, exposed as he was on the open wharf to what could turn to violence should Caroline's slaves learn of their freedom. He worried about no such thing. How could they possibly have found out rowing their way in a plantation boat downriver from Knightsford to Savannah? Anyway, no more than four Knightsford slaves were known agitators and only two of those had come down to work for him today.

An outright attack on the city itself plagued him far more than danger at the hands of the sweating Negroes doing his bidding now. Ever since the black day when Pulaski fell, one question had been on the lips of almost every man he'd met. Most business colleagues treated him with merely cool courtesy at best, but again and again he had heard them ask, "*Why*, with nothing but Fort Jackson and Fort McAllister and a handful of small batteries to protect us, doesn't General Hunter jump right in and take over Savannah?"

There seemed to be no answer. Leaning against the heavy frame of a warehouse door as he waited again for the crew of workers to load their backs with still more cotton bales, he wondered if there would ever be another real answer to anything.

Then from the wooden steps leading down to the wharf, he heard his clerk, Tom, almost frantically calling his name. "It's happened, Mr. Browning," Tom called. "It's happened, sir!"

"What's happened, Tom?"

Limping as fast as he could along the wharf toward Mark, Tom put a finger over his own lips and waited to reach him before he explained in a loud whisper: "Mr. Habersham just told me. I knew it would happen. I told you so! I knew if you was to come out here in the open this morning, those niggers would find out and they did! General Hunter freed 'em and they found out! They got a grapevine, you know. He freed the slaves in all three states yesterday!"

For a moment, Mark just stood there staring, first at Tom's terrified face, then at the open doorway that led into his warehouse, where six of the twelve slaves were now stacking cotton.

"We better get outa here, sir!" And with one quick glance at the men in the warehouse, Tom hurried as best he could to the nearest steps that led from the wharf up over the ballast rock wall to the safety of the Browning office. "Tom," Mark called after him. "Everything's quiet, Tom. Come on back and help me finish the job!"

He had shouted into the empty sunlight. Tom was out of sight up the steep steps. Heart thumping, Mark looked toward the straggling line of Negroes ambling back from the remaining bales on the wharf, toward the shadowy interior of the warehouse. Four men outside were just standing by the stacked bales, looking back at the man they thought of as their master. He wasn't. Because he could never bear the thought of owning another human being, Knightsford had never been put into his name. Caroline, who no longer openly resisted his anti-slavery beliefs but still thought it the only way to run a plantation, had inherited each man now staring back at Mark as well as those still inside his warehouse. To keep peace in his family, he had curbed making friends with most of Caroline's people, but he had certainly never feared them. For whatever reason, he feared them now.

A low mumble—men talking intently among themselves—from inside the warehouse caused him to look quickly again in that direction. Through the open front door eight strong black men were coming slowly toward him. Some stretched their arms, others rubbed their heads idly, one wore a smile which Mark could not have deciphered if his life had depended on it. He looked again at the group on the wharf. As with the gang making its way slowly from the warehouse, they, too, were acting like men whose day's work was finally over. They wiped their faces with bandannas, hitched up their baggy trousers, never taking their eyes off him.

I have to say something to them, he thought vacantly. I can't just stand here. I can't run away. "Have you been—set free, men?" he called as the two groups stood together now still facing him, their backs to the river. "Did Union general Hunter free you? I heard he was going to." When the men said not one word, Mark went on. "I'd be the most relieved man in Savannah if it turns out to be true, but I—I hope you make sure it is true. I don't see how an Army officer in command of three coastal states has the authority to do it. I'd think a thing like your freedom would have to come from the President of the United States."

Mark kept his eyes on them. They were still looking at him.

"I'm not at all sure just how you'll find out," he went on. "In case it's true, you certainly don't have to finish storing that cotton. You're welcome to take the plantation boat on back to Knightsford until—we know the facts. If it's true, I don't know what you'll do, do you?"

One of the group took his eyes off Mark long enough to glance at the Negro standing next to him. Slowly, they all exchanged looks, then a low voice—Mark couldn't tell whose—mumbled something he couldn't understand and, one slow step after another, the entire gang began to move in his direction. He had asked that twelve men come into town to do the work. Irrelevantly, he tried to count them now, but they were milling about among themselves wordlessly, always toward him, and he kept losing count.

"I'll get word to you at Knightsford as soon as all the facts are made known," he said, and a rising wind off the water blew his words back into his own face.

Two or three feet from where Mark stood, the men formed a single file and, one by one, they passed him on their way to the same steps up which Tom had just vanished. If he had been asked to describe the expressions on their faces, it would have been hopeless even to try. There were none.

From the habit of years, Mark went back to lock up his empty offices and began what was now the long, painful walk to the old Mackay house. He found Miss Eliza on the big side porch.

"Is it true, Mark?" she asked without even a greeting.

"That Nellie Gordon's uncle freed the slaves? Yes."

"Kate and Sarah hurried off an hour ago to their Women's Aid sewing. They were afraid to wait any longer for fear the—colored might be in the streets."

He sat down in the chair beside her. "But you aren't afraid to be out here on the porch."

"No."

"It's true, as far as I know," he said without emotion. "At least every single one of the men from Knightsford just walked away a few minutes ago. About half Caroline's cotton is still on the dock."

"I wonder what manner of man Nellie Gordon's uncle really is," she said.

"I hear he's nearing sixty. Extremely well respected, but my New York *Tribune* indicates he vastly overestimates the strength of our defenses here in Savannah. I read yesterday that General Hunter, just a few days after they took Fort Pulaski, reported thirty thousand Rebels on hand to defend us here. That's laughable." He looked out over her spring-green yard for a time. "Just saying 'Fort Pulaski' still sounds—unreal to me."

"Oh, dear boy . . . I know it does. Did you and Caroline make it out to see Jonathan's—new marker yesterday?"

"We did. I so wanted to have a handsome stone made for him, but markers don't matter, I guess. It seemed to have great meaning for Caroline that he be in the new part of Laurel Grove with the other Confederate soldiers, with a marker just like theirs."

She sat rocking slowly, deep in thought, then said in a quite firm voice, "Jonathan isn't out there anyway. Some days I feel as though I just can't wait to see the boy again. I'll be the first to see him, you know. Now, don't fuss at me for saying that. It's simply true. It helps me often. Put yourself in my place, then you'll know how it helps me."

"I'll do my best," he said, reaching to touch her hand. "Will Sarah and Kate be all right coming home, do you think?"

"Lucy Elliott and the Minis girls will walk home with them. Mark?"

He turned to look at her.

"I let them have a horse late yesterday. Nellie Gordon made such a strong case for how desperately the Southern boys need horses—just to get their pitiful food supply to them."

"Do you have any idea where Nellie Gordon really stands in this war?" he asked.

"With her husband, Willie. Oh, if her uncle, General David Hunter, ever came near Savannah from his headquarters at Port Royal, she'd welcome him right into her home—Sarah Gordon notwithstanding. But Nellie, no matter how she was brought up at home, *isn't* political."

"This—horror *is*—politics, isn't it?" he asked in a flat, hopeless voice.

"Jefferson, Adams, Washington, and Madison—didn't they do a splendid, risky thing? We're suffering the consequences of part of that risk now."

For a time no one spoke.

"Dare I ask how you feel today?"

"You may dare anything with me, dear boy. I feel the same. Old and weak and troubled and full of sometimes quite faithless prayer."

Not wanting to depress her further, he changed the subject. "I guess a lot of work is being done out at Fort McAllister these days. I only know what I read in the papers, now that—I can't talk to Jonathan. They seem to be throwing up quite a strong defense out on the Ogeechee."

"Yes. Such a beautiful spot. My Robert and I sometimes took his small schooner out there. I doubt that even God made a lovelier spot than the mouth of the Ogeechee River." She sat remembering for a while, then said, "You know, Mark, I've often thought what a breathtaking sight it must be to those Yankee soldiers up in their observation balloons sailing along through the air above that section of our land. If they're getting their defense information from the boys in those balloons, though, they must be seeing double when they look down. Did you say your New York paper reported *thirty thousand* men here protecting Savannah?"

"That's right. I think General Hunter made the estimate."

"The last our paper told about was thirteen thousand and I guess some six regiments of that pitiful number will be sent to Virginia early in June. I declare, I wonder why we go on trying to keep up with the papers. Some mornings I vow I won't. I'm so near—leaving. I'm sure when I get to heaven, Mark, I'll long to be able to tell you just how it is—watching all this horror and suffering and confusion from up there with my Robert and Jonathan—my father and mother, William and Jack . . ."

"Miss Eliza, please don't talk like that! I know you hate for me to say that, but—"

"No, I don't hate it. Saying it is natural." She looked directly into his eyes. "But it's getting to seem quite natural for me to talk about it—to wonder what it's going to be like. I'm—I'm not as afraid as I was. Doesn't that help you some? Maybe not a lot, but some?"

On the day Burke left for Roswell, June 3, Natalie felt almost as though he'd gone to war.

"Well, he hasn't," Miss Lorah said as she cleaned up after breakfast. "You got the mettle now to be truthful with yourself, Missy. I count on that. So does Burke."

Natalie could only stand at the kitchen window, her back to Miss Lorah, forcing herself in her new resolve to be a lifter, not a complainer, to hold her tongue. What she wanted to do was throw something and shout that she couldn't live without him for what might well be more than two long months. She said not one word, but picked so hard at a hangnail on her finger that she made it bleed.

"Don't it make you feel good to be counted on, Missy?"

"I don't know," she managed to say. "I guess it does." Then, from the direction she had watched Burke ride out of sight, she heard a horse clattering toward the cottage, along the river road. Without a word she raced out the door and was standing wide-eyed in the middle of the road, praying Burke was coming back for any reason at all, when she saw the old team and a loaded wagon. It was not Burke. Slowly, she turned away and was halfway up their pine-straw path when a man's voice with a Scottish burr called out, "Good morning, Mrs. Latimer! You people couldn't have prepared a more beautiful summer morning for my return."

On the driver's seat beside old Mr. Hammil, who rented wagons at the train station at Kingston, sat Andrew Low, bowing to her as he doffed his stylish, obviously new top hat.

She made herself nod her head in greeting, then turned and ran as hard as she could to her house.

"That was the final straw, Miss Lorah," she cried. "I've held on to myself up till now. It helped that I thought *I* might be able to make things a little easier for Mary Cowper when her baby comes in a day or so. Now that old coot has spoiled everything!"

"Which old coot, Missy? I heard a team and wagon. Who was it?"

"Old Redbeard. Andrew Low's out of prison and back to mess up everything I'd planned! Burke was going to visit Stuart Elliott at Marietta and it was going to help Mary Cowper so much being able to talk to me about Stuart, and now this stupid war has spoiled everything. Those dumb Yankees let him out of prison!" She picked up a sofa cushion and threw it across the room, knocking over Miss Lorah's vase of fresh daisies.

"Look what you did to my bouquet, Missy."

"I'm sorry I didn't break that ugly cheap old vase, too!"

"Won't take me a minute to mop up the water and I'm glad you didn't break the vase. I always thought it was right purty."

"Leave the water alone—the vase, too. You can fix your bouquet again later. I need you now!"

"I reckon that means you want us both to sit down at the kitchen table so's I can't get nothing else done."

"That's right, I do! Now that he's back, you're the only friend I have left anywhere around."

Sitting at the table in her accustomed place, Miss Lorah said casually, "Except Callie."

"Yes, except Callie." Natalie sat down, too. "Of course, Callie! But she's so like her father I can't—spew with her the way I can with you."

Miss Lorah's good chuckle only made Natalie angry, but she meant to wait at least long enough to refind her new, mature self. The silence didn't last long. "How many years is it going to take—if ever—for me to get so I even *want* to be calm and dull like everyone else?"

When, from the parlor, Mary Cowper saw her husband climb down from the wagon in front of her parents' home by the river, she hurried as fast as the child she carried would allow, then stopped just before she reached the front door standing open to the breeze. Her mother was at the quarters helping make children's dresses. She was thankful to be alone, thankful that Callie was with her children playing in the cliff caves down by the river, which she herself had once loved. Except for the house people, Mary Cowper was alone and it was good. She had stopped for these few seconds for one reason only—a kind of silent, sad goodbye to the awakened joy of her now close friendship with Natalie. They could still see each other, could still find some time to be together alone, but with Mr. Low back, it would all be different. The newly awakened joy had included Stuart, too, included him—dangerously.

At the open front door, she watched her husband, fashionably dressed in the expensively tailored clothes a man or a woman could buy only in the North these days—hat in hand—gesturing to the servants with the kind of elegant authority which was second nature to him. She breathed a prayer of thanks that he had come through enemy lines safely, that the children's father was here with them at last.

Aloud, as she straightened her aching back to go out to meet him, she whispered only one word: "Stuart . . ." And added silently, "Don't die—please don't die!"

Only two days later, on June 5, another Low baby—a girl—was born. At Andrew Low's urging, she was named Mary. That night, after she had made the lonely walk to her cottage along the river road, Natalie wrote to Burke: "Your dear first letter reached me today, and even though I long to be able to tell Mary Cowper about Stuart firsthand, I am relieved in a way that you have not yet had time to visit him. There's just a chance that he might have heard from Lucinda that Mary Cowper was expecting another baby. This way, when you can go, you can tell him that the baby has come and, although Mary Cowper is still quite weak, there were no tragedies. Do you remember long ago when we were young, Burke, and never thought about tragedy? Of course, we met during a tragedy—the wreck of the good old *Pulaski*—but even out there on the ocean with dying screams around us, our love threw up a shield and it goes on protecting me from too much heartache. Actually, my heart does ache as much as ever that I will never see my brother again and it aches still more for my dear parents. But the papers say there will be conscription soon and I give thanks that you are old! If such madness had occurred when you were still in your thirties, I'd simply have demanded that we leave the country and move to England! As things are now, you will be safe at your blessed age of forty-seven. I do not always agree with you politically—right now, I'd like to clobber everybody in both the Union and Confederate armies—but I'm more than thankful that we live in the Confederacy. Why? Because if we lived in the North, you'd be signing up of your own stubborn, Union-loving free will, just as Callie's Perry did.

"Miss Lib heard today from Kate Mackay. Their mother, Miss Eliza, is quite ill now. Miss Lib is so worried about her, I think were Mary Cowper not still in bed from giving birth, she would climb on a train and go down. And now I must tell you this: Don't write to me again here. Callie and I plan to leave on Monday, June 9, from the old Cass Station. After June 9, I demand as many letters as possible in care of my father in Savannah. And *do not worry about us being there.* If there's food to be had, you know Papa can afford it. Also, Papa wrote that new batteries and forts are springing up for the defense of the city. Fort Jackson has been strengthened and a new, smaller fort nearby is called Fort Lee. There's even a Fort Bartow on dear William Mackay's old plantation at Causton's Bluff! The poor, I'm sure, are suffering everywhere, but you need not worry about your wife and daughter in the mansion of Mark Browning, Esquire. You had better worry a lot, though, that your adored wife might well die of loneliness and missing you. Burke, it is not only dreadful never feeling you close to me, it is ridiculous!"

"*Your grandmother* and grandfather used to come all the way from Savannah to Etowah Cliffs by stagecoach, Callie," Natalie told her daughter as they rocked along over the smooth track that was taking them beside the Ogeechee River and on into Savannah. "That was real love for a naughty daughter, if you ask me," she added, enjoying Callie's failed efforts to imagine such a hardship.

"You and Papa would ride a stagecoach if that were the only way you could get to me," Callie said, giving her mother a good, sharp pat on the knee. "When Perry and I have children, I intend to see that they get smothered with love, too."

"We smother you, do we?" Natalie asked teasingly.

"Good smothering. I think that's the main reason the Low children like me so much. They know I love them and I had no trouble showing them, because I grew up in love—the special love of both my parents!"

For a while, they sat looking out the window, Callie excited over the clumps and clumps of swordlike palmetto growing beside the tracks. "It's hard to believe you enjoy plain old palmetto," Natalie said. "I guess you were awfully young the last time we came down to Savannah. This train certainly goes a lot faster than it once did. Do you know we must be going thirty or thirty-five miles an hour? The Central of Georgia did well in the old days to average seventeen." She looked at her watch. "I guess we'll be only about half an hour late, too."

"Who do you think will meet us, Mama?"

"Your grandfather, I'm sure. Maybe your grandmother, too."

"Do you suppose poor Mary will still be too—heartbroken to be there?"

"Oh, darling, Mary will be too heartbroken for the remainder of her life for—everything. But I never know about Mary, even though she and I are pretty close now."

"You weren't always close, were you?"

"Not always. Mary was in love with your father for years."

Callie laughed.

"Why not? Your father is the world's handsomest man. Excepting Perry, of course."

"Of course. Mary stopped being in love with old Papa, though, when she met Uncle Jonathan."

"Certainly, but just be glad your father isn't young. The silly government would try to force him into the Army if he were."

"You don't think much of governments, do you?"

"Very, very little."

"Mama, should we bring up Uncle Jonathan's name right off? Or would it be kinder to try to—stay on other subjects?"

"I don't know, darling. I honestly don't know. We'll just have to feel our way along. Miss Lib says we'll be amazed at how old and ill Miss Eliza Mackay looks. That means your grandfather's heart is already starting to break all over again."

"Will we be able to talk to Miss Eliza?"

"I hope so."

"Papa told me once that she loves the Union. Will it be all right for me to talk about Perry?"

"Miss Eliza does love the Union because she remembers when it was very young. But she's a Georgian through and through. You know I seldom discuss such things with anyone if I can avoid it. I'm dead sure she isn't a fire-eater, though, like Miss Lib and Uncle W.H."

"Does everyone in the North hate slavery?"

"Absolutely not! I don't think most care one way or another. Only the abolitionists."

"Papa hates it."

"He doesn't hate anything. He just believes in the Union."

"It can all get very confusing, can't it?"

"It doesn't just *get* that way, it stays that way!"

"Do you suppose my grandmother's Knightsford slaves went back out there after they just walked away from poor Grandpa Mark on the wharf that day?"

"We'll find out about that soon enough. None of it makes sense. Burke says only the President of the United States can free slaves. I guess everybody in Savannah hates old General David Hunter. Grandfather Mark told me in a letter that even though General Hunter may be right in principle, he was certainly the author of confusion when he freed those slaves. For days, people were afraid to be on the streets of Savannah and the slaves got hungry and had no place to sleep but the squares."

"Mr. Lincoln canceled what General Hunter did, I guess."

"So your father wrote, but I'm sure a lot of slaves didn't even know they'd been freed, whatever that means."

When the train pulled slowly into the station, Natalie and Callie were standing in the door already opened by the conductor. Callie saw the family first, and because her grandparents stood with Mary between them, she slipped an arm through her mother's, offering her courage, she hoped, in the face of everybody's grief.

"Mary did come, Mama," she said. "Mary's out there!"

It was hard to hear Mama's voice over the screech of the train wheels and the loud blast of steam as they came to a stop, but she did hear her mother say, as though just realizing it, "Jonathan—is really gone!" Callie was sure she'd heard correctly when Mama added, "Mary looks so lost . . . they all three look—so lost."

"Maybe having us here will help some."

As they rode through the summer twilight toward Reynolds Square in Grandfather Mark's carriage, Uncle Jonathan's name was not mentioned. The closest they came to it was a lot of hard hugging and holding when Callie and her mother hurried up to them on the platform. Mama had warned her that Miss Eliza was old and ill, but she had not been prepared for the way her grandparents looked. Both were still handsome, both looked older than she remembered, but in all her eighteen years Callie had never seen so much pain in faces that, in spite of it, found a way to smile.

They all went to bed early, but not before Mary led them into the room she'd shared with Jonathan to see her sleeping son, Little Ben. Natalie could only stare at the dark, dark head, the brown curled fingers of the hands that would surely someday be wide and strong and long-fingered as Ben McDonald's had been. A chill ran through her as she stood looking down at the child, remembering the last time she saw Mary's Indian brother—in her bedroom, kneeling beside her bed, declaring his love—just before he shot himself.

"He is like the other Ben, Natalie?" Mary asked, with the first real smile on her face since their arrival. That Mary was proud of the way her son looked, no one could possibly doubt.

"Yes, Mary," Natalie said. "He's exactly like Ben! That must help you—a lot."

"Next to being exactly like Jonathan, it helps." Mary touched the sleeping boy's thick black hair with unusual tenderness, even for Mary, and said, looking straight into Natalie's eyes, "I will—never touch Jonathan's head again until I die, too. Mama Caroline and Papa Mark know a lot, but—only you understand that." Tears streamed down over Mary's pale scar. "I pray you never be without Mr. Burke's head to touch."

They were all up early the next morning except Natalie's mother. Papa had already gone to his office when Natalie and Callie dressed a little before seven.

"This is my first time down at breakfast in so long," Mary said when Natalie and Callie joined her at the long table in the spacious dining room. "You sit in Mama Caroline's chair, Callie. She would like that."

Natalie took her own old place at the table, still marveling at how Mary had changed. Oh, she still lapsed back into flawed English when stirred deeply, as last night, but her day dress was worn with innate style and dignity. There was no sign of grubby hands and nails from replanting ferns as in the old days. Her brother's widow was a lady. Perhaps, she thought, Indian Mary had been born a lady.

"Is my grandmother not feeling well, Miss Mary?" Callie asked. "I thought sure she'd be down for breakfast on our first day here."

"After the late visit from the Knightsford overseer, I hope she's still sleeping," Mary said.

"What late visit?" Natalie asked.

"He roused your parents after eleven o'clock," Mary explained. "You two must have slept like pine logs not to hear him beat on our door knocker."

They both agreed that they did indeed sleep soundly, and Natalie immediately wanted to know if there was trouble at Knightsford.

"There is trouble on almost all plantations now," Mary answered, and then sighed deeply. "The–war. Everything bad is the war."

"Did Mama's slaves at Knightsford find out when old General Hunter freed them?" Natalie asked. "Was there any trouble out there?"

"Only one caused trouble," Mary said. "A man you don't know, Natalie. Papa Mark believes they should all be freed, but even he doesn't know how to make this man, Jasper, do right. Just yesterday, he held a gun on twenty other men and women at Knightsford and forced them to run away with him."

"Are the coastal slaves still free?" Callie asked.

"Not anymore," Mary said. "President Lincoln was furious at General Hunter. Only he can free slaves." She sighed heavily. "It is–the war."

"And the war is universal insanity!" Natalie sounded harsh and meant to. "I hate it. I hate all stupidity. What did Papa tell the overseer to do about it?"

"To go home and get some rest himself," Mary said, doing her best to smile at aging Maureen as she pushed through the swinging door from the kitchen with a huge silver tray. "Good morning, Maureen," Mary greeted her. "I hope you found something good to serve our guests. Even with Papa Mark's money," she explained, "this will be the first ham in two or three months."

"But today we have it," Maureen said proudly. "I've been saving it for you, Miss Natalie. My brother writes from Virginia that they can't get ham at all. Salt is up from two dollars a sack to eighty! The Lord have mercy–eighty dollars for a sack of salt!"

"We know, Maureen," Natalie said. "We can't get it either in the upcountry. Your brother's in Virginia?"

Maureen straightened her shoulders proudly. "Up in Virginia laying down his life every day for the Confederacy," she said. "I'm told the Irish from Savannah are among the bravest of soldiers anywhere!"

"I'm sure they are," Natalie said, the tone of her voice, from years of habit, dismissing Maureen, who served, then left muttering about how she and German Gerta argue night and day concerning the bravery of the Irish and the German soldiers.

"It must be very hard on Grandfather Mark," Callie said from what was obviously deep thought, "having to handle slavery problems when he doesn't even believe in it. I guess you know, Mary, that I'm engaged to be married. Perry Clay is in Kentucky, fighting for the Union. He doesn't believe in slavery either, but he's fighting because, above all else, he believes in the Union."

Natalie stole a quick glance at Mary, then said in a low voice, "It's much safer to—to talk about taking sides in the war up where we live, Callie. We're down on the coast now. My poor father is almost alone in town, I'm sure, being a Union sympathizer. So, while we're here, just be careful—very careful."

"Before Mama Caroline, yes," Mary said. "She is good with Papa Mark now on slavery, but they say little about it." Tears welled in her eyes. "It is hard to think that—if Jonathan were still here, he and your young man, Perry, might shoot a gun at each other!"

Callie seldom looked helpless. She did now and Natalie felt it was time for a safer subject. "Is this really your first time to come down for breakfast, Mary?"

"And did you come down because Mama and I are here?" Callie asked.

Mary only nodded yes. "Your mother and I are—real friends, Callie. I am happy you are real friends with Mary Cowper now, too, Natalie. She is *again* the mother of a new baby girl?"

"An adorable little girl named Mary," Callie said.

"Should anyone be surprised by now?" Natalie asked sarcastically. "She's married to old Andrew Low after all."

Seeming to ignore that, Mary said, "I do hope she can bring her baby in time for Miss Eliza to see another of her great-grandchildren." She took a deep breath as though her preparation for still another tragedy had already begun. "I must find still more strength for poor Papa Mark soon."

"Miss Eliza is really—dying?" Natalie asked. "I'm sure the dumb war has made her sicker than she might have been without it."

"I took Little Ben to receive her blessing yesterday. I longed for him to have it, but not later when she is too ill. She gave him a beautiful blessing. He will remember it someday, I pray."

"What did she say to Ben?" Callie asked eagerly.

"Her hand on his head and her face smiling, she said, 'Bless you, Little Ben Browning, for all the days of your life. Never, never forget that Jesus loves you and that He said, "Fear not, little flock, it is your Father's good pleasure to give you the Kingdom." One day you may ask why will you be given the Kingdom? The answer, Little Ben Browning, is that it is His *good pleasure*.' For one so weak," Mary went on, "Miss

Eliza made that very plain. I try to remember her words to Little Ben for all of my life, too." Her mouth trembled, but Mary added firmly, " 'His *good pleasure'* is somehow—*above* the war . . ."

Loving children as she did, Callie asked to stay with Little Ben while Natalie and her father walked together to visit Miss Eliza later in the morning of their first day in Savannah.

"The old city has certainly changed, Papa," Natalie said as they left Reynolds Square and headed up Abercorn toward Broughton. "I always think of Savannah as stately and quiet. Except the waterfront. Now the waterfront's like a tomb and the streets and squares are crawling with noisy soldiers and ammunition wagons and officers showing off their uniforms! People up where I live have no idea what war is like. I hate it. I don't know how you stand it coming out of the house into this bedlam every day. Even I feel all sealed off from the rest of the world here just because I know the city's surrounded by the enemy. I even feel sealed off from the—sky!"

He looked at her with the saddest, loneliest look she'd ever seen on a human face. "So do I, darling, and I find it especially hard to feel—cut off from Savannah's sky. I'm grateful to you for coming with me to see Miss Eliza today. I certainly hope she felt like getting up this morning. Sarah and old Hannah spend every night in her room now, watching over her. Hannah makes a pallet on the floor. Kate tries to spell Sarah, but she won't hear of it. I think it still has something to do with the hard time Sarah always gave old William."

"That doesn't make much sense, does it? It might help Kate to be able to take turns."

"Grief turns us all into—strangers, honey."

"Papa, what will you do without Miss Eliza?"

He kept his eyes straight ahead now. "I'm—managing somehow without your brother. At least, I'm still walking around."

In the few minutes Natalie was alone with Miss Eliza, she plunged right into what she found she just had to say to the lady who had sustained them all for every day of Natalie's life and longer.

"Can you hear me, Miss Eliza?"

"Of course, I can, dear girl. There's nothing wrong with my ears."

"You always called Papa 'dear boy,' didn't you?" The gray, curly head nodded against the stack of bed pillows. "Then I'm honored to be called 'dear girl.' I—I especially want you to know that I'm trying as hard as I know how to be—better these days. There's so much to make people sad. I figure no one needs me acting up the way I used to. You must have prayed a lot for me."

The dim old eyes looked off toward the faded brown floral print in the wallpaper at the end of the room. "I—do talk—a lot with the Lord, Natalie. Mark and his whole family are discussed with Him many, many times a day. Especially now do I talk often with God. Oh, Natalie, I'm proud of you and Burke and Callie. I hope Callie can visit me."

"She'll be here tomorrow with Papa. She wanted to stay with Little Ben today."

"I blessed Little Ben, although I don't know why Mary wanted me to."

"I've always believed every word you ever said," Natalie teased sweetly, "but I'd never believe for a minute that you don't know why she wanted your blessing on her son."

A genuinely distressed look crossed Miss Eliza's face. "Oh, all my life I've been so much occupied—with trifles."

"Miss Eliza," Natalie asked earnestly, "is there one thing that is never a trifle?"

"Yes, Natalie—*love is never a trifle.*"

When Mark and Callie visited her the next day, Wednesday, Miss Eliza asked two favors: "Please bring Caroline with you tomorrow and a little bunch of her Solfaterre roses from the back-yard garden."

On Thursday, when Caroline went softly into the shabby, but comfortable old bedroom, she carried the bright yellow double tea roses—as fresh and fragrant as when she'd cut them a few minutes ago before Jupiter drove her and Mark to Broughton Street. For a full minute or so, while Sarah stood watching at the foot of the bed, Caroline looked down at Miss Eliza. Her eyes were closed and although her breathing did not seem painful, it was labored.

"She had me reading the Scriptures again just now," Sarah whispered. "Mama loves one in particular: 'Fear not, little flock, it is your Father's good pleasure to give you the Kingdom.' "

Miss Eliza's eyes opened slowly and in a steady voice she said, "And *why* does He give us the Kingdom, Caroline? Because—because it is His *good pleasure.*" Then she smiled and lifted one hand to touch the roses.

"You brought them, didn't you? I knew my dear boy wouldn't forget the Solfaterres."

"Mark would never forget anything you wanted," Caroline said. "Go on, sniff! I'm holding them under your nose."

With enormous effort, but with much enjoyment, she took a deep, deep breath—deep enough, Caroline thought, to help her remember the delicate scent for all eternity.

"I must go now, Miss Eliza. Sarah and I will put your roses in a little vase while Mark's with you. He's waiting right outside your door in the hall."

Again the frail hand reached toward Caroline. "My dear, if I forget, please tell Mark that I said for him to 'trust and not be afraid.' " After another deep breath, she added, "Now, don't you forget."

"I won't, Miss Eliza. I'll tell him. I promise."

"Dear boy? Is that you, Mark?"

"Yes, Miss Eliza," he whispered, taking the rocker beside her bed. "I'm back again. I was here yesterday, too, but you were too snoozy to know it."

"My bad fortune. What day is this?"

"It's Thursday, June 12. Sarah said you've been sleeping a lot. Good for you."

"I'm—stronger today. Much stronger. Could you help me into my dressing gown? I know Sarah didn't sleep at all last night. She's too tired to—haul an old woman around today. I wish you'd—tell her to let—Kate stay tonight."

Lifting her from the high stack of pillows, he got her to the side of the bed and reached for her old blue dressing gown. "Are you sure you're up to this?" he asked tenderly. "I am if you are."

For a moment, she sat there rubbing her forehead. "My hair must look a sight—and no, I'm not sure I'm up to it, dear boy. Maybe you'd better—ease me back down in bed for a little while longer."

As though she were an infant, he picked up her frail legs and placed them back under the covers, pulling the sheet around her throat. "There, that's better for talking, isn't it?"

"Yes. Did you have time to read the morning paper?" she asked.

"I scanned it. I don't think it can be long before the Union forces control the entire Mississippi."

Her eyes stared vacantly at the ceiling. "My son Jack helped build a fort there—somewhere on the Mississippi—once, I think."

"You need to rest," he said, seeing the color drain from her face and hearing panic in his own voice. "Maybe I'd better go now. But we won't say goodbye. You know I'll be back."

"I know, dear boy." A fit of coughing wracked her and Mark sat holding the thin, soft, old body until the coughing subsided. " 'My flesh and my heart faileth,' " she whispered, " 'but God is the strength of my heart and my—portion—forever.' "

"Rest a while, dear friend, please rest!" A whisper was all he could manage now. "Oh, Miss Eliza . . . Miss Eliza . . ."

"The flesh and heart—will—fail—very soon now."

Unable to stop himself, he laid his head on her breast and sobbed.

The next morning, Mark was nearing the old Mackay house before seven o'clock. In sight of the gate, he knew she was gone. On the familiar front steps Sarah and Kate sat alone, chins cupped in their hands, looking for all the world like helpless, heartbroken children.

As he limped up the walk, Kate raised her plump, tear-stained face. "She's—gone, Mark. Mama's in heaven with Papa today."

Now Sarah was looking up at him, too, as he stood there at the bottom of the steps. "Once we saw her praying, but we couldn't tell one word she said. Then she tried to pull herself up in the bed. Sister and I did our best to—support her—one on each side. Mama didn't gasp for breath at all—she just—breathed out."

"That's right," Kate said in a voice as wooden as Sarah's. "She breathed out—her soul into the hands of—her God and Saviour."

Abruptly, Sarah jumped up. "Mark! Oh, I am worn out, I guess. How could I forget? She left a message for you!"

Mark's head was throbbing. He felt as though an enormous, crashing wave might choke off his own breath at any second. "She—left a—message—for me?"

"No one else has ever been her 'dear boy'—that I know of," Sarah said, almost in her old perky way. " 'Tell my dear boy,' she said about an hour before—she died, I guess it was—'that I promise to give his love to—Jonathan.' And—and then, she whispered, 'Tell him I'll do it—first thing!' "

SEVENTY-SEVEN

*T*he next morning as the Exchange clock was striking seven, Mark made his way numbly down his graceful stairs to the entrance hall, on his way, from habit and for want of anything else to do, to the office. Even going *down* the steps, they felt steep. The fanlighted entrance hall, its blue-and-gold oriental carpet streaked softly with June sunshine, seemed strange. The bustling sounds of Maureen in the kitchen preparing breakfast gave him no sense of anticipation for either food or what passed as coffee. He had shaved with a strange razor, and groomed his nearly shoulder-length hair into place with a brush that felt awkward in his hand, unfamiliar, as though he'd never used that brush before in his life.

His life . . . He still breathed. The pain in his legs was still there, he was going to reach for his own hat and cane and start the same walk along Reynolds Square to his office, but there was no reason for any of it. Habit had sent him on the same seemingly purposeless journey for over a year now. Today was different. He would go. He would pick up a copy of the *Morning News* as he had done every day for so long, but without a reason now. Miss Eliza hadn't been able to read the paper herself for weeks. Even the daily paper would seem foreign *if* he managed to focus enough to read it. What news there might be seemed suddenly irrelevant because his purpose in reading it before he paid his daily visit to her was gone. Today there would be no one with whom to share the news. In spite of Caroline's unwavering acceptance of their wildly differing opinions about the trouble in the land, he felt no freedom to discuss anything with her that wasn't purely personal. The closeness they shared now was far too precious to risk even the slightest misunderstanding between them. He could not, would not put his adored wife in the predicament of even attempting to take Miss Eliza's place. Mary would try to listen to him. Since Jonathan had gone away, she had shown signs of wanting to understand, but little sign that she did.

I could talk some to Mary, he thought, brushing at his gray top hat, but the news *is* the war and the war took Jonathan away from her, too. I can't bear Mary's pain today. Not today.

When Maureen appeared in the doorway to the dining room, he waved her away. Maureen knew when not to press breakfast on him. Her pride seemed no longer involved in his refusals. Food was so scarce, even Maureen had no illusions about her cooking.

Leaning heavily on his silver-topped cane, he turned the polished knob of the front door softly, so as not to rouse Caroline upstairs, still sleeping, he hoped.

As he took the first step outside into the June sunshine, he heard her call his name from the top of the stairs.

"Can you wait just a minute before you leave for the office, darling?" she asked, already starting down the stairs.

He stood watching her, the door open behind him. In the clear light, he thought she'd never looked so beautiful. She was exhausted, of course, also from lack of sleep, her graceful movements slow. Too exhausted himself from sorrow and lack of rest to tell her how he loved her, he could only watch her come toward him.

"No breakfast?" she asked. "Don't answer that stupid wifely question. I understand. I couldn't swallow either, I'm sure."

"I thought I'd go by for the morning paper and look in at the office," he said.

"I know. Would it help to get the *Morning News* and bring it back here? We could read it together." She touched his arm as he stepped back inside the entrance hall and closed the door behind him. "I know you don't feel as free to talk to me as to Miss Eliza but I'd like us to try reading the news together. I'm no longer afraid I'll—turn on you, beloved Mark." The smile she gave him was so full of love and confidence, he could only stand there staring. "I've wondered some about that

Union spy named Andrews who did such a daring thing by stealing one of our railroad engines in the upcountry," she went on. "Was the engine called the General?"

He was amazed that she could speak of the Yankee who had indeed managed, along with a handful of other Unionists, brazenly to ride off in the General while its crew ate breakfast at a place called Big Shanty. That had been back in April. Andrews and his men had been caught finally, but Mark had no idea Caroline even remembered having read of the daredevil exploit! He was still more amazed that she had brought it up–today.

"Yes," he said uneasily. "The engine was the General. It's conductor and engineer caught up with the Yankee, Andrews, finally–I think they ran on foot for more than two miles–then used a handcar and maybe another available engine or two. Anyway, all of Andrews's men are in jail. I guess he tore up some track, though, before the General's crew caught up with him, I think near Ringgold." Mark rubbed his own forehead hard. This must be some kind of dream! He and Caroline, at *her* instigation, could *not* be discussing a Union action in this almost calm manner. "I predict Andrews and all his men will eventually be hanged. Before the month is over, I'd think."

"It was a dreadful thing he did, but young Andrews was engaged to be married, Mark! I–I thought about the girl who loves him, who's waiting to marry him. I thought about her a lot last night when I couldn't sleep. You may not believe this, but even though they're Yankees–my heart aches for her this morning. Maybe for him, too."

Crazily, at that moment, he could not have relived more vividly the cold question with which Caroline had challenged Robert Lee over a decade ago–before the war–as they sat at dinner in Miss Eliza's dining room: "Sir, you're a Virginian, a Southerner–*is* there another solution to this despicable state of affairs–beyond the South separating itself from Northern aggression?"

The same Caroline who had been angered to bitter hysterics that night now stood looking at him with so much understanding he thought he might die of love for her. That long-ago night when Miss Eliza had said that prayer was the solution, Caroline had cried out: "And for what do we pray, Miss Eliza? For God to change *us* or *them?*"

The older, even lovelier face turned to him now was calm, the heart that had ceased struggling against their opposing beliefs held only unselfish concern this morning and a kind of steady patience that had, along with Miss Eliza's strength and wisdom, somehow made it possible for him to keep going after the ugly, useless war had taken his son from him. Had he, Mark, been the one still withholding himself from Caroline? Had he given only lip-service thanks that she seemed able and willing *not* to fly to pieces in the face of his opposing beliefs? Had he failed to believe that Caroline, even in their continuing disagreement, was indeed utterly open to him? Still a true Rebel, but no longer defensive? She clung to his arm, but he seemed unable to respond. She had asked that they read the *Morning News* together. He hadn't answered her. How could he without Miss Eliza's advice?

"Could you do that, Mark?"

"What?"

"Could you just go by the *Morning News* office and share the paper with me today? Here at home?"

With all his heart, he longed to say, "Yes! Yes!" Instead, he took her in his arms and held her in a hard, helpless, trembling embrace, then turned and hurried out the door and into the strangest day of all. The day they would bury Miss Eliza.

He had, last night, taken the notice to the paper. The few simple lines would be in today's *Morning News*. Lines which Miss Eliza would not see: "The friends and acquaintances of Mrs. Robert Mackay and the family are invited to attend her funeral this afternoon from her residence on Broughton Street."

SEVENTY-
EIGHT

*F*or *her parents'* sake, Natalie and Callie stayed on in Savannah long after Natalie meant to be home again. She had no real reason to go back, except that she kept worrying that Burke just might finish the Roswell job early and find her still gone. They had written to each other two or three times a week and Burke had never mentioned once that he might be through early, but what if he were? Every night spent alone in her girlhood bed in the family home on Reynolds Square had been an agony without him. All day long every day, she thought of things she needed to tell Burke and no one else. She was sure Miss Lib was terribly lonely in her mansion by the river with everyone gone but the servants. Miss Lorah must miss her and Callie, too, but Lorah Plemmons wasn't the kind of person for whom anyone felt pity. With all her might, Natalie had tried to cheer her parents, especially Papa, but daily her longing to go home grew.

By mid-July, her restlessness peaked and she marveled that her daughter could go about the house helping with Little Ben, sewing with Mary, cheering her grandparents in a hundred ways, and, except to dream of the day when she would see Perry again, never complain about being separated from him.

"I hold back all those selfish thoughts for night, Mama," Callie had said only this morning. "You and I are here to help my grandparents.

Why not visit Mary Cowper again today? Right now, in fact. I know you don't like to go over there when Mr. Low is home, but he'll be at his countinghouse at least until dinnertime."

Hurrying along toward Lafayette Square an hour or so later, Natalie refused to feel guilty because she wasn't as controlled as her daughter. We're two different people, she reminded herself as she walked right past talkative Fanny Cohen, who lived across the corner from the Lows, with only a pleasant nod. In the upcountry, Natalie met only Miss Lib's servants or someone she knew very well, so she felt no obligation for small talk. She would never really be at home again in social Savannah.

Sitting with Mary Cowper in the nursery while the infant nursed, Natalie scanned the latest letter from Miss Lib, who had written pages on how hard she was working with Miss Lorah and Mrs. Holder and the servants making military shirts, trousers, bandages, knitting socks and scarves—heavy ones now because everyone had given up hoping that the war would be over soon. "I guess it's a good thing I'm so busy," Miss Lib wrote, "because sometimes I miss Mama so much I almost wish I could die myself. I know rattling around in this big, lonely house makes it worse, but I'd give anything I own for just one more letter from her."

"Mary Cowper, I sometimes think I can't live one more day without Burke!" The outburst made Natalie feel ashamed. Mary Cowper had no hope whatever of seeing Stuart again on this earth.

No one would have guessed her friend's misery, though. The proper Mrs. Andrew Low mask was firmly in place as, calmly nursing his child, Mary Cowper mentioned that maybe Natalie should go home, since she and Callie could visit Burke on the way.

"You can take a train to Marietta, then rent a carriage as far as the Methodist Camp Grounds, a rather nice place, spend the night there, and go on to Roswell the next day."

"Might *you* be going back to Etowah Cliffs anytime soon?" Natalie asked.

"Not until Mary's a little older. We'll have her baptized here at Christ Church at the end of this month. We always like to get out of Savannah in August. Maybe we'll go up then, if Mr. Low can get away."

"Mr. Low, foot! Can't you go without him once?"

"I suppose so, but that isn't the way I live my life. You know that. I—I thought you understood now that you and I are close again."

The kindest thing Natalie could manage was silence. They *were* close, but she would never understand how anyone could work so hard at pleasing a husband she didn't love with all her heart.

When the baby was through nursing, Natalie placed her in the finely woven wicker crib and stood looking down at the tiny face. Two blue eyes–Mr. Low's eyes–looked up at her and little Mary smiled and flailed the air with her tiny hands.

"Smile now, little one," Natalie said. "Smile all you can. It gets harder, the older you become."

"Mr. Low thinks she looks a lot like my blessed grandmother Mackay," Mary Cowper said.

Natalie returned to her chair. "I think Mama is helping poor Papa believe finally that Miss Eliza is really gone. I'm proud of my mother these days. I feel quite close to her. I've always felt close to Papa, closer than he knew even when I was young and headstrong." Mary Cowper gave her an admiring smile and Natalie felt surprisingly pleased by it. "I don't suppose Mr. Low's going abroad again anytime soon."

"I certainly hope not! With the blockade, travel is just too dangerous. He isn't afraid, of course, but he is prudent. And, Natalie, how generous he is with our Southern Cause. Almost every male slave Mr. Low owns on any of his plantations around Savannah is hard at work on new fortifications to protect the city. Just last night, he was raving against Southern-born slave owners who seem willing to give their sons but not their slaves for freedom."

Natalie kept her mouth shut.

"Mr. Low says Fort McAllister is finished now and not a day too soon. I know you heard those Yankee gunboats shelling it again just before Mr. Low and I got back. It must have been ghastly."

"We heard the shelling," Natalie said without expression.

"Well, McAllister held. Mr. Low says it blocks the Ogeechee River, that the enemy is not going to get through to the old city."

"I don't think anyone can be sure of that. You know perfectly well, Mary Cowper, that I'm on neither side of this crazy war, but the Yankees are smart daring, too. You were still in the upcountry when a young Yankee named Andrews just up and stole a whole train engine right under the noses of the Rebel crew while they ate breakfast at Big Shanty."

The look on her friend's pretty face was more than gloating, it was vengeful. "Your young, daring Mr. Andrews is quite dead by now, though, and the General is back in full-time duty with the Western and Atlantic Railroad, carrying men and supplies for the South! Andrews and all his handful of brutes were not only captured but hanged!"

"We–must *not* argue, Mary Cowper," Natalie said, "not over this horrible war that's already caused so much grief and suffering. Do you think I've done my parents any good at all being here? I know Callie has, but I miss Jonathan so much myself, I only want to run to Burke's arms!"

Mary Cowper frowned. "You and I can't discuss the war at all, Natalie. I just want you to rest easy about your parents. The enemy is not going to take Savannah."

"Pooh!" Natalie scoffed. "Even General Robert E. Lee was sure the thick walls of Fort Pulaski wouldn't crack under their shells! He was dead wrong. How can Mr. Low or anybody else be so sure about all these little batteries they're building now?"

"I'm sure. Lucinda Elliott is, too. She told me so when she was here yesterday. She vows Stuart is. He urges her not to come to Marietta, to stay with the children because he feels they're all perfectly safe here."

"Stuart's too sick to make any sense! Almost nothing makes sense anymore," Natalie said, "but what makes the very least sense is how Lucinda can let a spoiled father and healthy young children keep her away from the man she loves!"

Mary Cowper's limpid, dark eyes looked evasively toward the window, away from Natalie. "We can't all understand everything about one another, Natalie."

"I'll say we can't!"

"For example, many here just don't understand why Mr. Low, a British subject, is so generous with his time and efforts and money in the Confederate Cause. I notice they're quick to lay hold of everything he offers, though—all the way from his slaves to the use of his British connections for guns and ammunition, to outright piles of cash. He attends so many meetings these days that he often can't get home for dinner or supper. We've only been back in town since the third of July and I wonder sometimes how they kept the Cause going while the dear man was in prison all those seven months!" Abruptly, Mary Cowper looked back at Natalie, her eyes vulnerable, beseeching her now. "Natalie, can't you even *try* to like him?"

With all her heart, she wanted to shout, "No!" What she said was: "I don't have anything against Mr. Low. I just—care so much about you."

"So does he. Mr. Low truly loves and respects me."

Now Natalie did say the only thing she could say, "He should." When Mary Cowper retreated again behind her long-practiced ladylike disguise, Natalie got up to go. "Callie and I will be taking the train back to Etowah Cliffs in a week or so," she said. "Please bring the children and come with us!"

"I've told you, I can't leave Mr. Low alone. I know how Mama misses us all, how lonely and worried she is about Papa in Virginia—Papa and Henry—and Bobby stuck somewhere in Florida, but I also know how lonely and worried Mr. Low was for all those cruel seven months in prison, Natalie. I'm not going."

"But Burke must have visited Stuart again. Don't you want a first-hand report on Stuart?"

Mrs. Andrew Low of Lafayette Square and Leamington, England, straightened her lovely shoulders, summoned her most formidable, noble look, and said, "Forgive me for being blunt, dear friend, but I'm staying right here with my husband."

When Natalie reached her parents' home a few minutes later, Callie met her at the door waving a letter from Burke. Together, they sat right down in the Browning drawing room and opened it:

25 July 1862
Marietta

Beloved Girls,

I have finished the Roswell job and am in Marietta five whole days sooner than I'd hoped. That means only a train ride back home after I've spent the night with Robert Goodman here. I am at the Goodman place on the Powder Springs Road as I write and Robert is due any minute, so I will get right to the point of this letter. On my way here today, I stopped again to see Stuart. The nurse was reluctant to let me in, but he saw me from his bed in the hall of the hotel being used as a hospital and motioned for me to come to him. The nurse went on yammering after me as I hurried to Stuart's bed. He still lay on bloody sheets from a hemorrhage just ended. His breathing was almost too labored to talk, but he caught my lapel. "You and Natalie and Mrs. Mackay are—my only—friends," he gasped. And when I told him Miss Eliza had died, I could have cut out my tongue. Talking was hard enough for him. He struggled against it, but broke down over Mrs. Mackay into hard sobs that brought on a violent fit of coughing. I was sure the nurses would get rid of me then, but Stuart prevailed, holding on to me. Evidently, he loved Miss Eliza more deeply than any of us knew. Finally, he said only, "That lady—helped—me find—God and forgiveness when I—killed Tom Daniell in that—duel. Because of her, I'll squeak into heaven, I'm sure." Natalie, it was all I could do not to put my arms around the poor fellow. But he had more to say: "My wife, Lucinda—wrote that—Mary Cowper was—giving birth again. Before I—storm heaven's portals, Burke, I've—got to know—about *her*." And when I told him Mary Cowper was fine and the baby, too, he closed his eyes and worked a while at getting his breath. I stood there waiting. Finally, his eyes opened and he looked up at me. "You're–sure she's–all right, Burke?" At that point, I couldn't help myself. Stuart seemed so alone, I just grabbed him in my arms and gave him a bear hug. "She's fine, just fine. Home in Savannah. Natalie has seen her almost every day." Eyes closed again, a little color back in his chalky, bearded face, he whispered, "Good! Good . . ." Then I left and rode out here to Goodman's. He sent no message to Mary Cowper and none to his own wife. The message I send to you and my beautiful Callie is that this old man misses you both so much, the pain of longing never lets up for even a minute. I wouldn't have tried to write anything so important had I thought we would see each other soon, but I have no idea when you'll be back and I leave for home tomorrow. Write your next letter to the cottage. I'll be waiting for it and for my two girls.

They sat looking at each other for a few seconds, then both jumped to their feet beaming.

"That's it, Callie. Mary will just have to take over here for us. We'll go just as soon as Papa's had time to get a letter that we're coming!"

Callie, unmindful as always of her crippled foot, whirled her mother round and round the room. "Let's spend all evening, Mama, persuading my grandparents and Mary to move to the upcountry with us. That's where we all belong now!"

When her father returned in the late afternoon from a carriage trip with Jupiter out to Laurel Grove to place two vases of the last Solfaterre roses of the season on Miss Eliza's still freshly mounded grave and on Jonathan's, he looked so lost, Natalie couldn't bear to urge him to leave Savannah. Because of Burke, leaving the city had been so easy for her, she had been slow, slow to accept the now obvious fact that her father would be only half alive anywhere else.

At the supper table, she said, "Callie and I had it all planned that we'd really beg you and Mama to go home with us, Papa. We're not going to do that now. It's safe at Etowah Cliffs, but somehow I don't think this is the time for you to leave Savannah."

"It's good to be wanted, darling," her father said, "but it will probably never be the time for me to leave. I've lost too much. I can't lose Savannah, too, no matter what happens."

"Try to understand him, Natalie–Callie," her mother pleaded.

"We do! Burke and Callie and I feel that way about our cottage at Etowah Cliffs, don't we, Callie?"

"We certainly do," Callie said with her loving smile. "Don't worry, Grandfather. We just thought maybe being up there with us might help. I know every time you walk into your office, you get a sinking feeling because Uncle Jonathan won't be there at his desk. I try to know how—awful it must be for you even to visit the Mackay sisters now."

For a long time, there was silence around the table, broken only by muffled noises from the kitchen and an occasional rattle as one of them set down a teacup or clinked ice in a water glass.

"I guess it's all right for me to tell you," Callie went on, "that Mama and I thought maybe because up there at least some people still believe in the Union, you might not feel so alone, Grandfather Mark." Natalie watched her daughter turn her smile now to her grandmother. "I certainly hope that didn't upset you, Grandmother. I know you're not a Union person. You've been wonderfully understanding that I'm going to marry a—Union man. Thanks."

Natalie's mother, once so volatile on the subject, was calm now. "I'm glad you don't remember me very well from the old days," she said sincerely. "I can't help what I believe, but I have learned—I'm still learning—how to give my love to your grandfather untouched by either his beliefs or mine. I find I have to love you and your young man in the same way, Callie."

Natalie looked from one to another, then said to her father, "You're blessed, Papa, to have Mama—as she is now, but if the rest of the fire-eaters in town make you feel too excluded, you know what to do. You know we'll be waiting for you."

"One day not long ago, Miss Eliza begged me to promise her that I"—his voice broke—"that I would never feel a stranger in Savannah."

"And did you promise?" Callie asked.

"I guess I did," he said. "But I break that promise most of the time these days."

When they waved Callie and Natalie off on the early train the morning of July 29, Caroline and Mark both allowed Jupiter to help them into their newly refurbished carriage for the ride home.

"Don't you think they did a splendid job fixing up our old carriage, Mark?" Caroline asked, smoothing the newly tufted upholstery.

"Yes. Even the creaking wheels look like new." Mark bit his lip, struggling against tears. "We'll miss the girls."

"Of course we will. I'm sorry Mary couldn't come with us to see them off."

"You do think Little Ben only has a sniffle, don't you?"

"I know it. I also know you're remembering that's what we thought about Willow, too, but Ben's been sniffling for four or five days now and not one other sign of any complications."

He sighed deeply. "Willow left us so quickly, didn't she?"

In response, she took his hand. Before the carriage had turned the corner into Reynolds Square, sudden, jarring explosions—distant blasts—one following the other, caused them both to sit bolt upright. It sounded much like the earlier bombardment at Fort McAllister, except that this time the firing was heavier. Caroline gripped Mark's hand and the side of the carriage seat as Jupiter laid a whip to the team in his effort to get them home fast.

"We're safe enough, Jupiter," Mark called. "I expect it's another bombardment down at Fort McAllister. Take it easy, my man! You're jerking us to pieces back here."

Jupiter, when he gave them both a hand down from the carriage, looked sheepish for having been so scared. "I'm sorry, Mr. Mark, Miss Caroline," he said, doffing his hat. "Looks like they jes' won't leave us be in Savannah no more."

"I think that's part of the tactic, Jupiter," Mark said. "It's always good strategy to keep the enemy guessing what you might do next."

Caroline whirled to give Mark a puzzled look. "I was just wondering, Mark," she said almost too pleasantly, "which enemy you meant—yours or mine."

Side by side on their favorite sofa, inside their own house, they sat tensely while the thunderous, steady blasting of naval fire went on and on and on.

Finally, Mark said, "I'm certainly glad Natalie and Callie are heading north, away from danger."

"So am I," she said. "At least there's no danger yet in the upcountry. Armies of both sides are moving up and down everywhere, though. Who can possibly know how long Savannah or the rest of the state will be safe?"

They had seen nothing of Mary through the entire bombardment, which Mark felt sure *was* again directed at Fort McAllister. Instinctively they knew she preferred to stay in her room with Ben. Long past dinnertime, Caroline finally heard Mary's soft footfalls descending the stairs. She was coming down the steps slowly and carefully, which meant she was carrying Little Ben, probably sound asleep.

The firing had stopped altogether and they both did their best to smile cheerfully at Mary and her son.

"He's almost too heavy for you now, Mary," Caroline said, as any mother-in-law might on any normal day.

"The bombardment has stopped, Mary," Mark murmured. "Is Ben's cold better?"

Mary nodded yes, and laid the sleeping child on a nearby love seat. After tucking his coverlet around him, she turned to face them. "Neither your side nor Miss Caroline's side—kill Jonathan again today," she said softly. Tears sprang to her eyes, but she kept her voice quiet, steady. "Jonathan—is safe now."

Twice more before the day ended, the big guns roared again, once for an hour, the last time until after nightfall.

Mark and Caroline retired early, but Mark lay awake, trying to capture some of Mary's relief that Jonathan was, at last, and forever, safe.

SEVENTY-NINE

*W*hen Natalie and Callie got off the train at Manassas Station, Burke was waiting. Once released by two pairs of wildly hugging arms, he took them to the far end of the platform, where his wagon and team waited to make the trip home.

"I mean to drive my wife and daughter myself in this magnificent vehicle." Loaded with their satchels and bundles and gifts from Savannah, he directed a hired man to bring the trunks and placed his own load into the wagon bed. Then he turned to Natalie. "Did you see Lucinda Elliott before you left Savannah?"

She frowned. "No. I didn't see her at all. We were never friends, so it wasn't rude of me. Burke, you know how I feel about Stuart and Mary Cowper." Then she asked, "He is—dying, isn't he?"

"Barring a miracle," Burke said. "The man may be gone by now. I—I wish his wife had been able to visit him at least."

"I do feel sorry for her," Natalie murmured as Burke helped her up onto the driver's seat, where the three of them would ride. "I guess she must love Stuart a lot, even though I don't understand the way she neglected him when he most needed her."

Within half an hour, the wagon was loaded and Burke was driving them along the old Cassville road toward Etowah Cliffs, so glad to be able to see them both again, he just kept looking from one to the other to be sure they were really there. Natalie did her best to tell him exactly how her parents were surviving Jonathan's death. She spent time trying to let him know that while she cried a lot, Mary struck her as being the strongest of the lot.

"I agree," Callie said. "Mary always ends up saying that they don't have to worry about Jonathan anymore. She's really sure he and Miss Eliza are together now, isn't she, Mama?"

Natalie sighed. "She certainly seems to be. I don't say she isn't right about that, but what good does it do Mary at night in that empty bed upstairs?" She grabbed Burke's arm. "I couldn't do it! I couldn't live through one night knowing you'd never be there again."

For a time, they rocked and jolted along in the wagon behind the plodding beat of the team as Burke did his best to guide the horses around gullies in the dirt road. The woods around them were nearly silent in the late summer way in which even songbirds rest.

"You haven't had much rain, have you?" Natalie asked idly. "This road is like riding over boulders."

"We need rain," he said. "But aren't we, out of all the people we know, the luckiest family anywhere?"

"I hope you don't forget and use that word 'luckiest' before religious Miss Lib," Natalie said a bit snidely. "She'd correct you and make you change it to 'blessed.' " She took a deep breath of the clear, light upcountry air. "Callie, how on earth did we manage to breathe in Savannah?"

Callie didn't answer. Burke could tell his daughter was deep in thought.

"Take a big breath of *our* kind of air, Callie," her mother ordered. "Take lots of them!"

Again, Callie said nothing. "I hope you heard from Perry while you were down there," Burke said.

Suddenly attentive, Callie told him she'd had two letters. "He's in Mississippi now, still under General Ulysses S. Grant, trying to take a place called Vicksburg. Perry says they call it the 'Gibraltar of the West.' So far, Grant and another general, named Sherman, haven't won. Perry is sure they will, though. And—he's safe so far. I just cling to that."

"I wish we could talk about happy things, at least on our first day together again." Natalie sighed. Burke was proud of her. She honestly hated the war for what it did to people's lives, but he could tell that living through still more grief from it with her parents had stretched her understanding.

"I don't think anyone is suffering more than Mrs. Stuart Elliott," Callie announced out of the blue, and Burke knew where her thoughts had been.

"Callie, what do you know about Lucinda Elliott that I don't?" Natalie asked.

"I'm sure I should have told you, Mama, but I'm eighteen and I do think of things on my own. I went to see Mrs. Elliott two days before we left."

Natalie sat up, startled. "You did?"

"I had to. She isn't the enemy, you know, just because Stuart married her instead of Mary Cowper. I know Mary Cowper wanted to marry him, and would have if Miss Lib hadn't butted in."

"That's putting it a little bluntly, isn't it, honey?" Burke asked.

"It's putting it the way it is," Natalie snapped. "Well, why did you tell Lucinda you were there, Callie? You'd never even met her."

"I told her the truth. I went because I felt so sure she needed someone to understand how she must feel being pulled apart the way she is. She seemed very grateful."

"Well, what on earth did she say? I'm sure she blamed her ailing father and the care of her children for deserting Stuart, but—"

"She didn't blame anyone," Callie said firmly. "She *explained*. She also said she would never forget me for coming. That she hoped with all her heart I would remember that, even though life often prevents it, nothing else matters as much as being with the person you love."

"Lucinda Sorrel Elliott said that?"

"Yes, Mama."

"Well, I never! It isn't as though the Sorrels don't have friends all over town and money. There are plenty of people who would take care of her children—and her father. If they can't find a Negro to nurse him because of the way they're all acting after Nellie Gordon's uncle freed them without permission, they certainly could afford a white servant. Papa's always found servants!"

"I think Callie's trying to tell us something beyond all that," Burke said gently. "Aren't you, Callie?"

"Yes, but I don't know quite how to say it."

"Well, try," Natalie commanded.

"I think," Callie began, "that it all proves that what you believe is right, in a way, Mama. You kind of expect life to bend to what you believe. Lucinda Elliott doesn't expect that. According to what she said, life gave her its greatest gift when Stuart Elliott married her in the first place. She feels she will have a better conscience if she stays responsible for his children now. What she wants, though—all she really wants—is to be with her husband. She just isn't like you, Mama, and you aren't like her. I guess we all have to make room for being different. Especially when, in the long run, we believe alike. You and Lucinda Elliott do."

Natalie turned to Burke and said so earnestly, he had trouble waiting to kiss her, "Burke, please don't stop loving me because our daughter is so much smarter and more Christian than I'll ever be!"

EIGHTY

A week or so later, Callie rode her own mare, Bette, with Sam to Cartersville for the mail and her father's newspapers, for which he waited daily.

"I'll bet you're coming along, Miss Callie, in case that Union man of yours wrote you a few lines," Sam teased.

She'd be sure to tell Miss Lorah, Callie thought as she and Sam pounded along the still hard-packed road, because Miss Lorah would be proud that Sam up and said something pleasant on his own. She loved Miss Lorah Plemmons and had thought a lot about how unselfish the woman was to bear the burden of Sam's slowness with such good grace and humor. Callie had always been able to talk to her parents about almost everything, but she could talk with Miss Lorah about absolutely everything.

"That shouldn't surprise you none, Callie, that we can talk," the graying, merry lady kept reminding her. "When two people suffer together the way we did when you were a baby—we worked every day together on that foot—they don't have room for walls to go up between 'em for any reason." Then Miss Lorah would cross two fingers and declare that for as long as she lived, they'd be just that close.

When Sam ambled, beaming, out of the Cartersville post office with the mail, Callie, still sitting Bette, flipped through the stack first for a letter from Perry. There was none, so next she looked through the death notices in Mr. Robert Goodman's newspaper, the *Southern Statesman*. She knew that's what Papa would do right off. Evidently Papa had found something to like a lot in Stuart Elliott, sick as he was when they met, because she'd watched her father scan the Marietta death notices daily since they'd been home.

On page two of the *Southern Statesman,* she found it: "Died in Marietta, August 3, 1862, Private Daniel Stuart Elliott of lung disease. He served briefly in Captain Charles Dubignon's Company, Phillips Legion, Georgia Volunteers. On October 30, 1861, he was discharged for medical reasons. Private Elliott was buried in the Presbyterian cemetery, Roswell, and is survived by his widow and two children in Savannah."

Without a word, she folded up the paper, stuffed it into her saddlebags with the other mail, and galloped toward home, knowing Sam would follow. All she could think as she rode over the miles was that Lucinda's name wasn't even mentioned.

~~~***~~~

In late November, Natalie anticipated the arrival of all the Lows, old Andrew included, with mixed feelings. That Mary Cowper needed to be comforted by her, she had no doubt whatever. Nor did she doubt that daily life for her friend since word came of Stuart's death had been an agony. No matter that Mary Cowper had once more withdrawn from Natalie's confidence behind her "fine lady Low" façade, Natalie knew her heart, and now that she realized that her own heart had far more space for the troubles of other people than she'd ever suspected, she suffered with Mary Cowper. Especially since the last letter from her to Miss Lib told them all that she was going to have still another baby! Giving birth to one after another of old Redbeard Low's children could only make the anguish worse.

Andrew Low would be furious, Natalie knew, because President Abraham Lincoln had, in September, issued a Proclamation that would eventually free all slaves everywhere. It wouldn't go into effect until the first of the new year, 1863, but Miss Lib was fuming and scared of the consequences, so Mr. Low would be, too. Natalie's father, of course, was relieved. "To me, Emancipation is an event for which I've prayed most of my life," he had written to Burke. "For selfish reasons, I only wish it had come before all the loss and bloodshed and while I was still young enough to celebrate. Caroline is taking it quite calmly, although I

understand how terrified she is that Negroes even contemplating freedom can well turn on their owners. I am convinced that Negroes are not
at all unlike us and by that I mean they are not homogeneous, not
duplicates of one another. Some will go wild with the unfamiliar
thought of being able to walk the streets at night, to sleep all day.
Others will remain loyal to their former masters, or just feel lost. That
freedom poses probably insurmountable problems, I have no doubt.
There is no way of knowing, but I predict some Knightsford people will
vanish, others will remain because some of the older ones still revere my
wife or because they dread hunger and lack of care more than they love
the prospect of freedom about which they have no clear knowledge. Of
course, Caroline's plantation and her people are my responsibility, but
on the whole, you and I, Burke, are fortunate to have hired those who
work for us."

To Natalie, the Knightsford slaves had always been just people in
the background of her life. She had never understood, had even been
annoyed at times with both her father and Burke for paying so much
attention to them. Now, at least, because she had been given a new
understanding—especially of Miss Lib and Uncle W.H.—she cared about
everyone.

Everyone? Well, everyone but old Redbeard Low.

"I don't like it one bit that you're stuck with taking old Low in our
carriage to Cartersville for the mail," Natalie said to Burke at breakfast
during the third week in December. "Why can't he go with Sam if he's
too high and mighty to ride a horse by himself? He can't get lost.
There's only one road."

Burke grinned across the table at her. "I'm not going because Low
might get lost, darling. I'm going simply to be courteous. He invited me.
No more work this week anyway."

"Are we going to be terribly poor?" she asked.

Now he forced a laugh. "We won't starve. I'm learning fast how to
make a good garden. Miss Lorah and I grew fine cucumbers and beans
and tomatoes last summer, didn't we? I'll be that much better come
spring. You watch."

"Being poor is no joke, Burke."

"I know it isn't, and although I'd have to upend my conscience to do
it, I can always find a job in Marietta or Atlanta making rifle stocks or

building boxcars for the Confederacy. I wouldn't like to, but neither would I let you and Callie want for anything."

"That's crazy talk. I could find work as a seamstress in Atlanta, too, if I knew how to make shirts for soldiers."

He grinned at her again. "For soldiers—or anybody," he teased. Then, suddenly serious, he said, "Don't worry, Natalie. You and Callie and I will do fine. Well, maybe not fine. That depends on how long the madness goes on, but we'll get by."

"If you're dead set on going with old Redbeard, you have to get on up the road to the Stiles house. He'd never consider meeting you here, I'm sure. But you've got to promise me you won't get into an argument with him over the war. Like me, old Low doesn't have red hair for nothing."

Burke and Andrew Low made it all the way to Cartersville and had started back, Low on the driver's seat beside Burke, without more than polite, almost gentlemanly barbs at the divergence of their tightly held beliefs about the war. An enormous stack of mail came for Low from Savannah and from Liverpool, forwarded from his Savannah office. For a mile or so, he excused himself and perused one or two letters, then laid the mail on the carriage floor at their feet and leaned back against the wooden seat.

"I can stop and let you stretch your legs anytime this hard seat gets too uncomfortable for you, Mr. Low," Burke said. "Sorry I don't have a driver so we could both ride back there on the cushions."

"Are you really sorry, Latimer?" Low asked with a half-smile.

Burke glanced at him, grinning, too. "No, sir. I like horses. Like the feel of the reins in my own hands. Always did."

"Few, if any, know it in Savannah, but I could handle horses, too, as a boy back in Scotland. Had to. What means I have now, I've earned myself."

Was Andrew Low about to speak confidentially? Burke wondered. Natalie had long ago told him that Low's boyhood abroad, his family, except for an uncle who had owned part of the old Low Company in Savannah before Natalie was born, were all shrouded in mystery. However the man came by his money, though, there was plenty of it to assure his place of eminence in Savannah. In Liverpool, too, and London. Heaven only knew where else. New York, Burke supposed, back before the war at least.

"What little I have, I earned, too," Burke said. "I'm glad."

"So am I. It gives a man a sense of power, don't you agree?"

"Power? Afraid I hadn't thought about that."

"I understand you're not finding much work these days, Latimer."

"That's right. Our housekeeper and friend, Miss Lorah Plemmons, would say work is as scarce as hen's teeth. It is."

"Can you build ships?"

"I worked in Baltimore in the shipyards before I came South. I know something about shipbuilding, why?"

"I can offer you a position in Savannah at a shipyard I own which will, especially in wartime, make you a rich man. Ships are desperately needed on the coast. I'm sure you know your in-laws live in a dangerous setting. The city could be attacked at any time from all those water routes. It will be if our Confederate Navy isn't strengthened. It occurred to me last night as my wife and I were getting ready to retire that it would mean much to the Brownings were you and Natalie to live for the next year or so in Savannah."

Burke gave him a long, serious look. He was in no way struggling with his answer, although if indeed he did have to hunt work in the Confederacy, compromising his loyalty to the Union would be as painful one place as another.

"There would be enough money in it for you and Mrs. Latimer to live well for the remainder of your lives if invested properly, and I would, of course, see to that."

"I'm most grateful," Burke said, "but no, thanks. I'm sure my wife's family does need her now that their son is dead. She and I are too contented right where we are, though, ever to think of leaving."

Andrew Low turned to look at Burke. "You really *are* a Yankee, aren't you, Latimer? I'd hoped it was only a passing influence from living up here among common men, small farmers who claim what they call 'spiritual kinship' with the much-vaunted American forefathers."

Burke was silent for a moment, then, peering ahead down the road, he said quietly, "I love my country, sir."

Andrew Low laughed. "Amusing, you Americans. You always have been."

"I'm aware, sir, that you're still a British citizen."

"But I have deep roots in Savannah, Georgia. My wife was born there, you know, as was yours. I let that fact matter to me."

"And you think I don't? My wife happens to feel exactly as I feel about where we live. We both love the Georgia upcountry."

Burke was still looking straight ahead, but he felt Low's eyes on him. "I fail to see what your wife's preference has to do with where you work, Latimer. A big, strapping, middle-aged man like you!"

"What Natalie likes is almost all I care about."

"I see. I also see that she quite evidently has been horribly marked by her Northern father, who is too softhearted to own a slave and whose ideas, at least, are indirectly ruining your chances for real success."

Burke snapped the reins to move the team along. He had heard enough. More than enough. He fully meant to take his time before responding to that gibe at Mr. Browning and Natalie. His revulsion at working for Andrew Low, cramped up in a city, had little or nothing to do with what he or Mark Browning hated about slavery. Plainly, Low disliked being crossed. Burke had not fallen instantly, gratefully into his plan for a way to get some good ships built for the Confederacy, and Low had lashed out with the first nasty comment that came to mind. He felt, suddenly, that he, along with Natalie, might really begin to worry about Mary Cowper's life with this arrogant man.

Wipe all that out of your mind, he scolded himself, and think straight. This man is an out-and-out Confederate at heart, British citizen or not. And to me, Confederates don't make too much sense. I know what's really eating Low. On January first of next year, a little over two weeks from today, all his slaves will believe themselves free to walk off his acres and out of his mansion and he won't be able to do a blessed thing about it! President Lincoln has finally stopped stalling around, waiting for the propitious time to free the slaves. The Lord knows I have no idea how they'll eat or what they'll do. It could be total disaster. But it will be the right thing to do and old Abe Lincoln is finally turning out to be the man I always believed him to be.

At last, after such a long silence from Burke, Andrew Low said in his most gentlemanly Scottish burr, "I do beg your pardon, Latimer. If an apology is in order, I suppose I should make it and I have. I consider you sixteen different kinds of fool, but I accept your refusal of my offer to put you in complete charge of my shipyards down on the coast. We will consider the subject permanently closed."

"I'm honored that you thought of me, sir," Burke said.

"And you were kind to drive me for the mail." After another silence, Low asked, "Is it out of line, now that we fully understand the extent of our disagreement on the subject of the War of Northern Aggression, to ask if it is indeed true that you have permitted your only daughter to agree to marry a Southern traitor?"

Burke glared at him. "No, sir, it is not true."

"But your Callie is planning to marry a young man from Georgia who went off like a tramp to join the Federal forces in Kentucky, isn't she?"

"Callie is going to marry young Sergeant Perry Clay, who is in the thick of the fighting now in Mississippi with General Grant because he agrees with me about loyalty to the United States."

"Of course."

"Why do you ask, Mr. Low?"

"To be able to tell my beautiful and staunchly Confederate wife the truth. No other reason. Mary Cowper has found the whole idea difficult to believe. You see, she's always felt as though your wife's family and hers were nearly blood relatives. It's appalling to her that Natalie could agree to her daughter's marrying someone who is plainly disloyal to the South Mary Cowper loves so passionately."

"My wife and Mary Cowper have seemingly learned how to be, if anything, closer than ever while disagreeing strongly over the war." He made himself smile drily. "I think you and I should be grateful for that, Mr. Low."

Back at the cottage, Burke was just beginning to tell Natalie of the odd conversation with Low when Miss Lib burst into the room in tears, waving a telegram.

"It's Henry—my son Henry," she sobbed. "Burke, Natalie—Henry's been seriously wounded at—the battle of Fredericksburg! Look—read it yourself, Burke!"

While Natalie tried to comfort the weeping woman, Burke read the ominous words: "Captain W. H. Stiles II, Lawton's Brigade, Ewell's Division, Jackson's Corps, wounded at Fredericksburg, on Prospect Hill, near Hamilton's Crossing. Condition feared fatal." There was nothing more. No word of where Henry might be now, nothing about the nature of his wound—nothing.

"Wait, I'm going home with you, Miss Lib," Natalie said, pushing her down into a chintz-covered parlor chair. "Don't argue. I'm going with you as soon as I get a coat. I know Mary Cowper's there and Mr. Low, but you need me. I know you do. And I'm going. Do you know where Uncle W.H. is in Virginia?"

"No—no, I don't, Natalie. I assume he was in the same ghastly battle with—poor Henry. Oh, my wonderful, strong, handsome son! I worry—

constantly," she went on, her words jerking out between sobs, "about W.H. because he's older and—not nearly as big and strong—as our son, but—yes! Yes, please come home with me, Natalie. I do need you. Mary Cowper will be so upset about her brother—"

"Does she know about the telegram, Miss Lib?" Natalie asked, pulling on a heavy coat against the December chill outside.

"Not yet. She and Mr. Low went for a walk when he and Burke got back."

"How did you get the telegram, Miss Lib?" Burke wanted to know.

"Mr. Holder, the overseer—just appeared with it. I—I didn't think to ask—how he got hold of it!"

EIGHTY-ONE

*T*hree *frantic* days later, on December 18, Sam brought a letter from W.H. which sent all of Etowah Cliffs into a frenzy:

14 December
Near Fredericksburg, Virginia

My dear Lib,

By now you know our valiant son Henry is wounded. It is but the next day after the battle as I write and I am not certain, but fervently hope that Henry is in the home of a kind lady not far from here. Her plantation is small, but not her generosity. I saw our fine son fall and rushed to his side, despite his protests that I, too, would be shot. "No," I cried, "but even if so, there is no better spot to fall than by your side!" I, as Henry's colonel, had him carried to the kind lady's small house nearby, where a musket ball was removed by the regimental surgeon. Henry was cared for all that first night–last night–by the chaplain and me. Due to command duties, I was forced to leave him this morning, with assurance that as soon as possible he would be moved to Richmond for further medical care. This morning, General Jubal Early sent for me and told me that I had covered myself with honor by my courageous charge at Fredericksburg, but that perhaps I had gone a little too far in my display of patriotism and love for my country. Be that as it may, I beg of you, dear Lib, to come as quickly as humanly possible to Richmond, where I trust our beloved son will have been taken for care. No care can compare with that of his wonderful mother, though, so come, Lib, at once. I will also send for his wife, Cliffie. I do not know who can escort you or how the journey can be made, but I beseech you, for love of your family and our glorious Confederacy, to make haste.

When Eliza Anne read her husband's letter aloud to Mary Cowper and Mr. Low, Andrew immediately offered his services as her escort. Natalie supervised the packing, along with the always practical help of Miss Lorah. Into the trunk, Miss Lorah placed a bottle of brandy–explaining that "it stirs the blood"–some wheat bread and biscuits, preserves, arrowroot, and a sponge cake.

While Eliza Anne hurriedly packed her own clothing, Miss Lorah went back to Natalie's cottage for a bundle of clean rags and the tiny loaf of sugar she'd been saving for some special occasion. "You and his wife, Cliffie, are going to nurse Henry, Mrs. Stiles," she said. "Sugar will give him strength and you'll need plenty of clean rags for sure."

Early the next morning, December 19, Burke and Callie drove Miss Lib and Andrew Low to Manassas Station, en route, by whatever conveyances Low might be able to manage, to Richmond.

After Miss Lorah went back to Natalie's cottage to finish her morning's work, Natalie and Mary Cowper walked slowly up the path to the Stileses' veranda, arm in arm.

"I'm so sorry, Mary Cowper," Natalie said. "I don't need to tell you that I can sympathize with how you feel over Henry."

"I know. And thank you. Dreadful things keep on happening, don't they?" She was fighting tears. "I can't let my children see me–cry. Could we take a short walk by the river before I go to them? Little Sinai seems quite dependable for a change. She's with them upstairs now. And Katie is old enough to want very much to help with the younger ones."

"If you hadn't suggested a walk, I was going to," Natalie said, dead certain that Mary Cowper desperately needed her this minute. How could she not need her? There had been no chance since the Lows had been there for the two to talk alone. Mary Cowper had to know Stuart was dead. She was friends with Lucy Elliott, and had undoubtedly spent hours with her in Savannah after word came that Stuart was gone. "I'm here," Natalie said, squeezing her arm. "I wondered if we'd ever find time alone to say all we both need to say to each other!"

They had retraced their steps down the path to the river road and were walking slowly toward the stables, away from the big house.

Mary Cowper stopped and looked straight at Natalie. "I–I've already done my weeping–I knew he would die before Mr. Low decided we would come up here. I was there to be some comfort, I hope, to Lucinda. She may never forgive herself for not going to him. Her guilt is as heavy as her grief. I understand guilt like that."

Natalie took her arm. "I know. I know you understand!"

After a time, Mary Cowper went on talking about Lucinda, the closest she dared go, Natalie knew, to mentioning her own grief over Stuart. "I hated leaving Lucinda, but nothing would do Mr. Low but that we get out of Savannah, up here, where it's safe. I had to come. I wanted to come. Little children can't protect themselves against enemy hordes!"

A plan had begun to spread like wildfire in Natalie's mind. She would need to be very, very careful–cautious, but she had already decided what to do. "You're right. Children are helpless," she said. "So are old people and–well, everybody. I try not to worry about my parents, who still refuse to get out. Mama would, I'm sure, but she's so protective of Papa these days. And she knows better than anyone on earth how much he loves the old city. How he hates to leave it. She writes so often that he always seems a little less troubled after he's just walked the Savannah streets for a while. Burke believes Savannah won't be attacked, so I don't worry too much about Mama and Papa and Mary and Little Ben. Burke says the Yankees will leave it alone, attack the forts around it, but not the town, as a part of their strategy. It keeps Savannahians on edge." There, she thought, that should be enough caution. "Mary Cowper," she went on, "was Lucinda's father really so ill she couldn't have gone to Stuart just for a few days?"

The dark eyes looked at Natalie in some surprise. "Yes, yes, I think so. And of course, the children . . ."

"Will Lucinda come up to Roswell as soon as she can to–visit his grave?"

"I–I'm sure she will. I know she will. The day we left the city she told me she'd give almost anything to be able to kneel there and tell him just once more that she loves him with all her heart."

Wanting so much to form the habit of thinking before she blurted, Natalie waited. Finally, she said softly, "Are you–speaking only for–Lucinda?"

Her eyes straight ahead, Mary Cowper whispered, "What?"

"You and I can go to Roswell while Miss Lib and Mr. Low are away. Burke worked there for weeks. He knows the Presbyterian church cemetery where Stuart's buried. Burke will take us, I know. There's no work now. What could possibly be wrong about—paying respects to the dead?"

Slowly, Mary Cowper turned to look at her. "But what—would I use as my—excuse for going all the way to Roswell—for leaving the children?"

"Don't you know some of the Bullochs in Roswell? I'm sure that's why Stuart is buried there. His stepmother used to live in grand Bulloch Hall."

"She's living in—enemy territory now, at the North—but Mr. Low and I have friends in Roswell where you and I would be welcome."

Natalie's heart was racing now. She hadn't dared hope that conventional, stoic Mary Cowper would even discuss such a trip!

If I go on being careful, Natalie thought, I think she'll go. I know she will. I know she'll be more peaceful once she's done it, too.

"Natalie, what good would such a wild trip do—anyone?"

Natalie thought fast, but carefully. "Wouldn't Lucinda like to know about where Stuart's—grave is? What it says on his marker?"

"Someone has surely told her by now." The old Miss Lib look of self-control masked Mary Cowper's face. "This whole thing is—wrong, somehow." Then she repeated, "What possible good could it do anyone?"

"Miss Eliza Mackay, your own grandmother, always said it would have helped her so much right after her husband died up in New York on a trip with Papa if she could have had a grave to attend. If she could have left flowers for him—just once even."

Tears filled Mary Cowper's dark, luminous eyes, looking off now in the direction of the river where winter sunlight tipped the tiny ripples in the shoal. "Natalie—could Burke go—right away, do you think? I'd need some time back here—before Mama and Mr. Low get home. I'll—need time alone afterward, I'm sure."

"We'll go tomorrow morning! That way we can get back here in time for Christmas with the children. I'll go right now and start packing. You, too. Then, as soon as Burke and Callie are home from Manassas Station, I'll tell Burke. And don't worry that he won't agree in a minute! Burke Latimer believes in love."

EIGHTY-TWO

*J*ust at sundown, three days before Christmas, Burke pulled the team and rented wagon to one side of the road in front of the Roswell Presbyterian church. For the past half hour or so, over the final miles from the Marietta Methodist Camp Grounds, where they'd spent the night at the preacher's home, Mary Cowper had seemed withdrawn. Not exactly melancholy, Natalie thought, just living somewhere deep inside herself. The Latimers respected that and so said little.

As Burke lifted them down from the high seat, he offered to wait by the wagon.

"No," Natalie said, keeping her voice very quiet. "Mary Cowper wants me to find the grave with her, Burke, and I want you there."

"Fine," he said. "Whatever you ladies say."

The trio walked slowly up the path toward the beautifully kept white clapboard church. Roseate sunset light reflected off the clear, small-paned windows except for the two under the Doric-columned portico.

In front of the church, Mary Cowper wanted to know if Stuart's funeral service was held here.

"Yes," Burke said. "That's what I read in the Marietta paper."

As though on a silent order, they began to walk along the side of the small church, then stood behind it for a moment, looking down into the lengthening day-shadows cast by tall oak and pine trees, into the cemetery, where varied tombstones—some old, some new—spread away and down over a fairly steep ravine. Burke reached for Natalie's hand to help her down the narrow path.

"I'll be fine," she said. "Help Mary Cowper. I'm used to steep places."

A splendid, tall monument stood at the foot of the first incline, near a thick-based, equally handsome marble marker. Brick walls encircled the few family plots—King, Pratt. The Roswell King family, Natalie guessed, since Roswell King had founded the town. Miss Eliza, whose husband, Robert Mackay, had been a Presbyterian in Savannah, knew about the Roswell church. Its people had Savannah ties.

She glanced at Burke, who was standing near Mary Cowper. Natalie had never loved him more. Only Burke would be doing this, she thought. Who else has a husband who would put up with such a strange journey for the sake of his wife and a friend she cared about?

When Mary Cowper began to walk ahead slowly, searching the names on each stone she passed, Natalie and Burke followed. Then Burke said, "Why don't we separate? We can all three look. Wouldn't that save time? These winter evenings are short. The light won't last long."

"Yes, Burke," Mary Cowper said. "I do want us to start back first thing tomorrow. You'll need to get rooms for us, too, at the hotel we saw at the edge of town." She tried to smile. "I'm very glad we decided not to stay with anyone we know."

Natalie was glad, too. They were certainly not on a pleasure trip. Mary Cowper needed to find Stuart's grave, to be with him alone for a few minutes . . . minutes that would have to last for all the rest of her life.

Keeping an eye on both Burke and Mary Cowper as she strolled alone through the family plots, Natalie read every name. Some families had erected brick walls, others iron fences around the graves of their loved ones. Can people still be together—out here? she wondered. In a way, I guess. In heaven, too. Since Jonathan's death, Natalie had begun to think more about what life might be like after this life ended. Was Jonathan with Little Burke now? And Miss Eliza? And William? And Ben?

When Burke called her, she turned to look in the direction he was pointing. Mary Cowper had found Stuart! Not beside another grave, not inside a carefully encircled brick wall or iron fence, alone, in the barest place around, a fairly level unplanted spot—but alone.

Mary Cowper was just standing by the new, plain stone, staring down at it. The marker's top was curved and a tiny matching stone stood just below it. At Stuart's feet.

Natalie looked at Burke, a few yards up the hill. When their eyes met, he loped quietly down to where she stood and took her hand.

"We'll go over there, honey," he whispered. "She might need us. But not too close."

"No. She'll want some time—to be with Stuart alone." Natalie's eyes stung with tears. "Oh, Burke . . ."

"I know, I know. Come on."

There was plenty of empty ground around Stuart's barely settled grave for the two of them to stand back and wait in plain view of Mary Cowper, who was still just looking down. Stuart was fairly tall, as Natalie remembered him, but how short the distance now between his headstone and footstone!

After a time, they saw Mary Cowper kneel. Her lips moved in a prayer or some secret message for Stuart. Then one hand reached toward the headstone to touch whatever inscription had been cut into the marble. At the sight of that touch, the pent-up tenderness of it, after the long, long wait for it, Natalie felt a sob catch in her own throat.

Mary Cowper looked around like a startled bird.

"It's all right," Burke called softly. "It's us, Mary Cowper. There's no one else here. Take all the time you need." To Natalie, he whispered, "Poor little thing's been holding it all back for so many years."

Burke knew! He really knew. Natalie threw both arms around him and held on for dear life.

Tree shadows touched one another now across the churchyard as the sun sank almost out of sight. Carrying Andrew Low's child, Mary Cowper was just standing, peering down, memorizing, Natalie knew, every letter of every word and date carved on Stuart's stone, as though promising herself never again to be totally without him.

Now she stooped and slowly traced each letter of his name with her finger, then turned to Burke and Natalie. "You'll both—want to see, I'm sure," Mary Cowper said, her voice thick with emotion, but without tears.

Hand in hand they walked slowly across the vacant area to where she stood and read the marker carefully:

Stuart Elliott
Born November 20th 1826
Died August 3rd 1862
Leaving this testimony
I die in Christ

The chill evening silence hung around them, with only a sleepy sparrow chirp to break it, until Burke said, "He told me that himself. Stuart was at peace with God."

"He told you, Burke?"

Natalie was sure Mary Cowper's lovely, perfect features had never been so full of light, and by now it could no longer be the sunset.

"Stuart gave Miss Eliza Mackay full credit for the peace," Burke said. "She got him to ask God's forgiveness for the duel with Daniell, and then to forgive himself. He told me forgiving himself was a lot harder."

For a long time, Mary Cowper just stood there, hands clenched. Then she said, "Grandmother Mackay saw him the way he really was, didn't she?"

"Burke did, too," Natalie whispered. "And so did I."

Allowing Mary Cowper to decide exactly when, the three reclimbed the shadowy hillside and passed again beside the clean white church. Natalie rode quietly between them as Burke drove into Roswell. Only the rattly wagon, a squeaking harness, and the team's hoofbeats broke the stillness.

Finally, Mary Cowper spoke. What she said was: "Thank you, Natalie. Thank you, Burke."

EIGHTY-
THREE

At home again by noon on Christmas Eve, Natalie, Burke, Callie, and Mary Cowper did their best to make a happy holiday for the Low children, but it was an anxious time for Natalie. She was worried, in particular, about her parents and Mary down in Savannah–alone.

"Uncle Jonathan couldn't have been with them anyway," Callie said. "By now, he would have been in prison with his friend Colonel Olmstead in New York."

"I know you're trying to help, Callie," Natalie said, too sharply, "but what can possibly help in the midst of this rotten war?"

The days dragged on and nothing did help. Everyone at Etowah Cliffs ate substantial food. Miss Lorah had "put up" half the summer garden, so they had plenty of corn, tomatoes, beans, and peas. And, of course, the eternal yams. They were sweet, though, and because Miss Lorah had sent their last tiny supply along to Virginia with Miss Lib for poor Henry, sugar was, by now, almost forgotten. Uncle W.H.'s cattle and hogs were dwindling, but they only did without a little meat of some kind for dinner a few times a week. Papa wrote that he and Mama hadn't had sweetened coffee in months. That now no amount of Browning money could buy coffee in Savannah. But they were all well and

Mary smiled a bit more often, especially the evening Little Ben finally caught on how to aim and shoot a marble.

"Papa's so proud that he taught Ben how to shoot marbles," Natalie said, handing her father's letter to Burke to finish.

"Don't you want to read it to me?" he asked.

"No. It's about bombardments. I'm sick of all that."

"I'm not," Callie said. "Read it, Papa. I'm trying so hard to keep up with what's going on. There's war just about everywhere but right here, isn't there?"

"Yes, Callie, there is."

"Perry thinks he can come back on leave as soon as General Grant takes Vicksburg. He's behind the lines now, though, because he's seen so much heavy fighting lately, so I don't have to worry so much for a while."

"Do you—worry all the time, Callie?"

Her face solemn, Callie said simply, "I cry myself to sleep most nights, Mama."

"But the next day you're always cheerful!"

"Why should I dump my worries off onto you and Papa? Finish Grandfather Mark's letter, Papa, please?"

"You bet, honey," Burke said, hunting the place where Natalie had stopped reading. "Your grandfather writes: 'Last month we really had a day of bombardment out at Fort McAllister. I was proud of Ben because he didn't cry once. After it was over on January 27, the paper said an armored Yankee ship called the *Montauk* had fired 61 five-inch shells and 35 fifteen-inch shells at McAllister. That, by the way, was the first time fifteen-inch shells had been used against a land battery. McAllister held. It held, too, when on February 1, the *Montauk* and an escort again shelled it for five solid hours without stopping! Natalie, your mother almost lost her nerve during this ghastly unbroken shelling. Major Gallie was killed—the crown of his head blown off—and seven gunners wounded. The Mackay sisters knew two of the wounded soldiers well and are helping nurse them now. That, along with unending work with their Aid Society, keeps us from seeing much of them, but considering the enormous emptiness in all our lives without Miss Eliza, the sisters are doing rather well. Better, I think, sometimes than I. I see no letup in the Northern attempts to take Fort McAllister, but then, what do I know about military tactics? We have had one short letter from Miss Lib in Virginia telling us of the trouble and hardship she and Low had in even finding Henry in a small house right on the battlefield. I am urging her to bring him here as soon as he is able to leave Richmond. With his mother and his adoring wife, Cliffie, nursing him, he will regain his strength soon. I know it is safer at Etowah Cliffs, but the trip from Virginia by water to Savannah would be so much easier on Henry.' "

Natalie reached for the letter. "Is that all the military stuff, Burke?"

"Except that now and then, under cover of darkness, a blockade runner manages to get through and citizens with money are able to buy food supplies, spices, even some yard goods. 'Our hearts go out to Eliza Anne and her soldier boys, Henry, Robert, and W.H.,' he writes. 'What a burden that woman carries these days, so far from the home she loves. Evidently, Richmond is crowded with friends and relatives searching for wounded loved ones who need care so desperately. Natalie, I know you want us up there and your mother and I promise we will consider it as soon as the authorities here are convinced that the attacks on Fort McAllister have ended one way or another. This will sound foolish, I'm sure, but with Miss Eliza gone, I cannot bear to leave Savannah if I'm not certain about being able to come back to her. Your affectionate father, Mark Browning.' "

"Poor Papa," Natalie whispered.

"I hope they can come," Callie said.

Burke mussed Callie's blond curls. "And *I* hope Sergeant Perry Clay will soon walk through that door!"

Callie went to hug him. "Oh, Papa, me, too, me, too!"

When their daughter limped from the house, tossing a somewhat forced smile over her shoulder at them both, Natalie said, "She is in love, Burke."

"Her old father certainly does not doubt that for one minute."

Natalie sighed. "I miss not being able to write to Miss Eliza when something important needs praying about. Nothing must happen to Perry. Callie doesn't deserve anything to happen to him!"

In Richmond, Eliza Anne and her spunky daughter-in-law Cliffie, who had come at once, spent their hours, night and day, nursing Henry. They were helped enormously by occasional visits from General Lee himself and the frequent attentions of his son Custis. Henry's every want was satisfied, as much as wants could be with the worsening shortages of everything that had once been taken for granted. The ghastly wound in Henry's chest healed rather nicely, she thought, but daily he suffered more and more from the wound in his left arm where the ball had lodged. "The ball was removed long ago," Eliza Anne wrote Mary Cowper, now back in Savannah with her husband and children, "but still the wound stays puffed and mean and so painful. Your brother's loving, gentle nature, so in contrast with his huge, muscular body, sustains us all. For every year of your life, daughter, you can be proud of Henry's courage and gentility even in his own sickroom. He is pale and weak still, but even so, I glow in his loving nature and manly beauty. And daily I pray your father can relinquish his continual desire for promotion in the Army and return with me to Etowah Cliffs, where he can far better serve the Cause for which we all risk our very lives and the lives of our loved ones. As soon as Henry is strong enough, we hope to come by water to you in Savannah, where medical care, I'm sure, will be better than in the crowded, harried capital here in Richmond. The hateful Lincoln blockade may prevent us, of course. I long to be with you in these days before the arrival of your child. A mother's place is with her daughter at times like this, but alas, a mother's place is everywhere and this mother misses her husband painfully and needs him. Your father has so many detractors in the Confederate Army and yet his intentions are entirely noble."

At the end of March, one of Sarah Mackay's faithful letters helped Eliza Anne make up her mind to take Henry to Savannah. "The Southern authorities in town assure us," Sarah wrote, "that after the dreadfully disturbing but futile attacks on Fort McAllister by the Yankees— one which destroyed the CSS *Nashville,* the other which went on for eight hours—we can be reasonably sure that, after the month past, all will be quiet here. If you and Henry will only come, Kate and I will assume full responsibility for his care and you will be free to spend as much time as you need with dear Mary Cowper, who, though growing large and cumbersome now, seems well. I know she needs her mother, and so once W.H. has visited you on his leave to Richmond, please, please come."

Eliza Anne was deeply troubled during the last three days in April as she waited for W.H. to reach Richmond. His return had always lifted her spirits, but lately his letters had been so filled with bitterness at his failure so far to be made a brigadier general, at his deep conviction that he was being wronged by those in the Cause he loved, she dreaded having to work at encouraging him again. Helplessly, she began to pray that their first night together might somehow, in the midst of so much suffering and chaos, bring back the old closeness. Heaven knew, she was exhausted. W.H. would be, too, if his complaining letters were any sign.

He was never a robust man, and the brutal hardships of life in Army camps had broken his spirit. She could nurse him if he were physically ill, but she doubted her own adequacy now in the formidable task of lifting his broken spirits. Henry would help. Cliffie would help. But in the long run, it would be up to her.

Her first sight of him as he plowed his way up the steps of the Gray house, where she and Henry and Cliffie were staying in Richmond, gave her some hope. His beautiful, proud head hung down, his shoulders were stooped, but W.H. looked far healthier than his letters had led her to believe. She breathed a prayer, even as he took her in his arms at the front door. Prayer had become a way of life for her—even gentle Henry teased her about being too religious. She prayed in W.H.'s arms that, by a miracle of God, she would have the strength to love him back to his old self-esteem.

He and Henry exhausted her and themselves that first night by reliving the bloody Fredericksburg battle where Henry had been wounded. When she gave up finally and told W.H. she would be waiting for him in the bed they would share, she despaired of anything happening that night beyond still more retelling of his troubles.

When, at last, he got into bed beside her, he seemed able only to cling, to press her to him, drawing her waning strength into his own body.

She kissed him and kissed him. He kissed back, but she could feel him straining to pull away and start talking again.

As though the whole matter of his status in the Confederate Army had been torturing him even as he kissed her, he began another tirade concerning a letter he'd written to General Jubal Early back in March, attempting to offset an unfavorable report to Early in which W.H., in temporary command of General Lawton's brigade, had been said to have kept no discipline and no order.

"I could endure such treatment no longer, Lib," he said, turning over on his back to stare at the darkened ceiling of Mrs. Gray's guest room. "I begged General Early for promotion to brigade commander and once more pointed out my qualifications. I think I rather dislike myself for having begged him, but I did tell him in a gentlemanly manner that if he could not see his way clear to promote me, I hoped he would forget the matter and destroy my letter. That in no way would his refusal diminish my esteem for him, that I would accept that he was motivated by duty to country and self."

For the first time in all the years of their life together, she could think of nothing to say to him.

"Lib?"

"Yes, W.H."

"Don't you have–anything to say to me?"

She took a deep breath and reached for his limp hand. "Only that I beg you to take sick leave and, as soon as we can both manage it, come back to Etowah Cliffs with me! I think it's too dangerous in Savannah!"

"I agree about Savannah," he murmured. Then there was a long uncertain silence before he said, "You still don't think me qualified as a military man."

"I–I don't think that's quite right," she answered, her voice trembling.

"Then what is right?"

"I know you to be perfectly qualified as a *statesman*. Look around you. The needs of the Confederacy grow more frightening every day. God knows, we need statesmen!"

With scarcely a pause, he asked eagerly, "And you need me to help you care for our valiant son, Henry, don't you?"

"Yes, oh, yes, darling, I do–I do! I need you–in every way! Can you arrange leave now–in time to go home with Henry and me? Straight back to our own place by the cliffs?"

He was propped on his elbow now, obviously so relieved by her urging that he already believed it was his idea. "What do you say, Lib, that when Henry is better we all go home to our river? Uh, for as long, that is, as my leave might be extended. I do long so to be back in our house. Why can't we just take Henry home? You can go down to Savannah for the birth of Mary Cowper's child . . . When is it, June? And I'll shoulder my responsibility as a father in seeing that Henry has his every need met at Etowah Cliffs!"

"Wouldn't it be far easier on Henry now to travel by water, though?" she asked carefully. "Unless you can use your influence to assure us some sort of safe passage to the upcountry."

That seemed to bring him quickly back to himself. "Of course I can use my influence and I will. I've been in regular, friendly correspondence with President Jeff Davis for a long time. I'll simply go by his office tomorrow right here in Richmond, and as soon as Henry can travel, we'll head for home!"

"Oh, thank you, W.H. Thank you!"

He embraced her. "What are husbands for, Lib?"

During the first week in May, W.H. managed to locate a new Richmond doctor, who discovered on his first visit to Henry why the wound in his arm had not healed. Whether President Davis had helped with that, too, Eliza Anne never knew, and she was too relieved with the results of the doctor's care to risk asking. By means of painful surgery, which Henry endured with expected bravery and in near silence, the new surgeon removed from the withering muscle in his normally thick upper arm the remains of a toothbrush carried into the flesh by the miniéball which had struck him in the chest!

"I'm sure," Henry whispered, still in excruciating pain from the probing, "I had my toothbrush in my shirt pocket—that day, Mama." Then he tried to smile. "That's—that's a Stiles thing to do, isn't it? Caring —right on the—field of battle—about my—pearly-white teeth?"

W.H. and Lib, at his bedside, exchanged proud glances, then Henry immediately fainted from the agonizing pain of the surgery.

Near the middle of May, Mark sat alone at his office desk reading the Savannah *Republican*, as he did every morning. His Northern newspapers had not come all week, and with the war worsening on all sides, there was now little difference between the local *Republican* and the *Morning News*—one as urgently pro-South as the other.

Savannah, for months entirely taken over by the Confederate military, still showed few signs of the romantic, sedate old city he and Miss Eliza loved. Why he kept reading the stories containing out-of-town soldiers' accounts of the place, he didn't know, but he read them all. Today's *Republican* depressed him more than usual: "Savannah is too hot, too damp." "The water not as good as the water back home." "Savannah is certainly not the fine city I expected," one upcountry soldier wrote. "The outskirts are filthy." "It is an old-looking place," wrote a boy from Athens, Georgia, "with ill-shapen houses and narrow streets on which the sand is a foot deep!" Another complained that "if the test that was applied to Sodom and Gomorrah was forced upon Savannah, she would barely escape the fate of those two cities."

Mark smiled a little, though, when he read a letter from a Macon lad who thought "the inhabitants of Savannah a set of stuck-up know-nothing fools. We came here as strangers and strangers we have remained. Nobody here gives a hoot about us."

He certainly hoped the Mackay sisters wouldn't read that. Mark had never known women to work such long hours or as diligently in their Women's Aid Society, the Ladies' Knitting Society, or at any other task they found to set their hands to. Nothing, they thought, was too good for a Confederate soldier. Both sisters had thrown themselves body and soul into the South's struggle. "We know you and Mama loved the Union," Sarah said one morning when he stopped by. "I guess Kate and I loved it, too, once, but the Union turned against us. We believe that our diligence is helping our own country and these days we both love the Confederacy."

That they did was obvious, and such dedication must be helping them live through these lonely months without their mother. "We're even thinking of starting a cartridge class, Mark," Kate said. "General Lawton's wife has her hall and parlors filled with flannel bags of cannon cartridges of every caliber, all made by the ladies of her class!"

During the first week in June, when Mark called at the dear old house on Broughton Street, in Miss Eliza's front hall and parlor sat the women collected by Kate and Sarah, patiently cleaning greased balls, filling paper caps with powder, and tying up missiles of death by the dozen! He bowed, backed up, and left as soon as he courteously could.

On his lonely walk home, Mark passed what was now known as the Wayside Home, run also by Savannah women, who furnished food, lodging, and other services to transient soldiers. He'd read that during a seven-month period last year, the Home had served more than five thousand men.

"I wish I felt up to working myself, Mark," Caroline said when they sat down to their meager dinner that day. "I know you wouldn't object if I joined one of those social cartridge classes, but I wish I could find energy enough to take a regular job!"

He stared down the long table at her still lovely face. "A–job, Caroline?"

"I read today that Lathrop and Company is hunting for a hundred additional tailoresses to make military garments of all kinds."

"But, darling," he said carefully, "poor women need those jobs. I admit our menus are scant. I know you need fresh meat for energy, but if it were available, we could certainly afford to buy it!"

"For heaven's sake, Mark, I don't mean I'd keep the money I earned. I'd turn it all over to the Wayside Home." Then she smiled. "Darling, do you realize that it relieves me as much as it does you that we can talk this way–so freely? That you accept my Southern fire, that I accept your Northern bias? Sometimes I think it relieves me more than it does you!"

Returning her smile, he said, "I doubt that, but it is good that we've both finally–grown up."

"I promise not to dive backward into self-recrimination. I know that upsets you more than anything, but I do know which one of us needed to grow up, Mark. Oh, dear, I'm getting so forgetful! We have a letter from Eliza Anne."

"Don't stop eating to get up, please," he said quickly. "I'm interested in all their affairs, of course, but not as much as in seeing you finish your dinner. Even foods like our endless yam concoctions and butterless corn bread give you energy. Did you feel tired when you got up today?"

"I'm much, much better, thank you. Eliza Anne is lyrical to be back by the river in her own house again and it's quite remarkable how quickly Henry's wound is healing now that it no longer contains his toothbrush."

"Poor Henry," Mark said.

"Eliza Anne says W.H.'s pride in Henry and his relief in being at home again himself have helped lift his depression. Even at home, though, she says he suffered enormously over the tragedy of General Stonewall Jackson's death at Chancellorsville. I know it saddened me a lot. Eliza Anne says General Lee is bereft, not only because he lost such a good friend but because Jackson's death is a dreadful loss to–our side."

"I know," Mark said. "Shot by his own men accidentally, the papers say."

"I'm afraid so. War is so ghastly!"

"It brings out the best and the worst in us all," he mused. "Kate Mackay told me this morning that Mary Cowper, only a month away from the birth of another child, is coming every day to sew at the Women's Aid Society."

"It's even bringing out more good in our daughter. Remember, she wrote just before Christmas that we can both be absolutely sure of the quality of her friendship with Mary Cowper now and forever. Such a proper kind of thing for Natalie to write. Of course, she explained nothing and, of course, I mean never to ask what she really meant by it."

"Isn't it about time for Eliza Anne to come down to be with Mary Cowper for the baby's birth? Andrew Low says she's coming and I think the baby's expected about the middle of June. Eliza Anne should be arriving around the first, I'd think."

"I'm trying," Caroline said, "in spite of our heat, to walk some every day, and this morning, on the other side of Reynolds Square, I met Lucinda Elliott. Oh, Mark, she struck me as looking so *old*, and even though we're mere acquaintances, she confided in me—rather detaining me to do so—that she will never be able to forgive herself that she allowed her children and Mr. Sorrel's illness to keep her from going to her husband before he died."

"She—told you that?"

"She most certainly did, and my heart went out to her so completely, I put my arms around her right there in public!"

"Well, good for you."

"Darling, we are so, so blessed to be together! And Natalie and Burke are equally blessed that he's too old for the conscription. You must read Eliza Anne's letter, because I've just remembered something else she wrote. It seems that W.H. is on fire now to raise another regiment up there of what he's calling Home Guards. He's very disturbed about the danger of a Union raid from Tennessee into north Georgia."

Mark frowned. "I've been worried about that all year."

"So have I—during my sleepless nights, but what troubled me so much was the thought that W.H. means to raise his regiment from men too old to be conscripted—men who wouldn't fight except to protect their homes."

"Burke," he said.

"Yes, Burke. Burke Latimer loves the upcountry enough to protect it. I know he's on your side, but he isn't a coward. How could I have forgotten to mention that part of Eliza Anne's letter?" She rubbed her forehead. "I get so disgusted with my pitiful supply of energy! Mark, I'm only sixty-eight. Is that old enough to be getting forgetful?"

He got up from the table and went to where she sat. "Don't confuse issues, my darling," he said. "It's been just a little over a year since you lost your only son. Grief is a—dreadful exhaustion—for us all."

EIGHTY-
FOUR

*O*n *June 7*, Eliza Anne arrived by train in Savannah and was met by Andrew Low, who informed her proudly that Mary Cowper appeared to be doing well.

"The new infant," he said as he helped her into his carriage, "should be joining us within just a few days. And I must add, Mrs. Stiles, that your daughter seems to be more at peace than I've ever known her to be."

Eliza Anne settled herself in the elegantly upholstered cab of his carriage and thanked him for his generosity and care of her daughter.

"It is I, my dear lady," Low said, climbing into the carriage to take his place beside her, "who thank you. I realize we have never openly discussed the matter, but I am well aware that it took some firm doing for you and Stiles to persuade her to marry me."

Eliza Anne was so startled by his remark that, for once, she felt inadequate to respond. She and Low had never been what could be called close acquaintances, even when he escorted her to find Henry, but this minute she felt that they might be. Her husband had owed Andrew Low money through all the years their daughter had been his wife. W.H. still owed him, but the now somewhat portly, still handsome Scot appeared truly satisfied. Mary Cowper had never confided in her since the marriage, but she chose to believe that Mr. Low could not look and act so contented if she were not contented with him.

"You couldn't have greeted me with better news, Mr. Low," she said as his driver took them toward Lafayette Square. "I have much to be thankful for. My husband is, at least for now, at home much of the time, and our son Henry is rapidly regaining strength. We—almost lost Henry."

"So I understand. The Cause needs such officers as Henry Stiles. I'm sure his father is proud that he is now a Major."

"So proud, but I'm afraid W.H. has a new worry."

"Your other son, Robert?"

"No. Bobby is still stationed in Florida, and he hopes soon to be sent here to Savannah. W.H. is sure Union forces will continue making raids into our part of Georgia. As I'm sure you know, we repulsed one such raid, an effort to cut the Western and Atlantic Railroad, our main source of supply for General Bragg. So W.H. is working hard to get permission from the Army or from Governor Brown to raise a regiment of Home Guards. Even small raids can be terribly damaging."

"They can, indeed," Low said. Then he turned to face her on the carriage seat, a rather sarcastic glint in his blue eyes. "Your illustrious husband simply cannot relinquish his delusions of military grandeur and heroism, can he?"

Eliza Anne stiffened. "I'm afraid I don't follow you, Mr. Low."

"The man's an author and, with enough funds, he could be an art collector of sorts. He's been a competent statesman. But, Mrs. Stiles, wouldn't you be eternally grateful if he gave up his ridiculous notion of riding a frothing horse into battle, no matter how becoming the uniform?"

For an instant her anger flared. Mr. Low was plainly making fun of W.H.! Then, remembering how much W.H. still owed him, she exerted every ounce of self-control and said quite calmly, "You must know, sir, that every wife prefers her husband to be a—statesman. The death rate is far lower!"

For the first several days her mother was there, Mary Cowper did her very best not to show that anything was wrong, but with this baby things were not the same as with the others. She felt well enough to go downstairs on the morning of June 15 and, although she wasn't hungry, kept up a cheerful conversation with her mother and husband at breakfast, asking innumerable questions about Natalie and Burke and Callie, giving Mr. Low a smile each time their eyes met from opposite ends of the long crystal- and silver-laden table.

Often, during the meal, she let one hand fall on her distended stomach, feeling for some sign of movement. There was none. Her mother sat to her right, so she took care not to check too often. One thing she meant not to do was cause Mama any more worry. Deliberately, she turned the table talk to Henry and listened until her head began to swim dangerously.

"Mary Cowper, are you feeling quite well?" Mama asked, reaching to touch her forehead. "Mr. Low, she's burning up with fever!"

Grasping the corner of the table for dear life, hoping to steady herself, Mary Cowper thought she'd never seen her husband's face so full of fear. Not even when the other baby had died. He jumped to his feet and cried, "Oh, my beautiful darling!" Then he lifted her to her feet, picked her up in his arms, murmuring, "No, Mary Cowper! Don't be ill, my adored one, don't be ill! I beg of you—I beg of you . . ."

Throughout the next day, she was too weak and feverish and dizzy to leave her bed. The doctor and her mother came and went, came and went. Through almost all the following day, June 17, Mr. Low knelt beside her bed, keeping his vigil. Mary Cowper felt oddly uninterested in why he wasn't at his office. The long day departed, darkness fell, and sometime after midnight, through a spasm of pain and cramped legs and weakness, she was sure Dr. Daniell had delivered her of a dead child.

Then, in a beat of receding memory, she was kneeling in the Roswell churchyard beside a lone grave with a pitifully simple, inexpensive marker. But on it her fingers were tracing the letters that formed his name, the date he was born, and the date he died "in Christ . . ." She didn't have any roses to leave for him. It was December. Roses weren't in bloom anywhere. And it was best because someone might have found them and discovered somehow that she had left them there. For a time, she prayed, and then out of a luminous, shimmering, faraway haze, she heard Mr. Low praying, too. Odd, she thought, that they had never prayed together before . . .

But then his voice beseeching God to let her stay with him faded, faded, and into the room strode Stuart—tall, his cheeks rosy with vibrant health, both arms out to her—beckoning. She smiled, oh, how she smiled at the sight of him!

A soft light flooded around them and, laughing as they'd always laughed, they left together on the journey they'd meant to take so long ago . . .

"If—it's any comfort to you," Andrew Low said to Eliza Anne, who was waiting at the foot of the stairs he now descended like a man sleepwalking, "she—smiled her way out of this life. I do hope the servants have served you coffee, Mrs. Stiles."

*C*allie *hurried* out to meet Sam when he rode up with the mail on June 20 and with a shout of excitement she ran up the path. Natalie met her on the cottage porch.

"You don't need to tell me," Natalie called as her daughter limped rapidly up the pine-straw path. "It's come! Sam brought a letter from Perry, didn't he?"

"Yes, yes," Callie shouted as though she were still ten years old. "He brought this stuff, too, but here—you take it, Mama. I'm going to sit by myself on Termination Rock and read what Perry wrote. Is that all right?"

"Of course it's all right. Go! It's exactly what you should do. But come back as soon as you can bear to and tell me what he says!"

When her daughter hurried away, faster, if possible, than a moment ago, Natalie flipped through the stack of other letters. One was for Burke from a business firm in Atlanta. That could wait till he got back in a day or two from Marietta. Another from Uncle W.H. off in Richmond again on regiment business of some kind and a letter for Natalie from her mother in Savannah.

Inside her cheerful living room, she called to Miss Lorah, who hustled in from the kitchen, drying her hands. "I got a letter from Mama! I thought you'd like to hear it."

"If I won't be nosin', I would," Miss Lorah said, taking the chair nearest where Natalie had plopped down on the green-and-white vine-print sofa. "You want to look it over first to be sure it's not too personal, Missy?"

"Whatever concerns Burke and Callie and me concerns you, too. Callie's gone off to Termination Rock to read a letter she got from Perry! Isn't that the most exciting thing?"

Lorah Plemmons's good chuckle told her she agreed, and as she broke the seal on her mother's letter, Natalie murmured, "My heart goes on breaking for poor Mary down in Savannah without Jonathan, but sometimes I think I'll burst with joy that Mary Cowper finally let me know she still loves Stuart in spite of—everything else. And now Callie has heard from Perry and . . ."

Laughing at her, Miss Lorah broke in: "And that fine man of yours is going to make a little money puttin' a new roof on the old part of the Stiles house as soon as he gets back from Marietta next week. I reckon you might just as well go on and pop with happiness! Never hurt nobody."

"One good thing about old Redbeard Low is that he does loan Uncle W.H. money to keep the rain from coming in," Natalie said, frowning at how short her mother's letter was. "My goodness, what a short note Mama wrote. I hope everything's all right."

"One way to find out."

"It's dated July 18. 'Our dear Natalie and family, I wish with all my heart that I did not have to write this, but your father and I felt you should know as soon as possible since Miss Lib may not be coming home anytime soon. Mary Cowper seemed to be doing so well carrying the new baby, but we are deeply grieved to have to tell you that the baby was born dead and Mary Cowper quickly developed septicemia or puerperal fever and died suddenly and peacefully, Mr. Low says, with a smile on her face.' Oh, Miss Lorah!" Natalie gasped. "I—really *loved* Mary Cowper!"

Lorah Plemmons reached to touch Natalie's knee, then to pat it slowly, rhythmically giving her time to cry if she needed to, to assemble herself, as Miss Lib sometimes said. "Missy, Missy," Lorah said at last. "Does it help to know she had a smile on her pretty face when she—went?"

Natalie snatched up the letter again. "Mama did say that, didn't she? I must have missed that part." Her cheeks were wet with tears now, but she looked up at Miss Lorah with an almost triumphant expression. "Maybe—maybe she—saw Stuart! Do you think she did? Do you?"

"Law, child, there isn't anybody can know what fine surprise the Lord might have fixed up for us once we get there. Or could be, He's got the surprise ready right when we first start out!"

They both heard Callie shouting long before she came crashing in the front door, her face glowing, Perry's letter in her hand.

"Don't shush her," Natalie ordered Miss Lorah when she saw her housekeeper put a finger to her lips. "It's all right, Callie. What did Perry say? Why haven't you heard from him? Is he all right? Is he coming?"

Ignoring her mother's questions, Callie asked, "Why were you crying, Mama? Is something wrong with my grandparents? Or Mary? Or Little Ben?"

"No. I haven't quite finished the letter yet, but—it's Mary Cowper. She's—dead and so is her baby." When Callie rushed to embrace her, Natalie sobbed, "I'm so—so sorry to have to tell you a thing like that just when you've had what must be good news from Perry!"

"Yes," Callie said, "it *is* the best news ever, but I loved her! Did giving birth to her baby—kill Mary Cowper?"

"It did," Miss Lorah said. "The baby was born dead, I guess."

"Like—Little Burke, Mama?"

Natalie could only nod her head. Finally she said, "You might never have been born, Callie, if—if I'd gotten the same dreadful sickness Mary Cowper had . . ."

"Septicemia—fever," Miss Lorah explained.

"But I *was* born, and I'm here to do anything in the world that might help you. I know only Papa could really help, but is there something I can do?"

Natalie forced a smile. "There certainly is. Read Miss Lorah and me the good news in your letter!"

"Could I just tell you?"

"Go ahead, child," Miss Lorah said.

"Perry's going to get leave! His regiment under General Grant has been laying siege to Vicksburg since last month. Just as soon as some Confederate general surrenders—and Perry thinks that could be far less than a month from now—he can start trying to slip back into north Georgia!"

"Oh, dear," Natalie said, horrified. "He does have to slip in, doesn't he?"

"Perry's the enemy in Georgia, Mama."

"I know that! But the poor boy had to sneak his way to the Union lines in Kentucky when he went. It's just so—unfair."

"I'd change that a little, Missy, if I was you," Miss Lorah said. "I'd say it's just so—manly of Perry. Must be bad enough to fight and then make your way home with the help of your own side the way the Rebels do. It's a lot worse, takes a lot more courage for Perry."

Callie was beaming again. "Miss Lorah, you're a brick! A solid-gold brick!"

"Is Perry well?" Natalie asked. "He's been through such hard fighting for such a long time now."

"He was all right when he wrote this, Mama. And we can all pray!"

"We sure can," Miss Lorah said, "but how do we pray for only one side? I make no bones about my love of the good old Stars and Stripes. But I can't help thinkin' about poor Mrs. Stiles. She's suffered so much over Henry. Now Mary Cowper's gone and I wonder where her boy Bobby is by now."

"He could be in Savannah soon, Papa thinks," Callie said. "There's a lot for Bobby's engineering regiment to do all around Savannah. Did Grandmother Caroline say anything about poor Miss Lib, Mama? She must be crushed over Mary Cowper."

"Oh, dear," Natalie moaned. "I haven't even finished Mama's letter yet! You read it, Callie. Read the first part to yourself. I'll cry if I hear that again. Miss Lorah and I can tell you where to start reading to us."

"The last you read, Missy, was about the smile on Mary Cowper's face."

For the time it took Callie to read to herself of Mary Cowper's death, Miss Lorah sat patting Natalie's knee again with her work-worn hand.

"All right," Callie said. "The next thing Grandmother writes is this: 'Your father and I are just back from the funeral at Christ Church. It was held at five o'clock this afternoon and the church was packed with genuinely grieving people, many of whom snubbed your dear father, Natalie, even in the face of his obvious grief. He is so terribly alone these days without Miss Eliza or Jonathan. When we reached home today, he mentioned missing William, too. I try to comfort him, but my own sorrow is very debilitating. My heart was deeply touched by Eliza Anne on the arm of Mr. Low at the church, with W.H. so far away in Richmond. Her face looked chalk white beneath her black veil. She, too, looked dead. When your father and I had supper just now, he said, so characteristically, "I confess Andrew Low has never been a favorite of mine, but his strength and poise impressed me today." We will keep a close watch on events here, hoping to visit you soon. We both send all of you so much love. Caroline Browning.' "

When Callie finished the letter, she, too, had tears in her eyes. "I– *always* really loved Mary Cowper," she said. "I loved her when I was a little girl, Mama."

"I know, darling," Natalie said. "Miss Lorah knows that, too."

Lorah Plemmons nodded, but said nothing.

After a long silence, Callie asked, "How can there be so much sadness right alongside so much–happiness? Can either one of you explain that to me? Is it terrible that with my dear Mary Cowper–dead– I'm still so excited and happy about Perry?"

"Absolutely not," Natalie said. "That's the way life is often, isn't it, Miss Lorah?"

"I reckon so," the older woman said. "If we never cried, nobody would know about a smile. The good Lord made us able to do both."

"But–at the same minute?" Callie persisted.

"At the same minute." Lorah Plemmons looked off out the open front door. "I'll never forget the purty clump of lady slippers I found growin' right outside the graveyard the day we buried my little girl and Luke. They'd been growin' there every year, likely, but I just never saw them before. I felt good just lookin' at them when we passed and I was bawlin' my eyes out!"

The three sat lost in their own thoughts for a time, then Natalie said, "I haven't been very kind to Miss Lib, but I could die over her today! And Uncle W.H.–do you suppose he even knows about Mary Cowper?"

"I'm sure Mr. Low sent him a telegram, Mama. Do you think he'll go straight to Savannah to be with Miss Lib? I know she'll stay on with the grandchildren. Do you both realize Perry could be here before Miss Lib gets back, now that this has happened?"

After more than two weeks of temporary work in Marietta, Burke was more than eager to get home. With an hour and a half to spare before his train left Marietta, he strode toward Robert Goodman's newspaper office for what had come to be a bright spot in his increasingly worrisome life.

Goodman, as always, greeted him warmly and vowed he wasn't busy. "I wish, in fact," Goodman said, "there were time to ride out to my place. We'd be more comfortable. But you have a train to catch. Squeeze into my private office, friend, and take your regular chair."

Burke glanced at a pile of papers on the desk. "Is that all news? Anything else good happened for the Union?"

Robert frowned, flipping through the dispatches and telegrams. "Only some fulfillment of my feeble predictions."

"You've been right a good part of the time so far," Burke said.

"Grant's had problems at Vicksburg. The Rebs kept General Sherman from getting to him not long ago. There was quite a battle at a place called Port Gibson, but Grant handled that and Sherman has joined him there this time, even though Rebel general Joe Johnston is advancing to the relief of Vicksburg. My prediction now is that Grant will be able, if his men keep fighting as they are, to get in between Johnston and the embattled city. I have no word of it yet, but I'd be willing to wager that the battle for Vicksburg itself is going on right this minute. Lee's Pennsylvania campaign is underway, too."

Burke frowned and shook his head. "Vicksburg hits close to home for me, you know. My daughter's fiancé is in the thick of it under Grant."

"Oh, yes," Robert said, leaning back in his chair. "The brave lad, Sergeant Clay of Macon. I enjoyed my visit with him. He was working for you, I believe, before he made his decision to fight with the Union. Will you take him back?"

"I will if I can. Perry's a number one carpenter, but he really wants a job with you on the paper."

"Well, that's quite possible, providing there is a paper." Goodman grinned. "I'm still alive. No one has taken a shot at me yet, but my paper barely is, Latimer, in spite of how objective I've tried to be in reporting only the straight news. Say, what do you hear from your father-in-law, Browning, in Savannah? Any chance he might be coming this way soon? I'd love to do a piece on how a Union man is faring down there in that hotbed."

"I don't know about writing him up," Burke said doubtfully. "The man has a hard enough time in town as it is. I certainly don't expect him anytime soon. I've tried to tell you the extraordinary way he loves the city. He's afraid that if he leaves, he might not be able to get back. Natalie and I have tried hard to persuade him to come to us, especially now that his only son was killed fighting as a Rebel right there at Fort Pulaski. The grief has really broken my father-in-law. My mother-in-law, too. She's a strong Confederate, so I guess in a way it's worse for the old man."

"Actually, what I'd like to find out is how far defection from the Southern forces has really gone down there. Some Rebels *are* defecting. Of course, your father-in-law may not know any more than he reads in the Savannah papers." Robert thumbed through a pile of clippings from both the *Republican* and the Savannah *Morning News* as he talked. "Rebel soldiers write letters to the Savannah papers, you know. Listen to this: 'Back in 1861 we reported that Irish soldiers are embracing the Cause with great spirit and ardor, especially the Catholics. Now we learn that there are some Irish among us who did not wish the Confederacy to conquer by any means. We find that no reliance whatever can be placed on the shipped men of foreign birth who are in Savannah now, many defecting.' That's from the *Republican.* Here's a story from the *Morning News* about a Thunderbolt soldier who writes: 'I believe that nearly all the people here think that we are whipped and I think that we are whipped, too.' Another wrote: 'Most of us have come to the conclusion that we have enlisted one time too often for our own good.' An editorial goes on to say: 'There is fear that the great weariness of the war and an absorbing desire to go home are rife among many of our troops. One firm support remains, however. The strong spirit of the women of Savannah. The very week after her daughter's funeral, Mrs. W. H. Stiles declared that "the Cause of the Confederacy is God's Cause and He will deliver our country in His own time." ' " Goodman looked at Burke. "Isn't Mrs. Stiles your neighbor?"

Burke was staring at him. "Yes, she is, and that sounds like something Miss Lib Stiles would say, but *when* did she say it? *In the week after her daughter's funeral?"*

"That's right."

"Mary Cowper? Dear Lord! Is there anything else about the death of —her daughter, Mrs. Andrew Low?"

"Let me look through an earlier paper. Yes, here's her funeral notice: 'The friends and acquaintances of Mr. and Mrs. Andrew Low are invited to attend the funeral of the latter from Christ Church, this afternoon, June 18, at 5 o'clock.' " Goodman paused. "That's a real blow to you, Burke, isn't it?"

Rubbing his hand over his face in disbelief, Burke said, "It is indeed. Mary Cowper Low was a close friend to my wife and me. Especially close, in fact, over the past six months or so. Since right before Christ-

mas of last year, actually. I'm sure her family has written Natalie, but—"
He got up. "I'd better not miss that train!"

Goodman looked at his watch. "You have all of forty-five minutes to walk about an eighth of a mile. Sit back down. We can just be quiet if you like. I can see you're terribly upset at what I just read." He shook his head. "Mrs. Stiles is certainly one of those spirited Rebel women, I'd say."

"She is indeed. More than that, she's a very great lady, actually. Her son-in-law, Andrew Low, is a strong Confederate sympathizer, too."

Goodman grinned. "Using his good British connections, I have no doubt."

"At one time, at least, yes. I would think that by now even Mr. Low has more or less given up on any foreign nation recognizing the Confederacy, though."

"Have the Stiles slaves left in any numbers since emancipation?"

"Only one that I know of. I'm not sure the Negroes up here even know about Lincoln's Emancipation Proclamation. It's a different story down in Savannah, my wife's father tells me. My belief is that slavery in the South is, except in a city like Savannah, pretty much as usual. Negroes are, after all, human beings like us. Capable of reacting in as many diverse ways. Some will remain submissively loyal, others will carouse and stir up trouble. Many won't know what to do." Still stunned at the news of Mary Cowper's death, Burke made a stab at polite conversation. "What about your slaves, Robert?"

"Loyal so far," Goodman said. "I'm a strong Unionist, but I need my people. I believe I treat them fairly. Many do, you know."

Burke looked at his own watch now. "I'm—I'm sorry to say this, but what you read to me about our dear friend's death has—muddled my thinking, Robert. She was only about thirty years old. Incredibly beautiful and full of life."

"My deepest sympathy," Goodman said. "Would you rather just walk around outside alone and not talk anymore? That might only make matters worse, you know. You do have the train ride back."

Burke rubbed his face with both hands now. "You're right. I'm better off here with you. I think I mentioned a moment ago that the South has surely given up on gaining recognition from a foreign power. Had you heard that one prominent Savannahian, Mr. Gazaway Bugg Lamar, instructed his son when he was abroad a few weeks ago to call on Ambassador Slidell in Paris?"

"No, why would he do that?"

"According to my father-in-law, to try to negotiate a French protectorate for the Confederacy. I'm surprised you hadn't heard."

"Well, I hadn't and I'm astonished at the whole idea! That is moving dangerously close to desperation, Latimer, on the part of the Rebels and not by an ordinary foot soldier either."

His mind still on how he would break the news of Mary Cowper's death to Natalie in case she hadn't heard, Burke said, "Desperation would be the hardest thing in the world for most Rebels to admit, but I see signs of it. Even up here. People are very, very weary of the war."

Goodman took a deep breath. "No one expected it to last but a few months. Here it is the middle of the third year. Is it any wonder they're tired? I know on your train ride back home, your mind will be on the loss of your young Savannah friend, Latimer, but give this some thought, too. By the end of this year, the North will hold not only Arkansas, Kentucky, a large part of Louisiana, Mississippi, Tennessee, and the Rio Grande frontier in Texas, but they'll have full control of the Mississippi *and* wind things up in Tennessee. Then what becomes of Georgia—what happens here in north Georgia? Won't the Yankees come straight down to Rome, Marietta—Atlanta? Your place could be almost on their route. Will you fight to protect your own land?"

Burke shook his head. "I don't know, Robert, I honestly don't know."

"Neither do I," Goodman said.

EIGHTY-SIX

The end of 1863 came and went, with both Natalie and Burke feeling helpless in the face of Callie's growing fears and anxiety. Only two letters had come from Perry Clay during the long, tense summer, one in June and the other in August. When she received the August letter, the three Latimers had held their own celebration in Perry's honor because at almost the same time Lee's men lost at Gettysburg, Rebel forces surrendered to Grant at Vicksburg on July 4. His leave granted, Perry's plans were to head for Bartow County and a reunion with Callie. But since August—nothing.

It wouldn't have been quite as sad or as trying, Natalie thought in February of the new year, 1864, if Callie weren't so brave. She was brave, though, and it shamed her mother, who found it almost too hard to bear that, until yesterday, Burke had been away from home doing the only work he could find to do at Confederate Camp McDonald in Marietta. Building for the Confederates was not easy for Burke, but he had to earn some money. They had used up their savings and neither would think of touching the nest egg they were keeping for the day when Callie and Perry could get married. The nest egg was what Burke had earned fixing the roof on the Stiles house last fall. She and Callie had loved having Burke work at home, but even now, Natalie felt furious with Andrew Low. Of course, it was generous of him to pay for the new

Stiles roof, but her heart ached for Miss Lib because old Redbeard Low had "loaned" Uncle W.H. the money by sending it straight to Burke as though W.H. might not pay him for his work.

When Miss Lorah joined her in the cottage parlor to help wind precious yarn, unraveled for reuse from the sleeves and back of one of Burke's old knit jackets, she was glad to have someone to talk to.

"Wouldn't you think Mr. Low might at least have mentioned his grief over Mary Cowper's death when he sent Burke that money?" she began as though the two had been discussing it all morning. "I know Mary Cowper's gone now and I also know it's a waste of time to keep on disliking the man, but poor Uncle W.H. doesn't deserve to be treated like an irresponsible child, do you think he does? He's changed, I know, but who hasn't changed in this stupid war? He and Miss Lib never did handle money very well and I wish they both didn't hate Yankees so much, but—" She jerked the yarn too hard and tangled it. "Now look what I've done by blabbing!"

"Yarn snarls sometimes, Missy," Lorah Plemmons said, quietly starting to work through the tangle. "And I know how hard it is for you with Mr. Low, but he's the way he is. Likely still too stricken over the pretty little thing's death to know much what he's doing."

Waiting for Miss Lorah to straighten out the yarn so they could start winding again, Natalie sat up very straight. "I also know that now, of all times, I need to be mature and even-tempered—and understanding. For Callie's sake, if for no other reason. I couldn't have acted as poised as Callie's acted since last summer! I had to wait and wait and wait after I knew I loved Burke before we got married, but I don't know now how I did it. I certainly don't know how Callie endures not knowing whether Perry's dead or alive!"

"Callie's young, Missy. You were young then, too."

"I hate it when anyone even hints that the young don't suffer!"

"They suffer all right, but our Callie's different from most. She knows her cryin' and fumin' around will only burden you and her pa and won't help Perry none."

"But where could Perry be all this time? Burke read that his troops had a big Fourth of July celebration when they won at Vicksburg, and he got his leave, but look how long it's been since then."

"I know you're tired of me saying this, Missy, but the boy does have to make his own way back to Georgia through Tennessee and it's not all clear of Southern forces yet, is it?"

"Oh, I don't know! I can't keep up with all that battle business. No matter who wins where, it doesn't seem to do anybody any good. Some general just thinks up a new place to start another battle. Burke thinks the Confederacy is doomed. The North has too many factories and too much money. People up there are living like royalty–parties and balls and plenty to eat and new clothes to buy."

Miss Lorah had no comment on that. She just handed the untangled yarn back to Natalie.

They worked in silence for a few minutes, then Natalie looked up at her. "Georgia is going to be–next, isn't it, Miss Lorah? What will we do if–they come here?"

The older woman took a deep, uneven breath. "I never in all my life felt like I know less than I know right now."

"Burke says most armies are in camp for the bad winter months now, but spring could be another story for us. Wouldn't it be tragic if they decided to come down into our upcountry just when the buds are swelling, when the birds have just laid their eggs?"

"I've thought a lot about how the little things must flutter and flinch everywhere when those guns go off in *their* woods and fields," Miss Lorah said.

"Another thing I don't understand," Natalie said, poking the loose end of the yarn deep into the ball they'd been winding, "is why my parents and Mary decided to make the trip up here from Savannah now, in February of all times. Papa's seventy-two, Mama's almost seventy. Neither one of them should be traveling in what could be icy-cold weather."

"I reckon they'll be here next week, though."

"Trains are either freezing cold or as overheated as August." She sighed. "I'll be glad to see them all, though, and we'll just have to keep them warm. At least our cottage is small. Yours, too. It was bitter cold in Miss Lib's big house yesterday when I went over there to check on her lazy people. I guess Mama and Papa might know how long Miss Lib plans to stay in Savannah with old Low and the children. I hope so. If it weren't for Callie overseeing things at the Stiles house, I can't think what might happen to it with Uncle W.H. away in Terrell County trying to buy still another plantation *and* raise another regiment! Sometimes I think military officers are monsters. They fight each other even when they're on the same side of the war."

"They don't all do that, I guess."

"Burke thinks Miss Lib's friend General Lee isn't driven by his pride, but who knows?" They were almost finished with the yarn and it would soon be time for dinner. She could sense Miss Lorah girding herself to get it started. Natalie heaved another huge sigh. "What's the use of fixing anything to eat, Miss Lorah?"

"Because it's time."

"Do you suppose Perry's a prisoner of war? Do you think he—might even be—dead? Or married to another woman?"

"Missy, Missy, *Missy* . . ."

"Well, you do have to admit this dreadful time of waiting to see what might happen next is—terrible, don't you?"

While she busied herself tucking the three balls of yarn they'd wound into her sewing basket, Miss Lorah said nothing. "I know you don't like it when I take time to study about something, Missy," she said at last, "but you're as right as rain. Waitin' is the hardest thing anybody is ever asked to do."

The temporary work ended at Camp McDonald, Burke was home in time to meet the Brownings at Manassas Station the following week. As he and Callie rode along together on the cold, windy driver's seat of his carriage, his thoughts were on his father-in-law. For the first time Burke fully understood how Mark Browning had leaned on his son, Jonathan. Because of the steady way Callie had conducted herself through her long months of agony over Perry, he understood how a father could come to depend upon his son as Mr. Browning had for all the years of Jonathan's life. Natalie agreed with him that indeed Callie was very like her Uncle Jonathan. Burke and Natalie both depended on their plucky daughter. She doesn't need a father leaning on her, Burke thought. She needs a father she can lean on!

"Are you sure you don't want to climb back in the cab, darling?" he asked. "No need for us both to freeze up here in the open."

The sunny smile came and she scooted closer to him on the hard seat. "And miss talking to you when finally you're close enough to hear me?" she joked. "Did you have a hard time working for the Confederacy at Camp McDonald, Papa?"

"I did. The work was all right, but my principles suffered some. I felt out of place with those hardworking, conscientious Rebel boys who are just as sure they're right as I am. I think that got to me more than almost anything. They're good Americans, patriots. They just come down on the other side of everything. I respect them, but I think I also felt dishonest. We needed the money, though, worthless as money is these days with prices so high. I didn't want to be short of funds with your grandparents coming."

"Grandfather Browning will give us anything we need."

"I know, but I've never had to take anything from him. He did mention that he wanted some work done on Miss Lorah's cottage while they're here. Her roof needs patching. She needs a new front-porch floor. These are not easy times for any of us, are they?" A quick glance at her perfect profile told him she was fighting tears. "Callie, there's a chance that your grandfather might know something we don't about where General Grant's troops are by now. Mr. Browning still gets Northern periodicals and newspapers, you know. Goodman in Marietta thinks Grant's going to be put in charge of all Union forces anytime now, since he did so well at Vicksburg and Chattanooga." Wanting desperately to reassure her, he added, "We'll talk to your grandfather about all that."

"But—he won't have any way of knowing where—*he* is. Papa, almost seven months is a long time to wait!"

"I know, darling, I know. Mr. Goodman gets casualty lists eventually, though, in his newspaper office—Union and Rebel. He vows Perry's name hasn't appeared."

She still hadn't allowed herself to cry, but she was clinging to his arm. "Does Mr. Goodman have any ideas where Perry might be?"

"Some theories, that's all. Perry could, of course, have been badly wounded, so that he had a long stay in a Union hospital. If not wounded, he isn't the kind of young man to quit fighting if he's needed, just because he'd earned leave. Sherman's forces joined Grant at Chattanooga. Perry could have figured he'd travel this way with Sherman sooner or later."

"If Sherman is going to Atlanta, we'll be right on his path, won't we?"

"I expect so."

"Will it make a difference to you and the way you love the Union, Papa, if Union forces invade the Georgia upcountry?"

Burke kept his eyes straight ahead. "I—I don't know, baby. Right now, I honestly don't know."

Greetings over at the train station, the Savannah visitors' baggage strapped to the rear rack of Burke's carriage, they bumped and swayed along toward home, Little Ben bundled in a fur coverlet, on the high driver's seat beside Burke, talking up a storm. Callie had, of course, been her open and honest self with Mary and her grandparents. She was never one to stir things up by keeping too much to herself *or* by overtelling. Her story of how hard it had been to wait for word from Perry was just right. At least, what Burke could hear of her talk from his perch up front. He marveled that while telling such a personal story, she seemed to stay aware of each one of her listeners, never once forgetting to include Mary. Burke knew how proud his father-in-law was of Perry's choice to fight with the Union, but most tactful of all, he thought, was Callie's sensitive inclusion of her Rebel grandmother.

"I know you'd prefer Perry to be fighting for the South, Grand-mother," Callie said, her clear, young voice carrying, as usual, like a bell on the thin, frosty air. "Papa and I understand that, so does Mama. Perry will understand, too, if—he ever comes back to me. He was pretty torn over the decision, actually, but his grandfather, like mine, loved the Union and taught Perry to love it." Burke glanced back at his passengers under two heavy woolen blankets just as Callie smiled at Mrs. Browning and said, "Somehow, I feel you'll like Perry a lot anyway, Grandmother. He's very intelligent and a natural kind of true gentleman, isn't he, Papa?"

Before Burke could answer, while he was restraining Little Ben, who had begun to wiggle, Mr. Browning shouted, "Burke! Slow down a minute! Look over there in that clump of bushes! Is that a man strug-gling through there or an animal of some kind?"

"It's a filthy, dirty man, Mark," Mrs. Browning gasped. "I can see his bushy hair and beard!"

Burke, holding Ben with one hand, reined the team and they all sat peering at the slow, stumbling movements in the stand of pine seedlings and leafless sumacs. It *was* a man! A rail-thin, broad-shouldered young man, Burke felt sure. "Hello!" he called. "Who are you?"

Callie's piercing scream startled them all. Burke looked around. She was standing up, and before anyone had presence of mind enough to stop her, she leapt to the ground and was running, as though she weren't crippled, toward the bedraggled man, half crawling now through the thick bushes. Only Callie's bright green winter coat could be seen as she knelt on the ground beside him. The man had fallen and was mostly out of sight in the undergrowth.

"Burke," Mrs. Browning cried, "Callie might be in danger!"

Jumping to the road from the driver's seat, Burke lifted Little Ben down, thrust the child into the cab to his grandmother, and ran to where

Callie knelt, calling back as he ran, "Don't worry about Callie! Give thanks—she's found Perry!"

Four-year-old Ben began to cry when his mother, Mary, also leaped from the carriage and ran like a deer to a nearby creek, her new velvet hat clutched in one hand, her new winter coat and velvet dress obviously forgotten. Burke saw her scoop the costly plumed bonnet into the stream of icy water, race back to where Callie knelt, and, in minutes, revive the bearded, dirty young man so that he opened one eye. Where the other eye should have been was covered with scarred, swollen tissue.

"Don't try to say anything, dearest," Callie was murmuring. "Just rest, Perry. Rest. More water, please, Mary—could you?"

Mary was already on her way back to the creek, to refill her grand hat.

His sensitive young face hidden under a thick brown growth of filthy, matted beard, Perry could only whisper, "Callie . . . Callie!"

"Sh." Callie smoothed the grimy forehead, black with smoke and dirt. "All that matters, Perry, is that you're here—you're here! And you're —alive. Rest, rest before you even try to say one other word. Do you hear me? Sh!"

Standing over them, Burke couldn't help thinking that she sounded exactly like Natalie giving orders. From behind where he stood, he could hear Little Ben chattering and the crackle of footsteps in the dry undergrowth. He turned to look. Mr. Browning and the boy were coming toward them—the old man's expression, Burke thought with a pang, was quite lost and confused.

"It's all right, Mr. Browning," he said, taking Ben's hand and guiding them both back toward the carriage. "I know this has been a shock to you, sir, but it's all good news. We've waited so long! Sergeant Clay's in bad shape. He may have lost an eye, but he's here."

"It's Perry, Caroline—Callie's happy!" Mr. Browning called out to his wife.

Back at the carriage, Burke lifted Ben up into the cab again. At once, the little boy began to smile, to examine and pull at the white ermine tails on his grandmother's muff. Burke helped Browning inside, too, but he had to be firm with him in order to convince him that he and Callie and Mary could get Perry out of the bushes and into the carriage without his help.

Burke hurried again to where Callie and Mary knelt beside Perry still flat on his back on the frozen ground. Carefully, he lifted the thin, emaciated body of his future son-in-law in both arms as though he were a tall, gangly child. Then he struggled along with his welcome burden, Mary and Callie on either side, back to the open carriage door. Summoning every ounce of energy, he hoisted Perry's inert form inside and straightened him out on the empty front seat. Quickly, he gave in to Ben, who shouted that he wanted to ride on the driver's seat.

"All right," Mary said. "Ben and I will ride up front with Mr. Burke. Callie should be on the seat with–*him*."

Catching his breath before he went around back to get an extra lap robe to cover Perry, Burke studied Mary's face as she helped Ben up onto the driver's seat. When he'd seen Mary first today at the station, she had looked so stylish, so like a fine Savannah lady, he had only bowed and smiled warmly. Now, the soggy, feathered hat dangling from one hand, her long, velvet skirt wet from the creek, cheeks flushed, he could feel the warmth of his long-ago affection for her. She looked almost like Indian Mary again–somehow younger, as agile as ever, and in spite of the sadness he knew would never leave her eyes, in full charge. In full charge as she had been in charge of cooking and cleaning and sewing for him and her brother, Ben, in their old Cherokee cabin so many years ago.

"Stop the wiggle," she called up to Little Ben, one of her hands still holding carefully to his short, fat leg. "Mama and Mr. Burke will be right up there with you." Then she turned to Burke with a determined smile. "We–back–we *are* back in Cherokee country again, Mr. Burke. We work together again–to help Callie."

"Yes," he said gratefully. "You bet we will!"

Without any help from him, she climbed up onto the driver's seat. She was smiling, but the sadness in her eyes almost overwhelmed him. "You're as–brave and–strong as ever, aren't you, Mary?"

She turned away, so that she looked straight down the road that, in two or three miles, would end at the old Etowah Cliffs river road. "No, I am not brave and I am not strong. I am only–still here on the earth." She shook her head in quick little jerks. "No, I make a mistake. I am–only *half* here on the earth–without Jonathan. But we will be sure, Mr. Burke, that Callie never be only half here. We work together to make her loved one well again."

Burke looked around to be certain his passengers were ready to go, scrambled up onto the driver's seat beside Mary and Ben, and started the team, suddenly unable to wait for the sight of Natalie's face when she saw that they were bringing Perry with them.

While they were still nearly a mile from the Etowah Cliffs river road, Callie, holding Perry's head on her lap, saw him open his one eye and try to smile up at her. As though her grandparents were not present on the seat across from them, she whispered, "Everything's all right now, dearest. I'm here to take care of you. You'll sleep in a nice, clean bed tonight—I've just decided, right in Miss Lorah's cottage. And when you wake up tomorrow, I promise to be there."

Speaking was such effort for him, she could tell, that she placed two fingers over his dear, raw lips, until she saw how troubled he looked. Obviously, he needed to say something to her. Callie took her fingers away. "What, Perry? What?"

With one thin, stained hand, he touched his torn, swollen eye socket. "I—had an eye—shot out. Will you—bring me a—book tomorrow morning? I've been—so afraid I—can't read anymore!"

EIGHTY-SEVEN

Early in March, Miss Lib's letter came with the news that in a week she and the Low children would be at Etowah Cliffs for a month or so. Natalie began immediate plans for putting the Stiles house in order.

"I'm sure Miss Lib is expecting you to spend a lot of time with Mary Cowper's children," she said to Callie just as Miss Lorah arrived to clean up the dinner dishes. "But don't let that change anything. Perry must always come first with you."

Natalie saw Callie and Burke wink at each other, then smile, but she cared not a whit that they teased her for being a romantic. She was and that was that.

"I reckon Perry will be along over from my place anytime now," Miss Lorah said, scraping plates. "He ate a whopping breakfast and dinner. If I'd had any more squirrel fried, I do believe he'd have gobbled it up. He nearly died of dysentery *and* pneumonia in Tennessee, I believe it was, but except for that ugly hole where his eye was, the boy looks as healthy now as a buck deer. And he reads better with one eye than I do with two."

"I'm riding to Cartersville today," Burke said. "I'll do my best to find meat of some kind, at least for Perry. Your father's going with me,

Natalie. We're planning to get something Miss Lorah can use to make an eye patch for Perry."

"Does Papa feel like riding a horse?" Natalie wanted to know.

"He says he does. If not, we'll take the carriage." Burke got up from the table, kissed Natalie and Callie, and headed for the door. "Take good care of our war hero, Callie."

Callie blew him a kiss. "My stakes in Perry are pretty high, Papa. I don't intend to let him out of my sight. He and I are taking a picnic to the river today. I made extra biscuits this morning and Perry's bringing a jar of Miss Lorah's honey."

"Some elegant picnic," Natalie scoffed, getting out a clean dish towel. "Blasted old war!"

When she and Miss Lorah were left alone, Natalie ordered Miss Lorah to sit down with her.

"Never could see why we can't talk and work, Missy. I got these dishes to do."

"Oh, all right, but I'm just about at my wits' end. I never paid much attention to things like politics or who's President, but war–especially this one–has to be the most insane thing even politicians have ever thought up!"

Sudsing the dishes in a pan of hot water, Miss Lorah said, "I doubt much real thought went into it, Missy."

"Take poor Perry, for example. He'd fought through all those other battles–so long, in fact, that he had a leave coming. Did he get it? No. On his way back here to Callie, he ran into General Sherman's men and went right back to fighting other young men who, like him, were born in the South, too. Perry was born in Macon, Georgia, Miss Lorah! And he's as strong for the Union as my father and Burke and look at both of them. Burke will never leave his beloved Georgia upcountry and my father is like a lost sheep away from Savannah! I tell you, the world is upside down. I have to believe Burke and Perry and Papa are on the right side, but isn't it all–crazy?"

"You know in your own heart that they're on the right side?" Miss Lorah said.

"I suppose so, because the North is winning. But a lot more than that makes me think they must be right. They're all three *pleasant*. Being Rebels seems to make perfectly well-bred, good people so disagreeable. Miss Lib and Uncle W.H. can get downright mean on the subject!"

"I don't see your mother as mean," Miss Lorah said with a sly smile. "She's a Rebel through and through, but look how she likes Perry."

Natalie stacked the dishes she'd just dried on a shelf. "I know, I know. She actually seems smitten with Perry and never mentions to Burke anymore that he's a 'benighted Union man.' I thought when Burke turned Uncle W.H. down at joining his Home Guard regiment, Mama might act the way Uncle W.H. did. Not so. Oh, Miss Lorah, poor Uncle W.H. is just another part of the madness, isn't he?"

"He's pitiful, if that's what you mean. Looks like, right or wrong, he's tried so hard and even the Rebels don't treat him with much respect. It's none of my business, but I'll betcha he's off over in Terrell County now buyin' up more land just because he's so flattened by not having much help with his Home Guard."

"At least he isn't just down the road nagging at Burke to join it."

"Burke don't need to join a regiment to protect our place here, Missy. That man of yours would never stand for even one of his own Yankees doin' us harm."

"I know he wouldn't—if he happens to be here." When Miss Lorah said nothing, Natalie threw down her dish towel. "Do—do you think they might come this way, Miss Lorah? Do you lie awake nights—worrying about that? We're standing here in the kitchen calmly doing dishes and those rough, dreadful men Perry fought with might be planning to come straight here! Men with guns in their hands! Guns that could kill us all. If they came marching in here, along our river road, how could we be sure they wouldn't do—awful things to us?"

Miss Lorah gave her a long, affectionate look, then a cocky grin. "They wouldn't get near *you*, Missy, as long as I could get my hands on this iron skillet!"

At the end of the first week in April, after Miss Lib and the Low children had been there almost a month, Burke took Natalie's parents to inspect the work he, Sam, and Perry had done on Miss Lorah's cottage. For the whole of her visit, Natalie had found Miss Lib so changed, so shattered, she had avoided time alone with her. Today, she sent word by Callie that she longed to talk—just the two of them.

"What's really wrong, Miss Lib?" she asked point-blank as soon as they sat down in Natalie's living room. "You seem so—beaten. Is it—Mary Cowper? I know you'd have given anything if Uncle W.H. hadn't gone off to Terrell County again yesterday just two days before you have to leave for Savannah, but the poor man told me himself that this time even he felt strange with you."

Tears swam in Miss Lib's eyes. "W.H. told *you* that?"

"I know you both still think of me as young and giddy and spoiled. I also know I acted like a buttinsky when you—arranged dear Mary Cowper's marriage to Mr. Low, but I'm not young anymore. I'm forty-one and everything is so crazy in our world, no matter which side people are on, I think we need to let go of old feelings. I've really tried to let go of my fury at you for breaking up Mary Cowper's engagement to Stuart Elliott. I think I've finally succeeded, maybe because, as much as I miss her, I now believe she and Stuart are together at last." She leaned toward her. "I'm talking a lot. Forgive me. If you're as—crushed as you seem, you don't need me to blather at you. Can't you forget being angry about the war for long enough to remember how close we once were? Are you so worried that Uncle W.H. might spend most of his first good cotton crop on that Terrell County land?"

Miss Lib dried her eyes. "Yes, I'm very worried about that. Thanks to Mr. Low's British connections, W.H. made his first real profit on that crop—over twenty-four thousand dollars."

"That's a lot!"

"But tomorrow, he undoubtedly plans to spend twenty thousand of it in Terrell County. Natalie, who's going to work the new land? Half of our people here have vanished. W.H. won't have enough money left to hire additional white hands to break new Terrell County land. Not if he buys seed and equipment—both at a premium." Looking genuinely perplexed, she studied Natalie's face. "You have really changed, haven't you? I mean, you won't go advertising what I'm telling you to Mark and Caroline, will you? I haven't even told my sisters in Savannah. I honestly never dreamed I'd be telling you!"

"Whatever I've been, you've never thought of me as a gossip, have you?"

"No. And I do need you to be my friend now. For more reasons than what W.H. might be doing today with his profits."

"I knew it!"

"You knew what?"

"That something somewhere is so wrong, it's changed you inside. You're no longer—sure you're almighty. You're not so bossy."

"Oh, dear . . ."

"I'm sorry to be blunt, but I think we *can* be friends again even if I'm not enough of a Rebel to suit you."

Hands clenched tightly together, Miss Lib said, "I can no more help resisting Northern aggression than your own mother can, Natalie, and sometimes all I can think of is—how will it all end? But yes, something else is wrong. There is something that has nothing to do with the war that is very, very wrong. I—I couldn't tell W.H. because he owes Mr. Low so much money."

"It's old Redbeard Low, isn't it?"

"It's—Mr. Low's—afternoon habit."

"What afternoon habit?"

"I know his business is slow in Savannah now. Factor's Walk and Commerce Row are deserted most of the time, but—I don't think that's the only reason he seldom goes back to his countinghouse after we have dinner. I know it isn't. The minute he excuses himself from the table, he heads for—the port bottle. By sundown, he's drunk as a lord!"

"Miss Lib! What does he—do to you?"

"Oh, he does nothing to me but act as though I'm not in the house taking every possible care of his children. When I'm forced to address him on some household matter, he either snarls or just sits there glaring at me as though I—symbolized some hated aspect of his life!"

Natalie's mind began to spin. Maybe Miss Lib *did* symbolize his grief over Mary Cowper! Maybe he much preferred to hire a nanny, to send Miss Lib packing back to her own house. That must be it! Seeing her every day in the rooms of his house, at his table, must keep his grief over Mary Cowper slashing at the man.

"Could—could he be drinking so much because of his—grief?" Natalie asked carefully.

"I've thought of that a thousand times," Miss Lib said. "I'm sure I remind him of—her, but I have no intention of leaving her children to fend for themselves with a besotted father!"

"Does—does he ever mention Mary Cowper to you?"

"No. It's as though she hadn't given her very life to bring his children into the world! He attacks me for spoiling little Willy, when he himself is the one who spoils the boy. He—he even accused me of giving the new housekeeper he just hired an emerald ring that had belonged to his first wife, when it wasn't mine to give! Of course, that lovely ring belongs to his daughters by Sarah Hunter Low. I haven't laid eyes on the ring since Mary Cowper's stepdaughters were last in Savannah years ago. He all but accuses me outright of stealing it, when I—I haven't even seen it . . ." She buried her head in her hands now and sobbed.

Natalie rushed over and knelt beside Miss Lib and began wiping her tears away. "Go on, cry it out," she said softly. "I don't blame you one bit. But he was—bemuddled when he accused you of such a thing, Miss

Lib. Try not to pay any attention to him or, better yet, just pack up your things and come home!"

Miss Lib looked up at her so helplessly, Natalie could have cried, too. Then, slowly, but surely, the old Miss Lib fire returned. "No, indeed. Thank you for understanding. But no matter what he does, I will never, *never* leave Mary Cowper's children there with him!"

"But what about Uncle W.H. and your house here?"

"Who knows what W.H. is going to do? He—he took pains to tell me that if he did buy the Terrell County land, he'd have to be there much of the time—months. At least until the clearing and planting are done. Oh, he's changed, too, Natalie. W.H. is suddenly old and very, very bitter over the war. I might as well tell you while I'm at it that, although W.H. can't admit it to anyone yet, General Howell Cobb has replaced him as organizer and commander of his cherished Home Guard!"

"Does Burke know?"

"No one knows around here but you and me. I wouldn't be at all surprised to learn anytime that my beloved W.H. has *resigned* from the Confederate Army. Like most of the rest of us, he was so sure the South would—romp to victory in a matter of months. Not just one but several government officials in Richmond, some generals as well, have harshly mistreated him, have told false stories about his selfless service to his country. Even President Davis has begun to ignore his letters. W.H. was dead right when he insisted that a Home Guard is needed here in the upcountry. Those boorish Yankees are headed this way. I have no choice but to take the children back to Savannah. Only God knows how long it will be safe down there, but for now it seems to be."

"I'd rather have Burke right here at home to try to protect us than off somewhere with Uncle W.H.'s Home Guard."

"I'm sure W.H. could have arranged to have Burke stationed here. Until Cobb replaced him, he wasn't without influence, you know." She frowned and looked down. "Now, he's—exhausted and crushed."

"I wish I could help you," Natalie said. "I do. I haven't felt close to you for a long time. I—kind of do now. Do you feel any closer to me?"

Miss Lib stood up and put her arms around Natalie. "Yes. Yes, I feel— closer to you again, and—even when you objected to me so strenuously at the time Mary Cowper married Mr. Low, I have to believe you meant well—and maybe you were right. Can we put that behind us? Every bit of it except—her dear sweetness always—with all of us?"

Natalie felt so near tears now, she could trust herself only to nod her head yes, yes.

"And I'm—glad Callie has her—odd young man back safely again."

"Perry isn't odd, Miss Lib. He's just loyal to what he believes to be right. Like you and Uncle W.H."

When later that day Perry was helping nail down the new joists that would support Miss Lorah's front porch, Burke asked him if he'd spent any time alone with Callie's grandfather, Mark Browning. Perry looked at him in surprise.

"No, sir, I haven't. I like him, though, and if you think it would be all right, I'll ask him to take a short walk with me this evening."

"You'll enjoy him. He's suffered some bad blows lately, but he's one of the most courageous men I've ever known."

"Callie has told me of his lonely time in Savannah. He must really feel strongly about saving the Union to have stayed so true blue when his own son turned Rebel."

"Worse than that," Burke said as he reached for his hammer to tap the last joist into place. "Yankee guns killed Jonathan and the man still stayed loyal. Rumor is that General Hunter's Federals failed to give the wounded Rebels medical attention. Mr. Browning didn't flinch even then. Be sure to take that walk, Perry. Callie will understand."

"I never worry about Callie, sir." Perry's smile showed laugh creases in the now clean-shaven face. "Sometime I'll get *you* off alone and tell you what a great lady your daughter really is."

"Perry?"

"Sir?"

"Having much trouble hitting those nails with—one eye?"

"Yes, sir, but I'll learn. I *can* still read. That's the most important thing."

"If you hadn't invited me for a walk this evening," Mark said as he and Perry strolled along the river road, "I'd have invited you. Mrs. Browning and Mary and I will be leaving in a few days. I've wanted to interrupt you and Callie long enough for a good talk."

"I'm honored, Mr. Browning. It's important to me that you know I love Callie with all my heart."

"She's—very like my son, Jonathan, her uncle," Mark said, hearing the tremor in his own voice in spite of his new vow to pull himself out of the despair which he had begun to abhor. "Callie seems to have my son's genius for *knowing* even before she's been told."

"Oh, yes, sir! It was her strength and confidence that brought me through all the fighting in Mississippi and Tennessee. I still find it hard to believe that a girl like Callie loves me, but I want you to know I'll always be good to her."

"A young man with your values would have to be."

"Excuse me, but how do you know that?" Perry asked.

"I've had nearly seventy-three years to learn about human nature, for one thing. Mrs. Stiles's mother, Eliza Mackay, taught me what I missed along the way. I wish you'd known her. She was a born Southerner, but Miss Eliza would have understood exactly why you chose to fight with the Union."

"I'm glad Callie knew her."

"So am I. Since you and Callie plan to marry when this is all over, I want you to know that I'm not always so—inadequate as now. I'm working hard at coming through two big losses." When the boy said nothing, Mark changed the subject. "I hear you're a writer."

"I mean to be, sir." Perry brightened. "I plan to work hard at becoming a real writer."

"Once this tragic war is over—and I guess it will be someday—our country will need writers to communicate intelligent ideas, Perry. Our people will need to learn to think again. I know from my own experience that genuine thought, for the past few years, has all but vanished. We're all so buffeted by emotion. All emotions aren't constructive, you know."

Mark's legs ached and he headed toward Burke's river-watching bench, where they both sat down.

"Go on, Mr. Browning. I'm interested in what you're saying."

Perry's urging at first seemed mere courtesy to an older man. Still, the boy had been living with death and exhaustion and hardship for so long, Mark thought, maybe he really means it. He has no father, Callie says. Except for what time Perry had felt strong enough to work with Burke, there had been no one to talk to. Noncommissioned men in either army were not usually brainy men, certainly not while sleeping on the ground or dragging along on marches of miles and miles over rough terrain. A sense of being needed surged in Mark. He turned on the bench to look at Perry.

"You—meant that, didn't you? You really are—interested."

"Oh, yes, sir. I haven't found it as easy as I've tried to pretend coming back from such a—different world. You're giving me real conversation and I need it. Don't misunderstand. Being with Callie is all I could think of even during the worst of the fighting, but . . ."

"But it isn't simple relearning how to live in such a tiny community in peace and safety."

"That's right." The crinkly smile, different, but as sunny as Jonathan's, came. "I still feel funny in—clean clothes. Especially ironed shirts. Callie insists upon ironing even my work shirts." The smile faded abruptly as Perry looked right at him. "I know how much you love Savannah, Mr. Browning."

Surprised by this, Mark could only say, "You do? I suppose Callie told you."

"Yes, sir. And I'd like to be selfish and urge you to stay on here, but . . ."

"But what, Perry?"

"I have no official information at all. I'm only a sergeant, but word gets around among the troops. I'm of the impression that now that General Grant is going to be put in charge of all Union operations, General Sherman will be in command of the Army of the Tennessee, and without meaning to eavesdrop, I heard him tell Grant one night when they were planning strategy in Grant's tent that what mattered was—destroying the railroads to Atlanta."

In the New York *Tribune,* Mark had read the exact same thing. What Perry was saying was that if he meant to get back to Savannah, he needed to go soon. "Which means that with Sherman near the Georgia border up in Tennessee now, he'll be coming down this way."

"Who knows for sure, sir, but from the Union side—our side—it makes sense."

"Yes."

"On my way back here, I did learn that Rebel general Joseph Johnston's forces are encamped up at Dalton, Georgia. To Sherman that's an invitation, I suspect."

Mark looked down over the forty-foot-high cliffs to the river, nearly crimson now in the afterglow of the sun already out of sight behind what was lately being called Stiles Mountain less than a mile away. Then he looked at Perry. "Do you have any idea how it makes me feel actually to hear another man call the Union forces—*our side?*"

"Callie told me how alone you are in Savannah."

"My wife is a Rebel, you know. My son's—widow, Mary, being half Cherokee, has no side at all. She's just—Mary, bless her. With Miss Eliza

Mackay gone, I am alone in Savannah. But strange as this is going to sound, our talk has given me what actually feels like—hope. It may not last. And I won't know for sure until I'm back there again, but right now, I almost feel that I will be able, from now on, to be—alone *with* Savannah. Not just—alone *in* the one place on earth I love more than any other."

"Your grandson, Ben, seems to thrive up here, doesn't he? He must be a great comfort to you."

In all innocence, Perry had managed to collapse the fragile hope Mark had felt. With all his heart, Mark wanted to find a way to allow himself to love Little Ben in a natural way—the way a grandfather should love his only grandson. The way he had loved Willow!

"Ben surely seems to dote on you," Perry was saying. "I never saw anything to equal the way he looks at you with those big, black, worshipful eyes. He told me you taught him how to shoot marbles. In fact, he proved it to me yesterday."

"He did?" Mark asked lamely. "Ben's a—fine, bright boy. I—I do the very best I can to be friends with him."

The next morning, while Miss Lorah and Natalie and Callie were working at home on making a black felt eye patch which Perry could tie around his head, Burke looked up from painting the Plemmons porch railing to see Mary coming toward him—for once, alone.

"Well, hello," he called. "Where's Ben? I wondered if he ever got a foot away from you, Mary."

"Sometimes it seems he only has me," she said, sitting down on the top porch step. "You can stop painting for one minute, Mr. Burke?"

"I think I could manage that," he answered, poking his brush into a can of turpentine before he sat down beside her. "What's on your mind?"

"Ben. My brother. He is so close to me up here."

"I'm sure he is. It must help a lot having his namesake."

She turned to look straight at Burke. "Papa Mark does not much like my son."

"What?"

"I know about his broken heart. I have it, too, so I know. He is—a stranger with Ben because of his dark skin. Because he looks like my brother, Bending Willow."

"Oh, there must be some explanation you're missing, Mary," he said, feeling genuine concern. "Mr. Browning liked your brother, Ben, a lot."

"He also taught my son to shoot a marble, but Little Ben is not—like my daughter, Willow—dear to him. Can you tell me why?"

"Where is Little Ben now?"

"With Papa Mark."

"Well, isn't that good?"

"Not when I have to ask Papa Mark to care for him while I come here."

"The man's not himself," Burke said. "You know it gets harder to bear loss at his age. He must feel bereft without Miss Eliza Mackay." He took one of her hands. "You're going to have to give the old fellow time."

"Two years, Mr. Burke? I cannot help it that my son looks like a full-blood!"

"Mary, it isn't that at all. I know Mr. Browning too well ever to believe that. The man's been hurt by so much, I'm sure he's just trying to protect his heart from still more hurt. He took Willow's death very hard, you remember. He may not even know that he's doing it, but I'm sure he's—trying not to get too fond of Little Ben."

Her look literally begged him to be right. "You are—still wise like long ago, Mr. Burke?"

He laughed awkwardly. "I'm—I'm pretty sure I'm right about this. You always thought me smarter than I ever was, Mary, but you're all leaving early next week, so promise me you'll be patient. And I think you did the right thing to leave Ben alone with his grandfather now. In fact, you should do that more often. Ben's a charmer! He's bright and funny and why not let Ben win the old gentleman himself? You just might be on the verge of overprotecting the boy. Of spoiling him."

In her enigmatic way, she seemed not even to have heard what he said. "Mother Caroline—love Ben."

"That's good, isn't it? She's changed a lot. Even I can tell that."

"Once she did not like my brother, Bending Willow. But now she is the one who loves Little Ben. I've learned a lot about living in Savannah away from—all this up here—but I haven't learned all I need to know about full-blooded white people, Mr. Burke. Only you."

Now he laughed easily. "I'll say you've learned how to live in Savannah! Do you realize when you first came here to talk just now you were speaking almost the way you used to speak?"

" 'Flawed English,' Natalie calls it."

"But the minute you even mentioned living down there, you began to sound almost like a real Savannahian."

"Does it matter?"

"I–I guess not," he said.

"I live now–for Ben. For Ben and Mama Caroline and Papa Mark– and you. But in Savannah for the three of them. Because they belonged to Jonathan. How can I tell Papa Mark how sorry I am that Little Ben– looks Cherokee?"

"You can't, Mary. You just have to wait for the old man to find himself again. I may be imagining this, but to me, he seems a lot better these last few days since he's decided you're all going back to Savannah."

"He loves it there so much," she said simply. "Sometimes I could cry for him." Burke saw tears fill her eyes now as she looked around at the tall pines and oaks, the gums and sassafras–all at their April greenest. "I could cry for Papa Mark because I–love this Cherokee country and long to be here–the same as he loves Savannah."

Just as Mary started up the pine-straw path to Natalie's cottage, her blood chilled at Papa Mark's cries for help. Running as fast as she could into the house, she searched every room. When she raced out onto the back porch, she could hear Little Ben crying. There he stood, Papa Mark kneeling helplessly on the ground beside him, mopping clumsily at Ben's bloody wrist with his handkerchief.

"Ben," she cried, reaching them quickly, "what happened? Papa Mark–how did he cut himself?"

"I don't know, Mary!"

She had never seen Papa Mark so frantic, so helpless. She pushed him aside not too gently, ripped off part of her petticoat, and tied a secure tourniquet around Little Ben's wrist. The tightness made him cry all the louder.

"Where were you?" she demanded of her father-in-law. "Where were you, Papa Mark? Were you not here with Ben?"

"No, no, I wasn't," he mumbled, gasping so for breath, she thought he might be ill. "Ben–Ben wanted to play in the yard. I said he could. I was–trying to read. He–he wanted to–shoot marbles!"

"I thought you might not mind watching him for just a little while," she said, still holding the tight cloth in place on her son's wrist. "Now, it's all right, Ben. You're more scared than hurt," she soothed. "At least, I hope you are—wait, let Mama loosen it a little." When she did, the blood began to flow so freely from the deep cut on his little brown wrist, she turned in her fright to face the trembling man standing helplessly by. "Look, Papa Mark!" She pointed to a large kitchen knife on the ground beside a half-whittled stick near where Ben stood, his face so scared and troubled, she felt all control leave her. "Where did he get that—knife? How did you allow him to play with such a dangerous thing?" She was screaming now. "How? How could you do that to—Jonathan's son?"

Her father-in-law could only stand there shaking his head from side to side, saying nothing.

"At least go for help, please!" she called back to him, Ben in her arms now, as she hurried into the cottage.

"I—make a—cane for Grandpa Mark," Ben sobbed.

"A—what?" she asked, soothing the child.

"A—new cane!"

"Oh, that's fine, darling. That was so—fine."

⁂

Burke met Mr. Browning stumbling along in the direction of Miss Lorah's cottage, managed to get shreds of the story out of him, and ran for Ben, thankful that his horse was already saddled for the mail ride to Cartersville. Seeing that there was no time to lose, he lifted Ben onto the horse in front of him, leaped in the saddle, and rode as hard as he could ride, praying the doctor would be in his office.

⁂

In the living room of Natalie's cottage, Callie, Mark, and Perry sat waiting for Burke and Ben to return. Callie thought she might die for love of her poor grandfather, who seemed so scared and so ashamed that he had chosen to read instead of staying right with his grandson. Callie paced up and down by the window, the curtains pulled back for a full view of the road Burke and Ben would ride down. To pass the time, her mother and her grandmother Caroline were out walking. Mary just sat there. Every now and then, Perry caught Callie's eye and tried to get her to smile. She couldn't, but at least he was there—just like one of the family—waiting with them.

"I—I guess I was—terribly selfish," Grandfather Mark said finally, his voice sounding old and flat. "I was reading my New York *Tribune*. I thought the boy would be safe enough in the back yard." When no one said anything, he went on, "Mary–I hope you can–forgive me."

Slowly, Mary turned to look at him. "I know you–shut Ben out of your heart, Papa Mark," she said in a quiet, dull voice. "Because–you still–miss Willow."

Callie watched her grandfather's stricken face. He opened his mouth as though to say something, then closed it, eyes staring at Mary as though he couldn't believe what she'd just said.

"Mary, Mary," he said finally. "Oh, Mary, my dear . . ."

"I know how upset you are, Mary," Callie said, "but can't you wait to rebuke him until Papa gets back so we can know about Little Ben?"

"I do not rebuke," Mary said. "I–understand that he cannot let himself be comforted by my son. It is too hard. Also, Ben's smile, even though he looks Indian, is too much like Jonathan's."

Callie felt weak with relief when right then she heard a horse trotting slowly up the road. "They're back," she cried, and ran outside, Perry after her.

Ben was asleep when Burke handed him down to Perry. "He slept most of the way home," Burke said softly. "He's going to be all right. Doc fixed him up. We just have to keep him from using that hand too much for a few days. Where's Mary? I thought sure she'd be racing out here."

"I think she and my grandfather Browning are having a . . ."

"Mr. Browning blames himself," Perry said, holding Ben in his arms.

"I suppose so," Burke said. "There's a–problem there, I think. I'm counting on Ben to solve it, though."

Only Natalie went with Burke when on May 14 their Savannah visitors took the train at Manassas Station.

"I feel as though I have a rock in my heart, seeing them leave this time," she said as they rode back toward home. "Something isn't right. I know Papa will be far better down there because he isn't happy anywhere else, but he surely worries Mary and Mama. My father isn't the kind of man to reject Little Ben. The boy's only four years old. He can't help the way he looks."

"That's going to work itself out," Burke said. "You wait and see. Right now, you and I have too much to be concerned about up here. They're fighting hard–'sharp fighting,' Goodman called it in his paper yesterday–up at Resaca. Natalie, that's only fifty miles or so from here."

She turned to look at him. "You're really nervous, aren't you? I mean, more than usual. I know I didn't sleep last night. If only someone would tell us what might happen! You think the Yankees are good, but those are Yankees fighting their way down into where we live, Burke! We're off the railroad. Will they bother us?"

"I doubt it's a matter of who's good and who's bad," he said in his thoughtful way that made her want to pound him.

"Then what is it? The slaves are supposed to be free—why are they all still killing each other?"

"A war has to be won or lost by one side or the other, Natalie."

"Why? You told me the other day that even Lincoln is putting out peace feelers. He's the President. Why doesn't someone down here take advantage of that?"

"He's not Georgia's President."

"You sound just like Perry! How can you both be so sure you want to preserve the Union when Union soldiers are coming after us?"

"If the Union still stood as it once did, nobody would be killing."

"But it doesn't!" She grabbed his arm. "Burke, I'm scared! I'm just plain scared. I'm a woman and women don't understand—killing each other's sons."

"Some women seem to. Didn't you hear that woman in the train station just before your folks left? She hates Lincoln. She made no bones about praying that he would be the one *killed*. And she was no backwoods ignoramus either. Her husband owns a sawmill and one of the finest mansions around here. I doubt that being a man or a woman has much to do with it at this point, honey."

"Why am I so mixed up? Why doesn't anything make sense anymore? I miss Mary Cowper so much because I really loved her, but she *felt* just like that blazing woman in the train station. You know Miss Lib feels that way. Isn't it enough to try to keep peace in our own households? Why do governments *do* these awful, ugly things to us?"

"I don't have an answer to that, Natalie," he said solemnly, "but I might as well tell you that it's likely we won't be making the trip into Manassas Station again anytime soon. Your folks just got out in time, as I see it. According to the paper, the Rebels are outnumbered at Resaca. That means Cassville is next when and if Rebel general Johnston has to retreat. I don't think there is any doubt but that Sherman's headed toward Atlanta. And we're on his route." He reached for her hand. "I hate to scare you, darling, but let's face it, we are only this short carriage ride from the W. and A. Tearing up that railroad is very, very important to General Sherman."

"I wish we were home so you could hold me. Put your arm around me now, please?"

EIGHTY-EIGHT

*A*s *the Western and Atlantic* left Acworth en route to Atlanta, where they would change trains to the Central of Georgia for home, Mark sat staring out the window, longing with all his heart to know what Caroline was thinking. Little Ben, with Mary in the seat opposite, had slept almost all the way.

"No wonder he's sleeping," Caroline said at last. "We had to get up so early this morning. Oh, Mark, wouldn't it be wonderful to be a child again–able to sleep without a worry in the world?"

"Yes, it would," he said. "I worry about Natalie and the rest of our family up there. There's no longer much doubt that Sherman is bound for Atlanta. Destroying this very railroad is one of his goals. They're calling the torn-up rails he left behind in Tennessee 'Sherman's neckties.' His men heat the rails and bend some of them nearly double. We–we won't be able to visit Natalie and Burke again by train, my dear, for a long, long time."

Mark still marveled each time she bridged the wide, deep disagreement between them over the war with gentle humor instead of the old panic. He should be accustomed to it by now. He wasn't.

"You sound like a Rebel, Mark," she said. "The last I heard, General William Tecumseh Sherman was a Union general."

He did his best to return her smile. He still lacked Caroline's courageous poise in the face of so much tragedy and he didn't like himself for it. This minute, he hated his own heavyheartedness. His shame at not having watched Little Ben more closely the day he cut his hand still depressed him. Plainly, Mark had expected too much of himself—at least, more than he had the energy or patience to live up to.

"I'd give my right arm, Caroline, if I could see Miss Eliza for just half an hour once we're home again!" He hadn't meant to blurt that. It had surprised him more than it seemed to surprise her.

"I know, dearest," she said, laying her hand over his. "She'd know exactly how to help you out of this. I wish I did."

"I'm sure it was Miss Eliza," he said after a silence, "who once told me that *seeing* one's faults and shortcomings is half the battle. God knows, I see mine lately. Maybe it was Aunt Nassie who told me that. It must have been one of the two."

"Does it matter, Mark? You *do* see and that means you're halfway—to where you long to be again."

"Grandpa Mark! I wanta sit with Grandpa Mark!"

Little Ben's low, husky voice, wide awake now, reached them both over the clacking train wheels, the steady squeak of the car, as did Mary trying to shush him, to get him to settle down and not bother them.

"Come on over, Ben," Mark called. "You can sit on my lap."

"Do you want to sit on your grandfather's knee, Ben?" Caroline called over the noise. "Come on—climb right over my feet."

"He won't be a bother?" Mary asked.

"Never," Caroline said, giving Ben a hug as he clambered over her and up onto Mark's lap.

"Let me see your eyes," Mark said, tilting Ben's head back for a closer look. "I still see some sleep in that one eye. Am I right?"

Beaming at first one of them and then the other, Ben laughed, expressing delight. He poked his grandfather in the chest. "You're funny," he declared, then fell immediately to inspecting his cut wrist. "I still have a bandage!"

"Yes, you do have," Caroline said, "but I think it could come off almost any day now, don't you?"

The boy looked stricken. "Not until I show it to Jupiter when we get home! Jupiter will be proud of it, too."

What should have been a light, amusing moment brought only pain to Mark. The little fellow needs a playmate in Savannah, he thought. Because their fathers don't approve of me in this frazzlin' war, their sons don't play with Ben. It was true. His driver, Jupiter Taylor, was Ben's best friend.

As though she'd read his thoughts, Caroline said, "Well, Jupiter is a splendid playmate, Ben, and I'm sure you're right that he'll be proud of your wound."

"I plan to get Jupiter to help me whittle another cane for you, Grandpa," the boy said.

"But my cane is just dandy," Mark said, and knew he should have sounded pleased instead of sensible.

"You—don't want me to make a cane for you?" Ben asked, his face both eager and disappointed.

"Oh, yes, I'd love to have a second cane, son," Mark said lamely, and longed to find within himself the spontaneous response he'd always felt for Willow. He had taken Ben on some walks around town, but as a sad duty most of the time since Jonathan's death, and he seemed helpless to do a thing about it. He had felt pride when the boy got the hang of shooting a marble, but there it had ended. Why didn't Ben stay clear of him, he wondered, for the boy's own sake? How was it that the lad went on adoring him, evidently even preferring his grumpy, sad-faced company?

"When we get home, can you and I go buy me the right kind of knife, Grandpa?"

"You bet we will."

"Mark, he's too young for a knife of any kind! Ben, isn't there something else you can do to please your grandfather? What about drawing him a picture?"

"A picture of me, Grandma Caroline?"

"Why, yes, I think that would be perfect!"

"I'll bet I'm pretty heavy on your knee, Grandpa."

"Heavy as a chunk of oak," Mark agreed.

"I wanted to whittle your new cane out of live oak. It doesn't grow in the Cherokee Nation. It does in Savannah, though."

Mary and Caroline exchanged looks. "But how did you happen to call where Natalie and Callie live—the Cherokee Nation?" Caroline asked.

"My mama," the boy said casually. "Her papa and mama lived in the Cherokee Nation. Mama was born there. I'm part Cherokee Indian, too. Mama says maybe the only Cherokee left in all of Savannah, Georgia! I got Uncle Ben's name. My Cherokee uncle, Ben, shot himself in the head a long time ago. Mama showed me his grave. She says my daddy was a white man. Like you, Grandpa. So, I'm mostly a white man, too. My dead sister, Willow, even looked white." The boy shrugged. "Can we buy me an apple when the train stops again?"

Mark stole a glance at Mary, then at Caroline. They had both heard Ben's every precocious word. Mary's eyes were so hopeful that he suddenly felt something like hope, too. She was smiling at him, determined now, it seemed, to keep pulling him until she'd pulled him all the way back to where he and she had been together when they still had Jonathan—close, real friends. Had grief come between them, caused him to move away from Mary, for self-protection against more hurt? Would he have gotten so far off the track if Miss Eliza had been there to keep him straight? For the short months he'd still had her after Jonathan's death, she had kept him from any deviation as wrong as shutting out his own little grandson. Was it already clear to Caroline, as it was coming clear to him, that losing Miss Eliza had pushed him beyond what he could endure and remain the Mark Browning he thought he knew?

He tried to smile across at Mary, then at Caroline. Had they been aware that he was just not man enough to work his way through losing both Jonathan and Miss Eliza? Did Mary or Caroline remember too clearly how he'd been with Willow? Did they despair of his ever reaching toward Ben—bright, innocent, unsuspecting little Indian Ben?

"Can I have an apple, Grandpa?" the boy asked again.

He swept the boy into his arms and sat holding him until Ben began to squirm. "Of course, son! Your old grandpa will buy you a whole bushel of apples if that's what you want . . ."

On the morning of May 18, Callie felt for the first time in her life the kind of panic a child experiences when parents argue.

"Mama has always been kind of bossy," Callie told Perry as they stood in the living room trying not to listen, but unable not to hear Burke and Natalie from their bedroom. "I've never heard her quite like this, though."

"That's not being bossy, Callie. It's plain old panic. She doesn't put any stock in Miss Lorah's Sam. Your mother's scared for the two of you to stay here while Mr. Latimer and I go to pick up our lumber at the sawmill at Spring Bank. It's only a short trip. We could be back in less than three hours, but . . ."

"But Mama would rather our back-porch floor caved in and the roof leaked than for us to be caught here by Sherman's men with only Sam. Anyway, Sam's hunting and we need wild game."

"We know Union troops are right now somewhere between Adairsville and Cassville–"

"Cassville is–*Manassas* now, Perry!"

"I know it is." He grinned. "When I was in the Army, we still called it Cassville. That's a good ride away, though. I'm sure your father and I will be back long before they could reach you here. We've got to try to think straight, Callie. We're off the railroad here. It would have to be a bunch of Yankee 'bummers'–fellows assigned to scrounge for food. They wouldn't be likely to harm you or anyone else."

"You don't know my mother very well yet, Perry, or you'd know she'd fly to the defense of her chickens or Papa's cow or one of the pigs or sheep just as soon as she'd fly to the defense of herself. I know these are soldiers you fought with–I'd try to reason with them. Not Mama!"

"That's what your father's being told right now," Perry said. "Listen to 'em go at it in there!"

"I never heard them really fight before. I don't want to listen!"

"Natalie, you're acting ten years old!" Burke shouted. "I'll see to it that six or seven of the Stiles people–good strong field hands–stay within calling distance of our house the whole time we're gone!"

"If you think," she snapped, "that six big buck Negroes are going to protect a white woman–Callie or Miss Lorah *or* me–when Lincoln says they're as free as I am now, you'd better think again, Burke Latimer. If you have a brain left to think with!"

"Old July wouldn't let anybody get near you!"

"Old July is at least a hundred and ten–what could he do?"

Burke crossed the room and took her firmly in his arms and began, quite against her will and her fists, to kiss her on the mouth. He so infuriated her that, trying to cry out over his kisses, to shout her disapproval, she made such weird sounds it brought Callie rushing into the bedroom. "It's all right, Perry," Callie called. "It's all over. Mama's subdued. Papa's kissing her!"

By the time Perry appeared somewhat shyly in the doorway, all three Latimers were laughing at themselves.

"I guess I haven't lost my magic," Burke said, squaring his shoulders, one arm around Natalie. "Have I, wife?"

"Not your magic, sir," Natalie said, "just your common sense.

You've lost all of that! But go on, both of you—go to the mill and get your precious old boards. See if Callie and I care! Just leave your gun where I can find it in a hurry. I don't care if you and Perry are both Union men—Papa, too—I'll put a hole in the forehead of any filthy unshaven Yankee who dares to set foot in this house!"

Burke and Perry hadn't been gone but an hour when Natalie, alone in the cottage because Callie and Miss Lorah were delivering eggs to the Stiles people, heard the distant thud of a rider galloping along the river road.

Before she did anything else, she ran to the back yard, chased down three of her chickens, and, carrying them by their feet, squawking their heads off, sped back into the house, dumped them in her kitchen, and reached for Burke's new rifle. He'd warned her not to fire it until he'd shown her how, but that didn't bother her now. The gun was loaded, she knew how to cock it, so what else was there except to pull the trigger. And she would if anyone on either side of this stupid war dared set foot in her house. Confederate soldiers were now also stealing food from their own people, she'd heard, and Perry had warned her that Sherman's men would be helping themselves to chickens and cows and pigs. Her heart pounded so, she was so scared and so angry, she couldn't think what else to do but wait and pray that somehow Miss Lorah or hefty Little Sinai could manage to protect Callie if soldiers broke into Miss Lib's house. Burke had finally told her how starved for women soldiers are in wartime. Well, so be it—if it were humanly possible, she would see to it that not one woman-starved soldier got any closer to Callie at the Stiles house than her cottage! They'd have to ride past her first.

At the open front door, she stood, rifle in hand, waiting, listening, as the horse came nearer. One lone rider shouldn't cause her too much trouble. She'd have a clear shot down her pine-straw path to the road when he passed.

I'll never admit it to Burke, she thought, but I wish I'd agreed to let him or Miss Lorah teach me how to shoot one of these things. Mary Cowper had been a crack shot—better, Uncle W.H. always said, than either of her brothers.

What, she wondered irrelevantly as the rider galloped closer, did Mary Cowper think about the war now? Did people stay political in heaven?

Out on the front porch, she could see the frothing horse and rider— one lone man in some kind of riding cap, whipping the horse as though he had a sure destination, one he needed to reach in a big hurry. Well, she thought, come on! Whatever you're after, I'm ready for you!

For a few seconds, the horse and rider disappeared behind the huge clump of bushes where the cliffs began, and her heart beat faster. Clutching the stock of the rifle, she could feel her hands tremble. And then the rider came in full view! Down the path she ran, rifle at the ready. Just as she took aim, the horse thundered by. Uncle W.H., a strained, agitated look on his face, made no effort to stop. He only gave her a cursory wave of one hand and headed straight for his own place.

The tearing fear vanished in a rush of the first young, headstrong Natalie fury she'd felt in years. She slammed the gun to the ground. It could have gone off, she thought. Forgetting that she'd just turned three chickens loose in her own house, she raced down the road after Uncle W.H.

When Natalie reached the Stiles veranda, Uncle W.H., Miss Lorah, Callie, Little Sinai and her birdlike mother, Old Sinai, were already packing armloads of Miss Lib's silver into a huge wooden crate. Callie saw her mother first and called, "We're going to bury the silver, Mama! Miss Lorah's wrapping it all in torn sheets. Uncle W.H. says the Yankees are heading for Cassville."

"We're not altogether sure of that," Uncle W.H. said, his face even more strained, "but our General Johnston's men seem to be retreating up there and we can't take any chances. Lib and I brought our silver from Vienna at great cost and trouble."

"But aren't the Yankees just trying to tear up the railroad," Natalie wanted to know, "to cut off Rebel supplies from Atlanta? Why would they come way over here? Burke doubts they will."

"I thought that too, Mama," Callie said, handing Miss Lorah a handsome pair of silver sauce tureens, "but who really knows? Uncle W.H. says they keep stopping to draw new battle plans, so we're just making sure of Miss Lib's silver anyway."

"They well may not come this way, Natalie," Uncle W.H. said, pounding a nail into one crate slat and looking awkward in the process, "but this silver is too valuable to risk those brutes finding it. Lib would never forgive me if I didn't do all I can to save her George III." Right then, he missed the nail and hit his thumb with the hammer. "Natalie, where in tarnation is Burke?"

"He and Perry went to the lumber mill over near Spring Bank.

They're repairing our front porch. *Our* roof leaks all over, too. Burke does have his own affairs to think of. He's repaired everybody else's house," she said defensively, taking out her fright and fury on Uncle W.H.

"I find it odd, to say the least, that he'd leave you at home alone at a time like this."

"He thought I'd be there with her, Mr. Stiles," Miss Lorah said, as always defending Burke. "Me and Callie here didn't expect to be at your place but a few minutes."

"Are you home to stay, Uncle W.H.?" Callie asked, ripping off a piece of old sheet so Miss Lorah could wrap a footed salver before it went in the next crate.

Uncle W.H. pulled himself up off his knees by the arm of a porch rocker and straightened his back. "I'm not staying any longer than necessary, Callie. I just closed the deal on new land in Terrell County. I'll be heading back there as soon as I can find transportation for the people I'll need to take from here."

"Don't you mean what people *agrees* to go, Mr. Stiles?" Old Sinai asked impudently. "I just hope you ain't thinkin' of my July, 'cause I can tell you right now, he's not leavin' the river!"

Natalie saw Uncle W.H.'s eyes narrow. The storm of anger that crossed his face because a Negro his family had owned for all her life would dare speak to him in such a flippant way made her glad Burke wasn't there. Burke had managed to hold his tongue time after time on the subject of Stiles's slaves, but if the Union won, they would no longer be slaves, and along with everyone else, Burke's temper was short, too, these days.

"I'm perfectly aware of the possible future state of things for you Negroes," Uncle W.H. said to Old Sinai, his voice icy. "I'll remind you, however, that Etowah Cliffs is still my place to manage as I please."

"Someday, you got to pay money to us, though," the elderly woman shot back.

Still glaring at Old Sinai, Uncle W.H. bit off his words: "If anyone is aware of that, I am." Back on his knees to nail down another wooden slat, he hammered so hard, the slat split.

"Burke will be glad to close these crates for you," Natalie said, hoping to change the subject. "He and Perry should be back soon."

"They must not have thought the Yankees would be way over here on the river today," Callie said, "or they wouldn't have gone."

Natalie saw Uncle W.H. give her daughter a withering look. "The enemy is indeed doing its best to tear up the tracks along the W. and A., Callie, which, if one thinks at all, indicates that they are no longer counting firmly on supplies continuing from Chattanooga—they're trying to live off the land en route south to Atlanta. What makes you think *our* chickens and livestock and silver and cornmeal and flour aren't good enough for them?"

"Oh, foot!" Natalie said, remembering the three chickens still shut up in her house. "I've got to get back home, Callie. You and Miss Lorah stay as long as Uncle W.H. needs you."

Scrubbing the kitchen counters, the table, and the floor after the chickens had messed, as chickens inevitably do, Natalie began to cry. Alone in the house, she made no effort not to. Uncle W.H. said a lot of wild things these days because he truly hated Yankees, even Perry, she was sure, but what he said about Sherman's men living off the land as they headed to Atlanta was probably true. Burke and Perry couldn't load their lumber and get home for at least another hour or more!

She'd heard people talk about being so scared, their necks prickled. It had been just a saying until now. A wasp must be crawling on the back of her own neck this minute! Her hand sudsy from the scrub water, she swiped at it. Nothing. Dear God, she thought, dear God, can't You get word to Burke somehow to hurry back to me?

Then, still on her knees with the scrub brush and bucket, she heard her chickens squawking in the yard—squawking in sheer, sudden terror.

At the kitchen window she saw why. Three big, burly men—two soldiers in filthy blue uniforms and with them a runaway slave—were chasing her chickens from one side of the yard to the other. And then she heard the black man call out to the others from the pine-straw path. "Looky here what I done found!" He had picked up the gun she'd thrown to the ground and was aiming it at the wooden tray Burke built back in the old days when they still had enough cracked corn to feed the birds.

"Hold it!" the burlier of the two white men yelled. "Don't fire that thing! You'll rouse somebody. We need to take us some chickens and get outa here."

That, she thought, was the answer to her prayer. "Go on," she whispered, unable to move away from the window. "Go on and take some of my chickens—then get right out of here!"

EIGHTY-
NINE

Three days passed before Burke could bring himself to accept the fact that he had indeed been fool enough to leave Natalie and Callie even for the short five-mile trip to the mill near Spring Bank. Worse yet, as it turned out, the trip had been fruitless. The new shingles were not ready, and today they would have to return—if the roof was to be repaired.

Alone with Perry in the back yard as they chopped enough wood for Natalie's breakfast cooking, Burke said, "I may have made a mistake not telling my wife or Callie what we heard from the Howard girls over at Spring Bank, Perry. What do you think? Should we tell them before we go back over there? Or should we forget the leaking roof and just stay close by?"

"With Colonel Stiles gone again, sir, and Miss Lib still in Savannah, I feel we should not leave them alone. I don't mean to be telling you what to do, but you could stay here and let me go back to the mill."

Enough wood split for now, Burke plunged his ax into an oak log and began to help Perry pick up what they'd chopped. "Miss Frances Howard is no nervous alarmist. I believe what she told us."

"Callie already knows, sir. I told her. I hope you don't mind that I felt someone here should be told that Johnston's Rebels are heading down this way."

"With the Yankees hard after them," Burke said, heading back toward the cottage, arms loaded with small oak pieces. "Just bring those pine splinters this trip, Perry. We'll finish chopping the rest of it later."

"I think Callie's mother is as poised as Callie down underneath," Perry said, filling his arms with pine.

"She is. She is. Seeing those three Yankees steal her chickens the other day was bound to scare her—get her dander up—but she laid low. You're right. We'd better tell Natalie at breakfast what Miss Frances Howard told us. Once Johnston's men pass through the Howard place, once Sherman's men march through after them, it may be safe enough for us to leave here for a few hours." At the back-porch steps, he stopped. "We might as well face facts, Perry. We're a little off the beaten path to Atlanta here on the river, but not very far. We'll try to give Natalie and Callie a clear picture of the state of things, as we heard it from the Howards. Then right after breakfast, I believe you and I had better run our sheep and the cow as far beyond the Stiles property as we can. The Yankees may not come this way, but they are living off the land."

Natalie listened without a single comment while Burke told her all he and Perry had learned three days ago from Frances Howard and her sisters: That the Howard girls' father had left the Confederate Army some days ago at Dalton and traveled the thirty or forty miles to his home at Spring Bank to warn his wife and daughters that Hardee's corps was retreating just ahead of Sherman's troops and that his family should leave at once because both armies would surely come that way. Callie, who already knew the frightening story, asked just the right questions. "Did the Howards refugee somewhere else, Papa?" When he answered no, that they had persuaded their father to let them stay and face the armies, Burke found it difficult to hide a smile. Callie certainly understood her mother! Natalie had said not one word, but her face plainly showed her approval of what the Howard family had done.

"If the Rebs did come past their place," Burke went on, "most likely it was sometime in the middle of last night. The Yankees could well be there by today. Spring Bank is only about five miles from here, Natalie," he said, turning to look straight at her. "Perry and I are not going back to the mill. We're staying right here—just in case."

"Nonsense!" Natalie exclaimed. "Just plain stupid nonsense! I'd much rather have a firsthand report of exactly how both armies acted when the Howard girls stood right up to them. I want you and Perry to leave at once. If you go this minute, you can be back by late afternoon anyway. Women have *some* rights in this world. Especially your own wife and daughter. We'd much rather know, wouldn't we, Callie?"

Burke saw Callie look at Perry for a hint as to what she should say. The young man nodded yes.

"I think maybe Mrs. Latimer is right, sir," Perry said to Burke. "An army corps on foot and horseback can't move very fast. But we should start now. Both the Yankees and the Rebs have been marching only a few weeks. They're not going to be particularly desperate for food. I— I've been one of them, you know. There are some bad eggs in every lot, but mostly they're satisfied if they just get enough to eat. We can bring back some firsthand information if we go."

Burke gave Perry a resigned smile. "All right. I want you to promise me, though, Natalie, that you and Callie and Miss Lorah will stay as far away from the Stiles house as possible—until we get home again. Most likely, if either side is of a mind to steal or if the Yankees mean to destroy, they'll go straight for a mansion before they bother a cottage." He got quickly to his feet. "I noticed they had some stout locks at the mill, Perry. I plan to buy all they'll sell me." He kissed Natalie lightly, then Callie, and turned to Perry. "Don't you think you'd better kiss your intended?"

At the cottage door, Natalie pulled Burke down to give him a real kiss. "You're being quite sensible for a man, Burke," she said, her face so brave and so beautiful, he marveled that he had been persuaded to leave her. "If those Howard women aren't afraid to stay right in the armies' path alone, you've got to trust Callie and me. Now go! Miss Lorah will be here any minute and she's all primed for trouble with her iron skillet."

By two that afternoon, the freshly cut lumber and shingles piled high behind them in the wagon bed, Burke and Perry heard shots from across the Etowah just as they turned onto the river road toward home. Reining the team, Burke listened, Perry listened. Neither spoke until five more shots rang out. Starting the horses with a whip, Burke whispered, "Hang on, Perry! There are men over there—shooting at the Stiles house!"

"That means they're checking to see if anyone's at home," Perry said, holding tight to the wagon seat. "Can you tell if they're Yankees, sir?"

"Would Rebels be shooting at a Rebel house?"

"I know they're stealing from them. All they want is food—no matter which army it is! Can't you tell with two good eyes what they look like?"

Peering across the narrow river, Burke could see now that there were at least five men and that they wore blue uniforms. "They're Yankees all right, I'm sorry to say."

"Not much we can do if the Stiles house is their target, so could we head straight for your cottage, sir?"

"You bet we will! I'm not fool enough to tangle with either side."

"I say we stay right with the ladies, Mr. Latimer. And keep watch. They stole your new rifle out of the front yard anyway. We've only got your old musket and a pistol."

"Don't worry. I'm not crazy enough to try to stop them—unless they bother Natalie or Callie or Miss Lorah!"

Inside the cottage, they found all three women huddled at the front window, peeping out, Miss Lorah gripping the handle of her iron skillet. In whispers, Burke and Perry told them how the Yankees had crowded onto the Howards' piazza, peered with "hideous faces" at their windows, broke down their locked doors and stormed inside, some of the men half nude, all filthy and noisy and full of curses and bawdy laughter. One Howard sister named Sophie took out a pistol she'd concealed in her gown and only Frances Howard's quickness in taking it from her prevented what surely would have been tragedy. At the peak of the "ill-mannered onslaught," as Janet Howard had told it to Burke and Perry, a Yankee lieutenant appeared "in the nick of time" at the door and yelled at the "brutish enlisted men," reminding them that Sherman's orders were that lone women were *not* to be molested. The young officer had then explained that they had believed the house to be unoccupied. When the Howard women begged to be helped through the lines at once, the lieutenant explained that the Rebs were fleeing south and that Sherman's troops were pursuing them and so there were no lines. He did put a guard on their bedroom, but all night long downstairs in the rooms of their fine house, the Howard women had heard the men carousing.

"Now listen," Burke went on, his voice as low as possible, "there are Yankees right now across our river—just on the other side. That's the shooting you heard. They're testing, obviously, to see if the Stiles house is occupied. Only the house servants are there, but the one sane thing for us to do is to stay right here behind locked doors and wait—and hope Sam doesn't ride up from the post office in the middle of something."

"We—we couldn't buy a new lock," Perry explained. "They were all gone by today." He reached for Callie's hand. "Your father is right, darling. The five of us will just stay put in this room no matter what until we see them go back across the river."

"Oh, Burke," Natalie whispered, clinging to him. "Do you suppose there's a—gentlemanly officer—in that bunch of Yankees coming across our river?"

"I wish we could see them," Callie said, her voice tight and scared. "I wish our house weren't set so far back from the road!"

"It is, though," Natalie said. "And—maybe they won't even pay any attention to our place—or us!"

For more than two hours, Natalie, Burke, Callie, Perry, and Miss Lorah watched in the direction of the Stiles house. Now and then Burke or Perry or one of the ladies would walk around inside the cottage or just get up to stretch. The road turned before it reached the big house and so little could be seen when the racket began over there.

"They've found Miss Lib's silver," Natalie breathed. "Oh, Burke, I was praying they wouldn't!"

"That's digging we hear along with all that yelling," Burke said. "No doubt about that."

"I told Uncle W.H.," Callie said, "he wasn't taking time enough to plant bushes to hide where he buried it all!"

"Do you suppose they've harmed Sinai or any of the other house folks?" Miss Lorah asked, eyes snapping. "I'd say it's a pretty pass when grown men just break in a body's house like that and help theirselves!"

"I thought you were a Union woman," Callie teased, trying, Natalie supposed, to lighten their mood a little.

"I am a Union woman, but bein' Union don't excuse meanness and bad manners!"

Right then, Perry grabbed Burke's arm. "Two of 'em are coming this way, Mr. Latimer—look!"

Two stripling soldiers had rounded the bend in the road and were shuffling almost aimlessly along in the direction of the cottage, both looking around, more as though they were on a stroll than a military raid.

"They're looking us over," Burke said, "but not very keenly. We don't look like we own much, I guess. If they were after meat, they've probably already found our cow and sheep. I didn't have time to move the hogs from out back. They'll just have to take their chances along with us."

"I'd say the hogs' chances are pretty good," Miss Lorah said. "Them boys looks tired to me—tuckered out. Whatever meanness they've done, they did it at the Stileses'. One of 'em just shrugged his scrawny shoulders and now I believe they're both headed back that way. I reckon we're no temptation." Her good chuckle comforted Natalie more than anything Burke or Perry had said all during the long, nervous wait.

"We'll be able to see them from here when they head down over the cliffs to their boat," Perry said. "But I think we'd better sit tight till they do. It'll take them some time to carry their loot and whatever food they stole down to the river."

"Don't worry, son," Burke said. "We won't make a move until we see them safely on the other side. Then we can go over and find out how much damage they did at the Stiles place. I wonder if Holder's missed his boat yet. They must have stolen it from his side of the river."

Up pacing the living room now, Natalie felt the old fury rise in her again. "I'll tell you what I wish, in case anybody's interested. I wish old Abe Lincoln and old Jeff Davis both had to go through this! What do you suppose they did to poor Miss Lib's house?" Abruptly, she began to sniff. "Burke, Miss Lorah! I smell smoke!"

"Dear Lord help us," Miss Lorah groaned. "You don't reckon they've set the big house afire, do you?"

His head out the open window, Burke sniffed, too. "I don't think so, Miss Lorah," he said. "That's the smell of rags burning—not wood. They're burning something, but I'm almost sure it isn't the Stiles house."

Within half an hour after they had seen the Yankees disappear with the final load down over the cliffs to where their stolen boat was docked, a sharp, quick knock came at the front door—still tightly barred.

"Want me to see who it is?" Miss Lorah asked Natalie.

"I'll go," Burke said, and Perry went right behind him. "Who's there?" he called through the closed door.

"It's me, Mr. Burke," the thin, cracked voice wailed. "It's Siney! For Lord's sake, open the door!"

"I think it's safe for you to bring us a cup of what we call coffee,

Miss Lorah, if you don't mind," Natalie said, hurrying to stand at the door beside Burke and Perry. "Help Miss Lorah, Callie."

When Burke lifted the wooden bar and opened the front door, Old Sinai ducked inside and stood in the middle of the living-room floor, wringing her hands.

"What on earth did they do, Sinai?" Natalie demanded. "They didn't burn the house, did they?"

"No'm, no'm, but they done all else a band of rotten Yankees could do to us! I dunno whether I'm live or dead! But they gone. They gone."

Burke pulled a chair up for the old woman and led her to it. "Try to calm yourself, Sinai," he said gently. "Sit down, get your breath a minute, then tell us all you know."

"We wanted to come and help you," Perry offered, "but we only had one old gun and we hoped when they found out no white people were at home, they might leave."

Fanning herself with her apron, Sinai mumbled, "They don't care what color we was. They took everything I had—all my treasures. I had me a bag of coins saved over years and years—gone, gone. I tried to hide Miss Stiles's dresses—tol' 'em they was mine. They grab ever' one an' laugh and say, 'These is too good fer niggers,' and—they set 'em all afire!"

"They burned Miss Lib's clothing?" Natalie gasped. "That must be what we smelled, Burke!"

"Burn 'em ever' one—even the things poor little Mary Cowper leave here." At that Sinai lost what small composure she'd managed, and began to wail. "I ain' got no bolster left on my bed, nor a piller, nor a sheet, nor a coverlid! I ain't got nothin' left." She stiffened. "They done run their dirty Yankee hands over Little Sinai's bottom, too, an' I like to kill 'em! I tell you, they's only one kind of good Yankee an' that's a dead 'un!" The wailing mounted. "An' here—I *sass* Mr. Stiles afore he lef' the last time. Lord forgive me, I may never see that good man again and I sass him bad! All us niggers thought when the Yankees got here, we'd be —in heaven. We ain't in heaven—they's spreadin' hell! Everybody say the Yankees gonna free us. Like a fool, I—believe it. I—I shoulda knowed better. What kin you 'spec' from a hog but a grunt?"

Burke and Perry exchanged looks. Natalie knew they both felt shame. She wanted to put her arms around each one of them and remind them of how many times Perry had told them all that war makes brutes out of otherwise kind, good-hearted young men, Union or Rebel.

This wasn't the time for her to say much of anything, though, except to try to quiet Old Sinai's weeping and remind them all that Miss Lorah and Callie would soon bring a cup of parched acorn coffee that might help a little.

NINETY

*T*he first letter from Etowah Cliffs after Mark, Caroline, and Mary returned to Savannah with Little Ben came to Eliza Anne,
who, as soon as she'd read it, hurried to the Brownings'.

"I came here instead of running to my sisters," she said, plainly
upset, "because Natalie wrote this letter! Have you heard from her?"

"Not a word," Caroline said as Mark led Eliza Anne into the drawing room. "What on earth is wrong? You look as though you've lost your
best friend! Sit down, Eliza Anne, please. Would you like some tea?"

"Nothing," Eliza Anne said, turning to Mark in what appeared to
Caroline to be—almost anger. "They've done it, Mark," she began. "*Your*
beloved Yankees have not only stolen us blind at Etowah Cliffs, they
burned all my clothes, all W.H.'s clothes and"—looking at Caroline now—
"I feel as though I've lost my best friend! I feel as though I've lost my—
husband, Caroline. W.H. wasn't even at home when they came. He had
been there only long enough to bury the silver and some of the china, I
guess, then hightailed it back to his precious Terrell County land. No
one was in the house but our house servants." Glaring at Mark now, she
hurried on: "Your splendid Yankees even stole from them—they took
poor Old Sinai's money she'd saved for years in a chamois bag! They're
worse than brutes! And don't tell me they only needed food, because
they didn't stop with taking off the sheep and hogs and beef cattle they

slaughtered, they shot dozens of others and left them lying there! They helped themselves to our garden and what they couldn't carry, they just pulled up." Tears streamed down her face now and she began trembling. "Worse yet, they found where W.H. had buried our silver and what they didn't take, Sinai said they threw off the cliffs into the river!" Hard, wracking sobs forced her to stop talking.

"Eliza Anne," Caroline said, going to her. "Oh, my dear friend, I'm so sorry! We're both—so, so sorry!"

"There's no need to dig down for what sounds like courtesy, Caroline, when you know perfectly well—Mark isn't sorry at all!"

Caroline looked at her husband. He only sat there, his head buried in his hands. She longed to comfort him, too, because she could almost feel his heart break not only for Eliza Anne—but for the country. For the ghastly, pathetic waste of it all. "Mark is sorry, but I—I guess it's too much to hope that you could believe that now," she said. "Eliza Anne, they—didn't burn your house, did they?"

"No. But—one thing they did could kill W.H.! They destroyed his library!"

Mark looked up. "They—*destroyed* it?"

"Natalie wrote that the entire downstairs of my home is littered with damaged books! The beasts couldn't carry off the whole library. It's too large. They're too ignorant to read W.H.'s kind of books anyway, I'm sure, but they just had to tear them up. Pages and pages are torn out and tossed over the house and yard. The dear cliffs, all the way down to the water's edge, are littered with the expensive volumes they tried to throw down into the river! Natalie didn't spare me. W.H.'s library is ruined—gone, and that—could kill him, Caroline! You'd both better begin to think about what you'll do with your treasures here." She made a sweeping gesture around the exquisitely furnished room. "Even if they know your husband is a Unionist, it won't stop them from smashing up your home—from stealing your possessions. After all, you live in Georgia! You both know Natalie is not a true Rebel in her heart. She believes in nothing, I think sometimes, higher than Burke Latimer, but even Natalie is infuriated at the Yankees—at what they did to us, to our beloved home!" She swiped at her tears. "So many of our treasures W.H. and Mary Cowper found during our years in—Vienna. Irreplaceable, all of them. Thank God I had my jewelry with me here."

Mark got slowly to his feet. "I can only be an irritant being here at a time like this, so I'll leave. I have an appointment at my office at ten o'clock anyway, with a gentleman from Marietta. Publisher of a newspaper. He just may have some fresh information to report."

Eliza Anne quickly dried her eyes, then straightening her shoulders, said in cold sarcasm, "I know your 'gentleman from Marietta.' I'm sure it's Robert McAlpin Goodman—one of north Georgia's flaming Union men! Burke's friend. You three have everything in common!"

Abruptly, the anger in her face was replaced by a look of sheer torment. She went to where Mark stood. "Oh, dear Mark, someday I hope you can forgive the ugly way I've—acted with you—over all this. We're both thinking the same thing this minute. I'm sure we are. You're thinking, and so am I, that for me to act in a hostile manner with you would break Mama's heart!"

Caroline felt she could not endure their pain. The torment on Mark's face equaled Eliza Anne's. "Do be careful, darling," she said. "And feel free to invite your Mr. Goodman home for dinner. Even in the face of what's just happened to Eliza Anne, I promise not to embarrass you." Tears welled in her eyes now. "I'm hurting inside for the two of you. And I'm frantic with worry over Natalie and Callie up there with—all that's going on. There's so little room left in me for my own opinions about anything. You'll be safe in bringing your Union friend home."

"Thank you," Mark said, "but Goodman is dining with Charles Green."

Eliza Anne frowned. "With Charles Green, Mark? I can't imagine what business Mr. Green might have with a—Unionist!"

"Well, he *is* a British subject," Caroline offered, and wondered why she said anything. She had heard from the Mackay sisters that Eliza Anne was having problems with Mr. Low. Of course, she thought, Andrew Low and Charles Green are no longer business partners and didn't like each other much when they were. Even conversation with close friends was becoming risky!

"I'm sure I don't know why Green and Goodman are meeting," Mark said. "I only know that Burke asked Robert Goodman to see me while he's here." Bowing to Eliza Anne as he went toward the front door, he said, "I am truly sorry, old friend, at what happened to your home up on the river. I hope you'll let me know if there's anything I can do. Anything."

Robert Goodman was waiting when Mark reached his countinghouse. As best he could on his stiff knees, he hurried across the footbridge from

Bay Street when he saw his guest standing before the locked door of
Browning and Son.

Hand out as he approached him, Mark said, "My apologies, sir, for
being late. You must be my son-in-law's good friend Goodman, from
Marietta."

"I'm grateful to you, Mr. Browning, for meeting me," Goodman said
as they hook hands. "I've been observing how deserted Savannah's
waterfront is these days. I'm in town, after all, to be able to give my
upcountry readers a firsthand report on the effects of the war in such a
normally busy port city."

"We're safe enough right now," Mark said, unlocking the double
doors and leading the way to his private office overlooking the river,
"but one glance out that window over there will show you how quiet
our waterfront really is some days." After hanging up their hats, he
motioned Goodman to a chair and sat down in his own. "I still come
here every day, but there's little or no work to do. Burke Latimer is
genuinely fond of you, sir. Your friendship means much to him. Do you—
do you have any recent news of where—both armies are up there?"

"Sherman and Johnston fought quite a bloody battle at what used to
be called Cassville several days ago. The two generals are fighting a
peculiar war, actually. I'm not sure it pleases President Davis, who
would prefer that Johnston go at the Yankees head-on, as Lee's trying to
do in the East. Neither Sherman nor Johnston seems to do that. Actually,
they could be said to be dancing a minuet with each other—however
bloody at times."

Mark nodded. "Flanking."

"That's right. Latimer tells me you're one of us, a poor, benighted
Southern Union man, Mr. Browning. That's why I came to see you first.
I thought perhaps you could guide me about the city."

"You won't find many Union sympathizers on the coast," Mark said.
"At the outset, I felt sure war broke out over sheer power, symbolized
by States' Rights. It's turned into far more now and runaway slaves
following Sherman are fanning emotions." He studied Goodman's intelligent, slender face for a moment. "Burke tells me you own slaves
yourself."

"I do. Most of my people have stayed with me." Goodman smiled
ruefully. "By the way, there's no need to be careful of expressing your
own views on slavery. Burke has set the table well for our talk today. I
even know you were reared from childhood by an abolitionist aunt."

"I was," Mark said. "Aunt Nassie was one of the early, convinced abolitionists in Philadelphia, but I've never felt it my place to condemn Southerners who owned slaves. I simply couldn't own any myself. My wife does, though. And I hope Burke also told you that she has managed to learn how to live with remarkable good humor in the midst of our differences. Oh, Goodman, other families are far more divided than mine. Almost impossible to understand, actually, the divisions are so erratic. Take James Moore Wayne, still a Justice on the United States Supreme Court. I once knew him. His family and mine share many Savannah friends. Justice Wayne at the time of secession was a slave owner himself, but one who loved the Union as we do and so held his place on the Court. His son, Henry Wayne, who also disliked slavery, nevertheless remained loyal to the South and has served brilliantly for the Confederacy all through the war. He's fighting in north Georgia now, in fact. The Wayne family is but one example."

"But you have been—still are—mainly alone in the city as a Union loyalist?"

"Now, yes. Others did try hard to block secession. In the end, they are staunch Confederates." Mark paused, then with an anxious look asked, "Sir, do you have any news of what might be happening to Burke and my daughter, Natalie, on the Etowah River? I know that a handful of Yankees did considerable damage at the Stiles place. Where are the armies now?"

Goodman leaned forward. "This is June 8. I'd say Sherman's men are gathering around the Western and Atlantic Railroad ready to close in with Johnston before my own town of Marietta about now. Of course, Sherman is being forced to weaken his forces some by assigning men to keep the railroad open back to Chattanooga. No matter how well a general knows how to fight, he fails if his men are hungry and poorly outfitted. My guess is that, barring an unusual move by Sherman, your family up there is fairly safe from raids by any more soldiers. Colonel W. H. Stiles and I do not see eye to eye on the war, but I deeply regret the destruction of his valuable library."

"So do I. W.H. and I have been friends since we were both young men. He was my attorney soon after I adopted this old city as the one place on earth I really wanted to live."

"If I were of a mind to leave my well-loved country place, I would surely consider Savannah—a beautiful city. But whether you pray as a regular habit or not, Browning, I'd advise you to start. I have no way of knowing for sure, but we know Sherman's orders are to take Atlanta and my guess is that once he does that—many bloody losses from now—he could head for the sea."

Mark sighed dejectedly. "And that means—Savannah." He looked straight at Goodman for a long moment, then said, "I do pray, but all I can bring myself to pray for is peace. Some, like Horace Greeley, are searching for peace in the North, too. I hope I'm not quite as eccentric as Greeley, but as impossible as his ideas often appear in the midst of all the bloodshed and killing, he is seeking a way to end it."

"I also read every word I can find of his. Actually, although I've been in Savannah only overnight, I've heard grumblings. People here are genuinely weary of the war." Goodman got up. "Thanks so much for giving me your time, Mr. Browning. I'll be in Savannah for most of a week. Perhaps we might meet again?"

Mark's face lighted as he stood, too. "I'd like that very much. I'd be more than interested to know how you fare today when you dine with Charles Green. He's a self-made man with one of the most impressive homes in town—and an open mind. His sympathies, as a British citizen, are with the South, but unlike some, Green seems ready to seek new ideas about what might be done."

"Has he told you that himself?"

"No. It's just something I sense about the man. You'll find him a real diplomat. So speak as freely as you like."

After the most delicious meal he had eaten in a year, Robert Goodman was convinced that indeed Charles Green was a most influential and erudite gentleman, one who surely could throw some light on the real state of affairs in Savannah. Green's wife had excused herself and the two men now sat alone together in one of the double parlors of Green's magnificent mansion on the west side of Madison Square. The house, on which Charles Green had lavished a fortune, stood close by the handsome Gothic Revival Church of St. John's. Burke had already given Goodman some of Green's background as Andrew Low's partner, and had told him that both men were still British subjects. "Low is a fire-eating Rebel in his sympathies," Burke had said, "but I doubt that anyone is totally certain about Charles Green. My father-in-law, Mark Browning, seems to believe that Green, while he did use his British influence in the purchase of guns and ammunition for the Confederacy, keeps open to all possible deals."

Burke has, for a man who lives in the Georgia upcountry, a remarkably clear picture of the seat of Savannah's power, Goodman thought as he accepted the vintage Madeira Green handed him. So far, he had been deeply impressed with Green's concept of the beautiful old port city. The man obviously knew what worked there, what had been done, what might be done if the right strings were pulled. Green's first question of his guest, however, took Goodman by surprise.

"I find, sir, that I want very much to know more about the character of General William Tecumseh Sherman. How much do you know? Have any of your connections in north Georgia given you insight into what the man is really like?"

Goodman sipped his wine, then said, "Well, I understand General Grant thinks highly of him. I know firsthand from a young man named Perry Clay, recently given a medical discharge from the Union Army because he lost an eye at Chattanooga, that Sherman's men respect him utterly."

"But Sherman himself," Green persisted. "No direct knowledge of his real character?"

"Very little, except what I learned through a clergyman I know well in Richmond who lately had a talk with General Grant about Sherman. As it happens, I received a letter last month from my clergy friend. Permission from Grant has not yet been given to Sherman, but on Grant's mind when my friend saw him was an urgent request from General Sherman to march his troops—once he's taken Atlanta—down through Georgia to Savannah. Grant raised objections over supplies. Sherman assures him they can live off the land. They would, of course, be cut off from their source of supply. Grant asked my clergy friend to pray about whether or not he should grant such permission. 'Sherman is a most superior general,' Grant told my friend. 'And a good, kind man, too, although he's absolutely unrelenting once his mind is set on a goal.' Beyond that, Mr. Green, I know little of the man." Goodman sipped his wine. "Am I out of order to ask why you want to know?"

"Not at all," Green answered. "I've just been doing some hard thinking. Now, Goodman, what of our chances for some kind of honorable peace? The South is in dire straits. Our money is virtually worthless."

"I was hoping for some light on that very subject from you, sir, and now that we know of Sherman's desire to move this way, peace is even more necessary. God knows I'm for it. God also knows, however, that most of my fellow journalists oppose any plan that might even appear to show the Rebels as weakening. Our own Governor Brown still resists

Confederate domination over the states, as you know. Brown is said to feel at times that President Davis is no less demanding than Lincoln would be. Brown really does believe in States' Rights. He's kicked and screamed at almost every Georgia soldier who's been ordered to Virginia or any front out of the state."

Green nodded agreement. "He kicks and screams at our farmers being ordered to plant mostly corn to feed Rebel troops, too. That is costly to coastal farmers when cotton brings far more income. I *am* a cotton merchant, you know. Brown also fought the Confederate take-over of Georgia's own railroad, the W. and A. The Governor vows he wants no trouble with Davis, but there *is* trouble. Growing trouble. Georgians are weary unto death of this war, Goodman. There are new resolutions which openly urge President Davis to make a fresh peace offer to Lincoln after every Rebel victory 'on the principles of 1776.' Whatever that means. My main concern, naturally, and I make no bones about it, is the city of Savannah. I'd appreciate your keeping me apprised of anything that might point to a peace settlement before damage can be done here. There is a special bond—social, emotional, and economic—between my native England and Savannah, Georgia."

"You must feel real attachment to the city to have built yourself such a magnificent home here."

Green laughed. "Especially my good wife believes that's true. A native Virginian, she sacrifices by living in Georgia. Virginians feel superior to Georgians, you know. And except for the city of Savannah, I understand why they do."

"Your love of Savannah is very like that of Mr. Mark Browning."

"Oh, not quite," Green said. "Browning's whole life revolves around it. We've been only business associates through the years, but the old fellow lives a very lonely life here now with his Northern ideas. I don't share those."

"I do, as I'm sure you know, although I am a slave owner. Browning and I love the Union, though, with the same deep-felt sincerity."

"I freely admit I've worked at helping the South," Green said candidly. "My former business partner, Mr. Andrew Low, is, on the other hand, a passionate Rebel. I happen to cherish Savannah, but my efforts on behalf of the Confederacy are purely economic. Does that surprise you?"

"Not at all," Goodman said.

"Then, may I hope to hear from you as things progress—or retrogress—up Atlanta way, Goodman?"

"You may indeed, Mr. Green, and I must go. I have an engagement in just a few minutes with a Savannah-born Confederate officer—an engineer, Captain Robert Mackay Stiles."

Green seemed genuinely surprised. "Young Stiles, eh? Interesting. You do mean to do a bit of investigating here, don't you?"

"Mostly I'm trying to take the measure of Savannah people. Young Stiles is a true-blue Confederate. I'm told he won't sit still for merely impertinent questions. I just want to get a grasp of the thinking of a hardworking Rebel officer with the enormous responsibility of an engineer in a complicated military setting like Savannah. He's invited me to his late grandmother's home."

"You'll find him charming. Far more lighthearted than his brother, Major Henry Stiles, or his brilliant, somewhat erratic father, Colonel W. H. Stiles. By the way, your Mr. Browning considers the Mackay and Stiles families as his own. So far as I know, they are the only family he has. And they're all—hot Rebels, poor fellow."

"I felt we'd be more comfortable here in my grandmother's house, Mr. Goodman." Square-shouldered, stocky Captain Robert Mackay Stiles strode down the steps of the old Mackay house to meet his guest on the front walk. "The only other place we could meet was my office at headquarters and it's dreary! Any friend of Burke Latimer's gets only the warmest treatment here, you know."

"A pleasure indeed," Goodman said as they shook hands and began to mount the porch steps. "For a man who's never lived in Savannah, Burke has thoroughly paved my way here."

On the wide porch, Robert motioned him to a weathered rocking chair and took one nearby. "As you can readily see by the decidedly gray color of my uniform, Burke and I are not exactly on the same side in the current unpleasantness, but we are close as men. He and Mark Browning's daughter, Natalie, have been our good neighbors at Etowah Cliffs for many years. Since I was a boy, in fact." The cheerful smile exposed a row of strong, white teeth. "Burke and Natalie are family and, of course, we're not the only divided family these days. You see, Mark Browning met up with my late grandfather on the boat coming down from Philadelphia when he was about twenty and became part of the Mackay clan right off." The good smile came again. Plainly, Goodman thought, Captain Stiles gets through these hard times on a cheerful spirit. "You and Mark Browning have a lot in common. Your reputation as a Union loyalist has preceded you, Mr. Goodman."

"I know and I've already had one good session with Browning. Just what is it you do here in Savannah, Captain?"

"I'm with Company E, Second Regiment, Engineer CSA."

"Yes, I knew that. But what exactly is the nature of your work at this point?"

Robert gave him a guarded, but not unpleasant look. "Too much desk work to be exact, sir. Otherwise, I oversee repairs on Savannah's defenses—I'm a general fixer when something breaks, needs to be redug, or collapses."

Obviously, there would be no divulging of important details by the captain. "Savannah's safety record has been quite remarkable since Fort Pulaski was retaken by the North," Goodman said. "There are Federals all around the city, but for most of two years it's seen no action beyond the coming and going of Confederate troops. Isn't that right?"

"Only the failed Northern naval bombardments of Fort McAllister," Stiles said. "That's a fine fortification out there. We feel no Northern invaders can get to us here in town as long as McAllister blocks the Ogeechee River." The smile flashed again. "What precisely can I do for you, Mr. Goodman?"

"Nothing precise, Captain Stiles. I just felt that now was the time for a bona fide news reporter to visit Savannah. I want to be able to write about the people here—waiting."

"Waiting, eh?"

"Isn't that what it amounts to?"

"According to some, Savannah's been in danger of attack for nearly three years. I suppose it has been, but most Savannahians have learned to live with the stubborn fact of the presence of enemy gunboats and troops at our doorstep. Threat of attack is an old story. Threat of attack from the east, that is." Young Stiles frowned. "New clouds do hang over us now. Darker, uglier, far more threatening. He's way up in your neck of the woods yet, but some here honestly believe they can feel the city shaking with the tramp of Sherman's boots. One of the most disturbing signs is the behavior of our Negroes."

"Oh?"

"Unruly on the streets by night and by day. They won't work if they can possibly help it. There are other signs, too. Outbound trains carrying refugees, crates of china, silver, bank specie—anything that can be removed from the city. Incoming trains are loaded with thousands of

Federal prisoners. Not all from Andersonville either. Handling and feeding all those prisoners of war is a heavy burden on a city already short of food. Our garrisons around town are, at best, manned only by pickets, so desperately do we need troops. Oh, I also have orders to oversee the building of a huge stockade next week to confine Yankee prisoners." He laughed softly. "Unless I miss my guess, the ladies of Savannah will take pity on them. Make no mistake, they'll despise what the Yankees stand for, but will undoubtedly toss what food they can come by over the stockade fences to the poor wretches. My two spinster aunts among them. I'm sorry you won't meet Sarah and Kate. Both are hard at work at a soldiers' hospital today—as usual." A troubled look passed over the handsome, open face. "I worry about my aunts, actually. They never let up. Their love of the South is that deep, but daily I can see them both growing dangerously weary."

"And do they ever question you about the wisdom of keeping on?"

He gave Goodman a sharp look. "Are you asking if my aunts grow so tired they sometimes think of—giving up?"

"I would quote no real names in my articles, of course."

"In that case, I'd have to say that Kate, the older of the two, cries a lot. She isn't showing a lack of patriotism—she's just so exhausted."

"Afraid of what might happen, too, I'm sure," Goodman said.

"They know, of course, what even a small band of Yankee raiders did to my parents' place on the Etowah River." He said no more.

"I know about that, Captain. That's why I long to write something that might somehow—bring a real desire for peace."

The smile Captain Robert Stiles gave him now was sad and ironic. "Good luck, sir. Good luck."

On June 14, the day before Goodman planned to leave Savannah, he took tea with Mark Browning in his town house on Reynolds Square.

"My wife is sorry you couldn't get here in time to dine with us again," Browning said. "She begs to be remembered to you. Caroline is sewing in the Mackay sisters' Aid Society today and apologizes for her absence."

With an easy smile, Goodman said, "I enjoyed meeting her. What a gracious and beautiful lady you have. I'm quite sure that one session where she was outnumbered two to one was quite enough for Mrs. Browning anyway. I must say, though, she isn't like some of the fiery ladies I've met socially since I've been in town."

"Caroline isn't like anyone else—anywhere on the earth," Browning said.

"I like you more than ever for that, Browning. And I understand. I feel the same about Mrs. Goodman. She's shown only patience with my Union views."

"There's no need, I'm sure, to apologize for serving you peppermint tea. We simply can't buy China tea anywhere at any price. My daughter-in-law grows her own mint in our back garden. Have I told you that Mary is half Cherokee?"

"No, but Burke did. I know the whole story of how he found Mary and her brother, Ben, living in a cave after they escaped the Georgia Guard's stockade. Ben's suicide really scarred Burke Latimer. I think he felt somehow he'd failed Ben."

"We both know he didn't." After a pause, Browning asked, "Do you ever spend time just thinking about Georgia, Goodman?"

"Lots of time. I've thought hour after hour since I've been here in the city you love, and about my own country place on Powder Springs Road in the upcountry . . . I love it the same way. We love her—in spite of the violence Georgia has stood for in the past as well as now, don't we? Some men actually thrive on violence, I believe. I don't understand it, but I accept it. Unless I miss my guess, the thought of violence can rather unbalance both of us."

The smile Browning gave him was certainly sad, but it was also grateful. A truly grateful smile. The man is so alone, Goodman thought. His son is dead and he's also lost other dear friends in the Mackay family with whom he could talk freely whether they agreed with him or not. He had the distinct impression that Browning had never been close to Charles Green, perhaps to no other business acquaintance. He's just plain grateful that I don't think him weak for hating violence, for loving the Union of all the states. He found himself compelled to try to tell the aging man of his admiration for him.

"Every soldier boy who has screamed in pain and fallen in battle in this terrible war, Browning, no matter on which side of the lines, has displayed enormous courage and strength. But none has shown more than you have shown me in the short time I've been here."

The words seemed to have embarrassed his host, but the smile lingered—and the gratitude.

"I know you can't stay long, Goodman," Mark Browning said, "but I want you to meet my daughter-in-law, Mary, and my little grandson, Ben."

"Ben, eh?"

"Mary named him for her beloved brother."

The words were barely out of Browning's mouth when from the entrance hall came the thud of running feet, and into the drawing room charged a chunky, dark-skinned lad of about four or five, with the blackest hair and eyes Goodman had ever seen. He appeared for all the world to be a full-blooded Indian child with a smile that miraculously lit the shadowy room.

Skidding through open sliding doors on a loose carpet, the boy stopped short, plainly surprised not to find his grandfather alone. "You got company, Grandpa Mark!" the child said, breathless.

"Indeed I have, Ben, and we were just talking about you. Come on in and meet our new friend, Mr. Robert McAlpin Goodman."

Pleased, the boy walked sedately to where Goodman sat and, in his most adult manner, shook hands with him.

"I certainly hope you feel well today, Mr. Calpin," Ben said.

Both men hid grins as Goodman thanked him and said he certainly hoped he felt well today, too.

"Yes, sir," Ben said, displaying his wrist. "I had a deep cut, but it's all well now. I cut it in the old Cherokee Nation when we visited up there."

"Mr. Goodman lives up there, too, Ben," Browning said. "And, son, his name is Mr. Goodman, not Mr. Calpin. His middle name is McAlpin."

Ben beamed again. "Oh. I was whittling a cane for Grandpa Mark, but I was too young then to do it right. He has a new cane now, though." Running from the room, he called over his shoulder, "I'll get it to show you! Wait right there."

In a few seconds, Ben was back with the sturdy, highly varnished cane Jupiter had helped him make and offered it to Goodman for closer inspection. "See? Jupiter and I first whittled the handle. It's shaped like the letter L. Grandpa Mark puts his hand right there," the boy went on, pointing with his own chubby brown fingers, "and then because it's so strong, he leans his whole weight on it and walks! I did most of the smoothing. Grandpa Mark uses it out on the street." For the first time the smile vanished. "My papa was killed in the war. I don't remember him very well, but we smile alike, don't we, Grandpa?"

"You certainly do," Browning said, tears filling his eyes.

"So, you smile like your father and look like your Uncle Ben," Goodman said, his whole heart going out to the disarming boy. "I'd say you're a pretty lucky fellow—having a grandfather like this to boot."

"As soon as you leave," Ben said, "Grandpa Mark and I will take our walk. We take one every day it isn't raining. We didn't used to, but we do now and sometimes we go to Forsyth Park and watch the troops drill. When Uncle Robert Mackay gets the new stockade built, we'll go see the Yankees penned up in it."

Goodman looked at Mark for a long time, then said, "I envy you this boy, Browning. I'm sure you know Ben is your bridge over—all this."

If he had tried, Goodman could not have written an adequate description of the look on Browning's face at that moment. Nor could he have told of it. He knew only that he was seeing the barest beginning of a kind of hope that somehow he was sure even Browning didn't yet understand.

"Grandpa Mark bought me a whole bushel of apples once when the train stopped for water," Ben said. "I only wanted one apple, but he bought me a bushel. They're in our cellar right now. Would you like one, Mr. . . . ?" He looked at his Grandfather for help. "Is his name Good Man?"

Browning hugged the boy. "Yes, son. And he *is* a good man. You and I can always be sure that Mr. Goodman is—our friend."

PART
V

June–December 1864

NINETY-
ONE

On Wednesday, June 15, Mark enjoyed the morning walk with Ben more than usual, but as soon as the boy begged to go to Forsyth Park to watch the pathetically awkward drill by young, green Confederate conscripts, he suggested instead that the two spend time together at his office.

Ben was surprisingly happy with the idea, and as he unlocked the door with the sign that still read Browning and Son, Mark wondered if, however inadvertently, he might have struck upon a future possibility of avoiding the sight of those stumbling, eager recruits. The child reveled in watching them. To Mark, it was sickening. He could only stare into their young, beardless faces and wonder which would be maimed or killed or taken prisoner. Jonathan was too freshly gone for added reminders of the ghastly events which were moving the horror closer and closer to Savannah.

Sharing the daily papers with Caroline had not been a good idea. She said little about either Union or Confederate losses, but Mark found the strain on himself too trying. He still made the hot, tiring walk to his office, still picked up both the papers on his way. A mention of Lincoln occasionally caught his eye, but his once keen interest in politics had seemed to die with Miss Eliza. No one depended on his opinions any longer. Few in Savannah thought of anything but the battles and skirmishes raging between Marietta and Atlanta. Military strategy had never been one of Mark's interests. It wasn't now. He'd never been able to join other men in their fascination with campaigns, with the wisdom or stupidity of this or that general. But if the rumors were true, General Sherman was indeed, as Goodman said, seeking Grant's permission to cut his army loose from its own supply line to the north and head for the sea. Everything, he supposed, depended upon how General Sherman fared in Atlanta.

Ben amazed him by standing quite contentedly at the office window that overlooked the waterfront while Mark read his newspapers. Just knowing the boy was there helped. It somehow took a bit of the edge off the ugly news stories which told of hideous human tragedy in such cold, lifeless words. He was sickened by the brief factual account of the sudden death of Confederate general Leonidas Polk, "during a conference of General Johnston's staff at their position on the summit of Pine Mountain near Marietta, Georgia, when Federal Parrott guns sent shells toward the summit from Sherman's new positions in the hills nearby. One of the shells killed General Polk instantly."

Mark buried his head in his hands. Someone loved Leonidas Polk. A whole family, a wife, must have loved the man, and abruptly, he was dead—not in the heat of battle—in the midst of a conference. He turned in his desk chair to look at Ben, still standing patiently at the window.

"Oh, son," he groaned. "Come here, please?"

The boy walked quietly to him and stood looking up into Mark's face.

"Aren't we having a good time?" Ben asked.

"Are you—having a good time?"

Two chubby arms circled his neck and squeezed hard. "Oh, yes, sir. Everything we do, I like best of all!" Slowly, almost caressingly, Ben rubbed his fingers over the smooth, worn patina on the edge of Mark's handsome old desk. "Did you bring this desk when you came to Savannah at my age, Grandpa Mark?"

In spite of his heavy heart, Mark smiled. "Yes, I brought it down from Philadelphia. You see, you were born right here in the city of Savannah, but I was born way up North in a city called Philadelphia. But I was older than you when I first came. A lot older."

"How old?"

"I was about twenty. Now, here—take my pen and write down on this piece of paper first a two and then a zero. Good! Fine."

"Does that say twenty? Did I write twenty?"

"You certainly did. Now, let me borrow the pen a minute and I'll show you something. Watch what I do with it. I'll put down your age, four, the numeral four right under the twenty and then we'll subtract it."

"What's that?"

"Subtract means take away from. Now, you're four years old, and if you take away the numeral four from twenty, that leaves sixteen. A one and a six. I was sixteen years older than you when I came to Savannah."

"I'm going on five!"

"That's right."

"Does subtract mean take away?"

"Yes."

"My papa was subtracted from us," Ben said thoughtfully.

"Yes, son. He was."

"And," the child went on, "that leaves you and me. We're still here in your office, aren't we, Grandpa Mark?"

He swept the boy into his arms and held him close. "Oh, yes! We're both still right here—together, Ben."

Within a week, the daily trip of the two Brownings to Commerce Row had, for Mark, become an anticipated habit. Even his appetite improved.

"I need to think of something for Ben to play with—something to amuse him at the office while I read the papers," he told Caroline as they sat over Mary's peppermint tea while Mary got Ben ready for the daily trip. "Do you remember seeing an old, old chamois bag full of marbles anywhere around in my stuff, darling? Just a plain old chamois bag with a leather thong as a drawstring. Marbles have always meant a lot to Ben and me. If I could just think what I did with that bag of my old marbles . . ."

"Mark, do you mean you've kept them all these years?" Her smile told him everything. She wasn't teasing. She was falling in with his idea wholeheartedly.

"It's around here somewhere," he said. "I bought new ones for Ben, but I'd never, never let go of that fine collection. I know I had it when I lived at Miss Eliza's in the old days. William and Jack used to play with my marbles, all except one special moon aggie. I wouldn't let them play outside with that. I prized it too much." He snapped his fingers. "Say, I wonder if they might still be in one of the drawers of my desk at the office. I kept them there when I was sixteen or seventeen—as soon as my father bought the desk for me."

So as not to disappoint the boy in case the marbles were lost, he said nothing to Ben as they walked toward Commerce Row a few minutes later, but as soon as Ben went, as he invariably did now, to the casement window to watch the boats on the river, Mark began to hunt, pulling out one drawer and then another, feeling all the way to the back of each, until he came to his last hope, the big bottom drawer.

"Did you lose something in your desk, Grandpa Mark?" Ben asked.

"Uh—I'm not sure, son," he said, amused, and pleased by his own suspense in the search, his own anticipation. Slowly, hating to hurry the possible disappointment, he eased his hand toward the very back corner, the right-hand corner of the drawer. His fingers closed on the beloved chamois bag with its round, hard treasures still intact!

He turned triumphantly to Ben, who stood by the window watching him. "Surprise!" he said, holding out the bag.

Ben was beside him in one bound, both hands out. "What? What is it?"

"Keep your hands out just like that and close your eyes until I tell you to open them." Both eyes squeezed shut, Ben waited.

"Now, sir, no peeping," Mark said, placing the marbles in the eager, open palms.

"Birds' eggs?" Ben asked, eyes wide open now. "No, it's too heavy for birds' eggs! Mama showed me a leather bag of birds' eggs she and Uncle Ben gathered when they were children, but they were light as feathers! What, Grandpa? It rattles! Can I open?"

"*May* I open," Mark corrected him.

"May I open?"

"Of course, but I'll tell you what we'll do. You pull open the drawstring while I spread my newspaper on the top of the desk, then slowly, being as careful as you can be, take out whatever might be inside and put each one on the newspaper. That way we can really examine them."

"But you haven't read your newspaper yet," Ben said.

Giving the boy a smile, Mark said, "Maybe I won't even read it today. Go on, loosen the drawstring."

"Careful—slow," Ben reminded himself as he pulled open the chamois bag and reached one hand down inside. And with remarkable control for a boy so young and full of life, who loved marbles so much, he took out just one, devouring it with his eyes. "Grandpa Mark," the boy exclaimed, "a bag of—marbles! A whole bag full of—pretty marbles! Did—did these come in your desk?"

Mark laughed aloud. "No, Ben, they didn't come with the desk, I've had them since I was your age. This morning I thought they were lost. I can't tell you how glad I am to find them. I could have bought you six times as many new ones, but they wouldn't have been real treasures like these. I had these marbles when I was as young as you!" Ben was still holding an ordinary green glassic, his eyes moving in sheer wonder from the marble to Mark's face and back again.

"That's not a very unusual one. Oh, they're all treasures because I collected them over a lot of years, but go on, reach in for another. See if you can come out with a moon aggie."

"A moon aggie?"

"Sure! Moon agate is the proper name, but I always said moon aggie. And if you can find one, I'll show you how to make still more moons in it."

"Moons–like in the sky?"

"Well, almost."

There followed such a display of boy joy and such strong excitement that Mark could feel the waves of it in the old office which had, till this day, been so empty, where he had felt so desolate and alone. Ben didn't show excitement in a noisy way, as did other boys, though. He was deeply silent, as his hand reached again and again into the bag, taking out the wonders one by one–plain, chalk kimmies receiving the same adoration as the blue- and- whites, or the tiny dark red agate that had been Mark's favorite as a boy–the one he always used to plunk his playmates' marbles all the way out of the ring. Ben's fingers were trembling with excitement. Too much excitement for any expression less eloquent, Mark thought, than the same deep Indian silence with which he'd seen Mary look at the Etowah River or an oak turned crimson in the fall.

And then Ben took out *the* moon aggie! Mark's favorite for more than sixty-five years–a brown-red agate, with no flaws and, just as he remembered, still covered with his proud collection of tiny spherical moons, plunked into the agate honestly–each moon there because Mark had hit another boy's marble hard enough to form it.

"Oh-h-h," Ben gasped, staring down at the marble, then up at Mark, the sphere lying rich and luminous in the palm of his hand. Finally, looking at Mark now with a film of tears in his dark eyes, he closed both hands over it and held it as though it were a rare jewel.

And he's not yet five, Mark reminded himself, entering Ben's awed silence. The boy's so young and he's capable of this kind of love and appreciation—and joy. Why have I waited so long to discover my own grandson?

Why have I waited so long?

Fully expecting Ben to demand that he show him at once how to make more moons in the aggie, he struggled to be rid of the memory of the time he'd wasted keeping the boy at arm's length since Jonathan went away. Ben was still speechless, still standing there, marveling at the treasure in his little hands.

"Do you see the moons in the aggie, Ben?" he asked.

Ben shook his head yes. He'd seen them, all right, but some primal clock had not yet chimed in the unplumbed recesses of the boy's being. Ben was in no rush for a game. He was content with silent awe and the moment of even wider grace.

~*~

Through July, Mark continued to receive his copy of Robert McAlpin Goodman's *Southern Statesman* in the mails, however erratically. The newspaper, now only a half sheet in size due to the extremely high cost of paper, arrived irregularly, but delays, Mark knew, had to do with the way Sherman's troops were destroying sections of railroad to the north. At least Goodman was still in business, a near miracle in itself since the man's strong Union views had created an enormous loss of advertisers and readers. Goodman had begun running a series of sketches about various prominent generals, though, both Union and Confederate, and although campaign strategy was of little interest to him, Mark read the sketches carefully. Their objectivity impressed him. Goodman was a journalist of integrity. The sketches about Rebel generals showed as much intensive research and work as did those of the Union forces.

He had found an article on Confederate general William Joseph Hardee of especial interest because Bobby Stiles had spoken so highly of Hardee. Callie's young man, Macon-born Perry Clay, although he fought with the Union forces, after maneuvering his way through Confederate lines two years ago had met some Rebel troops who truly admired Hardee. "They spoke of him," Mark remembered Perry saying, "by the affectionate nickname of Old Reliable." Hardee had been forty-five when the war broke out and had certainly advanced in both stature and respect through some of the bloodiest fighting in Kentucky and Tennessee, even though, according to Goodman's article, he had grown discouraged with his commanding general, Braxton Bragg. Hardee had, however, fought under Bragg uncomplainingly through Chickamauga and the Confederate disasters at Lookout Mountain and Missionary Ridge. When Bragg finally resigned, Hardee felt rewarded at last under the new command of General Joseph Johnston and was right now fighting along with thousands of Rebels in defense of Atlanta. Goodman's question was the question of all of Hardee's loyal men, because only days ago Confederate general Joseph Johnston had been abruptly replaced by reckless, daring General John Bell Hood! What would General Hardee do now? His record was such that he could, at his age, resign or ask for a change of command. "Hardee's loyalty to the Southern Cause," Goodman wrote, "will hold him steady through the Atlanta campaign, whatever the results may be."

Mark's admiration for his new friend, Robert Goodman, mounted daily, not only because of Goodman's love of the Union but for his courage and fairness of mind. Bobby Stiles had begun to stop by Mark's office now and then and, thanks to Goodman, Mark was able to converse with him in a more informed way. He'd always found W.H.'s younger son fair-minded, too. Bobby was a loyal Rebel, and perhaps it was only his reliable humor that made easy conversation with Mark possible, but he found himself looking forward to Bobby's visits. He felt they had become friends.

"If you think I come by just to talk to an old Union man like you, Mark," Captain Stiles said near the end of July when word of the maniacal hand-to-hand fighting at Peachtree Creek near Atlanta first appeared in the Savannah papers, "you'd better think again, sir. I know I need to keep my mind open to your odd political quirks, but the truth is, I stop by because this splendid young man is always here, too." The sturdy captain saluted Ben with a broad smile. "Not today, Ben, old partner, but tomorrow for sure, I'll challenge you to a game of marbles that may go down in history right alongside the battle for Atlanta."

Bobby Stiles never talked down to Ben. Whether Ben caught everything the captain was saying, Mark couldn't be sure, but the boy needed a strong young man to look up to and he certainly looked up to Captain Robert Mackay Stiles.

"I'll have all my marbles shined up and ready, Captain Bobby," Ben said, his bright grin matching Stiles's.

Bobby had read the news account of the Rebel loss under Hood in the hand-to-hand fighting at Peachtree Creek right there in the office with Mark. Atlanta's defenses were crumbling into disaster. Bobby had only looked grieved. He said little, except that "the whole encounter sounds just like General Hood's reckless tactics. The man never doubts his own daring impulses."

"I *dare* you to beat me tomorrow," Ben said.

"I wish I had time to take you on at marbles today, Ben," Bobby said as he started for the door. "I don't. There's a batch of Yankee prisoners coming in to take up a gentleman's life in my new stockade. I want personally to make them welcome."

Until Ben found out that Captain Stiles had engineered the construction of the new prisoner stockade, Mark had managed to keep the boy amused in his office every day, away from the terrible pathos of actually seeing penned-up, half-starved prisoners. The captain had changed that. On the day late in July when Mark had just read of a second wild attack near Atlanta ordered by General Hood—the vicious attack when General McPherson, one of Sherman's favorites, had been shot and killed while retreating—he saw no way out of taking Ben to see Stiles's stockade of prisoners on their way home.

As the two neared the high stockade near the heart of the city, Ben's eyes grew as big as saucers, but he said not one word. Mark would have given almost anything to know exactly what the child was thinking as they walked hand in hand, slowly—to Mark, painfully—around the pen in which hundreds of raggedly clothed men, too filthy, too emaciated, too bearded to show their ages, lay prone on the ground, sat and stared, or milled aimlessly about. The thought of exposing his grandson to such human misery, such human brutality to other human beings, sickened him. And yet, he had brought Ben himself. Only because the boy so wanted to come? Or because the stockade was inevitable if one moved at all about the now dilapidated town? There in the very center of the beloved city stood a stockade such as had held Ben's own mother and his uncle! *In Savannah?*

Mark stood there grasping Ben's hand so hard the boy wiggled it free and ran to the heavy fence to peep inside. Mark hurried after him, but Ben seemed fine. In fact, he'd found two of his good friends, Sarah and Kate Mackay, there, too, arms filled with baskets of bread and a few precious corn cakes, pieces of which they were tossing over the stockade wall to the desperate creatures lunging for them from inside.

Kate stopped when she saw Mark. "Oh, dear, isn't it just dreadful?" she gasped. "They're skin and bones, Mark! I know they're Yankees—

they brought it all on themselves, but—they're hungry, Mark! Those men are going to die of hunger if we ladies don't help!"

"I—I think it's fine what you're doing, Kate," he said.

"But isn't it awful?" she persisted, and pulled at Sarah's sleeve. "Here's Mark, Sarah—Mark brought Ben to see this ghastly sight!"

The moment was too painful for words, too painful for all three adults. Sarah turned around, but couldn't speak. She only looked down at Ben and shook her head in pity.

"He—he wanted so to come," Mark explained, clumsily, "because Captain Robert Mackay Stiles engineered—this."

Her plump face distorted in desperation, Kate said, "I know—we know he did. Of course, he was ordered to do it."

"Yes," Mark said, sounding helpless.

Tears were streaming down Sarah's gaunt red cheeks as she began tossing pieces of bread and corn cakes again. In fact, Mark thought, she's throwing that bread at them! She was. With all her might, Sarah was rearing back and throwing hunks of bread as though she were venting her full hatred of everything Northern. As though each bearded, stringy-haired prisoner inside Bobby's wall were General Sherman himself.

"There's no need to wear yourself out throwing so hard, Sister," Kate shouted.

Sarah couldn't stop. Grunting and perspiring in the heavy August heat, she was killing Yankees as hard and as fast as she could.

"Grow up to hate them—every one, Ben!" the normally ladylike woman screamed down at the child staring up at her. "I heard one of our soldiers say he aimed to teach his children to hate Yankees for as long as they lived." Still throwing frantically, hitting the tall board fence much of the time, she screamed again: "I thought he was wrong. I—know—now —he was—dead right!"

"Ben seems perfectly fine, Mark," Caroline said, obviously trying to calm him, once he had hurried home with Ben to the quiet and sanity of his own house. "Mary says Ben would have seen the stockade sooner or later."

"Maybe not," Mark said as he sank onto the drawing-room couch and sat staring at the floor. "Maybe no one would have taken him."

"I was going to take Ben," Mary said from the doorway. "Ben needs to know about a—stockade."

Mark lifted his head to look at Mary. "Why? He's only a–little boy! How can Ben possibly be expected to understand?"

"It is easier at a young age," she said, her voice steady. "Ben could stand there and think that his great friend Captain Stiles supervised its building. He could speak to his friends Miss Kate and Miss Sarah Mackay. Ben's mind was not feeling the horrors your mind felt, Papa Mark. Please believe me!"

Caroline, Mark knew, was paying close attention to every word Mary said. "And will you explain to him that you and your brother, Ben, were–thrown once into a–stockade, too?" she asked.

"I will explain when he is a year or so older. In time for him to remember what he saw today. I will go myself to see first. I will also take food if it is all right."

"Yes," Mark whispered. "Of course, take whatever we have, Mary. But I wish you wouldn't go. I don't want you to see it either, Caroline. I –I know they're Yankees, those foul, vermin-infested men–but they're human beings. It's–it's a ghastly sight."

"I didn't say I was going, Mark," she breathed. "I may go with Mary. I'm–not sure I could bear it, though." She crossed the room slowly and sat down beside him. "Is there any news of the fighting around Atlanta?"

He sighed heavily. "The same. Fighting. Sherman is–going to capture Atlanta, Caroline."

Still standing in the doorway, Mary asked, "And will that end the war, Papa Mark?"

He looked at her. "Only God knows," he said. "There are–peace efforts."

"The South will not give up!" Caroline spoke very, very softly, but Mark caught the desperation, felt her willing her beloved South never, never to quit.

They were already beaten. Even some Confederate statesmen were implying that privately President Jefferson Davis himself spoke of the heavy cloud hanging above his nation. Fighting on was beyond Mark's comprehension and yet Caroline had said it, too.

Oh, Miss Eliza, his heart cried out–cried out so loudly, in such despair–he half expected Mary and Caroline to have heard. Miss Eliza . . . *where is sanity?*

Mary was saying something to Caroline about washing Ben's hair before dinner, but Mark didn't really hear. As though a clear voice had begun to speak from far, far in the distance, words he needed to hear, Mark listened . . . listened:

". . . *thanks be to God which giveth us the victory through our Lord Jesus Christ.*"

The inscription on Miss Eliza's tombstone—newly in place with the words only she understood carved into it. *Victory?* Victory in a stockade swarming with only half-living, sore-encrusted men, all of whom only want to go home? There must be sanity in—victory. But where is it? Where?

NINETY-TWO

*B*y *the middle* of August, Mark, in common with many other Savannahians, kept up only in part with the general war news. Central in most minds, central to their very lives, was the raging battle for Atlanta, because by now almost everyone believed that unless God intervened, that all-important rail hub would soon be lost. In letters to the local papers, Mark read of a few who tried to diminish the possible loss of Atlanta, contending as a "loyal Savannahian" that it was too far inland to matter enough for such shedding of blood, but no thinking person believed that. Once western expansion could continue again, nothing would be as vital as railroads. Sherman's troops were nearing Atlanta by tearing up those rails, along with the killing and the maiming.

Gloom permeated almost every conversation. Eliza Anne, at dinner with the Brownings, repeated her valiant, but increasingly vain-sounding words: "Our Cause is God's Cause and He will deliver our country in His own time." At Christ Church, Bishop Elliott told them all that self-destruction was the only way the South could be conquered, that one of the great errors of the enemy was in believing that numbers and material power would win. "The enemy seems to think that the maintenance of our mighty principle is nothing," the bishop declared. "The Confederacy has seen its prayers answered so often that we come today boldly up to the throne of Grace, firmly believing that our prayers will return to us laden with blessings from the God of the armies of Israel."

Mary had sat with the family in the Browning pew, her head bowed. Of no one but Mary would Mark have dared ask, "Doesn't God care about the sons of Northern families, too?" Mary didn't answer. She seemed still to live only for Little Ben and for the parents of the husband to whose cheerful memory her heart still clung. He didn't ask Mary anything again after that sermon. What was the use? He simply watched her go about her days, giving. Giving to Caroline, to Ben, to Mark, even to Maureen in her grief over the death of her nephew who had fallen in the bloody fighting near Atlanta. She gave also, Mark knew, to others in town. Now and then at mealtime she would announce, much the way anyone might comment on the weather, that "Lucinda Sorrel Elliott today told me that she finally understood my relief that nothing more can happen to Jonathan. She now knows that nothing more bad can happen to Stuart, her husband. She finds comfort in that, too."

Mark, too, was finding some comfort at last in knowing that Jonathan was safe, that none of the savage fighting could hurt his son. Mary had spoken so often by now of Jonathan's safety with God that he finally believed it, but it was Mary's son who was leading him slowly, steadily back to life.

Caroline and Mark visited Colonel Olmstead's wife, Florie, often, and he paid close attention to the young colonel's words to his wife written from somewhere in the Confederate lines at Atlanta: "Georgia is in great, great peril." At least Jonathan's good friend Colonel Olmstead was still alive in late August, freed from prison by an exchange.

A new, sustaining habit seemed slowly to be forming in Mark's mind —the habit of giving thanks for every event or fact that might bless and not curse. He welcomed his own clearing mind. He was able now to read a little of what was taking place in Washington when, for months, he had been skimming over every news item having to do with the Union. Not once had he dared ask himself why he'd been doing that, but now he felt he was beginning to realize that in him there had simply been no room left for such reading. No ability to concentrate, to sort it all out. Lincoln's more radical Republicans were attacking the President hard. Certain members of Congress were accusing him of planning to go too lightly on the South when the time for reconstruction came. Only this month, Mark had studied what was being called the Wade-Davis Manifesto. Senator Benjamin Wade and Congressman H. W. Davis had issued a furious condemnation of Lincoln's pocket veto of their punitive reconstruction bill, proclaiming that it was Congress's right to check the encroachments of the executive on the authority of Congress. At issue, Mark knew, was whether Lincoln or the Congress would control things once the South was finally defeated and the country was struggling toward union again.

He could at least give thanks that he still believed in the fair-minded integrity of Abraham Lincoln, who would, Mark felt certain, act fairly toward the defeated South. He counted on that the way he counted on Lincoln's re-election in November.

On the last day of August, one of the hottest, most miserable months ever in Savannahians' memory, Mary mentioned at breakfast that she would be pleased if Caroline would go with her, while Mark and Ben were together at the office, to visit Florie Olmstead.

"Oh, dear, Mary," Caroline said. "It's so dreadfully hot! The streets smell so from all the rotting garbage. Is there a particular reason we should go today?"

"To me, yes. Maybe not for you, Mama Caroline. But I spoke to Florie yesterday at the market. In her latest letter from Charles, she said that he is, for the very first time, low-spirited and despondent. He believes that if the South is defeated at Atlanta, General Sherman could break away a force of men and carry terrible destruction to every corner of the land. That is bad! Florie is—afraid. She needs a friend."

"It is bad, but you're younger than I am," Caroline said. "I think you're also far more Christian. Would you mind to go alone this time?"

"No, ma'am," Mary said, and Mark marveled that the young woman seemed invariably to find a tone of voice that seldom if ever brought guilt to either Caroline or him.

A mighty scraping of spoon on mush bowl brought a light laugh from Mary. "Do you know, Ben Browning, what that loud noise means?"

Ben laughed, too. "No, what, Mama?"

"It means two things. One, bad manners to make such a noise, and two, the bowl is empty. The mush is gone."

Ben was still beaming as he and Mark set off once more for the countinghouse together, and Mark gave thanks because again the boy seemed perfectly content, even proud, to be with his grandfather.

By the time Mark had opened the office windows onto the river and skimmed through the mail, Ben had his chamois bag of marbles beside him on the floor and was contentedly sorting through them as though he hadn't been doing it every day all spring and summer. Mark watched as the boy happily took out *the* prized moon aggie and a steelie heavy enough to make dandy moons in the aggie when struck against it and soon Mark was smiling, too.

"Say, young fellow, you know the *right* way to make new moons is to shoot your taw at it in a real game, don't you?"

Ben let go his infectious, husky laugh. "But there's nobody else to play with me here but you. That means you get the moon aggie!"

"If you get any smarter, I won't be able to keep up with you. Do you know how smart you are?"

Ben scrambled to his feet and pounded across the floor to where Mark sat, threw both arms around his neck, and hugged hard. "Smart enough to have you for my grandpa Mark," he shouted too close to Mark's ear for comfort.

"All right, young sir, what is it you want?"

Stepping back a little, Ben looked him straight in the eye. "Nothin'," he said in a low, serious voice.

"You didn't say such a nice thing for—nothing, did you? Isn't there just one small thing you'd like me to do or buy for you now? Come on, tell the truth."

"I always tell the truth to you."

Mark grabbed him for another hug. "Oh, I know that. I believe you, too. In fact, if I ever caught you telling me a lie, I think it—might be the end of me."

Ben studied his face. "You might die—like Papa did?"

Mark tried to smile. "Something like that. And we'll play marbles and you can shoot real moons in the aggie in a minute or so, but first I want to talk to you about something." He got to his feet and walked to the open casement windows. "Come on over here beside me and take a good, long look out over the river."

"It's a brown river," Ben said.

"That's right and it flows all the way around that bend"—Mark pointed beyond the last building along Commerce Row—"all the way to the ocean."

"The Atlantic Ocean."

"Yes. Now, did you know that river out there is the reason Savannah was settled here in the first place? They settled on the river so big ships could come into port from across the ocean bringing us good things to wear and eat and so Savannah merchants could ship their cotton to other countries."

"You're a merchant," Ben informed him.

Mark smiled. "Yes, and your father and I were factors, too."

"What's that?"

"Men who keep track of foreign markets and see to the sale of Savannah planters' cotton and lumber and pine tar and other products. Factors loan money to planters, and try to get the best possible price for their goods. That river out there is—has always been until the war—a lifeline to the city."

He glanced down at Ben. The boy was looking up at him, patiently listening, but Mark realized he was holding up a game of marbles. The lad was listening because his grandfather was talking, but his mind was plainly on the game. Why had he really called the child to join him at the window that looked out over Savannah's waterfront? His clumsy little lecture was limping along, getting nowhere.

And then, he knew.

If he could interest Jonathan's son in Savannah herself, Mark would somehow be able to find *himself* in the city again. To find Savannah!

Ben was still looking at the river. "I love you, Grandpa Mark. Do you think you love me?"

The question was like a blow. Unable to answer, Mark leaned down to embrace him, seemingly for the first time, in full understanding of the way things had really been for Ben since Jonathan had died. He knew in that moment that Ben had somehow sensed the wall between the two of them. The wall—Mark's own creation—built with the bricks of self-protection. He had known such anguish, had fled so far inside himself to avoid still more hurt, the child had felt it. For nearly half of Ben's short life, he had been forced, as Mark himself had been as a small child, to live mainly inside his own world. Careful, sensitive attention from Mary had kept Ben cheerful and secure. Caroline had somehow turned her antipathy toward Ben's Indianness into genuine, freeing affection. She had certainly helped Mary keep Jonathan's memory alive for the child, as Aunt Nassie had kept the fragrant memory of Mark's own mother alive for him. But, what had Mark done?

Abrupt, smothering identification with his sturdy, dark-skinned grandson almost took his breath away.

"Yes, oh, yes, son, I love you! In fact, in a way I can't explain—this minute, I am loving you with a feeling of what I think we might call—*real adventure!*"

Beaming, Ben wriggled to be let loose from Mark's arms. "Oh, boy!" he shouted. "Adventure!" Childlike, Ben-like, he was rushing freely, headlong, into the deepest place in his grandfather's being. "Oh, boy,"

Ben repeated, thrusting out his chubby hand. "We sure do like adventure, don't we, Grandpa Mark?"

If Mark lived as long as had old Sheftall Sheftall, he would never forget their handshake. And Sheftall seemed as good a place as any to start the adventure. To begin to welcome Ben into what had really mattered in Mark's own life since the age of twenty—the adventure of learning Savannah.

Through the long, stifling month of August, the papers had kept Mark aware that three hundred miles away men were marching and bleeding and killing and dying and sleeping in mud in the battle for Atlanta, but the hot late-summer days for him were refreshed by his new adventure with Ben.

The two walked to the old Sheftall house on West Broughton where, as a young man new in town, Mark had formed the enjoyable habit of frequent visits, not only to brighten the old man's life but because he so enjoyed Sheftall Sheftall's mind and his every eccentricity. Ben, he knew, wouldn't understand the word "eccentric," so he described Sheftall's slippers with their ancient silver buckles, the equally ancient leather cocked hat, and the old, mended Revolutionary War uniform jacket.

"What's a cocked hat?" Ben wanted to know, eyes intense with interest.

"Men weren't wearing cocked hats anymore, but old Sheftall wore his proudly, because he had been a real hero in our Revolutionary War and three-cornered cocked hats were in style back then. The same was true of his silver-buckled shoes."

Beaming, Ben clapped his hands. "I like silver buckles! Mama has a silver buckle on a dress, but I never saw one on shoes. What's a revolutionary war?"

"Well, that's a longer story than we have time for out here on the street in this hot sun, but it was the war Americans fought to free themselves from the King of England."

"Are kings bad?"

"Not all bad, necessarily. Americans have just always longed to be free. To rule themselves, to govern themselves according to the will of the people. There's something God made in each one of us, son, that is always more at home, always better, when free. The only master—king—a human being needs is God. He wants us to be free, too."

"Were Americans slaves like at Grandma Caroline's Knightsford?"

"No, not all like that. Actually, those people who work Grandma

Caroline's plantation need to be free just like anyone else, and even though the war is still going on, they're almost free now."

"Are Cherokees free?"

Mark grinned at him. "You and your mother certainly are."

"But Mama says she misses that she can't run free in the woods anymore because we live in Savannah. Savannah is our home, though, isn't it?"

"I want you to decide for yourself, Ben, but I hope someday you'll choose to live your life in Savannah. I did, you know. That doesn't mean that you will have to come to love the old city the way I do, but the city will try always to give back to you far more than either of us could ever give to her."

"Is Savannah a woman?"

Mark laughed. "That's the expression people use. Just the way a ship —a sailing vessel or a steamship—is called a *she*. It would just seem funny to call either a city or a ship a *he*."

Ben laughed. "Lots of things are funny."

"That's right. Lots of people used to laugh at old Sheftall Sheftall, too. I never did. Miss Eliza's husband, Mr. Robert Mackay, never laughed *at* him either. We couldn't. The old fellow was too wise, too staunch in what he believed."

"Would he like our war?"

"No," Mark said, almost sharply. "Sheftall was a slave owner. But while the war may free the slaves, it isn't being fought only over slavery. Our war, as you call it, Ben, is being fought over power. The Southern states had dominated our national government by their own, familiar, aristocratic way of life—and when they saw themselves losing some of that power, they vowed to get it back. They're still fighting and it's a terrible, useless tragedy. Sheftall Sheftall's heart would be right *with the Union*."

Ben kicked a brown magnolia pod, then looked up at Mark with a restless smile. "You know a lot of big words, don't you?"

"Too many, maybe," he answered, vowing to stop thinking aloud to the boy in words Ben couldn't possibly understand. "Your father was very fond of Mr. Sheftall and the man loved to have him visit. Jonathan went every day until he had to leave for Yale College. He'd read aloud to him from the newspapers and discuss politics with him. Your papa really brightened his last days when the old patriot was too feeble to walk Savannah's streets anymore. Make no mistake about it, Sheftall was a real patriot."

"What's a patriot?"

"Men and women who love the country they were born in enough to die for it."

"Did my papa love his country like a patriot? He died for something."

"Yes, son. But, like me, Sheftall loved all of the United States. You see, in his war, he fought to make all the states free . . . free to become one nation."

"Did my papa love the whole nation?"

Mark, his knees too stiff to kneel beside the boy, stooped to lift Ben's earnest face to his. "When you're just a few years older, we'll have a good, long talk about your father. For right now, it should make you feel very, very proud that he gave his life for what he believed in. He followed his heart. There are thousands and thousands of Southern soldiers—like those we used to watch practice their drills in Forsyth Park —who are also following their hearts."

"Did some of them die, too?"

"I expect so by now. All you need to be sure of today, though, is that your father was brave and intelligent and good and happy-natured— like you."

Ben's smile once more lifted Mark's spirits. "It's happy for us to be together, Grandpa Mark. Will we have another adventure tomorrow?"

"Tomorrow and the next day and the next. My plan is to show you everything in Savannah that Miss Eliza's husband showed me when I first came here. Will you like that?"

Grabbing Mark's hand, the boy began to pull him along. "Yes, yes! Only I wish we could go to your office now and play marbles."

"I see no reason why we can't do just that," Mark said, trying to keep up with the youngster's eager pace, trying not to dwell even one more time on how much he'd missed by having built a wall against loving this most remarkable child. Was Ben brighter than most children his age? Could he be a born philosopher who knew how to savor, how not to compress everything into one day? Once they reached his counting-house, he already knew, Ben would, before the game began, take his time examining, admiring each marble, as though learning their characteristics, weighing their beauty, their value.

As they neared Bay Street and headed across the cluttered Strand toward Browning and Son, he had the distinct feeling that Ben saw deep, intrinsic value in everything Mark was showing him.

The boy is too young to express what it is he's seeing, Mark thought as he unlocked the double doors, but how it would help me if, by some means, I could enable Ben to see Savannah as—I'm beginning at times to see it again: without sadness, without feeling alone, without feeling a stranger. Of course, the same blood that gave Mary her longing still to run free through the upcountry woods ran in Ben's veins—at least some of the same blood. But Jonathan's blood, Mark's own, ran there too . . .

NINETY-THREE

Through the hot, humid days of the remainder of summer, their adventures included certain old Savannah houses which Mark had loved and felt a part of since his first sight of them more than a half century ago. Standing together outside, neither caring to go in, they first visited Mark's favorite, the house after which he and Caroline had rather patterned their own—the elegantly simple Davenport house on the once quiet northwest corner of State and Habersham.

"The same man built our house," Mark explained. "His name was Isaiah Davenport. Look here—come on over here and examine this downspout, Ben."

The child laughed at him. "You're teasing me!"

"No, I'm not. There are lots of these in town now because the city's so much larger than when I first came, but old Isaiah Davenport's dolphin downspouts are the best you'll find anywhere."

Ben ran his fingers over the open mouth of the cast-iron dolphin and said quite seriously, "You certainly do see things I don't, Grandpa Mark. I guess you're just lucky."

"I know I am, son," he said, taking the boy's hand as they walked along State Street toward Bull, where, in spite of the debris and garbage and gangs of noisy soldiers, he meant to attempt to interest Ben in some of Savannah's statues and monuments. Well, they would head toward cluttered Bull Street, but after all, his newfound friend was not yet quite five and no one monument, no one grand example of architecture had laid hold of Mark's own heart when he first found the city. He had simply fallen in love with the mystique of Savannah herself just by being there, by learning his way around her shaded squares, walking the peaceful, wide, sandy streets, by watching her embracing sky.

After a while, he stopped walking and looked up at the sky today, the ninth of September 1864. How much time had gone by since he'd taken the time to do that, since he'd even thought about Savannah's embracing sky?

"My own father, your great-grandfather, Ben, taught me to love the Savannah sky long before I ever saw it . . ." He hadn't meant to speak of his father to Ben, not yet. The words had come naturally, as though spilled softly from his own heart.

"Your father was my great-grandfather?"

"That's right and he loved Savannah more than any other city on earth. He traveled all over the world for years and years after my mother died, so he'd seen all the great cities. It was Savannah he loved, not only because he found my mother here selling produce in one of our squares but because of Savannah's sky."

The fact that the mother of the second-richest man in Savannah, his grandfather, had been selling produce in the square seemed not to register on the child at all. Ben was staring up at the overarching blue September sky—white-cloud-scudded—the whole embracing them both above the din of the war-distorted city, as though never to let either of them go.

No longer speaking directly to the boy, at least not expecting a response, Mark seemed only to listen and repeat aloud what his own father had told him all those years ago: "The only spot of its kind, Savannah has the charm and warmth of a village, but the elegance and dignity of a lovely English city. And the sky, son? I'll never, never forget the changing Savannah sky. Often floating with coastal clouds, often clear blue, often low and gray in the rain—but always the Savannah sky seems to be embracing the city."

"Does that mean the sky hugs us?"

"Yes," Mark said, pulling himself back quickly to the boy standing beside him, his head still way back, drinking in the sky Mark himself was also *seeing* again. The sky whose embrace he was beginning to feel again.

"You two appear to be cloud gazing," Mr. Charles Green said, stopping to shake hands with them both. "Is this old gentleman teaching you how to waste time, young Ben?"

"No, sir," Ben said quickly. "We're having an adventure!"

"Ah, so that's it, eh? By the look on your face, Browning, I'd say you have not yet read today's *Morning News*. I'm quite aware of your political viewpoint, but you seem so unperturbed, you must not know yet that Sherman has captured the entire city of Atlanta!"

"It's—definite?" Mark gasped. "You're certain, Mr. Green?"

Green nodded firmly. "Actually, it occurred on September second. Sherman cut so many telegraph lines, we only just got the news. These are trying times, Browning, whether we agree on the outcome or not."

The surprise meeting with Green, one of the few Savannah business associates who greeted him these days with anything but cold courtesy, and Green's news of the fall of Atlanta had so stunned Mark, he could only glance again at the sky, then down the quiet street stretching to the river. Ben was as quiet and gentlemanly as only Ben could be. It struck Mark that they all three seemed to be standing there—suspended in time.

"I—I have the strangest feeling, Green," he said flatly, "that we're—just waiting."

"Well," Green said, urgency plain in his cultivated British accent, "*I'm* not waiting! I'm positive, *if* General Sherman gets Grant's permission to cut his vast army loose from their supply base and communications up there, that eventually—before the end of the year—he could be right here in Savannah. I mean to have a hand in his arrival. I'm on my way to see newly re-elected Mayor Arnold and the City Council right now." He looked down at Ben. "Goodbye, young man. You're living through a bit of history today whether you're old enough to realize it or not."

Ben's glance at Mark was perplexed, but in his most courteous, adult manner, he bowed to Green and said, "I hope you'll give our regards to Mr. Mayor, sir."

Green appeared charmed, more charmed with the boy than surprised. He'd met Ben before. "I'll do that, young man. You have my word."

When Green hurried on toward City Hall, Ben, deep in thought, asked, "What did he mean, I have his word, Grandpa?"

"His promise. He promised on his word of honor to give the Mayor your greetings."

"Oh." Ben took his hand again and the two walked on.

Now and then, Mark saw him looking, looking at the sky, then down at his feet so as not to stumble. "Grandpa Mark, do you think you could sort of guide me so I won't fall down? Or bump into somebody? I'd certainly like to keep watching the sky all the way to wherever we're going."

"And why do you want to watch it, Ben? Because of what I told you my father said about it?"

"No. Just for me."

When they learned the following week that Atlanta was being evacuated, Mark tried to calm Caroline's fears that Sherman would indeed head toward Savannah.

"We simply can't believe every anxious rumor we hear in town, darling," he said as the two lingered at breakfast, Mark waiting for Mary to dress Ben properly for their daily foray. "Sherman's still in Atlanta. I'm sure he'll be there through the evacuation of the city anyway. Then who knows?"

"I know I dare not stop going, but those ladies at the Women's Aid gatherings tell me the wildest things! And why do you suppose the *Morning News* editor wrote as he did on Monday, Mark? It doesn't comfort me at all that he minimizes the importance of losing Atlanta. It scares me. 'Whoever heard,' the man wrote, 'of such a fuss being made over the fall of a twenty-year-old town three hundred miles to the interior?' That sounds to me as though he feels Sherman would consider Savannah far more a prize!"

"Oh, Caroline, don't make matters worse. It's all pure speculation. General Sherman didn't order Atlanta destroyed. He captured it, blew up an arsenal. Anyway, what benefit could it possibly be to him to harm Savannah, by far the most beautiful, most cultured city in Georgia?"

"Culture seems not to move generals—not Sherman or any other I've heard about," she said. "Even Savannah's beauty is hard to find now with batteries and stockades full of prisoners and her streets clogged with cursing, noisy troops!"

"Grandpa Mark and I think it's beautiful, don't we, Grandpa?"

Ben, dressed to meet any prominent gentleman, stood beside Mary in the doorway to the dining room, his face filled with anticipation.

"At least Ben will look like a Savannah gentleman," Mary said. "That is, if you two wanderers venture out again today, Papa Mark."

"Oh, we're venturing, all right, aren't we, Ben? I thought we'd go by the old Scarbrough place today, so I can tell him about all those fancy-dress balls where we used to dance away the night, Caroline."

"Do you really like just walking around with your grandfather looking at old houses, Ben?" Caroline asked.

"Oh, yes, ma'am," he said in his energetic, low-pitched voice. "I live right here with Grandpa in Savannah. He and I really have a good time!"

After they'd looked for a long time at the solid, columned opulence of the Scarbrough house on clamorous West Broad Street, the two made their way to South Broad and Barnard, a good place for a clear view a block away of what had always been, to Mark, the handsomest church spire in town.

"That's the Independent Presbyterian Church, son. It's where Miss Eliza's husband was a member. A lot of Scottish people go to church there."

"Mama's papa was Scottish."

"Yes, I know he was."

"Mama's papa was my grandfather, too—like you."

"That's exactly right. His name was McDonald."

"He had light hair, like Mama's."

"So I've heard, but all Scots don't have light hair. Miss Eliza's husband's hair was quite dark, the way mine used to be. Do you remember his name?"

"Mr. Robert Mackay."

"Good for you. Robert Mackay was certainly kind to me when I really needed a friend in Savannah."

"I'm your friend, Grandpa Mark. And you're my friend." Such a low, firm voice in a boy so young usually gave the impression that Ben was saying a lot more than the words he used. This time he seemed merely to be making one of his straightforward, typically Ben statements of truth. They *were* friends.

"I'd rather be a friend to you than to any other man on earth," Mark said.

Ben laughed. "I'm not a man!"

"Oh, yes, you are, son. In the very best sense. Now, look up. Do you think that church steeple as grand and beautiful as it's always seemed to me?"

The Independent Presbyterian Church stood on the corner of Bull and South Broad. At Barnard, they were far enough away for a good view and for a time they just looked, the child seeming to study the graceful, ornamental white spire towering against the sky. Finally, Ben said, "That steeple looks just like–Savannah."

This time, Mark thought, the boy had surely said far more than he yet knew how to say! Something very close to the familiar, old wonder at the once peaceful dearness of the city itself eased back into Mark's mind and heart. Savannah was little more than a filthy, bustling military camp now, but Miss Eliza, as always, had been right. The city hadn't left him. He had, in his pain and alien aloneness, hidden himself from Savannah. She hadn't cast him out after all.

Daily, while Ben played patiently by the office window, Mark kept abreast through his newspapers of Sherman's activities in Atlanta. The facts were that the Union Army had occupied Atlanta since September 3, and only a few days passed before Sherman notified Confederate general Hood that the city must be evacuated at once. Sherman's order offered food and transportation for Atlantans able to go to Tennessee, Kentucky, or farther north. Transportation was also offered as far as Camp Rough and Ready, a few miles south of Atlanta, for those who had no place else to go. One copy of the New York *Tribune* which got through the blockade published reports of an angry exchange of letters between the two generals, with Hood accusing Sherman of "an act of barbarous cruelty," but Sherman stood firm. Some 1,600 to 1,700 men, women and children had been evacuated.

Knowing how zealous Governor Brown had been throughout the war years in attempting to protect Georgia, Mark was not surprised when, almost at once, Brown withdrew from Hood's command all state militia, more than ten thousand troops, and gave them thirty-day furloughs, ostensibly for harvesting crops. Most knew the reason for the furloughs was to prevent state troops from being enrolled in depleted Confederate units of other states. About the middle of October, Mark read that Sherman was rumored to be attempting a daring move. With the militia on furlough and with the whole state practically at the mercy of the Northern army, Sherman had the idea that he might make peace! That he just might manage to induce Governor Brown to withdraw at least Georgia from the war.

Dear God in heaven, Mark thought, staring at the news account, if peace could be made with Georgia alone, Savannah would be saved!

He and Ben went on spending their days together, exploring the city, shooting marbles in his office, watching the ships that managed to get through the blockade as they inched into the docks along the waterfront, their hulks looming large. The now mostly black stevedores sang as they toiled at unloading precious foodstuffs, spices, a very occasional and expensive shipment of coffee and tea, which only a man as well-off as Mark could afford to buy.

"Were these rocks here when you first came to Savannah?" Ben asked one day as they stood alongside the high stone wall above Mark's own wharf.

"Oh, no, son. Our bluff was just sand in those days. I guess it must have been thirty years or more after I got here before someone was smart enough to begin using ballast rock to build a wall that would hold back the sand." In answer to Ben's inevitable question, he explained the meaning of ballast rock and told him of the day an ordinance was passed forcing ships to unload it on land because so much rock dumped into the river was causing shoals and a buildup of shoals blocked free passage for the all-important sailing ships which came to Savannah all the way from Europe and the Far East.

"Maybe we can take a trip to Europe someday," Mark said absently, his mind still clinging to the hope that Sherman might actually be able to make peace with Georgia.

"I don't think I'd like that," Ben said in his thoughtful way.

"What? You wouldn't like to make a long ocean voyage to London?"

Ben shook his head firmly.

"Why not, son?"

"Because we'd have to get on a big boat right here and go away from Savannah!"

For an instant, as Mark stared down at Ben's earnest face, the old glow rushed back. He felt the thrill of joy from his youth, his middle age —the joy he'd always felt in just being in this place. For him, being there had been more than enough until first Sheftall Sheftall, then William Mackay, then Jonathan, then Miss Eliza had left him. Especially when Miss Eliza went away, the city itself had seemed to desert him. But now there was Ben and the scrap of hope that Sherman might find a way to end the war in Georgia.

His hopes rose when, as the correspondence between Sherman and Governor Brown went on, the people of Georgia began to hold what they called peace meetings, especially in the piedmont and the northern parts of the state. There was even one poorly attended peace meeting in almost solidly Rebel Savannah, about which Mark didn't learn until too late. Just as well, he thought. My presence would surely have been only an irritant.

Nothing came of that meeting or any other, and Sherman's "audacity" had brought Confederate President Jefferson Davis hurrying to Georgia to visit Hood's army, to hold war rallies, and to express his contempt for what he called "croakers"—men who now refused to fight. Sherman's peace efforts failed utterly. Savannah's newspapers played down any talk of peace, insisting that Lincoln had no chance of being re-elected anyway. Of course, people all over the South were desperate; of course, they were sick and exhausted from the hopelessness of war. Desperation, he knew, always drove public opinion to extremes. "Once rid of Lincoln, peace will come!" The Southern newspapers ranted. According to a letter from Robert McAlpin Goodman in Marietta, most Georgia editors were declaring: "The mere whisper of peace is criminal. He who would entertain it is a traitor!"

Even the Atlanta *Intelligencer,* Goodman wrote, thought peace would come only after Sherman's defeat and even went so far as to contend, with Union forces occupying Atlanta, that "Sherman is indeed in danger of defeat."

Mark's frail hope vanished when Savannahians—even Caroline and Eliza Anne Stiles, still staying at the Low house with Mary Cowper's children—began to insist irrationally that Sherman *could* be defeated, that the South would indeed gain full independence!

During one of her rare visits to the Brownings', their old friend Eliza Anne wearily, but doggedly repeated her well-worn phrase that "God's time was simply not quite yet for the South." Mark kept still, as he'd been forced to do for years, but his heart ached for Eliza Anne. The burden of caring for her grandchildren, of living in the same house with Andrew Low, whom she now seemed almost to despise, the prolonged separation from W.H., all appeared to have flawed the intelligent woman's judgment. Anyone who faced facts as they were knew that "the reservoir of manpower in Georgia was nearly dry." Even President Davis conceded in a Macon speech that "we have not many men between eighteen and forty-five left." No troops at all could be spared from other fronts to oppose Sherman's fifteen infantry divisions. The total Union forces in Georgia now numbered over one hundred thousand men. The impoverished state had a tatterdemalion force of under ten thousand! And this included released convicts, militia, prison guards, one battery of artillery, and young cadets from the Georgia Military Institute. There was also the ill-behaved Wheeler's cavalry, which did number around three thousand, but under their erratic leader, they mistreated Georgians themselves and caused more harm than good in the collapsing cause of the South. Mark felt no satisfaction in all this. He still stood alone—as if he were outside the war itself—aware of only one truth: *He believed in the Union of all the states.*

He and his small grandson went on walking up and down Savannah's chaotic, piled up streets, while over and over again he was caught off guard by Ben's enthusiastic interest in what he called "Savannah surprises." The same "surprises" which had so charmed his grandfather. Ben charmed him now even in the infinite care and fascination with which he ran his brown fingers around the curls and loops and flowerlets and twining leaves hand-wrought into the town's magnificent ironwork forming fences, porches, handrails. Mark had taught Ben to tell time by listening with him for each throaty bong from the Exchange clock. Together, they climbed the tower, and the child showed keen curiosity in Mark's description of how much the city had grown since his own youth. From the Exchange tower, he patiently pointed and explained as Ben seemed to follow all he said about new squares and streets. Much of the time, Ben was silent, but his silences, which often reminded Mark of Mary's dead brother, Ben, were altogether attentive. Alone with his grandson, he thought a lot about what Ben McDonald must really have been like. Indian Ben, who loved Natalie too much to face living with the hopelessness of that love.

With Sherman now occupying Atlanta, he at least felt easier about Natalie in her cottage on the cliff beside the Etowah River. Sherman's men had already passed that way and Natalie had not been harmed. He despaired at the thought of W.H.'s destroyed library, of the damaged furniture, of Eliza Anne's heartbreak, and now of her debilitating bitterness.

On certain days, as the drier, crisper autumn air filled the streets and alleys and houses of his city, he thought deeply on the subject of hate, an emotion which had almost never touched his own life but which now filled the city as the rotting garbage and the smoky air filled it. If hatred could be fired as a weapon, he thought, Savannahians would be well armed. A letter printed in one of the local papers at the end of October chilled Mark's blood. A man named Graves had written: "I have vowed that if I should ever have children, the first ingredient of the first principles of their education shall be uncompromising hatred and contempt for all Yankees!" He read also of other people in town who were distraught because they'd just learned that in their own ancestries there had been the "vile poison of Northern blood." Not even the clergy was immune to the bitterness. With his own ears, one Sunday at church, Mark had heard a visiting rector shout: "The North is a stink and a byword among other nations. Blinded by their own fanaticism, they have elevated the Negro above themselves!"

Even his own groom and driver, Jupiter Taylor, who had for years been a free person of color, could not talk much with Mark about the hatred and confusion in the city. They were still good friends. Jupiter had always known of Mark's stand against slavery, but he did mix among his own people and within the Negro community in Savannah there was such a diverse jumble of opinions, loyalties, misconceptions, and varied emotions that even Jupiter seemed loath to discuss it. They did mention it now and then, but inevitably the talk ended with Jupiter rubbing his graying head and saying, "I don't know what's gonna happen, Mr. Browning. I just—don't know. They's some that hopes too much, some just—barely hope. Some gone crazy. A lotta folks, black and white—hates. I just—don't know. You an' me's just gonna have to wait it out."

Mark was touched by the word that finally spread across town that one of Caroline's close acquaintances had, for a few days at least, interrupted the steady scream of hatred against Yankees. A lady, called in the newspapers only by the name of Miss Marjorie, had cared so faithfully for a dying Yankee prisoner in Savannah during his final illness that when he died she purchased a cemetery lot and paid for the expense of a decent burial for him at Laurel Grove. The *Republican*, when it learned of the interment of a Federal officer in the same ground where Confederate dead rested, called on the authorities to put an end to such sacrilege: "It is outrageous to so pollute the sacred soil with the bodies of those who burn our houses, orphan our children, ravish our wives." The *Morning News*, Caroline herself discovered, disagreed.

"This should hearten you, Mark," she said at breakfast one rainy morning in early November. "The editor of the *News* contends the *Republican* article shows a 'shocking want of civilized feeling, a horrible misrepresentation of the noble Southern character.' "

As usual, Mark said nothing, but tried to give Caroline a noncommittal smile.

"I know you refuse to comment on any of it," she went on. "But I'm glad for what the *News* editor wrote. Miss Marjorie loves the South. We all know she does. She's simply warm, sensitive, very human. Anyway, I doubt that the young Yankee officer who died in her home started this ghastly war!"

Day after day, Caroline stayed beside him. Not once, in spite of her own deep devotion to the Rebel Cause, did she consciously provoke Mark. She seemed to know that while his Union loyalty never wavered, his fears for the safety of Savannah matched or exceeded hers. By now, after the long years of hardship and loss, they both considered it useless even to attempt to place blame. Doing so could lighten no burden; could, at this late, weary date, change nothing.

There was now only—more waiting.

What Sherman meant to do next, no one could know. He still occupied Atlanta.

NINETY-
FOUR

*O*n *Monday*, November 21, in Mark's mail was the half-sheet copy of Robert Goodman's *Southern Statesman*. Believing in Goodman's integrity as he did, he read his article first because Goodman himself had made a trip to Atlanta, in part by horseback because Confederate repair crews could not keep pace with Sherman's destruction of the railroads. Here at last was a chance to find out firsthand what Sherman was up to in Atlanta. Goodman had certainly picked the most newsworthy, most tragic moment to go in person to the captive city.

After two months in residence there during the evacuation, Sherman had ordered Atlanta burned. "But not all the city," Goodman wrote. "Sherman's orders were that only the principal buildings be destroyed: all railroad depots, warehouses, machine shops, and other buildings of use to the Confederacy. The troops were ordered *not* to burn dwellings, but when a machine shop and iron foundry were set afire, a nearby oil refinery ignited into a fierce, roaring inferno, then a warehouse filled with bales of cotton, so that soon large areas of the city were a fiery mass. I am told that the night of November 15 was made fearful and hideous by bursting shells and explosions which caused the very heart of the city to roar in flames all through the black hours. Now, more than forty-eight hours later, clouds of heavy smoke still hang above the doomed city. All homes but some four hundred are destroyed. All but a handful of mills, factories, and other places of business are gone. The streets are strewn with thousands of carcasses of dead animals—horses, cows, hogs, cats, dogs. Stores, hotels, Negro markets, theaters, and grogshops—burned to the ground. One aged resident told me," Goodman's report went on, "that the 'heaven was one massive expanse of lurid fire; the air was filled with flying, burning cinders . . .' An aide at Sherman's headquarters informed your reporter that all remaining citizens had fled, with the possible exception of fifty or so families and all of those deathly afraid of more violence. Looting is rife in the city. Sherman's troops seem to be doing their best to stop it, but there is such a madness abroad, order of any kind appears impossible. . . ."

Mark sat at his desk, as always, reading avidly with Ben nearby. Both were silent. He had learned long ago that, with his grandson, he was not hampered by being duty-bound to talk when he didn't feel like talking. Ben needed no special form of entertainment or attention. Mark meant, if possible, to keep the fiery fate of Atlanta from the child. At least until someone had a firm idea of where Sherman might go next.

From a Savannah paper, he gathered that General Hood, after evacuating Atlanta with his Southern troops, had moved north again toward Tennessee, hoping that Sherman would follow him in an effort to protect the Union's own line of communications. Sherman's men did follow certainly as far as old Cassville, which, this time, they burned to the ground. Mark's heart began to race. Cassville was close to Etowah Cliffs! He had been hopeful that, by now, Natalie and Burke and Callie and Perry were safe. He breathed a bit easier when he read that from Cassville the Union forces went on to Kingston, where the permission to head south was at last waiting for Sherman. He could now begin his long-anticipated march to the sea. Mark breathed easier for Natalie, but not for his own beloved city. Even now, as he sat in his quiet office with Ben, Sherman could be marching in the direction of Savannah!

Later reports speculated that Sherman's troops were moving south in two distinct divisions, some forty to fifty miles apart. No one seemed certain, but it was thought that the divisions would meet now and then and interchange directions so as to keep the people of middle Georgia confused, their nerves on edge. At other times, Mark read that the more than sixty thousand men were divided into four blue lines, each continuing to move steadily through the Georgia heartland toward the coast. Rations for twenty days went with them in wagons and carts, but cut off as they were from their source of supply, each brigade had an organized party of foragers, called "bummers," ordered to take necessary provisions from homesites, stores, and plantations en route, along with horses, mules, and anything else needed for the marching men to survive. Again and again, he read that they were ordered *not* to enter dwellings or commit any untoward trespass: to destroy buildings only if leaving them somehow disrupted their march. Still, Caroline kept hearing stories of horror perpetrated along the way, and even the Northern papers admitted that these orders were not always obeyed. "Sherman's soldiers," *Harper's Weekly* reported, "seem to believe they are at liberty to do as they please. Some go so far as to write in letters home that, undisturbed by Southern resistance, the march to the sea, though hard and dirty and long, is like a big, festive hunting trip!"

Mark, Caroline, and Mary agreed not to mention one word to Ben of what might lay ahead, and after days of anxious waiting, Mark stopped speaking of it even to Caroline. He no longer expected her resistance, but he was afraid of causing her fears to grow. "What gets our attention gets us," Miss Eliza always said. Talking about a thing forces attention to it, so except to discuss halfheartedly with Caroline and Mary how they could give Ben anything resembling a happy Christmas, he retreated again into near silence at home.

Out walking with Ben, he tried not to think beyond the fact that in the midst of crowds of milling soldiers in the streets of his city, with the noise and confusion of military emplacements, this place was still there for him. By some unexplainable means, Mark Browning had come back to Savannah. He had found her scarred, dirty, her streets strewn with trash, her river patrolled by gunboats, her shores raucous with shouted curses and commands, her fortifications bristling with pathetically inadequate armaments—but Savannah was there and he had reclaimed her.

He clung doggedly to the sites of familiar landmarks which had not changed. The tall steeple of the Independent Presbyterian Church still stood at the corner of Bull and South Broad, his own house stood, as did Isaiah Davenport's, the Scarbroughs', the Mercers', the Habershams'. The poor Habershams. Two sons had been killed in battle within an hour of each other.

Exhausted by the erratic leadership of Hood and the defeat in the Atlanta campaign, General Hardee, at his own request, had now taken command of the defense of Savannah. Most in town felt secure with the well-loved, experienced Hardee in charge, but Mark agreed with Bobby Stiles that no general possessed enough expertise to succeed with the ragtag army at Hardee's command. Captain Bobby Stiles came often both to the house and to Mark's office to talk, although the young man's time, now that the threat of attack had increased, was more limited. Still, each visit helped Mark because Bobby was as trustworthy, as cheerful, as honest as ever. He told no Confederate secrets, but he appeared to feel no barriers within their friendship.

"Wishful thinking is the latest style in town now, Mark," Bobby said at the end of the first week in December. "It's insane! Did you happen to see that the *Republican*'s editor had the brashness to call Sherman's army 'the *fleeing* army of the Union'? That's madness!"

Mark had read the *Republican* that day and also the *Morning News,* which a few days before, when Sherman's army was briefly halted at the Oconee River, had prattled that 'the skies are brightening!' "

"All wishful thinking," Captain Bobby repeated, then sighed. "You remember, I know, that my dear grandmother tried to tell us back when Georgia first seceded that it *wasn't* going to be over in a blaze of Southern glory within a few weeks. The lady was always right, wasn't she?"

That very afternoon, Mark asked Jupiter to drive him to Laurel Grove Cemetery. He knew Miss Eliza herself wasn't there. Wherever he went these days, she seemed closer to him than ever. Her thoughts, her hopes for him, for the country, seemed to beam down steadily on the bright path of God's own love. Still, going to the spot where her old bones lay beside William helped. For her sake, he was glad that she, like Jonathan, was safe now from anxiety over what lay ahead. William, too. Sherman heading this way would have raised William's Southern hackles, but as Jupiter drew the carriage up before the Mackay lot at the cemetery in a sunset glow of red and yellow gum leaves, Mark would have given almost anything for a good talk with William.

Jupiter's strong, warm, old hand felt comforting as he helped him down the carriage step. Neither spoke as Jupiter stepped back to wait, to give him time alone at the graves.

Mark went slowly to where William lay and stood in the deep silence for a time, thinking, Good William, I still miss you, old friend. Then he took the few steps toward the newer white marble marker bearing the name Mrs. Eliza Mackay. She never forgot that she went on being *Mrs.* Mackay, he mused, and wondered if she wouldn't have insisted upon the girls having Mrs. *Robert* Mackay carved into the simple marker instead of her own given name. He reached to touch it. The marble was cool in the November afternoon chill. And, once more, he read the inscription aloud softly: "In memory of Mrs. Eliza Mackay, who died on the 13th of June 1862, aged 84 years." Below was carved the Scripture she had repeated to Mark so often at the end:

> Thanks be to God which giveth us the victory
> through our Lord Jesus Christ.

He frowned, still desperate to understand exactly what she had really meant by repeating that word, "victory." Briefly, he glanced behind him, just to make sure Jupiter was still there, offering him support.

Again, Mark laid his hand on the rounded top of the white marker set on its brown base. Then, aloud, he said, "He's—coming, Miss Eliza. Sherman's on his way! Isn't there some way you can tell me *how* Savannah is going to hold me while she's an—occupied city? While she no longer belongs to herself?" He swiped at his eyes. "He burned Atlanta! What will I do—without you—if he burns our city?"

On impulse, he turned to call Jupiter to him. "What in the name of heaven did Miss Eliza mean, Jupiter, when she kept talking about God giving us—victory?"

In his low, rumbling voice, Jupiter said, "I reckon that kind of victory can't be put into words, Mr. Browning. If God looked after us all these years, most likely she meant He'll go on looking after us."

He stared helplessly at Jupiter. "I'm just—thinking about the city!"

"Oh, I know, sir. I do know."

Once more, Mark turned to read the inscription: "Thanks be to God which giveth us the *victory* . . ."

If she believed that, somehow so must he. And he felt that Jupiter did indeed know and that what he knew could not be put into words, either. He would never be able to tell Jupiter what it had meant that in each helpless time, through all the years of their friendship, Jupiter had always known about victory in the midst of trouble. Exactly as Miss Eliza had known. As she still knew.

The moment of reality, almost of discovery, didn't last very long. Before he reached the carriage, he felt tired again, but the moment had been true. Whatever Sherman did to Savannah, whatever happened to them all, he would keep searching for something he could recognize as Miss Eliza's "victory."

"I've come today," Burke said, taking his now familiar chair beside Robert Goodman's desk in the newspaper office in Marietta, "because my wife needs help. So many railroads are torn up, so many telegraph lines down, I can't find out anything and she's frantic with worry over her parents in Savannah—her little nephew, Ben, Mary, her sister-in-law, Mrs. Stiles and her grandchildren. Do you know of anything that might give me some assurance for her, Goodman?"

"Actually, I've been expecting you. Have you seen the destruction at Cassville yet?"

Disturbed by the indirect response from a man who normally was so straightforward, Burke said, "Yes, I've seen it. There's little left of old Cassville. Burned almost to the ground. Only Sherman monuments—lone chimneys—standing."

Goodman took a deep breath. "Sherman's making war against the people, Burke. Militarily, he didn't need to go back to Cassville. I think he burned it only because the citizens changed its name to Manassas."

"Probably," Burke said impatiently. "But that's done. Where is Sherman now? And do you think the same damage is continuing on down through the state toward the sea?"

"There's damage all right and he'll make Georgia howl, I'm sure, even though we know that renegade Confederates—some on orders, some not—have also destroyed property, stolen crops, robbed their own people. To me, that's unforgivable, except I'm sure Southern troops are hungry and they also destroy anything the Federals might use."

"Robert, I know we can't make any sense of all this. I'm not asking you to make sense. I just want to know something definite to tell Natalie. Haven't you heard anything about where Sherman's forces might be by now?"

Goodman shook his head. "No one seems to know for sure. Even Lincoln refers to them as 'the lost army.' The last I learned yesterday is that they're making quite deliberate progress through the intricate coastal waters and marshes, headed for Savannah. There is a rumor that General Grant has requested Sherman to pass up Savannah and go straight to Virginia to help defeat Lee, but it is only a rumor."

Burke frowned. "Would Sherman be likely to disobey an order from a superior?"

"My understanding is that it reached him in the form of a request, rather than an order. My guess is that Sherman is heading as fast as possible for your wife's birthplace."

Burke sighed heavily. "Not knowing is the worst part."

Goodman rummaged on his desk, then picked up a copy of the New York *Tribune.* "This was almost a week reaching me here, but let me read something, Latimer: 'Fort McAllister on the land side at the mouth of the Ogeechee River stands between Sherman and his source of supplies needed to capture Savannah. Again and again, Fort McAllister has been stormed by the Federal Navy in the past two years with no success. Sherman may try to take it with troops any day now because his ultimate goal is the destruction of South Carolina, the first state to secede, and Savannah is just across the river from South Carolina. Even if Sherman agrees to Grant's request to take his forces to Virginia, he'll have to wait somewhere for weeks until ships can reach him. That will give him ample time to take Savannah, then cross the river to destroy at least some of South Carolina.' The *Tribune* piece includes this quote from Sherman himself, Burke: ' "I attach much more importance to these deep incisions into the enemy's countryside because this war differs from European wars in this particular: We are not fighting armies, but a *hostile people,* and must make old and young, rich and poor, feel the hard hand of war . . ." ' I'm not sure he is going to be easily turned aside from a devastating march through South Carolina," Goodman added. "What the *Tribune* is also uncertain about is whether Grant sent a negotiable request to come straight to Virginia or an out-and-out order. I know from the aides I met at Sherman's headquarters right after they burned Atlanta that what the general's heart is set on is wiping out South Carolina. Savannah is merely on the way, but it *is* evidently one of his coveted prizes–the last in Georgia." Goodman's smile was bitter. "Don't forget, we've already been conquered up here."

Natalie's hands trembled so as she helped Miss Lorah dry the good china that she hit the handle of a cup against the shelf and broke it. "Now look what I did, Miss Lorah! I could cry–or cut my throat!"

"That's too bad, Missy, but I don't think I'd do either one, if I was you. You're too nervous to be handlin' good china right now. Anyway, we've washed it all twice already this month and haven't used it once."

"I know it. I'm so ashamed of myself."

"You needn't be. You love your folks down there in Savannah. Not knowin' is sometimes worse than knowin'."

"I've tried so hard to be contained and strong all these weeks. Do you suppose Burke will find out anything from Mr. Goodman? Oh, Miss Lorah, can't somebody somewhere *do* something?" Abruptly, she broke into tears. "My—papa could always—do *something!* Now, he's just an old—helpless man. What can anybody do against a whole, vicious army? I don't think I can—bear one more—day of—not knowing what's happening down there!" She fell into Miss Lorah's outstretched arms. "I really do love my parents. I can't even think—about Callie's wedding next January. Miss Lorah—what if Sherman—*burns* Savannah? It would kill my sweet father!"

NINETY-FIVE

"*Did you post* my letter to Natalie and Callie when you and Ben went out this morning, Mark?" Caroline asked at dinner on December 19.

"You know I did, darling, but we have no way of being sure they'll ever get it."

"I'm aware of that!" She had spoken sharply and was sorry, but her nerves were on edge. Fort McAllister, their last protection, had fallen in brutal hand-to-hand fighting to Sherman's troops six days ago and the whole city was distraught. Caroline had heard so many stories from panic-stricken women at the Aid Society, even from the wounded Southern soldiers she'd served at the Wayside Home. Wild, unbelievable stories of the atrocities suffered by helpless women and children and old people as Sherman's brutish troops stormed into their homes, ripped up mattresses and pillows, broke china and glassware—went roaring around family yards shooting down cattle, chickens, turkeys, and pigs—robbing their smokehouses of precious meat. The Yankees seemed bent on destroying far beyond what even all those thousands of soldiers could possibly eat. The thought of Sherman's "bummers" loose in Savannah robbed Caroline of desperately needed sleep. Every woman in town complained of long, anxious nights without rest. The men, too, she knew. Worse, the Yankees were burning houses for no apparent reason.

Everyone knew they had burned the heart of Atlanta almost to the ground. She had lived through blocks of raging fire in Savannah, but when Sherman burned, it was total. Her own fear of fire roaring through the city was acute, but what on earth would she do to comfort Mark should his adored city be burned?

"I'm sorry I snapped, darling," she said, her voice no longer sharp, just wooden. "I–I am afraid. I know you are."

"Yes, but it hasn't happened yet," he said, staring at his barely touched food.

"Sweet potatoes haunt your dreams, I'm sure. They do mine. I also know you don't really like collards."

He tried to smile at her. "They're what we have."

"Yes." After a silence, she asked, "Will you be seeing Bobby Stiles again today? And do you really think he tells you the truth about what he knows of our–possible fate?"

"I never know for sure if I'll see him, but I do think he tells me what he knows, what he's free as a Rebel officer to tell me. I know this sounds crazy, but I have a strong feeling Miss Eliza is nudging Bobby to keep us as informed as he possibly can." He put a forkful of sweet potato into his mouth, then laid down the fork. "I must pay Ben a little visit now, if you'll excuse me. Bobby could drop by soon. Mary says the boy takes his nap quite willingly as long as I pay him a visit when she tucks him in bed."

As Mark stood, she reached for his hand. "Ben has given you back your life, hasn't he?"

"Yes, what's left of it. I–I sincerely wish for your sake there were more life left in me." He kissed her hair. "We're both making the best of it, though, aren't we?"

When Mark preceded Captain Robert Stiles into the family drawing room, he sensed trouble. Until today, Bobby Stiles had managed to wear his sunny smile. There was no smile now as the two men took chairs, Bobby perched on the edge of his, letting Mark know that he had but a few minutes to talk.

"You're so good to keep coming by," Mark said, almost afraid of what his friend might have to say.

"Since McAllister fell, Sherman's supply ships are available to him now from Ossabaw Sound and he's demanded immediate surrender of Savannah by General Hardee."

Mark let his shoulders sag. "Well, I–I guess we've been expecting this."

"Yes, sir. Unless we surrender, Sherman threatens to shell and storm the city, with no effort to restrain his troops should they resort to the harshest measures." When Mark just sat there, Bobby went on. "General Hardee's reply went at once, refusing the surrender because our defense lines *are* intact, there are no Federal ships in the Savannah River yet and, should they try to get in, they'll find torpedoes everywhere. Even our city guns could blast the Yanks to bits on the river. That much is fact, Mark. Our defenses, such as they are, could hold them off a while. Even though Hardee refuses to surrender, my guess is that he's preparing a way for his forces to evacuate safely to the South Carolina side. All that racket you've been hearing down on the river is my engineering corps. We're constructing, as fast as we can, a pontoon bridge out of anything and everything we can lay our hands on."

Mark stared at him, his blood running cold, the truth of what Bobby had just said becoming real. "Hardee is considering *evacuation?* I know he has only a handful of men compared to Sherman and that they're too old or too young and almost all inexperienced, but–are you saying Hardee will just desert us here? Leave us to–Sherman's mercy?"

"General Hardee may not be able to manage an evacuation. If we can get even half the troops over such a rickety contraption as we're being forced to build, it will be a miracle."

Mark looked away from the handsome, young face, so like that of his old friend Robert Mackay, for whom Bobby was named. "I suppose just–building such a bridge is a fascination to you as an engineer."

"It's far more than that, Mark."

"But, Captain, can Hardee and his men make it across without Sherman knowing? Won't they hear them? The Federals are so close by!"

"We'll just have to find out, won't we?" Bobby stood up, his hand out. "This could be our last handshake for a while, old friend. I'll be going with Hardee, of course. Since I've been in charge of building the flimsy bridge, no doubt I'll be the last one to jump onto the end pontoon. I've written to my wife, Margaret, but there won't be time for me to walk to the Low house, so will you give my love to my mother and the children? To Caroline and Mary and my pal, Little Ben?"

Mark could say nothing. He threw both arms around Bobby Stiles and felt tears sting his own eyes as Bobby hugged him back–hard.

All day long, December 20, wagons loaded with Confederate Army baggage rumbled northward across the river over the rude pontoon bridge Bobby Stiles's men had constructed from barges chained to old flatboats which in turn were chained to hurriedly made rafts, all anchored to the river bottom by disused train wheels, then covered with a heavy layer of rice straw to dull the noise of wagons and marching boots. General Hardee had refused to surrender, but he was making a valiant effort to evacuate his troops.

Confederate cannon fire in the lines about the city, which terrified Savannahians had been hearing off and on all day, was louder than usual by late afternoon. First came the city troops, then at dusk, with a heavy fog rolling over the town, Hardee's men in the lines around the city began to file toward the Broad Street dock where the crude pontoons were fastened. Behind them, as they made their way toward what they hoped was safety, troops left spiked cannons, campfires, and a few pickets. The river battery garrisons crossed in boats to Screven's Ferry, Hardee's light artillery rattled slowly across, then, by the hundreds, more remotely stationed young and old Rebels moved through the unkempt city in a steady shuffling stream, stepped abreast onto the careening makeshift bridge, and headed over the river toward Hutchinson Island, then to the South Carolina shore, as a heavy gale began to blow and clouds hung heavily across the sky.

About midnight, as the lines of men kept coming, the Confederate ship, *Savannah* was blown up, then the *Milledgeville*. Later, Fort Jackson was fired upon and set ablaze, so that not only did the entire city hear the jarring explosions but every room in every home grew bright, then dark, then bright again. Few Savannahians made any effort to sleep. Most sat up wondering hysterically or numbly about what might lie ahead for them all. Fleeing soldiers with families in town said hasty, frantic goodbyes as all night long the men kept coming, kept plodding across the rafts and flatboats toward the other side of the river. At the first sign of overcast dawn, Bobby Stiles looked at his watch. It was 5:40 A.M. when he stepped at last onto the unsteady end flatboat and headed away from Savannah.

Unable to sleep, Mark and Caroline lay clinging together in their bed, trying to picture what might really be happening in the city outside. Neither spoke except in short, fragmented phrases of what each hoped was comfort for the other. Finally, right after dawn, a distant band struck up "Dixie" and Caroline sat straight up in bed.

"Mark, listen!"

"Yes," he said, still gripping her hand. "Yes, darling. I hear."

"What does that music mean?"

"I don't know. I—don't know *anything*, and I can't stand it another minute!"

In spite of Caroline's admonitions that the streets would surely soon be filling up with the first invading Yankees, Mark dressed quickly and headed outside just as sunrise began to push aside a little of the black and fateful night. Pockets of fog lay like smoke in the squares. Real smoke from the burning ships still hung over the city and mingled with the fog, but he kept walking, walking, walking—not to his office—toward Miss Eliza's house on East Broughton.

As he trudged along, the ugliest, most bedraggled bearded men he'd ever seen—conquering Union soldiers, if the ragged, weathered blue uniforms were any indication—began to fill the streets. Some fired their weapons into the air, others yelled and cursed, still others laughed or made feeble attempts to halt the looters—out-of-control Savannahians, Mark knew, who were breaking store and shop windows and carrying off armloads, wagonloads of chickens, bread, a few fresh vegetables, all making the semi-darkness hideous with their boisterous, hysterical noise and shouts. Mark dodged men on horses who galloped about with no object, while women of the streets roamed, obviously seeking customers.

In front of the Mackay house, he stood for a long time, listening to the sounds of the city gone mad, to the beat of hooves, the rumble of wagons, the crashing of glass and splintered doorframes as the looting went on.

"Savannah," he whispered. A mere whisper in such a din was ludicrous. Turning helplessly around and around in the street in front of Miss Eliza's house, he startled himself by crying out, "Savannah! *Savannah . . . !*"

Only one dim lamp burned in the familiar old Mackay place. What did he expect? Did he expect the city to find a way to answer his cry from the deep, long-beloved shadows of the old house that had sheltered him through the years—from the first night spent there—to the day they took Miss Eliza to her grave?

Devoid of reason, he began to walk along Broughton toward Bull Street. Maybe he'd find an answer there. Everything happened on Bull

Street. At the corner of Bull, he heard someone call his name and turned to see Charles Green hurrying toward him in the gloom of the dim, foggy morning.

"What on earth are you doing out?" Green asked, stopping for courtesy's sake. Courtesy, Mark thought, offered to a pathetic, confused, old man.

"I–I'm not sure, Charles," Mark said. "Couldn't sleep, of course."

"Of course. Who could? Sorry to rush off, Browning, but I'm on my way to the Exchange to meet the Mayor and councilmen."

"So early?" Mark asked irrelevantly.

"A gang of consarned Rebels stole the Mayor's horses last night, I understand. He had to hire a hack to go to the appointed place on the Augusta Road, where they surrendered Savannah to Sherman's representative, General John Geary, now that the last of Hardee's men have flown the coop."

Mark took a step toward him. "Charles," he asked, "which side are you on in this war?"

Green gave him a sharp look, then a sly smile. "I'm on the side of saving Savannah, Browning."

An unexpected, stubborn hope rose in Mark's heart as he watched Green walk briskly away. Standing there alone, *he* grew as stubborn as his hope. Then, as he watched, Charles Green returned to say something else.

"I see nothing wrong in telling you this, Browning. I'm so determined to show courtesy to Sherman *and* to Savannah that I'm offering the general my house as his headquarters."

Mark knew he could never catch up with Green, who once more hustled away, but he began to walk again, pacing himself, heading for the Exchange Building on the Bay.

By 6 A.M., thousands upon thousands of bedraggled, filthy, tattered Federal troops marched past him victoriously along Bull Street, their tramping boots strengthening the staccato beat of their drums. On order, the vast array of troops finally came to a halt before the Exchange and, with looters still breaking glass and racing through back alleys with stolen goods, General Geary began to address the troops from a position on the Exchange steps.

Mark moved as close as possible, as though loath to miss a single word that might give him some hint of the fate of his city. Scarcely daring to breathe for fear of missing one word, he listened:

"As representative of our brilliant General Sherman, who went over to South Carolina to make certain that the troops under General Hardee who fled the city last night will go no further, I have taken command of the city of Savannah!"

The roar that went up from the assembled Yankees was deafening. It subsided finally, and General Geary went on: "The distinguished Mayor of Savannah, Dr. Arnold, formally surrendered the city to me in these wise words: 'I respectfully request your protection of the lives and private property of the citizens and of our women and children and do hereby surrender into your care the city of Savannah, Georgia.' I solemnly vowed to the worthy Mayor," Geary went on, "that his request was promptly granted and that any violation of orders will be punished by death."

For a few more minutes, Geary then heaped praise on the soldiers in formation before him, for their show of determination and courage on the long, hard march to the sea. As he spoke, his men's cheers grew in volume until an enthusiastic young Yankee standing not three feet from where Mark stood began to shout from sheer joy: "We stand here at Savannah, boys, master over a hunnert battlefields which was bought an' paid for with our free man's blood—what we done will go down in history as one of the greatest achievements on record!"

The young soldier was then drowned out by such a roar and round after round of cheering from the others who had marched with him that Mark marveled at Geary's control and indulgence. The general let them cheer for a time and then held up his hand for silence. "As we meet here, looters—some members of the renegade Confederate Wheeler's cavalry, others Rebel deserters, all scum—are stealing goods from their own people out of the very stores and shops of the city we're obliged to protect. From this moment, such protection begins!"

When Mark reached his house at about 9 A.M., Caroline, frantic with worry, met him at the front door. He knew how distressed she'd been over him and that she knew why he'd gone out.

"Savannah is—saved," he said.

Caroline's frown was puzzled. "What do you mean, Mark?"

"Just that. The old city won't be destroyed. Charles Green and the Mayor and councilmen—saved it. Savannah has been surrendered into the hands of General Sherman. He will refit his army here. Savannah won't be burned like Atlanta. It's too valuable to the Union Navy."

Tears began to flow down Caroline's cheeks. He could almost hear her heart break, but for a time she spoke not one word. Then she asked, "Is it—all right down inside your heart now that you know Savannah won't be—burned, Mark?"

He nodded yes and, for the first time in a long time, did not have to force a smile. It was weary, but it came naturally.

At that moment, he saw Mary, holding Ben's hand, start down the graceful stairs. He saluted Ben. "Good morning, son," he called. "If it's all the same to you, I think we'd better stay inside the house today."

"Why, Grandpa Mark?"

"Well, for one thing, there are a lot of strangers in Savannah."

Ben broke away from Mary and ran to hug his legs. "We're not, though. We're not strangers, Grandpa!"

He gave the boy a hug. "You bet we're not, Ben!"

Still on the stairs, Mary cleared her throat, then said firmly, almost cheerfully, "I'd like to report—a victory during all that shooting and noise and fire and yelling last night."

Mark looked up at her. "A—*victory*, Mary?"

"I had just about decided to take Ben and go back to my upcountry to live for the rest of my days. But now, I've decided to stay here—with you. I don't have any words to explain, but all at once, I knew that with what we might have to face in Savannah now, it's time *I* stopped feeling like a—stranger in town."

Her smile could only have been sunnier, more radiant, Mark thought, if Jonathan had just walked through the gracious front door.

AFTERWORD

*G*eneral Sherman himself did not participate in the actual surrender of Savannah by Mayor Arnold and the City Council, because en route back to Georgia from a conference with Union officers at Hilton Head, his boat was stuck for hours in a mudbank. By the time the general reached the anxious city which Mark Browning so loved, Savannah was already in Union hands and courtesy was being shown to the conquerors by certain pragmatic Savannahians—especially Charles Green, who met Sherman at the Pulaski House and pressed the offer of his own mansion. "If you don't take it," Green said, "some other general will and I much prefer you." Sherman accepted and it was in his sumptuous second-floor suite that he composed the now famous telegram to Lincoln which read in part: "I beg to present to you as a Christmas present, the city of Savannah . . ."

On that Christmas, 1864, Georgians who suffered along the direct path of his march to the sea certainly thought of William Tecumseh Sherman as a monster. To this day, everyone everywhere agrees with him when he wrote: "War is hell!" I am convinced that he was first of all a soldier, not different from other generals bent on demoralizing the enemy. I agree with most thoughtful Georgians who, today, tend to find Sherman brilliant and provocative in his many-faceted nature. However, some older residents reared on family stories of his army's vandalism still bridle at the mention of his name. In the North, Sherman became an instant hero for what he did in Georgia and for his "imaginative telegram" to Lincoln, but his short visit in Savannah must have been, for him, a heady mixture of triumph and heartbreak. Savannah Negroes hailed him as their savior and came in droves to see him at Green's residence. The general, by the way, did not particularly like the people he helped free. Sherman entertained lavishly at Christmas, with Charles Green as an honored guest, but it was in the mansion now known as the Green-Meldrim house that Sherman read in a newspaper of the death of his six-month-old son, whom he had never seen.

He and his army were evidently firm but courteous to Savannahians, although the more rebellious among Savannah people declared not. Many Savannah women, in particular, remained hostile, and the Union troops' relatively peaceful stay was due largely to the realism of wise Mayor Arnold, who kept reminding Confederate diehards that "where resistance is hopeless it is criminal to make it."

Savannah herself was in a deplorable condition. The people were not only deep in poverty and need; the proud city showed the ugly consequences of four years of war. "Fences were broken down, sidewalks and wharves in ruin and Sherman's dead horses are laying in the streets by the dozen," wrote a Northern visitor early in January 1865. "The fact is, Savannah is a most miserable hole."

I have taken that quotation from *A Present for Mr. Lincoln*, by Alexander A. Lawrence, and my deep thanks go to Anita Raskin, owner of The Book Lady in Savannah, and to her assistant, Lonnie Evans, for efforts to find this invaluable out-of-print book for me. Lawrence wrote that when Sherman's men arrived, "the city was in a dilapidated condition . . . [but that] improvement was noticeable following the departure of the main Federal Army. In two months, 568 carcasses of animals were removed by the [Union] military, together with 8,311 cartloads of garbage and 7,219 loads of manure." Wharves were repaired, trees trimmed, and although many Savannahians remained bitter, hatred of all things Yankee was a bit less than might have been expected. After having worked my way through these four long novels that comprise the Savannah Quartet, I have concluded that nineteenth-century Savannahians were, in the main, pragmatic folk who loved their city and did much that they loathed in order to save her.

My office, as I write this, is stacked with reference books whose authors in many ways saved my sanity: Margaret Sanborn, James Mc-Pherson, James McGregor Burns, Burke Davis, Robert Durden, Burnette

Vanstory and countless others, along with a treasure of books and manuscript sources from Savannah's own Hodgson Hall of the Georgia Historical Society, without which I could not have done even one of these novels about old Savannah. In particular, I again salute my dear Bobby Bennett, who was there for me almost all the way through the Quartet, and since she returned to university for advanced studies, I have leaned especially on the cheerfully given expertise of Tracy Bearden. I also thank Ann Smith and Dr. Louis Bellardo, director. On the island where I live and work, Fraser Ledbetter at the St. Simons Public Library, Julie Shelfer and Mrs. Frances Kane were on hand when I needed them. I was also free to pester my revered friend Mr. Henry Green of St. Simons when I had use for authentic furniture and drapery research. And when I had to see a character through a particular illness and/or death, as always I called on one of my best readers and friends, Dr. William A. Hitt. Bill is my doctor when I can be persuaded to leave my office for his, but he helps and encourages me far more in the writing than he knows. At the Brunswick Library, Marcia Hodges, Dorothy Howseal, and Director Jim Darby again helped greatly, and I turned also to Earl McEachern of the Edo Miller Funeral Home in Brunswick, Georgia, for use of his research into the history of his profession. From Peterboro, New Hampshire, Tony Colby was kind enough to write to me for Mrs. Jane Meldrim Hewitt, who really knew the old Green-Meldrim house where Sherman stayed because she lived there in her youth.

From the riches of the Savannah Public Library, Judy Nichols and especially Susan Seay helped enormously with knowledge and enthusiasm for what I try to do. Even two of Savannah's expert tour guides were of immediate assistance: from the Helen Salter Tours, Mr. Manton Hester, and from Old Savannah Tours, Lorraine Bucher. My longtime friend and loyal reader, Mr. William H. Samuel, superintendent of Laurel Grove Cemetery, was again on hand to guide me to the burial sites I needed to see.

If I have captured anything of the character of the W. H. Stiles family, it is due directly to descendants, who helped me far more than they seem to realize: Hugh Golson of Savannah (credited by the others and by me with being the family historian), Elizabeth Layton of De Land, Florida, Margaret and Frederick Knight II and Julia and Frederick Knight III of Cartersville, Georgia, and Elise Heald of St. Louis. I curb myself for the sake of space when I try to express what these delightful, perceptive people have come to mean to me. They all have helpful

facts, but perhaps most important to me, they also have genuine unaf-
fected respect for and humor about their antecedents.

W. H. Stiles died while on business in Savannah, December 21, 1865,
one year after Union occupation of the city. This brilliant, restless,
extremely handsome gentleman, whom I came to admire in spite of how
often we would have disagreed politically, was certainly one of the
truly heartbroken Confederate loyalists. He and his beloved Lib (Eliza
Anne Mackay Stiles) were apart much of the time near the end of their
lives, since W.H. was determined to clear and plant his new land in
Terrell County. Eliza Anne, equally heartbroken and embittered, evidently took Mary Cowper's children to Etowah Cliffs sometime after
Sherman's Savannah "visit." She lived only two years without W.H. and
died in her home beside the Etowah River in the Georgia upcountry on
December 20, 1867. W.H. is buried in Laurel Grove Cemetery, Savannah,
in the Mackay plot with Miss Eliza Mackay, William, and the Mackay
sisters, and although Eliza Anne's grave is in the family cemetery in the
"little grove of trees" near the ruins of her upcountry home, this is made
known in a special inscription on the base of W.H.'s stone in Laurel
Grove, Savannah.

Along with his wife, Martha, my cherished friend Marion
Hemperley, for years Georgia's knowledgeable Deputy Surveyor General, continued his invaluable help to me. I must here also mention two
people dear to both Hemperleys, therefore to me—Jason and Miranda
Suggs.

The only speaking date I accepted during the writing of *Stranger in
Savannah,* was at the Atlanta Historical Society, through Dr. George
McDaniel. I not only belatedly became an instant member but found a
gold mine of information, especially on the natural surroundings at
Etowah Cliffs. The names of the roses used to decorate Etowah Cliffs
for Mary Cowper's wedding to Andrew Low were authentic roses of
that day, as were the Solfaterre roses brought by Caroline Browning to
Miss Eliza as she lay dying. I know this because of the expert help given
me by Margaret Brock of the Atlanta Historical Society's Tullie-Smith
House. For hours, I also studied the detailed journal kept by Kate and
Sarah Mackay as their amazing mother endured her final illness. This
journal was given to me by Hugh Golson, as was an account of Captain
Bobby Stiles's whereabouts toward the end of the Civil War.

The letter used by Natalie Browning Latimer in her effort to convince Eliza Anne Stiles that Mary Cowper should *not* be forced to marry
Andrew Low contains the exact wording from a letter Mary Elizabeth

Huger of South Carolina sent to the Mackay sisters in Savannah. Most of the actual wording of the letter to Eliza Anne from Mary Custis Lee, in which she showed the Lees' fury that South Carolina had seceded, has also been used. Many of William Thackeray's speeches are taken from his own accounts of his two lecture tours in Savannah. He did stay with the Andrew Lows at 325 Abercorn Street, a house I urge my readers not to miss seeing. You will be shown the unusual mansion on Lafayette Square, now owned by the Colonial Dames, by two charming ladies, Mrs. Joan Carter Bender and Mrs. W. C. H. Strong, who gave my research assistant, Nancy Goshorn, and me every possible help, including their enthusiasm and friendship.

If you have read the other three books in the Savannah Quartet, you already know of my respect for and delight in Mary Harty of Historic Savannah's classic Davenport House. I loved Mary and "her" house so much that I had Mark and Caroline Browning pattern their town house after Isaiah Davenport's masterpiece. No time spent in Savannah will ever now be the same for me. Mary Harty died during the writing of *Stranger in Savannah*. Some of the heart of the old city left for me with my beloved Mary. I miss her every day.

I am once more grateful for the friendship, fun, and sheer stimulation I find in being steadily supported by the interest and expertise of Scott Smith, director at Old Fort Jackson, and his brainy wife, Frances. Scott is my final authority on all aspects of the military emplacements around Savannah and will have checked the manuscript for accuracy before *Stranger in Savannah* goes to press. No one should visit Savannah without experiencing Old Fort Jackson. Thank you, Scott and Frances, for so much, and thank you, Tim Callahan, also of Old Fort Jackson, for original research. Especially do I thank you, Frances, for having put me in touch with the altogether unique Dr. Perry Cochran of the History Department of Georgia Southern College in Statesboro. Perry is all you said and more. In my incredible luck at finding Perry, I hadn't dreamed it would stretch to include his learned and attractive wife, Linda. Dr. Cochran is, at this moment, reading the manuscript and, as usual, putting me through the wringer of his vast acquaintance with American history and its people. I'm flattered that he thinks I did my homework!

At Fort McAllister, I also deeply thank Mary Worsham and Superintendent Daniel J. Brown. And at New Echota in Calhoun, Georgia, the director, Frankie Mewborn.

Aside from Miss Eliza and William Mackay, my two favorite characters among those who really lived, Mary Cowper Stiles Low and Stuart

Elliott, the lovers who could surely be called "star-crossed," have also captured my affections. Mary Cowper is buried in the handsome Andrew Low plot in Laurel Grove Cemetery in Savannah, and Stuart lies all alone to this day in the picturesque churchyard of the Roswell Presbyterian Church in Roswell, Georgia. I know he's all alone because my absolutely indispensable assistant and *friend*, Eileen Humphlett, and her husband, Dr. James Humphlett, found and photographed his grave for me. And I thank Ruby Ezzard, the church historian, for helping them. Lucinda Sorrel, the appealing young lady Stuart did marry, is with their two children in the Sorrel mausoleum at Laurel Grove. The arresting, still wealthy and successful Andrew Low left Savannah in the years following the Civil War and died at his country estate, Leamington, England, but his love for Savannah caused him to will that his body be returned for burial at Laurel Grove. If his "afternoon habit" continued, no one seems to know. I am indebted to Stephen Bohlin-Davis of the Juliette Gordon Low birthplace in Savannah for putting me in contact with a charming visitor from South Africa, Mrs. Jane Davidson, a descendant of Andrew Low, who, near the end of my writing, gave me rare photographs and still more detail about the gentleman himself. For much of my research here, as before and so many years after his death, I am once more indebted to my treasured friend the late Walter C. Hartridge, Savannah historian, whose papers were all at my disposal at Hodgson Hall, a gift from his beautiful wife, Susan, still my beloved friend.

I especially want to thank my former editor, Carolyn Blakemore, who stayed expertly and lovingly beside me through the other three novels in the Savannah Quartet and almost all the way through this one. If anyone knows my heart, Carolyn, it is you.

At my publishing house, Doubleday in New York, so many not only have supported me through the writing but seem now to welcome the idea, along with me, that *Stranger in Savannah* will be handed over to my new editor and friend, Nancy Evans, Doubleday president, and her assistants, Jean Pohoryles and Jennifer Brehl, who will take it the remainder of the way into the bookstores. I especially want to mention Jack Lynch, again my skillful copy editor; MarySarah Quinn, book designer; Michele Martin, managing editor; Jackie Everly, Ellen Archer, Michael Carter, Peter Schneider, and also the gentleman I felt I knew and trusted on first meeting, CEO at Bantam Doubleday Dell, Mr. Alberto Vitale. No recognition of support from my publisher would be complete without mention of the entire sales force and especially of my super southeastern sales representative, Ed Waters, and his Ruthie. I also thank Bebe Cole for having given me her rare friendship, understanding, and marketing know-how for more years than either of us has been at Doubleday.

The jacket for *Stranger in Savannah* is, without doubt, my favorite of any I've ever had. For this I must thank Nancy Evans and Bebe Cole, who sat at sunset with Joyce Blackburn and me and studied one handsome section of the superb ironwork on the Andrew Low house in Lafayette Square. At that moment we *saw* the jacket design, but Alex Gotfryd, my beloved art director, and Pamela Patrick, artist, "saw" it even more creatively from photographs taken for me by Eileen and Jimmy Humphlett, who, a few days later found the house under the same sunset glow.

Through still another book, I thank my superb agent and literary manager, Lila Karpf of New York, with whom I share far more than the contracting and marketing of books.

Because she is a part of my life, my heart moves again to my longtime friend Faith Brunson of Atlanta. I have her to thank for much more than having found Lila for me in the first place.

As soon as I finish writing this Afterword, I'll be calling one of my best friends, Easter Straker of Lima, Ohio, who, in spite of more than two years of traumatic hospital bouts, has gone right on holding me to my best and believing in me. And thank you, dear Mary Porter and Doris Shuman, for all you both do for Easter—and for me.

Genuine devotion and gratitude fly again to Mr. and Mrs. Fred Bentley of Kennesaw, Georgia, who not only cheered me all the way but did so much to help me keep perspective on the Rebel South, Sherman, and the colorful history of Georgia's upcountry. Through Fred, I met another true Southern gentleman, Mr. Robert McAlpin Goodman, Jr., great-grandson of the revered "Southern Unionist," Robert McAlpin Goodman, Marietta publisher of the old *Southern Statesman*. He seemed a natural friend—as indeed he came to be in my book—for Burke Latimer, Natalie's husband, who also held to his own belief in the Union of all the states. Meeting today's Mr. and Mrs. Goodman, Jr., in their lovely home was an experience I won't forget, nor will these thanks convey half my gratitude that they trusted me to write of their distinguished ancestor. Fred Bentley also arranged for the freely given help of busy Dr. Phil Secrist of Marietta and that of Ms. Carol McDonald, curator of Big Shanty Museum. I will certainly be bothering her again as I research the next two books, one of which will probably take place in Marietta, Georgia.

Early in the writing of *Stranger in Savannah*, my close friend—skilled at absolutely everything—Mary Wheeler of Nashville did expert work for me on the complex research of the political history of the decade leading up to the Civil War. You already know my high opinion of you, Mary, but thanks again from my heart.

A few names must be here for love's sake, for the value to me of their encouragement and loyalty, and they will each one know why: Jeanette and Ben Harnsberger, Del Ward Napier, and Terri Benson of Macon, Georgia; Millie Price of Nashville, Tennessee; Cindy and Mike Birdsong of Little Rock, Arkansas; Mrs. Lee Hark of Hampton, Virginia; Miss Ethel Jones of Hendersonville, North Carolina; Dena Snodgrass and Ann Hyman of Jacksonville, Florida; from St. Simons Island, Burnette Vanstory, G. G. Greneker, Frances Burns, Emma Gibson, Freddie Wright, Ruby Wilson, Sarah Bell Edmond, Alfonza Ramsey, Jean Alexander and the staff at St. Simons Chamber of Commerce, Gertrude Bradshaw and Elise Permar, co-editors of *The Islander*, Bill and Carolyn Sullins, and Betty and Chuck NeSmith of Insty-Prints in Brunswick, Georgia. I deeply thank my good neighbor and longtime friend Sarah Plemmons, who not only sees to my peculiar and unexpected needs but reads manuscript and is my source for nature research. From her own library, Sarah also kept feeding me excellent material on the Civil War in its most unusual aspects.

Now, an attempt at least to thank and show my love for my innermost circle of helpers, inspirers, and *tolerators*. Writers of long novels such as this one *have* to be tolerated much of the time. Joyce Blackburn, my closest friend for almost forty years, from whom I freely take all criticism and praise, has once more gone through every line on every page, making her always perceptive suggestions, her profound and humorous comments. She has also reminded me of things I just have to do in the twentieth century, kept me reasonably sane and believing in myself throughout. Writing novels is now my reason for getting up in the morning, but then, so is the steady pleasure and enduring stimulation of Joyce's company day in and day out. May I just thank you, Joyce? And will you know beyond that?

Joyfully, also an integral part of my inner circle is Nancy Goshorn, for years my late mother's friend and neighbor, who now lives nearby on St. Simons Island and goes on proving me right in my long-held belief that she is a born researcher! Nance, who, along with her aunt, the late Mary Jane Goshorn, took such loving care of Mother, now uses her "computer brain" and fine instincts to care for my professional and oddly human needs–without losing her sense of humor about me. Like me, she can be a workaholic and seems not to tire of checking me on dates, missed facts, nineteenth-century political happenings and, as with Joyce, fully accepts my vagueness when I'm writing. Welcome to St. Simons, dear friend, and to the sometimes wild world of creating books.

Even from faraway Duluth, Minnesota, my longtime favorite reader, Frances Pitts, stays a close part of my inner circle of support. Critically, painstakingly, understanding more at times than I do, she writes commentary on my manuscripts with her own unique literary flair. I trust her judgment and she has done more for my self-esteem and determination than she suspects. Thank you, dear "book person," for all you do for my confidence and occasionally flagging spirits. Let's both go on forever.

Finally, the hub of what a New York friend calls my growing "support group" is my full-time assistant in everything, Eileen Humphlett, to whom I have dedicated *Stranger in Savannah.* In my heart, every book I've done since *Margaret's Story* has been, in its own way, Eileen's book, too. She has not only mastered a computer (which scares me even to look upon!), she handles 90 percent of my mail with warmth and caring, all my business, my promotion tours, speaking schedule, is my frequent liaison with my publisher, and, like Nancy, is a born researcher when she has any time left for it. I have already written in another Afterword that Joyce and I call Eileen our Overqualified Keeper. She is far more than that. The special humor-lit bond between her family and the two of us makes life whole. Dear Eileen, if anything is amiss in this, *your* book, it's my fault, not yours. Accept *Stranger in Savannah* with my gratitude and love–for all that you are. Now that we're together, I marvel that I managed so long without you.

I confess dread at reaching this place in *this* Afterword, although at seventy-two, I am well and already planning the next novel. Still, the Savannah Quartet (the equivalent of a nearly 4,000-page manuscript!) has been my largest and most engrossing work to date. This last in the Quartet is not a book about military strategy or Civil War battles. I have tried to make it the story of the unique kind of anxiety and suffering felt by those forced to live on the edges of the actual fighting in this wasteful conflict. Even now, I miss all my people–painfully. It could be months before I stop wondering about them, trying to think what they will each do or say next. I will, of course, be doing future research in

Savannah, but already I miss the old city I've come to love much as Mark Browning loved her. In a way, some of me went into Mark, Natalie, Caroline, Indian Mary, Ben, Burke, and Jonathan. They are all my creations and perhaps that is why I miss them so keenly. The writing of these four novels spanning American history from the War of 1812 to the Civil War has given me a new and, I hope, more tolerant love of this uncommon, still relatively young land. I may not live to see it, but I do believe the day will come when Lincoln's vision of equality will be a way of life in these United States, in spite of the divisive scars which remain, but are now more subtly felt. Human divisiveness—which I see raging in new, less visible ways now—goes far deeper than racism of any kind. The writing has convinced me of that. It has also convinced me that the United States of America is still in desperate need of genuine, heart-deep *union*, the kind that is strong enough to care *through* differences.

As always, I offer my most inclusive thanks to booksellers everywhere and especially to my readers, one of whom wrote recently: "The only thing I don't like about your Savannah novels is that they end! But I take comfort in the fact that they are still on my bookshelves and I can simply start over again when I finish."

I wish I could.

Eugenia Price
St. Simons Island, Georgia
October 1988

Book Mark

This book was composed in variations of the typeface Caslon by Berryville Graphics, Berryville,Virginia.

It was printed on 50 lb. Glatfelter Offset and bound by Berryville Graphics, Berryville,Virginia.

DESIGNED BY MARYSARAH QUINN